They looked at each other for one half-serious moment, and then burst out laughing again. He wrapped his arms around her, and they kissed with an urgency that started off playful and grew more and more passionate. . . . He reached down and touched her thigh, where her thin dress had ridden high, and he caressed all around the firm, rounded curve of her bottom, until she bent forward and gasped in his ear.

They didn't even undress. In that elegant Central Park bedroom in 1921 . . . with the crackling strains of "Dardenella" and "Hindustan" faint in the next apartment, and the air delirious with perfume, they made love with an erotic grace that was rare, even for them.

"A VIRTUOSO ASSORTMENT OF DIRTY TRICKS . . . OF ROBBER-BARON OLD VELVET, A BOLT OF EXECUTIVE SUITE GAMING . . . A BEEFY WHOPPER, WELL DONE."
—*Kirkus Reviews*

RICH

GRAHAM MASTERTON

A KANGAROO BOOK
PUBLISHED BY POCKET BOOKS NEW YORK

Distributed in Canada by PaperJacks Ltd., a Licensee
of the trademarks of Simon & Schuster, a division of
Gulf + Western Corporation.

**POCKET BOOKS, a Simon & Schuster divison of
GULF & WESTERN CORPORATION**
1230 Avenue of the Americas, New York, N.Y. 10020
In Canada distributed by PaperJacks Ltd.,
330 Steelcase Road, Markham, Ontario.

Copyright © 1979 by Graham Masterton

Library of Congress Catalog Card Number: 78-9917

All rights reserved, including the right to reproduce
this book or portions thereof in any form whatsoever.
For information address Pocket Book, 1230 Avenue
of the Americas, New York, N.Y. 10020

ISBN: 0-671-81768-X

First Pocket Books printing February, 1980

10   9   8   7   6   5   4   3   2   1

Trademarks registered in the United States and other countries.

Printed in Canada

For Wiescka, my wife, with love,
and for Marty Asher, with very
special thanks.

1900

A WONDERFUL GARDEN PARTY

THREE HUNDRED FIFTY DOLLARS RAISED FOR SICK CHILDREN

By Our Society Correspondent

Mr. Frank Edmunds of Broughton threw a scintillating garden party for 250 celebrities and guests at his home on Saturday last, and $350.23 was raised for the sick children of Broughton and surrounding environs.

A notable newcomer to Broughton's social circles was a New Yorker, Mr. J. Cornelias, who has recently arrived in these parts to consider business investment.

—*The Broughton Sentinel*,
August 14, 1900

It was one of those days when the heat comes in suffocating waves, and you only had to leave your house and walk a few yards down Main Street, just to Scully's Hardware for a bag of beans or some washing soda, or maybe down to the little fish stall on the corner of Galveston Street for some snapper, and your clothes began to feel hot and sticky and uncomfortable, and your boots too tight, and you started to think about ice-cream sodas or lemon water ice, sipped at the shady tables of Howard's Refreshment Parlor.

There was no such person as Howard, never had been. The parlor was run by a small birdlike widow called Mrs. Grey, who ran up and down behind her high marble-topped counter in a rigid white apron, serving up sundaes and milk shakes in molded glass dishes. She served advice, too, if you needed it, or even if you didn't. Mrs. Grey considered that the free dissemination of worldly wisdom was part and parcel of the function of selling ices.

When Janet stepped across the scrubbed wooden floor that afternoon in August, the place was crowded, and the conversation tumbled warm and lazy through the cool filtered sunlight. Mrs. Grey was piling the last creamy layer onto a seven-layer strawberry ice, and talking to a big, sweaty-looking man in a worn blue jacket and patched-up trousers.

"If you want my opinion, young feller," she was saying, as she popped a final cherry on top, "you'll take yourself up North, and find yourself a factory to work in. There's regular employment up there, I hear the wages are better than ever. Things move slow down here, always have, and always will."

The man didn't seem to be listening. He was drawing invisible patterns on the cold marble counter with his blunt, workingman's finger.

"These days," said Mrs. Grey, "you have to know your onions if you want to make anything out of yourself. Time was, a pick and a shovel and a broad back was good enough. But these days, if you

9

don't know your onions, you'll finish your life as poor as you started it, and folks don't come any poorer than that."

A calendar on the pine-boarded wall flapped and flickered in the warm breeze that eddied into the parlor from the open front door. It read August 13, 1900.

"Janet," said Mrs. Grey in her hoarse old voice, "I do believe you come to indulge yourself again, at your mistress's expense."

It was a long-standing joke between them, but the big sweaty man at the counter obviously didn't realize, and stood back to look at Janet the way you'd look at someone's pet poodle when it wouldn't behave itself.

Mrs. Grey laid her hand on his arm. "It's a hot day," she explained, "and this here's just about halfway between the stores and the houses, and it ain't surprisin' that serving maids find themselves tempted."

Janet smiled. "It sure is hot, Mrs. Grey. I reckon a black-currant ice, with sweet syrup and a cherry on top, that'll do me. I swear I thought I'd melt to a puddle before I got here."

"Young girls like you shouldn't feel the heat," said Mrs. Grey, digging into the chilled black-currant sherbet. There was a delicious musty sour smell of black-currant leaves. "Wear more underthings, that's what I always say."

As she prattled on, the heavy-built stranger shifted himself around and took a long look at Janet. She was quite aware that he was watching, because she blushed slightly and lowered her eyes, but she didn't look back his way. Apart from anything else at all, he was a common workingman, and Mrs. Mulliner had spoken to Janet very severely about what she called "addressing herself" to butcher's roundsmen and general roughnecks. Janet thought it made her sound like an untidy parcel that insisted on being posted wherever it thought fit.

Janet was eighteen, and a housemaid for Mr. and Mrs. Mulliner, on Beaumont Street, where the houses were detached and painted white, and set back among palms and acacia and shady creepers. Down in the railroad area of town, they called it "The Racetrack," on account of its white-painted fences and its neatly trimmed turf, and the well-dressed young fillies who pranced up and down it. Mrs. Mulliner was one of the better-known fillies, even though she was a married woman. She went to Houston two or three times a year, and on every trip she bought herself several

10

hundred dollars' worth of fashionable clothes. Janet had heard that last season she paid nearly twenty dollars for one dress alone. But Mr. Mulliner didn't seem to mind his wife's extravagance; he was a good ten years older than she was, with peppery whiskers, and perhaps he thought his beautiful consort was worth a sizable slice of his profits. He ran a respectable and successful law partnership on Fifth Street, in the business district, and was considered a rich man.

Janet liked working for the Mulliners, and her contentment showed. She was a short girl, only five-feet-four in her military-heeled boots, and she had a pretty chubbiness about her that made her master's houseguests want to give her affectionate squeezes, especially after the brandy had been passed around for the third time. She had wispy brown hair that floated under her wide-brimmed straw leghorn in irrepressible clouds. Her cheeks were freckly, her lips were pert and pink, and she had wide slate-colored eyes that made her look permanently surprised at what she saw. In her cream percale skirt and her pink German linen blouse, she had a round-breasted curviness that made housepainters whistle as she bounced her way past, and retired gentlemen raise their eyeglasses for a longer and more appreciative look.

The heavy-built man in Howard's Refreshment Parlor was being more than appreciative, though. He was openly staring at Janet with his pale bulgy eyes in a way that made her wonder if her blouse was unfastened, or there was an unsightly smudge on the tip of her nose. He had a red, Dutch-looking face, with protruding ears as thick as gammon rinds, and rubbery lips. His hair was yellow and thinning on top; but for all his brutishness and his coarseness, there was something very powerful and masculine about him. He looked the kind of man who would see you out of trouble, or lift your cart out of a muddy rut with the strength of his own broad back.

He didn't say a word as Mrs. Grey topped off Janet's black-currant sherbet with syrup and cherries, tucked a long-handled spoon into the dish and handed it across the counter. Janet, still blushing, opened her purse and dropped five cents on the marble-topped counter. Mrs. Grey rang the money on the cash register, and gave her two cents change.

"Now, you make haste consuming that, Miss Janet, or else you'll get a scolding when you get yourself back. I just thank

11

heavens you ain't my housemaid, or else I'd be after you with a floor brush.''

Janet gave her a tight little smile and carried her dish of ice across to one of the tables. She chose it because it was the only spare seat, and she didn't want the heavy-built workingman to sit down next to her and make a nuisance of himself. She bent her head over her plate, and ate as quickly as she could. All of a sudden, all the pleasure seemed to have drained out of Howard's Refreshment Parlor, and she didn't even dare to look up, in case the fellow was still staring at her.

There were two young clerks at her table. She recognized them from Okram's Quantity Goods Store on Eighth Street. At first they were talking about fishing down at Harness Creek, but after a while they started making pointed remarks about her, as if she wasn't there. While she could usually have taken this kind of teasing in good part, and flirt back, she really didn't care for it today, and almost lost her temper.

"You have to make *one* concession," remarked one of the clerks, a redheaded boy in a tight brown suit. "She dresses nobby, even though she's working in the kitchen."

"Nobby?" said the other, who had dark wavy hair and plenty of dandruff. "She's a picture, I'd say, the kind men like."

She left her ice unfinished, which in actual fact she thought was a rather adult thing to do. Only small children and dogs licked the plate. She pushed back her bentwood chair, gathered up her shopping bag, and walked out. She didn't even turn around to call good-bye to Mrs. Grey, in case the red-faced workingman was looking, but she told herself that Mrs. Grey was probably too busy scooping out fresh dishes of ice cream to notice. Outside, on the boardwalk, the heat and the glare were like a great furnace door opening up.

Well, she thought to herself, *I'm glad I work for a respectable household. The way men behave, they're like wild dogs, only chasing after one thing. How can they be so brutish? They only have to sniff a pretty girl, and they turn into crude and horrible beasts. They treat a woman like a piece of raw meat.*

She crossed Main Street at the corner of Tenth Street, and walked in the shade of the wooden buildings, her heels rapping on the boardwalk and her long skirt rustling. A messenger boy on a bicycle whistled at her as he pedaled past, but she tilted her chin up

12

and ignored him. From now on, she decided, she wasn't going to have anything to do with men. They could stare and slaver as much as they wanted to. She couldn't stop that. But she could make sure that they didn't receive the slightest pinch of encouragement.

As she walked, she glanced at her reflection in the store windows, and saw a pretty little girl in a high-crowned straw hat and a crisp pink blouse. She straightened her back to make herself look taller, and to lift her breasts. A sizable frontage was fashionable this year, and she was quite proud of hers.

She waited at the corner of Ninth Street while a horse-drawn runabout rattled briskly past, and then she stepped out onto the hard-baked road. But she had only walked a few steps when she felt a strong hand pull at her left arm. She jolted her head up with surprise, and said: *"Oh!"*

It was the heavyset man with the red face. The crude brute had had the all-fired temerity to trail her down the street! Janet tugged her sleeve away, and said in a very high-pitched voice: "Take your hands off of me, you crude brute!"

The man actually laughed. "Come on," he said, reaching out his hand. "Let's cross the street first. I don't want myself sent sprawling by one of your local bumpkins on a bicycle."

Janet lifted her nose, picked up her skirts, and strutted across the street without looking left or right. When she reached the boardwalk on the other side, she was just about to keep strutting on, but the man grabbed her arm again and swung her around.

"Don't touch me!" she snapped, slapping his hand away. "If you don't leave me alone, and quit pestering, I'll shout out for help!"

The man blocked her way. "Listen," he said in quite a calm, reasonable voice. "I'm not trying to have my way with you. I recognize you from someplace, that's all, and when I saw you back there in Howard's, I was just trying to think where it was."

Janet turned her head away and did her best to look offended. In truth, she was quite intrigued to know where this mysterious stranger might have laid eyes on her before.

"I'll thank you," she said with a little quaver in her voice, "to let me pass by."

The stranger stepped out of her way. "I'm not detaining you, ma'am," he said.

Janet looked at him and frowned. He was simply standing

there, with a smile on his thick lips and a tiny mocking twinkle in his eyes.

"Well," she said uncomfortably, "thank you."

"It's my pleasure," he said.

She brushed her skirt down and adjusted her shopping bag. This man was too irritating! First he behaved like a brute, and wouldn't keep himself to himself; but now, when it seemed that he probably wasn't a brute, he kept himself to himself too much.

"I suppose you're not going to tell me," she said in the loftiest accents she could manage.

The man grinned. "I'm not going to pester you," he said obliquely.

"But you're not going to tell me, either?"

"Not unless you want to hear."

"Well," she said, giving in, "I can't remember having seen *you* before."

The man gently took her arm. "Let me tell you about it while we stroll along. I know you have an errand to run."

Janet was quite embarrassed, walking along Main Street with this big red-faced man in his working clothes, but she tried to look as composed as she could. She had seen Mrs. Mulliner going in to dinner with doddering old men, and if Mrs. Mulliner could escort unlikely-looking people with grace, then so could she.

"You work for Beatrice Mulliner, don't you?" asked the man. "I saw you out at Frank Edmunds' garden party on Saturday afternoon, but correct me if I'm wrong."

Janet blushed, for no reason at all. Perhaps it was the way the stranger referred to Mrs. Mulliner as "Beatrice."

"That's right," she said. "I'm housemaid at Mr. and Mrs. Mulliner's. I can't say I saw you at the garden party."

The man laughed. "No, I don't suppose you did. Not looking this way, anyhow. When I go to garden parties, I don't wear my working clothes."

She stared at him. "You mean . . . you went as a *guest*?"

He stopped walking, and gave a little bow. "In manner of speaking. Actually, I gate-crashed. I thought the food was good enough, but the conversation was pretty dull. Still, I guess I'm going to have to put up with it if I want to get on in local society. Is that whiskery old gent really Mrs. Mulliner's husband?"

Janet suppressed a smile. "Mr. Mulliner is older than Mrs.

14

Mulliner, yes, by a good few years. He runs a law business down on Fifth. He's a very amiable man, you know."

"Oh, sure," said the stranger reflectively. "I didn't say he wasn't."

Janet watched him for a while. She had never met such a curious person in her whole life. She knew she had to go, or else she'd be late back for the washing, but somehow she was reluctant to leave—at least until she had a clue about his identity and his extraordinary behavior. Why was a man who gate-crashed society parties walking around Main Street dressed like a common laborer? He was ugly and yet strangely fascinating, and she felt he had a power that was all his own. It wasn't just physical power, either. It was some kind of inside strength; some clear-cut definition of purpose that would never be deflected or slowed. The man ran his hand through his thinning yellow hair and looked back at Janet with a friendly grimace.

"Janet," he said, "I wonder if you could do a little thing to help me."

"It depends what it is."

"Well . . . I've been around this town for four or five days now, taking a look about. It strikes me that it could be the best place to set up business, and that's what I want to do."

Janet frowned. "There isn't anyone who's going to stop you."

The man moved aside to let a lad from the grocer's go past with a sack of potatoes. "I know that," he said. "But setting up business involves more than people tolerating you. They have to help you, as well. I need to know what goes on in this town, as far as business and society are both concerned, because I need to move fast and sure. Now, that's where your favor comes in."

"What is it?" asked Janet. "There isn't much I can do. I'm only the housemaid."

The man smiled. "You can spread a little gossip, that's what you can do. You can tell your mistress than an important fellow just came in from New York, aiming to set up in business here, and that his name is Johann Cornelius. That's all you need to say. Give it time, and everyone in town will want to know who I am, and where to find me."

"Is that all?" said Janet. "Just to say that Mr. Cornelius came to town and aims to set up shop?"

The stranger nodded. "That's all you have to do."

15

There was an odd pause. For a moment Janet wondered if Mr. Cornelius was going to give her some money, but when he kept smiling, and didn't make any kind of move to go for his pockets, it was plain that he expected the favor *gratis*.

She said slowly: "Don't think I'm not being neighborly, Mr. Cornelius, but free favors is something you do for your friends."

He smiled. "Aren't you my friend?"

"I've only known you for five minutes! Friendship is like a sheltering tree, Mr. Cornelius, but you can't shade yourself under half a twig."

He thought for a while. Then he said: "Okay, let's *make* friends. If you have a day off this week, I'll take you down to the meadow carnival."

She widened those surprised gray eyes. "Mr. Cornelius . . . you'll have to give me time to think about that. I do have . . . well, another admirer."

He took her hand and kissed it. It was a bit like being kissed by the red rubber ring around a pear-preserving jar. She glanced nervously around the busy streets to see if anyone noticed.

"Janet," he said. "All men, when they see you, are your admirers. Leave a message round at Howard's when you've made up your mind. Meanwhile, I have work to do, and so do you. It's been a great and cordial pleasure to meet you, and I look forward to seeing you again."

He smiled one brief smile, and then he strode off down the boardwalk, disappearing at the corner of Eighth. Janet stood staring after him for a whole minute, and then walked with uncertain steps toward Scully's Hardware.

"Something on your mind?" said Scully in the dim, soapy-smelling depths of the store.

Janet shook her head. "I'm not sure, Mr. Scully," she said quietly. "I think I just met someone very strange. Either that, or a villain. Or maybe both. I hope I don't ever have to find out which."

At lunchtime, hot and hungry, Johann Cornelius went into Parsons' Lunch Rooms on Second Street, on the peeling and impoverished side of the business district, and sat at a bare wooden table with a white basin of salt beef and dumplings, price eight cents.

Parsons' was a workingman's place, and unlike the middle-class restaurants in town, where conversation buzzed over the midday meal like a swarm of bluebottles, Parsons' was silent, as exhausted and ravenous men hunched over their food. Johann joined them, digging his cheap spoon into the solid dumplings, and breaking his rough brown bread with his hands.

He knew now, as a fact of life, that starting afresh in a new world·was neither romantic nor exciting. It was, instead, as lonely and painful and dispiriting as any human condition could be. Today—August 13, 1900—Johann Cornelius was twenty-seven years old, but the family celebrations that would have given his birthday any joy were absent, and so he studiously tried to think of it as an ordinary day, with no special significance at all. Growing older was not so important as surviving, and in any case the span of his life was already known and determined by the Lord, and nothing he could do would ever alter that. His only mission now was to set up in business and make money. The Lord helps those who help themselves.

Johann had been in America for a little over two years. He hardly thought at all about his family now, except in odd, unpredictable, and highly romanticized fragments. Johann, as a boy, had always had a passion for engineering—for anything mechanical, complex, and mathematical. His father, a dairy hand in Amersfoort, Holland, had worked for years to put Johann through school, so that he might become a great engineer. The year that Johann graduated, his father had a paralyzing stroke, for no apparent reason at all, while crossing a thundery field to fetch his cows. Johann had sacrificed his great engineering career to work at home and care for his mother, his debilitated father, and his six younger brothers and sisters.

No one knew how he really felt. No one knew that for all those years he sweated and labored in the dairy with a terrible gnawing frustration and bitterness, regretting his lost chance like a magnificently wrapped gift box that turns out to contain nothing but a badly knitted pair of khaki mittens. One day in 1897 he took his lunch of cheese and black bread from his mother, walked down the puddly lane, turned right instead of left, and never went home again. He still had dreams about his tired, plain-faced mother and his nodding, grunting, paralyzed father, but in the daytime he shut out such guilty visions with brightly colored pictures of Holland

17

with red-brick pavements, black-and-white cows, and pretty skies of chintz blue and puffy white clouds.

He had cadged a ride from a cheese wagon bound for 's-Gravenhage, and from there he walked to Scheveningen, and spent his last guilders on a boat ride to England. He knew two words of English—"yes" and "tolerance." "Tolerance" was an engineering word, and had nothing to do with religious freedom, which was why most Dutch people left their own country. He had found a job in Balham, a suburb of London, as a toolmaker and engineer, going back at night to a damp room which smelled of leaking gas and dirty bed linen. He remembered London for its huddled rooftops of rain-slicked slate, its yellow smoky skies, and a desperate feeling that life was always going to be like this.

In 1897, one rainy night in November, in Garratt Lane, Balham, he saw a poster in the window of a bootmaker's shop advertising passage to New York. There was a stirring etching of a White Star steamer, pennants flapping, bounding over a millpond sea on its way to the New World. The ships left Liverpool every Wednesday, and the steerage passage was four pounds. Johann went home that evening, opened up his tin money box, and discovered he had twenty-five shillings saved.

Through December, January, and February—a bitter London winter of deep snow and endlessly lead-colored skies—Johann starved himself for the price of a ticket. On Christmas Day 1897 he sat alone in his room and ate thin barley soup. By St. Valentine's Day 1898 he had the last threepence he needed, and the following day he went to the White Star office and bought his ticket.

The etching of the Royal Mail steamer sailing happily through calm waters turned out to be a product of artistic license. On a sloping, heaving Atlantic, Johann huddled under a sodden blanket, listening to the wretched crying of sick children, the coughing of old men, and the ceaseless pounding of the engines that bore them all relentlessly toward their unknown destiny. He felt exhausted and lonely, and he spent night after night in prayer.

With hundreds of other immigrants he was herded through Ellis Island. On his first day in New York, it rained from dawn until nightfall, and he was soaked through. But with time, and miles of painful walking, he found himself a job downtown with Nathaniel's Engineering, a small corporation that made brake systems for locomotives. Old man Nathaniel, an iron-haired German immigrant with half-glasses and a liking for canary-colored vests, had grown to like Johann, and had told him a few things about business, and particularly engineering business.

"It don't matter how good you are, you may be a genius," he used to say, lighting up his pungent meerschaum pipe. "What you have to do in engineering is make people think they can't do without you. Make them think you're indispensable. As soon as they start thinking that, you will be. Also, make yourself a lot of friends. It don't matter if you hate the sight of them. In this country, people give a helping hand to friends before they give a clenched fist to strangers, because this, my lad, is a country full of strangers."

Johann had kept his mouth shut, and nodded, and learned. In the late afternoon, when old man Nathaniel had gone home, he used to take out the corporation's accounting books and pore over them for hours at a time, until he knew the financial structure of Nathaniel's Engineering like the wallpaper next to his own bed. He learned the price of labor and the price of steel; the price of springs, screws, bolts, and spare parts.

At nine o'clock every evening he went to a night school on the Bowery, learning English from a fat Dutch spinster who wore black flannel dresses and black veiled hats. Over the weekends he took a brown paper bag with bread and sausage and walked around the streets of New York, keeping his eyes and his ears open. He explored the Battery and the ghetto; he pushed his way through the colorful crowds on Grand Street, and he mingled with the Italian festivities in Chatham Square. He also walked uptown and stood outside the magnificent mansions of the American rich. Once, outside 26 Broadway, he saw John D. Rockefeller himself, in his dark, perfectly tailored morning suit, and his heavy whiskers. What gave him the strangest feeling of all was that Rockefeller, so incredibly rich, was just the same size as he was—shorter, in fact.

During the months that he spent in New York, Johann tried as hard as he could to suppress his nostalgia for Holland, although one summer evening he sat in Van Cortlandt Park with tears running down his cheeks. He visited the Dutch graves on Staten Island, too, for no reason but to read their inscriptions under his breath.

He was desperately lonely, but he felt that his loneliness was an essential part of his destiny. Being alone enabled him to work twice as hard, with twice the intensity and the dedication. He made two friends at work—a young Irishman called Danny O'Sullivan and a

Jewish boy with a stutter called Ira Greenbaum—and sometimes they went out and ate their lunch together down at the docks. He also went out twice with a plump Italian girl he met at night school. The first time they went to a variety concert on Broadway; the second time she took him home to Washington Street to meet her parents. They fed him with *dolma*, plied him with muscatel, and then congratulated him, to his complete amazement, on his forthcoming marriage to their daughter. He skipped night school for two weeks after that, and when he plucked up the nerve to attend again, she was no longer there.

In the early summer of 1900 he was making $6.35 a week, and old man Nathaniel, one June morning, made a hint about promotion. That weekend he took a long walk up to the mid-Fifties, on Fifth Avenue, and for a whole Saturday afternoon he wandered among expensive carriages with top-hatted coachmen; women in furs and feathers and diamonds; men in starched white shirts and handmade shoes. He sat on one of the stone benches outside the Forty-second Street Library, with pigeons strutting around his ankles, and ate dry biscuits from his pockets. He made up his mind right then that he was going to be rich.

Johann had saved enough at Nathaniel's for two important things. One was a steam-packet ticket to Galveston, Texas. The other was a secondhand dress suit and shirt, which he bought from a pushcart on the East Side. He packed his worn-out brown suitcase and left New York without giving his notice and without saying good-bye to anyone.

Now, on his birthday, he sat in Parsons' Lunch Rooms, in Broughton, Texas, as poor as before but with his ambitions sharply defined. Not only his ambitions, but his techniques, too. As far as he saw it, the barrier between the rich and the poor was obvious. It was not much to do with hard work, and it was nothing at all to do with luck. To be rich, you needed to start off rich. Money could never be made without money. Wealth was created by the shrewd use of money itself; and great wealth could only be created by the use of lesser wealth. Once you had dollars that didn't need to be earmarked for shelter, clothing, and basins of salt beef and dumplings, you had the means to lift yourself out of penury and into plenitude. In finance, you needed money as your tool just as much as a carpenter needs his hammer.

Johann's problem was that he *had* no money. He had eleven dollars that he saved from his months of work in New York, and that was going to have to feed him and keep him for at least a month. But he had made up his mind that, in the absence of real dollars, imaginary dollars would have to do. He would give the appearance of reasonable wealth and hope that the illusion would be enough to attract the real thing. That's why he had gate-crashed the local society party on Saturday, painstakingly dressed in his carefully pressed suit and shirt, and that's why he was doing his best to make the acquaintance of everybody in Broughton who meant anything at all. The Mulliners, he decided, were a good bet.

The man next to him, a greasy-faced railroad worker, was covetously staring at Johann's piece of bread. He was obviously hoping that Johann had had enough to eat and would leave some behind. Johann raised his eyes and saw him. The man didn't look away. He had sunken cheeks and thin, callused hands.

Slowly and obviously Johann stuffed his bread into his own mouth and chewed it. The railroad worker watched every chew, as if Johann might change his mind halfway through masticating it and let him have a piece. Only when Johann swallowed did the railroad worker drop his eyes and carry on eating his thin red-cabbage soup.

Johann had made himself an unbending rule. Dollars could never be made by those who gave away pennies. He knew from his reading that if the richest man in America bought everyone in the whole country just one steak dinner each, he would go bankrupt overnight. Making money and *using* money was, in the long run, a far more charitable act. Even though the railroad worker stared at him resentfully, Johann knew that the Lord would understand, and was unshakably on his side.

He left his boardinghouse the next morning in his best suit. The house was a clean but shabby clapboard building on the corner of Lubbock Street, overlooking the stockyards. Broughton, above all, had been founded on the sale and transportation of cattle, although these days it also boasted a light engineering works that made kitchen ranges, and the T. F. Pusey Rifle Company. Johann had already been around to both of these factories, loitering near the gates in his workingman's clothes, and had formed some opinions about their production, their capacity, and their needs.

He was nervous, and he couldn't help sweating. At Sixth Street he took out his ragged white handkerchief and wiped his hands. Then he turned the corner into Fifth and made his way toward the Broughton National Bank, a solid and respectable-looking orange-brick building on the north side of the street. He pushed through the mahogany swing doors into the musty, marble-floored interior, and walked up to the high counter.

A clerk in spectacles said: "Yes?"

Johann said brusquely: "I have an appointment with Mr. Greaves. My name is Cornelius."

"Yes, sir," said the clerk, and went to tap on the manager's door.

Mr. Greaves was a tall, thin, and fidgety man with a habit of putting his glasses on and taking them off every few seconds, and of taking his pocket watch out of his vest and lifting the lid and snapping it shut, and then tucking it away again, and running his hand hurriedly through his thin gray hair, and coughing, and crossing and uncrossing his legs. He ushered Johann into his office, and offered him a seat, and then sat down himself behind his large leather-topped desk.

"Well, Mr. Cornelius, I've heard about you," said Mr. Greaves, shifting in his chair.

Johann raised his eyebrows. News obviously traveled very fast in a small town like Broughton. He lowered his eyes modestly and said: "Good things, I hope, Mr. Greaves?"

Mr. Greaves smiled. "Well enough, Mr. Cornelius. Well enough."

Johann smiled back. He knew that he was sitting too rigid in his chair, and that his hands were clenched tight on the brim of his hat. But he also knew that this interview could mean the difference between wealth and poverty. As he said years later to one of his children: "It was 'the crunch.' It was one of those moments when you know your whole life is at stake, and there is nothing you can do but fight for your own survival."

Johann tried to relax. He gripped the brim of his stiff black hat and said quietly: "I'm an engineer."

Mr. Greaves smiled patiently. "Yes. I heard you were."

"I'm thinking of starting up in business in Broughton. I came from New York, where I was partner in a locomotive brake company, and I heard that Texas was short on engineers, so down I came."

"I see," said Mr. Greaves in the manner of a man who patently doesn't.

"Texas, I heard, was a boom state. There's cattle, and oil, and a great need for good transportation."

"That's so," said Mr. Greaves. He crossed his legs, then

changed his mind and uncrossed them, and looked at Johann with an odd, impatient look, as if he wished he would finish what it was he had to say, and leave him alone to fidget in peace.

"I . . . er . . . I believe . . ."

Johann couldn't seem to find the words. Mr. Greaves twitched and fiddled and fidgeted, and the more he fidgeted, the more difficult Johann found it was to speak. He suddenly realized the enormity of what he was trying to do, and it seemed so impossible and ludicrous that he almost felt like apologizing, saying "good day," and walking out backward while the going was good.

"I . . . er . . . believe there's a healthy need in Broughton for a maintenance works . . ."

Mr. Greaves raised his eyebrows. "Maintenance works?"

"Yes. . . . I mean for engineering . . . there's all these machines—locomotives and lathes and steam presses and so forth—and I guess they break down quite often. They need maintenance, which is just where I come in."

Johann paused. He felt uncertain and embarrassed. He was trying to make a play for more money than he'd ever seen in his whole life before, and he couldn't even find the words to speak a simple sentence. He felt feverish and sweaty, and Mr. Greaves's neat little office seemed as airless and claustrophobic as a closed safe.

Mr. Greaves opened a silver cigarette box, passed it over, and said: "Smoke?"

Johann shook his head.

"I . . . er . . . feel that . . . er . . ."

"Yes, Mr. Cornelius?" said Mr. Greaves, lighting a cigarette himself and puffing smoke. The smell of it made Johann feel sweatier than ever, and he had a strong desire to walk out, leave the bank altogether, and stand in the street to breathe some fresh air. *Get yourself together,* he thought, staring at the brim of his hat. *Get yourself together and tell this man what you want. If you don't succeed now, you never will.*

"I believe that there's a need for such a works in Broughton," said Johann slowly. "And because of that, I'd like to get one going. I've spent a few days here now, and I've toured the factories and sounded out some real-estate agents, and I believe the whole thing's feasible. Not only feasible, but potentially profitable."

He spoke the abstract words he had learned in night school with immaculate care.

Mr. Greaves rested back in his chair, smoking. Even when he

was relaxed he couldn't stay still, and he passed the cigarette from one hand to the other, and twiddled it around and around, and sucked at it with the habit-ridden disinterest of a caged monkey sucking a grape.

Johann remained rigid, his back straight and his feet neatly together. His polished shoes were side by side, as if they were still in the box.

"Well," sniffed Mr. Greaves. "How much do you want to borrow?"

Johann licked his lips. It seemed, for one strange moment, as if he might actually get what he wanted. Magically and without fuss. But he reminded himself that lending money was, after all, a bank manager's job. Just because he was asking how much Johann wanted to borrow, that didn't mean he approved of Johann's ideas, or considered that Johann's credentials were adequate.

"About . . . ten thousand dollars."

"*About* ten thousand dollars? I see. Give or take how much?"

Johann nodded. "Give or take a nickel."

The bank manager laughed, until his laugh turned to splutters, and his splutters into a hacking cough.

"Excuse me," he said, wiping his mouth with his big green handkerchief. "I shouldn't smoke."

Johann shrugged nervously. "I've heard it's bad for the heart," he said. It was all he could think of to say.

Mr. Greaves said: "*Everything* about being a bank manager is bad for the heart. My doctor says I ought to spend six months on the Gulf, recuperating. He tells me to give up brandy-sodas and Havana cigars, and run around the goddamned lawn every evening. If I did what my doctor told me, I'd be dead in three days. I take sweet spirits of niter six times a day, and essence of pepsin four times a day, and I still feel sick as a dog."

Johann smiled politely. "Er . . . about this ten thousand dollars . . ."

Mr. Greaves crossed his legs again and gave two or three sage and serious nods of the head to show that they were back to business.

"Well," he said. "Ten thousand dollars is a great deal of money. I presume you have some kind of prospectus for this maintenance works of yours. Financial profiles, estimates of labor and materiél, employment requirements, that kind of thing."

Johann reached into his coat pocket. Out of a clean manila envelope he had bought yesterday afternoon, he took the pages of neat financial statistics he had laboriously prepared in New York, many of them based on the workings of Nathaniel's. He passed them across the desk, and for five silent minutes Mr. Greaves went through them, a tiny frown creasing the middle of his bony forehead, his fingers twitching the edges of the pages.

Johann relaxed a little and looked around the bank manager's office. There was an elaborately decorated six-hundred-pound Fireking safe in one corner, with a sepia photograph of Mr. Greaves's wife on top of it. In another corner stood a tall filing cabinet, with the names of local businesses on neat handwritten labels. Once you had your name in there, thought Johann, you were respectable. You had money. You had started off on your way to wealth. Sitting in front of Mr. Greaves as he was now, he felt like a shabby pauper, a penniless immigrant with nothing but the clothes he stood up in. He didn't yet understand the meaning of true wealth, but he knew, without any question, the meaning of poverty. He closed his eyes for a moment, and clenched his hands together, and prayed silently to God for guidance.

There was a rustle of papers. "Mr. Cornelius?" said Mr. Greaves. Johann, embarrassed, opened his eyes.

"These financial estimates seem to be excellent," said Mr. Greaves. "I haven't seen sounder prospectus work for years. Usually they come along with a few numbers scribbled on the back of an old sugar bag and expect me to lend them money on the basis of that."

He chuckled, and Johann, tense as a cat trying to stalk a bird twice its own size, chuckled with him.

"You say you've been talking to real-estate agents?" asked Mr. Greaves.

Johann nodded again. "There's an empty store down on Fourth Street that looks pretty useful. I went to see it yesterday. They're asking three dollars and nineteen cents a week."

Mr. Greaves sucked at his cigarette. "Well," he said, "I guess you could always beat them down a bit. Fourth Street isn't exactly millionaires' row."

"No, it isn't. But it's near the railroad yards and it's close to the factories, and that's what counts."

Mr. Greaves nodded. "Sure. Now, what about *security*?"

This was the crucial moment. Johann felt his heart rising and falling, and there seemed to be so much tight breath in his body he could hardly say anything sensible.

"We're not talking about an *unsecured loan*, I hope," chuckled Mr. Greaves, as if the idea of unsecured loans was the funniest thing since the Yellow Kid.

Johann tried to laugh, too. But then he had to say in a small, dry voice: "Mr. Greaves, I realize I'm asking you to take a great deal on trust, but the fact of the matter is that I am asking for ten thousand dollars without security."

There was a silence. Mr. Greaves stared at him for a moment, and then shook his head.

"Mr. Cornelius, I'm *very* sorry—"

Johann said: "Please. Don't tell me you're sorry. Please just listen to what I've worked out."

Mr. Greaves sighed. "Well, of course I'll listen. But you know, Mr. Cornelius, that we can never lend money without some kind of guarantee that it will ultimately find its way back to us. We take risks, like everyone else; but if I were to give you ten thousand dollars, on your say-so alone, well, then, everybody and anybody would be doing it, and where would I stand then? I'd have an empty bank."

Johann said: "Mr. Greaves, I am not 'anybody.' "

Mr. Greaves smiled. "I know you're not in *your* eyes, Mr. Cornelius, and I assure you that you're not in mine. But in the eyes of the bank's board of governors, I regret that you are. You don't even have an account here."

Johann took out his last ten dollars, ten creased one-dollar bills, and dropped them on Mr. Greaves's desk. "If that's your objection, I'll open one now."

Mr. Greaves shook his head. "That's not the objection, Mr. Cornelius. I have heard favorable things about you from several people in this town already. I'm sure you are a man of reasonable substance. But ten thousand dollars . . ."

Johann laid his hand firmly on Mr. Greaves's leather-topped desk. "Mr. Greaves," he said, "if you lend me ten thousand dollars, you will be doing something you will never, in the whole of your life, regret."

"With respect, Mr. Cornelius, if I lend you ten thousand dollars unsecured, and my governors get to hear of it, I may never even *live* to regret it."

26

"I will bring you a note," said Johann stubbornly.

"What kind of a note?"

"I will bring you a note from all the businessmen in Broughton, all the men who will want to use my maintenance works. Between them, they will guarantee your loan of ten thousand dollars."

Mr. Greaves sat back, twiddling his thumbs together, and thought about that.

"I think you're underestimating the businessmen of Broughton, Mr. Cornelius. They're a hard-baked bunch."

A week later Johann walked down Beaumont Street, head bent, like a man on his way to discuss his mother's funeral. The weather was cooler, and a fresh breeze was blowing from the Gulf, making the palms rustle, and the delicate flowers tremble on their creepers. He was dressed in the same dark suit he had worn to the bank, and the same stiff black derby hat, and his black shoes were very brightly polished.

He reached number 15 and stopped. It was a secluded, graceful house, surrounded by trees and white-painted wooden palings, with a wooden colonnade and a shaded veranda. There was a heavy scent of flowers, and from the leafy retreats of the garden a Negro woman was singing "Ella Speed." Johann walked up to the gate, looked up the pathway at the imposing entrance, and not for the first time felt a deep pang of hesitation and anxiety.

> *Come on, and ta-ake heed,*
> *Let me tell ya 'bout poor Ella Speed . . .*

He clicked open the gate and walked up the path. Out of his breast pocket he took a clean white card, and then he rang at the gleaming brass bell pull. Somewhere inside the house a chime went *binggg-bonggg*. He stood fidgeting on the veranda, tapping his card against his hand, waiting for someone to answer the door. A small tufty bird flittered onto the veranda rail beside him, chirped, and flew off.

The Negro voice sang:

> *Ella Speed was downtown, she was havin' her lovin' fun . . .*
> *Let me tell ya what Bill Morton done . . .*

The glossy black door opened up just a crack, and a white-faced parlormaid stared out.

"Yes?" she asked sharply.

"I've, er . . . I've come to call on Mr. and Mrs. Mulliner."

The maid opened the door a fraction more. She was a peaky little girl with a lacy apron and bright red ears.

"Mr. Mulliner isn't at home, and Mrs. Mulliner is resting."

Johann coughed. "Well, I only came to leave this."

He held out his card. He had had fifty printed, in the hope that they would give his name more authority. They read, in copperplate script: "Johann Cornelius, Gentleman Engineer."

The maid took the card and read it, moving her lips as she read. Then she said brusquely: "Very well, sir. I'll see that Mr. Mulliner receives it. Good day, sir."

Johann said: "Good day."

The door closed, and he was left on his own on the veranda. He coughed, and turned around, and made his way back down the path, his head still bent, and a persistent frown on his forehead. He was beginning to acquire the look of a man who, despite years of hopeful struggle, has come at last to realize that time is running out, and that his great and golden opportunity may never arrive. With his two years' work in New York, Johann had bought himself the chance of starting afresh, and of building the foundations of a fortune. But now, with only three dollars and seventy-five cents left, he was sliding inexorably toward that moment when he would be forced back into daily employment, for the basic wants of food, drink and a place to sleep. If it was God's will, though, he would have to bear it.

Johann was not an easy man to understand because he hardly understood himself. He was both shy and stubborn; ambitious and cautious; aggressive and defensive. He believed in his own strength and his own determination, but he was also resigned to the casual and even arbitrary intervention of God in his affairs. He never spared himself any discomfort; and he didn't particularly sympathize with the discomfort of others. But at the same time he was wholly entranced by visions of great wealth, and all the comforts and privileges that great wealth could muster. He didn't even stop to wonder whether he might *enjoy* riding in carriages, or drinking vintage wines, or dining like a gourmet, or not. He had no education in art and music, and very little understanding of history and culture. He knew a good tune when he heard it, and he knew the importance of a clean collar, but that was almost as far as his taste extended itself. When you talked to Johann Cornelius, you felt that inside his mind there was an unbending sense of belief, but after a while you began to ask—*in what*?

He stood on the corner of Beaumont Street, the shady and well-turfed racetrack of Broughton's superior citizens, and tried to decide what to do next. The truth was, he had spent four days making appointments with factory managers and railroad chiefs, and every one had turned him down. It was not that they weren't interested in the idea of a maintenance works. It was simply that investment money was short; and they would rather risk their capital in their own businesses than in his. Thomas F. Pusey, the riflemaker, had stroked his ginger whiskers, shaken his head slowly, and said: "If I had ten thousand dollars to set to chance, I'd just as soon take a ride on a Mississippi steamer, and gamble it all on faro."

Now, as a final effort, Johann was trying to make the acquaintance of Broughton's high society, in the struggling hope that someone of substance might underwrite his loan.

He was just about to cross the road when he heard a high-pitched voice calling his name. He turned around, and there was the parlormaid from number 15, and she was running toward him with her heavy skirts held up, waving his little white card.

"Mr. Cornelius! Mr. Cornelius!"

She reached him, panting and flushed. "Mr. Cornelius," she said. "I gave your card to Mrs. Mulliner, and Mrs. Mulliner asked if you would care to take some morning coffee with her."

Johann raised his eyebrows. "Coffee—now?"

"Yes, sir. And she said she'd be terribly disappointed if you couldn't come."

Johann said slowly: "Well, then, I guess I mustn't disappoint her. I thought you said she was resting."

"She was, sir," said the parlormaid. "But when she heard who it was who had called, she changed her mind, and decided to quit resting, and take some coffee."

"I'm flattered," said Johann as he walked with the parlormaid back to the house. "I believe I'm flattered."

The inside of the Mulliner house was dim, musty, and sumptuously high-Victorian. Dwarfing the hallway was a massive oak sideboard with ornate carving all over its doors and feet. fluting down its front, and brass handles in the shape of seashells. There was an umbrella stand made from an elephant's foot and a rigid-looking chair. On the walls hung a series of gloomy etchings of

Canadian forests, and an oil painting of an elk with some anatomical problem to do with its neck. Johann was led by the parlormaid into the morning room, and requested to wait. Mrs. Mulliner was "fixing herself," and would be down in a trice.

If the hallway was supposed to be impressive, the morning room was the *salle de résistance*. Heavily figured drapes of dark wine-red hung at the windows, and behind these were *point d'esprit* lace curtains, embroidered with baskets of roses, to strain out all but the mellowest of sunlights. Over the mantelshelf was a drape of green velour, decorated with a pond-lily pattern and trimmed with a knotted silk fringe. The shelf was crowded with daguerreotypes, pottery figurines, spider plants, paperweights, chiming clocks, silver candelabra, and souvenir knickknacks. The five-piece parlor furniture suite—upright settee, armchairs, and rocker—was carved out of gloomy and grotesquely Gothic oak, upholstered in crimson velour, and as uncomfortable to sit on as it was to look at. The walls were papered in a busy brown floral motif, and clustered with etchings, silhouettes, and embroidered samplers. It was clear that Mrs. Mulliner, apart from her talents with interior decor, also considered herself accomplished with needles and colored thread.

Looking about the morning room, Johann found himself knee-deep in occasional tables, aspidistra pots, side tables, parlor stands, and china cabinets—marooned amidst the washed-up flotsam of middle-class Texan taste. There was a cloying fragrance like pot-pourri, and an airlessness that made him perspire.

Johann waited for five minutes, pacing the Brussels rug, before Beatrice Mulliner swished aside the portiere and made her entrance.

"Mr. *Cornelius*," she breathed, greeting him like a long-lost friend, and lifting her hand to be kissed. "How *lovely* of you to call."

Johann touched his lips to her diamonds and sapphires, and attempted a bow. "The pleasure is all mine, Mrs. Mulliner. I was passing, that's all, and I remembered you and your husband from the Edmundses' party, and how charming you'd been, and wished to pay my respects."

"*Respects*?" said Beatrice Mulliner, fluttering her eyelashes. "What a wonderful man you are. Please sit down. I've heard so much about you, and I'm absolutely *agog* to hear more."

They sat—Johann very upright on the settee, and Beatrice Mulliner, with elegant poise, on a nearby armchair.

30

"Do you like walnut cake?" said Mrs. Mulliner in her provocative, husky voice. "I just *adore* it. I could eat it until I explode. But I must watch my figure, you know. I mustn't *always* overindulge myself."

Johann thought Beatrice Mulliner had a remarkable figure. She was a brunette, of medium height, with a thin, well-boned, and almost beautiful face. Her eyes were very large, with long lashes, and they had a feline tilt to them. Her mouth was a little weak, but her long and creamy-white neck, decorated with a seven-strand choker of sparkling jet beads, more than made up for it. She wore a cashmere tea gown of Chinese blue, with a wide lace-trimmed collar that reached to her shoulders, full sleeves and lace-trimmed cuffs. The gown was tied with ribbon at the neck, and a ribbon at the back drew it into her tiny waist. Johann could just see her toes, in gray silk slippers, peeping out from under her hem.

There was a quality about Beatrice Mulliner that, on first sight, attracted and disturbed Johann greatly. She was respectable, well-off, and an honorable lady member of Broughton's middle-class society. Yet she was magnetically and immediately attractive, sensuous and suggestive; the last woman you'd expect to find in a one-and-a-half-horse town in south Texas, married to a whiskery old buffer more than ten years her senior. There was no doubt at all that Beatrice Mulliner was a puzzle; although whether she was the kind of puzzle that a man would be able to solve in a God-fearing manner was another question altogether.

The parlormaid brought in coffee and walnut cake on rose-decorated plates and set them up on a parlor stand. Mrs. Mulliner dismissed her, and insisted on pouring the coffee herself. Johann, who expected a high degree of formality from upper-class society, was mildly concerned about this.

"You have a fine household here, Mrs. Mulliner," he said stiffly.

Beatrice Mulliner smiled, and Johann noticed that she had gaps between her teeth.

"You mustn't call me Mrs. Mulliner. That sounds too stuffy for words. Call me Beatrice, or Bea if you like. Some people do call me Bea when they're feeling *affectionate*."

"Oh," said Johann, taking a cake plate and resting it on his knee. There was something in Beatrice Mulliner's manner that made him feel extremely awkward and gauche.

"Mind you," breathed Beatrice, "in my firmament there is

31

never very much affection. Do you believe, Johann, that people can be starved of love, just as much as they can be starved of walnut cake?''

Johann had his mouth full. When he tried to answer, crumbs dropped on his lap, and he blushed.

"I don't know," he said, swallowing hard.

Beatrice sighed. "I believe that love is food, Johann. You don't mind me calling you Johann, do you? I believe that love is as much like food as beef, and curly kale.''

"I'm sorry," said Johann. "I don't understand.''

Beatrice shook her head. Her upswept hair was pinned and brushed, and shone in the soft sunlight that fell through the decorated lace curtains.

"It doesn't matter. It's one of those things that is of no particular consequence. Liddy, you see, doesn't *enjoy* discussing love, and so I have to do the best that I can.''

"Liddy?''

"Oh—that's my husband. I call him Liddy but his real name is Lidmore. Isn't it strange? Mind you, his parents were Irish, and the Irish are quite capable of anything. Do you know that he sings in his sleep?''

Johann sipped coffee. "No," he said. "I didn't know that.''

"He has a penchant for popular songs." Beatrice sighed. "The other night, after a dinner party with the Greaveses, he lay in bed and sang 'I'm Old, But I'm Awfully Tough.' And, can you believe it, he was deep asleep, and when I told him in the morning, he didn't remember a thing.''

Johann laid down his coffee cup. "Mrs. Mulliner—Beatrice—I can't help wondering if you're teasing me some. Pulling my leg.''

Beatrice smiled. "A little, perhaps. But it's so nice to have a man's company. I mean a real man. I suppose I get silly, and carried away.''

Johann said: "I don't know much about ladies' interests myself. I guess I've always had to put other things first.''

Beatrice looked interested. "Really? What on earth could you put before *that*?''

Johann lowered his eyes. He didn't answer.

Beatrice suddenly leaned forward and touched his hand with hers, and said: "Janet, my housemaid, said you chased after her down the street. She said you were dressed like a workingman. She was quite disgusted. Especially when you wouldn't give her any money to spread your little rumor."

Johann looked up. "She told you about that?"

"Of course she did. Janet's a little bit silly sometimes, and she's always slacking; but she and I get on quite well, considering we're mistress and servant. Janet doesn't even appreciate herself how good she is at keeping me informed. I like to know, you see, what's going on."

Johann laid his tea plate on the occasional table next to him. "And what did you conclude?" he asked. "I mean . . . after Janet had told you?"

Beatrice said: "I didn't conclude anything, except that everything everyone was saying about you was inconclusive. I've been watching you, you know, ever since you gate-crashed the Edmundses' garden party. You're an odd duck, if you don't mind my saying so."

Johann smiled.

"I think," went on Beatrice, still touching his hand, "that you're one of two things."

"Oh? What?"

"Well," said Beatrice, "I think that you're either very rich, and that you've come to Broughton to sweep us off our feet and shake us all up, or else . . ."

Beatrice paused. There was almost a look of regret in her eyes.

"Or else what?" said Johann throatily.

"Or else . . . you're extremely poor," said Beatrice in a very quiet voice.

There was a long silence. Beatrice looked at Johann, and Johann looked down at the small piece of uneaten walnut cake on his plate. The clocks on the mantelshelf, three of them, began to chime the hour of eleven. At last Johann said: "Beatrice, your husband is a man of means."

"Yes. Why? That's about all."

"All?"

Beatrice twisted a ring on her finger and smiled. "Poor Liddy—all means and no beans."

Johann coughed. "I'd rather not—"

"I know you'd rather not," interrupted Beatrice. "Everybody in the whole world would rather not. Liddy is a dear, respected gentleman. He is a pillar of Broughton society, and at

Thanksgiving we include him in our prayers. Everybody would rather not say anything about Liddy, because Liddy is a saint.''

"You sound bitter. What do you have to be bitter about?"

Beatrice gave a hard little laugh. "Material possessions, my dear Johann, are no consolation for emotional impoverishment. Look at this room. It's wonderful, isn't it? Grand luxury, the best that Liddy's money can buy. It has everything, and for your information we are even buying a horseless carriage. What it doesn't have is very much in the way of love.''

Johann said: "Beatrice, I don't think . . .''

She sighed. "I know. I'm talking about love again. You must think I'm such a bore. You wanted to talk about money, didn't you? Money is so much more fascinating than love.''

"I was simply trying to see if Liddy—your husband—might be interested in some investment.''

Beatrice said: "Investment?''

"Yes—that's right. I'm starting an engineering works in Broughton, and I'm looking for investors.''

"Do you want some more coffee?''

"What?''

"Do you want more coffee? There's plenty left.''

Johann held out his cup. "Thank you, yes. You see, I was wondering if your husband—''

Beatrice shook her head. "Liddy is not interested in investment. Liddy is not really interested in anything. You can try to persuade him, but you won't get very far. Are you taking Janet to the carnival?''

Johann watched Beatrice closely while she poured his coffee. He was beginning to feel suspicious about her motives in asking him here. She was obviously playing some kind of game with him, but he didn't have enough experience with women to be able to sense the tack of their devious ploys. He stirred his coffee with his tiny silver spoon, and didn't say anything at all.

"Janet said that you promised to take her," said Beatrice lightly. "As a kind of reward for spreading your reputation about.''

"Well—" said Johann, but Beatrice interrupted him.

"Why *do* you want your reputation spread about, Johann? Is it that you're trying to make us believe something that's true? Or is it that you're trying to make us believe something that's *not* true? Do tell, I've been dying to know.''

34

Johann coughed and lowered his head. Once again he felt like an amateur. He knew what he wanted out of his life, and he hoped he knew how to get it. But he had a great deal to learn about business techniques and intricate social maneuvers. Beatrice evidently knew where this conversation and this questioning were leading; but Johann didn't have an inkling, and simply stumbled suspiciously along behind her, hoping he would sense the inevitable ambush before it was sprung.

"I'm a businessman," he told her quite bluntly. "Every businessman wants his reputation spread around. You know what they say—'early to work, early to rise, stick to your job and advertise.' "

Beatrice laughed. Then she gazed at Johann very seriously, with her feline eyes wide open. She knew she looked her best when she made big eyes like that, and Johann felt an errant surge of attraction for her. There was no question that Beatrice Mulliner was a disturbing woman—both to look at and to know.

"Johann," she said in a throaty voice, "do you believe in the sanctity of marriage?"

He frowned. "I don't understand."

She leaned closer. "Johann, do you think it's right for married women, sometimes, to entertain admirers?"

"Well . . . I guess it depends."

"There's no love in my life, Johann. Liddy is a true and honest man, and he cares for me well. In every way except one."

"Mrs. Mulliner, I think this conversation is on dangerous ground."

She widened her eyes again. "Dangerous? There's nothing dangerous about me, Johann. Nothing dangerous happens in this house. This house is safe and secure and respectable."

Johann said nothing. The more he talked to Beatrice, and the more she coaxed and flirted with him, the more unsettled he became. He felt he could quite easily kiss her. He felt he could quite easily do more than that. But she was a temptation that the Lord had, quite deliberately, placed in his path, and he knew that if he succumbed to the urges of his flesh, he would probably be lost forever. Nonetheless, he had to place his saucer discreetly over his lap.

Beatrice stood up and went to the window. The thin sunlight made flower-basket patterns across her cheeks.

"I will be perfectly candid with you, Johann. I am a lonely

woman who is craving for affection. I knew when I first saw you that you were a strong and affectionate man. You were drinking champagne at the Edmundses' garden party, and you were standing in the shade of that old tree at the end of the lawns. The tree was strong and so were you. I compared you with that tree, and I think, in a way, that I fell in love with you. You're not a pretty man, are you, Johann?''

Johann, almost imperceptibly, shook his head.

"Well," said Beatrice, "I have no time for pretty men. I like men with their masculinity hewn on every feature. That's a lovely word, isn't it—*hewn?* Rough men, ambitious men, powerful men. Men with big hands and strong chests. Men with sturdy thighs. Those are the kind of men I like.''

Johann sipped coffee. "And what about Liddy?" he asked softly.

"Liddy?" said Beatrice. She came away from the window and rested her hand on the back of her chair, facing Johann with a wry, sad expression. "Liddy is a wealthy, genteel, well-spoken, well-educated, respectable bag of bones. I married him when I was seventeen. My parents lived in Galveston, you see, and Liddy was there for a lengthy trial. He saw me on the street, found out where I lived, and paid court. My father and mother were delighted, because I was a problem girl, and they always warned me that I would end up in trouble. They had no place in their lives for anyone passionate. They were mean-minded and shallow, and my life with them was nothing but conflict and frustration. I suppose I was just as glad to get away from them as they were to get rid of me. I never loved Liddy. But he was wealthy, and he gave me presents, and he made me feel like a grown-up woman. We were married in three months, and he brought me back here to Broughton. I have been here ever since, the prettiest lady on the Broughton social circuit, as well as one of the wealthiest. I'm young, well-dressed, overin-dulged, and miserable. Can you imagine, Johann, how bored and lonely I am here? I have been here for nearly ten years, and nothing has happened. A whole decade, passed by, and nothing to show for it!''

"No children?" asked Johann uncomfortably.

Beatrice closed her eyes. She spoke with them closed, as if reciting a well-known psalm.

"Liddy told me the night we were married that he did not

36

believe in the pleasures of the body, and that he hoped I agreed with him. He said that there was no greater virtue for a woman than to return to heaven as unsullied as when she left it. I have never *known* my husband, Johann. Do you understand that? All the happiness I have ever had has come from admirers. *Lovers*, if you prefer the word the local gossips use."

Johann knew what was coming next. His chest went tight, and he tried to remain as calm as he possibly could. But this sultry, husky-voiced lady in her Chinese-blue tea gown and her provocative perfume was stirring sensations inside him that he had never felt with such intensity before.

"Beatrice . . ." he said. "Beatrice, I feel I ought to leave."

Beatrice smiled. "You can leave if you like. But I know that you'll be back."

He stood up, brushing the crumbs from his best pants.

"I believe I know what you're going to suggest," he said, "and it cannot be. I must . . . I must thank you for the coffee."

Beatrice stood in his way, her hands on her hips.

"*What* was I going to suggest?" she said huskily.

"I can hardly—"

"What? What was it that you're so sure I was going to suggest? You can hardly walk out without explaining yourself."

Johann turned away. "Beatrice—Mrs. Mulliner—I think things have gotten a little out of hand. It's really better if I . . ."

He heard a rustle of skirts. He turned around again, and stopped in mid-sentence. His heavy mouth hung open like a startled porpoise's.

Beatrice Mulliner, standing by the coffee table, had raised her blue tea gown up to her waist. Underneath, apart from her gray silk slippers, she was wearing nothing at all. Her white legs were slim and shapely, and between her thighs was a dark triangular smudge. That was all Johann saw before he looked away again and covered his eyes with his hand.

"Mrs. Mulliner," he said. "Please lower your gown."

She didn't. She came up to him, with her skirts still raised, and stood only inches away. He could smell her perfume, feel the warmth of her body, and he had no idea of what he was going to do.

"Johann," she whispered. "Look at me. Do I look like the kind of woman who should lead a life like this?"

He didn't answer. He shut his eyes tight, and prayed earnestly that God would erase the persistent image of Beatrice Mulliner's nudity that kept swimming across his vision.

"Johann," said Beatrice again, "I liked you from the moment I very first saw you. I knew you were the kind of man for me. Johann, please say you like me. That's all you have to say."

"Mrs. Mulliner," he said, "*please*."

There was a moment's silence. Then she dropped her dress and brushed it straight.

"All right," she said. "But don't think you've gotten away with it."

When he was sure that she was decent, he turned around again. "I don't understand what you mean," he said heavily. "Mrs. Mulliner, this isn't right. It's all so *unusual*."

She sat down. It amazed Johann that she could seem so matter-of-fact just after displaying to him the most intimate parts of her body. She poured herself another cup of coffee, and even cut herself a fresh slice of cake.

"Of course it's unusual," she said, without turning his way. "The whole trouble with Broughton is that it's so *usual*. Liddy is usual, this house is usual, my life is usual. And so, it seems, are you. Have you ever had a love affair, Johann?"

He shook his head.

"Well, you ought to," she said. "If you were a man of any passion, you would have thrown me down on the rug and possessed me. Does that shock you, my saying that?"

Johann nodded. "Yes, I think it does. I have always tried to be a man of Christian principles."

She shrugged. "Well, if it shocks you, then I don't know what I can do to persuade you otherwise. But you must remember, Johann, that happiness is paramount. God did not create us to lead frustrated and worthless lives."

"Beatrice, your life is not worthless. Think what you mean to Liddy."

She laughed. "I know what I mean to Liddy. Liddy is possessive to the point of illness. To Liddy I am the pure lily of the valley, his one and only, his dream wife. Liddy would die without me."

"Does Liddy know? I mean . . . about your admirers?"

Beatrice shook her head. "If he even guessed, he would have taken to his sickbed and died of a broken heart."

Johann was silent for a while. Then he said: "Beatrice, I

consider you a beautiful and remarkable woman. You have shocked me, and upset me, but I don't want you to feel that, because of what's happened today, I think any the worse of you. I know what anguish you must feel, and I only hope that God gives you the strength to overcome it."

Beatrice didn't answer.

"You are a lovely woman, Beatrice," said Johann gently.

She looked up at him. There was a kind smile on her face, but it wasn't a smile of trust or belief.

"Many men have told me that, Johann."

He shrugged. "Yes, I suppose they have. But I want you to know that I'm not offended, and I hope we can continue our social intercourse."

"At a distance?"

He nodded. "I think it's better."

"Johann," she said. "How much money do you need?"

"What do you mean?"

She looked serious. "We had dinner with the Greaveses the other night. I mentioned you to Mr. Greaves, and he told me that you were trying to start an engineering company, a maintenance works, in Broughton. It seemed to me that you had asked him for money."

"Well?" said Johann.

"Well . . . is it impertinent of me to ask how much you need?"

Johann sat down.

"I think you have fathomed me," he said. "I am not a rich man. In fact, I am very poor. The reason I tried to get Janet to spread rumors about me was that I had little hope left of making myself wealthy and respectable. I come from a poor Dutch family, and that is about all. I have no connections, no friends, and no money. I was trying to borrow ten thousand dollars from Mr. Greaves to start an engineering business, yes. But so far, I can find nobody to underwrite my loan, and it looks as if I will never get the money."

Beatrice looked at him thoughtfully.

"I knew you weren't rich," she said. "I suppose that was part of your attraction. Other people may not have noticed, but I did. Rich men don't wear seven-cent collars and cuffs, and rich men don't eat cream cake with their fingers. I watched you at the garden party, remember? This," she said, lifting it up from the parlor stand, "is a cake fork."

Johann stared at the broad-tined fork, and felt more deflated by that than almost anything else Beatrice Mulliner had done.

"I see," he said dully.

"I wish," said Beatrice Mulliner, "that you would leave Liddy to me. As far as investments are concerned, anyway. If you're good to me, Johann, I'm sure that I can persuade Liddy to assist you."

"Good?"

Beatrice smiled wanly. "That's right, good. Are you still taking Janet to the carnival?"

Johann stood up. "I think I'd better go," he said hurriedly. "I think, really, I'd better go."

Beatrice kept on smiling. "Remember what I said," she told him huskily. "One good turn deserves another."

Johann called for his hat, and stood silent and rigid while it was brought. Beatrice Mulliner remained in her chair, a slight smile on her lips, while he stood there. He kept trying not to remember that she was stark naked underneath her tea gown.

When his hat was brought, Johann said "Good day," and Beatrice Mulliner offered her hand, silently, for a kiss.

Janet, in her frilly white maid's cap, was waiting for him by the front gate. He doffed his hat to her and smiled as much as he could.

"Tomorrow's my afternoon off," she said brightly. "And you *did* promise that you'd take me to the carnival."

He thought about his remaining three dollars and seventy-five cents. Then he smiled and said: "All right. I'll meet you at the pasture at three. Wear the brightest dress you have. I think we ought to celebrate."

Janet cocked her head on one side. "Celebrate what?"

Johann put his hat on again and straightened it. "Either the beginning," he said quietly, "or the very end."

The offices of Belliveau, Jackson, Strich & Mulliner, on Fifth Street, were imposing and respectable. Their shingle was painted in funereal black, with classic gold lettering, and it hung over a wooden portico and mahogany swing doors with shiny brass doorplates. Johann pushed his way in, and the swing doors swished quietly closed behind him. It was just after lunch, and the whole of Broughton was quiet and sleepy in the hot afternoon sun. A young law clerk in a green eyeshade was dozing behind the reception desk, head nodding over the racing papers, while flies hummed fitfully around the ceiling.

Johann pinged the bell on the clerk's counter. The boy blinked his eyes and raised his eyeshade.

"Sir?"

Johann took off his black hat and wiped his red perspiring forehead with his handkerchief. "I'd like to see Mr. Mulliner, if he's available."

The clerk stood up and tugged down his fancy vest. "I think he's still taking luncheon, sir. But you'll find him at Cade's Restaurant, on Sixth, if it's urgent."

"Thank you," said Johann. "I believe it is."

He walked back out into the glaring midday sunlight. Broughton was always sleepy at this hour, and there was nothing stirring in the street but a slow-moving business wagon and a dog disturbed by flies. Johann turned left at the end of the street, up to Sixth Street, and found the frosted-glass front of Cade's Restaurant about fifty yards along, on the right.

Cade's was one of the respectable restaurants in Broughton. Its front was freshly painted in green and gold, and there were heavy green drapes at the windows. It was a regular meeting-place for lawyers, gentlemen of property, merchants, and cattle owners. When Johann stepped in, most of the tables were taken. Men in flourishing whiskers sat over the green-check tablecloths, finishing their cigars and their coffee, and there was a rich aroma of steak and fried potatoes around.

A bald waiter in a long white apron came up and said: "You wanted a table? We have a table for one right down the back here."

Johann shook his head. "I'm looking for Mr. Mulliner. His office said he'd be here."

The waiter nodded. "Sure—he's right over there, with Mr. Croxton. Can I get you anything?"

Johann shook his head. "Not just now." With the money he had in his pocket, he couldn't even afford to sit down in this place. He made his way through the tables, until he reached Mr. Mulliner, and he stood beside him and coughed.

Mr. Mulliner, a tall and scrawny man with bushy gray whiskers, a long hooked nose, and receding hair, was deeply engaged in conversation with Mr. Croxton. Johann looked at Mr. Mulliner, at the hair sprouting out of his ears, at his shrunken body and his piercing, near-together eyes, and wondered how Beatrice could ever have considered marrying him, even for the sake of escaping from her parents. He was forty years old, but he looked ten years older.

41

Almost old enough to have been Beatrice's father, or her doddering old uncle. Johann tried hard not to think about Liddy and Beatrice Mulliner together in bed, and almost prayed his relief at Liddy's sexual puritanism. Johann believed in God, and the institution of marriage, but he also believed that marriage should be reserved for those who were physically and emotionally suitable, or no good would come of it. The marriage of Liddy and Beatrice Mulliner was a pertinent example.

"I *told* him," Mr. Mulliner was saying intensely. "I *told* him that if he attempted to bring an action, I would sue him from Dallas to next Wednesday, and I did. He settled for eight hundred dollars, and left the whole thing open."

Mr. Croxton, a cheerful and overweight Texan with a bootlace tie and a sweat-stained linen jacket, nodded his approval.

"I think you did the correct thing there, Lidmore. I always said he was all mouth and no spunk. Didn't I always say that?"

Johann coughed again, more pointedly. Mr. Mulliner heard him and turned around. The whiskered face that Johann saw then was the face of a hard, professional, and relentless lawyer. It didn't do much to ease his discomfiture, or his feelings of uncertainty and nervousness.

"You want something, sir?" said Mulliner. "Or are you just coughing from the dust?"

Mr. Croxton grinned. "I always take menthol drops myself," he said humorously. "Menthol drops and a stiff dose of rye. It don't do my cough no good, but it keeps me happy."

Johann attempted a smile. "I didn't mean to interrupt your luncheon, Mr. Mulliner, but the truth is that I have something important to discuss with you."

Mulliner shrugged. "Well, is it pressing? This luncheon I've been promising to Mr. Croxton here for nigh on twelve months."

"It would only take a couple of minutes," said Johann. "But I think you ought to know as soon as possible."

Mulliner frowned. "Know what? There isn't anything wrong, is there? Nothing wrong at home?"

"Oh, no—it's nothing like that. But I feel it would be best for everyone."

Mr. Croxton said: "Lidmore, if you want to spend a minute or two in private with this gentleman, I'm willing to occupy the next table for that time."

Johann said: "You're very kind, sir."

Mr. Mulliner sighed. "Okay, then, if it's only a couple of minutes. But you'll have to stop when the jambalaya comes, because I'm good and hungry."

Mr. Croxton moved to the next table, Johann sat in his place. He laced his hands together and tried to look as earnest and serious as possible.

"Well," said Mr. Mulliner. "Spit it out."

Johann coughed. "It's about business, sir. My name's Johann Cornelius, and I'm an engineer. You may remember me from the Edmundses' garden party."

Mr. Mulliner nodded. "I recall your face. Carry on."

"I came into Broughton to help out a few of the factories here. I want to set up an engineering maintenance works, because that's my line of business. The kind of work I can do is repairing machinery, testing new equipment, designing special parts. At the moment, Pusey's and Welward's and even the locomotive people have to send all their lathes and stuff away off to Austin, or even Houston. I can do that kind of work right here, and save them all time and money."

Mr. Mulliner sniffed and tugged at his whiskers. "I see. What's that to do with me?"

Johann bit his lip. "It's kind of delicate, sir. You see, I dropped by your house this morning to leave my card, in the hope of visiting you sometime and maybe discussing some investment in this works."

Mr. Mulliner said: "Yes?"

"Well," said Johann, "I'm a little short of the total capital I require for starting up, and I was hoping that a few local people might be interested in chipping in. Yourself included."

Mr. Mulliner said: "I don't quite see what you're driving at."

"Investment, sir," explained Johann a little desperately. "What I'm looking for is people who want to help me start up. People with money."

A waiter came past with a tin tray, bearing plates of Creole sausage and squab. Johann smelled the savory waft of food and felt distinctly hungry. All he had eaten all day was a rough breakfast of *flash un kas*, and if he didn't manage to settle his future soon, it looked as though dinner was out of the question.

Mr. Mulliner said: "*Money*? How much money?"

"Er . . . ten thousand, just about."

Mr. Mulliner puffed his breath out. "Ten thousand? That's a

43

lot of money. You won't find many people around here with ten thousand in loose dollars, just lying around. Most people have invested their loose money already.''

"The bank has ten thousand," said Johann.

Mr. Mulliner nodded. "Sure they do. If you're prepared to offer the bank the right kind of security, you can borrow as much as you like.''

"That's the problem.''

"What's the problem?''

"I don't *have* the security, and I'm looking for local people to underwrite me.''

"Is that why you've come to me? You want a note for ten thousand dollars?''

Johann shook his head. "Not exactly. It's your wife.''

Mr. Mulliner squinted his near-together eyes and said: "My wife? What has my wife got to do with this?''

Johann knew he was blushing. But it was better to try to forestall any sticky difficulties by telling Mr. Mulliner the truth than have Beatrice Mulliner ensnare him in her seductive ambush. His throat constricting, he said: "Your wife . . . invited me in this morning . . . and offered me coffee. I took coffee with her . . . and told her about my schemes.''

"Yes?" said Mr. Mulliner, looking sharp and intent.

"Well," said Johann, "I think she became a little overenthusiastic. I think she might try to persuade you to invest in my idea.''

Mr. Mulliner pursed his lips. "I see.''

Johann reached for his handkerchief and wiped his perspiring forehead.

"I just want you to know," he said unsteadily, "that I did nothing to encourage her interest. In other words, I don't want you to get the wrong idea.''

Mr. Mulliner toyed with his knife and fork. Then he arranged the cut-glass salt and pepper pots side by side on the green-check tablecloth, and lined up a bottle of sauce between them. All the time, he didn't take his glittering near-together eyes away from Johann's face. Johann sat upright in his chair and tried not to look shifty.

Finally Mr. Mulliner said: "My wife, Mr. Cornelius, is a woman who has bursts of enthusiasm." He made "bursts of enthusiasm" sound like boils on the neck. "She takes an idea into her mind, and chatters about it for days at a time, and then as soon as she has thought of it, it disappears. She is young still, and her mind is not constant. She is the same with people. She will take a fancy to someone, and for a while they will occupy the whole of her energies. But, like as not, they will soon be dropped for someone fresh."

He stroked his whiskers like a man stroking a particularly unpleasant pet cat.

"I want you to understand, Mr. Cornelius, that while your concern for my wife's excitement is appreciated, it is unnecessary. I am also afraid that I must let you know that I am not a man who cares to speculate, and that I could not ever consider underwriting your loan, no matter how much enthusiasm my wife brings to bear on me."

Johann swallowed. "I understand," he said quietly. "However, I did think I was doing the right thing by bringing this matter to your attention."

Mr. Mulliner nodded. Johann thought the lawyer had a strangely artificial quality about him, like a stuffed goat in a glass case. The bald waiter arrived with plates of jambalaya and hoecake, and Johann had to get up to leave.

"Despite everything," said Mr. Mulliner as Johann put his hat on again, "I want you to know that you have my very best wishes for the future."

Johann said: "Thank you. I hope I haven't disturbed your luncheon." Then he made his way through the crowded restaurant, and out into the street, before the fragrant smell of ham and tomatoes and prawns got too much for him.

That night, lying in his narrow iron bed under the sloping ceiling of his boardinghouse room, he heard a locomotive in the yards outside, sneezing and clanking as it waited for its boxcars. Reflections from the railroad lamps stalked and stirred across the wall, and he felt exhausted and empty. There is a dream of wealth in all men, and in Johann Cornelius its fulfillment was essential to his progress in life. Lying there, in his patched and faded blue nightshirt, he mumbled a short prayer to God for guidance and help, and hoped that God wouldn't think him too impertinent.

On the very brink of ruin, though, Johann somehow felt more hopeful about his future success than ever before. Perhaps he needed crisis to stir him into bold and desperate action. He slept for a while, and had a long dream in which he was being given stocks and bonds of immense value, only to discover that they were nothing more than instruction leaflets for patent medicines.

He woke again, and lay there for almost an hour thinking about Beatrice Mulliner. She disturbed him a great deal, and he kept trying to imagine the incongruity of Lidmore and Beatrice side by side in the same bed. They were actually there now, not more than a half a mile away. The stuffed goat and the goddess. Johann closed his eyes, and before he slept again, had a brief and haunting vision of Beatrice's thighs.

The next day was gray and thundery. The dust from the streets was whipped up into stinging clouds, and the horses tethered outside the Main Street stores were restless and bothersome. As Johann strode along the boardwalk past Seventh Street, he was beginning to wonder if he ought to invest a dollar-ten in an umbrella. Everybody else was carrying one, and the surreys and business wagons rattled past with their black hoods up.

He held his hat on his head as he crossed the breezy street past Howard's Refreshment Parlor and headed out toward Kyle's Pasture. The pasture was a small scrubby field on the outskirts of Broughton, surrounded by rustling windswept trees, where Barnet and Shenton's Meadow Carnival, according to the posters, was enjoying its second stupendous week.

When Johann reached the pasture, the carnival was almost deserted. The sideshows were open, but men were tugging tarpaulins over the sawdust rings where the trained dogs danced, and they were blowing out the popcorn lamps and tying down the tent flaps for a storm. A fresh metallic breeze was blowing out of the west, and the sky was the color of steel.

Johann walked across the tufted grass, looking around for Janet. She had promised to meet him at three, and it was already five past, according to the clock on Broughton's white-painted town hall. There was a greasy aroma of hot franks and onions, which reminded Johann that he hadn't eaten since yesterday morning. A few couples were wandering around the wind-blown stands and sideshows, but the weather was too brisk for crowds.

He looked around the back of the Mississippi Steamboat Ride, and into the boxing tent, where two fat bald pugilists were drinking bottled beer and laughing; he walked the whole length of the sideshows, where gypsy girls sat behind hoop-las and shooting galleries, chattering in high Romanian voices. Eventually he had covered the whole carnival, and there was no sign of Janet at all. Maybe the thundery weather had put her off. Maybe her mistress had forbidden her to go. Johann resigned himself to another tedious afternoon on his own, and started to walk toward the exit.

The flap of a small striped marquee was pushed open, not far away, and a woman stepped out. Johann glanced at her, then stopped in mid-stride and looked again. She was wearing a neat brown velvet-collared coat that reached to her hips, and a long brown skirt with braid patterns around the hem. Over her upswept brunette hair she wore an elegant turban hat decorated with feathers. It was Beatrice Mulliner. She smiled at him and gave him a little wave.

Johann stayed where he was while she approached him. In her walking-out clothes she looked even more attractive than she had yesterday. Her cheeks were flushed with a touch of *rouge de theatre*, but apart from that her face was elegantly white. She walked with a graceful sway of her skirts that showed beyond doubt she was a prime filly from The Racetrack.

"*Johann*," she said, extending her cream-gloved hand to be kissed. "What an unusual coincidence."

Johann lifted his hat. "Yes," he said flatly. "Is Janet coming, or have you come in her stead?"

Beatrice smiled. "Janet was indisposed, and sends her sincere regrets. I thought it would be most unkind if you were left on your own at the carnival. You must forgive me for keeping you waiting, but I just had to go and have my fortune read. That palmist is really quite a remarkable lady."

She took Johann's sleeve and they strolled hand in hand toward the roadway. Johann tried to remain as stiff and proper as possible, and held Beatrice Mulliner's arm as if it was a French loaf.

"Do you know what she said?" said Beatrice brightly.

"Do I know what who said?"

"The palmist, my dear! The palmist said I was to have a lucky day today, and that all who were dear to me would benefit from my affection."

"I see."

Beatrice stopped walking and looked up at Johann with a frown.

"Johann . . . I have the distinct impression that you are displeased."

47

Johann coughed. "Yes, Beatrice, I think I am."

"Don't you enjoy my company?" she said. "Isn't it just as good as Janet's?"

Johann nodded. "Of course."

"Then what's the matter? Are you worried that it might rain? Have you only one pair of socks? Have your shares fallen?"

Johann lowered his head. "I have two pairs of socks and no shares," he said quietly. "I am concerned that you are trying to use me for your own amusement."

Beatrice widened those feline eyes of hers. "Johann! I don't know how you could say such a thing!"

They resumed walking. Johann said: "I went to see your husband yesterday."

"Yes, I know."

"You know?"

"Of course. You don't think that Liddy isn't going to cross-question me about any man for whom I show the slightest enthusiasm, do you? He was quite annoyed, as a matter of fact, and said I had no right to invite a single man in for coffee without a chaperone."

Johann didn't answer. They reached the edge of Kyle's Pasture and began to walk back toward the town. Behind them, the steam calliope suddenly started up, and the roundabout with its red-and-gold-painted horses began to turn around, with nobody on it except one serious small boy in a sailor suit. His nanny, a dour woman in gray flannel, watched him go around and around with equal seriousness, and Johann, seeing them, wondered why the pleasure of others was always such a grave business. Certainly the pleasure of Beatrice Mulliner was a serious affair, in every sense of the word.

"You know something," said Beatrice, lifting her brown skirts out of the dust, "you are the first man about whom I can truthfully say that your financial situation means nothing to me."

"Does it usually matter?"

Beatrice laughed. "Of course it matters, my dear! The poor, besides having no use for toiletries, are not such good lovers as the wealthy. The poor man returns home each night exhausted from his toil, and if he does feel the needs of love, he satisfies them as quickly as possible. The wealthy man, however, likes to take his time, and dally awhile, and that is what makes him a more competent beau."

Johann said: "You speak very frankly, Beatrice, for a woman I hardly know."

Beatrice laughed again. "Is it necessary to know someone to feel fond of them?"

"I think so," Johann said. "Is that rain? We ought to hurry."

"I knew you were worried about the rain," said Beatrice.

"I am not worried about the rain. I am worried about what people may think. What did your husband say to you yesterday?"

"He said I was to be more discreet, or people would think I was behaving immodestly. He's a prudish old woman, and you mustn't mind him. And nor must you mind what people think. That's the first lesson in success. You want success, don't you?"

"I suppose so. It depends on the price."

Beatrice looked up at him. "Success costs nothing to the successful. You really ought to understand that success is always won from other people's failure."

They turned the corner into Main Street, and Johann began to feel distinctly nervous in case they were spotted by a friend of Lidmore Mulliner's, or even Lidmore himself. If he was going to have any chance of raising his ten thousand dollars, he couldn't afford the slightest twitching of local eyebrows, or the slightest whisper of gossip. Small towns like Broughton had a way of making life intolerably hostile and uncomfortable for unwelcome strangers. "Beatrice," he said, "I will walk you home to Beaumont Street, and then I believe it will be wiser if we do not see each other alone again."

"*Johann*," she said, pretending to be deeply hurt, "you are being so cruel to me today." She smiled politely at a passing friend, who made no pretense of her interest in Johann. "Hello, Mrs. Westmore!"

"This is very embarrassing," whispered Johann. "What if word gets back to your husband?"

Beatrice nodded to another friend. "Don't worry about Liddy. I know how to handle him, you know, even when he's really mad. You must have more courage, my dear, if you are going to make a fortune. Raise a little hell, my dear, that's my advice."

Johann said nothing. He didn't know what to say. As they passed Seventh Street arm in arm, he felt as sinful and outrageous as he ever had done in his whole life. He hoped that God would forgive him for this loose behavior, and he even tried to pray as they walked and talked.

49

"Johann," said Beatrice, "I do believe you're not listening."

"Of course I am. I'm just . . . concerned."

"Concerned? Or scared? Do I frighten you? You're not very smooth with ladies, Johann—did you know that?"

"I have no pretensions to smoothness."

"Johann, you're in such a dither! I *do* scare you, don't I? But do I do more than that? Do I make you feel good, as well? Do I make you feel lionhearted, and bold, and perhaps even savage?"

Johann was sweating. "I really can't say, Beatrice. I don't think we ought to speak like this."

"You don't like to talk about your passions, do you, Johann? But you must! I can see your passions boiling inside you! Why don't you let them out? Release them! They want to be free!"

"Beatrice," said Johann quietly, "please don't torment me."

They had reached the corner of Beaumont Street. It was quiet there. The sky was dull, and a few spots of rain were beginning to rattle among the leaves of the trees in the spacious Racetrack yards.

Johann took both her hands and said: "I must leave you here. It will do no good, otherwise."

She looked so beautiful standing there, with her dark uptilted eyes, her trim brown coat, and her neat figure, that it was as much as Johann could do to say those words. He was not used to emotional situations, and because of that, his feelings came on him like a storm of grit, unmanageable and unexpected. He had tears in his eyes, for no reason that he could even think of.

"I shall think of you," said Beatrice, "as one of those strange possibilities that never happened. Can I tell you something?"

"Of course."

"You are a man who doesn't even recognize the half of his potential. You are struggling for ten thousand dollars when you should be considering millions. You have the power, but right now you don't have the courage. You have the determination, but you haven't yet discovered what it is you should be determined about. All your energy is being wasted, because you are trying to live by other people's rules. I know what I'm talking about, Johann, because it has happened to me. I'm not the free, wild lady you think I am. I am as much trapped by this town and its narrow-minded people as you are."

Johann shook his head. "Beatrice—"

"I know," she said, a little sadly. "You have no money and you have to start somewhere. You and I, we have more in common than any of these dull and worthy townsfolk could ever understand. By God, I hate this place. I could raze it to the ground, and I would laugh while I was doing it.''

Johann said: ''I think we'd better say good-bye.''

''Must we?'' asked Beatrice. But then she took her hands away and said: ''I know we must.''

She paused for a moment, then stood on tiptoe and kissed his cheek. She smelled of heliotrope, and her cheek was so soft that he remembered what it felt like for days afterward.

''I will do you a favor,'' she said.

''A favor? I don't understand.''

''Like all favors,'' she said gently, ''it will have a condition attached. You see, you really need to learn that nobody, ever, does anything for nothing.''

Johann took off his hat. The wind blew his thinning hair up and down like a semaphore signal.

''What is it? The favor?''

She smiled faintly. ''You won't discover that until later. But the condition is that, in return, you never turn me away.''

''What?''

''The condition is that, if I come looking for you, at any time, in any place, you never turn me away.''

Johann stood stock-still and silent. He felt numb, like he felt when the New York dentist gave him chloroform to tug out his aching tooth.

''All right,'' he said hoarsely. He didn't understand at all.

Beatrice looked at him with a warm, regretful expression for a moment, and then she turned around and walked off down Beaumont Street. The last that Johann saw of her, she was turning into the gate of number 15. She didn't look around, and didn't wave. It occurred to him that they hadn't even said good-bye.

He stood there for two or three minutes. Then he placed his hat on his head and made his way back to the boardinghouse. That evening he had just enough money left for a plate of pork-and-apple pie down at Parsons'. He ate it very slowly, to make it last, and licked every scrap from his knife and fork.

The boy rapped cheerfully on the door of his boardinghouse room and stepped in. Johann was packing his white dress shirt and collars into his battered brown suitcase, and didn't take kindly to being interrupted. When it came to folding clothes, he was clumsy

51

and awkward, and somehow they always emerged from his suitcase looking as if they had been worn as loincloths by a whole tribe of unwashed Kiowa.

"Message for Mr. Corny-eely-ass!" said the boy cheekily.

"That's me," said Johann. The boy handed him a long crisp envelope sealed with red wax.

"Who's it from?"

"Dunno," said the boy. "Gave me a quarter for doing it, though."

Johann looked up. The boy was leaning against the doorjamb, obviously expecting the same financial favor from him.

"I'm sorry. I don't have a nickel. When I leave here, I guess I'll have to go live in a gopher hole."

The boy wrinkled his nose in disgust. "Don't ya believe in free enterprise?" he asked with high-pitched insolence.

"Sure," said Johann. "And that's why I'm not going to pay you for it."

"Oh, *swell*," said the boy, and went off, slamming the door so hard behind him that plaster dust drifted down to the floor.

Johann went to the window, where the light was better, and picked the red seal off the envelope. He opened it up and took out an official-looking letter. It was headed "Belliveau, Jackson, Strich & Mulliner, Attorneys-at-Law," but it was penned by hand. The writing was scratchy and intense, and the writer had obviously stopped after every few words to dip his nib into the inkpot.

"Sir," said the letter. "It has been brought to my attention that you have been making advances to my wife of a kind considered improper in respectable society. I have had the matter out with her, and it seems you have compounded the offense by encouraging her to fall into an affectionate humor as regards yourself. I consider it essential for my wife's good name, and the name of my business and my family, that you should leave the town of Broughton forthwith. In order to enable you to do so with the minimum of commotion, I have already spoken to Mr. Greaves at the Broughton National Bank, and informed him that I am prepared to guarantee your loan of ten thousand dollars, subject to those conditions required by state and federal law. Needless to say, I am only doing this under considerable personal duress, as the lesser of two evils, and my feelings are that you behaved like a roughneck of no character, and an adventurer. My wife wishes me to communicate to you that she has no further feelings of anything except revulsion and regret, and she trusts she will never lay eyes on you again."

The letter was signed "Lidmore Mulliner." It was a fierce, angry signature that must almost have snapped the nib.

Johann read the letter again, and then laid it down carefully on the green-painted wooden dresser. Outside, in the weak sunlight, a locomotive was moving out through the yards with a train of cattle. The pale sun gleamed on the crisscrossing rails, and long after the locomotive had puffed heavily northward, the boxcars clattered and rattled across the points. Fragments of steam and smoke drifted away between the fences and the telegraph posts, and across the untidy sidings and overgrown grass.

Johann stood there for a long time, silent and still. Then he turned back to his dress shirt, and with as much care and skill as he could, he started to fold it. There were wet stains on it where his tears fell, but even as he wept, he promised himself that he would never cry over anything ever again.

1902

THE EXCELSIOR HOTEL
"Where Nobs Stay"

offers

Accommodation of the
PLUSHEST SORT
Clean Beds, Hot Water
Flushing Closets

and

Our Special Steak Breakfast
with Two Eggs
Any Style

The sun had only just risen across the wide, windblown prairie when the motorcar crossed the rutted track that led across the Grant cattle spread and puttered its way westward by the water pump and the Mexican lean-tos in a plume of ocher dust. It was six o'clock on a March morning, and even though the breeze was dry and warm, the man at the wheel of the motorcar was dressed in a long white overcoat, with a knitted scarf and glass goggles, and his hands grasped the upright steering wheel in huge brown leather gauntlets. He had left Edgar, Texas, while it was still dark, and he wanted to be in Amarero in time for breakfast, which meant that he had traveled fifteen miles already in the chill of the false dawn.

His car squeaked and creaked over the ruts, but it was running well. It was a 1901 New Orleans 3½ which he had bought for one hundred dollars from the managing director of a bankrupt British shipping company in Galveston two months ago. He had painstakingly tuned up the single-cylinder 704cc engine; he had refurbished the two brass coaching lamps and the striped paintwork on the hood; he had nourished the buttoned leather seats with saddle polish; and he had rebalanced the elegant spoked wheels with their narrow white thirty-inch tires. This was his first long trip in it, and even though the leaf springs didn't do much to cushion his backside from the sun-baked Texas tracks, he felt magnificent, like a kind of motorized Nemesis bearing down on the horse-and-buggy world that science would soon sweep away.

As he passed the Grant spread, a herd of rangy-looking cattle, their coats ruffled in the wind, eyed him mournfully. The fut-fut-fut-fut of his engine rose and fell across the prairies, and a coopful of chickens squawked and squittered in fright.

Two Mexican workers in faded dungarees, trudging up to the house to hoe Mrs. Grant's vegetable patch, dropped abruptly to their knees as this unearthly mechanical apparition appeared around the corner by the paint store and roared past them in a blinding cloud of dust. They remained kneeling for almost five minutes, gaping toward the horizon where the car had disappeared, as if Jesus had just whizzed by on His way to a second coming, and had forgotten to say *buenos dias*.

But in his personal cyclone of sandy-colored dust, the automobilist himself felt cheerful. He liked to surprise people these days. In fact, he had gotten himself quite a reputation for it. He had surprised the whole township of Edgar, which was a roughish place with a pretty high threshold of surprise, when he had first moved in two years ago from nowhere at all and opened up the best-equipped machine-maintenance shop for hundreds of miles around. He had surprised his chief competitors, the sleepy and disorganized Perrot Oil-Rig Company, by purchasing 40 percent of their stock and 43 percent of their bonds and forcing them to sell out to him. He had surprised his landlady, old Mrs. Ottilie Hermann, by buying her rambling wooden boardinghouse from her for fifteen hundred dollars, by having it repainted red and replumbed with flushing toilets, and by letting it out again for five times the rent she used to charge in the old days. And he had surprised everybody even more by going to church not just once on Sundays but three times, and praying deeply and silently in his own pew, and by never drinking whiskey and by never paying court to any of the local girls, even though some of them were very pretty and all of them were extremely frustrated. They said about him in Edgar that he was a man who was destined for something, although they could never decide quite what. It didn't occur to them, of course, that he was dedicated to the making of money by scientific means; that he believed in luck and he believed in chance, but that most of all he believed in method and determination, those two, and that any man with the correct method who applied it with sufficient determination would become rich, as inevitably as any young man who visited Nelly Jones's fun house on Amarillo Street, Edgar, would catch himself a fearful dose of crabs.

Although he had a staff of two trained engineers, Sam Chivers and Jack Beak, and although he had three mechanics and a black man called Winston who oiled the lathes and swept up, he appeared to have no friends at all, and in company he was reticent and standoffish. They invited him everywhere, of course, because he was one of the most prosperous men in town. But at bake-offs and fetes, at church teas and men's social evenings, he stood large and quiet, as if he had his mind on other things; and if he hadn't been

58

the fastest and most efficient supplier around of drill bits, Corliss valves, dynamos, Neurnst lamps, and Vernier transit compasses, and if he hadn't been able to repair oil-drilling equipment sounder and better than anyone in the whole of the Lone Star State, then they probably would never have invited him anyplace at all.

On this warm March morning, he crossed the prairie under an empty sky, with empty horizons stretching out on every side, and he felt chosen, and alone. And as the hours and the prairie went by, hours of jolting and bouncing and dust and flies, he sang to himself in a deep, croaky voice, which nobody had ever heard him do. He sang "Where the Sweet Magnolias Bloom."

While he sang, on the horizon, great castles of cumulus clouds grew, pile upon pile of elaborate white towers, and terraces, and boiling bridges. His eyes were sore from the dust, and his arms ached from clutching the automobile's steering wheel for so long, but he felt an inspirational strength, and he sang louder.

It took four hours of bumping and squeaking through the dust and the heat before Amarero appeared in the distance—a shabby clutter of wooden houses, stores and hotels, surrounded on all sides by oil rigs. The rigs from several miles away looked like the masts of a strange fleet of ships which had anchored mysteriously on the prairie. Oily black smoke smudged across the sky, and Johann, stopping his automobile on a low and eroded ridge, knew that he was back in wildcat country.

He took out his handkerchief and dabbed his grimy face. Johann had been fascinated by the oil operations in Amarero ever since he had first visited the town last year, trundling an overhauled rotary power force pump on the back of his horse-drawn business wagon. It was a hard-bitten town, populated by oilmen, whores, and shopkeepers, apart from a doctor who drank and a priest who appeared to be under the impression that he was Saint Sebastian. Up until the fall of 1901, Amarero had been nothing but a railhead for West Texas cattle, and the woodburning locomotives used to come up from Broughton and the Gulf only four or five times a year. There used to be little more than an auction room, a boarding-house, a diner that offered pork and beans or sausage and beans only (home fries extra), and a railroad yard that didn't amount to more than a few rickety cattle enclosures and a rusted set of buffers. Then a middle-aged wildcat prospector named Kyle Lennox arrived in town—a man with great black droopy whiskers, brocade vests, and an unpleasant reputation for brawling and taking his teeth out during poker games. He had drilled in the area for four or five months, as well as drinking himself insensible every night and having an intermittent and very noisy affair with the widow of the auctioneer before last, who lived in a peeling house on her own at the northwest end of Main Street, which was the only street there was. One morning in October, miraculously, Kyle Lennox's drill bits released the Amarero Number One well, a moderate-sized gusher that eventually pumped out thirty-five thousand barrels a day. The only problem was that the land on which Lennox was drilling belonged to the widow, and to safeguard his interests he had to run up Main Street in the heat of the eleven-o'clock sun, burst into her house, and fall on his knees on her Berlinwork rug in his oily dungarees to propose marriage. She clucked at him for making the rug dirty, but when he promised her ten thousand rugs, she said yes.

Kyle Lennox and the woman he still called "the widow" had sold out Amarero Number One to a young businessman from Houston called Jimmy Makepiece, who together with an investment group from New York had promptly founded Amarero Oil. As a bonus, Lennox was guaranteed dividends and lump sums, and appointed president of the company, which didn't give him much influence but conveniently meant that he had to stay in Amarero, well out of Makepiece's way. From his low vantage point on the ridge, Johann could already see Lennox's three-story Gothic house, set a quarter-mile out of town to the north, with its gilded dragon-scale roof gleaming in the morning sun.

The discovery of oil had transformed Amarero overnight. Johann arrived on Main Street with his New Orleans automobile fut-futting and his goggles thick with dust. He pulled up opposite the Excelsior, applied his brake, and shut off the engine. There was a hot, swallowing silence, interrupted only by the click of his car as it cooled down, and the wind swinging the sign saying "Excelsior Hotel—Good Eats & Clean Beds." He took off his gauntlets and his goggles and unbuttoned his motoring coat.

An old fellow with a white walrus mustache and dusty breeches came walking up the boardwalk next to him, and stopped. He was smoking an eagle's-claw pipe, and he wore a weather-faded derby hat. He said: "How do," without taking his pipe out from between his teeth.

"How do you do," replied Johann, smiling briefly in acknowledgment. He was looking tanned and healthy these days, although his cheeks were blotchy from the sun, and his thin blond hair, under a panama hat with a green puggaree, was stuck down with lavender pomade. Beneath his motoring coat he was wearing a light linen suit, with a green bow tie and a fresh percale shirt.

The old man inspected Johann's car. Then he said: "Happen you're looking for John Kummer."

Johann lifted his mock-alligator briefcase out of the back seat of the car. He didn't answer.

The old man said: "You ain't the first, of course. There's been creditors galore. Grocer's men for the chuck he ate; haberdasher's men for the overalls he wore; dry-goods men for the dry goods; and hardware men for the nails and God alone knows what else. Why, he's even run hisself a slate up over yonder."

Johann turned and looked at the Excelsior Hotel, a wooden monstrosity painted green and gold. On the first-floor balcony, shaded from the morning sun by a parasol, was a young prostitute with red wavy hair and a black basque which forced her breasts into a low and provocative line. She waved her fingers at Johann, and he turned away.

"Do you know where to find him?" asked Johann.

The old man coughed. "I can tell you something," he said. "I once scouted for Robert E. Lee."

Johann stepped into the cooler shadow of the boardwalk. "You and every other old storyteller this side of the Brazos. Is he out at the oil camp, do you know, or has he come into town?"

The old man took off his derby hat and knocked it back into shape.

"Could do with a fill," he said uncommunicatively.

Johann said: "I'll give you a nickel for a fill if you tell me where he is; but you tell me first."

The old man thought about that. He wasn't in any particular hurry.

Kummer was one of many wildcatters who hadn't struck it rich out at Amarero, and he owed Johann $732.08 for maintenance work, gasoline engines, and spares. This trip was a debt-collecting trip, and Johann intended to get his money.

"Well," said the old man at last, "how about a fill and a slug?"

"A fill," said Johann. "And not until you tell me."

The old man shrugged. Then he said: "It sure wasn't like this in the old days, you know, when folks recalled the war. There was a time when you only had to say to someone that you'd seen Robert

E. Lee hisself, and more than that I once touched his coattails, which I did. I touched his coattails and said 'God bless you, general,' and he looked down with that gentle bearded face of his, this was in Pennsylvania, and do you know what he said to me?"

"No," said Johann wearily, "I don't."

"Lee said to me, 'Take your goddamned filthy fingers off of my coat,' and that was all. And that's why I ain't been too partial to great heroes ever since, because they never go around making great and gentle speeches like they're supposed to."

Johann leaned forward and laid his hand on the old man's shoulder.

"Supposing you just tell me where John Kummer is, huh?"

The old man nodded. "You could try the oil camp."

"And what if he isn't there, like I suspect he's not?"

"Then you could try the church. Maybe he's praying to God to make it rain money."

Johann shook his head.

The old man sighed. "You could, if you had a mind to, try Room 26 at the Excelsior Hotel, where you might find a man who's almost packed and ready to leave town with his sweetheart, who's a reformed whore of sorts, name of Dolly Jarvis, from Abilene originally."

Johann gave the old man's shoulder an affectionate pat. Then he reached in his vest pocket and produced a nickel, which he pressed into the creases of the old man's leathery hand. He then straightened his tie, picked up his briefcase, and walked across the hot morning street to the entrance of the Excelsior Hotel.

Next door, the front of the firehouse was open, and the fire chief, in shirtsleeves and suspenders, was polishing the steam-pumper. He was sweating so profusely that his withered crimson face looked as if it were jeweled with rhinestones. It was hot in the firehouse because the pumper had to be connected at all times to the basement boiler, and it was only when it was called out to a fire that the chief would toss an incendiary rocket into the pumper's own furnace to set it alight.

Johann paused for a moment to watch the fire chief at work. There was a hot smell of horses, brass polish, steam, and incandescent coal that made the firehouse seem like the waiting room to hell. After a while the fire chief came over to the door, wiping his hands on a rag.

"Howdy," he said, admiring his handiwork and hardly glancing at Johann.

Johann nodded. "How do you do. Looks like hot work."

"You bet."

Johann walked around the gleaming pumper respectfully. In every handle and bracket and pipe he could see his own face, brass-colored and distorted, and he could even see a ghostly red image of himself in the shining scarlet paintwork. The chief continued to wipe his hands.

Johann said: "You keep this thing polished all by yourself?"

"Sure do."

"Seems like an awful lot of unproductive time. I mean, if they made pumpers with less brass and more steel, you wouldn't have to furbish them up so much, would you? There's your helmet, too. That doesn't have to be brass. Up in New York they have black leather."

The fire chief rested his hands on his hips and stared at Johann with the expression of a man who's just taken a mouthful of cold coffee and doesn't quite know in which direction to spit it.

"Mister," he said, "a fire pumper without brass just ain't what a fire pumper *is*. Anyhow, using up time, that's what it's all *there* for. It's there to keep me busy, in between fires. A fireman's life ain't all chasing after burning chimney stacks and spraying water around the shop. No, sir! As they said to me back in the old days—a fireman's duty is to keep a good firehouse, and that's what counts."

Johann almost felt embarrassed at being so crassly ignorant of firehouse ethics. He said: "I'm sorry. I'm not an expert, you know. I don't know much about fires."

The fire chief hung up his rag. He was scrawny and potbellied, like a tough old turkey. "Well, friend," he said, "you'd learn yourself a great deal about fires if you stuck around here."

"Why's that?"

"Huh! Firetraps, these houses are. It only takes some drunken foreman from out at the camp to snooze off to sleep with his pipe going, and you've got yourself roast family before you can spit in the wind."

"Sounds dangerous."

"It sure is, and that's what I'm here for. Aside from the polishing, of course."

Johann stepped out into the street again and squinted up at the Excelsior. "That place must be a worry to you," he said.

The fire chief was blowing his nose. "What place?" he asked.

"The Excelsior, next door."

"Oh, that! That's the devil's own playground, that place is! We've had three fires there this year already, and one of 'em real serious. A fellow from Amarero Two was up there with a lady, and they was tussling around or something of the kind, her foot kicked the oil lamp by the bedside and spilled oil all over his back, and set him alight like a torch! That whole room smelled like pork cutlets for days."

Johann wiped the sweat from his forehead with the back of his hand. "If I was *in* that hotel," he said, "and I wanted to get *out* of there quick, because of a fire or suchlike, where would I go?"

The fire chief came out into the street too. He pointed with his polish-whitened fingers up to the second-floor balcony.

"That's easy," he said. "That balcony runs around the back of the building, and round the back there's an iron fire escape, bought from the old Magnificent Hotel at Dallas when they pulled it down, or it fell down, I don't recall which."

Johann nodded. "Thank you," he said. "And I wish you well with your fires."

"Won't you come in for a shot?" asked the fire chief. "Or there's some ginger wine if you're a temperance man."

"Thank you, no," said Johann gently. "I have some business to attend to."

He left the firehouse and walked around to the front of the Excelsior Hotel. The front doors of mahogany and patterned glass were hooked ajar to create a draft, and in the gloomy lobby Johann could see potted aspidistras, plush red sofas, and two or three well-dressed men standing around talking and smoking cigars. At the long marble-topped desk, which ran along the length of the right-hand wall, a desk clerk in a gray uniform braided with fraying gold cord was picking his nose. Johann stepped in, and walked with measured footsteps across the black-and-white-tiled floor. The desk clerk, a greasy-faced man with a brilliantined mustache, didn't even look in his direction. Johann pinged the bell.

"When you've finished prospecting for oil up that nose of yours, perhaps I can have some service," he said loudly.

The desk clerk turned, eyed him up and down, and said: "Okay, mister. Don't get yourself all riled up. What's it to be?"

"What's on offer?"

The desk clerk shrugged. "Well, that depends if you're staying or if you're just passing through, and it depends on whether you want breakfast with bacon and cream in your coffee, and it depends on how long it's been since you last got your leg over a lady. Where did you come from?"

"Edgar."

"And how did you come?"

"By automobile."

"Well, in that case, I guess you won't be as keyed up for a woman as some of them that have come all the way from Abilene by horse."

Johann rested his elbow on the counter and beckoned the desk clerk nearer. Then, when the man was close enough, he said: "A dollar bill says I'm looking for John Kummer."

The desk clerk stared at him without answering for almost half a minute. Then he said: "Five dollars has already said he ain't in."

Johann thought for a while, then stood up straight and nodded. "That's all right. Just make sure he knows that Johann Cornelius called and that Johann Cornelius won't be put off his debt for any longer."

"You ain't raising the ante?"

"Why should I? I'll catch him, sooner or later. That's what I came here for."

The desk clerk looked at Johann's muscular shoulders and thick-lipped, determined face and said: "Yes, I guess you will." Then he said, more cheerfully: "I don't suppose I can interest you in our latest acquisition?"

"What's that?"

The desk clerk made a clumsy circle out of finger and thumb, and kissed the air. "It's a peach, if you must know. A quadroon girl from Piedras Negras. Twelve years old and willing to learn anything you want to teach her. A clean slate, so to speak."

Johann looked at the man but said nothing. A tiny nerve pulled at the underside of his left eye, but otherwise he remained motionless.

"There she is now," said the desk clerk, leaning across the marble counter and pointing toward the far end of the lobby. Johann turned.

She was sitting in the faded light that fell through the frosted glass window onto the plush settees. The "Ex" of "Excelsior," a shadow from the hotel's name on the grimy pane, was patterned across her soft dusky cheek. There was another girl down there—a bleached blonde with dark roots and mottled acne scars on her cheeks—but the quadroon girl sat by herself, staring at the tiled floor as if she were waiting patiently for a train that was already four hours late. She was exceptionally pretty, with long dark eyelashes and curved pouting lips, and she was dressed in an incongruously quiet and elegant lace-waist dress of coppery brown Japanese silk, with elbow sleeves and collar trimmed with Valenciennes lace. Her black hair was brushed upward and tied with brown ribbons, leaving one or two stray curls around her ears. She did not look up when Johann first turned around, but after she became aware that he was staring at her, she lifted a small white Marcelaine silk fan and gazed at him bashfully over the top of it.

Johann turned back to the desk clerk.

"That girl there? She's a . . .?"

The desk clerk smoothed his mustache. "Most certainly is. Twelve years old and very clean. Ready for anything, if you want to know."

Johann felt an extraordinary sensation in his stomach that he had never felt before. He also found he was short of breath. He looked again at the girl, fascinated and horrified at the same time. She was so pretty, and so young, and so unspoiled, that it seemed electrifyingly disturbing to him that she should be a whore, and that she should be available to whatever stinking greasy middle-aged oilman wanted to put her price down on the desk clerk's counter. How could she allow herself to do it? She looked so delicate and respectable, she should have been sewing in a milliner's or still learning her lessons at school. Did she enjoy it, or was it the only way she knew how to make money? She was so poised, as if she came from a good family, and that was what made it even worse.

"Well?" said the clerk, drumming his fingers idly on the open register. "What's it to be? Two dollars fifty the half hour, eight dollars all night."

Johann said huskily: "I didn't come here for that. I came here for John Kummer. Just tell him I'm here in town, and if he wants me I'll be waiting outside in my automobile."

"Automobile, huh?" said the clerk. "Pretty fancy! Wish I was in the debt-collecting business."

66

Johann ignored his gibing, and turned around to leave the hotel lobby and return to the street. But when he reached the doors, he couldn't resist one last look back at the quadroon girl, who was still sitting there meek and pretty in the slanting light of the sun. She saw him looking, and this time she didn't hide her face behind her fan, but returned his gaze boldly.

He stepped out onto the boardwalk and took a deep breath. Then he straightened his panama hat and walked slowly around the side of the hotel to the alley where the kitchens were, and where the hotel laundry was dripping on long washing lines to dry in the noon sun. The kitchen door was open, and Johann could hear the clattering of pans on the range, and when he passed he saw a black kitchen-hand turning the handle of a bread mixer and singing "Tenting on the Old Camp Ground."

He checked his pocket watch. It was getting on for ten o'clock. When he had found John Kummer, he was going to get himself some late breakfast, and with any luck John Kummer would be picking up the check. He squinted up at the shabby back of the Excelsior Hotel, and he could see where the ornate iron fire escape ran down from the second floor into the backyard.

Kummer was even more predictable than Johann could have hoped for. It was at moments like this that Johann knew, without question, that he had that radiantly simple view of life that makes millionaires what they are. While ordinary mortals sweated and struggled to enmesh themselves in more and more complications, Johann Cornelius refused to perceive any problem as complicated, and he dealt with everything in a straightforward way that was sometimes crude but always brought the hogs home with their noses clipped and their ears marked. He knew that subtlety was something that only those who were content to remain poor could possibly afford. That was why he was standing at the back of the hotel, perspiring slightly in the prairie sun, as John Kummer came hurrying around the second-floor balcony in a cheap check summer suit and a haircloth hat, carrying a bulging carpetbag. Just behind him, with flouncing red skirts and all her possessions stuffed into a worn velvet bag, came a big-nosed girl with reddish hair all awry, and Johann gathered this to be the whore of sorts, Dolly Jarvis.

John Kummer came clanging down the iron fire escape, and Dolly Jarvis came clanging down after him. They pushed their way through the lines of wet bedsheets hanging on the washing lines, and reached the alley hand-in-hand, looking back up at the hotel as they went, for fear that Johann Cornelius had already discovered their room was empty and that they had taken to their heels.

Johann was standing there with his hands in his pants pockets, and John Kummer almost bumped into him. Johann said: "Hallo, John! Nice of you to come down so prompt."

Kummer was a bulging-eyed man with a sad mustache and enormous ears. He was so startled when he saw Johann that he froze in a pose of complete shock, like someone playing statues at a birthday party, and Dolly Jarvis stared at both him and Johann in complete bewilderment.

"I was thinking of taking some breakfast," said Johann calmly. "I drove over from Edgar this morning in the New Orleans, and I haven't had a bite since last night's supper. Won't you join me?"

Kummer licked his lips. He had a marked Minnesota accent when he spoke, which didn't improve his general desirability, and made him seem even shiftier and cheaper than he really was.

"That's real nice of you, Mr. Cornelius. But the fact is, the train's in from Broughton before too long, and I really have to catch it."

Johann took out his watch again. "I don't want to detain you," he said, "but the Broughton train isn't due until three this afternoon, and I usually reckon that five hours is enough for breakfast, don't you?"

"John," put in Dolly Jarvis, "is this that Cornelius man? Is this him? Tell him to get lost!"

John Kummer patted her arm and gave her an uneasy little smirk. "It's okay, Dolly. Mr. Cornelius here is a very understanding man."

Johann smiled at Dolly and nodded. "I'm known for my understanding," he told her.

"In that case," she said, "why are you keeping us here? We want to catch that train, and we've got a lot to do beforehand, so unless you've got anything important to say, I suggest you get out of the way and let us get on with it."

Johann adjusted his panama hat. "John," he said quietly, "I can't let you go without the money."

John Kummer said: "Money?"

"The seven hundred and thirty-two dollars and eight cents. The

68

money you owe me for rig maintenance and two four-stroke gasoline engines and everything you put into that dud oil well of yours and never paid me for."

John Kummer smiled and then abruptly stopped smiling.

"I'd appreciate settlement before you get on the train," said Johann. "Broughton's a long way off, and Mexico's even longer."

Dolly Jarvis said shrilly: "What do you know about Mexico? Who said we were going there?"

"Ma'am," replied Johann, raising his hat, "it's the natural place for anyone to go that owes seven hundred and thirty-two dollars and eight cents, and doesn't have the necessary capital to pay for it."

John Kummer suddenly said: "All right, Cornelius. That's enough. Out of our way."

"Not without the money, John," warned Johann.

"With or without. I'll pay you next month. Just get out of the way, that's all."

There was always a kind of code to arguments like these, but Johann didn't obey it. Instead of waiting for John Kummer to provoke him any further, he took one step forward and punched him, as hard as he could, in the mouth. He felt Kummer's teeth on his knuckles, and then Kummer fell over backward into the dust and lay there like a checkered log. Dolly Jarvis lifted her hands in surprise and shock, but all she could manage to say was a squeaky little "Oh! You've killed him!"

Johann inspected his knuckle, which was bleeding. "Oh, no," he told her, "I haven't done that."

John Kummer sat up. He didn't look at all well, and he spat three teeth, in strings of blood, onto the dusty alleyway. "Oh, fuck," he moaned.

Johann hunkered down beside him, and spoke in very soft, insistent tones. "John," he said, "I've invited you to breakfast and I recommend that you come. If you don't have the money to pay me, then I think we're going to have to work out a deal between us that satisfies everyone, especially me. You could use some ice water on that mouth, anyway."

"Oh, my God," said Dolly Jarvis. "Oh, my God, you're so *brutal*. Do you hear that? You're a brute!"

Johann turned around and looked at her. "I may be a brute, ma'am, but you're a harlot, and speaking for myself, I'd rather

69

make my money through honest brutality than spurious love."

"John!" shrieked Dolly Jarvis, pointing a grubby white glove at Johann. "Hit him!"

John Kummer wiped his mouth and climbed painfully to his feet.

"Hit him!" snapped Dolly. "Go on!"

John Kummer shook his head. "Come on, Dolly, let's just be sensible, huh? If I try to hit him, he's going to knock my head off, and for that pleasure I wouldn't exactly walk a mile."

"What are you?" said Dolly. "Some kind of a coward?"

Johann said: "I think he has a right to be, Miss Jarvis. I intend to get my money out of him even if I have to boil him down and sell him for laundry soap. I also have an Iver Johnson revolver in my automobile, and I will shoot him if necessary. A man's property and money may not mean much in Minnesota, but it's the law down here in Texas, and whatever people here may think of me, they've accepted me as a Texan."

"You're big enough and dumb enough," said Dolly sarcastically.

Without much further argument, they walked across the street to the Amarero Lunch Parlor. It was only two or three buildings away from where Johann had left his automobile, which was now being solemnly inspected by half a dozen scruffy small boys and a man in a plaid shirt and black Texas Ranger pants who looked like the Amarero idiot.

The lunch parlor was quiet at this time of day. It was a small white-painted place that used to be a hay-and-feed store, with white-painted wooden tables and bentwood chairs. There was a high counter with a glass case of pastries and crackers at one end, and an elaborate stack of cans of Doris Brand molasses at the other. As they sat down, a big woman with forearms like Kentucky hams came out from behind the counter and set down three glasses of ice water. In one corner of the parlor, a thin man in a derby hat sucked his coffee out of his saucer.

John Kummer was distinctly not hungry, although Dolly Jarvis ordered corned-beef hash and beans because she knew from experience that if you didn't eat free meals when they were offered you might end up paying for the next one. Johann asked for pancakes, bacon, Virginia links, fried eggs, hash, syrup, and cream. His taste in food was as straightforward and unpretentious as his business technique, but that didn't prevent him from eating a great deal of it.

Kummer was looking pale and bruised, particularly in the pallid light of the lunch parlor, which was filtered by cream paint that came halfway up the windows. He sipped his ice water and winced, and Dolly Jarvis sighed and crossed her legs and turned away, as if to say that at least he could have been a man and taken *one* swing at Johann Cornelius, even if it had missed.

While they waited for the food, Johann lifted his alligator briefcase onto the table and opened it.

"John," he said seriously, "I've got a proposition to make to you. You can take it or leave it, but if you leave it, I'll have to warn you that you'll go straight down to the sheriff's office and I'll have you thrown in jail for taking money by fraud."

John Kummer gave a seasick smile.

"I'm glad you're giving me the option," he said weakly, and Dolly Jarvis sighed dramatically and clucked and flounced even more.

"You have a hundred and six acres of land out there at Sweetwater Trail," said Johann. "You're entitled to it, all correct and legal, although I did hear that it was Indian land once, and that you didn't exactly pay them a whole mint for it."

John Kummer shook his head. "I paid two dollars an acre, fair and square. They took it, and if they took it, that's their problem, not mine."

Johann shrugged. "Your love of your fellow man really doesn't interest me. What I am interested in is how you're going to pay me back. I suggest that it might be fair and square if you *gave* me those hundred and six acres. I work that out at six dollars and ninety cents an acre, exclusive of rigs and engines and other equipment which I'm repossessing anyway, and when you look at it that way, you realize that you've actually made a profit of four dollars and ninety cents an acre, which is five hundred and nineteen dollars and forty cents."

John Kummer put down his glass of ice water. He appeared to be a little confused.

"You're telling me that I've actually made a *profit* of five hundred and nineteen dollars?"

"That's correct."

"So how come I wind up with no land, no machinery, and no

71

cash? If I made five hundred and nineteen dollars, where is it? Huh? I don't have any five hundred and nineteen dollars."

"And forty cents," added Johann.

Dolly Jarvis protested vociferously at this. "What kind of adding up is that?" she said harshly. "You're a first-quality, out-and-out stickup artist, and that's the whole truth of the matter in one word!"

Johann didn't even look at her. As the big woman with the muscular forearms brought their plates of food, with soda bread and fresh tomato salad, he picked up his knife and fork and said to John Kummer in a level and utterly calm voice: "There's your choice, John. Give me the land and get yourself out of Amarero a free man, or else it's down to the lock-up as soon as breakfast's over."

John Kummer looked miserable. He said: "What about my other creditors? What are they going to say? I might be paying *you* off, Mr. Cornelius, but I owe for the food and the clothes and the tools I used, and a whole lot more besides."

Johann crammed his mouth with pancake and sausages. "That's all right," he said. "No need to worry about that. You just go around to the people you owe, and tell them to come to me, and I'll pay them off in full."

Dolly Jarvis, who was forking up corned-beef hash as voraciously as if she expected to find a diamond necklace underneath it, stopped eating for a moment and regarded Johann suspiciously.

"You'll pay off all his debts?"

"That's what I said."

"How much are your debts, John?"

"Oh, I don't know. Four, five hundred bucks."

Dolly Jarvis wiped her mouth with her hand, and stared at Johann hard. Johann simply smiled at her affably, like a man on a pleasant Sunday-afternoon trolley ride smiling at his fellow passengers.

"Oh, you're a rat and a half," she said softly.

Johann kept on smiling.

"You're the sneakiest low-down dirty rat that ever took breath," she continued.

John Kummer frowned at her and said: "Come on, now, Dolly. Mr. Cornelius has made an offer that's going to get us out of

72

trouble. Don't let's strain the *entente cordiale* around here. Please?''

Dolly pushed away her half-eaten plate of corned beef.

"Are you so dumb, John Kummer, that you don't realize what game this man is playing?" she said scathingly. "Don't you understand what he's doing, and don't you understand what a mistake you're making?"

John Kummer scratched his head. Dolly gave an exasperated cluck, and then turned back to Johann. "You know something that John doesn't know, don't you, Mr. Cornelius?" she said. "You know that there's oil out there at Sweetwater Trail, and just because John ain't found it yet, that doesn't mean to say it ain't there. The minute we step on that train for Broughton, you're going to be out there with your pick and your shovel, and you're going to make yourself so much money that four or five hundred dollars won't seem like nothing more worthwhile than a red cent.''

Johann neatly mopped up the egg yolk from the side of his plate. "You should have been a businesswoman, Miss Jarvis," he said warmly.

"You forget," said Dolly Jarvis, "I am."

John Kummer didn't like that. "You mean you *were*," he told her. "You said you were giving it up."

Dolly turned and snapped: "How can I give it up when I'm hanging around with a penniless no-good booby like you? This is the first time in your whole life you ever made a profit, and besides the fact that you've spent it already, you have to give away a gusher to get it! You dumb bastard!"

Johann finished his meal and called for some fresh coffee.

"You can shout and scream all you want, Miss Jarvis," he said blandly, "but even if you kept that land for yourselves, you'd never find that oil in a million years, even if you knew where to look. You don't think I'm that simple, do you, that I'd give you the slightest inkling of what I was doing if I thought you'd be able to prospect it for yourselves? I like things plain and honest and out in the open, and what I'm saying is that I'll take the land in lieu of my debt, but that if the debt isn't paid, I'll make sure our mutual friend here spends the rest of his life breaking up rocks for the county."

John Kummer said: "It's hopeless, Dolly. I'm going to have to give it to him. Listen, Mr. Cornelius, I've got the papers here. There's an attorney on the next block, and he'll fix it for us."

"You worm," said Dolly Jarvis.

Kummer turned on her and banged the table with his fist. "Don't you call me no worm, you henna-haired whore! I'm doing this because I don't have no option! If you're so all-fired courageous, how come you're not back in Abilene, giving yourself up to the bail bondsmen?"

"Oh, nuts," said Dolly Jarvis.

Johann Cornelius stood up, took his hat off the hatstand by the wall, and pushed his chair back in.

"Thanks for the breakfast, Dolly," he said. "You're a generous woman."

Dolly glanced at the empty plates and cups and then back up at Johann, and flushed.

"What do you mean?" she said. "I thought this was *your* treat, not mine!"

"Let's just put it this way," Johann said. "It's sometimes easier to shell out for a late breakfast than it is to find a bounty hunter on your doorstep looking for ten percent of your bail money."

Dolly opened her purse, took out a dollar, and laid it on the table. She said quietly: "They used to tell me in Sunday school, when they found me behind the bushes with my drawers down and all the little boys looking, that I didn't have no morals. Until I met you, Mr. Johann Cornelius, I believed them. But now I've met someone who has no more morals than this table, and it's a frightening thing."

Johann didn't reply at first, but tipped his hat to the woman behind the counter, and ushered Dolly Jarvis and John Kummer out into the street. He stood for a moment on the boardwalk, screwing up his eyes against the glaring sun and the heat of approaching noon.

"I'll tell you something about morals, Miss Jarvis," he said as he watched a horse-drawn runabout jangle past, driven by a fierce-looking woman in an old-style bonnet and a floral print dress. "Morals are a way of anticipating the divine justice of the Lord on earth, in the hope that when the Day of Judgment finally arrives, that our hearts and our affairs will be in reasonable order. I live my life by a far greater morality than you because I have a far greater task to perform, and one day you will be able to think to yourself, with a considerable amount of pleasure, that you bought me my breakfast."

74

Dolly Jarvis gave Johann a long, expressionless stare, as if trying to capture this moment on some Lumière dry plate in her mind. "Come on," she said. "Let's get this over. The sooner we send the Reverend Cornelius on his way, the better I'll like it."

"The attorney's just down this way," said John Kummer.

Johann nodded. "If you're so anxious to be rid of me, I suppose we'd better go."

Dolly Jarvis, walking arm-in-arm with John Kummer, the heels of her button-up boots tapping on the boardwalk, turned around and looked at Johann and gave a sardonic little laugh.

"Oh, I'm not anxious to be rid of you," she said. "I just hope that one day the Lord grants me the pleasure of having you as a customer, and then, by God, I'll bite you where it hurts, and you won't forget Dolly Jarvis in a particular rush."

Johann said: "You shouldn't talk that way, you know. You're making our mutual friend nervous. A man should never be nervous when signing away his rights to anything, don't you agree? It makes the nib tremble, and forever after the deeds will show just how frightened he *really* was."

At three, Johann saw Dolly Jarvis and John Kummer off on the southbound train, and he stood by the side of the track, his thumbs in his belt, until the locomotive and its three-carriage train had almost disappeared into the distance, leaving nothing but a ringing reverberation in the rails and a series of black puffs of smoke which drifted away westward, expanding and opening like funeral plumes.

Then he left Amarero station, with its freshly painted signal box and its new maroon ticket office, and crossed the sun-baked yard to where his automobile was waiting. He took out the starting handle, cranked her up, and then climbed aboard to go and inspect his property.

It took twenty minutes to reach Sweetwater Trail, a remnant of one of the old cattle trails that had made fortunes for beef barons in the days before gasoline engines and lubricants. Johann stopped his car by a slabby butte that protruded out of the prairie, and sat there for ten minutes or more, looking around the hundred sloping acres of scrub and dust that a large sign optimistically announced as "Kummer One." It was a blazing afternoon, with only a few clouds on the horizon, and there wasn't more than a warm whisper of wind to relieve the heat. Johann took off his panama and wiped the sweatband with his handkerchief.

About six or seven hundred yards away, John Kummer's main drilling rig stood, silent and deserted. There was a small hut with a tin chimney stack, a wagon with a broken wheel, and a litter of ropes and tackle and abandoned tools. There were no shadows, and only lizards moved in the sun, staring at Johann with blank beady eyes.

There was only one job to do today. He got down from the car, making its springs creak, and walked over to the sign that said "Kummer One." He pushed and pulled it backward and forward until it eventually fell flat, with a clatter that seemed unnaturally loud. Then he went back to the automobile and took from the back floor a black-and-white sign that he had painted for himself three days ago. He found a hammer among the abandoned tools, and banged the new sign into the ground just a few feet away from the drilling rig. The sign said: "Cornelius Oil."

He used his sleeve to mop the sweat off his forehead. Then he swung the hammer around and threw it in a long tumbling parabola toward the oil camp. It struck the side of the hut with a hollow thump.

He knew there was oil out here. It would take him a little while to locate the best site for drilling, but he had already done enough casual experimental surveys around Sweetwater and Amarero to convince him that there was more black gold under the ground here than Kyle Lennox and all the other wildcatters dreamed of. Johann believed in science, not the hard-bitten spit-in-the-wind type of guesswork that had brought in Amarero One and most of the other wells in this part of the prairie. That was why he had spent a few hours of every visit to Amarero with a seismograph, popping off small charges of dynamite here and there, and recording his readings in a carefully written notebook—the same notebook that he had used to write down his analyses of Nathaniel's Engineering in New York. There wasn't any sense in buying a new notebook until this one was used up. They cost two cents each.

Johann had studied the whole subject of oil prospecting for almost two years—ever since he had arrived in Edgar. With weighty geological books imported from Europe by Kernbaum's Bookstore, he had spent night after night sitting in his apartment in the old red rambling house on Grange Street, gradually learning by the light of his glass reading lamp that the presence of oil was

76

indicated by underground salt domes. American opinion was that these salt domes were formed by the expansion of salt crystals or deposits from rising columns of brine which came up from deep and volcanic sources. But European theory attested that the salt flowed because of the weight of overhanging rocks. Johann read more and more, and eventually came to understand what geological features to look for, and how to use a seismograph, a torsion balance, and a gravimeter to test the formation of underground soil structures. It was the crust of the earth which told you whether there was likely to be oil under the ground or not, and Johann made sure that he could systematically and accurately find out where it was.

It was five months ago, on his last trip out to Amarero, that he had set off charges not far from Sweetwater. He had suspected then that John Kummer was in financial difficulties, and apart from being academically interested in whether there was oil under Kummer's property or not, Johann was also trying to safeguard the cash that Kummer owed him. He still wasn't sure how copious a well was there, and he wasn't at all certain where to start drilling. But the stuff was there all right, and he counted himself lucky that there were more than four million square feet in one hundred and six acres, and that John Kummer had picked all the wrong ones to drill in.

He stood there for a while, hands on his hips, looking around the dusty land in the afternoon heat. This was his beginning. This was where he came in with a chance to make some real money. He kicked the ground like a man testing a cartwheel to see if it was sound. He felt pleased, but at the same time he felt calm and detached. It wasn't luck that had brought him John Kummer's land. It was the culmination of all of his years of planning and study and hard work, plus the ten thousand dollars that Lidmore Mulliner had paid him to get out of Broughton and never return.

After a while he went back to his automobile and started it up. He backed the New Orleans up the slope by the butte, paused for a couple of minutes just to take a last satisfied look at the fresh-painted sign that said "Cornelius Oil," and then engaged the gears and drove northward in a billowing trail of dust.

He hadn't, to begin with, aimed at going back to Amarero. There was a shortcut he could have taken two or three miles outside of town, where the northbound track divided and one branch wended its way diagonally east across scrub and sand to join the

Edgar trail not far from the ridge where Johann had sat that same morning, looking at Amarero from way off. The shortcut would have saved him a good two miles, but when he reached the turnoff he kept heading due north, despite the nagging in the back of his mind that said *What are you doing? What are you doing?*

As he bounced over the rough track in his automobile, he kept telling himself that he needed to go to Amarero to top up his spare gasoline can. He was pretty sure he had enough fuel to get home, but you never knew for sure with automobiles. They were temperamental devices at the best of times. The last thing he wanted to do was camp out on the prairie all night with an empty gas tank.

It was only when he was actually driving down Main Street that he began to admit to himself what he was really doing. Even then, he felt as if he was completely helpless, completely unable to change the course of events by turning around and going straight home. Usually, he felt as if he was the master of his own destiny, but when it came to women, he lost his grip like a swimmer in the Colorado rapids losing his grip on a lifeline, and he was swirled away into the current.

He drew up right outside the Excelsior Hotel, and left his motor running. He stepped inside through the decorated glass doors, removing his hat, and walked up to the counter along the wall, where the desk clerk was now reading a copy of *The Broughton Sentinel* and picking his nose with even more industry than before. The quadroon girl was not there, and the plushy sofas were empty. An abandoned cigar butt still burned in a brown onyx ashtray, its blue smoke twiddling and twirling in the late-afternoon sunlight that fell through the windows.

Johann pinged the bell. The desk clerk looked up.

"Oh," he said, "you're back."

Johann felt cold and sweaty, and desperately uncertain about what he was going to say. The desk clerk waited expectantly for him to state his business, twisting the brilliantined hairs of his left mustache and blinking with disconcerting regularity.

"It occurred to me," said Johann, "that you might be open to certain financial arrangements."

The desk clerk raised an eyebrow.

"The thing is," Johann continued, "I wish to make you a proposition. This is only if it's economically suitable to you, and, well, romantically suitable to the person in question."

The desk clerk said: "Romantically?"

Johann nodded. "That's the only way I can think of to say it."

"I see," said the desk clerk.

Johann fingered the brim of his panama hat nervously. "This may be impossible," he said. "I'm not a usual visitor to this kind of establishment, and so I'm not sure of the etiquette. It may be out of the question."

The desk clerk said: "You're quite right. It may."

Johann swallowed. "On the other hand," he said, "the person in question may be amenable to it, and find it a satisfactory way to settle all sides of the problem."

The desk clerk dug in the corner of his eye with the end of his forefinger and then examined the speck of sleep that he had excavated, with apparent connoisseurship. "It sounds to me like you've got someone in mind," he suggested. "A lady?"

Johann fumbled with his hat. "A lady, yes. The . . . the young one. The quadroon who was down here earlier."

The desk clerk swiveled around in his chair and checked the clock on the wall behind him. "You're too late, I'm afraid."

"Too late? You mean she's already—"

"She's gone for her supper. She'll be back soon."

"Listen," said Johann. "I want to buy her."

The desk clerk sniffed. "All right. How long for?"

Johann came forward up to the counter and said: "You don't understand. I don't just want her for half an hour."

"All right," said the clerk. "It's eight dollars the night."

"No," said Johann. "I didn't mean that, either."

The desk clerk, pen poised over his guest book, looked up at Johann warily. "I can give you the night for seven-fifty," he said. "But no less. Not a cent less."

"You don't understand," said Johann, flushing. "I don't want her for just one night. I want her for good. I want to buy her from you completely."

The desk clerk laid down his pen. "In other words, you want to book her every single night? Three hundred sixty-five nights a year? Mister, that's going to cost you. I ain't so sure she's worth it. She's only thirteen, you know, and she don't have that much experience. Not much meat on her, neither."

"Well," said Johann, smiling a little with embarrassment, "I expect the meat will fatten up later. But you still don't understand what I mean. I want to purchase her for myself. I want to take her away from here, and have her live with me."

At that, the desk clerk stared at Johann as if he thought he was quite mad. In most ways, Johann thought he probably was. But he knew this was one compulsion which he would have to follow through. The quadroon girl had somehow moved him so deeply. that he *had* to have her. He didn't know if he wanted to save her from her sordid fate or if he wanted her to satisfy his own fleshly desires. He would have to think about that later. At the moment, all that concerned him was taking her away.

"Mister," said the desk clerk cagily, "that girl belongs to Mr. Kyle Lennox, the same way this hotel does, and the same way most of this town does. I don't believe that Mr. Lennox would take too kindly to the downright sale of one of his girls. I don't believe that at all."

Johann said: "In other words, you don't want to take the responsibility?"

"Well, no, sir, I'm not sure that I do."

"In that case," said Johann, "I'll go speak to Mr. Kyle Lennox myself. Do you happen to know if he's in town today?"

The desk clerk nodded, and closed his guest book. "Mr. Lennox is always in town. But take it from me, I don't think he's going to take too kindly to the downright sale of one of his girls."

"Well, leave that to me," said Johann. "Tell the girl to wait, and not to go with any customers, and I'll be back in a half hour."

"Okay," said the desk clerk. "It's your funeral."

Johann left the hotel and climbed aboard his automobile. It was growing cooler now, and the sun was touching the top of the Red Star Stores & Ironmongery opposite. The dusty street was striped with shadows, and someone in an upstairs room was playing a trumpet. A surrey clattered past with its horse sniffling and jangling its bridle. There was a dry, aromatic smell of prairie in the air, mingled with the strong aroma of fatback and beans.

With a loud backfire, Johann's automobile jerked forward and futtered up the street. He steered the motorcar out through the few stables and stores that dotted the northern boundary of the town, and then drove across the hard prairie track that led to Kyle Lennox's mansion.

It was a three-story Gothic house of uncomely proportions. Kyle Lennox had ordered it built from a drawing in a magazine, and while the Amarero carpenter had done his best, he was more used to putting oil rigs together, and the house had finished up impressive enough but oddly disturbing to look at. None of the windows seemed to be in quite the right place; none of the doors were sufficiently wide; and the carvings and decorations were only as good as an enthusiastic stick whittler could have done with a small penknife. The front yard was surrounded by a neat green pale, although nothing grew there but three or four tough, stunted bushes.

Johann switched off his engine, dismounted from his car, and went up to the front gate. He paused for a moment before he walked up the red-ash path, and he thought about the risk of what he was doing. He was well-known around these parts, and respected. It wasn't that he cared what anyone thought of him; it was just that for now, he depended too much on local approbation and support in his efforts to make money. If the tale of this day's conversations got around, and there was always a risk of that, he wasn't at all sure that he could still command the same influence in Edgar, or anywhere about. When he struck oil, the townsfolk of Edgar could choke themselves with their own tongues as far as he cared, but tonight called for discretion.

He squinted at the fading sun. The trouble was, he didn't even feel that he had any choice. The moment he had set eyes on that girl, he had known that he wanted her. There wasn't any question of going back now.

He walked up the path, mounted the two wooden steps that led to the porch, and knocked on the narrow mulberry-colored door. Inside, he heard a dog barking, and the sound of footsteps.

It was Kyle Lennox himself who opened the door. Johann had seen tintypes of him in *The Amarero Citizen*, but he had never met him in person. He looked older and oilier than he had in print—a fat dissolute man in a purple silk smoking jacket, with a broad sweaty face and a heavy walrus mustache. He was smoking a cigar and carrying a cut-glass tumbler of bourbon, and he stood there looking at Johann as if he'd been expecting him, but wasn't quite sure if he was real.

"Mr. Cornelius," he said, in a phlegmy voice. "How grand of you to call."

Johann took off his hat. "The hotel called you, did they, on the telephone? I saw the wires, and wondered."

"Well, actually, they did," grunted Kyle Lennox. "But I would have known you anyway. The reputation of Johann Cornelius has made itself felt in these parts, and don't you know it."

"May I come in?" asked Johann.

Kyle Lennox swung wide the door, and Johann stepped past him. Lennox's breath stank of drink and anchovies, and as he bowed with mock formality to welcome Johann into his house, Johann could see that his hair was dyed black and was growing silver at the roots.

The hall was musty and dark, as if nobody ever opened a window. It was hung with florid late-Victorian oil paintings of women with immense thighs and cascading bosoms, and the furniture, though sparse, was dark and immense. A German shepherd with one ear bitten to shreds was lying panting on the rose-patterned carpet next to the umbrella stand. Even though the usual annual rainfall in Amarero was something less than four inches, the stand was crowded with gold- and silver-knobbed umbrellas. In society magazines, Kyle Lennox had seen umbrellas in the homes of all the leading socialites, and he considered at least ten of them essential equipment in any high-class residence.

"The widow's resting, I regret," explained Kyle Lennox, following Johann unsteadily into the drawing room. "She has *turns* these days, not being as young as she was, and she finds the only way to get rid of them is to lie in bed with drapes drawn, and cover her face with Creme de Java."

"I'm sorry about that," said Johann politely, looking around the room.

"I'm not," said Kyle Lennox. "It gives me a chance to read my French magazines. Do you want a drink?"

"No, thank you."

"A cigar? They're good, you know. An old gambling buddy of mine brings them direct from Havana."

"No, no. I don't smoke."

Kyle Lennox sat himself down in a big red plush Morris rocker with swan's necks carved on the arms. The whole drawing room was furnished in this style, with a massive davenport of quarter-sawed oak, a gigantic gondola couch, and various armchairs of ill-assorted sizes. There were more paintings and engravings on the walls, but they were so awkwardly arranged that it always looked as if some were missing, or there was one too many. The carpet was dark tan with a floral pattern and pictures of castles on it.

"Well," said Kyle Lennox, crossing his fat legs in their gray grease-spotted pants. "You don't drink, and you don't smoke. I gather you're a first-class attender of church too."

Johann sat down on the edge of the davenport, with his hat on

82

his knee, and said nothing. Kyle Lennox eyed him, and puffed more smoke into the stale drawing-room air.

"If you're as good a fellow as all that," said Lennox, "what *do* you do for fun?"

Johann coughed. "If they've already called you on the telephone, Mr. Lennox, they would have told you why I'm here. I want to make this as brief and as modest as possible."

"I'm sure you do."

"The fact is, you employ a young quadroon girl down at the Excelsior Hotel. I would like to employ her myself, permanently, as a housekeeper and companion. This would be subject, of course, to her approval, and to whatever price you would care to ask for her transfer."

Kyle Lennox scrutinized Johann with an amused smile.

"I want you to know," added Johann, "that she would be well looked after. She would be cared for, and fed, and her general education would be continued."

"Aha," said Kyle Lennox.

"I can pay well," said Johann, "and I would hope that between us we could reach a quiet and satisfactory settlement. A gentleman's agreement to the benefit of all concerned."

Kyle Lennox swallowed some more bourbon, and then stretched back in his chair, setting it rocking on its lion's-claw feet. The whole idea of Johann Cornelius wanting to buy one of his girls seemed to tickle him enormously.

"Mr. Cornelius," he said, "you don't seem to grasp the nature of the girl's business. As the old saying goes, whoring is the world's greatest industry. You have something, you then sell it, but having sold it, you still have it to sell again. Carina is not a cake of kitchen soap or a half-pound of cheese. She's going to make money for me for the next twenty or thirty years, until her hair goes white and her teeth drop out and she has to spend the rest of her days fornicating with circus mules to make a few pennies for food. That's the way it is, and that's the way it always will be."

Johann said: "How much do you anticipate that she will make for you in her working lifetime?"

Kyle Lennox noticed the tenseness in his voice, and looked less amused than before.

He said: "Twenty dollars a night for three hundred sixty-five nights is seven thousand three hundred dollars. Seven thousand three hundred dollars times twenty years is one hundred and forty-six thousand dollars. The girl, you see, is a little gold mine.''

"You're not saying that you want a hundred and forty-six thousand dollars?''

"You're a friend. You can have her for one hundred and forty.''

Johann lowered his eyes. "That's out of the question.''

Kyle Lennox laughed. "Let's face up to it, Mr. Cornelius. You just can't afford her.''

"I could pay you by installments.''

"In which case, I would give her to you by installments. A few minutes each week at first, and only full-time when you had paid everything off. Mr. Cornelius, it's only fair.''

Johann rubbed his chin thoughtfully for a moment, and then stood up.

"I don't think we can do business, Mr. Lennox,'' he said huskily. "You'll excuse me for taking up your time.''

Kyle Lennox shrugged. "Well, if you can't see your way to the price, that's very sad.''

"Will you show me out?''

Kyle Lennox didn't answer, but puffed at his cigar, with a frown on his face, the frown of a man who is trying to work out something complicated in spite of three-quarters of a bottle of bourbon.

"Will you show me out?'' repeated Johann.

"Wait a moment,'' said Lennox, waving his hand. "Supposing we put it this way. Supposing you give me ten percent of whatever you find on the Kummer land out at Sweetwater Trail. Supposing you agree to do that.''

"Then you'd give me the girl?''

"Certainly. No question about it.''

Johann looked at Kyle Lennox closely. There was a toadlike look about him that Johann found repulsively fascinating. If ever a man had his character advertised on his face, it was the oil magnate of Amarero. But as Johann had already discovered, it didn't do in Texas to hide any of your lights under any of your barrels, and if Kyle Lennox was going to do business like a toad, then it was all the better if he looked like one.

"You think there's oil there?'' asked Johann.

"No doubt about it,'' said Kyle Lennox. "If there wasn't, why should you want it?''

Johann kept his eyes on the floor. "It could be that I'm thinking of raising myself a few cows."

"At Sweetwater? Don't make a sick man laugh. What are they going to eat out at Sweetwater? Lizard mornay, with cactus juice for dessert?"

Johann still didn't look up. "Could be that I'm thinking of opening myself a new engineering works."

"Sure," admitted Kyle Lennox. "Except that you don't go looking for building land with dynamite charges and a seismograph. When you go looking with dynamite charges and a seismograph, you're looking for oil, in the approved fancy up-to-the-minute Frenchified way."

Johann, looking thoughtful, walked back across the drawing room to the window. This side of the house faced west, and the dazzling orange sun was sinking toward the horizon in a haze of indigo dusk. Almost silhouetted against it, the thin outline of Kyle Lennox's Negro gardener worked at the dried-up rows of broccoli with a spindly hoe, and the chop of metal against hard soil reached Johann where he stood. He glanced down at the small carved side table beside him, and there was an open copy of *La Vie Parisienne*, with a two-tone drawing of a pretty girl pleasurably startled by two butterflies suckling her nipples.

"Eight percent," said Johann in a low but decisive voice.

Kyle Lennox didn't turn around.

"Nine," he said, by way of reply.

Johann came away from the window, and sat down again on the edge of the davenport. He looked Kyle Lennox straight in the eye, and he said softly: "Mr. Lennox, you care for money so far above the welfare of the girls you own, and you are so convinced that there is oil out at Sweetwater Trail, that you know in your heart and your mind that eight percent is more than a generous price."

"Eight and a half?" suggested Kyle Lennox.

Johann sat back and simply stared at him without any expression at all. Kyle Lennox looked back at him twitchily for a few moments, and then uncrossed his legs and said: "All right. Eight percent it is."

Johann extended his hand. "Let's shake on that, Mr. Lennox, and let me say one more thing."

"What's that?" joked Lennox. "Seven and a half percent?"

"No, the price is agreed. But I just want to say that this is a private bargain, between men of honor. If you so much as whisper the news of this to anyone at all, I shall be round here in what I can only call a less than forgiving humor."

"You have a fine way of putting it, Mr. Cornelius," said Kyle Lennox. "Would you care for a drink?"

"No, thank you. If you would just kindly call the Excelsior, and tell the girl to get ready, I will collect her on my way back to Edgar."

Kyle Lennox set down his bourbon glass and walked out to the hallway where a five-magnet telephone in a heavily decorated mahogany case was hung on the wall. He picked it up and gave his instructions to the desk at the Excelsior in a soft mutter, in case the widow heard from her sickbed upstairs. Johann heard him saying: "That's right, trunk, hatboxes, and all. In ten minutes."

Lennox then came back into the drawing room and stood for a while with his cigar in his mouth and his hands in his smoking-jacket pockets, smiling at Johann in an odd kind of way, as if he couldn't make out what manner of person this Cornelius fellow was at all.

Johann said: "I shall be off, then," and he put on his panama.

Kyle Lennox kept on smiling. "I wish I knew what you were going to do with our young Carina," he said. "A man like you—well, it doesn't seem usual, somehow. Mind you, the priest around here, Father Pankhurst, he's had a few strange moments. Maybe it's all those years of going without."

"Mr. Lennox," said Johann, "what I now do with Carina is none of your business. Our deal is settled."

"Okay," replied Lennox. "I get the hint. But you can take your little girl along in the happy knowledge that anything you want her to do, she'll do. Why, if you even asked her to open that pretty mouth of hers so's you could—"

"I said, it's none of your business!" snapped Johann.

"Okay, okay, no offense meant," said Lennox soothingly, raising his hands in mock surrender.

Johann said: "I apologize. I didn't mean to lose my temper. I'd better go now."

Together they walked through the hallway to the front door. As Johann stepped outside into the warm evening air, Kyle Lennox stood by the porch rail and breathed in the aroma of dust and weed. "Can't say I care too much for oxygen," he said. "I've heard that it rots the mind!".

Johann walked down the ash path to the gate and opened it.

"I'll say good-bye, then."

Lennox gave him a wave of the hand. "Good-bye, Mr. Cornelius. It's been a pleasure to do trade with you. I hope you're happy with your goods, and I know that I'm going to be happy with my eight percent."

"Yes," said Johann, and went across to his automobile.

As he mounted the step and sat down in the driving seat of the car, something moved him to lift his eyes from the purple figure of Kyle Lennox on the porch and glance up at a lace curtain that was twitched in an upstairs window. For a few seconds he saw a pale unlovely face peering out at him through the glass, and then the curtain fell back again. He looked down again at Kyle Lennox, who was still grinning and waving, and he felt terribly disturbed. If Lennox had condemned himself to live in this grotesque house on the prairie, with this wan woman in her face creams, then his dissolution and his greed for money must have surpassed anything that Johann had ever felt. He just hoped that, in his own way, he wasn't another Kyle Lennox in the making. Often the ugliest visions are the visions which appear in the mirror. He didn't wave at all, but turned his automobile and drove back into the center of Amarero with the sun on his right cheek and the first chill of evening on his left.

He pulled the New Orleans to a shuddering stop right outside the hardware store and stepped down. The proprietor, a tall mournful young man with a brown storekeeper's apron and a heavily scented walrus mustache, came out onto the boardwalk wiping his hands. He stood there and looked at the New Orleans and said nothing. Then he looked at Johann and said nothing. The pale evening sky was reflected in the store window behind him, and a price tag on a Dutch hoe handle whirred and flapped in the breeze.

"You stock gasoline?" asked Johann at length.

The young man nodded. "We surely do. You want some? We got some good cheese, too, just came in from the coast."

"Just the gasoline, thanks."

"You're the boss," said the young man, and walked around the back of the store to bring the gasoline. While he was gone, Johann paced up and down the boardwalk, checking his watch again. If he'd had a mind to, he could have bought a long-tine alfalfa fork for sixty-nine cents.

The young proprietor came back around the store with a red-painted enamel can of gasoline and a brass funnel. Johann unscrewed the cap of the fuel tank for him, and he began to pour the gasoline in.

"How'd you like her?" he asked. "Reckon she's pretty bumpy out on these roads."

Johann wasn't really listening, and he said: "What?"

"Pretty bumpy," repeated the young man.

Johann frowned at him, and brushed back his straying hair with his hand. "Oh, sure. I see what you mean. No, she's not too bad."

The proprietor sniffed, and jerked his head over to the northwest. "Old Jack Hulton, one of his boys had one. I don't know what make it was. But the first time he took it out, it overturned in a dry ditch and he busted his neck. It didn't kill him, mind, but they have to wheel him around in a basket chair now, and feed him with mushed-up oats."

Johann gave a brief, uninterested smile. The gasoline gurgled and splashed into the automobile's tank, and the simmering fumes distorted the darkening evening air.

"Saw a fellow was killed in Broughton, too, by his own machine. Got himself run over."

Johann said impatiently: "Listen—how long is this going to take? I have to meet someone."

The young man sniffed. "You want it filled up, don't you? I have to take it slow, on account of it's inflexible."

"Inflammable, not inflexible."

"You bet. You sure you don't want some cheese?"

Johann shook his head. "Just fill the car and I'll get going."

Eventually the young man had emptied the red-painted can. He shook out the last few drops with a flourish, and then screwed the top back on.

"There you are, sir. Filled to the brim. Just mind you don't do what that fellow in Broughton did. Squashed flat like a bug, he was."

Johann paid him, and then climbed back up into the driving seat to set the spark and the throttle. The hardware-store man watched him, and added: "It just goes to show, doesn't it, that God can strike you down no matter what kind of man you are, storekeeper or sodbuster or attorney-at-law.''

Johann raised his head. "Attorney-at-law? What made you say that?"

The proprietor blinked, as if he couldn't even remember what he'd been talking about. "Well," he said slowly, "the fellow in Broughton that was squashed flat, he was an attorney-at-law. Least, that's what it says in the *Sentinel*."

"Do you have a copy?"

"Well, uh . . . sure. It's inside."

"Will you go get it for me?"

Puzzled, the storekeeper disappeared inside the doorway of his store, ducking down to avoid the cheese graters and nutmeg scrapers and Hunter's Old Reliable flour sifters that festooned the frame. He came back with a crumpled copy of *The Broughton Sentinel* on which somebody had obviously been blacking their boots, and handed it over. He pointed to a story at the foot of the front page, and then stood back and watched with undisguised curiosity while Johann read it.

For a while the only sounds in the street were the flapping of the newspaper in the breeze and the fitful whirring of the price ticket on the hoe.

The headlines read "Tragic Automobile Accident Kills Broughton Lawyer," "Crushed to Death by Own Vehicle," "A Most Heart-Rending Scene on Beaumont Street."

The man who had died was Lidmore Mulliner. According to the newspaper, which was written in the most flowery and melodramatic way, he had been taking his wife, Mrs. Beatrice Mulliner, for a first run in his new Pierce Arrow, just delivered. Toward the end of Beaumont Street the automobile had stalled, and Mr. Mulliner had climbed out of the car to restart it. Just as he had managed to get the engine going again, the emergency hand brake had slipped, and the automobile had jumped forward and knocked Mr. Mulliner to the ground, running over his chest with its right front wheel. By the time three passing accountants had been able to lift the Pierce Arrow from his prostrate body, he was at the point of death, and had expired without even passing on the combination of his office safe.

Johann laid the newspaper down. His face showed no emotion at all, but inside he felt as if something extraordinary had happened, as if pages had fallen from the calendar in scores, as if the sun had come up again, and set again, as if the ground beneath his feet had stirred.

He handed the paper back to the hardware-store proprietor. Farther along the street, in the gathering shadows, he saw the door of the Hotel Excelsior open, and a small figure step out onto the boardwalk. He said in a distant voice: "Thank you. I appreciate your kindness."

The hardware proprietor said nothing as Johann started up his automobile and moved off down the street toward the corner. But he stood there and watched for a long while before ducking back into the shady, soap-and-leather-smelling interior of his store to light up the lamps.

She was waiting for him on the hotel steps. She was wearing the same brown dress of Japanese silk, only this time she wore a fawn spring cape over her shoulders, decorated with brown piping, and a brown mushroom hat with ribbons. At her feet were two hatboxes and a smallish basswood trunk. The faded light of evening made her look even younger and slimmer than Johann remembered her, and as he drew his automobile up to the corner and applied the brake, she turned toward him with the intensely beautiful face of a dark child, and he felt that same shortness of breath that he had felt before.

He climbed down from the car. He was broad and heavy, while she, even in her velvet-and-patent Blucher boots, was only a little over five feet. He held out his big hand and said as gently as he could: "Carina? I'm Johann Cornelius."

She nodded, without speaking.

"Are these your boxes? Your trunk?"

She nodded again.

"Okay, then," he said uncomfortably, and he picked up the luggage and stowed it along with his briefcase in the back seat of the New Orleans. Then he turned and helped her to mount to the front passenger seat, where she sat with her hands demurely together on her lap.

He climbed aboard himself, and released the brake. "You're not frightened, are you?" he asked her. "This thing's noisy as all hell, and if you're not used to it, it can shake you up. But it won't hurt you."

Carina looked at him, and inclined her head almost imperceptibly to show that she understood.

"All right, then," said Johann, revving up the automobile's engine and engaging the gears, "let's get going."

He was ready to start when the desk clerk appeared at the door of the Excelsior Hotel, waving a piece of paper. Johann disengaged the gears again and turned around in his seat. The desk clerk came down the hotel with a particularly insolent smile.

"What's this?" said Johann, as the clerk handed him the paper.

"Speaks for itself," answered the clerk, and then said: "Goodbye, Carina. Have fun!"

Johann took off one of his gauntlets and unfolded the paper. It was a regular bill from the "Hotel Excelsior, Fine Food & The Telephone, 27 Main Street, Amarero, Where Nobs Stay." On it was written: "For one girl, 8% gross oil rights at Sweetwater Trail, rec'd with Thanks."

When he read that, Johann felt for the first time in his life that he had gone against God. He tucked the bill away, and drove off.

They drove for hours across the prairie. The moon hadn't risen yet, and they had been making their way by the dim yellowish light of the automobile's lamps, bouncing and creaking over ruts and hard-baked cattle tracks, and almost choked sometimes by dust. Carina had taken off her hat and wrapped a fascinator around her head, although she remained silent, and hadn't said a single word to Johann since he had first collected her from the hotel steps.

Sometimes they saw lights of homesteads and ranch houses from way off. They twinkled through the huge prairie night like the lights of ships far away at sea, with the whole night sky glittering with stars above them. The wind was cooler, but still gentle, and the barking of dogs carried for miles.

Johann cleared the dust from his throat and said: "It makes you feel lonely, doesn't it, out here at nighttime?"

Carina said nothing. He could see by the reflected sparkle of the lamps in her eyes that she wasn't asleep. But she didn't even turn her head or acknowledge that he had spoken.

He drove for while longer, and then he said: "I discovered today that someone had died, someone whose death could have meant a lot to me, if it had happened a while sooner. I was thinking about death, too, and how it must leave you all alone, like being on this prairie at night. I was thinking . . ."

He paused. She didn't even seem to be listening. But then he said: "I was thinking that you have to take your chances when and where you can find them. I mean, your chances of not being alone."

He didn't know what else to say after that, so he fell silent. Over the lip of the prairie, a curve of light appeared, as white as a frightened face, as the moon came up.

Not long before they saw the lights of Edgar, Carina unexpectedly reached her hand over and touched his thigh. It wasn't a sensual touch; but more a touch that sought reassurance, and companionship. Johann turned his head and saw that her eyes were glistening with tears. She was muffled up in her knitted fascinator, and he could hardly see her face, but he suddenly realized that her long silence had not been hostility, or aloofness. She was a thirteen-year-old girl who had been packed off without warning with a hefty twenty-nine-year-old engineer, and even though she might have been a prostitute, and been prepared to do anything at all with anyone, Johann wondered how much of that was simply because she knew nothing about life and what was expected of her, and had no friends.

"Was it someone you loved?" she asked him. She had a soft, lisping Mexican accent.

He squeezed her hand kindly. "Not really. I met him once, but I didn't know him well. It's nothing to worry about. It was a shock, that's all."

"I thought . . ." she said, and then stopped herself.

"What did you think?"

"When you went to Kyle Lennox, and bought me, I thought you loved nobody. But you do, don't you?"

Johann steered the automobile across a rough patch of rocks and ruts. "What do you know about love?" he asked her.

"I don't know much," she said, shaking her head.

They drove in silence for a little while longer, and then Johann said: "Did it surprise you, when you heard what I'd done?"

"A little. I was frightened, though, because some men are very strange."

"You've known . . . a lot of men? *Muchos hombres*?"

She nodded.

Johann, in spite of the empty feeling that her nod provoked in his stomach, attempted a smile.

"Well," he said as cheerfully as he could, "that *was* your business."

"You don't like it," she said.

"I didn't say that. I just said, that *was* your business."

She dropped the fascinator so that the wind and the dust blew in her dark upswept hair. "You are jealous, though, aren't you? You want everything to be your own, to belong to you. You don't like to think that I went with many men."

"I didn't say that either."

"You didn't have to. I can see."

Johann said: "It doesn't matter now, anyway. It's all in the past. It's forgotten."

"I can't forget," argued Carina. "All those men, I was with them. I can't forget them."

"Well, you'll have to try."

"Why? Because you want me to? You bought my body. That was all. You didn't buy what's in here." She tapped her head.

He looked at her wildly. "It's for your own goddamned good! The sooner you . . . wipe those things out of your memory—"

"The better you'll like it?"

He looked at her again, and he suddenly realized she was deliberately teasing him. He started to laugh, and then they were both laughing. He was laughing so much he almost drove into a scrub of bushes, and he had to twist the wheel around to get himself back on the track.

"You must stop yourself from feeling jealous," she said, holding his arm. "If you want me to live with you, you must stop yourself. I cannot change what happened now. All those men who put themselves inside me, nothing can change that."

Johann said: "Was it many? I mean, was it fifty, or a hundred?"

Carina stroked his chin with her hand. "Does it matter?" she asked him. "Why is a hundred worse than fifty?"

"I just—"

She raised her hand so that it sealed his mouth. Then she leaned over and said quietly: "Don't worry. If you have bought me, then I will learn how to love you. You can teach me."

Johann drove in silence for a while, and then he turned to gaze

93

with increasing strangeness and wonder at her gentle profile, her soft parted lips, and the tears that sparkled in her eyes. He felt terribly afraid, as if he had stepped off the straightforward path that God had set for him, and indulged desires without regard for anyone's feelings but his own. He knew that he had committed a sin by buying Carina, although he wasn't quite sure which sin it was. He didn't lust after her or even want to touch her. He just wanted to *own* her because she was a beautiful thing. He knew without question that he was going to pay for this day's disobedience, and yet his desire to have Carina was so strong that he never once considered turning back to Amarero, delivering her back with her trunk and hatboxes to the Excelsior Hotel, and forgetting that she had ever taken his eye.

"I don't know," he said, "if I can teach you love. I have had very little love myself. I can teach you friendship."

She touched his hand. "Perhaps we can learn it together. Two people who don't know, trying to learn!"

"You're so young," he said. He coughed in the clinging dust.

"Young!" she exclaimed. "I'm thirteen next week!"

He stared at her uneasily. "But that's so young. You're nothing more than a child."

She sat there in her cape and fascinator, so upright and ladylike, and said: "I *used* to be young. I was young when I started. I was ten when I started. My tenth birthday! But now I know more. I've found out which men are the sons of bitches and which men aren't."

Johann said: "I'm afraid there's more to life than that."

"You think so?" she answered. "I don't think so. I think if you can tell a man for a son of a bitch the first time you lay your eyes on him, then that is all you have to know."

"What about me? Am I a son of a bitch?"

Carina put her head on one side and smiled at him sweetly.

"Yes," she said. "You are the biggest son of a bitch of all."

He laughed. "What makes you say that?"

"Because you will always get what you want, no matter what, and you will always get it cheap. Mostly, you will get it for nothing."

"I didn't get *you* for nothing."

"What did you pay? Can I ask?"

Johann said: "Of course you can ask. I gave Kyle Lennox eight

94

percent of the oil rights to the hundred acres I own out at Sweet-water Trail.''

"And how much is that?''

"It depends. It might make him a wealthy man for the rest of his days, it might not. Until we bring the well in, we don't have any idea how much crude is down there at all.''

"And, just for me, you will give him all that?''

"That was the deal.''

She lowered her head. "I didn't think I was worth a fortune.''

Johann was embarrassed. "Don't flatter yourself,'' he said. "He was originally asking for ten, and I knocked him down.''

"Ah,'' she said, "but that is the way you are. In the end, you'll see you will get me for nothing. No—I don't mind. That is just the kind of man you are. One day, I think you will be very rich.''

"Well, let's hope so. Look—there's the lights of Edgar. Now let's see what you think of the way a budding rich man lives.''

Carina leaned closer against him, and held him near as he drove, and he was glad for the sake of his reputation that Edgar's streets were almost deserted as they drove in, and that the lighting on most corners was dim enough to make it difficult for anyone whose curtains parted to see what that goddamned futtering was—at this time of night for Lord's sake—or to make out who they were.

He pulled up on Grange Street, by the white fence of his big red house with white shutters, and he reached into his vest pocket to find his front-door key. As they reached the porch, Carina turned and smiled at him happily, excited with her new life, and that made him feel even guiltier than ever.

Johann, being the owner, had the largest apartment in the house. He occupied the whole of the third floor, which included a sitting room, a dining room which he usually used as a study, a kitchen, a bathroom, a main bedroom, and a smaller bedroom which opened out into the Gothic turret on the northwest corner of the house. Carina went up the stairs first, carrying her hatboxes, and Johann came clumping up behind with her basswood trunk and his briefcase.

The door from the landing opened straight into Johann's cramped little hallway, with an ugly hall stand that was all protruding coat hooks and cheap varnish. He dropped everything

95

there, and ushered Carina through to the sitting room, where he went around lighting the lamps and opening the two wide windows. This evening he drew the red velvet drapes as well, although he wasn't in the habit of it. What does a puritanical engineer do on his own that any passerby is going to find of burning prurient interest?

The floors in the apartment were dark-stained oak, laid with red-and-brown rugs which he had picked up as a bargain from a traveling carpet salesman. In the sitting room, the walls were papered in green fleur-de-lis patterns, and hung with black-framed sepia photographs of views of Holland. Johann's furniture was all solid, functional business pieces which he had bought at an auction of effects from a cattle broker's office at the respectable end of Amarillo Street. Brown leather armchairs, each uglier than the last, were crowded around an enormous golden oak desk with brass handles, a high-backed davenport in brown plush, and other odd and uncomfortable knickknacks that belonged more in an office than a private home, like a Bank of England swivel chair and a varnished filing cabinet.

Across the corridor, as she peeked around the apartment, Carina could see the small dining room. The table was piled high with engineering books, and a greasy part of a steam piston lay on the sideboard on a piece of folded-up newspaper.

"The first thing to do is get yourself into the tub," said Johann. "Have yourself a good long bath, and get rid of the dust. There's no scented soap, I'm afraid, only plain, but I'll put a clean towel out for you, and you can borrow the bathrobe that's hanging on the back of the door if you need it."

While Johann lit the cylindrical gasoline water heater beside the bath, Carina unpacked her trunk in the small turret bedroom. There was a narrow brass bed in there, and a veneered wardrobe which smelled of mothballs, and a rag carpet. A print of Loch Lomond hung above the bed. Carina hung up her six silky dresses and put away her shoes. She had stockings to put away, too, and petticoats; but no underclothes, because she never wore them. On the windowsill she laid her cheap Russian-bristle hairbrush and comb, and a creased and faded photograph of a Mexican woman peering into harsh sunlight.

Johann rapped on the door and said: "Water's hot now, Carina."

After Carina had padded into the bathroom, and rather disconcertingly left the door ajar, Johann went into the kitchen and stoked up the cooker with corn cobs ready for supper. He was only a bachelor cook, but he could put together a good plateful of bacon and eggs, with hunks of bread and fresh butter from his little ice chest, and that was the fanciest food that anyone could want after jolting on automobile springs all the way from Amarero.

The cobs were burning up nicely when the bell in the hallway rang. Wiping his hands on a grubby towel, Johann went out and opened the front door of his apartment, and said: "Yes?"

A woman was standing alone on the landing, in a large plumed black hat and a black spring coat.

Johann peered into the shadow under the veiled brim of her hat.

"Yes?" he said again.

The woman didn't move. She remained dark as a raven on the landing, accoutered in jet beads and black gloves, like a visitation from the grave.

"I don't know you," said Johann. "Did you want another apartment?"

The woman shook her head very slightly.

"Never," she said. "Never in a *thousand* years could I want another apartment. Don't you recognize me, Johann? It's Beatrice."

Without another word she stepped into the apartment, funereal and regal, and into the sitting room. Johann closed the door and went after her as quickly as he could.

She was standing in the warm lamplight, already removing her mourning hat and peeling off her black leather gloves. She turned to him, and although she looked a little older, and a little more tired, it was the same slender brunette Beatrice, with her beautiful slanting eyes and her sensuous lips. He could even smell that same fragrance on her that he had smelled the last time he saw her, at the Broughton carnival. Heliotrope, delicate and nostalgic.

Johann stood there unable to speak. His chest felt like a steam boiler under extreme pressure, and he could hardly draw breath.

"Johann," said Beatrice, reaching out her hands. "It's so good to see you. You look so well."

"Beatrice," said Johann hoarsely.

She came up and took his wrists, and kissed him on the cheek. Her lips were warm and moist, but his own jaw appeared to be paralyzed, as if he had kept it in the ice chest all night, and his eyes were wide open and staring.

"I'm staying with an old friend of Liddy's, just three streets away, here in Edgar. Do you know Mrs. Elvira Russell? She's been so sweet to me. I moved in yesterday. Mrs. Elvira Russell said I should wait, but I had to see you. You're looking so prosperous!''

"Yes," he said faintly. "Times are better."

"I thought it would be so wonderful to be near you while I mourned. I need your strength, Johann, just like you once needed mine. And when my year's over, when I put aside the black—"

The sitting-room door creaked slightly. Johann raised his head at the sound and looked across the room. The door creaked again, and then opened.

Beatrice looked up, too.

It was Carina, and she was quite nude. Her body was slim and dusky-skinned, with tiny brown-nippled breasts, narrow hips, and only the tiniest curls between her legs. Her hair was dripping wet, and hung over her shoulders in ragged tails. She wore a single gold chain around her bare stomach.

"Sir?" she asked, obviously intimidated by Beatrice. "Sir? I think I have nits."

1903

CORNELIUS (ENGINEERS)
of Edgar, Texas

Specialists in the supply and repair of equipment for the prospecting of oil and the survey of land, and General Engineers for farm and railroad machinery.

Propr: J. Cornelius

He walked across Main Street with the edgy, restrained step of a man who has set out for an appointment too early, and has to file away at each long and obstinate minute with the rough edge of his own impatience. He stopped at the drugstore on the corner, and in the dim interior, shaded at this time of day by green blinds, he went up to the candy counter, with all its glossy home-dipped toffee apples and twists of jawbreaking barley sugar, and paid two cents for a small pack of violet cachous, which he opened as he stepped back out onto the boardwalk, and crunched between his teeth.

As he continued his walk to Kearney Street, the dust filmed the toes of his well-polished shoes. He was unusually smart today, even for such a visit. He wore a light gray linen suit, and a dove-gray hat. He smelled of Roberts' Cologne, and carried a cane. Several townsfolk, as they passed him by, said: "How do, Mr. Cornelius," but most of them seemed to mutter it out of the corner of their mouths, and all of them stopped in their tracks once he had passed, and stared at him. He was, after all, the richest man they had ever known.

On the corner of Kearney Street, he raised his hat to Miss Beckinsale, from the Edgar Town School. She was a young, pale woman much given to black-and-white shepherd-check skirts and wide, plain hats.

She said, in her wan voice: "You're looking finer than ever, Mr. Cornelius. Life seems to agree with you here."

"I wish love did, as well as life." He smiled.

Miss Beckinsale sighed. "You know what Lord Byron wrote, Mr. Cornelius. He wrote that 'man's love is of man's life a thing apart, but 'tis woman's whole existence.'"

Johann smiled uncomfortably. "Perhaps I should remember that," he said, and raised his hat again. Miss Beckinsale looked at him for a moment, as plain as a clothespin on which someone had painted a face, and then sighed quite loudly and went on her way.

As he continued his walk, Johann felt disturbed, but not unpleasantly. It occurred to him that his increasing wealth and his greater experience in dealing with people and business was giving him a mastery of himself which made him more interesting and attractive—in spite of his continuing tendency to hit first and ask questions later, and in spite of the fact that he was obdurately male rather than handsome.

A horse-drawn buggy rattled past, taking sacks of cornmeal out to the Mesquite Ranch, and he put another violet cachou between his front teeth and bit it.

Beatrice had timed her afternoon promenade to the second, and was waiting for him on the corner of Kearney and Maple. She was dressed in black, as always, although she was shielding her pale complexion from the sun with a gray parasol. She smiled when she saw him, and lifted her hand, delicately and perhaps a little mockingly limp-wristed, so that he could take it and press his lips to her black cotton glove.

They were walking now, arm-in-arm, back along Kearney Street toward Main Street, where they would go into the lounge of Edgar's only hotel, the Superior, and take tea. It was a ritual they observed two or three times each week, during these long, respectable months of Beatrice's mourning. Beatrice may have been sexually outrageous by the standards of many of the citizens of western Texas, but never openly, and even during her most impassioned affairs when she was married to Lidmore, she had maintained the outward appearance of a woman of the correctest kind. Now that she was living in Edgar, which was a far smaller town than Broughton, she had to make particularly sure that she conducted herself by the standards of Christian etiquette, and that meant keeping her friendship with Johann within circumscribed limits, at least until a prudent period of time had passed. Johann did not really see the necessity for postponing his courtship for so long, but he tended to forget that Beatrice was not as thick-skinned as he was, and that she needed, as a woman, to have a leading place in Edgar's social circle, such as it was. So while she had made it known to the ladies of the town that she was an old friend of Johann's, and that she was staying in Edgar under his protection, she remained at the house on Kearney Street of the widowed Mrs. Elvira Russell, who had been a playmate of Liddy's sister back in the '70s, and who had albums and albums of sepia pictures of Lidmore as a serious young man.

As they crossed the square toward the pillared wooden frontage of the Superior, they were greeted with polite "how dos" and "good afternoons" from almost everyone they passed. Johann opened the swing door of the hotel, and they went inside.

The Superior in Edgar was as much like the Excelsior in Amarero as a loofah resembled a saguaro. It had a creaky carpeted floor, plenty of aspidistras in pedestaled planters, a high mahogany desk, and ceiling fans that went around and around tirelessly and uselessly. The whole place smelled of Garland's glycerin antiseptic soap, known as "the farmer's bar," and Johann often complained that even the tea tasted of it. They went through glass doors into the hotel lounge, where some of Edgar's leading ladies were already perched on their bentwood chairs nibbling at sand tarts, and a waitress in a long black skirt and white apron showed them to their accustomed table by the northern window, away from the sun.

"Well," said Beatrice, setting her reticule at her feet, "have you had a good day?"

Johann shrugged. "I'm seeing Phil McKeogh in a few days. He's been stock-taking, assessing how much the whole business is worth. Oil, engineering, the lot. He says we already have liquid assets well over half a million dollars."

"My dear," rejoined Beatrice. "Does that mean you could be a millionaire?"

Johann shook out his napkin. "I suppose it's possible."

"But you don't seem very excited."

"Why should I be? It's what I set out to do."

Beatrice reached across the table and took his hand. "But, my dear—a millionaire! It's simply wonderful!"

He lowered his eyes. "I suppose it is, yes."

"Oh, my darling," she said, in the quietest voice she could, so that the sharpened ears of Mrs. Dunphy couldn't pick up her endearment from the next table. "I'm so glad for you. So very glad. I always knew that you had it in you."

He looked up at her. Her expression was very soft and gentle, but somehow, for some reason he couldn't quite grasp, she seemed curiously distant. He said: "Millionaires are supposed to get what they want."

She paused. She could guess what was coming next. The pause was communicated to the people at the next table, and Mrs. Whitehead, a bulky woman in taut lavender satin with the profile

103

of Geronimo, turned obtrusively in her chair to see what was afoot. Johann glanced across at her and gave her a vinegary little grin. She turned away.

"I have to admit you've been very patient," said Beatrice. "I want you to know that I admire you for that."

"It's been well over a year now," insisted Johann. "And you told me yourself that Lidmore wasn't much of a husband to you."

She nodded absently. "I know."

"Well, if you *know*," insisted Johann, "then why don't you come out of mourning? I love you, Beatrice. You're quite aware of that. I believe you love me. You came here, didn't you, to be close to me? The moment you say the word, we can marry, and you can come live with me."

She looked at him. A carriage went past outside their window, with jingling harness. Johann could see the tall waitress sweeping toward them, bearing their tea tray. He coughed.

"Once you say the word," he continued, "I can go out and buy us a house. A real mansion. Or have one built to order. But you have to say the word."

The waitress set down their teacups, their plate of cookies, their thin-sliced bread and butter. Beatrice poured, her hand perfectly steady, and then replaced the rose-patterned teapot on its china teapot stand.

"I don't want to appear to be *hasty*," she said, without looking at Johann. "After all, I'm chairman of the Women's Art League."

"What does the Art League have to do with us getting married?"

She put her finger to her lips. "Please, my dear. Not so loud. I couldn't bear gossip."

"What does the Art League have to do with us?" Johann hissed. "I don't want to marry the goddamned Art League. I want to marry you."

She brushed one of her high-curved eyebrows with the tips of her fingers, as if she had a slight headache. "I'm not sure," she said at last.

"You do *love* me, don't you? You still love me?"

She looked up at him, and smiled tenderly.

"I think I'm just afraid," she said.

"Afraid? Afraid of what?"

"Afraid of getting married again. Afraid of being caged up. The little blackbird in the wicker lantern."

Johann stirred his tea, and tapped the spoon once against the rim of the cup.

"You can't mourn forever," he said in a husky voice.

"Well, I know that. But I don't want to rush. And, please, I don't want you to rush me."

"I'm not rushing you. I've waited more than a year already."

Beatrice turned her head. Johann sat there and watched her, looking at the way the pale light from the north window touched her high, curved forehead, her long upswept eyelashes, and the perfect curves of her lips. At her throat was a black velvet ribbon with a black carved flower of ebony, set in silver.

He said: "I love you."

She didn't turn back. Instead, she lowered her head, and he suddenly realized that her eyes were moist.

He said: "You're crying. Beatrice, you're crying."

She reached down for her reticule, and took out a black-edged handkerchief. "It's nothing," she said. "It's simply the dust."

"It must be something."

"I don't know," she whispered. "I'm just being ridiculous."

"You're never ridiculous."

She wiped her eyes. "Oh, yes I am. All human beings are ridiculous sometimes."

"Not you."

Beatrice stared at him with watery eyes. There was a sad smile on her face. "I need time," she said. "That's all."

"Time for what? More mourning?"

"No, I'm past mourning. Past real mourning. But I'm still not sure about myself. I thought when Liddy died that all my problems were over; but it was only after a few weeks that I realized they were just beginning. You can't solve any problem by trying to destroy the cause of it. We are all wedded to our problems, Johann, until we overcome them by our own human logic and our own human strength. Liddy died, but now there is you. That's one of the reasons I'm holding back. I couldn't bear it if you became Liddy, all over again."

The muscles in Johann's jaw tensed, and then slowly relaxed. He laid the fingertips of all ten fingers on the edge of the table, as if he were trying to push it away from him, and then he said: "Do you want me to show you?"

Beatrice looked pale. "Show me what?"

"Show you that I'm not like Liddy."

"I don't know what you mean."

"Of course you do. You remember that day you invited me into your parlor."

She touched her forehead. "That was different," she said quickly.

"Why was it different? Don't you think I haven't had that picture of you burned onto my eyes ever since? If you looked into my eyes now, you could still see it."

"Johann," she said weakly, "I think I feel faint."

He grasped her wrist. The fierceness of his gesture didn't go unnoticed at Mrs. Whitehead's table. Scarcely moving his lips, he whispered: "I adore you, Beatrice. I need you. Don't you understand how much I have to possess you?"

Beatrice blinked. She looked at him like a woman who has just been rescued from drowning in a public boating pool.

"I think you're too much for me, Johann. Perhaps that's the truth. You have so much . . . energy. So much power. And yet you lay it all at my feet, as if it meant nothing. I'm not at all sure that I'm capable of controlling it. All my lovers before you were such boys."

Johann released her wrist. "I'm not your lover," he said baldly. "I only wish that I were."

Beatrice took a sand tart from the dish, and laid it on her plate. She made no attempt to eat it. The lounge of the Superior was very hushed, and Johann wondered if they'd been talking too loud. On the far wall was a print of Winan's "Mud Digger" locomotive of 1844, and for some reason it made Johann strangely nostalgic for his days in New York. He felt churned up inside—passionate, aroused, but fearful, too, because he did desperately love and worship Beatrice, and the thought that she might not love him, the idea that she might be slipping away, receding from him with every month that passed, almost made his millionaireship seem worthless.

Two nights later, after he had closed the green-and-gold door of his workshop behind him, Johann went to the corner drugstore and drank, standing up, a single cold glass of lemonade. Then, instead of turning right as he left the store toward Grange Street, where his red-and-white house was, he kept walking straight ahead, along Mountolive Street, where the houses were smaller, but neater, and fenced off with white-painted palings.

A few houses along, he stopped, and looked up and down the street. Then he opened the gate of a tidy one-story weatherboard cottage, and went up to the front door, in the shadow of a narrow veranda. He took out a key from the breast pocket of his brown suit and let himself in.

Carina was waiting for him in the small parlor, which was decorated with figured wallpaper of emerald green, and crowded with knickknacks which she had collected during her months as Johann's protégée. There were cases of South American butterflies and moths, bedraggled stuffed warbling vireos in dusty glass domes, mournful prints of villages in Portugal, and ugly china plates with chipped edges. Everything was treasure to Carina, as long as it looked exotic and colorful, and Johann often complained that her cottage was more like an auction room than a young girl's home.

She was sitting gracefully in a small curved chair, her hair pinned up with a glittering cut-glass slide, dressed in a pink taffeta gown with net over the sleeves. Her face was as oval and mystically beautiful as ever, and her dark eyes were lifted to Johann with such mesmerizing liquidity that he could only stand by the door when he first came in, and smile at her. A porcelain clock, heavily over-decorated with fruit and cherubs, chimed on the mantelpiece.

"I expected you at seven," she said, with very young solemnity.

"Yes," he said, setting his hat down on a side table, next to a collection of seashells glued into the shapes of frogs and horses. "I had a late order for the Amarero rig. I have to get over there next week. Amarero, I mean."

She stood up from her chair with a rustle of petticoats, and came over to kiss his cheek. He bent forward so that she could do it.

"Would you care for a drink?" he asked her. "I brought a bottle of port wine."

"All right." She smiled.

There was an easy, relaxed silence between them as he went to the corner cabinet and took out two crystal wineglasses. He uncorked the port and poured them each a modest half-glassful; and then he came over and sat down beside her next to the brick fireplace.

"What shall we drink to?" she said.

He shrugged, still smiling. "I don't know. Maybe to friends."

"Why not to business?" she asked him. "You love your business."

"The business is taking pretty good care of itself right now. And in any case, I love you, too."

She looked wistful. "Not properly."

"Of course, properly."

She gazed down at the amethyst and carnelian rings on her thin, delicate fingers.

"Not as a husband might," she said softly.

He sat back, tugging up the knees of his pants so that they wouldn't get baggy. He sipped his wine and looked across at her with an expression of gentleness and concern that would have amazed and disconcerted most of his friends and business colleagues. Beatrice saw Johann's face when he was trying to express his adoration of her. Only Carina saw the face of simple, uncomplicated affection.

Turning his glass between his thick fingers, he said: "I like to think that I rescued you. How could I treat you the same way as the people I saved you from?"

"You never thought of making love to me?"

He looked away.

"Love . . . making love . . . doesn't always have to be painful," she said in a voice so calm and demure that he didn't realize what she was saying at first.

He cleared his throat. "I know. But regardless of what most people seem to think, there are other things that a man may want from a young girl like you, apart from making love. I bought you, Carina, but the day I brought you here, I made you a gift of yourself. You're not my property. I ask only to be your good friend."

"You are my good friend," she said, gently reaching across and touching the back of his hand. "You are."

He was silent for a while, and then he stood up and paced around the room, picking up odd paperweights and postcards that Carina had arranged on the shelves and tables.

"I may be deceiving you, and I may be deceiving myself," he said in a thick voice. "Perhaps, when I bought you, I was just trying to prove to myself that anything could be bought. An oil well, or an automobile, or a girl. I can't pretend that money isn't important to me, Carina, and that I don't want all the power and the luxury that money can bring. You know, when I first came to Texas, I went to a bank with my cap in my hand asking for ten thousand dollars, and they refused. Last week, the same bank manager came back and asked me if I would care to deposit any of my funds there.''

''What did you say? Something nasty?''

''Not really. I just told him that he seemed to have forgotten his own lesson—neither a borrower nor a lender be. Then I accidentally, or maybe not accidentally, trod on his foot.''

Carina laughed. ''You make me feel so safe,'' she said.

He shook his head. ''None of us are really safe. But money can make us safe from some things. Like hunger. Or humiliation.''

Carina frowned. It was growing dark now, and the duskiness of her skin seemed to be part of the grainy shadows in the over-decorated parlor. Johann had the strangest feeling that, many years from now, he would remember this day, remember this moment, and think of it with unbearable sadness.

Carina said: ''Are you that much afraid of Beatrice?''

''I don't know. Maybe it's not Beatrice at all. Maybe it's just my feelings that make me concerned. Whenever we're together, I can't stop myself from acting like an idiot.''

Carina set down her wine, and turned in her chair so that she could look at him with that soft, tender warmth that he treasured her for. She was still very young, which made her direct and naive; but her years of selling herself for the clumsy and rancid satisfaction of old men had given her a sharpness and sense of human absurdity from which Johann often unashamedly learned. She rode around town in her dogcart every evening after the heat of the day had cooled, her matchless profile held high, her expression unalterably calm and self-possessed, and she relished every whispered word, every turned head, and every frown of Baptist disapproval. They knew, you see, that she had something to do with Johann, but they could never quite figure out what. And sometimes she stopped at the drugstore to buy herself peppermint ices, which to the townsfolk seemed to make matters even worse. Whenever she met Johann after work, she would tell him about everything that had amused her, and she described some of Edgar's most sober citizens so wickedly that he laughed until he almost choked.

He loved Carina's company in the way that some men grow to love the company of college friends; but even more than that, she was like a younger sister. She was precious to him, and yet approachable. She brought out in him a capacity for warmth and a feeling of delightful kinship that he could hardly contain. He had

109

no desire to marry her, or to make love to her. That would break the feyness of her spell. But he knew that if he lost her, he would probably lose the dearest person he had ever known. He couldn't describe or understand it any more than that.

Although Edgar was a small town, where gossip flew faster than dry alfalfa in a September wind, Johann's regular visits to Mountolive Street had fortunately escaped Beatrice's attention. She knew of Carina, of course; but only as the orphaned daughter of a Mexican wildcatter to whom, as the man lay crushed under a collapsed rig, Johann had once faithfully promised to act as Carina's protector and guardian. That was the explanation he had given Beatrice the night she arrived to find Carina naked in his apartment ("Poor child, she was filthy from neglect"), and that was the explanation he continued to give, with occasional minor elaborations. It wasn't surprising that Beatrice knew nothing of the whispers and the raised eyebrows that followed Carina wherever her dogcart trotted. The ladies of Edgar were as keen to keep themselves in her good books as she was keen to keep herself in theirs, and apart from that they were extremely fearful of what Johann might do if Beatrice were told the truth. Johann had the kind of intolerant masculinity that made them all flutter and tremble and wish (in their wilder moments) that they weren't already married.

Carina said: "I can never understand why Beatrice frightens you. You're not scared of anybody else. Everybody else is scared of *you*."

Johann took another sip of wine, and stood before a cracked case of hawkmoths with an expression of resignation.

"She's a beautiful woman," said Carina. "But she never makes you happy, does she? She never will, either, because she doesn't really love you. Not as I do."

"You don't think so?" asked Johann, turning. "I don't know."

"If I were her, and I loved you as she says she does, I would come out of mourning tonight. I would show you all the tricks that I ever learned with men, and make you happier than you could ever dream. Have you heard of the trick called the Mohawk Claw?"

"Carina," Johann admonished her.

"But it's true," insisted Carina. "When she refuses to come out of mourning, that means that she doesn't love you."

110

Johann blew some of the dust from the glass moth case. "She's frightened, that's all. She can't make up her mind."

"But how can she love you, if she treats you so bad?"

"She doesn't treat me bad. She's just confused."

Carina smiled, and shook her head. "She doesn't love you, Johann. One day you'll have to face it."

Johann looked away. He suspected that what Carina was saying was true. But somehow, with the dogged refusal to surrender that characterizes those who love but are not loved in return, he supposed, he guessed, that Beatrice was shy, or that she was simply uncertain, or that maybe Liddy's death had affected her more than she had ever revealed.

"Carina," he said huskily.

She came over and held his arm. He pressed his fingers to his forehead, and he had to swallow before he spoke again.

"She made me shed tears once," he told her. "I hope I won't ever have to shed tears again."

"Johann," whispered Carina, "you're not a man of wood and iron. You're a man of skin and blood, like all the rest. You mustn't drive yourself this way."

He looked at her, and then, very gently, he kissed her braided hair.

"To be rich, I have to be made of wood and iron. Men of skin and blood stay poor."

She stroked his cheek. She said: "Tonight, will you stay?" In the gloom of the parlor, he could see a tear on her cheek, glistening like the reflection of a single star on a dark beach. She kissed his cheek, soft lips against the taut gloss of close shaving.

He put down his empty glass. He answered: "No," so quietly that she wasn't sure he had spoken at first.

Early the next morning, he dressed in a blue wool suit and a derby hat, and went out to be shaved at Tatum's Barbershop. This was his sole extravagance, his only self-indulgence, and he would sit back in the big leather-and-iron chair while Jack Tatum lathered his blond prickly chin with a badger brush and then shaved him close and sharp with one of George Wostenholm's Original and True hollow-ground pipe razors. In later years, Johann would often remember Tatum's place at odd and unpredictable times; the sharp smell of the surgical alcohol in which Tatum soaked his teeth

111

at night, the clipping of shears, the bland aroma of shaving soap and the way the early-morning sun fell across the mirror and across the Brown & Bigelow calendar of "Colette"; and the reason he recalled it was that having himself shaved each morning by a barber was his first outward display of wealth. After Jack Tatum, nothing on which he spent his money would ever have quite the same tang of success.

Freshened up, he walked down Congress Street to the workshop. It was a corner premises, with green-painted window frames and handsome gold lettering that said "Cornelius (Engineers)." When he opened the front door, the bell tinkled, and Sam Chivers came out to the front counter in his greasy brown apron, bald but whiskery, his half-glasses perched on the end of his reddened nose, like Santa Claus making some last-minute adjustments to his sleigh.

"Hallo, Sam," said Johann quietly. He closed the door behind him, and walked across the worn boards of the shop toward the counter, taking off his coat as he came. Sam raised the flap for him, and he came through into the inner office, which in turn led out to the stores and the workshops. There was a reverberating clang of hammers on metal, and when he glanced through the glass windows of the office, Johann could see that work on his latest oil-pumping equipment was well-advanced.

Phil McKeogh, his accountant, was sitting waiting for him. He was a painfully thin young man with brilliantined hair and silk socks, and he held his briefcase on his lap like a pet spaniel. Johann said: "You're up early. I thought accountants slept until sunset."

McKeogh snickered. "Today, you'll be glad I didn't. I finished your valuations last night."

Sam should have gone back to the workshop, but he knew how crucial these evaluations were, and he waited there, his wrench held loose in his hand, and he looked at Johann expectantly.

Johann sat down. On his desk was a leather-edged blotter, a brass calendar with yesterday's date on it, a ledger, and a jar of pencils. He clasped his big hands together on top of the blotter and said: "Well?"

McKeogh grinned, opened his briefcase, and handed over a sheaf of accounts. "Congratulations," he said. "You're a millionaire."

Johann took the papers and flicked through them. He didn't feel elated, but then this moment had been anticipated for so long, through so many months of hard work and setbacks, that he hadn't expected to. What he did feel, though, was a sense of self-vindication, a sense that he was right, and that God *knew* that he was right.

"It was that well you spudded on the eastern edge of the site that clinched it," explained McKeogh. "That's brought up more barrels of crude in two months than the rest of them have in six. And having those new storage tanks is going to help plenty."

Johann couldn't help smiling. He said: "Well, Sam, that's it. We made it."

Sam reached out his hand. "I'm real pleased for you. I'd just like to say that I hope it brings you what you want."

"Let's have some brandy," Johann suggested.

"Not for me," said McKeogh. "I have old man Sharp's books to go through this morning, and I can tell you for nothing they need the concentration of Hercules himself."

They shook hands all around, and then Phil McKeogh left, leaving the doorbell jangling behind him. Johann went to his veneered filing cabinet, took out a bottle of brandy and three glasses, and poured a nip into each.

"Let's have Jack in here, shall we?" he asked Sam. "I think this is one day we ought to celebrate."

Sam wiped his hands on his apron. He said: "You're happy?"

Johann filled the last glass, and then looked up, puzzled. "Why shouldn't I be?"

"I don't know. It's just that you've been pretty glum of late. And folks are beginning to ask how long the widow-woman of yours is going to stay in her weeds."

Johann raised his eyebrows. "So that's it."

Sam looked a little embarrassed. "I don't mean to pry. You know that. But we've been working together for a long time now. And I sometimes wonder if you might do yourself some good unburdening yourself. It helps to have a friend to talk to."

There was an awkward silence, and then Johann said: "Yes, Sam, I know."

Sam sat on the edge of Johann's desk. He picked up one of the glasses of brandy, but he didn't drink any. He said: "You're a rich man now, Johann. You can travel anyplace you want, meet any woman you want. It doesn't seem to make much sense, fretting over a widow-woman like that."

"Sam, I love her."

Sam sniffed. "Maybe you do. But does she love you? That's what folks are asking."

Johann got up from his desk and walked across to the window that overlooked the workshop. He could see Jack Beak, thin and wiry with dundreary whiskers, hammering away at a metal crossbeam. He said: "Sam, there's love in her heart somewhere. I know there is. But the woman's a goddess."

"No woman's a goddess, Johann."

Johann swiftly shook his head. "This one is. She has the strength of a man, and the wit of a man, and yet she's a beautiful woman. She scares me to death sometimes. I don't know if I hate her or worship her. But she's got me right here, Sam, right in my heart and my mind, and I can't do anything about it."

Sam put down his brandy. "It isn't any of my business, Johann. I'm only trying to tell you what it seems like to me. And it seems like to me that you're chasing after some kind of shadow that isn't there."

"Well, maybe I am."

Sam reached into his apron pocket and took out a briar pipe. He slowly packed the bowl with negrohead tobacco, and then he struck a match on the window and lit up.

"Have you bedded her?" he asked softly.

Johann shook his head. "She wouldn't have it. Not till her mourning's over."

"Well, do you think it might be some kind of idea to try?"

Johann's eyes widened, but he didn't look up.

Sam said: "I know it sounds blunt. But a cousin of mine in New York was after a widowed lady in much the same way, and it was only because he got himself drunk one Washington's birthday and took her off to bed that he ever found out she was feared of the physical side of things, not having had them for so long."

Johann grunted. "I'm not a drinker. One glass of brandy is enough for me."

"I'm just giving you help, Johann. Sometimes us old people look at things a little more salty than you young ones. There's a time for manners and there's a time for going out there and taking what you want."

"Sam, you just don't know Beatrice. You don't know her."

"All women are pretty much alike. It's only moonstruck lovers think they're different."

"Sam, for Christ's sake!"

Sam shrugged and put his pipe back in his mouth. Then he took it out again and said: "Listen, I'll have one more word on the subject. If you want to get yourself around to Mrs. Mulliner's place one evening, and you want a few hours uninterrupted, I'll ask Mrs. Elvira Russell to step out with me for the fiddle concert. I reckon she's always cast an appreciative eye my way, and that's the best I can do."

Johann lifted his glass. "That's what I call devotion, Sam. I don't think I'd step out with Mrs. Elvira Russell any more than I'd step out with a bald eagle."

"Do you want me to do it?"

There was a long silence. Then Johann said: "I don't know, Sam. I don't think so."

Sam stuck his thumbs in his apron. "Okay, Johann. But the offer's always there."

"Anyway," said Johann, "I believe I'm more interested in business right now. It's time I went to New York."

"New York? What about the business here?"

"Slobodien's quite capable of looking after the oil rigs."

"But this place?"

Johann frowned, and looked around the workshop. "You can run this place for a couple of months, can't you? You and Jack? You can always call on Phil McKeogh if you have trouble with the books."

"I don't understand why you're going. Just when you're doing so good."

Johann stood up. "It's very simple. I have a million dollars and it's time to make use of them. If you stay still, you get rusty. I want to keep going, keep making more. I want to get into insurance, and shipping, and maybe buy some railroad stock. I want to fix up a better price for refining my crude. I want to find out what goes on in Wall Street. I want to stop being a rich rube and start being a businessman."

"What about Beatrice?"

Johann paused. "Well, I don't know. Maybe she'll want to come along. Maybe she'll wait here. A couple of months without me might help her to make up her mind."

"You really think so?"

Johann looked at him. "I don't know what I think. But I'll have to find out, won't I? I can't keep dancing on the end of her mourning ribbons."

Sam leaned forward on the desk. "Listen, Johann, just let me ask Mrs. Elvira Russell to step out with me. Just let me do that once. Then, when you're alone with Beatrice, seize your chance. Do it before you go away to New York."

"Sam—"

Sam tilted his head on one side. "I know what you're thinking. You're thinking that I don't understand how sacred this lady is to you, that I don't understand anything at all. But sooner or later you're going to have to do something, Johann. You can't spend the rest of your natural life standing around like a cigar-store Indian."

Johann fingered the edges of the valuation reports which told him he was a millionaire. Then he said: "You'd better call Jack. Let's celebrate before we spend it."

Late the following evening, Thursday, he was still at his desk by the time it grew dark. The last act of the day was to write a long letter, by hand, to the headquarters of Amarero Oil in New York. Ever since he'd struck crude out at Sweetwater Trail, Johann's relationships with Amarero Oil had been cordial and constructive. He had lent them equipment on several occasions, and he was on good terms with their crews and their foremen. He did little business with them. All his crude oil he sold to the Colton Oil company for refining, simply because Colton's prices were better. But he had the kind of business mentality that looks way ahead into the future, and it occurred to him that the day might come when he needed to buy an outfit like Amarero Oil, and it would help if they were already amenable.

The letter concerned Kyle Lennox. It was a friendly letter that belied what Johann was actually trying to do. Now that Johann was worth well over a million dollars, and now that Jerry Slobodien had reported that the eight rigs out at Sweetwater Trail were bringing in twenty-five thousand barrels a day, Kyle Lennox's eight percent was fast becoming a small fortune in its own right. It was not that Johann begrudged Carina her price. It was just that enough was enough, especially as far as a cheap toad like Kyle Lennox was concerned, and after Phil McKeogh's valuations Johann had made up his mind to elbow Lennox out of his way.

In sentence after sentence, he praised Kyle Lennox's abilities as a manager, even though he was quite aware that Amarero Oil considered him unreliable and disagreeable. He called Lennox "upstanding and discerning" and said that he was "worth his salt." And then, almost as an afterthought, he asked if Amarero

116

Oil would care to help him out by transferring Lennox's contract to Cornelius Oil, and thus affording Johann the services of a "true veteran of the oilfields."

He sealed the letter, addressed it, and then put on his coat and closed up the workshop for the night. He knew that Amarero Oil would find his suggestion irresistible, and he was even humming to himself as he turned down the lamps on his desk. Once he had Lennox's contract in his own safe, things would begin to look very different. Lennox's eight percent would be discontinued immediately, and if Lennox complained—well, the circuit judges didn't think much of employees who griped about their employers, especially when their employers were as rich and as potentially influential as Johann.

He left the office and locked the door behind him. Out on the dark street, a cool evening breeze was blowing, and there was a distant yowling of wild dogs. He heard a footstep on the boardwalk, and he turned around to see Sam Chivers leaning against the veranda post, smoking his pipe.

"Sam. I didn't see you there."

"I haven't been here long."

"Why didn't you come inside? There was some brandy left over from yesterday."

Sam stepped forward, and the light from an upstairs window fell across his brushed velour hat and a smart powder-blue suit that Johann had never seen him wearing before. He smelled strongly of lavender.

"To tell you the truth," he said, "I was kind of embarrassed."

Johann smiled, a little quirkily. "You look like you're dressed for a Spanish funeral."

"Well, not quite. But I *am* dressed up to take Mrs. Elvira Russell out for an evening stroll."

"I thought you were taking her out to a fiddle concert."

Sam prodded at the bowl of his pipe. Across the street, in the shadows, a tethered horse restlessly shook its harness. Sam said: "The fiddle concert isn't till Wednesday next. I thought you needed your help a little more urgent than that."

"Sam," said Johann, "I'm *not* going around there. You can walk Mrs. Elvira Russell till your legs drop off. But I can't go near Beatrice with any kind of personal proposition until she comes out of mourning. And that's all."

Sam sighed. "Johann," he said, "you're pretty dumb for a

millionaire. Can't you get it through that head of yours that Beatrice is chewing the strings of her stays, just waiting for you to go around there and pull her out of those widow's weeds headfirst? She wants you to do it, Johann. She *needs* you to do it. Otherwise there won't be any feeling that she's been chased, and catched. A woman needs to be catched, Johann, and that's one of the first facts of life."

Johann took a deep breath. "I'm taking this letter to the Wells Fargo office, and then I'm going across to Walsh's for supper. After that, I'm going home to bed, and I'm going to go through the cracking analyses until I fall to sleep."

Sam gripped his arm. Under the shadow of his hat, Johann could just make out the rheumy gleam of his eyes. The old-timer paused for a moment, not certain what kind of words could cajole Johann into taking a chance with Beatrice, but then he said dryly: "How old are you, Johann?"

"Thirty. Why?"

"Just asking. It seems to me that thirty's kind of old to stay unwed. What happens if you pass away without an heir for all that money of yours?"

"I'm not planning on passing away."

"Nobody ever is."

"Well, even if I do, I won't be too worried about my money, will I? I'll be dead."

Sam sighed again. "You take a hell of a lot of persuading."

"I'm not going to see Beatrice tonight, Sam, and that's my last word."

"You'd let me suffer a whole evening with Elvira Russell for nothing? I've promised her now. I can't go back on my promise."

"Sam, I'm not going."

"You're scared."

"Maybe I am."

Sam pushed back his hat. "Well, will you walk along with me to Mrs. Elvira Russell's door? I kind of hate to face the old crow alone."

Johann looked at him for a while, and then nodded. "Okay. But next time, ask me first before you go asking old ladies out for decoy walks."

They stepped off the veranda and crossed the street in the cold light of an early moon. There was a smell of sausage and dust and mesquite in the night air. A piano was tinkling "My Love from Level-land," and someone in an upstairs room was arguing loudly.

"I was thinking," said Sam, as they walked side by side down Kearney Street. "This town is too small for you now, when you come to consider it. I guess you're right to think of New York."

Johann was looking ahead, toward the lighted veranda of Mrs. Elvira Russell's two-story weatherboard house. He said: "It's not so much New York, Sam. It's the whole world."

They walked up to the front door, and Sam rang the bell that hung down beside it. "I was considering taking Mrs. Russell down to the church hall. I hear there's a singing practice tonight."

Johann smiled. "Rather you than me."

They heard footsteps inside the house, and then Mrs. Russell appeared at the door. She was a very tall woman with wide shoulders, from which her high-buttoned dresses were draped across her bustless chest like a tarpaulin over an old gun carriage. Her face was big as a buffalo's, and her hair was twisted and knotted into an iron-gray confusion of braids. She saw Sam, and pursed her lips in incongruous flirtation.

"Sam Chivers! And early, too. And you too, Mr. Cornelius! I didn't know you were coming along."

Johann coughed. "Well, I'm not. I was just taking a short stroll with Sam. I'll say good night now."

"I'll fetch my wrap." Mrs. Russell bustled. "Do you step inside here, Sam Chivers. I won't be more than a moment."

Johann said: "Good night, Sam. Good night, Mrs. Russell," and he was about to turn to leave when he heard Beatrice's voice call: "Johann! Is that Johann?"

Johann turned, and glanced at Sam tautly. Sam hesitated for a moment, and then said: "That's right, Mrs. Mulliner. He's just leaving."

Beatrice came through the lamplit hallway, and paused by the front door. She was wearing a long simple dress of dark brown cotton, which for some reason reminded Johann of the dress that Carina had worn the first day he found her. In the glow of the oil lamps, Beatrice looked more goddesslike and more beautiful than ever.

"Don't go," she said. "Why not stay for a sherry-wine?"

Mrs. Elvira Russell was busily arranging a fringed wrap around her broad shoulders, and pinning her hat on. "If Mr. Cornelius stays, Beatrice, then I'll have to stay, too, and I must say that I'm not inclined to. I've been looking forward to this walk with Mr. Chivers all the day."

"He can stay for five minutes, Aunt Elvira. I *am* a grown woman."

"That's what your cousin Coreen used to say, and she was assaulted by fish porters."

Beatrice gave that small, mystic smile. "Aunt Elvira, there are no fish porters for three hundred miles."

"Very well. But for five minutes only. I don't want my house connected with scandal."

Johann, hat in hand, felt disturbed and discomfited. He said: "I have some work to catch up on, as a matter of fact."

"You can spare five minutes," insisted Beatrice. "Come inside, and let me have your hat."

Sam, as he passed, gave him a quick squeeze on his elbow. He paused in mid-step, uncertain, but then he followed Beatrice inside, and into the dowdy little parlor. The windows had been closed all day, and the parlor was uncomfortably stuffy.

Beatrice sat down at one end of the leatherette settee and said: "The sherry-wine is to your left of the two decanters. A small one will be quite enough for me."

Johann opened the cabinet, took down two glasses, and poured the sherry. Beatrice said: "I was thinking of you today."

He looked around. "Oh, yes?"

She smiled briefly. "I was thinking of how you came into my life, in need of my assistance; and how I came back into yours, in need of your assistance. It shows that life has a certain ironic balance, don't you think?"

Johann handed Beatrice her glass. Behind him, the front door slammed shut as Sam Chivers and Mrs. Elvira Russell went off for their stroll and their singing practice. Johann wondered how long they were going to stay out. He coughed, and perched himself on the opposite end of the settee.

"Here's to your million," said Beatrice, raising her glass.

"And here's to you," replied Johann, much more quietly, raising his.

They drank, and then exchanged embarrassed smiles.

"It seems strange to be on our own," remarked Beatrice. "I am so used to having Aunt Elvira hovering over me. She is very particular, you know. I sometimes wonder what on earth she would have thought about all those misbehaviors of mine.''

"Does the brown dress mean that you're out of mourning?"

Beatrice glanced down at it. Then she shook her head. "No, it means that all my black dresses are in the laundry."

Johann looked down at his glass. "Why don't you consider it?" he asked her.

"Consider what?"

"You know what I mean. Coming out of mourning."

"But I've told you. I'm simply not ready."

Johann lifted his eyes. "I have to go to New York, you know."

She gave him a quick sideways glance. "New York?"

"I can't stay in Edgar forever. This place has been good to me, but there's more to business than pumping up a little oil and mending broken-down compressors."

"Well . . ." said Beatrice. She sounded put out. "I suppose it had to be."

Johann didn't answer. Beatrice put down her drink and stood up, brushing the creases out of her dress. She went to the fireplace and looked at herself in the mirror over the mantelpiece. She saw, in her own eyes, the face of a woman who was probably born too comely, at least for the life she was destined to lead. And seeing herself in this dingy parlor, with this rich but clumsy man, she suddenly felt very sorry for herself. When she looked down at her hands, she was twisting her wedding ring around and around with almost feverish nervousness.

"Well," she said, "I expect I shall get used to it."

"Used to what?"

She turned, with a tight smile. "Used to living out my life in godforsaken towns in the west of Texas, taking my tea by myself, and wondering whether life ever did have anything else to offer me."

"Beatrice—life has a whole storehouse of things to offer you."

She lifted her hands as if it was all hopeless. "You're a man," she said. "A man is a free agent. He can go where he pleases, do what he likes. He can go to saloons and drink. He can drive automobiles, and curse out loud. He can vote. But what can a woman do, even if she has the spirit? She has to rely on a husband for all things. She even has to rely on him to provide her the means to be unfaithful."

Johann rubbed his chin. He didn't know what to say.

Beatrice came over and offered her hands. She said, more gently this time: "I don't mean to hurt you, Johann. You know that, don't you? But I'm no longer sure of my feelings. Your work and your money seem to mean so much to you. I feel when I'm with you that your mind is always somewhere else, always thinking about business, always thinking about making more money. If we're to have any kind of life together, if I'm to have any kind of life with you, I must know that you're not going to lock me up in a house on my own, fretting for love, while you go off to New York and Washington and San Francisco, chasing your dollars and forgetting your wife. That's what happened with Lidmore. He put me in prison while he went off to work. Don't you see that a woman can only be free when her husband's there beside her?"

Johann cleared his throat. "You don't think that I could make you happy?"

"Johann—I need *reassurance*. I need to know that you wouldn't treat me like Liddy. I need to believe that, whatever happens, your feelings for me will always come before business. *Always*, without question."

He looked at her, confused. He couldn't understand her at all. She had come to live in Edgar so that they could be close during her mourning, and eventually marry. At least, that was the way he had believed things to be. Yet she had prolonged her mourning indefinitely, and as the months went by, he had gradually grown to believe that he would be best occupied in making as much money as he possibly could and biding his time. Now that he was off to New York, however, she seemed to have changed her mind altogether, and was actually setting out her terms for marrying him.

What he didn't know was that Beatrice was deeply afraid. She had privately postponed the day that she was to come out of mourning again and again; not because she was afraid of marriage, but because she was afraid of marriage to Johann. He was a different man from the poor young hopeful she had first coquettishly entertained in her parlor. Since then, he had made his own money, and learned to handle it, and grown sharper and quicker and wiser. Whereas she had once been able to control him, and twist him around her finger, he was now quite capable of doing the same to her, and would have done if he had realized just how pale her influence over him had faded. He still adored her, still loved her,

122

but she knew that once he saw real society, and real wealth, she would probably lose him forever.

The alternatives kept her awake nights. If Johann left her behind in Edgar, she would be beached in this stuffy plains community without means, apart from what Liddy had left her, and without an escort. But if she married him and went with him, she knew that her social skills, no matter how grand they seemed to the ladies of Edgar, would seem hopelessly gauche in comparison to the celestial etiquette of big-city hostesses. Only Beatrice herself knew how overwhelming her fear of social humiliation was. It was almost greater than her fear of being left alone.

She said: "I need to feel protected, Johann, and cosseted as a wife should be. I need the security of my own house, and to know that you're not going to leave me alone while you go off on business. I don't want to be an oil-well widow, or a compressor widow, or even a Wall Street widow. If we are to marry, I want you to be here by my side, as my attentive husband."

Johann reached out for her hand. "Haven't I been attentive up until now?"

"You're attentive to your business, too."

"Of course. What man isn't?"

Beatrice smiled sadly. "I told you when I first met you that I was starved of affection. I am an affectionate woman, Johann. But a woman cannot decently go in *search* of affection, as a man can, and that is why I need to know that you will build me a house, and in that house be constantly more attentive to me than anything or anybody else in your life. You want me to be faithful, don't you?"

"Of course."

"Of course! But that means that I want you to be equally faithful to me!"

"I shall be. I swear it."

She sat down next to him on the leatherette settee, grasped his hands, and kissed him, very lightly, on the end of his nose.

"Then you won't go to New York?"

He looked at her narrowly. "I *have* to."

"Even if it means we can't marry?"

"Beatrice, I don't understand!"

"Johann, it has to *be*! I have been mistreated in love all my life! I have never known what it is like to live with pride and affection with the man I desire! I need to be loved, Johann, all the hours and

123

all the minutes and all the seconds of my life! If you wish to marry me, if you wish me to cast aside my weeds, then you will have to promise that love forever and ever!''

Johann was silent. He could feel his own heart beating, tight and slow. The brass clock on the mantelpiece whirred softly and then began a ridiculously elaborate chiming that went on for almost a minute.

Beatrice whispered: "You may kiss me, if you wish."

He blinked at her.

"Do you want me to prove myself to you?" she asked, her voice soft but heated. "Are you concerned that your love will be demanded but not returned?"

"I don't know," he said uncertainly. "It seems that you're not yourself. One moment it was almost impossible to persuade you to talk about marriage, and now you're insisting on it."

"Perhaps I've realized what a prize might be slipping out of my grasp. Perhaps I've made up my mind."

"Made up your mind about what?"

"You. That you're really the man I need."

"I don't understand what made you suddenly—"

She smiled, and then gave an odd little laugh. "Does it matter? Does anything matter except for us?"

"Well . . . some things do."

She shifted herself nearer to him, and he could feel that tightness in his heart squeeze even tighter. That perfume of hers, that heady scent of heliotrope, seemed to affect his mind. Through the brown cotton of her dress, her body felt very warm and enticing, and he felt, quite unexpectedly, a sensation of passion for her that soaked over his emotions like syrup over a stack of dry pancakes.

"You won't go, will you?" she whispered.

"Beatrice, Bea, you can't hold back the natural course of a river. If I have to go to New York, I have to go. It's what my life is about. It's *me*."

She put her arm around his neck. He felt very short of breath.

"Don't you love me?" she coaxed him. "You said you adored me."

"My God, I do."

"Then say you won't go. Say you'll marry me, and stay with me forever. Promise me that much."

124

"Beatrice, that's *everything*."

"Won't you give me everything? Don't you adore me?"

"Of course. More than my life. Don't you believe me?"

She kissed him, first his cheek and then his lips. Her mouth was indescribably soft and luscious to him, a sweet fruit that he wanted to bite into and devour. He could feel her breasts against him, heavy and taut in their stays. Deep down, he had a hotness and a hardness that threatened to overwhelm him.

He held her back. His hair was ruffled, and he felt as if he were trying to hold back a landslide.

"Your mourning," he breathed. "What about your mourning?"

"It's over," she said. "All you have to do is say it, say you'll marry me, say you'll stay with me, promise, promise, promise, and it'll be over."

Her fingers brushed against the tautness in his lap, and he shivered.

"Oh, my darling Johann," she whispered, holding him close again, and licking at his ear. "All you have to do is promise."

"Beatrice, that's—"

His head dropped, and he shut his eyes tight. He was torn inside by such lusts and such fears that he could hardly think.

"Promise," she said softly. "Please promise."

He opened his eyes. "You're asking for everything," he told her in a croaky voice. "I love you, Beatrice. You can't even understand how much I love you. But you're asking for everything."

She nestled closer. "Oh, promise," she begged him. Her hand stroked his thigh, and her wrist kept touching his hardest and most sensitive spot. He took a deep breath, and raised his head.

"Look," she said, and she reached her hand inside his coat and took out his brown leather wallet. She had given it to him herself, last Christmas, and had admonished him to fill it to bursting. She opened it up now, and took out his money—five or six hundred dollars in singles, fives, and tens, and twenties. She stood up, clutching the money in her hand.

"Is *this* what you want, instead of me? More of this? Don't you have enough already? You're a millionaire! You have oil wells! If you stay here in Edgar, if you marry me, you can have us both! Money and me—both!"

Bright-eyed, she tossed the money up into the air, and the

parlor was filled with floating, swooping bills. Then, as they scattered over the rug, she raised her brown dress, and sat down among them, a saucy curtsy amidst a shower of greenbacks.

Johann looked at her, electrified. Her long, well-shaped legs were gleaming in their black silk stockings. Then he could see her black stocking supporters, and the lace-trimmed edge of her corset cover. She wore no bloomers, and against the dull carpet he could make out the faintest suggestion of dark curls.

She smiled at him. "Oh, Johann. Don't change. Let's be just the way we were, on that day you first came to tea. We had walnut cake, remember?"

He stood up. His head was pounding. He tugged off his coat; then, even more rapidly, he unbuttoned his vest, and loosened his cuff links. As he did so, Beatrice lay back in the litter of money, and held up her arms toward him, enticing him. His muscles were trembling with anticipation, and his broad chest was flushed. He felt as if he had completely lost control of himself, and was acting like a stiff and jerky puppet in a paper theater. Dressed in nothing but his close-fitting white cotton underwear, with the front of his fly unfastened, his red hardness bare, he knelt down on the rustling dollars and grasped her silk-sheathed thighs in both of his broad muscular hands, parting them wider.

"Take me now," coaxed Beatrice. "I have had so many, Johann, but none like you. Take me now."

He leaned over her, panting with strain and passion, and presented his crimson head to her moist black curls. She pulled his face down toward her, and kissed him, savagely and fiercely, as if she wanted to tear his ears off, or rip the flesh in tatters from his cheeks.

"Promise," she gasped, as he was about to thrust for the first time. "Promise you'll stay. Promise you'll love me, and keep me, and promise you'll never go away. Promise you won't go to New York."

Johann's eyes were tight shut. He felt as if he were nearer to Beatrice than he could ever imagine possible, and yet a thousand thousand miles away. He loved her so much that he could scarcely take a breath, and he could feel her warmth and wetness touching his glans like a siren's kiss.

"*Promise*," she insisted.

He made a noise that, even to him, sounded like a suppressed

126

sob. Then he said: "I promise," and she opened herself up to him, and he pushed inside her so hard and so big that she actually jumped.

It was short, greedy, loud, and so overwhelming that both of them screamed at each other in their lust. The dollar bills, fives and tens and twenties, flurried around them as Johann thrust and thrust and thrust with all of his masculine strength, thrusting against everything that had been crowded inside his mind for so long, thrusting against the passion he felt for Beatrice, thrusting against the world that threatened to fall in on him and crush him.

Then Beatrice shrieked like a coyote bitch, and tore her fingernails all the way up his back, inside his cotton combinations, and the pain of it triggered off an endlessly sharp, pumping ejaculation that finally, finally, when the last tremors had shaken him, left him feeling as if he had departed the world altogether, left Texas, and spun around distant stars.

The next he knew, Beatrice was lying beside him, kissing him over and over, and saying: "You promised. Oh, you're beautiful. You promised."

Johann felt stunned, elated, and awash on waves of love and disbelief. He held her in his arms, touching the miraculous softness of her face and her ears. He kissed her with great tenderness, and whispered hoarsely, "I love you. My God, Beatrice, I love you more than I could ever say."

Beatrice's lashes were moist with tears. She kissed him back, as lightly as a butterfly alighting on his lips. There was a slight mark of worry on her forehead, but she was flushed pink with the excitement and the exertion of their lovemaking, and no matter what fears the future held, she knew that she could never explain to Johann what it was to have a man after so long.

"We'd better dress now," she said softly. "Aunt Elvira will be back soon."

Johann kissed her again, and held her face against his chest. "I was beginning to think this would never happen," he told her.

Beatrice sat on the floor, with one silken calf bared, while he collected his clothes and his money and dressed. As he tied his necktie in the glass above the mantelpiece, she said: "I shall announce tomorrow that my mourning is over, and that we are courting. Then perhaps we can look for a place to build our house."

127

He tugged at the bows of his necktie, and then turned around to look at her. He was about to say something when there was a knock at the front door.

"That must be Aunt Elvira. She's forgotten her key. Quick, Johann—let her in, while I button up my dress. Look, you've left some money on the floor there."

Johann went to the front door and opened it. On the porch, in the dim light of the moth-riddled lamp, stood a Western Union boy with cockeyed spectacles and tousled blond hair. He stiffly held out an envelope and said: "Wire, sir, from New Orleans. Addressed to Mrs. Mulliner."

Johann frowned, and reached into his vest for a nickel. He didn't know that Beatrice was acquainted with anyone in New Orleans, let alone anyone who might send her a wire.

The boy, quite gratuitously, said: "Her sister is dead. Died of consumption. They're sending her nephew up to stay here in Edgar."

Beatrice, pinning up her hair, came out into the hall and said: "Who is it, Johann? What's happened?"

Johann turned, and handed her the wire with a cold feeling of misgiving. "Before you open that," he said, "I want you to know that I love you."

The boy stood on the boardwalk of Broughton railroad station in his tan double-breasted English suit with elasticated breeches, his shoes brightly polished and a clean white handkerchief poking from his top pocket, and all around him the long shadows of a fall evening in Texas stretched across the street. Beside him was a cardboard valise with cheap tin locks. It had a manila label, as did the boy. The train had long since clanked and chuffed its way out of the station, and disappeared around the bend by the sun-bleached palings and the freight yards. Since the boy had been waiting, almost two hours, the sky had darkened from clear blue to dusky indigo.

The man who served as master of the station, as collector of fares, and as sweeper and sluicer of the station premises, a friendly ginger-haired fellow with a peaked cap and a large railroad watch, came out from the station building and approached the boy slowly, his hands planted irremovably in his pockets, and he stood for a while just a few yards away, whistling "Who Put the Overalls in Mrs. Murphy's Chowder?" through the gap in his front teeth.

"Your folks coming to get you?" asked the stationmaster. "Seems to me you've been waiting a powerful long time."

The boy looked up. He was pale and serious, and about nine years old. He touched his tan rep cap before he answered, which showed the stationmaster he was well-reared. He had very blue eyes. He looked tired and thirsty.

"A friend is coming to collect me, sir. My aunt's new gentlemen, in his automobile."

The stationmaster rocked backward and forward on his heels. He had an elderly mother at home, senile but still blessed with a hilarious line in piano-salesman stories. He said: "So that's it. Well, you can bet your pants to a pile of snow that he's broke down. I always said those automobiles wouldn't stand the pace, because I'm a railroad man myself, and I don't believe in travel without rails. My pappy was a railroad man before I was, Texas and Pacific, in the days of Dodge, and he used to say that if folks was intended to travel wherever and whenever the mood took them, then God would have laid rails here, there, and every which place."

"The name of my aunt's new gentleman is Mr. Cornelius, sir," said the boy to the stationmaster.

The stationmaster turned and looked down at him. Then he looked around and said, "Come inside."

He picked up the boy's valise in case anyone should take a fancy to it, which was unlikely, since it contained only clean undervests and a book that the boy's father had given him when he was six, about famous desperadoes of the West. Then he pushed open the brass-handled door of his office, which was a dusty and stifling little room with a cluttered rolltop desk and dozens and dozens of railroad dockets and timetables pinned to the walls in curled-up sheaves. There was a gloomy railroad clock which measured time so grudgingly that the boy kept thinking it was about to stop, but it never did.

"Sit down," suggested the stationmaster. There was a wooden crate of oil-rig spares by the side of the desk, and the boy did so. The stationmaster opened and shut almost every drawer until he found a box of stale Spanish-peanut candy. He offered some to the boy, but the boy declined, and so he chewed off a piece himself, and everything he said was accompanied by a great deal of munching and swallowing and sticking his little finger between his teeth to clear out the sticky pieces.

"I guess your aunt is Mrs. Beatrice Mulliner, the widow lady," said the stationmaster.

The boy whispered: "Yes."

The stationmaster leaned forward and read the boy's label. "Well, that's a good guess. 'Master Daniel Forster, c/o Mrs. Beatrice Mulliner, Kearney Street, Edgar, Texas. To be collected.' "

The boy said: "Is there anything wrong? Has something gone wrong?"

The stationmaster sat back in his swivel chair. "Not in so many words, Master Daniel Forster. But I guess you're old enough to know what folks hereabouts think of Mr. Cornelius, your aunt's new gentleman, and you'd be well-advised to hold it in mind."

Sitting on the crate, the boy suddenly began to think of his mother, and even though he was listening to the ginger-haired stationmaster, he began to feel an uncomfortable lump in his throat, as if he were going to cry. After waiting outside the station for two hours, he was beginning to miss his usual teatime milk, and he couldn't help feeling a painful yearning for the quiet house in the genteel suburbs of New Orleans with its orchards and rambling gardens, and if he closed his eyes he could almost see the blue gingham tablecloth where he used to sit and drink his beaker of milk before going out for a last play.

"You mustn't think I'm being ill-natured," said the stationmaster, "but I like you. You're a good old boy, and I guess forewarned is usually forearmed, and I reckon you could do with some of that forearming. You take my word for it, J. Cornelius is a hard man, hard as rocks, hard as nails. He's rich as all hell, but the way I heard it, he got that way more through cheating than hard work, and anyone who gets in his way gets pulled up and tossed aside like tumbleweed. I've heard some odd tales of his tricks, I can tell you, and I reckon you'd be doing yourself a favor, and Mrs. Mulliner too, if you kept your ear to the rail."

The boy said anxiously: "Nothing's gone wrong, has it?"

The stationmaster sucked at his teeth to get out the candy. "Not in so many words. But you go see for yourself. Now you're forewarned, you won't let nothing take you by surprise. And if you ever feel the need, pass a note to Jack Beak, he's an old railroad buddy of mine, from the Santa Fe, and Jack'll make sure it gets to me."

Biting his lip, the boy said: "I'm not quite sure what you've warned me about. I'm afraid I don't quite understand."

The stationmaster reached over and laid his hand on the boy's shoulder. "Master Daniel Forster," he said, "You've got yourself

130

a whole lot of growing up to do before I can tell you all there is. But you keep your ear to the rail, and you'll be ready when the train comes."

Almost at the moment, there was the regurgitating sound of a motor horn outside. The stationmaster said: "That'll be him. Are you ready now?"

The boy said: "I'm afraid, a little."

"No you're not," chided the stationmaster. "Here, take this. Keep it by you, and in emergencies, blow it like billy-o."

He handed Daniel a real metal railroad whistle, with a brass ring and a green cord. Daniel took it hesitantly, but then he realized it was actually his, and he put it eagerly into the pocket of his tan suit. He said formally: "Thank you, sir. Your generosity is much appreciated."

The stationmaster cuffed him lightheartedly. "You get along now. Here's your bag. And remember your old friend if you ever feel unhappy, and come down here and see me again soon. The name's K. Jones, stationmaster."

Daniel solemnly shook hands with the stationmaster, and then hefted his valise and walked out into the late-afternoon sunlight. Johann's automobile was waiting in the yard, juddering and shaking as its engine ticked over, and Johann himself was sitting at the wheel in his white motoring coat, his eyes concealed by small dark-tinted goggles. Especially after K. Jones's dire warning, his aunt's new gentleman appeared to Daniel like some kind of bizarre ogre, and it didn't help the boy's nerve much when Johann sat there, silent and unmoving, while he tried to lift his valise into the back of the car.

Daniel climbed up to the front seat, and sat there waiting for something to happen. Over at the station door, the stationmaster stood with his hands in his pockets whistling his favorite tune and watching what went on.

Johann said dryly: "Do you know who I am?"

Daniel said: "Yes, sir," in a very small voice.

"What did you say?" asked Johann, louder.

"I said, 'yes, sir.' "

Johann regarded the boy for a long moment, his eyes invisible behind his dark goggles. He said: "Well, if you know who I am, why don't you raise your cap?"

The boy colored, and raised his cap. "Sorry, sir."

Johann, quite unexpectedly, gave a small, lopsided smile. He said: "You don't have to say sorry. I was taught to do the same when I was a boy, and cuffed when I didn't. When you're a boy, manners are worth having. They help you survive in a world made for grown-ups."

Daniel was completely perplexed. But he didn't have much time to think about Johann's peculiar words, for Johann said: "Hold tight!" released the hand brake, engaged the gears, and drove out of the railroad yard with three loud backfires.

Johann drove as if there were only two possible speeds—halted or flat-out—and over the ruts and gullies of Broughton's sun-hardened roads, Daniel bounced up and down in his seat like the needle bar on top of a sewing machine. He had never traveled in an automobile before, and he was thoroughly alarmed by the dust and the noise and the terrible speed. Beside him, Johann was hunched over the four-spoke steering wheel as if bending double was an essential part of increasing the automobile's velocity.

"The fastest machine around!" shouted Johann, as they came clattering around the corner into Broughton's main street. "What do you think of it?"

Daniel, white-faced, could do nothing but stare at Johann and try to smile.

They drove through Broughton's neat and respectable center, past Howard's Refreshment Parlor, past houses and stores and stables, and headed northward across flat ranch country, under an engulfing sky the color of purple laundry ink, the wind and the dust blowing in their faces. Daniel had to screw up his eyes to prevent the road grit from making them smart, and keep his pocket hand-kerchief pressed to his nose and mouth.

Johann said: "There's nothing like it for blowing out cobwebs, a ride in an automobile. You don't have time to be gloomy, like you would in a carriage."

Daniel didn't know what to say to that, or whether he was expected to say anything at all. Whatever K. Jones had told him about his aunt's new gentleman, Johann Cornelius appeared to be tolerably dashing, and quite friendly. Whether he was really as hard as rocks was another matter, but Daniel was old enough to suppose that a man could be as hard as rocks to his business partners, and yet civil and amiable to his friends.

"I think Texas looks very wild," he ventured to say. "Are there still desperadoes here?"

Johann thought about that, and then laughed. "There are always desperadoes here," he said, "and not all of them have guns."

132

Daniel waited for Johann to say something else, or explain what he meant, but that seemed to be all. They drove in silence for another two or three miles, across a breezy plateau with only a faint violet smudge on the horizon to suggest there might be mountains in the distance, or clouds, and then Johann suddenly reached in his pocket and handed Daniel a greaseproof-paper packet.

"Cold beef sandwiches. Beatrice made them for you."

Daniel took them gratefully, and opened them up. "Would you like one, sir?" he asked politely. Although Johann didn't say very much, and seemed to speak in conundrums whenever he did decide to talk, Daniel was beginning to like him He was a man's man. He drove and drove at top speed, and there was something larger than life and heroic about him.

Johann said: "Much obliged," and took a sandwich, and crammed it into his mouth as he drove. Daniel bit into his, and made a neat semicircle with his teeth.

Johann said, with his mouth full: "This place is going to be good for you, do you know that? It's wild all right, and that's just what you need. Start up a new life, put all the past behind you. I'll help you. Forget about the sad things that happened before, and start fresh."

Daniel swallowed his sandwich before he spoke, the way his mother had taught him. It seemed strange that Johann should be so insistent on him raising his cap, and yet could blithely talk and eat at the same time. He said: "The stationmaster told me you were hard as rocks."

Johann turned and looked at him with those piggy-eyed goggles.

"He said that? Those were his actual words?"

"Yes, sir. 'Hard as rocks,' he said. And he said you cheated people."

"Cheated people? What did he mean by that?"

Daniel frowned. He wasn't sure now that he should have betrayed K. Jones's confidence. But at the same time, Johann was Beatrice's gentleman, wasn't he? And if Beatrice was fond of him, and if Daniel himself felt that he was friendly, then what could be the harm? Maybe K. Jones had exchanged cross words with Johann Cornelius, and bore a grudge. You could never tell with stationmasters.

"I'm not sure," he told Johann uncertainly. "He didn't really explain himself."

Johann looked at Daniel for one moment more, and then

133

turned his attention back to the wheel of the car. The last glowering rays of the sun touched his goggles, and sparked off them as if his eyes were godly lances of fire.

"Well," he said at last, "I suppose what he says is true."

Daniel took another bite of sandwich, and then quickly had to put it down and cling to his seat. The track across the plateau was crusted with the hoofprints of cattle, baked into the mud, and the automobile shook and rattled as it crossed over them.

"This is a land of hard men," said Johann. "They came here when there was nothing but prairie and dust. They're proud of their hardness, and if you want to best them, you have to be harder still. I've been trying to make my fortune here, Daniel, and that's why I conduct myself the way that I do."

He was silent for a while, and then he said: "When I came to America, I had nothing and nobody. I was worse off than you are now, because I didn't even have aunts or friends. Well, when you're alone like that, and you have to make your way up from the basement, you learn to keep yourself to yourself, and to show nobody that you're hurt, or disappointed, or angry, or even when you're happy, if you ever are. If you do show them, just once, then they'll turn your weaknesses against you, and you'll be back down to the basement before you know."

Daniel believed that he understood this. He would have liked to hear more, but Johann didn't seem to have any more to say, and so for the next few miles they sat side by side without speaking.

"Is Aunt Beatrice well, sir?" Daniel asked at last.

Johann glanced at him. He had been thinking about Carina. He said: "Saddened by your mother's death, but otherwise well."

"Is she a good friend of yours, sir? A very good friend?"

Johann took out his handkerchief and loudly blew dust out of his nose. "We were to marry, as a matter of fact," he said, sniffing.

"Were to, sir? Does that mean you won't?"

"Well, I'm not so sure. We couldn't wed up until now because she was mourning your uncle Lidmore. Now she's mourning your mother, and that has postponed things for a while longer. I suppose we shall marry eventually. She's a very attractive and self-willed lady, your aunt."

"I don't know Aunt Beatrice very well, sir. She only came down to see us once, and I was just a child then."

134

Johann nodded. "You'll get to know her now. She's a lady in a hundred thousand, I can promise you that."

Daniel looked serious. "You do sound as if you like her, sir, I must say."

Johann didn't turn around this time. He remained bent over his wheel, his eyes fixed on the dusky distance.

"Well," he answered, "that's as may be."

It was almost dark by the time they arrived in Edgar. Daniel thought it looked a very shabby and broken-down place indeed; but then, he was used to the lush tropical gardens and elegant wrought iron of New Orleans. A few men in unfashionable suits were talking on a street corner, and when Johann passed in his white coat and goggles, they swiveled on their heels and stared until he was out of sight. Daniel turned and looked back at them once, and he was surprised to see that they didn't appear friendly at all. Perhaps Johann had treated some of them as hard as rocks, and they didn't like him for it.

They turned off at the main square, and puttered slowly down Kearney Street. It looked, to Daniel's eyes, a very desolate little row of weatherboard houses, and he had to swallow very hard to stop the tears from filling his eyes. Johann said: "Here we are. This one on the left, with the lighted porch," and slowed the automobile down.

As they came nearer, and drew up outside, they saw that another car was already parked there, around the side of the house. It was a white Daimler-Benz, coated with dust, as if it had been driven very far and very fast. Johann, climbing down from the New Orleans, pulled off his goggles and stared at it hard.

He was still looking at it when the front door of the house opened and Beatrice came out with Mrs. Elvira Russell. Beatrice called: "Daniel, my poor little boy!" and came down the veranda steps toward him, her arms outstretched.

Beatrice was wearing a black evening dress of silk mull, overlaid with wide Gibson shoulders. Her soft dark hair was pinned up as usual; and when Daniel reached the veranda and caught the scent of her perfume, which seemed so like his mother's, he burst immediately into tears, and clung around her waist, trying uselessly to blot out what had happened.

Johann stood a little way away, holding Daniel's cheap valise and regarding the Daimler-Benz with a humorless face. Mrs.

135

Russell called out: "You have a visitor, Mr. Cornelius. He tried to find you at home, but you were still out, so one of your tenants directed him here."

Johann brushed the dust from his motoring coat as he came up to the porch. Beatrice smiled and lifted her head from comforting Daniel to give him a light kiss on the cheek. She said: "It's Mr. Lennox, from Amarero. I don't know what he wants. He said he had to talk to you urgently."

"Yes," said Johann, and Beatrice frowned briefly as he walked past her into the house, and set down Daniel's case in the hall with an expression of darkly engraved anger.

Kyle Lennox was waiting in the parlor with a glass of sherry. He looked sweaty and red, as if he'd been drinking. Johann came into the room and stood there silently for almost a minute, while Lennox eyed him with greasy discomfort.

"Well," said Johann, taking off his motoring coat. "What do *you* want?"

Kyle Lennox grinned and sat back. He was even more disheveled than Johann remembered him, with a food-spotted vest of shiny quilted green silk, and his hair pomaded flat to his head. He said: "That's a hard drive, that, Mr. Cornelius, from Amarero. Lots of dust, lots of flies. It's one of those trips you'd only make if you had to."

"Oh, yes?" asked Johann guardedly.

Kyle Lennox raised his glass of sherry, and then tipped it all down his throat in one swallow. He wiped his mouth on the back of his sleeve. "A nice sherry-wine, that," he said. "Widow-women always keep a good sherry-wine, and I speak from experience."

Johann stayed where he was, his pale blue eyes fixed on Lennox's sweat-glossed face. He said nothing.

Lennox sniffed. "The truth is," he said, lacing his fingers together, and then waggling his long black fingernails. "The truth is that something appears to have gone awry. You know what I mean by awry?"

Johann almost imperceptibly shook his head.

"Well," said Lennox, taking out a cigar, "what I mean by *awry* is not so much *awry* as *astray*. Something seems to have gone astray. Not a cow in this case, nor a girl, but a payment. A payment of eight percent, as agreed between us, and which was regularly placed in my bank until now."

Johann raised an eyebrow. "You drove all the way from Amarero to tell me that?"

Lennox tugged at his earlobe. "I wouldn't have, not normally. But then I heard rumors."

"I always say that people who listen to rumors get to hear what they deserve," said Johann quite coldly.

Kyle Lennox shrugged. "Maybe you're right. But maybe I deserved to know that you'd fixed my contract before it got to *be* a rumor, and maybe I deserved to hear that you'd decided to welsh on our deal."

At that moment, Beatrice came in. She said: "Would you like another drink, Mr. Lennox? Johann, what about you?"

"Is Daniel all right?" asked Johann.

"Oh, I think so. He's tired, mostly, and overwrought. Aunt Elvira's cooking him ham and eggs in the kitchen. Poor little child. He was so fond of Sally, and she was so fond of him. I could cry for him."

Johann said tightly: "Mr. Lennox is just leaving, so he won't need another drink."

Kyle Lennox raised his empty glass. "On the contrary, I'd love one. I wasn't planning on leaving straightaway."

"What you're planning and what you're going to do are quite different kettles of fish," said Johann.

Beatrice looked at him anxiously. "Is something wrong?" she asked. "Have you two had an argument?"

Johann shook his head. "Mr. Lennox is leaving, that's all. Right away."

Kyle Lennox's smile looked a little more rigid, but he didn't move from the leatherette settee.

"We have a small matter of eight percent to settle first. I won't leave here without it, nor without your signed bond that you won't default again. I know what you've done with my contract, Mr. Cornelius, but there's a law in the Lone Star State, and that law says that a man has to have rendered unto him what is rightly his."

Johann didn't answer. Beatrice had never seen him looking so fierce, and she was almost frightened of him herself. But Kyle Lennox didn't seem impressed. He sat there picking his variegated teeth, still watching Johann in the way that a toad watches a mountain lion: *You may eat me, but by hell you won't like the taste.*

"Surely eight percent is not such a great amount," suggested Beatrice, trying to be conciliatory.

Kyle Lennox flicked a scornful glance at her. "Eight percent of a million dollars is eighty thousand dollars," he said in a dry voice. "And if it strikes you that eighty thousand dollars is not such a great amount, then I'd say that you probably owe me even more than you're admitting to."

Beatrice turned to Johann, flushed and confused, but Johann didn't take his eyes off Lennox, although he reached out and held her wrist in a strong, comforting grasp. He said quietly: "Mr. Lennox is right. But eighty thousand dollars, whether we admit to it or not, is eighty thousand dollars more than he's going to get."

Lennox stuck his cigar between his teeth, took out a match, and struck it against the sole of his shoe. As he lit up, he watched Johann coldly and unblinkingly through the clouds of blue smoke. For a moment, all three of them were motionless, and Johann felt again that strange sense of destiny, as if the history of his life was bearing down on them all, and he knew that what was going to happen next was as unavoidable as his purchase of Carina. This, for some arcane reason, was a crucial moment in Johann's career.

Kyle Lennox said: "You're forgetting yourself, aren't you? You're forgetting what those eighty thousand dollars paid for."

"I suggest you get out of here, before you cause this lady any further offense."

"Offense? You're talking to me about offense? Does the lady know what favor I did you that was worth all that amount of money?"

Johann could feel his heart beating in slow, suffocating bumps. He knew then that he loved Beatrice more than he had ever imagined possible, and it was all he could do not to look down at the rug where he had actually possessed her, for the first and only time. He held her wrist so tight that he hurt her, and when she prized his fingers off her, he had the dreary, frightening sensation that he had touched her for the last time.

She said to Lennox: "Favor? What favor? What are you talking about? What possible favor could Mr. Cornelius have wanted from you?"

Kyle Lennox stood up. It was only then that they realized how drunk he was. He leaned toward Beatrice at an alarming angle, and pushed back his greasy hair with his ring-covered fingers.

"Ask Mr. Cornelius. He's your beau, madam, unless the gossip has it wrong. Surely a beau shouldn't have secrets from his lady."

Beatrice glanced at Johann uneasily. "Johann?" she asked. "What is this favor? What does he mean?"

Johann said slowly: "It was a small private matter which Mr. Lennox, on careful reflection, has decided not to speak about."

"Johann," insisted Beatrice, "I want to know. Surely we shouldn't hide anything at all from each other. Not if we're to—"

"It's a matter of no importance," snapped Johann. "Now, Lennox, you can leave. And I mean *now*."

"Oh, no." Lennox laughed, and then coughed thickly. "You don't get rid of me that easy. I want your signed note right here in my hand, or I don't take a single step."

"You're my employee now. Don't forget that. And you're not getting a brass button. Now, get out before I toss you out."

Lennox picked up the sherry decanter and poured himself another drink with hands that shook so badly that Beatrice was afraid he was going to shatter both his glass and the crystal decanter. Then he raised his glass, contemptuously toasted Johann, and downed the sherry in one.

"You don't leave me much of a choice, Mr. Cornelius. No choice at all. I've tried to play the game, tried to do it fair, but if you don't stick to your bargains, then there's nothing else for it."

Beatrice said: "This is absurd! Surely we can know what this favor was supposed to have been?"

Kyle Lennox coughed, sniffed, and then grinned. "It seems, since we haven't been paid for holding our tongues, that we *can*. The favor, if you can call it a favor—"

Johann took a deep breath. "*Lennox*," he warned.

But Kyle Lennox was too drunk with whiskey and sherry, and the intoxicating sensation of taunting the richest man in Broughton County. "The favor," he said with a sloping smile, "was a girl."

Beatrice frowned, and blinked.

"She was a young quadroon girl, from Piedras Negras," continued Lennox. "She was sent to me for employment in my hotel, the Excelsior, as a common prostitute. As *fodder,* if you know what I mean, for the baser tastes of the Amarero oilmen."

The silence was as thick as dusty velvet drapes.

Kyle Lennox continued: "The girl was said to be thirteen years old, but the wetbacks don't know counting from horse manure. I saw her myself, and she was eleven or twelve at most."

Lennox glanced up at Johann, and gave a little smirk. It was.

part pleasure, and part fear. Johann's face was stiff with suppressed rage, and Lennox knew that he was going to hit him.

Strangely, though, the atmosphere changed. Lennox glanced toward the door, and Johann, turning, saw Daniel standing there, pale-faced, in his shirtsleeves and tan breeches.

Daniel looked from Lennox to Johann to Beatrice, and then said in a small voice: "Aunt Elvira sent me to say good night."

Beatrice said quickly: "Good night, Daniel. I'll be up in a moment to tuck you in. I just have to—"

Lennox drunkenly raised a finger. "Even though she was only eleven or twelve," he continued, his voice very slurred. "Even though she was only eleven or twelve—"

"*Lennox!*" shouted Johann. He reached forward and tried to seize Kyle Lennox's lapels, but Lennox was so ridiculously drunk that he fell sideways on the leatherette settee, and then slipped onto the floor. Beatrice pulled Daniel protectively into her skirts, and screamed: "Johann! *No!*"

But in any case, Johann couldn't reach Lennox in time. Lennox staggered up onto his knees and shouted: "He bought her! For eight percent of his oil! That was the favor! He bought the girl and he set her up here in Edgar! He gave her a house and fancy clothes! And better than that, he uses her night after night in the way she is accustomed to!"

Johann barked liked a mad dog. He took one stiff stride across the room, seized Kyle Lennox by his green vest, and flung him back against the fireplace. Lennox half-climbed to his feet again, but it was then that Johann reached back his arm and punched Lennox so hard in the mouth that teeth and blood burst out of Johann's fist like a magic trick. Lennox said: "Grargh," and dropped back onto the floor, but Johann was insane with rage and wouldn't let him go. He plucked the man up and hit him in the face again, dislocating his jaw. Then he hurled him back against the glass-fronted cabinet, and in a shower of broken teacups he kicked Kyle Lennox again and again in the testicles until Lennox shrieked like a woman in labor.

Beatrice was screaming: "*No! No! Johann! No!*" and Daniel was whimpering in terror. But Johann was ablaze with fury, guilt, and grief, and he was unreachable and unstoppable. He stood over Kyle Lennox, who was twisted under a chair, and he raised the heel of his coltskin shoe and stepped on Lennox's nose with his entire weight. There was a snap as loud as a chicken's leg breaking, and blood ran over Lennox's upturned face in a dark spidery gush.

Johann turned around. Beatrice was standing there, her hands raised in almost comic horror, and Daniel was clinging to her skirt.

"Do you see that man?" quaked Johann. "Do you see that filth beneath my feet?"

Beatrice said: "My God, I'm sure you've killed him. Oh, my God."

"Killed him?" shouted Johann. "And what if I have?"

"He said . . . he said you *bought* that girl . . ."

"Yes!"

"Johann . . ."

"You want to know if it's true? Is that it?"

"Johann, you must calm yourself. Johann, please."

"You want to know if it's true? You want to know if I've deceived you? You don't trust my honor? Is that it?"

"Johann, no!"

Johann turned away, still breathing heavily. He looked down at the glass-littered floor for a moment, and then at his swollen knuckles. He said in a low, quiet voice: "It's true. Her name is Carina, and I bought her from Lennox for an eight-percent share in the oil pumped up from Sweetwater Trail. She wasn't the daughter of a Mexican oil worker at all, not like I told you. That was just a way of making it easier for you to understand."

There was a white, rigid silence. Then Beatrice said: "And do you *use* her, as Mr. Lennox said? Is that why you bought her? To *use* her?"

On the floor, Kyle Lennox gargled and groaned.

Johann said: "I suppose I bought her because I needed affection, and I needed love. I also bought her because she is very beautiful, and I couldn't bear the thought of her spending her life in that fleabitten hotel, being abused by oil workers, night after night, and getting old before her time. I bought her because . . ." He paused, searching for ways to explain to Beatrice the sad mystical sensations that Carina gave him. But all he could say was: "I bought her because I wanted to have her, like a possession."

"Then she's your mistress?"

Johann shook his head numbly.

"Then she's *not* your mistress?"

He looked up at her, cautious and suddenly tired.

141

"I promise you, I have never touched her," he said.

Beatrice stood there with her face as white as an alabaster statue. She whispered: "My God," and then she raised her arm to her forehead and fell to the floor in a rustle of black silk, swooning gracefully across the tasteless carpet. Daniel, distraught, fell on his knees beside her, and patted her cheeks in a vain attempt to wake her up.

Johann took three or four deep breaths, and then walked over to Beatrice. He gently pushed Daniel aside.

"She's dead," wept Daniel. "She's dead!"

Johann said: "No, she's not. I just think she couldn't face any more. She's fainted."

Quite unexpectedly, Daniel took out his real railroad whistle and blew a long and piercing blast. Johann stared at him in amazement. He said: "What was that for?"

"It's an emergency," said Daniel. "The stationmaster told me to blow it in case of emergency."

Johann lowered his eyes back to Beatrice. "I don't think all the whistles in the world could help with this emergency," he said, so softly that Daniel could hardly hear.

At that moment, Mrs. Elvira Russell appeared in the doorway, her hair tied up in curling papers. She looked around her ravaged parlor, and at Beatrice and Kyle Lennox, and whispered: "Heavens. Is anything wrong?"

Johann stood up. "There's nothing wrong, ma'am, that a good earthquake couldn't set right. I think you'd better call for the doctor."

He waited until the doctor came, and stood uselessly by while Kyle Lennox's nose was examined and pronounced crushed, and while Mrs. Elvira Russell climbed furiously up and down stairs with hot towels and sal volatile for Beatrice. At last, at ten o' clock, Mrs. Elvira Russell frostily suggested that he might have outstayed his welcome, and he found his hat and left.

He drove around to Carina's cottage, and parked outside. All the lights were out, which must have meant that Carina was asleep. He desperately wanted someone to talk to, but he didn't want to wake her. So he sat in his silent automobile in the cool Texas night, listening to the wind from the prairie and wishing that the needle-pointed stars would drop from the sky. The metal hood of his automobile ticked and pinged as it cooled down.

142

He knew what he had done to Beatrice. He supposed that the only surprise was that she had taken so long to find out. Even though it hadn't really mattered up until now, because nobody in Edgar had had the nerve to say anything openly about it, he knew that Beatrice would find it intolerable to live with the pity and the mockery that she would sense behind every smile.

He didn't cry. He had promised himself that he would never cry again. But he felt such misery that anyone passing by that night would have heard a single, held-back sob, and known that Johann Cornelius was hurt.

The following afternoon, Friday, he called around at Mrs. Elvira Russell's house just after luncheon. He was dressed in a plain blue suit and a blue hat, and he was carrying a box of crystallized fruit tied up with yellow ribbons. He was surprised to see that Kyle Lennox's white Daimler-Benz was no longer parked outside, but he presumed that his toadlike adversary of the previous night had driven off back to Amarero and his washed-out wife.

Mrs. Elvira Russell was not amused by his call. She stood in the doorway and said: "Yes?"

Johann coughed. "If it's possible, I'd like to see Beatrice. I think I need to apologize. And to you, too."

"She's not in."

"Are you sure? It would mean a lot if I could. I think there were a whole lot of misunderstandings last night."

"Yes. But she's not in."

Johann held out the fruit with a stiff arm. "Could you give her this candy, then?"

Mrs. Elvira Russell made no move to take it.

"Please?" asked Johann.

Mrs. Elvira Russell said: "It won't do you no good. She's left for permanent."

"Permanent? What do you mean?"

"She left with Mr. Lennox this morning. She said to tell you it was all she could do. She wasn't going to stay here to be laughed at. She's going to put up with Mr. and Mrs. Lennox for a while, in Amarero, then she's taking young Daniel to the Gulf, and you won't see hide nor hair of them from then on."

Johann stared at her in horror. "She left with *Lennox*?" he asked her.

"That's right. Mr. Lennox kindly offered to take her home, and take care of Daniel, too."

"When did they leave?"

"An hour since. You won't catch them."

Johann stood on the porch, numbed. How could she leave him without even a letter or a message? How could she leave him for *Lennox*? He lifted his box of sugared fruits and looked at them bitterly. She hadn't even given him time to explain.

He said: "I'd better pay you for the broken cabinet."

Mrs. Elvira Russell shook her head. "You needn't trouble."

"But that's ten dollars' worth of damage there."

"That's all right. I found twenty dollars under the settee a while back, and I guessed whose it was, and how it got to be there. So that will see me right."

Johann bit his lip. Behind him, out of the shade of the porch, it was a bright clear day, with a sky as blue and wide as America's best. He turned and, without a word, walked back to his automobile.

Friday afternoon was a bad day to travel to Amarero. It was the day that the Amarero Oil Company and the Cornelius Oil Company paid their men, and those that didn't go straight to the marble-and-mahogany fastnesses of the Wonderful Elk saloon to watch themselves fade into drunken gloom in the mirrors that surmounted the bar, like underexposed photographs of long-forgotten faces, took themselves to the Hotel Excelsior for quick sexual relief. Friday night was a rowdy night, with fights and fires and oilmen having bizarre accidents, like the time an Oklahoma-born wildcatter had leaped from the second-floor window of the Red Star Ironmongery to greet an old drilling buddy from Damn-right who was passing in the street below, and he died impaled on the upright handles of three self-wringing mops that were standing on the boardwalk.

But Beatrice had been determined, with the kind of determination that only those who have been gravely humiliated can understand. And with Kyle Lennox impressed to take the wheel, regardless of his grotesquely bandaged nose, she had sat straight-spined all day in the rear seat of the Daimler-Benz, with Daniel beside her, as they traveled across the miles and miles of dusty deserted prairie between Edgar and Amarero, and the sun circled above them like the gleaming arc of a polished sextant.

It was a day of heat, blowflies, and dust. They ate chicken that Mrs. Elvira Russell had prepared for them, and drank tepid lemonade from a stone bottle, although Kyle Lennox had two quarts of bourbon in his carpetbag, and he consulted them more and more frequently as the doctor's pain-suppressing tablets wore off. By the time they saw Amarero in the distance, under a distended red sun that was fat from the week's shining, Lennox was singing "I'm Wearing My Heart Away for You" in a high nasal trill, and the white Daimler-Benz was bouncing and jolting from one side of the track to the other.

Beatrice attempted several times to shake Kyle Lennox back to sensibility, but as the sun finally settled behind the low distant hills, he was scarcely able to drive at more than a stuttering crawl, and the automobile's motor cut out time and time again. Eventually, only half a mile away from the rundown shacks and stables that surrounded the town, the car veered into a low, stony gully and came to a sharp halt against the fallen truck of a checkered-bark juniper. Lennox fell face-forward over his steering wheel and began to snore loudly, a long string of bloody saliva hanging from his open lips. Beatrice stood up in the car, the evening wind blowing the ribbons of her hat, and Daniel sat worriedly beside her, holding his valise against his knees.

"We shall have to abandon him here," announced Beatrice. "I am sorry for the poor man, but his condition *was* rather self-inflicted. We can always send someone back to fetch him."

"Where shall we go?" asked Daniel.

Beatrice descended from the automobile, her skirts held up in case the hem was snagged by the Daimler's brake handle.

"Hand down the cases," she said. "We shall walk to the railroad station and inquire about suitable lodging for the night."

As evening faded into darkness, Beatrice and Daniel, hand-in-hand, hurried as fast as they could along the dusty track into Amarero. Beatrice turned around once, but she could hardly make out the white shape of Kyle Lennox's car, and it was plain that he hadn't stirred.

Ahead of them, in the mournful prairie night, they could see the lights of the Excelsior and the Wonderful Elk, and they could hear shouting and shrieking and every now and then a volley of pistol shots. It was an ordinary Friday night in Amarero, and Beatrice felt a tug of alarm and anticipation, because even an ordinary Friday night in Amarero was riotous. She clutched Daniel's hand tighter, and tried not to think about her fear, even when she heard a woman screaming and screaming in the distance, out by the old Indian

145

huts. Daniel said: "Can we go slower? My legs are quite tired." But although she slackened her pace for a little while, her anxiety soon got the better of her, and she began to hurry along as quickly as before.

To reach Main Street, they had to pass through the dark and shadowy tangle of huts and rundown stables where Amarero and the even prairie reached an untidy compromise. Old ramshackle doors and windows creaked and banged in the steady wind, and the sun-whitened remnants of fences and signposts poked through the darkness like the bones of a carcass. Beatrice gripped Daniel's hand so tightly that he cried out, and held her shawl to her throat as if it could protect her from whatever demons, human or supernatural, might lurk in the night.

She felt afterward, in what afterward there was, that she willed her fate upon herself by being so frightened. She wondered if her fear gave off a scent that men could detect; or if it glowed luridly in the dark. But the inevitability of what happened was more to do with her broken association with Johann Cornelius than it was to do with her own fear.

She remembered very little. A bunch of men in plaid shirts and working trousers were gathered at the corner of the old livery stables, laughing and jostling each other and passing a bottle around. She saw the bottle shine, and heard the liquid sound as the men lifted it up to their bearded lips. She remembered that she made up her mind to pass them by without looking at them and without comment. There were probably ten or eleven of them, and they looked a hard-bitten bunch. They were drunk already, and one of them was singing a coarse and raucous song about drilling for oil. There was a smell of rough pipe tobacco on the wind.

As Beatrice and Daniel hurried past, one of the men called out: "Hoi!"

Beatrice didn't turn around, but tugged Daniel along even faster.

"Hoi, lady!" shouted the man again.

Beatrice started to run. She held up her black silk skirts and went as fast as she could along the soft, dusty track. Daniel ran beside her, panting.

She thought she had escaped; but the men, though drunk, were faster. She heard them running up behind her, and almost as she reached the rhomboids of lamplight that fell across the street from the Wonderful Elk saloon, she was seized by the skirts, and she fell,

146

shrieking and beating her fists, into the dusty roadway. Curious faces, whiskery and red, appeared at the windows of the saloon, but nobody attempted to come out and help her. She shrieked: "Leave me be, for the love of Our Lord!" but two of the sweaty and sour-breathed oilmen lifted her bodily up from the ground and carried her, with legs kicking and petticoats flying, back into the darkness. There was only Daniel, whining and crying as he ran around and around, helpless and desperate, hitting at the legs of the oilmen while they made away with his aunt. One of them—a black-bearded fellow in a balding beaver hat—eventually turned around and went after Daniel like a bow-legged spider, and snatched him by the arm.

"Let her go!" wept Daniel. "Let her go! She's not yours!"

The man in the beaver hat shook Daniel hard and said roughly: "We didn't never say she was, boy! We didn't never say she was! All we aim to do is to borrow a lend of her for just a while!"

Daniel kicked at the man's shins with his pointed boot, and the man boxed Daniel's ears so hard that the boy fell over backward in the dust. His head sang, and he ripped his tan breeches on a stray tag of barbed wire.

Singing and laughing, the bunch of oilmen carried their prize away into the shadows behind the dilapidated livery stables, and they only laughed the more when she shrieked for mercy in the names of her saints, Saint Agnes and Saint Bartholomew, in her high, well-bred voice.

Daniel picked himself up and trotted, his cheeks smudged with tears, to the building where he thought they had taken her. Even though the men were making such a row, he trod as carefully as he could so that they wouldn't hear him. He skirted around the stables, and down a narrow alleyway overgrown with tough wild grass. Something shifted suspiciously in the shadows—a prairie rat or a disturbed lizard—and the boy went cold all over with fright. But now, through the gaps in the dried-out timber walls of the livery stable, he could see the darting beam of an Ever Ready flashlight, and heard the men roar and guffaw, and Beatrice beg all the more insistently for clemency. So he tried to ignore his fear of the invisible creatures in the dark, and he stepped up to the shaky old wall and put his eye to the knothole.

By the quixotic light of the electric torch, the scene he saw was of such extraordinary vividness that he remained still and silent, a boy poured from alabaster. It was the *colors* that he would remember for so many years afterward, as if what he saw was a rich Rembrandt tableau, a painted anatomy lesson in the murky night of a Texan oil town in the 1900's. He did not recognize what he saw, because he was an innocent boy, as boys could be in those times, and he knew his catechism better than he knew what rabbits did when their tails twitched. But he was luridly conscious of the grisly desecration that was taking place before him, and although he remained still, his spirits sank within him until he felt that he was lost to the real world forever.

He saw Beatrice's legs raised, in their shiny gray silk stockings, and parted wide. He saw a dark motif of hair, and what appeared to him to be a glistening scarlet wound. Her black dress was bunched up around her waist, so that he could not see her face. The oilmen appeared to have tied her with frayed cord to the top of an old kitchen table. They were huddled around her, with sweaty and bearded faces of strangely gentle curiosity. One after another, as they passed the bottle around and some of them sang, they unbuckled their heavy belts and dropped their pants to their knees. Then they stood between Beatrice's opened thighs, and from his spy place at the knothole Daniel could see their big hairy buttocks jerking backward and forward in a way that disturbingly brought to mind a wooden monkey he had been given by his mother as a smaller boy, which jerked its way up a string. Beatrice prayed at first, in a quiet voice, but after the fourth or perhaps the fifth oilman had presented himself between her legs, she remained silent, except for an occasional mewl. The Ever Ready flashlight was direct at her red and shining gash between each bout of monkey-climbing, and Daniel saw that it was basted with gelatinous white.

This proceeding went on for two or three hours, and the oilmen were as unconcerned and jocular about it as if they were crowded in the ginger-beer tent of a meadow carnival. They opened more bottles of whiskey, and sang some more; and one of them even produced a mouth harp and played a few bars of a popular song. Now and then, one of them would return to Beatrice and stand between her legs again, although as time wore on their exertions grew less vigorous, and they panted and puffed, and sometimes gave up with shouts of self-derogatory laughter. Several times Daniel heard Beatrice say: "Please, I'm a widow." But all they did was grin and tell her: "That's all right, ma'am. In that event, your husband won't mind, will he?"

Toward midnight the oilmen grew so drunk that two or three of them passed out on the ground and began to snore. One of them was violently and noisily sick, and because of this, the others decided to make their way back to the Excelsior Hotel, since they still had sufficient money for paid fornication, their first relief of the evening having been free. Daniel heard them stumble away, and after half an hour he was quite certain that they had gone. It was only then that he stood away from the knothole, his arms by his sides, his face blank and shocked. He was not a boy who found it easy to hate people, or even to dislike them. Although he was only nine, he had a precociously developed sense of pity and forgiveness, which may have come from his mother's constant and eventually terminal illness. He did not blame the oilmen for what had happened so much as he blamed Johann for having obliged a defenseless widow and a small boy to venture into a rowdy boom town on pay night. He saw Johann as the author of everything bad that had happened.

He heard Beatrice sighing. Long, extended sighs. He tugged at one of the boards, and it came out with a squeak of rusty nails. Then he squeezed through the wall into the livery stable, and approached Beatrice softly and gently, averting his eyes from her lifted skirts and the bloody smears of fluid on her parted thighs.

He held her hand. He whispered: "Beatrice, it's Daniel."

She turned and stared at him. There was only moonlight now, from a freshly risen moon, and she wasn't sure if he was real or not. She said: "Daniel?"

He pulled at the cords which bound her and eventually worked them loose enough for her to get free. She laid a heavy hand on his shoulder as she lifted herself painfully up from the kitchen table, and stood in the gloom of the stables, breathing in irregular gasps. The mess of her rape slid stickily down her legs, and she felt as if she was going to vomit, but she held her head high, and said to Daniel in an unsteady and husky voice: "You must find the sheriff."

In New York, in the opulent smoking room of a substantial stone house overlooking the East River, two men sat crouched over a table and spoke to each other in soft, carefully enunciated whispers. The room was enormous and suffused with brown afternoon light. One wall was ranked with green and crimson leather books, all with gold lettering on their figured spines. A globe rested in antique mahogany gimbals. What seemed strange about the way the two men were huddled together was that the smoking room was empty apart from them, and nobody could possibly have overheard what they were saying. The man with the hand-carved meerschaum pipe and the round, brandy-mottled face was none other than Percy F. Colton, the oil millionaire, and the man with the pale gray suit and the unfashionably clipped mustaches was Arnie Styvers, who had been acquitted only last month of the manslaughter of the Polish actress Irena Womack. Styvers was known to his friends as "The Vent," for the way in which he talked without apparently moving his lips.

They met together seldom. It was not in Percy Colton's interest to have it known that he was a friend of Styvers', and in any event both men had enough messengers and minions to keep up an almost daily dialogue. As they talked, Styvers kept looking at his long clean fingernails. He hardly ever looked up.

"I talked to Jimmy Makepiece today," said Percy Colton quietly.

"Umh-humh?"

"Amarero's fine, by all accounts."

Styvers splayed his fingers, and then buffed his nails on his lapel. He didn't answer. He knew that Percy Colton had more to say.

"The only problem seems to be Cornelius Oil. Have you heard of Cornelius Oil?"

"No."

Percy Colton picked up his pipe from the leather-topped table and stuck it between his teeth. Right now, he didn't know whether he was going to light it or not. He said: "Cornelius Oil is bringing up twenty-five thousand barrels a day, maybe more. They're pumping oil from the same pool as Amarero One. It's a snappy little outfit, from what I hear."

"Who's in charge?"

"His name's Johann Cornelius. One of your hardheaded immigrant types. Strong-tempered, by all accounts. It seems he makes it a specialty to lease or buy up land where other wildcatters have run out on their luck. He uses his head, you see, and a whole lot of fancy instruments, and he brings up oil where other people can only find gophers."

"You're worried?"

Colton shook his head. "Not really. He doesn't have the refining. All of his crude he sells to us. If he gets too uppity, or too

150

lucky, we can simply smile and say sorry. I'd rather give him some rope, though—let him keep spudding wells while fortune smiles in his direction. Then, when he's up to his ears in crude, we can refuse to buy any more."

"Sounds sensible."

Colton took his pipe out of his mouth and sat back. "It's known as forward planning, so they tell me."

Styvers nodded vaguely. "What do you want me to do?"

Colton produced a small gold penknife from his vest pocket and began to dig at the caked dottle in his pipe bowl. "Nothing at the moment," he said. "That's the essence of forward planning."

"You sound like you've got something up your sleeve."

Colton chuckled. "I shouldn't really tell you."

"Is it that bad?"

"It's bad enough."

Styvers waited for Colton to tell him. He was a patient man. A ship hooted on the flat silvery river outside.

"You know Kyle Lennox, don't you?" asked Percy Colton, his voice crammed with amusement.

"Sure. Big whiskers, bad taste in vests. He started off with a three-card table on Hester Street. Years ago, that was. Then he went west and gambled on the riverboats. He's Jimmy's manager down in Amarero, isn't he?"

"That's right. And that's what makes this whole thing so funny."

"Go on," said Styvers, without moving his lips.

Percy Colton leaned forward conspiratorially. "Kyle Lennox sold Johann Cornelius a twelve-year-old girl."

Styvers' eyes flickered, but he didn't seem particularly surprised. He wasn't the most shockable man in New York City.

Colton leaned back again. "For some reason, Cornelius took a fancy to this twelve-year-old girl down at Lennox's cathouse, and he made Lennox a deal. The deal was that Cornelius took the girl, and in return Lennox got eight percent of his gross profits."

Styvers glanced up. "Eight percent of twenty-five thousand barrels a day? For a twelve-year-old girl?"

Colton said: "Ours not to reason why—ours but to take advantage. It just seems that Cornelius felt a burning need for this young lady—if that's not too polite a description of her—and that was the price he was prepared to pay. For a while, anyway. When the oil really started to gush up, he wanted out. His accountants wrote to us here in New York a very serious and solemn letter saying how much Cornelius Oil would like to take Kyle Lennox off our hands, and use Lennox's expert talents in Amarero for themselves. This, of course, was before we found out about the girl.''

Styvers grunted in amusement. "Poor old Kyle. So you let Cornelius have him?''

"Of course! Lennox is nothing but a drunken vegetable these days. It was a pleasure to see him go.''

Styvers scrutinized his fingernails with even greater concentration. "That's not all, though, is it?''

Colton grinned. "Oh, no, that's not all. Lennox got to hear what Cornelius had done, and so he paid him a visit, and understandably protested, and Cornelius understandably broke Lennox's nose and four of his ribs.''

Styvers said: "I've heard they're very uncultured out west.''

"Wait!'' said Colton with overflowing pleasure. "What happened after that was even better. Cornelius had his fiancée with him, and his fiancée's young nephew, a boy of eight or nine, and they were so scandalized by his behavior that they decided to leave Edgar, and travel to Amarero with Lennox. On the way into Amarero they were set upon by a gang of rowdies, and the fiancée, can you believe it, was raped. Not once, which would have been bad enough, but *twenty* times, with the boy watching. Or so Jimmy informs me. Now, don't you think that's distressing?''

Styvers didn't appear to be particularly distressed. "Sure, it's distressing,'' he said. "Where do I send the flowers?''

Colton tapped his head. "You have to think, Arnie. Think! And you have to know that Johann Cornelius is in a real interesting situation right now. He's fixed his eyes on three more plots of land, two to lease and one to buy. Even if he strikes a runt of a well, he's going to have thirty or forty thousand barrels of crude every day for refining.''

"And that's more crude than you can refine for him?''

"Can or will.''

"And what does that mean?''

Colton opened his desk drawer and took out a Delft tobacco jar. "It means that all the crude he can't refine he has to store. Storage is very expensive, even if you can find the tanks. And oil has to be transported from the well to the tanks, and that's expensive too. And all the time you're storing crude, you're making no more money out of it than you would be if it was still lying in the ground, and so you run out of fluid cash and you go bankrupt.''

Styvers considered this. Then he said: "Okay, but Cornelius must know this as well. So what's his way out?''

Colton was so pleased with himself that he couldn't stop himself from smiling. "He can do one of several things, Arnie. He can sell out his business to us for a fair and reasonable price, and make something out of it, which is better than nothing at all. Or else he can store up his crude in the slender hope that we'll change our minds, or that Shell or someone else will agree to refine it. Or else he can do what he's doing now, and that's try to interest the Houston-West Refinery into starting a partnership. He's on his way to New York right now, so Jimmy tells me, to talk to their major shareholders.''

"Houston-West? Who are they?''

"They used to be a branch of Schmettens Oil. Schmettens went to the wall, but the Houston-West plant was bought up by a small group who were looking for investment in petroleum products.''

Styvers said: "You've lost me. What does all this have to do with Lennox getting his nose busted and Cornelius' fiancée getting herself raped?''

Colton rose from his seat like a classical conductor bringing his orchestra into the last movement of Beethoven's Seventh. "It has plenty to do with it. Especially when you know that the small investment group who bought Houston-West are all Quakers, and that if they ever discovered they were doing business with a molester of twelve-year-old children, or a monster who could surrender an innocent woman into the hands of a gang of drunken rapists, they would consider their deal at a very firm end. When Cornelius arrives here, I shall have him discreetly informed that we know all about his aberrations, and that his wisest course of action would be to forget about Houston-West and enter into some kind of amicable arrangement with us.''

Styvers' fingernails traced out the gilt leaf patterns that bordered the desk. "Amicable, huh?''

"Of course! You think I'm going to upset such a talented discoverer of oil? I shall be happy for him to continue what he's doing, employed by Colton Oil, and to pay him five hundred dollars a month.''

Styvers said: "That's good money. Unless you happen to own the wells yourself. Do you think he'll agree?''

153

"That's where you come in," said Colton. "Cornelius has an obvious weakness, and the weakness is his twelve-year-old girl. When they arrive in New York, I want you to abduct her for just as long as it takes to persuade Johann Cornelius to change his mind."

"And if he doesn't?"

"He has to."

"But if he doesn't?"

"Then the East River is deep and wide."

Styvers was silent for a moment, and then he rose from his chair and neatly pushed it back under the table. He was a slight man, with an appearance of almost constant tiredness, as if he had to keep books late at night, or send a promising young daughter through ballet school. He ran fifteen gambling-and-booze dens in New York City alone, and three of the most notorious bawdy houses. He often dined with the mayor, and he occasionally went fishing with the chief of police. There had been several incidents of death by shooting or drowning which had been rumored to be "Styvers' jobs," but the judges had always looked down favorably so far on a man who did so much for New York commerce, and whose fingernails were always so immaculately clean.

Styvers said: "Keep in touch about the timing. When Cornelius is expected to arrive, and so forth. Then leave all the rest of it to me."

Colton said: "I still have some of that good brandy, if you'd care for a snort."

Styvers shook his head. "Save it for yourself, Percy. The cunningest bastard deserves the finest drink."

They had arrived in the foyer of their hotel, the old Plaza on Fifty-ninth Street, amid mahogany and marble and brass, and they stood with their trunks at their feet, severe and quiet, not speaking to each other because each was submerged in different and particular thoughts. They were booked into two separate but adjacent rooms as Mr. J. Cornelius and Daughter. They did not look like father and daughter, but neither did they look like man and whore.

Johann was dressed in a light gray fall overcoat with black velveteen lapels, and a light gray hat. He carried a black cane, and his pointed shoes were black and gray. Carina wore a black turban-style hat decorated with German braid and spangled jet, with a black lace veil across her face, and she was sophisticated and discreet in a plainly cut black coat. They held their heads high in the

154

way that close friends do as they wait in the foyers of strange hotels.

Later, they dined by lamplight on oysters and plain roasted quail at Eduard's, a fashionable restaurant that Johann had once passed by when he worked for Nathaniel's Engineering. The waiters had starched white fronts, and plied them with sauces and vegetables as if they were children to be spoiled. Carina said very little, but ate a black-cherry bombe in enchanted silence. A violinist with white wiry hair stood next to an aspidistra and carefully sliced up Mozart like a grocer's assistant slicing up ham. At the next table, a ginger-haired man in a high white collar was saying "That Hetty Green is the meanest woman alive. Mean! She has more ready cash than J. P. Morgan, some say, and yet she walks around like a ragbag, and argues over sixteen cents for a pair of shoes."

His companion, a finely dressed young lady with a very large nose, laid her white hand on his sleeve and said: "Yes, dear. But wouldn't it be marvelous to be able to *afford* such meanness?"

Johann listened, and watched. His face was alive with quick secret smiles. He was back in New York, but now he was sitting on the solvent side of the window, and he wanted to learn names and connections and prices. He wanted to discover who had power and who had not. He wanted to know who could be levered and who was strong. He was quite aware that in this city of Cabots, and Coltons, and Rockefellers, and Vanderbilts, his one million dollars was inestimably puny. Hetty Green was conservatively valued at one hundred million, despite her parsimony and the aged black dress she wore day after day and year after year. And lesser though his fortune was, J. P. Morgan, with his passions for yachts and European art treasures, was worth at least sixty-eigh* million. Johann was conscious of his own brute ambition and his almost religious fervor for making himself rich; but he was also conscious that the wealth of New York's four hundred dominated every industrial endeavor and every hall of politics and influence, and that he needed more than fervor to break into the fortressed walls of trusts and monopolies and fixed prices.

Carriages clattered outside the restaurant window, and appeared to blaze in the reflected flames from a flambé dish across the room. There was an aroma of cigars and grilled lobster and Benedictine which Johann inhaled as if the very inhalation of it could enhance his wealth. Carina said: "I love New York. It makes me very happy."

Johann was not aware of any particular sensation of happiness; but he was certainly aware of feelings of renewed strength. There had been many days in Texas when he had been ready to despair. Days when the dusty wind blew, and he was short of money and work. But now he felt that real wealth was within his grasp. He had producing oil wells, and a billfold of ready cash, and when he tied up his first big-business deal with Houston-West next week, he would be ready to take over more land, and more oil, and he would be blizzarded with dollars like a Yukon prospector struggling through the snow. He was unnaturally excited, and flushed.

He held Carina's thin wrist across the starched tablecloth and said: "I'm pleased that you're happy. Sometimes you seem a little sad."

"Yes," she said simply.

He didn't ask her why she was sometimes sad, because he knew. He lifted his glass of mineral water and drank it slowly, watching her face in the light of the table lamp, his eyes giving nothing away.

She said: "Will we ever be elegant, like these other couples in here?"

He smiled. It was a wistful smile, which she hardly ever saw.

She said anxiously: "You'll try to love me, won't you? As long as I know that you'll try."

He used his napkin to pat away the perspiration which glistened on his forehead. He shook his head. He asked for the check. For the oysters and the plain roasted quail, as well as the bombe and the mineral waters and the coffee, the total was twelve dollars and six cents. This was more than Carina used to earn for giving herself to a drunken oilman. They rose and walked with dignity through the tables of laughing and chattering people. It was eight-thirty, and Carina was surprised that so many people were up so late. The waiter came hurrying after them and said: "*Monsieur, le pourboire.*"

Johann frowned at him. "What?"

"The gratuity, monsieur. You have left no tip."

Johann looked down at the expectant silver plate. A few of the people at nearby tables could see what was going on, and they were watching with amused interest.

The waiter said: "It is customary, monsieur."

Johann reached into his inside coat pocket and produced his billfold. He undid the snap fastener and carefully removed a single dollar bill. He held it between finger and thumb, and waved it slowly backward and forward in front of the waiter's nose.

"This dollar," he said, "was not earned by begging. It won't be spent on beggars, either."

Then he returned the bill to his wallet, took Carina by the arm, and walked out of the restaurant to collect his hat and his coat. There was a murmur of shock and laughter behind him, but he took no notice. In this life, nobody deserved anything for free. He had once refused bread to a railroad worker, three years ago in Parsons' Lunch Rooms, in Broughton, and he certainly didn't intend to betray himself or that railroad worker by handing out free money.

The restaurant manager, a short Armenian with a gleaming bald head, caught his arm as he pushed his way out of the front door.

"Sir, excuse me . . ."

Johann turned. From the uncompromising expression of Johann's face, the manager could see that it was probably advisable to let go of his arm. He said in a high voice: "Sir, I regret you are no longer welcome here."

Johann stared at the man for a long while with a look that was both patient and violent. Then he said: "What is the name of this place?"

The manager said: "Eduard's, sir."

Johann nodded. "Very well," he said. "I shall make a particular point of buying this place in the near future, and of throwing you out on your ear."

The manager gave a high, supercilious laugh. "Empty threats don't worry us here, sir. We expect a gentleman to behave like a gentleman. Now, please go."

Johann led Carina out into the night. He hailed a cab, and they returned uptown through the dimly lit streets. Halfway back, Carina asked: "What will you do with a restaurant?"

Johann looked at her. "You really believe that I'll buy it?"

"Yes."

Johann squeezed her hand and laughed. "You're right," he said. "I probably shall."

She kissed his cheek. He thought nothing of the kiss at the time, except that it was pleasantly affectionate, but like many human events of which we think nothing at the time, it was the last. She would never kiss him again, nor would he ever kiss her. He saw her smiling to herself in the occasional squares of light that fell across her face. Outside, a shower began to spot the streets. It was the third Friday in October, 1903.

They abducted her with efficiency and skill. In the first slate-colored light of morning, there was a knock at Johann's door, and a bellhop entered with a sealed envelope on a tray. Johann, tousled and bad-tempered, took the envelope and tore it open. The boy waited for a nickel. Johann read the letter slowly while the boy waited, and then ripped back his bedsheets and stalked, in his long striped nightshirt, to the connecting door which joined his room to Carina's. He banged on it loudly.

The bellhop said: "I must be cutting along now, sir."

Johann ignored him. He banged on Carina's door again. He shouted roughly: "*Carina!*"

There was no reply. Johann stormed furiously back across the room and tugged open his wardrobe door. The boy hovered nervously in the background, anxious to leave but unaccustomed to anyone who didn't tip. He cleared his throat, although it didn't need clearing.

Johann turned to him and snapped: "Get the hell out of here!"

The bellhop was almost grateful. He went quietly and closed the door, while Johann struggled out of his nightshirt and pulled on his black pants. He was angry and frightened, but his expression was one of sour determination. When he was dressed, he went into the bathroom and ran the faucets to shave. This might be an emergency, but he wasn't going to face any extortionist with a stubbled chin and a soiled collar. He worked up a lather in his rose-decorated shaving mug and began to spread the soap on his chin with his badger brush.

The letter was written on good vellum paper by a typewriter. It said: "*Your lady companion is safe with us. You will proceed instanter to the Waldorf Hotel, where you will by met by our representative and negotiations for her release commenced. Come at eight. Do not inform the police.*"

He looked at his red, lathered face in the steamed-up mirror. He said to himself, quite loudly: "Stay calm," but calmness was impossible. The best he could do was suppress his fear and keep his hands steady while he shaved. He knew Carina would probably be safe. After all, it must be his money they wanted, and they certainly

158

wouldn't get any if they harmed her. But she was so precious, so much his own, that he felt as if his whole emotional life had been burgled and ransacked, and his dearest secret spoiled.

Carina, and the affection she so freely gave him, were all that he had of the world in which people liked and loved each other. Without her, now that Beatrice had left him, he was alone, with only his sense of historic mission to keep him going. And even for a financial demigod, there were plenty of empty and lonesome hours when a sense of historic mission was a pretty cold substitute for a laughing dinner companion, although Johann may have been hard put to admit it.

His Tree-brand razor cut through the shaving soap in quick, geometric patterns, and he thought of Beatrice, too. Perhaps he should have been kinder that terrible night in Edgar. Perhaps he should have curbed his temper, or tried to lie his way out of it. He knew that he still adored her, but he wasn't sure now whether he could have married her. She was a woman of strange, tantalizing force. Maybe they would have been happy together, once she had learned to love him again; or maybe they would have quarreled and fought until they sought divorce, or chosen to live together in icy noncommunication. He wondered where she was this minute, and what she was doing. He had left Edgar early Saturday morning, taking Carina with him, and had driven to Broughton for the noon train east. He knew nothing of Beatrice's rape, and he certainly wasn't aware that news of his private affairs had preceded his arrival in New York.

He finished dressing, tucked the typewritten letter in his pocket, and left his room. As he crossed the foyer, the bellhop who had woken him that morning blew a raspberry, and was promptly cuffed by the bell captain.

He arrived at the Waldorf a little before eight. He entered the hotel cautiously, and with an upright back. Although it was quite early, the foyer was crowded with fifty or sixty gentlemen in frock coats who had assembled for no apparent reason, and were talking to each other in almost embarrassing earnestness. Johann kept away from the crowd, and circled the lobby slowly, his eyes flickering around in search of his mysterious correspondent.

When a hand touched his elbow, he knew that his correspondent had found him. He did not turn around at once, but said in a quiet voice: "You are risking your neck, I hope you know."

An equally quiet and composed voice replied: "I trust we won't

159

have to risk *anyone's* neck, yours or the girl's. This is something we can settle with great promptitude."

"You wish to speak here?" asked Johann.

"Here is the best place possible," answered the voice. "This is a meeting of numismatists. They have it annually. Nobody will notice that out of all these enthusiasts, only we are discussing coinage of a different breed."

Johann coughed. "Is this extortion?"

The voice chuckled. "Certainly not. Not unless you consider that all business is extortion of one kind or another."

Johann at last turned around. The man he saw was Arnie Styvers, "The Vent," in a sagging morning suit. He looked the gangster up and down without saying a word.

"Do you want to open discussions?" asked Styvers. "Or do you want to be heroic? It's up to you, really."

"What do you want?" asked Johann hoarsely.

Styvers smiled. He still didn't open his lips, though, and Johann considered that he probably had rotten teeth. There was a diamond stickpin in Styvers' necktie that was probably worth eight or nine thousand dollars. It could have been more; Styvers' weedy physique had the effect of cheapening everything he wore.

"Let's sit down," Styvers suggested. He indicated two gilt-painted tapestry chairs, either side of a potted palm. He sat himself down on one of them, and waited for Johann to sit down on the other.

Johann said: "I want to know where the girl is."

Styvers examined his fingernails. "Of course you do. That's why I'm keeping mum. If you agree to the deal, you get the girl back unharmed. If not, we'll have to think of some way to parcel things up. You understand that, don't you? It's not businesslike to leave loose ends."

"You'll kill her?"

"I didn't say that."

"I know. But you meant it, didn't you?"

Styvers looked almost coy.

"All right," said Johann. "Tell me what you came here to say."

"I wish you'd sit down," said Styvers. Johann, testily, sat. Then Styvers said: "It's a question of financial cooperation. It's a sound plan, when you consider it, and there's no reason why you should lose out. All I need is your say-so."

160

"What's the plan?"

"It's like this," said Styvers. "A friend of mine hears you're in town to talk to some people called Houston-West. It seems like, in Texas, you're striking oil just about everyplace you park your automobile, and you're looking for refinery facilities."

"What if I am?"

Styvers gave a sickly shrug. "I keep telling you, it's very easy. Houston-West are mainly Quakers, and the way I hear it, they don't take too kindly to doing business with people who lead immoral or scandalous lives. If you try to do a deal with Houston-West, then the chances are that they're going to find out about the girl, and also about the rape."

Johann squinted at him. "Rape? What are you talking about? What rape?"

Styvers smiled. "You know what rape," he said sardonically.

Johann stood up. "Now, listen here," he said fiercely. "Whatever you say about the girl, there's never been any question of rape."

Two bespectacled numismatists turned and blinked at him. Johann said: "Listen, mister, you'd better spit out what you've got to say pretty damned quick, or I'm going to tear your head right off your shoulders."

Styvers started to clean his ear out with his finger. "I don't advise it. Not all of these people are coin collectors. One or two of them work for me, and they can all shoot straight when it's called for."

Johann turned and stared ferociously around at the assembled men. It was impossible to tell if Styvers was telling the truth or not. But the way he had things organized, he probably was. A man who could silently kidnap a girl from under his nose was bound to make sure that he had a bodyguard. He took a deep breath and then sat down again.

"I know what you mean about the girl," he said quietly. "But I don't know what you mean about the rape."

Styvers examined the end of his finger. "Maybe my information is awry," he said blandly. "But the way I heard it, you KO'd Kyle Lennox, and then your old lady got herself raped twenty times by a bunch of oilmen, out in the streets."

Johann's face went gray. He said: "Beatrice?"

"I don't know," said Styvers, unconcerned. "Twenty times, though—that's what they said. Just after you belted Kyle Lennox."

Johann stared at his feet. He felt numb. He whispered: "I didn't know."

Styvers began to clean out the other ear. "Well, that's too bad. But whether you knew or not, Houston-West ain't going to like it."

"You're going to tell them?"

"If we have to."

"And what's the alternative?"

Styvers grinned. "The alternative is actually very attractive. The alternative is that you sell up to Colton Oil for a favorable price and leave all your cares and woes to good old Percy F. Colton."

Johann stuck his hands in his pockets and let out a long breath. "I see. It's Percy Colton."

"He's only trying to do you a favor," put in Styvers. "He knows that you've struck more crude oil than you know what to do with, and he knows you've been looking for someone to take it all off your hands."

Johann nodded. Then he said: "How long do I have?"

"What do you mean?"

"Well, Colton doesn't expect me to make my mind up right away, does he? I need a few hours to think."

Styvers took out his pocket watch. "We've got the girl, you know," he reminded Johann. "Any dawdling, and she's a stuffed goose."

"Just a couple of hours."

Styvers thought about it. "All right," he said after a few moments. "Call this telephone number at eleven o'clock on the nose, and give them your answer. If it's yes, then you get the girl back straightaway. If it's no—then she's a stuffed goose."

Johann said gently: "I understand."

He rose from his seat, and without looking back at Styvers, he walked through the numismatists with the straight back and set of a man who has reached a terrible crisis in his life, from which he may not turn back. In the street outside, an unpleasant crosswind was blowing, and a news butcher on the intersection was trying to hold down his flapping placard and keep a hand on his cap at the same time. Johann ignored the Waldorf's doorman, who tried to hail him a cab, and walked uptown toward the park, his hands dug deep in his overcoat pockets.

During those three hours of grace, he did several things. He sent a cable to Mrs. Elvira Russell's address in Edgar, beseeching Beatrice

162

to cable him back with news that she was safe. He also wired Sam Chivers, inquiring "How's tricks?" He took his Iver Johnson revolver out of his suitcase, loaded it, and put it into the bedside drawer of his hotel room. He telephoned the nearest police precinct and informed them that his half-caste adopted daughter was late in returning from a walk in the park, and that he was worried. The desk sergeant told him to remain optimistic, and to call again if she hadn't returned by midafternoon. Then he walked down to the Dutch church on Forty-fourth Street and sat for ten minutes in silent prayer. At eleven o'clock "on the nose" he telephoned the number that Arnie Styvers had given him, and said he needed more time. The soothing voice on the other end of the line gave him two more hours to think it over, but that was going to be all. There was a lengthy silence, and then the telephone went dead.

He never discovered what really happened, although he was still paying private investigators three years later to look into it. He was only ten minutes away from calling up and surrendering to Styvers when the telephone rang and a police officer told him that his adopted daughter may have been found. Unfortunately, the circumstances were not happy. His throat went very dry, and he sat on the edge of his bed like a man who has just woken up from a bad dream to discover that reality is worse. His adopted daughter (if it was actually she) had apparently fallen or jumped from a sixth-floor window on Fifty-fifth Street, two doors away from the Gotham Hotel, where a young man called John Warde would leap to his death from a seventeenth-floor ledge in 1938. His adopted daughter had suffered from fractured ribs which had pierced her lungs, and she had died on the way to the hospital. The police were very sorry. A Jewish pediatrician who had attended her while she lay on the sidewalk had reported that she said only two things—first, that she had gotten away from them (whoever "they" were); and second, that she should have stayed where she belonged. Johann heard these words with such pain that he bent forward as the policeman told him, clutching his chest as if he had agonizing heartburn.

It took him a long time to recover from the shock. He stood by the hotel window for almost an hour, not moving. Then he checked his watch and realized it was almost time for him to leave. He went to the door of his room as if his leg and arm joints had seized up from lack of use. Only as he walked along the long carpeted corridor did he begin to understand what Carina had saved him from, whether she had died accidentally or sacrificed herself deliberately. Without Carina, Colton had no proof of any misbehavior whatever; and even if the news about Beatrice were true, it was hardly enough on its own to stand up against him.

He went down in the elevator and asked the doorman in a whisper to hail him a cab.

As he had expected, no one had spoken to the board of Houston-West. Their office was darkly paneled, and their elderly faces were almost invisible in the gloom of this October morning. Behind them, a brass-faced, long-case clock chimed every half hour, and their discussions had to pause each time while the chimes died away. Johann sat at the far end of the massive oak directors' table with his papers and plans spread out before him, and explained his operations and his finances; and after three hours of careful examination of his written plans and detailed schedules, the board agreed informally to a working partnership to refine his crude oil from Sweetwater, Emmett Heights, and the West Amarero fields. They shook hands with him. Their hands were old and dry.

The morgue was chilly and tiled in olive green. He didn't stay for long. A German student in a white coat folded back the sheet over Carina's body and Johann identified her at once. She looked quite peaceful, and he remarked on it. The student said that falling from a height was quite a happy death, compared for instance with burning or mangling. She had been so heavily concussed that she probably never felt any pain. Johann thought of her sitting next to him in his automobile, her beautiful face framed by her fascinator. Here in the morgue she was no longer quite so beautiful; but whether it was her life with Johann that had done that, or her fall from the window on Fifty-fifth Street, he couldn't be sure.

Outside, in an uncomfortable draft, he was interviewed by a policeman. He was able to give an exact account of his own movements at the time of Carina's death, and to produce his telephone accounts from the Plaza to prove it. The policeman made copious notes in very round handwriting with a blunt pencil, and then let him go. He went straight to the Plaza to pack.

He knelt by his bed when his suitcases were all closed, and said a short prayer for Carina. He told her he loved her dearly, and he gave her soul to the Lord. He said a prayer, too, for Beatrice, hoping that she was safe, and that she would understand and forgive him. Before he left, he took a last look around the rooms to make sure that he hadn't forgotten anything. On the bathroom shelf, next to the mirror, was one of Carina's hair slides, in the shape of a butterfly. He picked it up and put it in his pocket; but then changed his mind, and set it back on the shelf. Maybe some other young girl would find it, and wear it in unconscious memory of someone who had made him realize that love is often more magical than human beings can bear.

1909

CORNELIUS OIL PAYS TWO
MILLION FOR EAST INDIANA
CHEMICALS

"A bargain buy"

Ninety new jobs for local men and women

From P. K. Lomas, Industry Reporter

Cornelius Oil, the wealthy and expanding concern from Texas, has paid almost two million dollars in stocks and bonds for the East Indiana Chemical Corporation, and has immediate plans for expanding the factory's production of nitrates and phosphates.

Mr. Johann Cornelius, the millionaire owner of Cornelius Oil, expressed the opinion to this correspondent that the price he had paid for East Indiana was "of the bargain-basement variety."

—*Indianapolis Star & Citizen,*
February 9, 1909

They had been walking through the trees almost all afternoon, and eventually, when the sun began to lose its warmth, they meandered back toward the house across the long wild meadow where the poppies blew, and through the squeaky iron gate into the walled kitchen garden. There, they went hand-in-hand along the mellow brick pathways, talking in quiet, affectionate voices; while the June breeze rustled the leaves of ripening corn and summer squash, and butterflies danced around the beans and sweet potatoes, and rosemary and thyme and tarragon nodded in their separate beds like enthusiastic operagoers in a private box.

Reaching the lean-to greenhouse, where pale Polish tomatoes were fattening behind the misted glass, she spread her skirts and sat on a low wall; and he stood protectively beside her, and took his pipe from the breast pocket of his linen jacket, and began to pack it with tobacco.

She said: "You've made me so happy, Jack. I can hardly believe that it's true."

He smiled and said: "Ellie." He didn't have to say much else, because she knew for a factual certainty that he felt the same way. Only three hours previous, he had knelt on the mossy floor of the woods that skirted her parents' home, as the green stain on his pants still bore witness; and he had taken her hand and kissed it once, and asked her to be his bride. Since then, they had walked and talked about love, and money, and where they were going to live, and the day had circled its shadows around them like a pleased parent encircling them with her arms. Now, in the kitchen garden, a few hundred yards away from the white-painted plantation house where she had lived all her life, they basked in that gingery evening light that is almost peculiar to Williamsburg County in South Carolina, and the birds chirped and the bees droned and their happiness was so ridiculously full that they spoke with tears in their eyes sometimes, and sometimes with laughter, and once, on the sloping hill that led away toward the neighboring estates, they had

169

waltzed together, an impromptu waltz that had taken them around and around until they collapsed breathless and hilarious in the waving grass.

He took out matches and steadily lit his pipe. After three matches, the rich aroma of Balkan tobacco mingled with the scent of climbing roses, and after a couple of satisfied puffs he rested his elbow on his knee, and took the pipe from his mouth, and looked at her tenderly.

"Making you happy, that's what I'm here for," he said. "And besides, making you happy makes me happier still, and so I guess that I'm only being selfish anyway."

"Oh, come on. You're *never* selfish."

He leaned forward and kissed her forehead. A gentle, reassuring kiss that barely touched her. He said: "I'm sure of my love for you, Ellie, and that's the way it's going to stay. Because if I thought that our love would go sour, the way that their love did; if I thought we were going to scrap all the time, and wind up scratching each other's eyes out, then I'd take up my hat right now, and I'd turn on my heel, and I'd be three hundred miles away from here before the week was out."

"Jack," she whispered. "Nobody could stop us loving each other but the devil himself."

He kept on smiling, so pleased and so happy that he couldn't stop himself. Ellie looked deliciously cute and grave, sitting on the wall in her blue-check gingham jumper, with her coppery hair brushed up into a gingham bow, and he had to touch her soft cheek to convince himself that she was real, and that she was really his. She was the prettiest of Earle Jackson's four daughters, and the youngest, and that meant she'd been spoiled all her life, but spoiling hadn't spoiled her, and as her father used to say, in a low voice so that she wouldn't hear: "She hands out twice what she's handed, and in my accounts that's credit." She was a small girl, with a round, almost childish face; and her eyes were wide and gray and dreamy. But her manner was confident and poised, and her voice was vibrant, and the words that she spoke could raise even skeptical eyebrows; so that when a man talked to Ellie Jackson, he knew he was talking to a woman. Maybe, at nineteen, she was precocious. Maybe she rode her chestnut mare a little too showily; and maybe the French that her governess had taught her was a little too flamboyant. But the Jackson family possessed both gentility and gentleness, and their wealth and fortune had been long enough established in South Carolina for them to find social savagery unnecessary. Maybe they weren't as rich as they'd been in antebellum days, when Earle Jackson's grandfather had seen the hills of Fortuna so thick with slaves that a visitor could have believed they were growing black wool instead of white cotton; and maybe life in the South had lost some of its elegance as the century had turned and the automobile had opened up the countryside. But in this summer of 1909, the days were still balmy, and the dresses still swept the well-cropped lawns, and there were still parties with parasols and punts on the lake, and Ellie Jackson was pretty and kind, and more than anything, happy.

"We'd better get going," said Jack, opening up his watch. "Your mother wanted us back for tea."

"Tea and wedding cakes?"

He kissed her. "That'll come soon enough. And then you'll be Mrs. Jack Field, and you'll have tea parties of your own."

"Tea parties? I shall have champagne parties, every day. Just to show people how happy I am."

"Not on my salary, you won't. Not until Father makes me a partner."

"Well, it's time he did," asserted Ellie. "You're doing very important work now."

"Defending a squatter charged with stealing two hundred head of cabbage isn't exactly Supreme Court stuff."

"Yes, but you're going to Rhode Island to enter that plea for Husman and Welch."

"I wish I weren't. I'm going to miss you."

Her eyes softened. "I'm going to miss you, too. But one day you're going to be a great and famous attorney, and we won't regret it then."

He took her hand, and they left the kitchen garden and walked across the grass to the back veranda. The house, Fortuna, was shadowed by elms, but the sinking sun lit up the figures of Ellie's mother and father and sisters as they sat admiring the gardens, and they looked in their white lawn dresses and wide white hats like famous society figures on the deck of a yacht. Ellie waved, and her father waved back.

Earle Jackson had been cautious of Jack at first. The boy had seemed determined and energetic, but inclined to rush at whatever he wanted to do without thinking first. He was a handsome boy, yes. He was tall, with wavy brown hair and a fine straight nose, and his dark eyes rarely seemed to lose their humor. His father had sent him to Harvard, and he had returned to the South with a reasonable degree in law and a reputation for healthy practical-joking. But what had disturbed the conservative Mr. Jackson when Jack and Ellie had first exchanged glances at a coming-out dance for Ellie's sister Annette was that Jack had made it plain he wanted to practice law out West, in Texas or Oklahoma, where the big oil companies were. He had told Mr. Jackson with intense conviction that "If the future of business is to be steeped in oil, then the future of business attorneys is bound to be steeped alongside of it."

Mr. Jackson hadn't denied the truth of what young Jack Field was saying; but with Ellie so sweet on the boy, there was always a chance that he would ask for her hand; and Mr. Jackson knew that he wouldn't be able to find it in himself to refuse his darling baby Ellie anything. However, he couldn't take to the notion of Ellie being marooned in a Texas cowtown or one of those wildcat shanties on the Oklahoma Red Beds, and no more could Mrs. Jackson, who was warm and sympathetic to the flutter and flush of true love, but knew how important it was for her daughter to take her place in South Carolina society.

So behind today's proposal of matrimony, there had been a little friendly maneuvering. Mr. Jackson had invited Jack's father, Duncan P. Field, the respected Kingstree attorney, to have lunch at his country club; and there, over a damask tablecloth and filet of sole marguery à la Diamond Jim, Mr. Jackson had broached the suggestion that if Jack had marriage to Ellie in mind, then he might do better to remain in South Carolina for a while, particularly if part of Ellie's dowry were to include the passing of all Mr. Jackson's legal business to the offices of Field, Field & Sobers, of Kingstree.

Mr. Field hadn't wanted to sell his son down the river, not even for the price of ten or twelve thousand dollars' worth of new business. But for his part he had always believed that Jack would be wise to pick up a few years' legal experience in Carolina before he tried to take on the boisterous law of the oilfields; and there was something else, too, which he rarely spoke about, and that was his own painful and martyred marriage to Jack's mother, who had died of pleurisy when Jack was ten. He wanted Jack to be happy, above all, and he knew that Ellie could make him so.

Now, as Jack and Ellie came across the lawn toward the house, Mr. Jackson stood up from his seat on the veranda and raised a glass of champagne. "I am drinking to your future good fortune," he announced. "And so would your mother, but she feels she may have already had sufficient."

Mrs. Jackson, a poised, straight-backed woman in a white summer shirtwaister and a picture hat with white roses on it, let out a tinkly laugh. She approved of Jack, partly because he was easy on the eye, and relaxed, and would make himself a respectable amount of money, and partly because he smoked a pipe, which she always found irresistibly masculine.

"Sit down, sit down," invited Mr. Jackson. "We have apees and butter drops if you're partial, and gingersnaps if you're not."

The table on the veranda was laid with a white lace cloth, and was elegantly set out with dishes of cookies, a Georgian silver tea service, and a magnum of Bollinger, green and beaded with dew, in a large silver cooler. Annette was there, and Esther, the oldest of the four sisters, and Esther's two-year-old son, Christopher, was perched on three cushions, with a huge white napkin tucked into his neck to save his white Russian romper suit from crumbs. They were all excited and flushed, and they had all been drinking champagne, and Jack found himself bubbled along on a tide of laughter and flirtatious admiration from Mrs. Jackson and her daughters, and irrepressible friendliness from her husband.

"When Earle came to my father and asked for my hand," said Mrs. Jackson in her cultured Southern accent, "my father said, 'You couldn't take her sister Alexandra instead, could you? She's the one who really gets on my nerves.'"

They all laughed, and Ellie poured some Darjeeling tea, and under the cool roof of the veranda and the whispering leaves of the flowering clematis they spent the afternoon in family celebration. For Jack, having a family like this was something completely new; and even though he started off with caution and reserve, he soon found himself brought so affectionately into the Jackson circle that he felt as if he'd known them for most of his life.

Earle Jackson rose to his feet. He wasn't a tall man; in his light gray summer suit he stood about five-feet-nine. He tousled the hair

173

of his grandson, whose mouth was now brown as a nigger minstrel's from eating chocolate cake, and he spoke in a low, happy voice. He said: "I just want to drink a toast to us, because we're real contented today at Ellie's betrothal to Jack. I know that Jack had his heart set on going out West and making his fortune in the oilfields, but I think Jack realizes now that by staying here in Carolina he's going to prepare himself mighty well for any future challenge that he might encounter. To my mind, one of the best preparations he's making—and I'm highly biased—is marrying Ellie. Ellie, like Annette and Esther and Caroline, has been brought up to live her life fully and to give her heart to everything she does. Well, I'm pleased to see that she's finally given her heart to a young man that we can all be proud of, and we wish all of ourselves happiness because of it."

Jack, a little dizzy from champagne, and blushing, got to his feet. He said: "I want to thank you for your words, sir. I know that I'm going to do my best to fulfill them, because you've all shown me kindness that's over and above what anyone could have expected. I love Ellie, and I'm going to do everything I can to make her happy; and I hope that by making her happy, I'll make you happy, too."

He sat down, and Ellie kissed him, and they all laughed some more and applauded, and maybe for the first time in his life Jack began to have some kind of inkling of what happiness really meant.

"Well," said Margaret Jackson, "we're going to have to settle a date. Sometime in the spring, of course."

"And guests," enthused Annette. "We'll have to decide on guests. My Lord, there are going to be hundreds!"

"What about the cake?" asked Esther. "How many tiers?"

Ellie went pink. "We haven't even *thought* about children yet. Jack said as long as they're healthy, and have all their toes, then he's quite content."

They stayed on the veranda until it began to grow cool, and then the ladies went inside to change for dinner, while Earle Jackson took Jack into the smoking room, and they stood by the tall window looking out over the trees and the fields of Fortuna plantation, and talked of money and law.

Earle Jackson said: "You're off to Rhode Island tomorrow, then."

"That's right, sir. It's a special hearing. One of our oldest clients got himself mixed up in a land-restraining order up there. It's going to be big stuff. Well, for me, anyway."

Earle Jackson coughed. "That's good. I always like to see a keen young man getting ahead. As a matter of fact, though, I was wondering if I could impose on you while you're up in those parts. I have some valuables, jewelry and paintings and suchlike, that I inherited from my mother when she died last year. I've been meaning to take them up to New York for auction, but I haven't had the occasion, and the way things are going it looks as though I won't for some time. Short-staffed, you know, especially out in the fields. Perhaps when you've finished in Rhode Island, you could stop off in New York for a few days and take them along to the auctioneer's for me. All expenses paid for, of course."

Jack was a little embarrassed. He hadn't made himself any firm commitments for the rest of the summer vacation, but apart from stepping out with Ellie as often as possible, he'd also been planning to fish in Lake Marion with a college chum who was working for the season in Columbia.

"Well, sir," he said, "I'm not sure that I can."

Earle Jackson shrugged. "If you can't, then I'm out of luck. But it would have helped. It would only take a few days—just long enough to see the jewelry sold, and you could stay with some friends of mine at the Ritz-Carlton on Forty-sixth Street. The Forbeses, you'd like them."

Jack had to admit that the trip sounded pretty tempting. He'd only been to New York twice—once as a small boy, and once from Harvard—and the idea of staying at the Ritz-Carlton and taking a look around the city with all his costs paid for was a darn sight more attractive than angling for lake fish with Oliver Talmadge, who was good fun when you had nothing better to do than sit in a small boat and hope the trout would bite, because he could do bird calls and moose calls and imitate President Taft, but when you *did* have something better to do, which was almost always, Oliver Talmadge was one of those pests who didn't know when he wasn't required. He'd miss Ellie, of course; but Earle Jackson had been so generous and friendly that it seemed pretty churlish to say no.

"I'd have to make a few rearrangements," said Jack. "But it sounds like kind of a pleasant diversion. I'd like to do it."

"Well, I'm pleased." Earle Jackson smiled. "I wouldn't like to trust that jewelry to the mails or the railroads, and in any case I need someone to take it around to Parke-Bernet personal. And since I have a beautiful hostage waiting for you here, I'm pretty sure you're not going to run off with it."

Jack grinned. "The day I run away from Ellie is the day I lose my senses."

An engraved brass clock on the mantelpiece struck seven, in prissy, whirring chimes. Earle Jackson said: "How about a bourbon before we change for dinner? I have my own special blend brought down from Kentucky, and if anything ever made your hair stand to attention, this will."

That night, after a rich dinner of turtle soup, ham mousse, baby turkey bordelaise, and orange sherbet, and after a lot more laughter and champagne, Jack and Ellie took their coffee on the veranda, with Mr. and Mrs. Jackson sitting a discreet distance away, and they watched the fireflies dancing in the darkness, and listened to the sad rustle of the trees and the distant sound of fiddle music from the servants' cottages, across by the stables.

Ellie, in an evening gown of lace over alice-blue silk, sat as straight-backed as her mother, and Jack relaxed with his pipe and watched her with all the secret pleasure of a man who's newly in love. It seemed to him then that she was just perfect. Those wide-open eyes, the tilt of that nose, those slightly parted lips. The light from the veranda lamps reflected from her diamond-and-sapphire engagement ring, a spark of blue fire on the small hand that lay in the shadows of her lap.

She said: "Do you ever feel scared?"

"Scared of what?"

She turned and looked at him, and the moths that flickered around the lamps threw patterns across her cheek. "Scared of growing up. Scared of having to fend for yourself."

"I don't think so. I've been fending for myself for a long time."

She said: "I'm scared of being a woman, in a way. Instead of a girl, I mean."

"I don't believe there's anything to be worried about. And in any event, you'll have a husband to care for you."

She smiled. "I don't want you to care for me *too* much. That's one of the things that I'm scared about. It just seems to me that women should be more independent these days. We're not wax

176

dolls, you know, to be wrapped up in tissue paper and kept at home. I think women should do their best to match their husbands.''

Jack sucked at his pipe doubtfully. "You don't mean *work*, surely? I wouldn't expect a wife of mine to work.''

"Of course not. But I'm sure I could find plenty of respectable and profitable things to do. I'm very educated, you know. I can breed horses and I can grow flowers, and I can even sail a dinghy.''

"You'll be saying you want to vote next.''

"Well, don't be surprised, that could come. I bet I know more about politics than most men. I take an *interest*, Jack, and I want to be the kind of woman you can talk to, and respect, as well as love.''

He tamped down the tobacco in his pipe. "I'd still love you, even if you couldn't speak a word.''

She reached across and touched his face, as if she was touching something very rare and precious, and she gently wound his hair around her finger. "You won't object, though, if I try to have a mind of my own? It won't ever mean that I'm less loving, or that I won't obey you as the marriage vows say. But Mama and Papa have always brought us up to have opinions, and tastes, and to think for ourselves.''

Jack held her wrist, and then leaned forward and softly kissed her lips. "Whether I liked it or not," he said, "nothing could stop you from being my own dear Ellie. It's just for yourself that I want to marry you, and if you have opinions on anything, whether it's American foreign policy in the Caribbean, or the color of a baby's layette, then whatever you say will be as welcome in our home as you are.''

He sat back in his high-backed wicker seat and looked at her warmly. "As a matter of fact, I've been concerned about what you were going to do all day, once we were married, and once I was off working at the office. I used to see my mother sitting around in her housecoat, reading library books and eating candies all day, as bored and fretful as a mouse in a cage; and when my father came home she used to burst out with all of her stored-up boredom and all of her fretfulness, just because she was too idle to get up and do something interesting on her own account.''

He stopped, and looked away. He hadn't meant to slight his mother, but it was so difficult to explain what he was and how he felt without bringing her into it. He said quietly: "I love you, Ellie. If you want to breed horses or grow flowers or even climb mountains, I'll help you. I want to know that you're happy, and that you're doing what you want to do. I can't say that I won't ever be jealous of you, or that I won't feel protective toward you. But I promise you that I won't try to coop you up, or make you live a life that you secretly despise."

She kissed him, glancing quickly over her shoulder to make sure that her mother and father weren't watching. Then she whispered: "And what would you do if I was very naughty, and wouldn't behave?"

"Independent girls aren't supposed to *be* naughty."

"Oh, they are sometimes. Just because I have a mind of my own, that doesn't mean that I don't want to be treated like a defenseless female sometimes."

He grinned. Then he said: "Well . . . if you're naughty . . . I shall have to reprimand you."

She giggled. "And what if you reprimand me, and I'm still naughty?"

He pretended to think deeply. Then he kissed her on the tip of the nose and said: "In that event, I shall be obliged to spank you."

Her eyelids drooped coquettishly. "I shall have to be naughty quite a lot then, won't I? After we've talked about your work, and the political situation, and the color of baby's layette."

They looked at each other for a long, silent moment, both with perplexed expressions. Then they burst out laughing, so loud and so long that they had tears in their eyes, and Mr. Jackson came across the veranda and stood over them with an amused face, not understanding their hilarity at all, but pleased with their joy, so pleased that he turned back to grin at his wife, Margaret, as if to say: Look at this happiness that we ourselves created.

Johann Cornelius came out on deck just after the steamship had passed Shutes Folly Island in Charleston harbor, and was beating its way out to sea. He stood for a while holding the varnished rail, the cool Atlantic breeze ruffling his hair, and he watched the afternoon sun sparkling on the water, and the tree-lined shore of James Island sliding slowly past. A small tugboat with a shiny brass ring around its funnel bounced over the waves on their starboard side, pooping its whistle with a puff of white steam that chased

178

away inland; and seagulls wheeled and dived all around them. He took out a green handkerchief and solemnly blew his nose.

Although the railroad was quicker, he still preferred to travel from Texas by sea. He had two first-class suites, complete with a desk and a comfortable bed, and he could keep in touch with any part of the continent by ship's telegraph. What was more, apart from a coaling stop at Charleston, the SS *Galveston Bay* remained at sea, and he could keep himself isolated from pests and spongers and litiginous rivals. To his fellow travelers, he appeared like a dour and wealthy eccentric, whiling away his time on a small coastal steamer, and whenever they politely inquired why he spent so many hours secluded in his cabins, he would simply reply: "Canasta," as if that answered everything. But in reality his cabins, while he journeyed to New York, were the headquarters of the whole of Cornelius Oil, and from his huge mahogany desk, with its green-shaded lamps and its single sepia photograph of a sad-looking woman in a boa, he kept daily and nightly reins on his oil properties in Texas and Oklahoma and California, his insurance interests in New York, his chemical works in Indiana and Illinois, and his political involvements in Washington. There were many Republican senators and congressmen who were beginning to notice his steady financial rise with interest, although the Rockefellers didn't like him one bit, and J. P. Morgan had once said that "given the choice of having Johann Cornelius on this earth or of not having Johann Cornelius on this earth, it would take me several hours of considered thought to put up any kind of argument in favor of the former, and then I'd be damned if I could get myself to agree."

Johann was living between a large white house at the better end of Washington Avenue, Houston, and a seventh-floor suite at the two-year-old Plaza Hotel in New York which he was increasingly anxious to move out of, partly because it cost one hundred dollars a day even when he wasn't there; and partly because Mrs. Clara Bell Walsh, widow of the Royal typewriter tycoon Julius Walsh, lived right along the corridor, and insisted on keeping a motley collection of dogs which yapped when he was trying to work. He had already been upstate a couple of times to view a number of mansions, and he liked the look of a sober, symmetrical house on Lynwood's Island, in the Hudson.

During these years before the Great War, he seemed more

179

remote to those who knew him than at any time before or after. Only two people stayed close beside him—his oil manager, Jerry Slobodien, a sarcastic professional rig worker with a thin, chiseled face, a permanent five-o' clock shadow, and a taste for ruby signet rings and shoestring ties; and his manservant, Carl, a baffled white-faced Swede who spent all his off-duty hours sitting in an upright chair on the boat deck, reading *The Katzenjammer Kids* out loud, slowly and ponderously enunciating such phrases as "und all of a sudden, bang, und anodder vun, bang, und Sir Reginald Wienerschnitzel rolled into der swamp und vas seen no more except vunce und dot vas der last time."

Johann's closeted life was the subject of considerable Wall Street speculation. Some said that he was a business genius who was eventually going to tower over Morgan and Rockefeller and Vanderbilt. Others said he was an eccentric who ate dandelions for breakfast, slept in full evening dress, and would never amount to anything. J. Paul Getty probably came nearest to the truth when he remarked that with Cornelius rigs pumping up millions of barrels of oil each day at Sweetwater, Muskogee, Seal Beach, and Checotah; with Cornelius nitrate plants in Gary and Peoria and Normal churning out tons of fertilizers and explosives; and with Cornelius underwriters in New York and Baltimore bringing in thousands of dollars of daily premiums—that with all this headlong rush of expansion and investment and complex management, Johann Cornelius didn't have *time* to socialize.

Handling a multimillion-dollar business that was running away with him was certainly exhausting, particularly since Johann had an ingrained reluctance to delegate. He hunched over his desk almost eighteen hours every day, and still had to leave work undone, papers unsigned, and contracts unread. He went to bed in the gray tight hours of the morning and read business documents until he fell asleep, and each day he was haunted at dawn by his own face in the tortoiseshell shaving mirror—red-eyed, lined, and weary. He would soon be thirty-six, but he looked like a man of fifty.

There could have been something else, though, that kept him so much to himself. He would never speak about it, but the waiters on the *Galveston Bay* sometimes walked into his office and found him sitting back in his leather chair, biting thoughtfully at his thumbnail and staring at the photograph on his desk. One of the waiters had once had the courage (after five straight bourbons and a six-dollar bet) to ask Johann who the lady was. But Johann had done nothing but look at him as if he was transparent, and whisper: "Ask Lennox." Since the waiter hadn't the slightest idea who Lennox was, the identity of the beautiful but wistful woman had remained a secret.

Johann liked to come up on deck once in a while and take the air, particularly when land was still in sight. It also gave him the opportunity to check out his fellow passengers, of whom there were usually very few. He rarely spoke to them, but liked to observe them: the wilted would-be carpetbaggers returning North after failing to make their mark on an increasingly industrialized South; the widows who had buried their husbands on unfamiliar Southern soil going back to the bosom of their families with their faces as stiff as writing paper; the odd-job men, the out-of-work sailors, and health-conscious people in shapeless clothes who felt for reasons best known to themselves that a trip up the coast might be salubrious.

Today, though, as Johann stood by the rail, he saw a young man who looked nothing at all like an unemployed sailor, nor an odd-job man of any description. The boy was tall and very wholesomely good-looking, as if life hadn't chipped him yet, nor any unhappiness scoured him. He had wavy chestnut hair, this boy; and a fashionable sack suit in gray worsted with a shadow check. His face in profile was fresh and sharp, and if he shaved more than twice a week, then he used better razors than most. There was something about the boy that interested Johann, and he stood for a while watching him, his hands deep in the pockets of his wool frieze overcoat, his eyes watering in the wind.

After a while the boy turned away from the rail and walked along the deck, crossing the shadow of the smokestack in which Johann was standing. As he passed, Johann said: "I shouldn't worry. It won't be too rough."

The young man reddened slightly, and raised his hat. "I've traveled by sea before, sir," he said politely. "I don't think a few choppy waves will put me off."

Johann looked at him for a while and then said: "So you're not afraid of the sea?"

"No, sir."

There was another silence. The sea breeze sang through the wires above Johann's head. Johann said: "You'll forgive me saying so, but you look as if you've left something behind of great importance."

"Do I look like that?" asked the boy.

"Well, yes. It was the way you were standing. I take these trips quite often, you see, and I know when someone's left something quite important behind."

The young man brushed back his hair. "It seems that you're a very sensitive person."

Johann shrugged. "There are plenty of people who wouldn't agree with you."

The young man turned and looked back toward Charleston. "Actually, I've left my fiancée behind. Just for a few days, while I take a trip to New England, and then New York."

"You would have been back sooner by train."

"Yes, sir. But, for this trip, my future father-in-law believes that trains are not to be trusted."

Johann gazed out across the light turquoise sea. "Your future father-in-law is probably right. Trains, on the whole, are not to be trusted. A train came in once, and a train went out, and one took fortune while the other brought dismay."

The young man obviously didn't understand a word of this, and gave a polite grimace. "If you'll excuse me," he said, "I'm going below to my cabin."

Johann touched his arm. "There's plenty of time for that. Come and have a drink. If you're engaged to be married, then perhaps we ought to celebrate."

The young man looked unhappy. "I regret, sir, that I have no idea who you are."

Johann smiled. "That's probably all for the best. But my name is Johann Cornelius, and I dabble a little in oil."

The young man extended his hand. His handshake was as firm and crisp as the rest of him. "I believe I've heard of you, sir, and I'm pleased to make your acquaintance. My name's Jack Field, and I'm an attorney."

Johann raised an eyebrow. "I'm gratified to hear it. The Lord defends those who defend themselves. Come along, the bar's just here. You'll find that Errol can mix up the best New Orleans Sazerac you ever tasted. Not that I'm a drinker. I was simply told it was so."

Jack smiled uncertainly as the bulky, Dutch-looking man in the dark blue frieze overcoat ushered him toward the varnished double doors that led inside to the restaurant and bar. It was only a small bar—six feet of polished red marble flanked by two huge Bordeaux lamps engraved with bunches of grapes. Behind it stood the sour-faced Errol in his starched white bartender's coat, his mustache waxed into rigid upright spikes. Errol was the pride of the small Galveston steamship line, although it was only because of an unmentionable incident at the Bank Exchange bar in San Francisco in 1904 that he wasn't still mixing drinks with the renowned Duncan Nicols, instead of tramping it up and down the coast shaking up cocktails for customers who usually disposed of them straight over the ship's rail at the first heaving of unsettled seas.

Jack Field and Johann sat on leather-topped stools, and Errol immediately poured out a small brandy for Johann and passed it across the counter. Then he said to Jack: "You're a bourbon man, sir, if I'm not mistaken."

Jack glanced at Johann, but Johann's face remained un-communicative and blotched by the wind.

"Well, yes," said Jack. "I'll take an old-fashioned."

Errol mixed the drink so fast it looked as if he had eight pairs of hands. He set it on the bar, and said without any hint of expression in his voice: "That's the best old-fashioned you'll ever taste, and that includes the Pendennis Club in Louisville, Kentucky, where they invented them. If you ever want another old-fashioned as good as that, come back here. You won't get one no place else."

Johann grimaced. "Every barman in the world believes he's the best barman in the world, and the only thing different about Errol here is that he probably is."

Jack was tempted to ask "Then what the hell is he doing here?" but he was sensitive to the feeling on the SS *Galveston Bay* that most of its regular passengers and crew had pasts they would rather forget and presents they weren't particularly keen to face, and so he contented himself with a grin, and raised his glass in a toast.

"To smooth sailing," he said.

Errol polished his cocktail shaker with an immaculate cloth. "There's the tail end of a hurricane supposed to be blowing itself out off Cape Hatteras, so don't bet on it."

Johann lifted his brandy. "In that case, I think it's worth drinking to. Smooth sailing."

They sat in silence for a while, and then Jack said: "You'll

183

excuse me saying so, but it seems that you take this trip pretty often.''

Johann grunted. "Too damned often. Two or three times a year. If I didn't like to keep a personal eye on my business in Texas and my business in New York, I wouldn't go near this tin punt for money.''

Errol muttered: "Me neither,'' but when they turned to look at him, he was assiduously pouring chilled lemon juice into a flagon, and he didn't even raise his head.

"You're quite a famous name in oil these days,'' said Jack.

"That's right,'' said Johann. "Oil and chemicals.''

"I was trying to get into the oil business myself,'' Jack explained. "You know, the legal side of the oil business. It seems to me that it's wide open right now, and that a good sound attorney could make himself a lot of money.''

Johann gazed at Jack with pale, unexpressive eyes. Jack felt that he was being weighed and scrutinized like a sack of sugar. He said: "Do you have many attorneys working for you, Mr. Cornelius?''

"More than I'd like,'' Johann replied. "Up until now, I've used regular established law firms. McErrow and Johnson in Texas, and Orris and Nussbaum in New York.''

"I've heard of Orris and Nussbaum. They're pretty impressive people.''

"They seem to do their best,'' remarked Johann. He was biding his time, waiting to see what this young man was going to say next. He had the interesting feeling that Jack Field was something special, that Jack had taken the SS *Galveston Bay* to New York because Johann's destiny had ordained it. Johann never doubted for a moment that fate ordered other people's lives around his own; and it was for that reason he had stopped Jack Field on the deck and introduced himself. He never usually felt inclined to speak to anyone on these trips, and he hardly ever spent time in the bar. But today seemed to be different, and so did Jack Field.

Jack said: "Personally, I've always believed that an industry needs lawyers to match the way it does its business.''

"Oh?''

"Well, if I was representing an oil company, I'd get out to the oilfields and learn the business from the bottom up. I'd take a look at the major leasings for myself, and see what the problems of

184

drilling and pumping and storing and refining really are, so that whenever I stood up in a court of law I'd know what the hell I was talking about. There are too many lawyers who represent their clients without the remotest understanding of their clients' business. Oil is a rough, tough, technical business, to my way of thinking, and I think it needs rough, tough, technical lawyers."

Johann sipped his drink and ran the tip of his tongue across his thick lips.

"You seem to have very strong views about it," he said.

"Well, that's the way an attorney has to be."

Errol set a small dish of sesame cocktail cookies on the bar, and Johann picked one out and bit into it carefully. All the time, he kept his eyes on Jack.

He said: "If you're so opinionated, and if you're so worked up about the way an oil attorney ought to work, then what are you doing about it? Have you talked to anyone? Shell? Standard Oil? Why haven't you talked to me?"

Jack smiled. "Well, it's a long story. But it's all to do with my engagement."

"Tell me."

Jack didn't want to say anything about Ellie at first; nor about Mr. Jackson's stipulation that if he wanted to have her hand in marriage he would have to stay in South Carolina. Explaining something like that to a man as hard-bitten and isolated as Johann Cornelius seemed to make him sound as if he was all milk and water. But, on reflection, Jack reckoned that if he'd made the decision, then the decision must be defensible, and Johann would probably understand his choice.

"I guess the problem is that I'm in love," Jack said. "Not just infatuated, or swept away by romance. I'm in *love*. I can feel my emotions as strong as if I could distill them and bottle them and set them on the shelf. The way I see it, a love like that only comes once in a lifetime, whereas oil will always be there."

Johann listened to this, and then ran his hand over his thinning, pomaded hair. Errol said: "Another brandy, sir?" but Johann shook his head.

"Mr. Field," he said, "you've made a poor decision."

Jack colored. "I don't think marrying Ellie will prove to be anything of the kind, sir. She's a beautiful and intelligent girl. And independent, too, which is rare enough."

"I didn't mean that," said Johann. "Of course she's beautiful and intelligent, or you wouldn't have fallen in love. I'm not denigrating your fiancée, Mr. Field. I'm sure she's lovely. But I *am* criticizing your decision. No woman, no matter how exquisite, can give you back the business opportunity that you are so gaily throwing away."

Jack laid his glass on the table; and Errol, without being asked, mixed him another old-fashioned. Jack said: "I'm not sure that I like the way you're saying that, Mr. Cornelius. You hardly know me."

"I know you better than you think, my boy, because I know myself. I also know about oil, and you are wrong about oil. Oil will not always be there. Or rather, the same opportunities to get into the oil business will not always be there. This is a tough, grabbing business and the big boys are going to have it sewn up in two or three years. That includes me. No, if you want to work in oil, then you must start right now, because if you don't, you'll be a South Carolina attorney for the rest of your days."

Jack swallowed bourbon. "Maybe you're right," he said, "but at least I'll be happy."

"Come on," said Johann impatiently, "you know that I'm right, and you also know that you won't be happy for long. Her family may have pressured you into thinking that life is fine and genteel in Kingstree, South Carolina, but where's the challenge? Where's the money? What you just said to me about oil attorneys makes sense. If you worked that out for yourself, then you've got a good head and you can see a business opportunity when it's there. Do you seriously believe you're going to be content to mince up and down the sidewalks of Kingstree for the rest of your life, lifting your hat to elderly ladies and remarking on the way the dust from the lime trees spoils your velvet collars?"

Jack said fiercely: "Do you know what it's like to love someone the way I love Ellie?"

There was a pause. Then Johann shook his head. "I probably don't," he said softly. "But do you know what it's like to be rich?"

"I know what it's like to be comfortably off, yes."

"Not comfortably off. *Rich*. When you're rich, you're never comfortably off. You're . . . you're . . ."

Johann raised his right hand, his fingers curled as if he were clutching a mass of banknotes. He could hardly articulate what he felt about wealth, especially to someone who had just turned down wealth in favor of marriage. He could see Jack watching him expectantly with those brown alert eyes, but he knew that if he described his desire for money the way it really was, the boy would not only fail to understand, he would probably be shocked as well. One day Jack might grasp what he was saying, but not today.

"You're addicted," he finished baldly.

Jack watched him for a while. Johann couldn't make up his mind if the boy was afraid of him or not; but when Jack eventually spoke, Johann decided that he wasn't. He liked that. The boy was young, and not ashamed to admit it. If there was one thing that Johann couldn't take, it was a green young smart aleck.

Jack said: "In that case, I'm obviously not an addict. Well, not a complete addict, in any event."

"There's no such thing as a halfhearted addict, Mr. Field. Not where money's concerned."

"Oh, I think there is, Mr. Cornelius. In fact, I think there are many of us would go halfway for money, but not the whole way."

Johann sipped the last of his brandy. "What do you call 'the whole way,' Mr. Field?"

"Giving up Ellie. That, as far as I'm concerned, would be the whole way. Then, I'd also say that giving up one's religion for the sake of money, that would be going the whole way. Or murdering for it."

"Then it's wrong to kill for the sake of money, in your opinion?"

Jack frowned. "Not just in my opinion, Mr. Cornelius. I believe that it's also in the opinion of most civilized people."

"Really."

Behind the bar, Errol said, quite apropos of nothing: "That Duncan Nicols, he could mix you one of his Pisco punches in 1880 A.D., and mix you another one of his Pisco punches in 1903 A.D., and you couldn't tell the damned difference."

Johann commented: "Errol, that's probably an indictment of the public palate, more than proof of Duncan Nicols' matchless barkeeping, and I'd be pleased if you'd keep your mouth shut."

Jack said: "I don't understand. How can you possibly justify murder for the sake of money?"

Johann rubbed his forehead. "You can't understand that at all?"

187

"No, sir. I can't."

"Well, let me put it this way. Supposing that I had committed murder for money. How would you defend me in a court of law?"

Jack shrugged. "It's very hard to say, not knowing the circumstances."

"Well, let's say that in my pursuit of money, I let a woman die by willful neglect. What tack would you take with the jury? What philosophical points would you raise to convince them that what I'd done was in the best interests of America?"

Jack took his pipe out of his coat pocket and absentmindedly fingered the bowl. "Personally, I wouldn't raise *any* philosophical points. I don't think that a court of law is the right place to make abstract appeals to notions like 'greater good' or 'best interests.' You see, what really counts is winning the sympathy of the jury, and what a great many lawyers don't seem to understand is that juries are made up of ordinary people with a very limited grasp of what's going on."

"Go on," said Johann, his eyes narrowed.

Jack Field shrugged self-consciously. "Of course, I'm only a junior attorney. I'm not even a partner yet. But this is the way it seems to me. I've been along to hear cases where a famous attorney makes a historic speech on a fine point of law, bringing in all kinds of obscure precedents and high-flown references, and you can see the jury sitting there with their mouths hanging open, for all the world like a pen full of pigs, and they plainly don't understand a word."

"So what would you do?" Johann asked.

Jack Field stuck his pipe in his mouth while he found his tobacco. Then he took it out again, and said: "I'd appeal to things that the jury could understand. I'd bring in old soldiers, and have them testify that you gave money to the veterans' hospital. I'd bring in the mayor, and have him say that you'd always served your community well. I'd bring in honest-looking workmen, to tell what a good boss you were, and how you lent them money when times were hard. And, of course, I'd bring in a widow whose husband had died in your service, and have her say that you'd looked after her ever since. Then, and only then, I'd have someone from your company explain why you had to neglect this woman in favor of making money."

Johann half-smiled. "You sound quite cynical for such a young man."

"I'm not cynical at all," said Jack, shaking his head. "I wouldn't be trying to mislead the jury, or defend an action that couldn't be defended. All I'd be doing would be to show the jury why you'd behaved the way you had, but I'd be showing them in terms of real life, rather than terms of law. I believe in plain speaking, Mr. Cornelius, that's all."

"I see. And what would be your own views on such an offense? Could you think, yourself, that letting someone die could be justified in the interests of industry?"

Jack, taking out his tobacco pouch, paused and looked worried. "Do you mean, could I believe myself that making money for the good of the nation is a valid mitigation of fatal negligence?"

"Yes. I mean exactly that."

Jack turned this one over in his mind. He stalled for time by slowly stoking his pipe, because he had a curious feeling that a lot more depended on his answer than the outcome of a hypothetical argument. He was not insensitive to personal auras; and Johann Cornelius had a gravitational attraction about him that drew lesser particles like Jack, and Errol, and everyone and everything else that wasn't screwed to the floor, inexorably and inevitably toward him.

From the restaurant, while the ship swayed and tilted into the Atlantic, they heard the clatter of knives and forks, as the two black stewards laid the tables for lunch. The marine engines pulsed steadily through the red-carpeted floor beneath their feet, and Jack Field looked at Johann Cornelius and wondered what he ought to say. There was a smell of pea soup in the air.

Jack said: "I think I would have to know you better before I answered you truthfully."

"But surely you have an opinion?"

"What can I say? You might be a saint, Mr. Cornelius, and the person in question might have brought her death upon herself. On the other hand—if you'll forgive my impertinence—you might be a terrible cad, and have driven her into an early grave by your own callousness."

For a moment Jack thought that he might have annoyed his host. But then Johann gave a small nod, and turned to Errol and said: "Fix me one more brandy, Errol. I think I might have something to celebrate, too."

Jack could sense a subtle change in Johann's demeanor. It seemed that the questioning session was now finished, and that

Johann was about to make some remark about Jack's performance. What Johann actually said, though, made Jack's hair prickle, and his white rubber collar feel uncomfortably tight.

"I think our meeting today was no lucky chance," said Johann. "In fact, I think it was one of those strokes of fate that make life stride forward in the way it does. You and I, Mr. Field, are going to do great things together."

"I beg your pardon?"

Johann laid a thick-fingered hand on Jack's shoulder. "You came on board celebrating an engagement. Well, I think you will disembark at New York with a great deal more to celebrate. I would like you to work for me, in Texas and Oklahoma, on the oilfields."

Jack stared. "I'm afraid that I don't follow," he said in a small, congested voice.

Johann took his brandy from the bar. "I need a young attorney who can immerse himself in the oil business and turn out to be the best oil attorney there ever was. I want a man who knows about crude and cracking, salt domes and sand beds; and at the same time I want him to hold his own in a court of law. In other words, Mr. Field, I want you."

"Mr. Cornelius, you've only known me five minutes."

"If I couldn't judge a man's integrity in five minutes, then I'd never survive in the oil business."

"But, Mr. Cornelius, I'm afraid it's out of the question."

"Isn't it just what you wanted?"

"Well, yes, but if I go to work in Texas, then I can't marry Ellie. I mean, that's the whole point of my staying in South Carolina."

Johann looked at Jack over the curved rim of his glass. The ship rose and sank in the Atlantic swell. Across from the bar, the deck doors opened, and one or two passengers in mackinaw coats came in for their lunch. One of them said: "Lamb cutlets, is it? What about a flank steak?"

Johann said: "It's time you learned, Mr. Field, that there is nothing in life that can't be fixed."

"What are you saying? That you can fix it for me to marry Ellie *and* work in Texas?"

"Why not?"

"Because Mr. Jackson expressly forbids it, that's why not. He doesn't want Ellie starting her married life in an oil town, and that's all there is to it."

Johann lowered his head and looked down at the brass bar rail, and the gleaming copper spittoon. "Do you agree with Mr. Jackson?"

Jack stared at Johann hard. "I suppose so," he said cautiously.

"Well, *do* you, or *don't* you? You seem clear enough in your mind about matters of law. *Do* you think it's right for this Mr. Jackson to have such a hand in your career and your future fortune, or *don't* you?"

"You have to understand that I love Ellie, and I also respect her family. There's nothing amiss with Mr. Jackson, I can assure you. We're already friends."

"Friends? What kind of a friend won't let you go off and make your way in the world, just because he doesn't want his daughter to get downwind of a few roughnecks? Oil towns are tough, Mr. Field, but you won't be spending all your waking days in oil towns, and most of the time you'll be sitting in an office that would make Mr. Jackson's look about as dandy as a bench in the park."

Jack got off his stool. He knew that Johann was deliberately provoking him, but at the same time he couldn't help himself from being provoked. He said, with as much control as he could manage: "Sir, that's my future father-in-law you're talking about."

Johann smiled. "I know. And I admire the way you're defending him. But he's not right, is he, even though he's kind? If he's prepared to have you marry his daughter, then he's got to accept that you're going to become her husband and her master, and that if you want to take her to Texas, or Oklahoma, or even the moon, then that's your right and your privilege, and it has nothing to do with him."

"Mr. Cornelius, I don't want to fall out with my parents-in-law, and that's all I can say. I've given my word to Mr. Jackson already."

Johann raised his eyebrows as if to say: *Ah, well, it can't be helped,* and downed the remainder of his brandy. At that moment, Jerry Slobodien came in from the deck in a shiny gray jacket with a velvet collar, and a shoestring tie with a diamond stud. His black hair was grown long for 1909, and combed back in glossy wings of bear grease.

"This is my business manager, Mr. Slobodien," said Johann. "Perhaps you'd like to have luncheon with us, and we can talk some more?"

Jack hesitated. He felt indecision stirring around inside him like a potful of greasy stew. If it hadn't have been for Ellie, he would have taken Johann Cornelius' offer there and then. But he believed in honor; and if he'd given his word of honor to stay in South Carolina, then stay in South Carolina he would.

He said: "I'll eat with you, Mr. Cornelius. But I must warn you that I won't change my mind."

"That's all right," said Johann. "People who change their minds easily can change them back again just as quick, and what I prefer is dedication."

They went through to the ship's dining room, a pale cream-painted salon with twelve circular tables covered with white cloths, where some of their fellow travelers were noisily sucking pea soup. Outside the windows, the gray sea rose and fell, and the last few seagulls swooped for scraps. One of the black stewards came forward and pulled back their chairs for them, and they sat facing each other with stiff smiles while the second steward brought the day's menu. It was pea soup, with lamb cutlets to follow, and persimmon pie.

"Generally, I take my lunch in my cabins," Johann explained. "The cook's a Chinaman, but he can sometimes be bribed to make a passable Welsh rabbit."

"I think I'll skip the soup," remarked Jerry Slobodien, glancing at the diners at the next table. "It sounds like it's too damned loud."

One of the diners, a mild-looking bespectacled man in a green tweed suit and a canary-yellow bowtie, dabbed his lips with his napkin and stared at Jerry Slobodien balefully. But the oil manager gave him a silent dark-chinned grimace in return, and the man returned to his soup like a startled turkey.

"Incidentally, Mr. Cornelius," said Slobodien, reaching into the breast pocket of his coat and producing a crumpled scrap of paper. "We just had a message from Orris and Nussbaum. It seems that we have been legally restrained from breaking ground at Sapulpa Bluffs."

"Restrained? Why? By whom?"

"Mr. Spizak doesn't know yet. He only found out when he was trying to clear the final details of the lease. Some party acting on behalf of some other party has persuaded the district courts to hold up our drilling operations until the deed and title of the lease can be properly established."

Johann's mouth tightened in annoyance. "That's ridiculous.

We leased those oil and mineral rights fair and square from the Baptist church."

"Not according to this mysterious party who's taken out this restraining order. This mysterious party seems to think that all rights in land at Sapulpa Bluffs are still owned by Seminole Indians, and this mysterious party has even produced a certain Chief Wewoka, from Boggy Depot, Oklahoma, whose rights we're allegedly infringing."

The steward came up with his pad and his pencil and said: "What'll it be, gentlemen? The cutlets is ecstasy itself."

"Ecstasy itself? Where did you ever learn yourself a phrase like that?" demanded Jerry Slobodien.

"Mr. Abraham Ruef, sir. He traveled on this steamer once, sir. A fine man, sir, but Jewish."

"You're not exactly a white man yourself, Dudley. Just bring what you have, and we'll eat it."

"Very good, sir."

"And bring us a bottle of that red wine the captain drinks, and three glasses."

"Two glasses," said Johann. "I've had enough for one day."

"Yes, sir."

Jack, who had been sitting very silently, unfolded his napkin and said: "There is a way around it, you know."

Johann looked up alertly. "A way around what? You mean this snag at Sapulpa Bluffs?"

"Well, I think so. One of my subjects at Harvard was land registry and titles."

"And?"

Jack colored. "I'm not entirely sure about this. I mean, I'd have to check it up in the law books. But the way I remember it, the Seminole Indians signed an agreement with the U.S. government in 1867, revoking all their mineral rights in the state of Oklahoma."

Johann looked at Jerry Slobodien and raised a meaningful eyebrow.

Jack said: "I don't like to guess at things without knowing the facts, but it seems to me that this 'Chief Wewoka' is probably a fraud, and that someone's obtained this restraining order just to delay your drilling."

Johann thought about this, and then nodded. "That could make sense. Colton and Moffat have both been interested in

Sapulpa. But what can we do? This order's been granted in a district court.''

"That doesn't matter," said Jack. "Even if Chief Wewoka is genuine, he can't possibly have any claim on your oil rights. You could have that restraining order overturned by suppertime.''

Johann sat back in his dining chair with a grin.

"You know something, Mr. Field. You're wasted in South Carolina. Wasted. You're a natural-born oil attorney if ever I came across one. What do you think, Jerry?''

Jerry Slobodien was lighting up a thin black cheroot. "Whatever you say, Mr. Cornelius. It all sounds like good news to me.''

"I'd have to check on my facts," said Jack doubtfully. "I'm only speaking from memory. It could be that the agreement with the Indians has been rescinded by now.''

"Not a chance." Johann smiled. "The day we give anything back to the Indians is the day we've scraped this country's resources down to the bare bone. Don't doubt your legal talents, Mr. Field. You have just the kind of fighting spirit I like.''

Jack toyed with his knife. "I'm very flattered by your comments, Mr. Cornelius. I really am. But I've already explained the position I'm in, and there's nothing I can do, or want to do, to change it.''

Johann smoothed back his sparse blond hair. "You think I'm trying to tempt you away from the straight-and-narrow path?''

"No, sir. I know that your offer is fair, and I believe that I could make a good oil attorney—and probably will, when the time is right. But the circumstances cannot be altered. I have given my word, and Ellie means more to me than any career possibly could.''

"Well," said Johann, "your love for your bride-to-be is admirable. If only your love for your work were equally strong.''

"Ellie is the most beautiful creature on God's earth, Mr. Cornelius.''

"In your opinion.''

"Love is always a matter of opinion, Mr. Cornelius. Like honor.''

The black steward, Dudley, arrived with the pea soup. Johann picked up his spoon at once and began to drink it. Jack watched him in surprise; and Jerry Slobodien, his cheroot still dribbling smoke, watched Jack.

Jack licked his lips. Then he clasped his hands together and

194

closed his eyes and said quietly: "For the food and drink that we are about to receive, we thank Thee, O Lord, amen."

He opened his eyes. Johann had paused, with his spoon dripping soup into his plate. There was an uncomfortable hiatus, while the ship creaked and rolled, the engines vibrated through the deck, and the knives of the diners at the next table grated and squeaked on their dishes as they tried to dismember the tough little lamb cutlets that were ecstasy itself.

"Are you ready to eat now?" asked Johann, and there was a serrated edge on his voice.

Jack said: "Quite, thank you, sir."

Johann laid down his spoon, and wiped his mouth with his napkin. "You mustn't think that I'm irreligious, Mr. Field, but if there's one thing I cannot bring myself to do, it's to give thanks to a higher authority for what I eat. All the food that goes into my mouth gets there because of my own efforts, no matter how wonderful the Lord is for stocking the earth with abundant lunches."

Jack said nothing for a moment. He found it almost impossible to work out what manner of man Johann Cornelius really was, and the feeling unnerved him. It wasn't only the deck that was rising and falling beneath his feet; it was his self-assurance as well.

"I think," said Johann, "that you and I are going to get along fine. What do you think, Jerry?"

Jerry Slobodien crushed out his cigar, and winked across the dining room at a prim young girl in a velour bonnet who had just come in from the deck. She looked like a governess on her way home to New York. Jerry Slobodien said: "Oh, you'll get along all right. It's just a question of terms. Isn't that right, Mr. Field? Terms."

Jack, at that moment, felt more uncomfortable than he ever had before in his whole life. "I beg to disagree," he said quietly, and he couldn't understand why Johann Cornelius and Jerry Slobodien exchanged such self-satisfied smiles.

Just before dawn the next morning, the SS *Galveston Bay* began to run into rough seas. In South Carolina, the previous night, Ellie had heard rain on her bedroom window just before she fell asleep, but out here, six miles off Cape Hatteras, the rain came with the whiplashing tail of a hurricane. It had already shrieked its way across southern Florida, forcing the palm trees to lash and grovel, lifting off rooftops, and stirring up fishing boats so that they

195

champed and foamed at their moorings like rabid dogs. Now, ailing and ill-tempered, it was twisting out eastward across the Atlantic, bannered with dirty skies, and it was still fierce enough to raise the ocean into thirty-foot peaks. It tilted the SS *Galveston Bay* across massive gray-green slopes, and drove the ship through tumbling buttes of spray, until the marine engines whined and rumbled and strained, and the bulkheads groaned like old men having bad dreams.

During the storm, Johann Cornelius remained at his desk under a dim green-shaded lamp, bent over a long report on the geological conditions of a new lease in California. Jerry Slobodien stayed with him for a while, but then went up to the observation saloon to smoke a cheroot and amuse himself at the discomfort of the other passengers. Most of the early-morning coffee and kippered herring had long since disappeared over the rail, and now the *Galveston Bay*'s guests sat with plaid rugs around their knees, their cheeks the color of newspaper, silently praying to the gods of abdominal equilibrium, if there were any, to deliver them from nausea, and lead them not into regurgitation.

Jack Field, who hadn't eaten much breakfast, looked a little better. He was standing by the starboard window, watching the seas rise and plunge all around them, smoking his pipe. Jerry Slobodien came over and leaned his back against the handrail next to him, casually puffing out smoke.

Jack said: "Quite a blow."

Jerry Slobodien nodded. "Ass-end of a hurricane. Nothing to get excited about. We've been through worse than this."

"I think I'm glad I said no to the bacon, all the same."

Jerry Slobodien laughed.

The ship turned in the sea, paused, and then dropped twenty feet into a trough. Rain slashed against the saloon windows, and even through the thick glass Jack could hear the wind screaming in the masts and the wires. Deep beneath them, within the ship, he heard another sound, too, like a cartload of logs being delivered down a cellar chute. He glanced at Jerry Slobodien, but Slobodien either hadn't heard it, or had, and didn't care.

"Mr. Cornelius is really regretful that you haven't changed your mind," remarked Jerry Slobodien.

"Oh? I thought he was just playing games."

Jerry Slobodien shook his head. "Mr. Cornelius never plays games. I've known him six, seven years; and I've never seen him play any games yet. He doesn't have that kind of humor."

196

Jack gripped the rail tight to keep his balance on the heaving deck. He was beginning to wish that he hadn't started this pipe, but then, to knock it out in front of Jerry Slobodien and all the rest of the seasick passengers was an awful admission of landlubberliness. A suppressed burp that tasted of coffee and Balkan tobacco rose in his throat, but he managed to keep smiling.

"Does Mr. Cornelius have *any* humor?" he asked.

"Oh, sure. But not the style that many people understand. He's amused by what-do-you-call-it."

"I don't know," said Jack. "What *do* you call it?"

"Poetic what-do-you-call-it. Justice."

Jack wedged his pipe in between the varnished rail and the saloon window. "You mean that he likes to see people getting their just deserts?"

"That's correct."

"Has he ever thought that he, too, might one day get his just deserts?"

Jerry Slobodien grinned wolfishly. "Jack," he said, "I like you. But I'll tell you one thing. If Johann Cornelius ever gets his just deserts it'll be nothing more nor less than he runs out of people prepared to be bought."

"But that will never happen. Most men have a price."

Jerry Slobodien shrugged. "In that case, he won't get his just deserts."

Jack, alerted by the oddity of this conversation, and indeed by the oddity of the whole day's conversations, had half an inkling of what Jerry Slobodien was trying to say. But he wasn't at all sure whether Slobodien was trying to provoke him into changing his mind about working for Johann, or trying to warn him off altogether.

The SS *Galveston Bay* shuddered like a locomotive trying to get itself a grip on the rails. Jack said: "Before I met Ellie, I would have considered working for Mr. Cornelius as a great privilege. But I'm afraid that I can't be shaken. I respect Mr. Cornelius, but I also respect my future father-in-law, and that's the way it has to be."

Jerry Slobodien said: "Well, it's your funeral." But just as he said "funeral," the ship's engines stopped, and the deck of the saloon suddenly tilted their way, so that bottles and glasses rushed off the top of the bar and smashed against the mahogany paneling. Several of the passengers dropped their plaid rugs and shouted: "What's happening? Steward—what's happening?"

The ship rose and slid and wallowed, and for a few moments it was almost impossible to keep a footing on the deck. Jack felt himself thrown with a bang against the saloon window, then back again, and he saw his pipe sliding twenty feet away across the carpet. Outside, tall spires of foam rose above the deck, and as far as Jack could see, the ocean was a greenish landscape of restless mountains under a black sky.

An alarm bell started to ring. Jack said: "We're sinking! My God, do you think we're sinking?"

Jerry Slobodien put a spindly leg out and stamped on his cheroot. "No such luck, if you ask me. They're just trying to scare us into paying double fare."

The alarm bell kept on ringing. The ship heaved around between the waves with a sickening aimlessness, and the girl in the velour bonnet vomited across the patterned carpet. Jerry Slobodien said: "That's *her* off the list. I can't take a woman who can't hold her breakfast."

Jack said: "For God's sake! We ought to get to the lifeboats!"

"You think a lifeboat's going to do any better than this tub?"

"Dammit, Mr. Slobodien, this ship's helpless!"

At that moment, one of the ship's officers, a fat Spanish-looking man in a gold-braided cap, gold-braided pants, and a woolen undervest, hurried erratically through the sloping saloon with a bullhorn. He wrapped an arm around one of the mahogany pillars and called out, in unnecessarily stentorian tones: "Ladies and gentlemen! The captain says to regret the ship's cargo is shifted! We are therefore listing! Seriously! Therefore, we must make haste to the lifeboats! Ladies first!"

One man shouted: "What about my belongings? All my papers?"

"Sorry, sir! No time!"

"But I've got thirteen thousand dollars down there! That's five years' work!"

"Sorry, sir! The captain says to make all haste! The cargo is shifting quick! Maybe the whole ship turn over!"

Jerry Slobodien said: "Where's Carl? We have to warn Mr. Cornelius."

Jack gripped his shoulder. "You find Carl. I'll go for Mr. Cornelius. I have to go down there anyway. There's a box in my cabin I can't leave."

"You heard what he said!" snapped Jerry Slobodien. "There's no time! Just warn Mr. Cornelius and get on up here!"

The SS *Galveston Bay* creaked and dipped alarmingly, and the lights dimmed to a faint unhealthy orange. Through the salt-crusted windows, Jack saw a gray glassy cliff that seemed to move toward them as if it was on rollers, and he felt the ship pause in a trough, preparing itself to receive the tons and tons of sea water that were towering over it.

He made his way across the crazily angled saloon to the ship's main stairs. Engravings of Lily Langry in carved teak frames beamed at him beatifically on each side. Clinging on to the brass handrail, taking one tilted step at a time, he looked down and saw water coursing across the red floral carpet on the deck below. Behind him, he heard Jerry Slobodien shouting: "Carl! *Carl*! We have to get out of here!"

The ship suddenly swayed, and Jack was thrown across the staircase, tumbling over and over, bruising his back on the edges of the stairs, and he landed on all fours in the seething, gurgling waterfall that ran across the carpet. Coughing, hurt, he picked himself up and climbed toward the corridor where Joahnn Cornelius' first-class staterooms were. There was blood coursing from both his nostrils and mingling with the sea water that ran down his face, and a livid bruise on his forehead where his head had struck a brass lamp bracket. But he knew that he couldn't leave Johann Cornelius to drown, and neither could he lose Earle Jackson's family jewels. He managed to stagger ten or twelve feet down the corridor, with the rolling of the ship throwing him heavily from side to side. But then the *Galveston Bay* turned sidelong against the seas, and the howling force of the hurricane tilted her over so violently that Jack found he was skidding across the wet mahogany paneling of the corridor walls. He grabbed for a door handle, and held on to it tight, while the vessel shivered and shook all around him, and thousands of gallons of ocean collapsed through the doorways and hatchways all around him.

The ship rolled again, and Jack saw a door swing open a few yards farther down the corridor. It banged open and shut a few times, and then the bulky shape of Johann Cornelius emerged, pulling himself out of his cabin like a man rising out of his coffin. Johann made his way toward Jack on his hands and knees. The ship was heaving so desperately that there was no possibility of staying upright, no matter how rich you were.

"*Mr. Cornelius*!" shrieked Jack. "*The ship's turning over! We have to get to the lifeboats*!"

"Well, get on with it!" Johann shouted back. "*I'll follow*!"

"*I have to go to my cabin*!"

"Don't be so goddamned foolish! This goddamned ship's going to fall apart in a moment!"

"But I can't leave the jewels! I have all of my fiancée's family's heirlooms in there!"

Johann had reached Jack now. The Dutchman was soaked through, and his face was cut from a toppling lampshade, but it was rigid with determination. He managed to heave himself up to his feet as the ship slopped uneasily into a trough, and he bent forward and offered his hand.

"Come on, we'll get out of this together!"

"But the jewels!" Jack protested frantically. "I was entrusted with them! I can't leave them there!"

Johann pulled Jack roughly upright, and Jack seized the brass rail that ran along the side of the corridor to steady himself.

"I must!" he shouted.

Johann pushed him savagely toward the stairs. "Get going! Don't argue! If you're that worried about your damned family jewels, I'll pay you for them! I'll give you whatever they're worth! Now, let's go before we damned well drown!"

Two of the Galveston's crew had come climbing and scrambling down the main staircase to look for them, and so they half-slid and half-crawled through the rushing shallows that poured across the deck, with Johann shoving Jack ahead of him, and reached out for the sailors' hands.

"Up on deck to your left!" ordered one of the crew. "And make it quick as you like!"

Jack hesitated for one moment, and turned, but Johann pushed him again and said: "I'll pay! Now, get up those stairs!"

Outside on deck, in the slanting rain and the shrieking wind, the lifeboat was already being winched up on its davits. The pale, frightened faces of the passengers and crew, of whom there were only twenty-three altogether, were swinging to and fro in the boat like a gallery of colorless portraits. Jack and Johann were helped up over the boat's slippery side, and they found seats next to Carl, Johann's manservant, who was holding a wet comic paper and looking alarmed and confused. The green seas that rose around them were so immense that Jack couldn't believe that they would possibly stay afloat.

With pulleys clanging in the gale, the lifeboat was winched out and lowered down the rusty, leaning side of the steamship toward the ocean. Eventually, the waves slapped at its keel, and then caught it and tossed it away from the *Galveston Bay*, and then back again, and Jack clung on to the narrow seat, his eyes tight closed, hoping that Ellie would never have to be told that he was drowned.

The last crew members slid down the swaying winch lines and clambered on board. Then they pushed the boat away from the hull of the SS *Galveston Bay* with oars, and they were swept off into the canyons of green and gray, too scared for their lives to shout to each other, or sing, or do anything but grip their seats as hard as they could, and pray to God for the hurricane to blow itself out.

The last Jack saw of the steamship was her black-painted stern, streaked with rust and clustered with barnacles, her brass screws raised to the filthy skies, as she sank quickly beneath the Atlantic. Then there was nothing but sea, and wind, and gray clouds that rushed eastward over their heads.

They sat in the dark hotel drawing room under an old cracked oil painting of the frigate *Merrimack*, before she was turned into an ironclad. Through the gardens, lined with orderly plane trees, they could see the wide shining stretch of Hampton Roads, and the flags fluttering in the distance at Newport News. They had ordered brandies, and they sipped them with the quiet appreciation of men who know that the world is a man's world, and very regulated, and that life would remain as stable and as dignified as this even when the painting over the mantelpiece was twice as old as it was today. It was a light breezy afternoon, but the drawing-room windows were all closed, so that inside, where the two men sat, it was silent and still.

Earle Jackson said: "I can't stay for too long, I'm afraid. We're taking the three-o'clock train back to Charleston."

Johann, dressed in a borrowed and badly fitting gray suit, answered: "That's all right. I'm leaving on the New York mail train myself at four. How's Jack?"

"The doctor said he was lucky not to have fractured his skull. But he's more cheerful this morning. I just thank God you're all safe. You should have seen my daughter's face when the intelligence reached us."

"Jack's a fine fellow," said Johann. "Very shrewd for his age, but pleasant, too. Your daughter's a lucky girl."

Earle Jackson gave a brief smile, but nothing else.

Johann said: "I think this is going to put me off steamers for good. My manager's been spending the morning trying to persuade

201

me to purchase a railroad car. I can't say that I'm entirely against the idea, either."

Earle Jackson nodded. There was a silence that wasn't altogether comfortable. Outside the window, out on the Roads, they could see a naval escort at anchor, and a flurry of yachts leaning into the wind.

Earle Jackson said: "I really came here to thank you."

Johann looked at him. "Thank me? What for?"

"Well, for saving Jack. He says that you saved him. He was all for going to rescue my family heirlooms, but he says you pushed him back up on deck."

Johann coughed. "Anyone else would have done the same. And, quite incidentally, I promised to pay for those heirlooms, whatever they were. You must give me some idea of how much they were worth."

Earle Jackson shook his head. "No, I won't hear of it. Jack's life is worth more to my family than any jewels or paintings that ever were. To me, too. Ellie was so relieved—well, I have to say it brought the tears to my eyes."

"Ellie's your daughter? The one who's going to marry Jack?"

"He told you?"

"Oh, sure. We had quite a long talk on the boat, before the Lord God intervened and sank us. But listen, I did promise Jack that I'd pay for those jewels—really. If you fix a price, I'll have my bankers send you a certified check in the morning."

Earle Jackson looked down at the Kashmir carpet. He said, in a low voice: "I'd rather you didn't. It's really not necessary. It was just some jewelry that belonged to my mother."

"Was it insured?"

"Of course. For less than its auction value, I suspect. But quite enough."

"Well," said Johann, "it's up to you. If you want to be recompensed, I gave my word, and I'm willing to keep it."

Earle Jackson said: "What I had in mind was something different. I wanted to offer something to *you*. As a way of saying thanks for saving my daughter's happiness."

Johann looked at Earle Jackson with pale, narrowed eyes for a while. For some reason that he couldn't pin down, Earle Jackson seemed unduly unsettled, almost *shifty*, especially for a man who had sought an audience with him in order to thank him for saving the life of his future son-in-law. Johann was intrigued by Earle Jackson's discomfort, but at the same time he was quite prepared to take advantage of it without knowing its cause. He recalled forcing a Californian landowner down to a rock-bottom lease deal a couple of years back, simply because the man was betraying, for whatever private reason and however unconsciously, a deep anxiety to sell out.

Earle Jackson said: "I was thinking of offering you a horse, as a matter of fact. My plantation, Fortuna, is also one of the finest stud farms in South Carolina. There was a particular chestnut I had in mind, a yearling. It's called Charleston Lightning."

Johann sipped at his brandy without taking his eyes away from Earle Jackson's face. Then he got up from his seat and walked across to the fireplace, where he stood for a while and examined the painting of the *Merrimack*.

Finally he turned around. He said, with heavy kindness: "I'm very flattered by your offer, Mr. Jackson, and very gratified. But I'm afraid I don't really have any use for horses. I rarely have any time to myself, and when I do, I catch up on my sleep. I'm a businessman. Paper, ink, accounts, money. I wouldn't know what to do with a horse."

Earle Jackson was a little put out. He said: "Oh. I was hoping you'd kind of like it."

Johann smiled. "I would. Don't get me wrong. But I'd rather you kept the horse yourself, and made good use of it, than give it to me. I wouldn't like it to go to the glue factory for lack of use."

"Well," said Earle Jackson, taking a short breath, "I'm afraid that I don't have anything else to offer. It's no use giving you money."

"No," said Johann, still smiling.

There was another awkward silence. Johann stood beaming down at Earle Jackson's bent head as if he were about to lay a blessing on him, or bestow a knighthood. Earle Jackson lifted his brandy glass and tipped back the last of his brandy.

"There is one thing," said Johann.

"Yes?"

"I don't want you to misunderstand me. I'm not trying to interfere in your life, or in the way you run your family's affairs. But right now you have the last word on something, on some*one*, rather, whose services could be more than useful to me."

Earle Jackson stared at him, uneasy.

Johann sat down again, still smiling. "What I'm saying is that young Jack seems to me to have the qualities that I've been looking for in an oil attorney. Apart from which, he has some very radical notions about oil, and the profits of the oil industry, and some even more interesting ideas about oil and law and business morals. He's young yet. Inexperienced. But oil's a hard business, and a young man can learn quick."

Earle Jackson said faintly: "Jack still has his training to finish. He's indentured to his father's firm in Kingstree."

Johann looked poker-faced. "Is that a handicap?"

"Well, no, but Jack's father thinks that—well, and I agree with him that Jack should stay for a while in his home state."

"What does Jack think?"

"I presume that Jack agrees. Nobody's forced him to stay in Carolina."

"And Ellie?"

Johann was watching Earle Jackson closely with every question, and when he asked about Ellie, he knew at once what Earle Jackson's sensitive spot was. Earle Jackson flinched, almost as if Johann had struck him a playful pat on the cheek. The muscles around his mouth tightened, and he couldn't smile for a hundred dollars.

"Ellie's place is in South Carolina society," her father said quietly, "growing up gracefully alongside of her mother and me. I know you've made your wealth in oil, Mr. Cornelius, and I don't mean to speak offensively, but there is no place for Ellie in a boom town on the Western frontier, amongst wildcatters and suchlike."

Johann remarked: "You seem uncommonly fond of your Ellie. Most parents these days would give a chestnut yearling and a year's supply of feed just to see the back of their daughters."

Earle Jackson looked away. He said quietly: "Yes, Mr. Cornelius, I am uncommonly fond of Ellie. But then, to me, Ellie is a very uncommon daughter. She—well, she reminds me of her mother, when she was young."

Johann grinned. "I see. But I don't think you have any cause to worry. Boom towns are not all mud and whiskey, you know, and wildcatters can be quite human once you get to know them. Some of them have even been heard to pass the time of day."

"I realize that, and I didn't mean to cause you offense. But I'm afraid that I had to stipulate that if Jack and Ellie were to marry, then Jack should stay in South Carolina and finish his training, with a view to taking up a partnership with his father."

Johann lifted an eyebrow. "So it's a chestnut yearling or nothing?"

"I'm afraid so. But you're still very welcome to that."

204

Johann was silent for a short while. Then he put down his glass, and laced his big fingers together, and said: "There was a time, years and years ago, when I wanted to own somebody too."

"I don't follow."

"She was a girl," explained Johann. "Younger than Ellie, but very beautiful. And just like you, I wanted to have that beauty, actually have it, all to myself. I bought that girl, because in those days and in that place you could still do things like that. I kept her in a case like a specimen of butterfly, or bird. I loved her in a way that I didn't believe anybody else could ever understand. But I believe *you* understand, Mr. Jackson, because it appears to me that you love your Ellie in very much the same kind of way. Not profanely, but possessively."

Earle Jackson tried to look fierce. "You're not trying to suggest that—"

Johann raised his hand. "I'm not trying to suggest anything, Mr. Jackson. I'm just telling you that beautiful young girls can make a man behave in jealous and irrational ways that maybe he shouldn't. Even daughters. Maybe *especially* daughters."

He lowered his eyes. "Regrettably, I know from my own experience that beauty is infinitely fragile, and that it can't be put in a case and breathed over. You can sigh for it and you can ache for it, but you can't own it, not ever. I tried to, and I wound up crushing it."

"What do you mean—*crushing* it?"

Johann shrugged. He could hardly believe it, but even after all this time, he still felt a lump in his chest for Carina. He said, in a tighter voice than he'd meant to: "She died, mostly because of me. I wasn't even there to see it happen."

Earle Jackson blinked, but then he recovered himself a little and said: "Well, I'm sorry. But I'm afraid that it's really nothing to do with me. I made my decision for Ellie's own protection, and for Jack's own protection, too."

"Protection against what?" asked Johann. "Protection against experience? Protection against smallpox, or bad food, or the timetables of the Southern Pacific? Protection against life? You can't protect people from their own talents, Mr. Jackson."

"I'm not attempting to. I simply believe it's wiser if Jack bides his time."

Johann gave one sharp, decisive shake of his head. "Then you're wrong. Jack is the right age, with the right talents, and he's keen as mustard to get into the right business. If you let me hire

Jack Field as my oil attorney in Texas, without letting it stand in the way of his happy betrothal to your daughter, then you're doing Jack a favor, and you're doing Ellie a favor, too. Jack's going to be a wealthy man if he comes into oil right now, there's no two ways about it. But if he doesn't, then he's going to stay a South Carolina mouthpiece for the rest of his life, and Ellie's going to stay a South Carolina mouthpiece's lady.''

Earle Jackson looked exceedingly discomfited, as if he'd climbed into a pair of briar tweed pants without remembering to put his long johns on first. He said awkwardly: "I don't really want to argue about it, Mr. Cornelius. I came here to thank you, and I believe that I have. If you don't feel able to take my horse, then that's the way it is. But I can't offer you anything else."

Johann said: "That's all right. But let me ask you to think about what I've told you, just for a day or two. And do something else, too. Ask Jack what he really feels, and Ellie. And then think about yourself. Just how long can you keep Ellie cupped up in your hands, Mr. Jackson? You're going to have to let her go someday. She's not a bird, and she's not a butterfly. She's a young woman, with a right to her own future.''

For a moment, Johann thought that Earle Jackson was going to lose his temper, and tell him to stop interfering. But there were heavier pressures on Earle Jackson's conscience than Johann Cornelius—Ellie herself, for one—and he lifted himself from his club chair as if he were a carrier taking up his backpack after an unaccustomed rest.

"Very well, Mr. Cornelius," he said in a thin tone. "I'll agree to think about it. When I've made up my mind, I'll have one of my friends in New York call around to give you my answer. Is that fair enough?"

"Fair enough."

Out in the hotel garden, Johann could see Jack and Ellie promenading between the trees hand-in-hand; Ellie with her candy-striped parasol, and Jack in a brown suit as badly fitting as Johann's. On board the SS *Galveston Bay*, Jack had told Johann that he would never understand how much he loved Ellie; but then, the SS *Galveston Bay* was resting now on the bed of the Atlantic Ocean, alongside the wreck of the *Merrimack* and a dozen other ships; and declarations of love, unlike ships, are rarely commemorated in oils, or hung above the mantelpiece as souvenirs.

Johann smiled, and pointed out of the window at the happy couple. All that Earle Jackson could do was turn away, leaving his empty brandy glass on the table, and close the door behind him.

The girl was waiting for him in the foyer of the Plaza as he came back from a long and difficult meeting with Du Pont. An unexpected summer shower had slicked the sidewalks outside, and the hotel was crowded with wet umbrellas and chattering people hoping for taxis. Johann walked across the patterned carpet to the gold-painted gates of the elevator bank, and stood patiently while an elderly woman in furs was helped out of the car.

The girl was sitting in one of the two elegant little armchairs in the foyer, about ten feet from where Johann was standing, and she made no attempt to get up. She said clearly: "Mr. Cornelius?"

Johann turned. She smiled.

"Did you call me?" he asked.

"You *are* Mr. Cornelius?"

"That's right."

She lifted an arm. She was very petite and pretty, and she was dressed in an expensive summer coat of beige wool. She couldn't have been older than eighteen or nineteen. Johann suddenly realized that she expected him to go across and take her hand.

He came over with a slow, even walk. Then he held her hand, in its matching beige glove, and kissed it.

"Well?" he said with a cool smile.

"I have a message for you," she told him. "My name is Hester Forbes, and my father is a friend of Mr. Earle Jackson, of South Carolina."

"I see."

"Well, you don't, really. Father was going to bring this message himself, but he had to go to the doctor for his piles."

"I beg your pardon?"

"Aren't they an occupational hazard for businessmen?"

Johann looked down at her seemingly innocent heart-shaped face. "I suppose so," he answered, amused.

"Anyway," she said, "I was going across town myself so I said that I'd deliver it. The message is—'Texas it is.' Do you understand that?"

Johann nodded. "I think so."

"I'm pleased about that, because it's double-Dutch to me. Do you want to buy me tea while I'm here?"

"I wish I had time, Miss Forbes. But I regret that I have a meeting in fifteen minutes' time."

She pulled a face. "Oh, well. Father did say that you made your money by sheer hard labor. It's been nice to meet you, all the same. Most millionaires are so small. You're very big for a millionaire, do you know that?"

Johann couldn't help grinning. "I didn't know there was a national size-to-wealth ratio."

"Of course there is. There's a ratio for everything. By the way, what religion are you? You're not Jewish, by any chance?"

"I'm Dutch Free Church. Why?"

Hester took a small notebook with mother-of-pearl covers from her bag, and penciled a few words in it.

"Nothing," she said. "I'm just working out another ratio."

"Not an eligibility-for-marriage ratio?"

She looked up, and went a little pink. "How did you know?"

He took her beige-gloved hand and squeezed it. "Miss Forbes, you're an eligible-looking girl yourself, and every eligible-looking girl in the USA is searching for an eligible-looking millionaire."

"I wasn't going to propose," she said. "Leap year was last year."

Johann held her hand for a moment longer, and then let it go. He raised his hat.

"Thank the Lord," he said, "for small mercies."

It must have been a season when wheels turn, when doors open and close. When Johann came down to the desk the following morning, the receptionist handed him, among his usual mail, a long white envelope postmarked Boston, Massachusetts, and inscribed "strictly private." He tucked the rest of his letters into his inside pocket, and carried this one, unopened, into the dining room where he sat down at his accustomed table by the window, overlooking the park, and propped the letter against the salt and pepper.

He knew nobody in Boston that he could think of. He had done no business in Boston. The handwriting, an even blue-black copperplate, was unfamiliar. The letter remained untouched while the waiter brought him coffee, and while he ordered two poached eggs, with bacon and toast.

Eventually, he picked the letter up, and tore it open with his butter knife. There were two sheets of white bond, sharply folded, each filled with the same even handwriting. He sipped his coffee and began to read.

After the first three lines, he set his cup of coffee back in its saucer. He laid the letter on the table, and smoothed it out with his hand, as if he were trying to erase what was written in it. When the waiter came up with more coffee, he didn't even notice.

The letter read:

Dear Mr. Cornelius,

It is six years since we last saw each other, although I have followed the progress of your career quite assiduously in the newspapers. I am afraid that I have to bring you intelligence that is both bitter and sad. I can only hope that you mourn when you hear it with just a fraction of the grief that you caused yourself by your own cruel actions.

On the last day of April, Mrs. Beatrice Mulliner was found dead in the bathroom of her apartment in Roseland, Tangipahoa Parish, Louisiana. She had retreated to Roseland after the shame and dishonor you caused her in Edgar, Texas, hoping to find a fresh beginning, and to build again her broken hopes and self-esteem, but apparently this proved beyond her capacity. She took her own life by cutting her wrists and her throat with an open razor, and she bled to death within a very few minutes.

I am writing to you now because of what Mrs. Mulliner said in the note which she left behind. She said that she was taking her life because the assault she suffered at the hands of oilmen from your own corporation was a greater pain and besmirchment than her soul could bear, although in a manner which she felt you could not understand, she loved you still. She had tried to form a liaison with an oculist who practiced in Roseland, but when he proposed matrimony to her, the disgust she felt at her past was too great for her to bear, and she could not accept. It was then, despairing of her future, she decided to take her life.

She made one suggestion, sir, which I trust you will not take as an impertinence from me but as a last request from a lady who loved you and who died in the cause of that love. She asked that in her memory, and as a way of atoning for the agony you caused her, you should pay me a regular allowance, and to give me letters of introduction to

209

whichever railroad officials might best help me to further my intended career in the railroads.

She said that I must not make such a request appear as a threat, but that you should consider your personal involvement with members of government, society, and business most carefully before coming to your decision, since I have in my possession her manuscript letter which describes in detail everything about your conduct in Edgar and elsewhere, with the names of corroborating witnesses.

I can be reached at any time at the above address. I hope that the Lord enables you to find peace of mind, and some respite from your guilt.

Yours,
Daniel Forster

Johann was shaking as he laid down the letter. He felt cold and queasy, and he seemed to find it impossible to rise from his chair. All these years he had lived with some kind of hope that Beatrice still loved him, that she was still alive and safe; and he could have counted in scores the dreams he had dreamed of meeting her in strange places, in ornamental gardens and at railroad stations. He could feel her body in his hands even now, a warm ghost. He could almost reach out and touch her hair. He could almost hold her.

The waiter, a white cloth over his arm, came up with his bacon and eggs, and stood waiting for Johann to remove the pages from the table.

"Sir?" he said, at length.

Johann looked up. He was very pale.

The waiter said: "Are you all right, sir? Shall I bring your breakfast later?"

Johann found the strength somehow to sit up straight and give a tense, humorless smile.

"No, no," he said. "It's nothing. I think I've just discovered that one has to pay for one's past mistakes."

"Very true, sir," nodded the waiter. "Would you like the pepper?"

1921

America's present need is not
heroics but healing; not nostrums
but normalcy; not revolution but
restoration; not surgery but serenity.
—Warren G. Harding, Boston, 1921

It was Jack Field's first free Saturday for nine weeks; and so he took Randy to Riverside Park, where they punted a ball around for twenty minutes, and then sat on a bench in their overcoats, sharing a paper poke of hot chestnuts, and watching the N.Y. Central freight trains as they clattered ceaselessly backward and forward in wreaths and curls of white smoke. Jack enjoyed the noise and the bustle. Most of the incoming trains sounded like traveling farmyards—cackling and bleating and lowing—as animals were brought in from the Western states for slaughter in Manhattan's abattoirs. And then there was the honking and parping of motor horns from the Dodges and Maxwells and Briscoes that teemed up and down Riverside Drive; and the echoing hoot of ferries from the 129th Street pier. It was a bright, snappy, blue-skied day in November, 1921—the year that Jack Dempsey knocked down Georges Carpentier at Boyle's Thirty Acres in Jersey, the year that Babe Ruth raised his home-run record to fifty-nine, the year that a bathing belle scandalized spectators at Washington's Potomac Beach by rolling down her stockings past her knees, and most important of all for Jack Field, it was the year that Warren Gamaliel Harding was inaugurated President.

In a few days' time, on November 19, Jack Field would have been working for Cornelius Oil for twelve years. He owned a five-bedroom apartment on Central Park South, tastefully decorated in warm golds and browns by André Manche, and hung with paintings by Sisley and Degas; and a seven-bedroom colonial house in New Hampshire, with nearly two hundred acres of woodland and pasture. For Jack and Ellie Field, money had brought furs and servants and automobiles, but it had also brought calm and satisfaction, because they both enjoyed their small family and their leisure, and money had given them the opportunity to indulge their happiness in both. Ellie still liked to bake cookies and prepare dinners (her deviled turkey was mouth-watering), and there were still plenty of times when Jack enjoyed taking Randy out on New

213

Hampshire lakes in early fall, when the leaves were rusting off the trees and the still waters mirrored the far peaks of the White Mountains, to fish and talk and munch cold chicken and fruity kolaches in the crisp fresh air, and never think about Johann Cornelius or oil or chemicals all day. Those days of freedom weren't so frequent now, especially since the slump in oil prices and Harding's inauguration in March. But Jack and Randy's closeness wasn't strained; and Jack could sit back now on this bench in Riverside Park and look at his nine-year-old son with a fatherly warmth and affection that reassured him he was human, even after nine straight weeks of exhausting legal negotiations in smoky hotels and offices.

Jack hadn't changed much in twelve years. He was broader, and looked better-fed. But he still had that sharp, Mount Rushmore profile, and that brown wavy hair that had first attracted Ellie. He wore a well-cut camelhair coat with a tie belt, and a dark brown suit from Savile Row, London, but he hadn't remembered to put his shoes out for cleaning last night, and he could never tie his necktie straight. Randy had inherited the wavy hair, but there was a softness in the boy's face that always reminded Jack of Ellie, and there were times when he could put his own hands around Randy's thin wrists and marvel at his son's half-elegant, half-awkward childishness.

He didn't know what Randy was going to be when he grew up, and right now he didn't much care. But he could look across at his own black touring car parked at the curb, with his black-uniformed chauffeur, O'Hara, stretching over the mudguard to polish the hood, and he could only pray that Randy wouldn't get himself involved in the same business.

A ferry went by, strung with bunting, and blew its whistle. It reminded Jack disturbingly of that day on the SS *Galveston Bay* in 1909, as the ship had moved slowly out of Charleston harbor. Randy, who was peeling a chestnut with his thumbnails, said: "You're not going to doze off, are you, sir?"

Jack blinked at the boy, and then smiled. "No, no. I wasn't dozing off. I was just thinking."

The boy brushed chestnut shell from his navy barathea coat. He wore gray knee socks and a gray tweed cap. He frowned at Jack in concern, and said: "You weren't thinking anything awful, were you?"

214

"What makes you say that?"

"Well, sir, you had an awful face on."

"Did I? I guess I've been working too hard."

Randy bit into the soft amber flesh of his chestnut, and chewed it. A maroon-painted freight train from the P&P Railroad clanked past, carrying coal. Randy said: "Will you *always* have to work so hard? We haven't been out to the lakes for weeks and weeks."

Jack dry-washed his face with his hands. "Things have changed," he said tiredly. "These days, the oil business is really getting to work, and when the oil business gets to work, *I* have to get to work, too. Did I ever show you an oil contract? They're as thick as a Webster's dictionary, some of them, and the only difference is that they don't explain what they mean."

Randy said solemnly: "Mother thinks you ought to take a vacation, sir."

Jack grinned, and affectionately straightened the boy's cap. "I know she does. And *I* think so, too. Just as soon as things settle down, we'll take a trip to the mountains and do some skiing. Now, how would you like some tea at the Claremont?"

"Oh, yes, please," said Randy; but then he frowned again and said: "Is it the President, sir?"

"Is what the President?"

"Well, I heard you talking to Mr. Cornelius on the telephone. I didn't mean to listen but I couldn't help it. You said the President was as dumb as they come."

Jack looked at his son in surprise. It was hard to believe that only a few years ago this serious-faced small boy had been lying in his crib in their house in Tulsa, sucking a red-rubber rabbit and watching the nursery curtains rise and fall in the morning breeze. He said: "When did I say that?"

"I don't know, sir. Last week, I think. *Is* the President dumb?"

Jack leaned forward on the park bench. A long freight train with Pacific Fruit Express cars, and stock cars from Chicago, and cars with the old Chesapeake & Ohio cat symbol, and Erie Lackawanna cars, came clanging and clattering by. When it had passed, he said: "Well, the President's not dumb exactly. He was smart enough to get himself elected, and he knows how to make people like him. He's a good-looking man, you see, and he's sociable, and he talks plain English."

"But he's dumb?"

Jack grinned. "Let's put it this way. When Mr. Cornelius and I went down to Washington that time to talk about the Navy oil reserves, we were invited around to the White House to meet Mr. Harding, and we had a real pleasant chat. We talked about theater, and sports, and all about Mr. Harding's dog Laddie Boy. He cracked a few jokes, too. You couldn't help but like him."

Randy said: "So what was wrong with him?"

"Well," answered Jack, "he may be a very cheery kind of a fellow, but he's not much of a President. A President has to do more than look good and talk good and make people feel happy. It seems to me that he really doesn't know very much about anything at all, and when all the jokes are over, you can suddenly see that he's the kind of man who doesn't really have a mind of his own. In my opinion, all the thinking that's going on in Washington these days is being done by the President's old cronies from Marion, Ohio, and *they're* sharp, I can tell you. Mr. Cornelius says they're sharp as corkscrews, and twice as twisted."

Randy licked his lips against the cold. "Does that mean they tell lies?" he asked his father.

Jack shook his head. "Not in so many words. But they're always ready for what they call 'a little deal,' or 'a business proposition'—and that usually means that some of the money that should have ended up in someone else's pockets winds up in theirs."

"Then they're robbers! Are they robbers, sir?"

Jack took out his cigar case. After all the years he'd been working as chief attorney for Cornelius Oil, after all the conferences and caucuses and negotiations and understandings, after all his professional efforts to use shades of language that would make "pressure" seem like "persuasion," and "diversion of funds" appear to be "legitimate outlay," this was the first time that anyone had ever come out cold and said what inwardly he had always felt. He was working, no bones about it, amid saw-toothed tigers in business suits.

He clipped his cigar, and fumbled in his coat pocket for his lighter. He still preferred a pipe, but when you worked as intensely as he did, there wasn't time for any of that leisurely stoking and lighting up and relighting.

He said: "You can't really call them robbers, Randy. But I guess you could call them opportunists. They make the most of any

216

chance they get, and once they've sunk their jaws into something, they won't ever let go. It's a tough world, and that's all there is to it."

Randy looked up at him. He was feeling a desperate sympathy for his father that he didn't know how to express. He said: "Sir? Are you sad, sir?"

"*Sad*?" said Jack. "What do you mean by sad?"

Randy tried to think. But all he could say was: "I don't know, sir. You just seem to be sad."

"Well, I guess I'm tired, more than anything. I've just spent nine weeks solid talking oil business with the government, and believe me, *that* can make you feel sad."

Randy swung his legs aimlessly. Then he pointed out across the Hudson and said: "Look at that ferry! It's got flags and balloons!"

In spite of the cold wind, the boat was packed with people, and they could hear the faint strains of "My Rambling Rose" wafting across the water. The ferry's black-and-white-striped funnel was pouring out twists of brownish smoke, and down on the open rear deck there was dancing and singing and laughter. Jack wouldn't have been at all surprised if there was beer on board, too, although a passing police launch did nothing but toot the ferry a greeting on its whistle.

Jack said: "That looks fun, doesn't it? Maybe we should take the ferry across to the Palisades one day, and fry some bacon down on the beach."

Randy nodded, without answering. He seemed to have gone quiet, as if he felt that some of the trust between them had been taken for granted. And maybe it had, thought Jack. His son had been sensitive enough to see that he was sad, and all he'd done was fob the boy off with the same kind of crocodile smile and meaningless words that he used for the people at work.

He said: "Randy?"

"Yes, sir?"

Jack sat around on the bench, and looked at his son squarely. "Randy, if I tell you something, can you promise to keep it to yourself? It's something important—something to do with the reason I'm feeling sad. But it has to be a secret, and that's honest Injun."

Randy looked up. When he saw the boy's face, Jack wondered

217

how he'd even had the gall to ask him to keep it quiet. This is your son, he reminded himself caustically. Not Warren Harding or Johann Cornelius or Albert B. Fall. Your own son, Randy Field.

Randy said: "Honest Injun, sir."

Jack coughed. "It's to do with these people who work for the government. These people you said were robbers. Well, over the past nine weeks, I've been working on one of these 'little deals' of theirs for Mr. Cornelius, and believe me, it's one of the trickiest pieces of work you've ever heard of. It's been my job to clear up the legal side of it, so that what we're doing is all legitimate, or at least *looks* that way."

The ferry boat whistled loudly, and a shower of red balloons bobbed up off the deck and tangled with the afternoon wind. There was the sound of three cheers, almost swallowed by distance and traffic.

Jack said: "When we wrap up this deal, a lot of people stand to make a great deal of money out of it, and that includes me. I could come home with sixty or seventy thousand dollars. But what I really have to ask myself is—do I deserve the money, and do they? Or are we really swindling it from someone else?"

Randy didn't say a word, but looked at his father and knew that he was unhappy. Unhappiness, up until now, had been nothing more severe than a pedal car that had shed its wheel; or no more shoofly pie at suppertime; or perhaps the day that Mother had wept because grandfather had packed his trunk to go see God. But what Randy saw in his father today was a very different mood of unhappiness. It was (if only he could have recognized it) the distinctive pain of a man who realizes, after more than a decade of hard work, that he has probably made the wrong choice of career, and that he should have given all those years and months, all those sweltering summers and sharp winters, to some quite different occupation, something which would have brought him up to the threshold of middle age in one whole piece. Instead, Jack Field was just finding out that his loyalty and his integrity had been wrongly invested, and that the last man on earth with whom he should ever have associated himself, let alone devoted himself, was Johann Cornelius.

Jack lifted his son's chin with a gentle hand and looked at the bright eyes and the snub nose that was blanched by cold. Across the street, a flag snapped in the wind, and a motorcar indignantly hooted at a horse-drawn wagon.

"Randy," he said, "you're only nine years old, but I want you to try to follow what I tell you, because there are going to be times in your own life when you come across problems like this. Times when you have to make up your mind whether you're going to do the honest thing or the easiest thing. Times when you have to turn around and say, well, I'd like to be richer, but I'm not going to do what it takes to be that way."

Randy nodded. Jack wasn't sure whether he'd really grasped what he was trying to say, but he went on anyway. Apart from Ellie, he had nobody else to tell, and right now Ellie was worried enough about Margaret, her mother, who was hospitalized in Charleston with chronic sciatica.

Jack said: "Years ago, before you were born, and I was just started at Cornelius Oil, Mr. Cornelius asked me to buy up oil rights in a piece of land in Oklahoma. Now, it was fine land, this— all forest and field—right by the Kiamichi River in Pushmataha County. Mr. Cornelius had done a few surveys up there, and he reckoned there was good Oklahoma crude lying deep down at six thousand feet. So, I bought up the rights."

He sucked at his cigar a couple of times to keep it alight, and then he said: "The trouble was, when we came to set up drill rigs, the county authorities stepped in with a conservation order and wouldn't let us drill there. They said they wanted the land for a public park and a nature reserve, and when we appealed, the state supreme court upheld them. They said—and I guess they were partly right—that an oil town right slap in the middle of a beautiful place like that would've looked like an eyesore. Rigs and pipes and storage tanks and raw pine huts aren't the prettiest scenery you can think of."

"So what happened?" asked Randy. Jack could see that his son felt gravely honored to have his father's confidence on such an important matter, and he was clasping his cold thin knees like young Walter Raleigh listening to the wise old salt on the beach.

Jack said: "Up until President Harding was sworn in, nothing happened at all. I tried almost every year to have that conservation order changed or overturned, but the county authorities kept on saying no, and besides them there were plenty of people in

Washington under Woodrow Wilson's administration who didn't like Mr. Cornelius one bit, and they made sure we were blocked off time after time.''

A 4-8-2 freight locomotive came wuffing and clanking by. It stopped for a moment to wait for a signal, and then slowly moved off, with a lot of dripping and steaming and hissing.

Jack lowered his eyes. "Things certainly changed, though, when Mr. Harding was sworn in. You see, Mr. Wilson was always such a lonesome kind of a man. I only met him a few times, but he was sick, and he was tired, and he was still clinging to some kind of notion that we could all live in a peaceful perfect world, if only we worked ourselves hard enough. Because of that, he was always sticking his oar into business matters, and making business life harder than I guess it needed to be. But Warren Harding—well, Warren Harding is a different breed of biffalo-buffalo-bison altogether. He says he wants to help American businessmen go their own way, and all of a sudden it's all back-slapping and folksy talk, and the government is actually wheeling and dealing alongside of us."

Randy took off his gray tweed cap and scratched his short wavy hair. "Isn't that good?" he asked his father. "Don't you want wheeling and dealing?"

"Well, some of us do," answered Jack. "But, just like I said before, it depends what that wheeling and dealing is going to cost us, as far as doing the right thing is concerned. Somebody once said that President Harding was the same size and smoothness all the way around, but the way I figure it, that's only because he always turns to face you, no matter which quarter you come at him from. I've been talking to some of the men behind him for the past nine weeks, and believe me, there's nothing smooth about them."

He stuck his hands in the pockets of his camelhair coat, and he remembered the smiling, persuasive expression of Albert B. Fall, the Secretary of the Interior, leaning over a walnut table so polished that his face was reflected upside-down, like the two theatrical masks of tragedy and comedy.

Jack said, in a thick voice: "Quite soon after we met Mr. Harding in May, the Secretary of the Interior called me up and suggested that we should open talks about the land at Kiamichi. Well, those talks are what I've been doing for the past nine weeks."

"Are they going to let you drill there?" asked Randy.

"Yes, but only if we do something for *them*."

"And is that what's making you sad?"

"In a way. What we have to do in return for drilling clearance is to pay Mr. Fall, or lend him, a very large amount of money."

Randy pulled his cap back on. He said: "Is that wrong, sir? To lend him money?"

Jack nodded. "A government official is supposed to represent the interests of all the people, and if he takes money to represent one person's interests against the rest, then that's wrong. Can you see that?"

"Even if it's you?"

"Yes. Especially if it's me. And that's because I ought to know better."

Randy said: "I *think* I see what you mean."

Jack put his arm around him. "It doesn't matter if you do or you don't. One day, you'll remember this, and you'll remember what kind of a choice I had to make."

A hooter sounded from a construction site not far away, and Jack suddenly realized how chilly it was. The sun was settling into a low bank of mauve clouds over Weehawken, and the Hudson was purplish-gray now, and coldly restless. Jack stood up and held out his hand. "Come on, let's go get that tea. I could just fancy a hot raisin bun."

Hand-in-hand, father and son walked across the grass toward the touring car. O'Hara, the chauffeur, saw them coming, gave a last *hah*! of breath to the gleaming bodywork, and tugged his tunic straight. Behind him, the fading sunlight had turned Grant's Tomb into a pale Grecian stage set, as pink and chalky as almond dragées.

"We're going to the Claremont for tea," said Jack. "Then we'll make our way home."

O'Hara, his cap tucked under his arm, his carroty hair ruffled by the wind, opened the door for them; and they climbed into the leathery interior of the touring car. With his usual bland face, O'Hara remarked: "It's passably fresh, sir," and arranged a heavy plaid blanket over their knees. Then he closed the door and got up behind the wheel. It was a standing family joke that O'Hara never used a committal word when a noncommittal one would do. He had once amused Jack by describing a torrential downpour as "moistness," and even the most hilarious comedy show or song to him was only "diverting."

221

It wasn't more than a few yards to the Claremont, of course; but Randy had just gotten over the grippe, and Jack knew just how much displeasure he would have to face from Ellie if he brought the boy home with the snuffles. But as they settled back in their seats, Jack began to wonder what life would be like without chauffeured automobiles to keep them warm; without steam-heated apartments and furs and good food. Once you've shopped for your jewelry at Cartier and Van Cleef, once you've dined at the finest restaurants, once you've mixed with the most glittering names in New York society, how can you ever be satisfied with shopping at the neighborhood markets, or looking for a cheap overcoat at Macy's, or taking the trolley car with everyone else?

Jack said: "Would you miss all this, if we didn't live this way? Having a man to drive you around? Having all the food you wanted, and always staying warm?"

Randy lifted his head and looked at him. The boy was genuinely puzzled. He didn't answer, but simply shook his head, and it was only then that Jack realized he couldn't answer, because the question to him was quite meaningless. For all Randy's grown-up ways, for all his seriousness, he was plainly unable to understand that life could be led without luxury, and that those ragged boys who danced and played kazoos outside the Carlton and the Rialto picture palaces on Broadway were real boys, actual living boys, like himself. As O'Hara stuck out an arm that was rigid as a signpost, and pulled smoothly away from the curb, Jack sat back with the feeling that he was living a precarious charade, and that he was beginning to make his mimes too obvious to be mistaken. Sooner or later, Cornelius was going to turn around with that taciturn face, and challenge his loyalty; and he knew what he was going to have to say. And if Albert B. Fall pushed him any further on the Kiamichi lease, it was going to be very much sooner than later. There was a crucial meeting scheduled for November 17, at the Hotel Vanderbilt, and that was just days away. At that meeting, Fall had promised, "all would be revealed," and Jack Field was going to have to make up his mind whether he could swallow that "all" or not.

Outside the Claremont, O'Hara opened the touring-car door for them, and they stepped out. They walked inside, and a waitress showed them a table by the window, where they could sit and look out over the river, which was twilit now, and strung with lights from the Jersey shore. A ferry went past in the half-darkness, leaving V-shaped rippling shadows on the water, and the lights of the automobiles on Riverside Drive rushed past like glowing beads.

Jack ordered a milk shake, a pot of tea, and two hot raisin buns. Then he sat there and smiled at his son, who was sitting opposite with such seriousness and gravity, and wished there was some way he could tell him how much he loved him without sounding sentimental or mawkish.

Instead, he said: "It's just possible that we might have to leave New York. It depends on what happens over this oil business."

Randy said: "Will I have to leave school?"

"I'm afraid you will, if I lose my job."

"You could always get another job, sir."

"Oh, yes?"

"Well, you could drive a train."

Jack sat back and laughed. "Yes, I guess I could drive a train."

The waitress arrived with the tea and the toasted buns, and they spread the butter on thick and sat for a while in silence while they ate. Then Jack said: "In the next week, I'm going to have to make up my mind. Do I stick with my job, and Cornelius Oil, or do I stick with what's right? And I can tell you, Randy, that's not an easy choice to make, because I love you and your mother, and I always want to give you the best."

Randy said, in a matter-of-fact voice, with his mouth full of bun: "You do, sir."

"I do what?"

"You *do* always give us the best. It's like today. I've had the best day today that I've had for ages."

Jack looked at his son, and hardly knew what to say. Instead, he buttered himself another bun, and ate it with a lump in his throat. He remembered what J. Paul Getty had once said to him, out in Oklahoma, when one of their wells ran prematurely dry. Getty had poured himself a drink, downed it, and then looked around with that lemon-drop face of his, and said: "If there's one thing you shouldn't worry about, it's poverty. It's good for you, once in a while. Lord Byron once said that adversity is the first path to truth; and truth, Jack Field, is a whole sight more valuable than oil."

223

Jack reached across the tablecloth and laid his hand on Randy's. He said softly: "How would you like to go fishing tomorrow? Just you and me?"

And the way that Randy looked then made him take out his handkerchief, and wipe his eyes, and invent some story about hot buttered bun going down the wrong way.

Ellie was sitting with her feet up reading *This Side of Paradise* when the front door opened and Jack and Randy came noisily into the hallway, laughing and breathless from their obligatory race down the corridor, which the long-suffering Mrs. Vandersteen from the opposite apartment called "the elephants' Olympics."

Ellie laid down her book on the reading table and went to meet them. Jack was trying to throw his hat across the hall so that it landed on the coat peg in one toss, and Randy was hopping around with his scarf over his face pretending to be the Masked Bandit. Ellie leaned against the doorway and watched them with a tolerant smile.

Jack said: "Hi, darling. We've had a terrific time. Really terrific."

Ellie shook her head. "How you two can turn a simple thing like hanging up your hats and coats into the *circus maximus*, I'll never know."

She leaned forward and kissed Jack, and then helped Randy with his shoelaces. "Would you like a cocktail, Jack?" she asked. "And you, my freezing cold boy, what would you say to a hot malted?"

"Has Ethel gone home?" asked Jack.

"I let her go early. It's a long ride up to the Bronx."

"Okay, then," said Jack, rubbing the circulation back into his hands, and walking into the drawing room, "in that case *I'll* make the malted. I make the best malted this side of the Rocky Mountains, don't I, pardner?"

"Yes, sir!" agreed Randy, stooping to pull up his long gray socks.

"And I'll have an old-fashioned," Jack said, and he took Ellie's hand and kissed her again, more lingeringly this time, a kiss that finished up with a smile.

Their apartment was up on the ninth floor, fronting Fifty-ninth Street. Through the open drapes you could see the twinkling lights of automobiles and carriages, and the winter trees of Central Park standing in lamplit drifts of curled-up russet leaves. It was a warm apartment, with soft quiet carpets, and fine mid-Victorian antique furniture, upholstered in dark brown velvet. There was a sparkling chandelier, and velvet drapes the color of clover honey, and around the walls, apart from the English and French impressionists they loved so much, were pencil-and-ink sketches by Kandinsky and Modigliani. In the corner overlooking Fifth Avenue and the Sherry-Netherland Hotel stood Ellie's grand piano, brought up from South Carolina when they first moved to New York.

Jack went down the corridor into the kitchen and took milk out of the icebox. The kitchen was decorated in a fashionable combination of cream and pale green, and they had an electric washing machine which their maid Ethel worshiped as if it was a South Sea island god.

"Albert Fall telephoned again," said Ellie, as Jack poured the milk into a saucepan.

"Did he say what he wanted?"

"He said it wasn't urgent. He was just checking to see if you could make it on Monday. I think he wants to run over that Kiamichi contract again."

"Again? We just spent two months running over it."

"Well, call him back if you like."

Jack lit the gas flame. "I'd rather not. I'm giving myself a weekend vacation, and Johann Cornelius himself couldn't get me to leave my family right now. Where's the sugar?"

"Where it always is. You talk about Johann as if he's your lord and master."

"Well, you have to admit that he's got the right initials. What's that book like?"

Randy came in with his clockwork locomotive, and said: "Excuse me, sir, but I think the spring on my train's broken."

Jack hunkered down to take a look at Randy's bright blue tinplate engine. He wound it up with the key a couple of times, but each time there was a rasping noise, and the wheels refused to turn. Ellie said: "Jack! The milk's boiling over!"

Jack rescued the saucepan and carried it across to their new electric blender. "Don't worry, Randy. If we can't get the old loco to work, I'll buy you a new one."

Randy glanced at his mother, and then back to Jack. "Will we be able to afford it, do you think?" he said seriously.

Ellie looked at Jack in surprise. "Afford it?" she said. "A two-dollar train? Of course!"

"I won't have one if we can't afford one," said Randy. "I can always push the carriages along."

Ellie ruffled his hair. "You won't have to push the carriages, darling. We'll buy you a new train the minute the store opens up on Monday. Now, look, here's your malted. Take it along to your room and drink it there. Ethel left you some supper in the oven, and it'll be ready in a half hour."

Jack switched off the kitchen light and they went back into the drawing room. Ellie went to the cocktail cabinet to fix him an old-fashioned, while Jack eased himself into a plump button-back chair and reached for his pipe and his matches.

"What's all this about not being able to afford things?" asked Ellie. "What ideas have you been putting into Randy's head now?"

Jack shrugged. "It's nothing."

"Well, it must be something. He doesn't normally worry about the household budget."

Jack rubbed a slice of tobacco between the palms of his hands. "All I did was tell him that he shouldn't take wealth for granted."

Ellie came over with his drink.

"Why shouldn't he take it for granted?" she asked. "He's never going to have to eat stale bread and dripping, is he? There are some things you *have* to take for granted."

"I didn't mean that. But this business with Fall is getting pretty parlous."

"*Parlous*? What do you mean by that?"

Jack tried to smile. "It's really nothing to worry about."

Ellie said: "Jack?" and frowned. She came and knelt beside him, and he knew then that he'd hidden his anxiety about as well as a bearded goat under the bed. Her face was as soft as always, with those wispy coppery curls and those eyes as gray as flaked slate; but she was looking cautious and concerned, and that meant she had sensed his awkward husbandly efforts to protect her from something harsh. He averted his eyes. He always felt embarrassed when he tried to keep things from her, and he made a fussy, fiddly performance of stuffing his pipe with Virginia. Ellie was always open and fresh, and she tried daily and energetically to prove herself independent, no matter how much their men friends smiled in pained condescension, or her girl friends tittered in disapproval.

So when he attempted to protect her, like now, he felt as if he was selling her out, instead of performing a virtuous and spousely duty. Now that she was over thirty, and now that women had had the vote for over a year, Ellie had become self-possessed to the point where she could argue with Johann Cornelius over dinner until he coughed and went red and thought up some excuse to leave early; and she had once told Grover Whalen, that dapper young man who devised so many of New York's extravagant welcoming ceremonies for visiting celebrities and returning heroes, that to be greeted the Whalen way must have made many famous men suspect that they had unwittingly drowned on their way across the Atlantic, and that they were being received in the front lobby of Pandemonium. But, in spite of her assertiveness, Ellie was still graceful and pretty, and as she sat beside him in her short loose housedress of strawberry-colored silk, Jack was as much stirred by her femininity as he was by her strength.

He confessed: "It's too early to say anything, really. But I get the feeling they've maneuvered me into an impossible situation. And this week Fall's going to lift the lid off his latest mess of stew, and expect me to dip in as hearty as the rest."

"I don't understand," she said.

He lifted his eyes. "It's very simple. Albert Fall is going to push through permission for Cornelius Oil to start drilling operations at Kiamichi, provided Mr. Fall himself isn't entirely unrewarded."

"Then he wants a *bribe*?"

"Essentially, yes. But it's more complicated than that. He doesn't want to be paid out of company funds. He wants us to raise the money through some bright new scheme he's just worked out, which he's going to tell us about this week at the Hotel Vanderbilt. He wants us to run some kind of a racket that enables him to clear his money free of any suggestion of conspiracy or connivance, and pay it straight to him."

Ellie listened to this, and then reached out and brushed her husband's forehead with her fingertips, as if she was touching something very precious and fragile.

"You know me," said Jack. "You know I'm not opposed to incentives. When you're in the business, you always have to drop a dollar here and a dollar there if you want people to do you any favors. But this is worse than bribery. This is beginning to look to me like deliberate and systematic swindling."

Ellie brushed back her short copper curls, and looked worried.

227

Alongside her diamond-and-sapphire engagement ring was a wide gold wedding band engraved with the intertwined initials "J&E." She said: "What's going to happen if you say no? What if you won't bribe him?"

"Then we lose the Kiamichi lease and I lose my job."

"Johann wouldn't sack you, surely. Not after all these years."

Jack tamped down his tobacco with his broad thumb. "Johann sacked Jerry Slobodien, remember? And Jerry was with him a darned sight longer than me."

"Jerry was drunk all the time."

"That wasn't why Johann sacked him. He sacked him because he held up production at Sweetwater to rescue a trapped burro, and he lost us eight thousand barrels of oil. Johann doesn't give a nickel for your morals and scruples, you can have them or not have them and he doesn't care. But if they start losing him money, then that's the end of it. You're out."

Ellie held Jack's hand, and looked up at him anxiously. "Is that what's going to happen to you?"

Jack set down his drink. "I don't know. It depends what Fall is going to ask us to do."

"But you've gotten involved in some pretty greasy things before, haven't you? I thought they were part and parcel of the oil business. There was that awful Sinclair proxy business you set up in Washington, wasn't there? What makes this one so different?"

Jack pulled a face. "I don't know. I guess what really shocks me is the way that the government is giving such barefaced encouragement to anybody who believes in making a fast buck, and the way they make damned sure that a good share of every fast buck ends up in their own pockets. I'm not an idealist, Ellie. You know that. And I'm not an innocent, either. I've done a few legal deals that would have made my father's hair fall out, especially when we were having all that trouble with Woodrow Wilson. But I believe in drawing a line somewhere, and I think I believe in government that's at least reasonably honest."

He paused for a moment, and then he said quietly: "I guess I've compromised myself just once too often, too. A time does eventually come when all the dollars in the world can't pay you back for your lost integrity."

Ellie stood up. She was still his petite, pretty Ellie; although there was an over-thirty softening in her skin which reminded him of Margaret Jackson, her mother.

He said: "I didn't want to tell you until I knew something for certain. But the way Fall's been working these past nine weeks . . . well, I'm pretty certain he's cooked up a dilly."

"Jack," she said gently, "you could have told me."

He rubbed his eyes. "I could have, and I guess I should have. But what with your mother—"

"My mother's my mother. Nobody could ever replace her. But you're my husband."

"How is your mother?" he asked.

"She's feeling much better, as a matter of fact. I had a telephone call from Dr. Shura today."

"Well, that's good news. At least something's going right."

She said: "We won't have to leave the apartment, will we?"

He shrugged. "I don't know. Not right away. But if I leave Cornelius Oil and strike out on my own, it's going to take a big chunk of capital and we're going to have to cut out the chauffeur-driven limousines and the big parties. I'm a rich man, Ellie. I guess I must be richer now than Johann Cornelius was when I first met him. But I'm only going to stay rich if I get my money working, and that means much more creative investment, and much more financial risk. The bank balance is going to take a heavy knock without that annual two hundred thousand coming in like clockwork."

Ellie thought of Randy's tinplate locomotive. "Clockwork breaks down sometimes, Jack, but the railroads keep on running."

Jack smiled. "Randy said I could always take a job as a railroad engineer."

"Maybe that's not such a bad idea. I met that young Daniel Forster a couple of weeks ago. The shooting star of P&P Railroad. He said they were looking for good legal executives and management."

Jack sighed. "I feel like an out-of-work vagrant already."

"You could always start a private practice, like you were going to do when you were younger."

"It's too soon to think about that," he said tiredly. "If there's any way I can work around this problem, instead of meeting it head-on, then I will."

"But you don't think you can, do you, my darling?"

He stared across the room for a moment, clenched in his armchair like a man on the Rocket-to-the-Moon ride at Coney Island. Then he said: "No, I don't believe I can."

She smiled, but she wasn't very happy. "Well," she said with a tight little breath, "it looks like we'll have to start economizing."

He said: "Would you miss it very much? New York?"

She nodded. "I'm very happy here, Jack. I guess it's the kind of city where a woman can do things and be things that nobody would tolerate anyplace else. And then there's all the parties and the dances and the dinners. I'd miss the theaters, too."

He looked down at his knees. They seemed to belong to somebody else altogether, and he half-wondered if he still had the power to walk. He said in a throaty voice: "I could always tell Albert Fall yes."

She turned. "And come back home without your honesty? Just for the sake of parties and dances? I wouldn't let you do it!"

Ellie came and perched herself lightly on his lap, and kissed his forehead with three kisses. Then she looked right in his eyes and said: "I married you because you were straight as Abraham Lincoln, and good-looking as Rudolph Valentino, and a better lawyer than Arthur Garfield Hays and Clarence Darrow rolled into one. Don't you ever disappoint me by saying yes to a carpetbagger like Fall unless you know you're really doing the right thing."

He lowered his eyes. "You'd miss the jewelry, too, wouldn't you? And having your new fur coats every fall."

She placed one finger across his lips and shushed him. "I love you," she whispered. "That's all that counts."

He felt tears in his eyes even though he didn't want to show how worried he was. She brushed them away for him, and hugged him close, and said: "Don't you ever fret about money, my darling. If I have to live in a cabin in the Blue Ridge Mountains, and cook succotash every night but Sunday, when it's roast raccoon—then just as long as you're there, and Randy's there too, then I'll be happy. I might even learn to cook up white lightning."

He couldn't help laughing through his tears. "My wife, the bootlegger."

She stroked his forehead, and kissed him again, and then said: "You mustn't underestimate me, you know. I love you, and I think I can share your worries as well as your good times. If we end up with our pants hanging out at the back, well, that's too bad. At least people will know that we're honest."

"I don't know. I'm beginning to wonder what's honest and what isn't."

She shook her head. "You know what's honest. *You're* honest. You always try to do the best thing and the fairest thing, and the only time I've really seen you act tricky is when it won't hurt anyone at all. Oh, and crosswords. You're always tricky when you fill in crosswords."

He picked up his matches. "Well, if I haven't acted tricky up until now, this could be my big chance, right?"

She plucked his pipe out of his mouth. "Don't light it now. Come to bed."

He said: "What? What about Randy?"

She grinned and tugged at his arm. "Randy's playing with his fort. He's going to be hours."

"Ellie, I come home and tell you my whole career's on the line, and you want to go to bed?"

"Don't be so conventional! Don't you think it's the best tonic?"

"Why, sure, but—"

Ellie pulled him upright. "Come on, then."

They walked arm-in-arm through to the corridor, and peeked through the doorjamb into Randy's playroom. Randy was kneeling on the floor, his malted milk forming a crinkly skin, while he set out dozens of lead soldiers in ranks of four. Jack circled his arm around Ellie and whispered: "Looks like Bull Run. That should take at least another half hour. He's pretty short on Yankees."

Silently, with that slow hurry that only lovers know, they went to their own bedroom and locked the door behind them. It was a high-ceilinged room, with a wide four-poster bed hung with a figured cream silk canopy like a Moorish tent. The rugs were thick and white and soft, and all around there were mirrors in gilt ormolu frames in which their faces were reflected like a gallery of gentle portraits. Outside the window, they could hear the faint sounds of juddering taxicabs waiting for fares from the Savoy-Plaza, and the leisurely clopping of horse-drawn hansoms; and someone in another apartment was playing "I'm Always Chasing Rainbows" on a Victrola. But Jack and Ellie were quiet within their love for each other, and they stood for a moment and kissed in the shaded light from the bedside lamps like a honeymoon couple at some grand hotel in Europe.

Jack kissed Ellie's forehead, and eyes, and lips, and he held her close, feeling her warm skin through the thin slippery silk of her

231

dress, his eyes lowered, so that all he could see was a close-up of her pink moistened lips, her teeth just parted by the tip of her tongue.

He said: "How come it's always like the first time with you?"

She butted him very gently and affectionately with her forehead. "Because it always is. And because each time is always the best."

"You think I'm crazy, don't you?"

"Why should I?"

"I don't know. For the first time, we've gotten ourselves a government that wants to bend over backwards to help us. And all I can do is throw myself off the edge of a cliff because I'm so damned burdened with principles."

She outlined his lips with the tip of her finger. Her gray eyes were staring into the future, or maybe the past. She said: "Would you be happy if you said yes to Fall?"

He shook his head.

For a moment she looked at him with her head on one side, and then she smiled and said: "In that case, what the hell are you so worried about?"

The musical fanatic in the next apartment put on "Smiles," and Jack took Ellie's hand and foxtrotted around the bedroom with her, humming in an off-key tenor. He circled her around to the bed, and then plunged sideways onto the white brocade bedspread, like a man pitching himself into the surf, and he pulled her over with him. They bounced and laughed, and he lay chuckling on his back while she straddled him and kissed him all over his face.

"Freud says that everything we do has its roots in sex." Ellie grinned. "Perhaps you're acting so firm and upright at work because you're so firm and upright at home."

They looked at each other for one half-serious moment, and then burst out laughing again. He wrapped his arms around her, and they kissed with an urgency that started off playful and grew more and more passionate. He felt her warm saliva slide from the side of his mouth onto the bedspread. Then he reached down and touched her thigh, where her thin dress had ridden high, and he caressed all around the firm rounded curve of her bottom, until she bent forward, and gasped in his ear.

They didn't even undress. In that elegant Central Park bedroom in 1921, in a dim unfocused light that transformed them into soigné fantasy characters from a White Star poster for first-class travel aboard the *Majestic*, with the crackling strains of "Dardanella" and "Hindustan" faint in the next apartment, and the air delirious with perfume, they made love with an erotic grace that was rare even for them. She arched over him, her back curved, her Vaselined eyelids glistening, her mouth open; and beneath her he lay with his muscles tensed in the lamplight, and his face tightened into the expression of a man who hears or sees or touches something so close to perfection that he can hardly bear it. Sometimes they whispered or cried out when they made love, but this evening they were almost silent. Ellie moved up and down on Jack, and what she felt for him then didn't need sounds or words. What he had said tonight hadn't frightened her, as he had thought it might. Instead, it had given her fresh faith that he was a man of great honesty and self-discipline—qualities which she had begun to suspect might be slipping out of his grasp at Cornelius Oil. So the rigidity she felt inside her was more than physical. It was the hardness of a man who could act like a man, and she loved him for it. He held her waist tight in his strong hands as he began to approach his climax—so tight that he hurt her. But all she craved was oneness with him, closeness with him, and she forced herself down on him harder and harder until he was touching her sensitive womb with every thrust, and she winced with the strange painful pleasure of it.

They came so close, for just a few dark and dazzling moments, that Ellie could feel the tears in her eyes. She didn't know where her own body ended and Jack's began. It seemed that he was her and she was him, and that she could blissfully spend the rest of her life with his penis sheathed inside her, and his hairy testicles hanging between her own thighs like odd proud jewelry. But then her mind blinked—like looking into the black back of a Kodak camera and pressing the shutter—and she knew that they were almost through, almost there, and she was still desperately trying to cling on to the closeness as Jack dug his fingernails into the soft flesh over her hips and said: "Ellie, oh Ellie. Oh, Ellie," and his warmth flowed into her in three quick pulses.

It was a long time before they opened their eyes, and when they did, they felt as if they'd just returned to their apartment from a three-month trip abroad. They lay side by side, kissing and stroking each other, and talking in whispers. They talked about Randy, and about a winter vacation in Florida, and about Johann Cornelius. Ellie, lying back, said: "Do you think Johann really loves Hester? I always get the impression they're pretty remote from each other. I mean, remoter than us."

233

Jack twined her hair around his finger. "It's impossible to say. In any case, it's none of my business."

Ellie propped herself up on her elbow. "You know what the Kubceks think, though, don't you?"

"No, I don't know what the Kubceks think. What do the Kubceks think?"

"Well, Mrs. Kubcek at least is quite certain that Johann has another woman. A secret mistress tucked away someplace."

Jack shook his head. "There's no chance of that. He doesn't have the time. In any case, I don't think he loves anyone or anything except himself, and money."

"Perhaps he had a passionate love affair when he was younger."

"Sure. And perhaps you can run automobiles on peanut butter."

Ellie picked up a pillow and playfully hit him with it. "You never take anything seriously," she said.

He held her tight, and kissed her. "I take Johann Cornelius very seriously," he told her. "Because if I didn't, I'd wind up more than jobless, and more than broke."

"What do you mean—more than jobless?"

"It's difficult to say. But Johann's one of these people who bring out the best in you and the worst in you, both. He can make you feel that you can do anything, make any amount of money, conquer the world in five minutes flat. But he also makes you feel as if you've got to sell yourself out to do it. I think he knows what morals are, although some people believe that he doesn't. But he seems to believe that if you're going to be rich, and stay rich, you have to change your idea of morality to suit your financial ambitions, if you see what I mean."

Ellie sat up. The curve of her breasts, limned with light from the bedside lamp, held Jack's eye while he spoke.

He said: "Johann makes you understand that nothing is sacred and nothing is safe—that's if you *really* want to be rich. Maybe you're right, and he did have a passionate love when he was young. But if he did, he's buried it under ten tons of concrete and he's not letting it out. He's fond of Hester, sure. But I always get the feeling that he married her to bear his heirs and to run his household and to walk into official dinners on his arm, and for not much else."

Ellie snuggled against his chest. "And how do I know you didn't marry *me* to do that?"

Outside, in the study and the sitting room, their telephones began to ring in jangling chorus. Jack kissed her, and answered: "Simple. If that was all I'd married you for, I'd hop out of bed right this instant and pick up that phone. As it is . . ."

He pushed her gently back on the pillow, and lifted himself over her, breathing as he did so: "Ellie . . ."

On the morning of November 17, 1921, Jack took a taxi down to Wall Street to have a talk with Johann Cornelius. He was due at the Hotel Vanderbilt later, for the oil meeting which Albert Fall had described as "essential and crucial." He wore a brown overcoat of marled tweed, and a brown hat with a wide band. He was still handsome, but he was pale, as if he needed to take a few weeks' vacation in the sun.

Johann was sitting behind his desk in his dark oak-paneled office looking morose. He had been trying to float a new bond issue in cooperation with the House of Morgan, but the financiers were proving picky about the terms of the issue and the total capitalization required. He greeted Jack with a snappy "What time do you call this?" and shuffled papers around as if he was tired of the whole business.

Jack said: "It's only eight. Did you expect me earlier?"

Johann didn't answer. He was wearing an unusually severe black suit and a white gates-ajar collar. Behind him, on the office wall, was a photograph of the Texan town of Amarero, now one of the most industrialized oil centers in the whole state, with rigs and storage tanks and a brand-new cracking plant. A leafy house plant languished on the window ledge.

"I'm pretty sure that Fall's going to come up with the big one today," remarked Jack. "I have all the papers on Kiamichi here if you want to see them."

Johann tapped his gold propelling pencil on the green leather of his desktop. "I wish those Bolsheviks had blown up the whole damned building," he said petulantly.

"You mean the Morgan Building?" asked Jack. "Are they giving you trouble with the Seal Beach issue?"

"You name something they're *not* giving me trouble with."

Jack sat down opposite in a comfortable brown club chair. He never understood why Johann didn't leave his stocks and bonds negotiations to himself and the rest of their legal and financial staff. Apart from the fact that Jack had several close friends at Morgan, he was on good terms with William H. Remick, the president of the Stock Exchange, and he could have handled the Seal Beach issue with a great deal more diplomacy and speed than Johann himself. It was a complicated ruse to whip up over seventy million dollars for a quick Cornelius expansion program, and it needed both timing and subtlety. Maybe the only real difference was that Johann, despite his financial thuggery, would probably wind up with better investment performances than any of his staff, but as Nathan Frank, Jack's young deputy, said: "Being asked to buy bonds by Johann Cornelius is like being asked by your rabbi to buy tickets to the B'nai B'rith dance. You just don't say no."

Jack said: "They'll come around. They just need to feel they're being magnanimous."

"It seems to me that there's too much damned magnanimity around and not enough sound investment. I'm going to have another try at Western Banks while Morgan's are sitting on their hands."

Jack shrugged. "That's up to you. In any case, this meeting at the Vanderbilt is a little more urgent."

"Who's attending?"

"Harry Sinclair, for certain, and James O'Neil. They've been thick with Fall since way back when."

"Anybody from Standard?"

"Bob Stewart probably."

Johann rubbed his eyes with his knuckles. "It sounds to me like Albert's setting up some kind of mutual-benefit society. What does it sound like to you? All the old gang who dug deep in their pockets for Harding and Cox last year, paid back with interest."

"I think it's a little more than that. Fall's been taking a pretty unnatural interest in oil."

"There's nothing unnatural about an interest in oil."

Jack picked out a sheaf of paper bound with red legal ribbon. "It depends which oil it is, and what form your interest takes. Supposing, for instance, we were talking about oil which was being held in reserve for the U.S. Navy."

"Supposing we were? There are three naval reserve fields, aren't there? Buena Vista, California, Elk Hills, California, and Teapot Dome, Wyoming. So what?"

Jack looked at his shoes and wished that he'd remembered to

236

have them polished. "Well, let me put it this way. Under whose jurisdiction would you expect these naval reserves to fall?"

"Are you playing games?"

"Not at all. You'd expect them to fall under the jurisdiction of the Secretary of the Navy, right?"

Johann said nothing. His hard, cautious expression was enough. It told Jack Field that what he was saying had better be good, or else. At forty-eight years old, Johann was probably at his most abrasive, at his most competitive, and he had the harsh maturity of granite. Jack, like everyone else in Cornelius Oil and its associated industries, had often skinned his hands against the granite, and he knew how uncompromising it was.

Jack said: "During May, President Harding transferred custody of all these naval oilfields from the Secretary of the Navy to the Secretary of the Interior. No particularly cogent reason was given."

Johann raised an eyebrow. "So the oil is now at the disposal of Albert Fall—every oilman's friend?"

Jack pulled a wry face. "*Some* oilmen's friend. Not so much ours. I still think he bears a grudge about your campaign contribution, and what you said about Hughes being a sheep in sheep's clothing."

"I like to be apolitical," said Johann, pronouncing the word "apolitical" with peculiar relish. "I don't like my business to go in and out with the political tide. That's all."

"Well," said Jack, "whatever Albert Fall felt about you in the past, he's obviously going to forgive you now. From all of our talks on Kiamichi, it's pretty clear that he's prepared to be nice to us if we're prepared to be nice to him. Just *how* nice, and what we have to do in return, remains to be seen."

Johann got out of his chair and went to the window. Through the grimy rain-washed glass he could just see the corner of the Morgan Building, and the Corinthian pillars of the Stock Exchange. The Morgan Building was still pitted and scarred from the window-sash weights that had been blasted into it by last year's anarchist explosion.

He said: "Albert's playing some kind of game. Now, what do you think it is?"

Jack lifted out a closely typewritten report. "I had my people give me a rundown on these naval oil reserves. They were set aside in 1909 to give the Navy a protected supply of fuel oil in case of war. The trouble was, though, that several oil companies, including us, took up leases right on the edge of the government fields, Elk Hills in particular, and we've been pumping up oil that, very likely, comes from underneath Navy land.''

Johann turned around, his hands clasped behind his back. "What was the trouble? They could have put offset wells along the boundary of their land to neutralize the drainage. That's what *we* do.''

"*They* did, too. But now something else has come up. The military are getting themselves all jittery about a war with Japan, and they don't just want their oil protected, they want it up out of the ground where they can lay their hands on it. That means that Fall is probably going to ask for competitive private bidders to pump up the oil, keeping some of it back as a royalty to meet the needs of the Navy.''

Johann thought about this, and then nodded. "So Albert has at least three plum leases on his hands?'' he asked.

"That's right.''

"And he's trying to set up some kind of back-scratching society of oil executives, with the probable prize of Elk Hills or Teapot Dome or Buena Vista to whichever executive scratches his back the best?''

"That's the way I see it.''

Johann tapped his pencil against his teeth. "Well,'' he said at last, "what line are you doing to take when Albert puts this proposition in front of you?''

Jack took out his folded handkerchief and patted his forehead. It seemed desperately hot in Johann's office, and he would have done anything to take his coat off. He said uncertainly: "That's why I came to see you. I need to know what line *you* want to take.''

Johann looked at him. "You're my legal adviser,'' he pointed out. "You tell me.''

"I can't—not until I know what Fall's going to suggest. I just wanted to know how far you were prepared to go along with him.''

"You mean, would I like the Teapot Dome lease, or the Elk Hills lease?''

"Well, yes.''

Johann nodded. "Of *course* I'd like them. They're choice tracts of oil-bearing land.''

238

"Even if we have to get involved in something less than strictly legal?"

Johann went back to his chair. "Has Albert suggested anything illegal so far?"

"Not in so many words. He keeps talking about 'mutual interests,' but he hasn't made it plain what these really are."

"Then he hasn't?"

"No."

"In that case," said Johann, "I can only presume that he's not going to suggest anything illegal now. But it's up to you. You're the business lawyer, and this is one particular area where I bow to your judgment. You go along there today and work it out for yourself. Just make sure that whatever you decide, it's in the best possible interests of Cornelius Oil."

"Supposing he wants an immediate answer?"

"Then give him one. But make certain it's the right one."

Jack took a shallow breath. "That's what I wanted to know," he said unhappily. "What *is* the right one?"

Johann sat back and inspected Jack through slitted eyelids. "The right answer," he said dryly, "is the answer that you can bring back here and have a raise for."

"And the wrong answer?"

Johann shook his head, and gave a small smile. "I don't threaten people, as a rule," he remarked. "Threatening people lets them know where they stand, and that inhibits their performance."

Jack looked down at the heap of paper on his knees. Slowly, thoughtfully, he began to collate it and tidy it up.

"All right," he said at last. "Shall I call you when it's over?"

Johann glanced at the clock above the door. "No. I'm out of the office later this afternoon, talking to Fishman's. Meet me at the Gotham at five sharp."

Jack stood up. He felt as if he'd been sent out with a rolled-up copy of *The Wall Street Journal* to do battle with mythical monsters. He cleared his throat, as if he was going to say something else, but he knew that he had nothing else to say, and he turned around and left the office with his head bent in thought. Johann's receptionist called after him: "Your hat, Mr. Field! Your hat!"

During the afternoon, pale sun penetrated through to Johann's office, and he laid down his pencil and went to the window again.

For some reason that he couldn't quite put his finger on, he'd been feeling restless lately, out of sorts. It wasn't just that business was going through a difficult time, and that the market was alternately boisterous and suicidal. It was something to do with himself, a feeling that he had left some decision about his life undecided.

He had been married to Hester Forbes Cornelius for almost ten years now, and their anniversary was approaching. He thought he might buy her ten exceptional diamonds to mark the occasion. He was contented with his marriage, and proud of his three children, and yet he felt as if going home to Hester when business was through, dining with her, talking to her, even sleeping with her, was an oddly unimportant part of his life. She was there to soothe him, and there to run his household, and there to make sure that they attended the right parties with the right people. She knew about French impressionists, Mozart, and the care of opera hats. She had decorated the house lavishly and expensively and in taste that had aroused the admiration of *Ladies' Home Journal*. She knew diplomats and socialites and celebrities, and spoke with equal confidence on H. G. Wells's *Outline of History*, the best-selling book of the year, as she did on art or education or business. But, to Johann, it was like a shadow theater, this marriage; an experience that comforted and entertained him, and yet which he never seemed to live in the round. Whenever he talked about himself and Hester, it always sounded as if he were talking about another couple whom he happened to know quite well. This wasn't because he didn't feel affection for Hester. She was pretty and self-assured, and she had a particular knack for making him feel both masculine and reasonably cultured, and less like a rough-cut robber baron. He was more confident in her company, and more likable, than at almost any other time. But he still suspected that real life had come to a twilit close in 1903, when Carina had fallen from the sixth-story window on Fifty-fifth Street and Beatrice had deserted him; and that every day of marriage and child-rearing and dinner parties that had happened since then had been acted out by a well-paid extra who looked and spoke exactly like Johann Cornelius, and who kept his outward life going while the genuine Johann Cornelius still sat in the empty waiting room of 1903, with the magazines growing older and dustier on the table, hoping that time and fate would prove to be nothing more than dreams, or mistaken calendars, and that the door would open and there would stand Beatrice.

240

He could never explain, even to himself, how much he had adored Beatrice. He was prepared to admit that what he had loved, what he still loved, was a hazy and romantic picture of Beatrice which she had never actually lived up to. But if she had made him happy, what did it matter?

As he stared sadly out of his window, watching the sun behind the gray November clouds, he wondered if his relentless appetite for money and power had really been responsible for what had happened to Beatrice and Carina.

His desk telephone rang, and he went over to pick it up. His receptionist said: "Mr. Cornelius? Your wife's here. She wants to know if you have five minutes."

He looked down at his desk. There were heaps of letters to sign, and two thick folders of stock assessments to go through. But he said: "Okay. Show her in."

Hester came through the door in a low-belted camelhair coat and a small cloche hat. She came over and kissed him, fragrant with Chanel, and put down her big red-and-black snakeskin bag on the chair.

"I've been shopping," she said. "I thought I'd call by and ask you what you wanted for dinner. The Daughertys aren't coming over till nine."

He said: "Oh. Well, whatever you like. I seem to remember that Mal likes his lobster."

Hester made a pencil note in a small diary. "Lobster, that's right. And maybe some entrecote steak. You look thoughtful."

"What?"

"I said you look thoughtful."

"Oh. Well, I have been."

Hester gave him a funny look, and sat on the edge of his desk. Physically, Hester and Johann were an ill-matched couple. Where he was beefy and built on a large scale, she was small and detailed and very pretty. She had a heart-shaped face, a long and graceful neck, and her hair was shingled. Her eyes gave her most of her character, because they were round and brown and enormous, and her dinner guests would gaze into them mesmerized until she looked away, and then they'd wonder what on earth she'd been talking about.

She was the elder daughter of Mr. and Mrs. James Forbes, originally of Wakefield, Massachusetts, and in her day she had been the most eligible young lady in New York. Her father, a humorous and inventive man of Scottish descent, had made an appreciable fortune out of royalties for his patents for color-printing machinery, and although he lived in Manhattan, he still farmed in Wakefield as a profitable hobby. He had been well-heeled enough to send Hester to private college, as well as dispatching her to Zurich for a year to finish her off.

Her second (and romantically decisive) meeting with Johann had been quite accidental. Johann, against his will, had been dragged off by Latham T. Jolley, the Minnesota mineral billionaire, to join a weekend party at his "hideaway," as he called it, in Norwalk, Connecticut. If it hadn't been for an imminent contract signing worth eighteen million dollars, Johann wouldn't have even contemplated going. But, as it was, he spent Saturday and Sunday pacing the corridors and reception rooms of Jolley's distinctly unjolly mansion, trying to feel that he was doing his duty, and drinking too much brandy.

He had come across Hester in the library, sitting in a big leather armchair asleep. It had been a warm afternoon in 1910. The coincidence had intrigued him so much that he had sat himself opposite her, and watched her as she slept, and thought how pretty she was in her rose-colored day dress, with her hair tightly braided and pinned up. The dusty sunlight had crossed the room from the skylight above them, and gradually she had woken up, and seen him sitting there, relaxed in his chair, his pale blue eyes regarding her fixedly from over the hand that he held in front of his face. He could even remember her first words to him. "Oh," she had said, "it's you. Didn't you know that only married people should watch each other sleep?"

She was nineteen and he was rich. He wasn't like the New York boys, either. He was blunt and direct in business and he knew what he wanted, although he had a baffling evasiveness about him, too, which intrigued her. He never spoke about his background, nor his past loves, but she felt sure that she could winkle it all out of him in time.

Perhaps they had fallen in love. It appeared that way. There were visits to concerts, where Hester sat with eyes sparkling and Johann sat beside her so rigid that he could have been an advertisement for someone's patent starch. There were weekends at Wakefield, and these days Hester often leafed through the albums of sepia photographs, showing Johann in his shirtsleeves poling a punt, or Johann sitting cross-legged on the grass, squinting into the sun as he ate a sandwich.

That, in any event, was their courtship, and their marriage had seemed inevitable. There wasn't much passion, but it seemed right that culture should marry money, since by their union both could be enriched. They had a set-piece wedding in New York, with showers of confetti, and an organist who believed that sheer volume was the essence of good music. Afterward, as they were driven away by carriage, Johann had kissed Hester and said: "You're going to make me a wonderful wife," and he was right, she had. When they had come home, she had established herself as chatelaine of all his houses, particularly Lynwood's Island, and with an extraordinary sense of realism for a girl so young, she had counted herself lucky that she was rich, and that Johann was fond of her, even if he wasn't a tiger.

Their sex life was proper, and quite polite, and involved the lifting up of nightshirts and nightdresses. It wasn't untypical of 1911, though, and it was quite enough to produce Roderick, and then John, and then Hope. Roderick was at private preparatory school now, seven years old with plump legs, and poor at games. John was four, and serious, and Hope was two, a willful little girl in flounces and bows.

Johann said: "I may be late this evening. I have a meeting with Fishman's."

"Is that why you're thoughtful?"

"Not really. I was thinking about us."

"Us?" asked Hester, raising an eyebrow. "What do you mean by 'us'?"

"Well, you and me."

Hester took out another notebook and tried to decide what wines she should order up from the cellar that evening. "I hope it was something flattering," she said, ticking off a Pouilly Fuissé.

Johann shrugged. "It wasn't anything much. I suppose I was just trying to work out if we'd had a good marriage or not."

Hester put down her book. She gave a short, uncertain laugh.

"I don't know what you mean," she told him. "Of course we've had a good marriage. We still do."

He came over and stood close to her. "But you are happy?" he asked her. "You don't feel I haven't been loving enough?"

"Of *course* not," she said lightly. "Why, what on earth brought this on?"

"I don't know. I was just beginning to wonder if I was neglecting you."

"Of course you're not neglecting me. What woman could have half what I've got?"

He sat down in his chair. "I didn't mean that kind of neglect. I meant as far as love was concerned. I sometimes feel that I haven't been paying enough attention to you. Not the right kind of attention."

"My dear, if it's bed you're talking about—"

"No, no, I don't mean bed. I mean, don't you sometimes feel that there's something between us—like a window, or a closed blind—and that all we can see of each other is silhouettes?"

Hester looked quite mystified. Johann didn't often speak about his emotions, and the trouble was that whenever he did, she couldn't understand a word of what he was saying. She twisted her mouth into an odd little smile and said: "Hmph."

Johann rested his head against his hand. "You're right, I guess. Maybe I've been cooped up in this office too long. I'm going stir crazy."

"You could take a vacation."

"Where? I don't fancy sailing. The last damned ship I went on sank right under me. The good ship *Galveston Bay*."

Hester glanced at him archly. "You could fly."

"Fly? You're joking."

"No, I'm not, actually. I've been thinking it's time you had your own airplane."

Johann lifted his head. "I beg your pardon?"

"I said, 'I've been thinking it's time you had your own airplane.'"

"What do I need an airplane for? What's wrong with trains?"

"They're slow, that's what's wrong with them. Anyway, an airplane would suit you—suit us. You could fly on up to Lynwood's Island after work, and it would only take you a half hour."

"Hester . . ."

She smiled, and fixed her big brown eyes on him. "You know it makes sense, Johann. You could get around the country in a tenth of the time it takes you now."

Johann pulled a face. "Well," he said, "I'm not sure. I hear people get pretty airsick."

She shook her head. "Haven't I always been right?"

"Well, sure, but—"

"Wasn't I right about taking over Haymann Drugs after the additive scandal? And wasn't I right about buying the *Kronprinz* from the Navy? And wasn't I right about Knut Insurance?"

244

Johann couldn't help grinning. "Very well," he said quietly, "I have a wife who's always right. Maybe I should retire and let my wife take over the business."

Hester looked at him, and he wasn't sure whether she was serious or not. "I don't have your strength," she said plainly. "And I don't have your determination."

"Hester . . ." he interrupted.

Hester pecked him on the cheek, put her bag over her arm, and went to the door. But as she was about to leave, she said: "Johann . . . there's nothing wrong is there?"

He shook his head. "No. I guess I just need a break."

"Well, I'll start finding out about your airplane. That will give you something to look forward to. Maybe Curtiss or Ford or one of those people. You can give it to yourself as an anniversary present."

He said: "Okay," and then she left, waving to his receptionist on the way out. She took the elevator down to the street, and Johann's long black limousine was waiting for her, attended by their patient chauffeur, Carl, the same white-faced Carl who had escaped with Johann and Jack Field from the SS *Galveston Bay*. It was only when Carl had closed the door for her, and the car had moved away from the curb, that she allowed herself to sigh and look out of the window at the crowded New York sidewalks with an expression that could have even been pain.

Jack Field walked from the Vanderbilt to the Gotham, in spite of the cold. It was dark now, and he turned the collar of his tweed overcoat up against the night wind. All around him, New York was busy with home-going traffic, and the sidewalks were crowded with young stenographers leaving their offices, most of them fashionably dressed in short skirts and coats, with striped woolens and long scarves. Hot-chestnut and bagel vendors stood on the street corners, shuffling their feet and prodding their fumy coke. There was a sharp smell of winter in the air.

Jack reached Fifty-fifth Street, and went up the front steps of the Gotham. Only twenty feet away, in 1903, Carina had lain dying on the sidewalk, a Carina who would remain forever fourteen years old. Jack pushed his way through the engraved glass doors and crossed the lobby to the front desk. He said: "Mr. Cornelius here? Tell him it's Mr. Jack Field."

The desk clerk rang up to Johann's suite. Then he said to Jack: "All right, sir. You can go on up."

In the elevator, Jack watched his face in the small dim mirror. He had already decided what he was going to do, but it was curious to watch himself doing it. Reflected in store windows along the streets, glimpsed in the windows of passing taxis, and now in this elevator mirror at the Gotham, was the face of a man who had probably made up his mind years and years ago that business was not the divine mission that Dr. Cadman was professing it to be, and that businessmen had no more right to consider themselves the chosen vessels of the Lord than anyone else, no matter how many jobs they created, or bonuses they gave, or babies they kissed.

Jack was not a Red, and never could be. But what he had heard today at the Vanderbilt Hotel was more than sufficient to persuade him that, if such corruption had to exist, then he would rather not be part of it. If that meant his resignation, he could make enough money as a criminal counsel, or as a family attorney, or as anything else at all. But even if there was no other way to make a living than to accept the proposals that Albert Fall had come out with during today's meeting, then Jack would have preferred to panhandle on the Bowery rather than say yes.

The elevator stopped. Jack stepped out and walked along the overheated corridor to Johann's suite. He pressed the bell.

Johann came to the door himself, in a bottle-green bathrobe. His legs were bare, and he smelled of soap. Jack said: "I hope I haven't disturbed you."

Johann closed the door behind him. "Not at all. I just finished a meeting with Fishman's, and I felt like a bath. Do you want a drink? You look half-frozen."

"An old-fashioned would go down well."

"Help yourself. The bar's over there."

Johann went and sat down on the wide velour settee while Jack took off his scarf and his overcoat and propped his briefcase against the side of a chair. The suite was dimly lit and hushed, with thick mushroom-colored carpets and closed drapes. Two cigar butts were crushed out in a modern stainless-steel ashtray.

"Well, then," said Johann, as Jack poured out his cocktail. "How did it go?"

Jack shook Angostura in his drink, and stirred it. He could see half of his own face in the mirror in front of him, and Johann's white, blond-haired leg. He said: "I think you're probably going to ask me to quit."

There was a short silence. Johann sat up and reached for his

246

brandy. He said: "I don't ask people to quit unless I have a good reason. You know that."

"What about Jerry Slobodien?" asked Jack, knowing that he was reckless to ask.

Johann glanced at him sharply, then shrugged. "Jerry was a special case. Jerry was cheating for years. And, besides, he didn't take it personal."

Jack turned around. "Well," he said, "that's as may be."

Johann watched him. "Why don't you just tell me what you did that makes it so probable that I'm going to sack you?"

Jack sat down in one of the wide, soft armchairs and loosened his tie.

"No, don't tell me," put in Johann before Jack could speak. "You said no to Albert. Albert put something up and you turned it down. He offered you Teapot Dome, and you turned it down."

"Not quite," said Jack, "but nearly."

Johann swallowed brandy. "You'd better tell me, in that case."

Jack nodded. "I'd kind of guessed what was going to happen. The trouble was, Fall never trusted us as much as he trusted Sinclair and O'Neil and all of those others. We were too . . . well, non-political."

Johann smiled when Jack said that, but he didn't interrupt.

Jack set down his drink. "As far as I can make out, it's going to work this way," he explained. "Humphreys has agreed to sell out of his Mexia field thirty-three million three hundred and thirty-three thousand barrels of oil, at a dollar-fifty a barrel."

Johann frowned. "What's wrong with that?"

"Nothing. Except that he doesn't sell it to Sinclair Consolidated or Prairie. He sells it to the Continental Trading Company of Canada."

"The what?"

"That's just what *I* was asking. But wait. The Continental Trading Company of Canada then resells the same oil to Sinclair Consolidated and Prairie Oil, but at a dollar-seventy-five a barrel, and that makes a profit of twenty-five cents a barrel."

Johann's face went rigid. "Twenty-five cents multiplied by thirty-three million is what?"

"Albert Fall worked it out for us. Eight million dollars, plus. That's after commission and kickbacks."

Johann nodded slowly. "Eight million dollars. I see. And I don't suppose I can guess who the joint shareholders of the

Continental Trading Company of Canada might be.''

Jack coughed. He felt as if he might have caught a cold on his way up from the Vanderbilt. He said: ''You're absolutely right. Bob Stewart, Harry Blackmer, Harry Sinclair, and Jimmy O'Neil. And us, if we're game. They're prepared to split the money five ways if we want to, and that's cash on the nail that doesn't get reported back to directors or stockholders. Pocket money. Or pocket *bonds*, actually. The money will all be paid off in Liberty bonds.''

''What does Fall stand to make out of it?''

Jack took out his handkerchief and wiped his nose. ''That's the really tricky part. If any of us feel generous enough to part with any of these bonds in Mr. Fall's direction, he might be favorably inclined toward us when it comes to allocating private leases for Teapot Dome and Elk Hills. He might look on us with even further favor if we lavished a few bonds on Will Hays. The Republican National Committee seem to have found themselves stuck with a campaign debt for Harding and Cox that won't go away.''

''They're going to pay off their campaign debt with Liberty bonds? *Those* Liberty bonds?''

Jack shook his head. ''Of course not. They'll persuade a few of their wealthier friends to contribute to the campaign fund, and slip them Sinclair's Liberty bonds in return. Hey presto, dirty bonds become clean bonds.''

''What about Kiamichi?'' asked Johann gruffly.

Jack shrugged. ''Kiamichi gets cleared for drilling if we opt into Continental Trading. Otherwise, no.''

''And you've already opted out, on our behalf?''

Jack didn't answer. He felt flushed, as if his temperature was up above normal. Down in the streets below them, he heard the screaming of a police siren.

Johann sat silent for a long time. He toyed with his glass of brandy, swirling it around and around. Jack watched him closely, sipping his old-fashioned, and sweating.

Eventually Johann said: ''Do you want to leave Cornelius Oil?''

Jack looked puzzled. ''Of course not.''

''Tell me the truth.''

Jack paused, and then nodded. ''Well, if you want to know the truth, I guess I've been worried about it for quite a long time.''

''I know that.''

''You *know*?''

Johann looked at him fixedly. "Of course I know. You're one of my top executives and I hate to delegate. Do you think I walk around with my eyes shut? I'm supposed to have a hide like a bull and a bite like an alligator, but don't you understand just how much of that is bluff? I'm God in that office, Jack, and just like God I have to know everything and everybody, and just how they feel."

Jack said: "If you *knew*, then—"

Johann waved him into silence. "You're one of the best people I've ever had. You're a talented lawyer and a good businessman and you're also a nice guy. I wanted to get as many years out of you as I possibly could, and that's why I haven't asked you this question before. I knew you weren't happy, but I needed your skill. That's what we call intelligent use of available resources."

He put down his drink, and added: "As soon as I knew you were discontented, I put up your salary, remember? It wasn't a bribe to keep you, Jack, but I hoped it was some kind of recompense for doing a job you didn't really enjoy."

Jack lifted his hands in surrender. "This sounds like you're getting around to firing me."

Johann gave him a sloping, half-humorous smile. "I will if it makes you feel any better."

Jack said: "I told Fall and Sinclair no. I told him there was no possibility of Cornelius Oil getting involved. That's good enough reason for kicking me out of the door, isn't it?"

Johann stood up. Jack could hardly see his face against the soft shine of the lamps. Johann said: "Did you think no was the right answer?"

"Well, yes. I did. I wouldn't have said it otherwise."

"Why did you think it was right?"

"Because the profit doesn't add up in the long term. One-fifth of eight million dollars is only one million six hundred thousand, and *that's* only supposing the whole deal goes through. Apart from that, if we're expected to hand that out to Hays and Fall in the expectation of leases at Teapot Dome and Kiamichi, then the math just doesn't make sense. Not for us, anyway. We can raise money for bribes and backhanders with much less risk. This administration is too damned thick with wheelers and dealers and good old pals from way back. It's creaking with corruption and before long it's going to get itself found out, and if that's going to happen, the last place I want Cornelius Oil to be is damn slap in the middle of it."

Johann listened to this, and then slowly nodded.

"I think Diogenes could stop here, if I understand my *Pocket University* correctly," he said, in a gentler voice than Jack had ever heard him use in his whole time at Cornelius Oil.

Jack said nothing.

"You made the right decision for the right reasons," Johann went on. "I was worried this afternoon that you might muff it, because you thought that I wanted Teapot Dome and Elk Hills at any cost. But you didn't. You did right. This whole government is going to get itself in a deep and serious mess pretty soon, and it's going to count in our favor with the Senate if we made a point of keeping our hands clean. Apart from that, lost causes are never completely lost."

"What do you mean?" asked Jack.

Johann grunted. "Watch this," he said, and picked up his telephone. There was a long silence, and then he said: "Moira? Get me Albert Fall on the line. He's probably round at the Mellons'."

For almost five minutes, neither of them said a word as Johann waited for his assistant to find him the Secretary of the Interior. At last Johann said: "Albert? It's Johann. I thought I'd find you there."

Jack could hear a tinny, diminutive voice on the other end of the line. Then Johann said: "Albert, I've just been talking to Jack Field. Yes. Yes, that's right. Well, I know you're disappointed, but that's the way things work sometimes. No. I respect his decision. Well, I'm sorry."

Johann traced a pattern on the telephone table with his fingertips while Fall answered him, and then he said: "My real worry is Kiamichi. Yes, that's it. You see, the thing is, Albert, I'm pretty keen to get my people started out there. Well, I know all about give-and-take, Albert, and that's why I've called you. I know we're not taking part, but the point is that what you're all doing with Continental Trading Company—well, it's the kind of operation you'd like to keep hushed up, right? Top security, right?"

Johann glanced across at Jack and winked. Then he said: "The way I see it, Albert, we can keep our mouths religiously sealed for you, but only if you do something for us in return. Something like clearing the problems on Kiamichi. No, Albert, don't say that. What do you mean? No, it's not like that at all. It's just a plain and simple deal. We make sure the Continental Trading Company stays

250

a secret between us, and you give us a little help in Oklahoma. Now, what's so terrible about that? Okay. Yes, I know. But Senator Walsh might be interested, mightn't he? I mean, he's really hot on that kind of thing right now. Yes. Well, that's all I'm asking. Yes. Okay. Well, call me tomorrow. That's all right. But, Albert—make sure it's yes. All right. Good night."

Johann set down the phone. He was obviously amused. He walked across to Jack with his hands in his bathrobe pockets, and he was smiling broadly.

Jack said: "You've got quite a nerve."

Johann nodded. "It's the only way to get ahead."

"Well," said Jack, "what do I do now? I came here expecting to get fired, and now it seems that I'm not."

Johann rubbed his chin. "No, you're not fired. But maybe this is as good a time as any for you to get out of this business. If you're not happy, then there's no point in kicking your heels around here for the rest of your life."

Jack coughed. He didn't know what to say.

Johann sat on the edge of the table beside him, and rested a big hand on Jack's shoulder.

"What you did today was good work," he said, "and I appreciate good work. So let's say that I pay you for that work, and that I give you a small parting gift to help you get along in whatever kind of lawyering takes your fancy."

He got up, and went over to the desk, which was littered with letters and papers and stock reports. He opened his checkbook, unscrewed his pen, and wrote out a check. Then, flapping it to dry the ink, he came back to Jack and handed it to him. Jack didn't mean to look at how much it was, not in front of Johann, but he couldn't help dropping his eyes and glancing at it.

"It's ten thousand dollars," said Johann. "It's not a fortune, but it's the same amount that somebody once gave to me, to start me off. I couldn't let you leave with any less than that. Or any more, for that matter."

Jack said softly: "Thank you. Ten thousand is plenty. If you made a million out of it, I guess I can, too."

Johann said: "I'm going to miss you, you know. I want us to stay friends."

Jack nodded. "I'd like that. I guess it hasn't been too easy for us to get along together lately, the way things have been."

"Well, let's talk about that later," said Johann. "Right now I suggest you get back home to Ellie. You look like you're coming down with a head cold."

Jack stood up and gathered his coat and briefcase together. He still felt as if he had to say something else, even if it was only goodbye. He went over and offered his hand to Johann, and they shook.

"I won't forget any of this," he said. There was a catch in his throat that might have been his oncoming cold.

Johann grunted. "You'd better. Because if you ever tell anyone else what happened here tonight, I'm going to ram that oil rig up where it hurts the most."

On the way home, Jack made two stops. He went to a Greek store on Third Avenue, which was the only store he could find open, and bought a red tinplate train. Then he stopped off at the next corner and bought himself a hot bagel, which he ate as he walked back across town to Central Park South. It was a freezing night in November, 1921, and the cold brought tears to his eyes.

1927

When Your Guests Are Gone—Are You Ever Sorry You Invited Them? Be Free From All Embarrassment! Let the Famous *Book of Etiquette* Tell You Exactly What to Do, Say, Write, or Wear on Every Occasion!

—Advertisement, 1927

Spring, in that small corner of Pennsylvania, always seemed to arrive early. You could have motored up from Johnstown or Altoona, and the trees there may still have been bare, but here in the valleys of Robinstown, the buds were already sticky and fresh, and the clouds seemed to roll warmly across a sky that was promising summer when everyplace else was still paying off the debts of winter.

That day in March, 1927, it had rained a while before dawn, but now the sun was out, and the puddles in the tracks were reflecting the sky like pieces of broken blue china. There was a fresh smell of wet grass and the dew clung on spiderwebs beneath the overhanging trees. The shadow of cumulus swam leisurely across the rounded hills that kept Robinstown safe from the bitterest northeasters, and secluded from strangers and traveling brush salesmen.

Down by the village store, Martin Levon, the storekeeper, was heaving barrels of beans and sacks of red potatoes from the back of his Ford pickup. A maroon flivver came chugging slowly down Main Street, its narrow tires splashing in puddles and mud. It drew up alongside him and coughed to a stop.

"'Morning, Martin," said the driver.

Martin didn't turn around, but hefted the barrel up against the wooden store wall.

"'Morning to you, Grover."

The driver, Grover Bean, climbed carefully out of the car and limped across to the boardwalk. He was one of the most important men in town, since he owned most of the grazing land north of the Asquahanna River, and all the mineral rights besides, and his herd of dairy cattle had won prizes every year from 1922. He was lean and tall, with a wide-brimmed hat over a face as long and mournful as a bloodhound's.

Martin finished unloading his pickup, and chained up the tailboard. Grover sat down on one of the old kitchen chairs outside the store and lit himself a thin cheroot. The morning breeze blew the smoke away over his shoulder.

"'It's going to be a fine spring day," said Grover, leaning back. "I reckon that we could do with such a day, too."

Martin wiped his nose with the back of his shirtsleeve. "Guess so, but I prefer to have her *wet* than to have her *dry*. Wet days, folks hang about the store longer, and gen'rally purchase more."

The two men sat for a few minutes, smoking and appreciating the day. It wasn't considered proper in Robinstown to come out and state your business straightaway. The community (Pop.: 350) was too small for that. You discussed family matters first, and hemmed and hawed, and in the end you finally got around to saying what was on your mind.

Grover said: "I was reading last night that they can send moving pictures through the airwaves like the wireless these days. Seems they're going to test it out soon, this year maybe. It's the television, they called it. Now, that sounds interesting, doesn't it?"

Martin sniffed. "Don't see the use of it. It don't make no difference if you just hear a feller play the banjo, instead of seeing him, does it?"

"Oh, there's more to it than that," said Grover. "They reckon they can bring you sports, right into your own home, right the moment it happens. And you could see the President speak, clear as day, when he's in Washington and you're home."

Martin scratched the back of his head. "Now I *know* there ain't no use for it! It's bad enough having Coolidge in the White House, without having him setting in my own home, without as much as a please or thank you."

Grover, who was a firm believer in Republican "normalcy," and had once been invited to a charity buffet in Philadelphia which Calvin Coolidge was supposed to attend (he hadn't, because of flu), started to laugh.

"There isn't any turning *your* head, Martin. Not by wireless nor television, nor any gimcrackery or hokum going. You're a good man!"

Martin relit his dwindling cigarette and shook out the match. He looked at Grover hard, as if he sensed that the farmer had something important to say.

"It ain't often you're free with the compliments, Grover."

Grover's face abruptly went serious, like the creases dropping out of a tablecloth.

"No," he agreed. "It isn't. But then, it isn't often we get the chance to make anything out of ourselves."

256

Martin said nothing but waited for Grover to continue. He had all day, and all tomorrow, and all the day after that, and so there wasn't any point in rushing it. Grover Bean had something important to say, and because he was a gentleman, he was going to say it in the way a gentleman should.

"Last month, I had myself a letter," said Grover. "It was written from Pittsburgh, from the Kruyper Dye Works. All official, headed notepaper and all. It seems they're planning on setting up a factory here, at Robinstown, and they want to use the Asquahanna River for the dye process. They'll bring in a railroad spur, and build houses for the workers, and expand the whole place like you'd never believe it."

Martin stared at him. "They want to build a *factory*? Here—in Robinstown?"

"They sure do. They made an offer for the Slope Meadow and the South Hill, and two or three of those old pastures we don't use anymore, and they say they're going to bring in work and money and make Robinstown into a boom city."

Martin frowned. "It sure sounds like something. But what about the farmers hereabouts? What's it going to do to them? They're my regular customers, Grover, and even if I get more customers, I don't care to see my old friends sold down no river, dye works or dammit."

Grover shook his head. "You don't understand. See there—along the river bend—that's where the factory goes. The workers' houses go up beyond the woods, and you'd never even see them. It's all on my land, and most of it's land I don't use no more, and woods, and the top of the Rabbit Ridge. Why, the Rabbit Ridge is so steep you can't get cattle up there unless you carry them up on your back. It isn't any use to me."

Martin stood up and walked over to the edge of the boardwalk. He shaded his eyes against the sunlight, and looked out over the valley of the Asquahanna, at the soft valley with its blossomy trees and its little cluster of painted clapboard houses.

"I guess it would liven things up, as far as business goes," said Martin slowly. "I mean—think of all the folk who would live here regular, and come to buy at the store day by day."

"That old cash register wouldn't stop ringing," said Grover enthusiastically. "You could be a wealthy man, Martin, if you worked hard and you played your hand right."

"They wouldn't have no company store?"

257

"I could make them promise that, as a condition. I haven't signed any papers yet. I wanted to see what the town said first."

Martin turned around, and he was emphatic. "Well, you make 'em promise that. No company store, and then they can come in here and build themselves a hundred dye works! Even two hundred, if they've a mind to!"

Grover laughed. "I'm glad you like the idea, Martin. There are going to be plenty who don't."

Martin grinned. "You get old-fashioned folks in every community. But I'd say this dye works calls for a celebration. I've got myself a couple of bottles of L. L. McKenzie's special out back, if you'd care to step inside."

Grover shook his head, but smiled. "I prefer to keep my brains where they belong at this time of the morning. Anyhow, it seems that the Kruyper people may be up here today, to talk over the land sale, and I wouldn't want them to think I was anything but temperate, would I?"

Martin nodded. "I guess not."

He coughed, and shuffled his feet for a while, and then he said: "I guess they're giving a fair price."

Grover shrugged. "That's something that everybody in the whole of the county is going to want to know. How much did Kruyper's grease old man Bean's palm for the dye-works land? Well, I'm going to say it out straight, so there's no gossip and there's no exaggeration. What they've asked for here is a package of land taking in all that area like I said, and what they're paying is two hundred and fifty thousand dollars."

Martin whistled. "That's a quarter of a million bucks! They're going to pay you a quarter of a million bucks for the Rabbit Ridge and the Slope Meadow and a few bits of old scrub? They have to be nuts!"

"Hold on there," said Grover, lifting his hand. "That's all good land, with good rich soil, and what they don't want to build a dye works on, they could use for grazing, or growing, or whatever they wanted."

"You just said yourself the Rabbit Ridge was no good for grazing. If *you* ain't ready to haul a cow up there on your back, do you think *they* will?"

Grover pulled a face. "How should I know? They asked for it, so maybe they got ways and means."

"A quarter of a million dollars," said Martin huskily, and had

258

to sit down on the bean barrel again. "That's more money than I ever saw. You know something, Grover, I always said you was a gentleman, and I was absolutely right. If you won't take a small drink with me right now—well, I suggest you take a large one!"

Grover Bean, pleased with his news and his imminent wealth, at last relented. Martin went in to fetch the moonshine out of the long-case clock in the hall, and he called to his wife, Katherine, to fetch glasses, because this was celebration time, whether it was ten in the morning or not. They were going to have more customers in their store than a dog has fleas, and everyone around was going to be rich.

As the spring morning warmed up, they sat around a barrel on the porch, and Martin poured them stiff shots of L. L. McKenzie's home-brewed stuff, and they laughed and smoked some more, and anyone who passed by was told the news. As Grover had predicted, it wasn't every member of the Robinstown community who was pleased to hear that their houses were soon going to be overshadowed by a dye works, but most of them recognized that it was going to give them financial security at a time when financial security was getting a little thin on the ground.

It was just past eleven when they saw three large black sedans glittering in the sunlight as they came slowly up the rough Asquahanna road and through the ash grove farther down the valley. Almost silently, the cars drove toward them in the mud, and pulled to a halt beside the village store.

"Looks like a funeral t' me," said Martin, and then cackled out loud.

Grover Bean looked more serious. "Maybe it's the Kruyper people, come to talk about the works."

Across the street, the gingham curtains of old man Johnson's house were obviously atwitch, and George Purvis, keeper of the peace, switchboard operator, and savings-bank manager, came trudging across the street in his plaid shirt and his suspenders with his ginger mustache awry and ready for anything.

The sedans had darkened windows, and it was impossible to see who was inside. For a moment they stayed there silent and unmoving, like sinister apparitions from another planet, but then the doors opened, and three chauffeurs stepped out to open the rear doors.

Out of the first car climbed a sharply dressed young man in gray with a briefcase and rimless spectacles. He had that smooth, well-fed look of successful junior attorneys, and the fact that he didn't care about stepping into the thick black mud of Robinstown's Main Street showed Martin that he must have enough money to own more than one pair of shoes. He came across to the store, and raised his hat to them, "for all the whole world," as Martin said later, "as if he was going to sing us a song."

"Is either of you two gentlemen Mr. Grover Bean?"

Grover stood up hastily, almost knocking over his tumbler of moonshine. His long doggy face was purpler than usual, and he wiped his palm on his breeches before he shook hands.

"That's me, sir. I'm Grover Bean. I'm honored to make your acquaintance."

"How do you do," replied the young man in gray. He had a peculiarly tart way of smiling. "My name's Oswald Stone, and I represent the Kruyper Dye Works. I suppose you received my letter about the final negotiations for the sale of your land?"

Grover said: "Yes, I did, yes, thank you," in a kowtowing kind of way that really disturbed Martin, who was unusually clear in his perceptions after two and a half glasses of L. L. McKenzie's special.

"We can go over the details later," said Oswald Stone. "In private."

Grover said: "Surely. By the way, this is Martin Levon, who runs the store here, and this is George Purvis, our law officer and manager of the Asquahanna Savings Bank."

The Robinstown men said: "How do," a little suspiciously, and made no effort to shake hands.

Oswald Stone stepped up onto the boardwalk and scraped the mud from his feet. He noticed the half-empty hooch glasses on the barrelhead, but he didn't remark on them. Instead, he turned around and inspected the town and the valley as if he was planning on converting the whole place into a holiday camp.

"Nice township you have here," he said briskly. "Real nice."

George Purvis put his big head on one side and said: "That's the way *we* like it."

Stone smiled. "Of course you do. And we aim to help you keep it that way. If anything at all, what we plan to do here is going to be an improvement. It'll bring some life into the place, pep it up a bit."

Purvis said: "Happen we don't want it pepped up? Happen we prefer things the way they are?"

"Well"—Stone smirked—"that's something that you and Mr. Bean here are going to have to thrash out between you. Mr. Bean has offered us the land, straight and legitimate, and nobody can blame him for doing that."

Purvis looked steadily at Oswald Stone for a moment, and then turned around and looked with equal weight at Grover Bean. For some reason, Grover seemed embarrassed, and he couldn't hold George Purvis' stare for more than a couple of seconds.

"It seems to me," said Purvis, "that the sale of a man's land is a man's own business. But it also seems to me that if a man's land is going to be used for something that's going to make waves all over town, like this is, then I reckon it's the town's business, too."

Martin Levon scratched his spiky hair. "That's all well and good now, George," he said gently, "but you have to think of the trade. There ain't nobody round Robinstown who's done good for themselves since the war, and with all them dairy prices dropping every day—well, maybe we got to fix to do something. The future ain't in farming, and that's for sure."

George Purvis spat onto the road. "That's hogwash and *you* know it. As long as there's people who need feeding, there's going to be farmers. So there's surpluses of grain, and there's surpluses of butter, and there's more meat than Calvin Coolidge can stuff in his mouth at one go. But I heard there's a bill in front of Congress for selling surplus stuff abroad at low prices, and clearing the surplus, and *then* you'll see if the future's in farming or not. You'll sit here in Robinstown, with black smoke choking your cattle and dye poisoning your river, and you'll wish to the Lord Almighty that you never done what you done this day."

Oswald Stone didn't seem to be the slightest bit perturbed by this speech, but he beckoned to one of the chauffeurs standing by the three limousines, and when the man came across to see what he wanted, he whispered something in his ear.

The chauffeur nodded, and walked back to the second car in the cortege, trying to avoid the puddles in his shiny brown boots.

Oswald Stone said to George Purvis: "There's someone here that I'd like for you to meet. Maybe, when you've talked to him, you'll change your opinions."

George Purvis shook his head. "There's only one thing that's going to change my opinion, and that's the end of the world. When that day comes, you can put up dye works till you bust."

The chauffeur opened the rear door of the second limousine,

and a man climbed slowly out. When he stood up to his full height, Martin Levon realized, almost immediately, who it was. The man was broad-shouldered and heavily built, like a prize bull in a well-fitting vicuna coat, and he wore a gray hat over a broad, mature, but rather reddened face. He came walking toward them with his head lowered, touching the muddy road with the tip of a black cane, and it was only when he stepped up onto the boardwalk that he lifted his head and looked them all in the eye. Not one of them had spoken, and even now they didn't know what to say.

The man removed one gray kid glove and extended a chunky, stubby-fingered hand. George Purvis shook it first, and it made him wince, because the man had a hard grip and three heavily engraved gold rings.

"I'm Johann Cornelius," said the man, looking from one to the other. "I'm the owner, in a way, of the Kruyper Dye Works."

Oswald Stone smoothed back his hair. "Mr. Cornelius will be pleased to answer any questions. You have some questions, don't you, Mr. Purvis?"

George Purvis looked suddenly small and shabby next to Johann. His open-necked work shirt was faded and patched, compared with the white pristine gates-ajar collar of Johann's shirt, and Johann's impeccable necktie, and his hands were rough and scarred.

Still, he managed to find his voice. He looked defiantly at Johann and said: "I don't have no questions, Mr. Cornelius, no questions at all. All I have is objections. The way I see it, you've led Grover Bean here astray with money, and now he's prepared to sell you land for a purpose that won't suit this township. That's the way I see it."

Johann nodded.

"What makes you think that a dye works won't suit this township, Mr. Purvis?"

George Purvis coughed. "I'm not a rich man, Mr. Cornelius, not like you, but I've lived in this township most of my life and I know what suits it and what don't. When Congress passes that bill for selling farm surplus abroad, why, this place is going to start to come to life again, slowly, and that's why we don't want no factories here, poisoning our rivers and pushing us out of our rightful land."

Johann's face was expressionless. "Do you really think that Congress will get that bill past the President?"

George looked fierce. "Why, he don't have no choice."

Johann remained bland and unmoved. "He does, I'm afraid, and I'll bet you five hundred dollars that he vetoes that bill straight out."

"Aw, come on . . ." said George. "He don't have no choice."

Johann turned on him. "No, my friend, it is *you* who have no choice. You don't have a choice at all. You're going to be pulled by your ears into the future of this nation whether you like it or not. You're going to be part of what makes America great, and what makes America great is nothing to do with squabbling farmers and antitrust laws and softheaded, softhearted meliorists."

He reached out and seized George Purvis' shoulder. He pointed up the valley, toward the distant woods and the hazy curves of the Rabbit Ridge. "What do you see there?" he whispered loudly. "When you look up that valley, what do you see?"

George was uncomfortable, but he didn't have the temerity to shake free from Johann Cornelius' grip.

"I see trees," he said awkwardly. "Trees . . . and grazing land."

"And what else?"

George squinted. "I don't know. Clouds?"

Johann let him go. "You see trees, and grazing land, and clouds?"

"I guess so," said George, rubbing his shoulder.

Johann shook his head, like a fond uncle shaking his head at the ignorance of a dull nephew.

"I see those things, too, Mr. Purvis, but I see something else besides. I see a river, and whenever I see a river I see power, and water for factory work. The power is free, and the water is free, and that means economy, and profit. I see something else, too, but that something else is a secret, because that something else is going to make this town rich and me richer. Come on, Mr. Purvis, this is America. This is the land of opportunity. Didn't it ever occur to you to become rich?"

George Purvis opened his mouth and then closed it again. Martin Levon was looking at him, and so was that lawyer fellow, Oswald Stone, and he just didn't know what to say. Sure, he used to dream about riches, and buying himself a fancy automobile. But that was just foolishness, and as he grew older, it faded out of his mind. He knew that big money wasn't for him, and he grew to be satisfied with his small musty office, his black cylinder stove, and his blue pot of quietly simmering coffee.

"Well, now," said Johann Cornelius with a thick-lipped smile. "I think it's time we settled this property transaction for good. Would you care for a ride, Mr. Bean? Maybe we can talk over the final details and get this show on the road."

Grover Bean tugged his jacket straight, and nodded in acquiescence. But even as he walked toward the long black Cornelius cars, he turned back toward George Purvis, who was staring at the boardwalk with the stunned, hopeless look of a priest who wonders if his faith has somehow gotten itself entangled in selfish desires and worldly conundrums, and he felt he wanted to say something to George, just about anything at all, even if it was only "Sorry."

Inside the limousine, it smelled of deep-buttoned leather and brandy. The tinted windows made it gloomy, like a traveling sepulcher, and it was hard to distinguish the faces of all the men who were sitting there. Someone opened a briefcase, and there was a rustle of papers and deeds. The door was closed to exclude the breeze and the world outside.

"Sit down," instructed Johann Cornelius, pulling out a jump seat for him. "Make yourself at home."

Grover sat, biting his lip with nervous concentration.

Johann quickly ruffled through the papers, refreshing his memory. Then he looked up and said: "I trust there's nothing here that you object to, Mr. Bean?"

Grover coughed. "Well, sir, there's the question of fencing on the south, and I'm asked to make a couple of inclusions on behalf of the townsfolk."

"What are they?"

"Well, I want it stipulated that all the dye-works people spend their money at the local store, and that you have no company store in competition; and I also want it made plain that the river is not to be poisoned by dye, since two herds of cattle drink out of it below the ash grove."

Johann turned the pages of the contract until he came to the relevant pages. He read them carefully, and then looked up again at Grover.

"Those are your stipulations, are they?"

"Yes, sir, they are."

Johann sighed, and rubbed his forehead. Oswald Stone, sitting next to him, recognized the signs of his impatience, and gave one of his bitter little smiles.

"Mr. Bean," said Johann in a weary voice. "We are offering you two hundred and fifty thousand dollars for your land. Is that enough, or is it not enough?"

Grover looked at Oswald Stone, and then to another Cornelius aide sitting in the limousine's darkest corner.

"It's enough," he said. "We've agreed to that."

"Well, then," said Johann, "if it's enough, take it. Just don't try to impose ridiculous sanctions and stipulations on me, because if I make a contract I make a contract, plain and simple, and there's to be no frills and exceptions and odd clauses to make it into a pig's dinner. Either sell me the land, or don't sell me the land. It's up to you."

Grover swallowed. It hadn't occurred to him for one moment that Johann would face him with a choice like that. The truth was, he desperately needed the money, because his farm had been through three bad years, and he was seriously in debt. To allow the bank to foreclose on his outstanding loans was out of the question, especially to a gentleman, as he considered himself to be, and the only way he could raise the capital was to sell.

"Well . . ." said Grover uncertainly.

"Well, what?" retorted Johann. "Are you going to sell me the land, or aren't you?"

Grover lifted his head. "Yes, sir, I will," he said clearly.

"That's what I wanted to hear," said Johann. "Oswald, pass Mr. Bean a pen, and let's have his John Hancock down on the dotted line."

The contract was unfolded and laid out for Grover on a small walnut table in the back of the limousine. Oswald Stone handed him a pen, and Grover held it poised for a while, pretending to examine the contract for one last time, although the words were unfocused and blurred. The men in the car waited patiently for him, and when he had signed his name in blue-black ink, there was no disturbing haste to take the contract back. When the writing was dry, Oswald reached out for it and said: "Satisfied?"

Grover nodded, without looking up. "Yes, sir, I am."

"Then here's your check for two hundred and fifty thousand dollars, as agreed."

Grover took the check without looking at it. He tucked it into the pocket of his jacket, and mumbled: "Thank you."

He was just about to open the limousine door when Johann Cornelius caught his arm.

"Mr. Bean," he said. "I would rather you examined the check."

Grover Bean said: "I trust you. There's no need."

"No, no, you must," insisted Johann. "I would hate you to think that you'd been tricked, or cheated. Just make sure that it's right."

Grover took out the check and peered at it closely. "It seems fine to me, thank you," he said.

"That's very good," said Johann. "I want to thank you for your helpfulness, and I want you to remember me with good cheer, no matter what happens next. These days, there isn't enough good cheer."

"No," said Grover, uncertain and anxious as he stepped out of the car. "I suppose there isn't."

The limousines drove Johann back through the Pennsylvania hills as far as Altoona, where his Ford Tri-Motor airplane was waiting for him, at four o'clock in the afternoon, on a rough field strewn with daisies. As the engines coughed and droned into life, ruffling the grass back and scattering a flock of finches, Oswald Stone came aboard to give Johann a final briefing on the Robinstown deal.

The interior of the plain silver airplane had been built as a small office, with a cushioned basketwork chair for Johann, and four more basket chairs for his passengers. The inside of the fuselage was lined with walnut veneer, and there was a cocktail cabinet with engraved glass doors. Johann's desk was neat and almost bare, and everything on it—pens, ink, and paper—could be secured firmly into place with brass clips. On this flight back to Lynwood's Island, he was working on a complex transfer of preferred stock, and the papers had already been laid out for him by his secretary, Henry B. Keith, a sniffy young man who accompanied him in badly pressed linen suits wherever he went.

266

Henry Keith was up front talking to the pilot, while Johann's Negro traveling valet, Lester, was preparing a light salad at the back of the plane—opening up lunch baskets and porcelain jars, and laying out Novia Scotia smoked salmon, fresh cold asparagus, crisp Chinese lettuce, peaches, and white wine.

Oswald Stone checked his pocket watch and said: "There's only one difficulty left."

"What's that?" asked Johann. "I thought you said the whole thing was ready to roll."

"Well, it's not a *new* difficulty. It's the railroad."

Johann didn't look up, but unclipped a gold propelling pencil from his coat. "I thought I told you to settle that," he said, almost as if he wasn't listening.

"I *tried* to settle it. I spent the whole of yesterday with Mc-Farlane. But they still have reservations. I don't know why, and I've been trying to find out why. But all the way along, their board of directors has been extremely hostile, and they still won't give us any of the assurances we want."

Johann said: "I'm not moving one bucket of earth until we get those assurances, do you understand that?"

"Yes, sir, I do. But I can't say right at this moment that it's going to be easy."

Johann was already giving most of his attention to the stock-option figures in front of him. Oswald had to speak very loudly to make himself heard over the rattling of loose plates and bottles of ink and pens and the overwhelming *grroowwrr* noise of the motors.

"Sir," he said, "I get the feeling that the railroad wouldn't lose any sleep if we didn't get this operation rolling at all."

Johann sniffed, and wrote a question mark next to a list of oil holdings. "What makes you think that?" he asked quietly.

"I beg your pardon, sir?"

"What makes you think that? *Why* wouldn't they lose any sleep? And why can't you handle a two-bit operation like the P&P Railroad without whining and moaning and making excuses?"

"I'm sorry, sir," said Oswald, embarrassed. "But it seems to me that they have a vested interest in keeping our Robinstown operation right under their thumb. They've been haggling for months over freight charges and quantities, and we still haven't been able to resolve an economic carrying structure."

"Why don't you speak English?" said Johann roughly. "You mean they want too much money for hauling our output."

"Well, that's right. And they won't come down. They're still talking thirty dollars a short ton."

"That's out of the question. What do they think we're running—a railroad benevolent fund?"

"I asked them that, sir, but they wouldn't give way. They say they want thirty dollars and that's final."

Johann laid down his stock reports and thoughtfully pulled at his thick red lips. His thin hair was oiled to his scalp with brilliantine, and parted in the center, like the sparse mane of a child's rocking horse.

"Thirty dollars, huh? Now, why should they want that much?"

"I don't know, sir," said Oswald. "It seems to me that they're pricing themselves right out of the market."

Johann nodded. "Yes, it does. But why should they? The only reason people do that is because they don't really want the work in the first place, or they only want it on very specific conditions. Why shouldn't the P&P Railroad want the work of carrying our product from Robinstown?"

"Maybe they don't want us to open up at Robinstown at all."

"But why not? I thought we had everybody straight on that."

Oswald stood up. Seeing people off in airplanes always made him afraid that he was going to be inadvertently trapped on board and flown to some place that he distinctly didn't want to go. His wife, Janina, was cooking Schnitz-und-Gnepp tonight, too, and it was one of his favorites.

"I was thinking, sir, that if I can't get P&P to cut their rates—"

"*Cut* them? I want them *halved*! And on the same guarantees, too!"

"Well, sir, yes," said Oswald. "But if they still won't come down, I was thinking that maybe we could discreetly call in a couple of private detectives. Everybody's supposed to be straight, but somebody's obviously holding out. We should find out who."

Johann sat back in his creaky basketwork chair. "Hmm. I don't usually care for that. How much stock do we hold in P&P?"

"A little less than nine percent, sir."

"Who's the majority stockholder?"

"It's supposed to be a holding company based in New Jersey called . . . here we are . . . TransMechanic."

Johann scribbled down the name. Then he said: "Okay, leave that side of it to me. Meanwhile, keep pressing them. Give them twenty-four hours to make up their minds, and if they still can't halve their rates by then, call in a good detective and have him sniff around the board. I'm not having any half-raw bunch of Dutchmen make a monkey out of me, and that's all there is to it. Oh, and something else. Get a man up to Robinstown to watch that Purvis guy. See if he can't be persuaded to soften up some of his attitudes. When this thing takes shape, the last thing I want is a bad press. I'm not having another Ludlow massacre."

"Sir, I don't really think—"

"*Do* it, Oswald, will you? Soften him up. We're going to have enough problems when they all find out that the dye works isn't even a dye works, without Bolsheviks like him giving us a hard time."

"Okay, sir, whatever you say. I'll try to cable you out at the island if I hear anything before the end of the week."

Henry Keith came back from the cockpit in his rumpled suit and announced that they were ready for takeoff. Oswald tried to think of some parting words he could say to Johann to make him feel that he was doing a great job down here in Pennsylvania, but couldn't. He grabbed his papers and his briefcase and clambered down the little alloy ladder to the grass, holding his hat against the roaring draft from the propellers.

The Tri-Motor's door was closed, and the airplane bumped around into the wind. The pale afternoon sun turned the propellers into slanting curves of light, and there was a brief smell of kerosene in the air. Oswald stood in the field waving as the airplane gathered speed and began to trundle away from him, but he was quite sure that Johann wasn't waving back. Johann was such a sour, practical bastard that he wouldn't waste the energy. He was the first rich man that Oswald had ever worked for, and even though Oswald was elated by the prestige, and very much better off than he had ever been before, he was sometimes driven to such depths of servitude and humiliation by Johann's criticisms and demands that he went back to his suburban home in the better part of Pittsburgh and wept and shook on Janina's shoulder.

The plane picked up speed and its tail wheel lifted from the grass. Then, with a throttled roar, it tilted itself awkwardly into the air and began to climb toward the west with the ungainly look of a large goose trying to waddle up an icy slope in winter. Oswald watched it for a few moments more, until the sound of its engines had almost completely dwindled away, and then he turned back to his sedan.

Two and a half thousand feet in the air, Johann was drinking one frugal glass of chilled Meursault and cutting wafer-thin slices of well-peppered salmon. Opposite, Henry Keith was making do with a quick cold beef sandwich—not because Johann objected to his sharing the salmon, but because he himself always felt so uncomfortable sitting at a luncheon table with his taciturn employer. These days, Johann talked business when he did talk, and he never saw the purpose of putting other people at their ease, with the result that many of his dinners and receptions were bristling with agonized silences. When Hester had once asked him why he didn't try to make more conversation, he grudgingly answered: "The only word that's worth speaking is the word that makes a buck."

Henry knew that Johann wasn't as totally insensitive as that remark made him out to be. For a man with so many employees, and with his finger in so many pies, flans, turnovers, and pasties, Johann was unusually introspective. John D. Rockefeller Jr. had called him "that fellow with the hard heart and soft head," and the very first time that Andrew Mellon had met him, at a reception held in 1925 by the Secretary of Commerce, Herbert Hoover, Mellon had been struck by the way that Johann wandered about as if he were the victim of an automobile accident, in a state of suppressed shock. Johann was, in 1927, as rich as Irénée Du Pont, and a powerful political figure. He owned banks and chemical plants and his opinions appeared regularly in the three Southern newspapers he controlled. He was beginning to buy into aviation, and his position as chairman of the Federal Commission on Foreign Trade Restrictions gave him a unique opportunity to influence foreign markets, particularly Germany, in favor of his own corporations. Yet—as an emotional being—there was something about Johann Cornelius that unsettled almost everybody who met him. A terrible wound-up tension, as if he was holding back some pain, or some fear, or some anger, and would never release it.

As the Ford Tri-Motor droned across the border into New York State, Johann paused from his work for a moment to look out of the little rectangular windows, and watch the sun settling smokily into the evening clouds. He enjoyed flying, because it gave him a sense of what he owned, and the potential which he still had to realize. He could look out over the endless fields and highways of America, fading into soft dusk in the western distance, and hear the chilly rush of the evening wind on the plane's wings.

Henry Keith, seeing him staring out of the window, had a look

270

too. He coughed and said: "It's a great sight, isn't it, Mr. Cornelius?"

Johann didn't answer at first, but then he sat back and looked at this pale-faced young man with his creased suit, his polished brown hair, and his long bony nose, and he said flatly: "Yes, it's a great sight."

Henry sat back too. "Are you through with the oil-stock papers, Mr. Cornelius? Because if you are, I'll double-check them alongside the Daylong figures."

"Nearly through," said Johann absently. He was twiddling with his gold propelling pencil as if he had something on his mind. Henry Keith had never seen him quite so preoccupied.

"Mr. Cornelius . . . is anything wrong?"

Johann continued to twiddle. "I'm not sure," he said slowly. "I was just thinking about the Robinstown setup."

"You mean the P&P Railroad? I'm sure that Oswald can handle it. I know he's kind of green, but he knows what you want."

Johann shook his head. "It's not that. I just want to know why they're being so goddamned awkward. Someone, somehow, is trying to throw a monkey wrench into this, and I wish to hell I knew who it was."

"TransMechanic?"

"It could be. Do we know who TransMechanic are?"

"I've heard of them," said Henry. "They're a holding partnership for several different engineering and railroad interests, but I'd have to dig a little deeper to find out who the *éminence grise* might be."

Johann nodded. They were flying into some broken cloud, and he had to reach out and steady his glass of wine.

"Henry," he said after a while, "what do you *think* about Robinstown?"

Henry, who had been shuffling papers together and clipping them into neat stacks, was taken by surprise. Johann hardly ever asked him his opinion of anything, and even when he offered it, he was usually ignored. Perhaps it was the Meursault, or perhaps Johann was tired, but he seemed to be in a dark brown, thoughtful mood. Henry sat up straight in his basket chair and tried to think of a sensible, moderately impressive answer.

"Well, sir, I think it's . . . it's *good sense*. It gets us into a new district in a new field of endeavor, and it . . . well, it's an exciting beginning . . . I mean, for all of us . . . and, well, it's . . . it's very exciting."

Johann rubbed his eyes.

"I know its exciting, Henry," he said patiently. "Profit, by definition, is exciting. But what I want to know is what you *think* of it. What your *entrails* say. Is it distasteful, for instance? Or immoral? Have you thought about that?"

Henry Keith frowned. He was a little nearsighted, but he thought eyeglasses made him look too much like Dwight Morrow and so he preferred to sit near things and squint at them.

"You're frowning," said Johann in a critical voice. "Don't you know what 'immoral' means?"

"Well, sure I do," said Henry. He tugged his crumpled jacket around himself and looked unhappy. "I just don't really understand how 'immoral' fits in with the Robinstown setup."

Johann stared at him for almost a minute. Then he said: "Henry, you are a pretty good secretary. You sharpen my pencils, you fill up my inkpots, you keep everything neat and tidy. You know how to pass on instructions, and you don't make mistakes."

Henry said: "Thank you, sir," but very uncertainly.

Johann lowered his head. "Your trouble, Henry, is that you will never understand power, and if you don't understand power, you will never understand money. The two are completely and irrevocably interlinked. If you have money, but you disregard the power that it brings you, then you will lose that money, as sure as the leaves fall off the trees in September. The exercise of power is the only safeguard against theft, swindle, takeover, inflation, and economic decay."

Henry said: "Mr. Cornelius, I didn't know that you found my work to be unsatisfactory."

"It's not your *work* that's unsatisfactory. It's your soul. You have an unsatisfactory *soul*. Maybe you're young, and you haven't even realized you have a soul yet. That could be it. But it's about time, because you're in the major leagues now, Henry, and there is no room for a man who doesn't have a satisfactory soul."

"Sir?" said Henry. He was more baffled now than he could ever remember. He was beginning to sweat, in spite of the chilly air that was blowing through the airplane, and for a moment he seriously wondered if Johann was actually sacking him.

Johann sipped the last of his wine. He dabbed his lips with a clean Irish-linen napkin and signaled to Lester to clear away his dishes.

"Henry," he said slowly, "you can't deny that most people think I'm a tyrant."

"Oh, sir, I wouldn't say—"

Johann waved a thick-fingered hand at him. "Come on, Henry, don't be such a goddamned ass-licker. Everybody in the world thinks I'm a tyrant, including my wife, and that's the way it has to be. But what they don't know, what they never guess, is that I'm only half the tyrant I could be. The reason for that is that *power*, unless it's handled with great care and responsibility, is the kind of tool that can fly out of your hand and hit you straight in the eye. Nobody with great power uses all the power at their disposal. You think Junior does? Or Mellon? Power is only effective when it's used sparingly and with consideration for morals and principles; and the more sparingly you use it, and the greater consideration you show for morals and principles, then the more powerful you can become. If I used all the power I could muster against you—you personally—then I could break you. But what's the use of that? It's far more profitable if I use only a fraction of my power, and have you working for me."

Henry scratched his head. "I'm sorry, sir, but I still don't see how this applies to Robinstown. I'm sorry."

Johann rubbed his forehead like an uncle trying to explain simple geography to a cretinous nephew.

"Henry," he said, "we have misguided Mr. Bean into believing that he has sold us land for a dye works. A dye works won't go down too well in Robinstown, but at least it's on the margin of what the people will swallow. The question I'm asking you is concerned with the morality of buying land for a dye works, using borrowed federal funds for the purpose, when our real intention is to strip the whole place bare and dig up coal. You know as well as I do that if we strip the ridges and the pastures around there, the farmland will erode, and in five years you won't be able to feed a Colorado beetle around there, let alone a cow."

Henry swallowed. "I see," he said, nodding at last. "I see."

"You *see*, Henry, but what do you *think*?"

Henry looked down at his lap. It was piled high with papers, and he stared at them as if they had dropped from nowhere.

"I think, sir, seriously, that morality doesn't come into this

273

particular deal. I mean, morality is one thing, but what you're doing is for the good of the most people, and that's moral, surely? There'll be coal, and work for hundreds of men, and with the way that farm prices are going, a mine has to be worth much more than agricultural land. Apart from that, sir, you have to drag these people into America's future, by their ears if necessary.''

Johann listened to all this, and then closed his eyes. He was beginning to feel like fifty-four. His heart seemed to beat deeper and slower, like a heavy swimmer churning his way through tidal troughs. His blood seemed to run more tiredly, and his head was almost permanently aching with the strain of remembering the scale and the extent of his investments and his properties.

Henry wiped his nose with his handkerchief. The Ford was now vibrating and bucking between the clouds, and he was glancing nervously out of the window to see what was happening, and where they were.

"I have . . . well, I guess I have one question. If you don't mind my asking it.''

Johann said: ''Be my guest.''

"Well, sir, can I please ask what *you* think about Robinstown? Do *you* consider it moral? I'm sorry if that sounds kind of impertinent, but you did say that—''

Johann laughed, once, out loud. There was no humor on his face at all.

"Henry,'' he said, "you haven't understood a single word.''

"Sir?''

"Listen, Henry, I was born on a farm, the son of a dairy farmer, just the same as those people up in Robinstown. My father died of a stroke, and from working too hard. Farming is a tough, miserable, badly paid existence, especially these days, and it's thankless, too. But look at mining! Miners might get paid more, but then mining's tough and miserable, too, and miners die young from dust on the lungs, and collapsing shafts, and floods. They never see the sun and it's grinding hard work.''

Henry said: "You make one sound just as bad as the other.''

"They *are*, Henry, and that's the whole goddamned point! The only thing that isn't quite so bad is sitting here, comfortable and rich, and telling all those poor bastards what to do, and even *this* can be hell. Life is an accident, Henry. An accident! A serious accident in which people really die. The only morality of the

Robinstown deal is that it's not as bad an accident as it could have been. And *that's* the point."

The two men sat and stared at each other in the curious half-darkness of the cabin. Then the lights flickered on—a pair of bronze lamps in the shape of Olympic torches—and the pilot called back from the cockpit: "Some pretty rough weather up ahead, sir! I suggest you stay in your seats!"

Johann leaned over and peered out of the airplane's windows. The sky outside was that odd green-black color that gun barrels go when they've been rubbed too slowly with charcoal. Rain was rapping against the glass, and outside the motors sounded as if they were groaning and grating their way through a mixture of cornmeal and broken glass.

The Tri-Motor swayed, and dropped fifty or sixty feet to starboard. A bevy of pens rolled off Johann's desk and scattered on the floor. The motors strained and pulled, and the plane was buffeted from side to side by an angry, cross-tempered gale.

Johann gripped the arms of his chair firmly. "*Lester!*" he called.

The black man appeared from his seat at the back. He was obviously frightened, but he was doing his best not to show it. Nobody showed emotion in front of Johann, not even his own children.

"Yes, sir?"

"Lester, pull the drapes. I don't want to look out of the windows just now, and neither does Mr. Keith."

"Right away, sir."

He went around the swaying cabin, holding on to the brass handrails on each side, and drew the small brown velvet curtains. Soon—except for the pitching and tossing and the grinding drone of the motors—they could have been sitting in a small office anyplace at all.

It took them twenty minutes to battle their way through the storm, and they only cleared the last of the heavy clouds as they made their descent toward Lynwood's Island. Henry Keith was very white, and hadn't said a single word during the whole experience. To him, it was oppressively claustrophobic to fly with the airplane's curtains closed, as if he was being forced to run blindfolded through a strange city, in the pouring rain. But Johann had simply bent over his desk and continued to check column after

275

column of figures, until he was satisfied that the stock negotiations were ready.

The Ford Tri-Motor, with its marker lights blinking, moaned across a calm night sky, pale with clouds, toward the gleaming Hudson. Close in to the west shore, thickly forested, was the dark pear shape of Lynwood's Island, and as they circled around it, Henry Keith could make out the white square cottage and the ornamental gardens.

On the ground, a row of white lights was switched on to show the pilot where to land, and he turned into the wind again to bring the airplane down. They bumped hard onto the turf, bumped again, and then they were trundling quickly past the end of the long gardens and toward the trees. The motors popped once or twice, and then stopped.

Johann rose stiffly from his seat and stretched his back while Lester brought his hat and coat. Henry Keith was busy gathering up papers.

"Henry," said Johann, as his secretary went forward to talk to the pilot.

"Yes, sir?"

"Henry, you must never confuse morality with fate. One has nothing to do with the other, and if you understand that, then you may stop being frightened when you fly."

Henry blinked. Then, for the sake of settling the whole discussion, he said: "Yes, sir. I see. I'll remember that," and went through the curtains to check how much fuel the homeward trip had cost them. It was probably just as well he went quickly, because he didn't see Johann Cornelius grin.

Hester had heard the airplane circling around the island from the sewing room. She lifted her head for a moment to make sure it was Johann, and not a mail plane or one of those people on their way to Pocantico, but then she carried on with her embroidery with the small smile of a wealthy Protestant wife who knows that her husband is about his business as he should be, and that all is in domestic equilibrium.

Hester didn't particularly care for embroidery, but the fact that she didn't care for it made her needlecraft into a kind of decorative self-imposed penance. At the moment, she was sewing an elaborate pillow cover in a traditional pattern of roses and leaves and forget-me-nots. She spent very little time on her own, except for her hour of sewing in the white oval sewing room, and somehow she felt it was important to undertake some task that was both difficult and dislikable.

Her age may have had something to do with it. She would be thirty-six in August, and she had been married to Johann for sixteen very uneven years.

As she heard the Ford Tri-Motor land, she laid down her embroidery and rang a small silver bell. Her personal maid, Marise, a quiet and rather sophisticated young French girl with a bun in her hair and lips that Johann always called "cupid's cushions," came into the room. She was dressed in gray, like most of their staff, with white lace collar and cuffs.

Hester, sitting on her Sheraton sewing chair, said: "You've been smoking."

"*Pardonnez-moi, madame*?"

"You heard, Marise, quite clearly. You've been smoking and I can smell it from here. How many times do I have to tell you that young ladies do not smoke, and that I forbid it?"

Marise bustled across the room to help her mistress clear away the silks and the needles.

"I apologize, madame."

"You will do more than apologize. You will promise me, upon your oath, never to do it again."

Marise closed the sewing basket with its gilded clasps and put it away. "Yes, madame, I promise upon my oath."

Hester stood up. Because she was only five-feet-two, she looked quite diminutive next to Marise, like a wind-up doll on a souvenir jewelry box. She was wearing a pale lemon afternoon dress, with long silk fringes, and strings of perfect Indonesian pearls. She said: "You have probably heard the airplane."

"Yes, madame."

"I will say hello to Mr. Cornelius in the morning room, and then I will dress for dinner. I shall wear my oyster dress, I expect, and I want the peacock brooch and the diamond bracelets I wore last month at Newport."

"Very well, madame. I shall have them laid out."

"Good. Is Stainer around?"

"I think he brings brandy for Mr. Cornelius."

"Oh. Well, when he's done that, tell him to set dinner in the garden room."

"Very well, madame."

277

Hester left the sewing room and walked across the square central hallway, her yellow shoes tapping on the polished mosaic, and went into the morning room. It was high and rectangular, this room, with a view from its tall ranks of windows down the long slope of the garden to the Hudson. At night, its rich russet drapes were drawn, and if it was cold, a log fire was built up in the formal steel Victorian fireplace, as it had been tonight. The walls were the color of pale spring primroses, and the floor was polished herringbone parquet, with antique Indian rugs. There were Early American paintings of Iroquois settlements and Puritan villages around the walls, as well as two Cubist pictures of guitars by Georges Braque.

Hester sat by the fire in a small crinoline chair. The butler, Stainer, had left Johann's usual silver tray of Napoleon brandy ready for his arrival, along with ice and soda.

After a few minutes, she heard voices in the hall, and the door was opened. Johann came in, laughing about the storm they had flown through, and ribbing Henry Keith for his fright; and Henry himself followed afterward, looking bilious and ready for bed.

"How are you, my dear?" asked Johann. He came across, leaned over like a toppling redwood, and kissed her. She kissed him politely back.

"We hit an electric storm just a while back, and poor Henry was getting himself ready to meet his Maker!"

Hester raised an eyebrow. "I suppose we should all be ready to meet our Maker, at any time."

"Henry isn't!" Johann laughed. "Henry has a great deal to confess before he's ready for the pearly gates!"

"Johann," admonished Hester. "Remember that Henry is your secretary."

Johann sat down. Suddenly the burst of humor and enthusiasm seemed to leave him, and he said nothing more for a while. Henry, embarrassed, sat himself down in the most uncomfortable chair in the room, and gave Hester a short series of weak smiles. She was used to it. Because she was very pretty, and because she was so much younger than Johann, the men who had to work for the Cornelius empire would often turn to Hester for sympathy and help. It was only when they had spilled out their hearts to her, as most of them eventually did, that they realized she was almost as hard-shelled, in her own way, as Johann was. She never betrayed their confidences, not even to Johann, but then she never betrayed her husband, either

278

Johann unlaced his black Peal's oxfords. It was a habit of his that Hester deplored, but she allowed him to do it when he'd been working particularly hard. Stainer, the English butler, an infinitely mournful man with silver side whiskers and blotchy red cheeks, came squeaking in on evening pumps to pour his drink.

"I omitted to tell you, sir, that a Mr. Lindbergh telephoned, and requested that you telephone him back."

"What did he want?"

"I had the impression, sir, that he was seeking funds for some scheme of aviation, but further than that I could not say."

Johann took his brandy and sipped it.

"I must say I think I've heard of Lindbergh," he said. "But I'm damned if I can remember why."

Henry said: "Do you want me to call him, sir?"

Johann shook his head. "Right now I want to get this Robinstown deal sorted out. It worries me."

Hester said: "I thought Robinstown was all arranged."

"It was supposed to be," answered Johann, leaning back on the big velvet-covered Chesterfield. "All the right pressures have been applied on all the right people. All the proper palms have been greased. But I get the feeling that somebody's being awkward, and I get the feeling that they're being awkward for their own personal reasons."

Henry shrugged. "We could easily find out who it is. All we have to do is check with Grossmith."

Johann said: "I don't want to do that unless I can help it. What I really want to know is the real truth about TransMechanic."

"I could find out now for you, sir. It would only take a call to the office."

Johann thought about that, and then nodded. "All right, Henry, that's a good idea. Tell them to track every proxy as far back as they can. I don't particularly want to take any action until I know who I'm up against."

"Very good, sir."

Henry seemed to be glad of the opportunity to slip out and leave Johann and Hester alone.

"Did I tell you that John's at home?" asked Hester.

"He's *home*?" said Johann, surprised. "What's he done now—played hooky from school?"

"They've had Spanish influenza. One junior boy has died of it, apparently, and they've sent the rest of them home for the term."

Johann sipped some more brandy. "But what's he going to do?

279

He can't slope around here for six months. How about some private tutors?"

Hester said quietly: "I thought you could handle that."

"Handle what?"

"A little private tutoring. Take him around with you—show him how you work. He's got to see you in action someday. Why not now? I think it's a golden opportunity."

"I think the school needs to be sued bankrupt."

Hester stood up and walked across to the window. She parted the drapes and looked out at the dark garden and the distant glitter of the Hudson River. Her own pale reflection was superimposed on the night, like a ghost seeking admission to the real world.

"He'd adore it, you know," she said coaxingly.

Johann sipped brandy and pulled a face.

"You've no idea how much he respects you," she added. "He defends you to the death, even when they're teasing him at school."

"Why should they tease him at school?"

"Well, of course they do. He's John Cornelius, isn't he? He's rich and famous, and his father's well-known as a financial tyrant."

Johann smirked.

Hester came across and sat beside him, perched on the edge of the Chesterfield. She thought that Johann was looking very tired and much older, but at the same time she wanted him to know the truth.

"You can't be a whole man, Jo, unless you take some time out for your children. Your business won't be a whole business, either, because when they're old enough they should come into Cornelius Oil and help you. If you don't have time for them now, if you don't show them the ropes, you'll have to spend three times as much time with them later."

Johann fixed an eye on her. "They're *my* sons," he said. "They've got *my* brains, and *my* strength. *I* managed to make a fortune without any help from my father. Why should *I* mollycoddle *them*?"

"Oh, Johann, I'm not talking about mollycoddling. But times have changed. Nobody can make big fortunes now the way that you did. There isn't the land, and there isn't the oil, and apart from that, there isn't the legal opportunity. You know that."

Johann stared at the fire. "I remember what happened the year we got married. The Supreme Court dissolved Standard Oil New Jersey. But I don't remember anyone saying then or ever that it was illegal to go on making money. John and Roderick will make money, don't you worry about that, and they won't need their father holding their hands, either."

Hester said: "You're wrong, Johann. Have you talked to them lately?"

"Of course not. They've been at school."

"Well, it's about time you did," said Hester. "I mean it, Johann. You're assuming all kinds of things about them without even knowing what they're really like."

Johann blinked in surprise. "But they're like *me*!"

Hester shook her head. "They're not entirely like you. Not as much as you seem to think they are. Roderick, for instance, doesn't have half of your strength, and he'll never be ruthless as long as he lives. John's got a bit more energy than Roderick, but he's not a business fanatic. He likes swimming and riding and things like that, and books, too. As for Hope—well, Hope's a handful. I can't imagine what she's going to be like when she's older."

Johann said: "Hester, why are you telling me this? It's going to be *years* before those children are ready to understand business."

Hester twisted her pearls around, and said nothing.

Johann said: "I come home, and suddenly everyone's accusing me of being a bad father. I mean—why?"

"Because it's got to be said sometime, and because I've been talking to John this afternoon. You just don't realize, do you? He wants to get to know his father, he wants to understand you, he wants to be close to you. You're so remote to him, Johann. You're a mysterious stranger who sometimes asks him how his schoolwork is going, and that's all."

Johann thought for a moment. The clock above the steel fireplace chimed seven, very prettily.

Hester said: "Go and talk to him, Johann. Now, before dinner. Just give him a chance to know that you care."

Johann looked up. "All right," he said quietly. "If you think it's necessary." He drained his brandy glass and set it back on the tray, and then he silently and thoughtfully tied his shoelaces up again.

John was upstairs in the children's library, reading a book about famous automobile races. He was a short little boy of ten years old, with a brown corduroy buster suit and very close-cropped hair. When Johann walked in, he immediately jumped up and said: "Oh! Good evening, sir!"

Johann said: "Hello, John," and spent a few moments pacing around the library and peering at some of the books on the shelves. John stood there rigidly, licking his lips in apprehension, while Johann picked up the illustrated volume he had just been reading.

"Automobiles, huh? You like automobiles?"

"Yes, sir. I do."

"Hmm," said Johann, "I see."

Johann paced some more, and then he sat himself down on the edge of Hope's old school desk.

"Sit down, John."

John, a little uncertainly, sat down.

Johann coughed. He gazed for a while at this odd little boy in his brown breeches, and he wondered what in the world he was going to say to him. The strangest thing of all was that Hester had assured him that this boy, his own son, wasn't even like him at all, but a completely new and individual person. In a funny kind of way, that struck him as rather ungrateful of John, and lacking in respect.

"Your mother and I thought we should have a talk together, you and I," said Johann. His voice seemed to stick, and he cleared his throat. "Your mother seems to think that you'd like to get to know me a little more, and maybe find out what it is that I do for my living."

"Yes, sir," answered John in a very small voice.

"What did you say?" asked Johann.

"Yes, sir. I would like to."

Johann reached forward and awkwardly patted John on his bristly head.

"Do you like school?" he asked.

"Yes, sir."

"And what's your best subject?"

"Singing, sir."

Johann nodded, and then frowned. "Singing?"

"Yes, sir. I came top."

"You came top in singing?"

"Yes, sir."

Johann blew out a loud brandy-flavored breath. "*Well*, John, I suppose that's something. But, tell me. What do you think is the *use* of singing?"

John lowered his eyes. Two crescents of dark eyelashes on two pale cheeks.

"I don't know, sir."

"You don't know? You made the effort to come top in something, and you don't know what use it is?"

"Yes, sir."

Johann got up from the school desk and paced about the library a little more. He hadn't been into this room for two or three years, and he felt uncomfortable, as if he had trespassed. But this business with the children, what Hester had said, had irked him. He felt he had to carry out some fatherly commission, but he wasn't entirely sure what it was, and whatever it was, it was bound to be irritating. He scratched his scalp.

"John," he said, in his gentlest voice, "it's a big hard world out there."

John bit his lip and nodded, glancing out of the darkened library window as if he expected to see actual fighting on the lawns.

"It's a big hard world and you have to be prepared for it. You have to be *strong*. You have to know your field. That's the only way you're going to survive. Do you understand me? You have to be tough!"

"Yes, sir."

Johann stared at the boy for a while, and then he said: "How's your math? Is it good?"

John dropped his eyes again. "Quite good, sir."

"How good is quite good? What position in the class?"

"Tenth, sir."

"And how many boys in the class?"

"Ten, sir."

Johann didn't answer at first, but began to tap his foot on the floor. Why was this boy so dumb? He came from a clever mother, and a financial genius of a father, so why did he act so dumb? Johann recognized that he was beginning to grow angry, and he had to make an effort to parcel up his anger and put it aside, at least for the moment.

"Tenth out of ten isn't 'quite good,' John," he said quietly. "It's disastrous. Don't you think so?"

"Yes, sir."

"Well, if you're no good at math, what are you good at? Apart from singing? There must be some talent in that thick little skull of yours, surely?"

"Composition, sir."

"You mean writing? You're good at writing?"

"Yes, sir. I came second in composition with two gold stars."

"Well, that's something. What kind of things do you write?"

"I wrote 'My Father,' sir. We all did."

Johann bent his head down toward the boy for the first time. "You wrote a composition about me?"

"We all did, sir. It was 'My Father.' "

"Could I see it?"

John looked up at him.

"Please, John, could I see it?"

Without a word, John went over to a small brown leather suitcase and opened it up. He handed a sheet of lined paper to his father, and then stood there and watched his father's eyes flicker over the few lines of round, penciled script.

It read:

> My father is very rich and is the Cornelius Oil billionair. He is very old and does not have much hair. I like it when he goes away because my mother lets us have dinner in the garden room and sometimes eat squob. My father is stric and we have to do what he says. I would like to buy him a nice wig for his birthday because even though he is stric I do love him because he is my father. He has an airplan called the Ford Tri-Motor.

Johann read the composition twice. Then he laid it carefully on the edge of John's writing desk, and stared at it for several silent minutes. John stood with his hands behind his back, waiting expectantly for his father's comments. It seemed as if, somehow, time had arrested itself, and Johann was unable to move.

Johann swallowed, and then said stiffly: "Did you mean this?"

John didn't quite understand him, but nodded.

Johann turned away. He didn't know why the composition made him feel so disturbed. He took out his handkerchief and blew his nose, and for the first time in years he felt as if he was going to cry.

John said: "Do you like it, sir? When I wrote about not much hair, I didn't mean—"

Johann shook his head. In a hoarse voice he said: "I like it. I want you to write some more, when you have the time. Get to be the best in your class."

He ruffled his son's hair with his big hand, and then he turned around without another word and closed the library door behind him.

Henry Keith was waiting for him in the hall.

He said: "Mr. Cornelius? It was easier than I thought it was going to be."

Johann, still preoccupied with John's composition, stared at Henry as if he was a time-traveler who had suddenly materialized from another century.

"What? What was easier?"

"Tracing the stock proxies, sir. I got the office onto it right away, and they had a stroke of luck."

"Well?"

Henry consulted a long list of names. "A great many of the TransMechanic stockholders are small private concerns with excellent *bona fides*. But the controlling interest, and *ipso facto* the controlling influence in the P&P Railroad, is a corporation from Delaware called BM Industries."

"Oh, yes?"

"BM Industries is under the personal control of a man called Daniel Forster."

Johann stopped in mid-step, his hand poised to open the morning-room door handle, his mouth half-open as if to speak. It was like a spell, the name "Daniel Forster"—a spell that could paralyze a man where he stood.

Johann turned around. His voice was very thick, like surf through gravel on the beach. "Are you sure about that?"

Henry looked worried. "Well, yes, sir. Of course. We've been through fifteen different . . ."

Johann's eyes dropped slowly toward the mosaic floor. He obviously wasn't listening to a single word.

Henry said: "Mr. Cornelius? Is there anything . . .?"

Johann shook his head. "No," he said roughly. "There's nothing wrong. Why don't you go get yourself something to eat now? I want to speak to my wife."

Three days later, in Robinstown, Grover Bean left his red-painted house soon after breakfast and decided to walk down the wide sloping meadow that fell toward the Asquahanna River and check on his young Freisian. The weather was a little colder now, and he wore a thick overcoat of green speckled tweed and a knitted scarf.

The sun was just up over the Rabbit Ridge, falling through the trees in long shafts of light, and Grover's breath smoked as he trudged through the grass.

There was a muddy track that curved up toward Grover's house from his main gate above Robinstown, and when Grover walked along the highest ground he could see most of it, and almost down to the Asquahanna besides. The birds were cheeping and chirping in the branches, and high above his head the cirrus clouds were lazily trailing their white hair in the sky. Grover whistled as he went, an off-key repetitive whistling that echoed from the ash groves.

It was quite by accident that he saw George Purvis's car. He was beginning to descend the slope now, and he might have missed seeing it altogether if a rabbit hadn't scampered out of the grass, and Grover Bean hadn't climbed onto the higher ground again to see where the rabbit might have sprung from. The rising sun glinted from the flat windshield of George Purvis's old Briscoe, and Grover paused and squinted downhill to where the car was parked—strangely askew and with its offside door hanging open.

He jogged as fast as he could through the tangled grass until he reached the track. He couldn't see inside the car because the sun was shining off the glass, but when he came close he realized that George Purvis was still in the driving seat. He stepped up nearer and said, "George?"

The morning was very quiet and still. His feet crunched on the rough cinders that he'd put down in the winter to help his flivver through the mud. When he reached the car door he saw that there was blood on the cracked leather seats, and that it was dripping from the car and forming a rusty pool on the road.

He didn't want to look at George Purvis, even in death. He walked quickly and stiffly down to Martin Levon's store and telephoned the sheriff of Asquahanna County from there. Martin Levon stood by the phone while he made his call, wiping his floury hands on a cloth and staring at Grover Bean in silent stupefaction.

Eventually, Grover hung up.

"Is he coming up here?" said Martin, awed. "The sheriff, I mean?"

"He has to," said Grover. "He said it would take him a good hour, and we weren't to touch nothing at all in the meanwhile."

"I wasn't planning to," said Martin. "I can't abide the sight of human blood."

"Well, me neither."

Grover stepped out onto the front boardwalk and took a deep breath of cold morning air. Martin followed him, still wiping his hands.

"Who d'you reckon could have done it?" asked Martin. "You don't reckon it was them dye works people, do you? Just because he wouldn't say he liked it?"

Grover gripped the rail of the boardwalk and stared down at the muddy street.

"I don't know, Martin. I'm beginning to wish I never signed that land away. It seems to have brought more trouble than it was ever worth."

Martin sniffed. "Well, you can say that," he said. "And the trouble with trouble, as my old grandfather used to say, is that it begets more trouble."

Grover looked across at him oddly. "I remember your grandfather," he said, as if it were suddenly and terribly significant.

Daniel Forster was washing his hands in the men's room of the Harvard Club on West Forty-fourth Street in New York City when Walter Grossmith, class of 1907, walked in. Grossmith took the next basin to Forster, and proceeded to hang up his coat and remove his cuff links. Their reflections faced each other side by side in the mirrors above the faucets, two smooth-faced and successful men who were approaching middle age with the assurance of comfortable incomes and society friends.

Grossmith filled up his basin and began to wash his hands. As he soaped them, he began to glance at Forster from time to time as if he recognized him. Then he said: "Excuse me, sir, but don't I know you?"

Forster was dabbing his face with a towel. He paused, and looked at Grossmith with the usual cautious expression that people with hundreds of friends and acquaintances reserve for faces they can't quite place.

"I know," said Grossmith, as if a divine light had illuminated his memory. "You're Dan Forster, the railroad man! Correct me if I'm not one hundred percent right!"

"Yes," said Forster, still a little baffled. "You're absolutely right."

"I'm Walter Grossmith," said Walter Grossmith. "These days I work for the Department of Commerce. Excuse me if I don't shake hands."

"Pleased to know you," said Daniel Forster.

"You know something," went on Grossmith conversationally, "I never even realized what it took to run a railroad until I went on a tour of the Union Pacific sheds, and then I was absolutely amazed. I saw the whole shebang—the boilers cleaned out, the schedules made up. It was real interesting stuff."

"Yes," said Forster, as the washroom attendant helped him on with his coat. "It's very interesting, isn't it?"

"Mind you," continued Grossmith, "I don't suppose you see much of that kind of thing in your job, do you? I guess you're mostly a desk driver, right?"

Forster brushed his hair, and then laid down the brushes.

"That's right," he said. "I have other interests as well."

"My grandfather was a railroad man, way back in the seventies. He used to sit me right down on his knee and tell me about the times they had to slow right down to hardly any speed at all, because the tracks were thick with buffalo."

Forster was ready to leave now, and he looked impatiently at his pocket watch.

"Did you ever know that August Busch had Busch beer piped into every room of his private railroad car?" said Grossmith, lavishly rubbing suds between his fingers. "Now, that's the kind of railroad style that seems to have died out these days, don't you think? Whatever happened to the old private railroad cars like they used to have in the nineties?"

Forster shrugged. "There are still one or two of them around. And you can always rent a private car from Pullman."

"That's very interesting," said Grossmith. "Now, what would a thing like that cost?"

"Well, that's very hard to say," said Forster testily. "You have to pay the rental plus eighteen first-class railroad fares. It depends on how far you want to go, and how you want to travel. Now, if you'll excuse me—"

"I wasn't thinking of traveling anyplace special," interrupted Grossmith. "I just wondered if such things were still possible."

Daniel Forster looked at his watch again. "Yes, quite possible," he said. "Now I really must go."

Walter Grossmith, his hands rinsed and dripping, turned around to face him. For some reason, Forster paused again. There was some quality about Grossmith that caught his attention; something curiously unnatural, as if Grossmith was talking and working to some prearranged plan. Dan Forster had always been sensitive to atmosphere, and it had helped him more than once, like the time he had walked into a railroad board meeting and *known* instinctively that there was a heavy power play in the air. It was an instinct which had been sharpened by his constant awareness that Johann Cornelius was always someplace behind him, and could always take back what he had once handed out, with interest.

Forster was thirty-three; a tall and cultured man with a tendency to leanness and the arch inflections of a Southern accent. He had a roundish, intelligent face, and clear blue eyes which reminded his wife, Betty, of Tom Mix. Despite his neat dark business suit and his crisp white turn-down collar, and despite the sheen of a barbershop shave, many of Dan Forster's friends felt that he would have looked better on a horse, in a tall white hat.

"Mr. Grossmith," he said, "it's been a pleasure to meet you, but I have business associates here for luncheon, and I really have to leave. Maybe we can talk about railroads some other time, if you come here regular."

Walter Grossmith dried his hands. He was a short, fortyish man with bright yellow suspenders and a bulky, big-nosed, funny-papers face like Huey Long's. He said: "Okay," quite affably, but then he said: "Will you do me one favor?"

"What's that?"

"Will you just tell me what you think about railroad rebates for coal transportation?"

Daniel Forster looked confused. "*Coal* transportation? Any *particular* coal transportation? I mean, rebates are possible for heavy freight users. That's been a regular deal with Standard Oil and other corporations for years. But you'd have to talk to one of our freight managers about that."

Walter Grossmith put on his coat, brushed his short curly hair, and stepped out of the washroom into the club's lobby with his arm interlinked with Daniel Forster's like an old buddy. Forster was too polite to pull away, but he looked around him in embarrassment, particularly when he saw two or three of his friends coming in off the street.

"It's really the *principle* that concerns me more than anything," said Grossmith. "Why should some users be given preferential rates while others are squeezed out?"

"I don't know, without having the details in front of me," said Forster, flustered. "Listen, you really must—"

"Oh! Look who's here!" said Grossmith brightly, as a small man with a striped suit and a neat mustache came in through the door and crossed the dingy carpet. "If it isn't my old friend!"

Walter Grossmith released Forster's arm and put out his hand. The small man twinkled his eyes and said: "Hi, Walter," and they shook hands. Then Walter said: "This is Dan Forster. You know Dan Forster, the railroad man?" and the small man shook hands with Dan Forster.

At the moment Dan Forster gripped the small man's hands, and at the split second that his smile was at its widest and most welcoming, a man who had been standing in the darkest corner of the lobby, apparently waiting for a friend, lifted an Eastman camera out of the folds of his overcoat and took a flash picture. He then walked quickly out of the club and disappeared into the street.

"What the hell was that?" snapped Dan Forster. "What the hell's going on here?"

Walter Grossmith stepped forward again. The small man seemed to have disappeared as magically as the cameraman. He took Forster's arm once more, and said in a low voice: "We're very sorry about this, but it seems you've made a pretty silly kind of mistake."

"Mistake? What Mistake? Listen—what is this?"

"Calm down, Mr. Forster. There's no point in losing your temper."

"What the hell are you talking about? You can't come in here and take pictures of people without their permission! I'll have you tossed out of here and blackballed!"

Walter Grossmith hushed him down. "Mr. Forster, please. It wasn't *me* who took the picture, now, was it? Just calm down."

Daniel Forster gripped Grossmith's lapel and held him close. Several other members turned around to watch, and there was a disturbed murmur of conversation in the background.

Forster whispered: "Unless you tell me what's going on here, I'll tear your head off. I mean that. Now, talk."

Grossmith didn't even look up at him. "It's very simple, Mr. Forster. You've made a bad mistake. You remember the old Crédit Mobilier scandal on the Union Pacific? Well, it's at least as bad as that. I'd say it was almost twice as bad as that."

Forster's round face was bright crimson with anger and confusion. He said: "Who *was* that? That friend of yours? Who *was* it?"

"Friend of mine?" said Grossmith. "I don't know what you're talking about. I never saw the fellow before in my whole life, except in the newspapers."

"You shook his hand! That's the only reason *I* did!"

Grossmith gently eased Forster's fingers away from his lapel. "No, Mr. Forster, I think you're mistaken. *I* didn't shake his hand. Why should I shake the hand of a man like that? I'm an influential man. I have my reputation to think of. I can't be seen shaking the hands of men like that, particularly in a place like this. Why, what would people say?"

Forster took a deep breath. Then he said: "Very well. It's all beginning to fit into place. Just tell me who it was so that I know what I'm up against."

Grossmith took his arm again and led him toward the club room. A couple of friends passed by and said: "Hi, there, Dan!" and Daniel Forster had to give them a tight smile and a nod.

"This can be very painless if you take it nice and gentle and see things real reasonable," said Walter Grossmith.

"I'm listening," Daniel Forster told him tersely.

"Well," said Walter Grossmith, "it appears that you've been kicking up some dust with the P&P Railroad over the Kruyper Dye Works out at Robinstown, Pennsylvania."

Forster stopped walking and stared at Grossmith with his intense blue eyes. He knew what was coming next; it was as plain and obvious as a P&P locomotive coming around a Pennsylvania curve, and there was nothing at all he could do to step out of the way.

Grossmith said: "It would be kind of appreciated in some circles if you had a quiet word with the P&P freight people and told them to think about a rebate for Kruyper's product. After all, we don't want to hamper good old United States commerce, do we? And we don't want to stand in the path of progress."

Forster said: "Is that all?"

Grossmith grinned benignly. "It would be pretty pleasant if it were, wouldn't it? But I'm afraid there's something else. All of a sudden, you feel like disposing of some TransMechanic stock, just because it makes sense these days to allot the right shares to the right trust, and you feel like doing it at giveaway prices."

"And what if I *don't* feel like doing it?"

Grossmith chuckled. "Mr. Forster, you're a vulnerable man! The New York papers would have a real ball with that picture of you, particularly when they read the captions that go along with it."

"What captions?"

"The captions that say: 'Pennsylvania Railroad Owner in Cahoots with Mobster.' "

Forster pulled out a club chair and sat down. A waiter came over and said: "Would you like to order, sir?"

Forster said: "I'll have a sidecar. This gentleman isn't staying."

Grossmith waved his hand. "Of course I'm staying. Make that two."

Eventually Forster said: "All right, Grossmith. What mobster?"

Walter Grossmith leaned back and reached in his pocket for a cigarette. He made a big fuss of lighting it and puffing out smoke before he answered.

"That little fellow you seemed to be so friendly with in the lobby was Jackie Morello, who is not a particularly enormous mobster in his own right, but is recognized by all and sundry, and particularly by the New York Police Department, as a close business associate of Frank Gizzi. Gizzi—as you're well aware—was unfortunately involved in that business of corrupting officials of the Baugh-Menominee Freight Corporation to transport illegal liquor across the state line."

Forster, staring dully at the floor, said: "Go on."

Grossmith tapped his cigarette in the ashtray. "There isn't much more to say, is there? Mr. Cornelius recognizes that he is beholden to you from way back, but Mr. Cornelius also feels that he has done you proud and given you everything you ever asked him for, and any further attempts on your part to interfere with his life or his business will not be taken particularly kindly. My personal advice to you is that you should go about your business, forget this has ever occurred, and live a long and happy life. Are you married?"

"Yes," said Daniel Forster. "Two children."

"That's very nice," said Grossmith. "I'm always glad to do business with family men, because they're so amenable."

"Is that a threat?" snapped Forster. "By God, if you threaten me—"

Walter Grossmith laid a soothing hand on Forster's arm. "You've been paid your price, Mr. Forster. Don't think you're going to improve on it, because you're not. Everybody has their limit, and when you started playing coy with the P&P Railroad, that's when Mr. Cornelius reached his. Now, please. Let's just talk about railroads, and forget about all this unpleasantness, shall we?"

Daniel Forster stood up. He tugged down his vest, and stared at Walter Grossmith as if he were the devil, or at least a fairly prominent demon.

"I'll be damned if I'll ever speak another word to you, Grossmith. And I'll be damned if I don't see that you get what you deserve, one day, whenever it is, and however it's done."

Grossmith smiled, and shrugged. "If nothing else," he said, "I think I deserve a medal for tact."

1934

DAVID BOOKBINDER TO
CORNELIUS OIL AFTER
COLTON FURORE

Mr. David Bookbinder, chief legal executive for Colton
Oil up until the shareholders' meeting debacle two
weeks ago, has taken his Golden Smile to Cornelius Oil,
where Mr. Johann Cornelius is reported to be "more than
happy" with his new associate. Informed sources say
that Bookbinder, 47, a onetime legal eagle for Cullings
Maidment Sparks, has a substantial share of Cornelius
stock, and a salary that should keep him in law books for
at least three centuries.

—New York Daily Post,
August 17, 1934

Later that year, Dutch Schultz, who had been a fugitive from justice since January 25, 1933, was to walk into the office of United States Commissioner Lester T. Hubbard at Albany to surrender himself. It was not to be revealed in the publicity statements that he had been driven to Albany from Lynwood's Island in Johann Cornelius' own Rolls-Royce; nor was it revealed where Schultz had been hiding so successfully for almost two years.

It was the twilight of the Prohibition era and of all the gangsters and racketeers who had thrived on it. In less than a year, federal agents had shot to death John Dillinger, Pretty Boy Floyd, Homer van Meter, and half a dozen lesser public enemies; and on the day that Schultz surrendered, Lester M. Gillis (better known as Baby Face Nelson) was to be found lying dead in a ditch at Niles Center, Chicago, with seventeen bullet wounds sustained the previous night in what the newspapers called "a sanguinary encounter."

The changing mood was probably no better illustrated than by Commissioner Hubbard, who didn't recognize Schultz when he came to give himself up, and had to have his memory refreshed on Schultz's case by his attorney. Nineteen thirty-three had been more than a year away; it had been a whole era away. This was 1934.

It was a year that opened with Mae West in *I'm No Angel* and Katharine Hepburn in *Little Women*. It was a year when trolley cars gave way to motor buses on nine New York City lines, including Madison, Fourth, and Lex. Mrs. Anna Antonio, a twenty-eight-year-old mother of three who had murdered her husband for his $5,000 insurance, was executed in the electric chair at Sing Sing. She said: "I'm not afraid to die." It was a year that began with a savage winter in New York, and then saw temperatures rise to 117 degrees in Oklahoma, with thousands left homeless and destitute in the blizzards of dust that swept the West. John Jacob Astor married Ellen French, fifty strikers were wounded by police bullets in Minneapolis, and President Roosevelt went looking for swordfish in Hawaii. In Louisiana, the Kingfish, Huey Long, was joking

297

that he'd bought himself a silk shirt with a collar so high he had to stand on a stump to spit, and on Wednesday, May 23, a warm and fair day in that same verdant state, Texas Rangers and sheriff's deputies ambushed Clyde Barrow and Bonnie Parker outside of Gibsland and reduced them, according to eyewitnesses, to a "smear of red, wet rags."

That same day, forty or so miles to the west, in Shreveport, Johann Cornelius was standing in the burned-out ruins of the first Cornelius Oil gas station on Jewella Road. The ashes smudged his brown-and-white two-tone shoes, and dirtied the cuffs of his cream linen pants, but he stood there stolidly with his hands deep in his coat pockets, his eyes shaded by his panama hat, staring at the charred timbers and the twisted metal framework, and he looked unmovable. Not too far away, on the black-streaked sidewalk, Henry Keith talked to the city fire marshal, but both of them treated Johann's grief as something personal, and made no move toward him until he called them.

The sky was almost cloudless, except for a few smoky puffs of cumulus over Cross Lake, and even though it was only half after eleven in the morning, everyone could tell that it was going to be another roastingly hot day. Leaves of a scorched ledger peeled away one by one from their burned binding and fluttered across the street.

After a while Johann said: "Henry."

He said it softly, but Henry heard him at once. He came across the smuts and the ashes on tippy-toes, and stood beside his employer, holding his pants legs a couple of inches off the ground.

"You wet yourself?" asked Johann.

Henry Keith blushed. "No, sir."

"Then don't stand there looking as though you have. If you need a quarter to have your pants cleaned afterward, I'll lend it to you."

Henry Keith let the cuffs of his pants drop. "Thank you, sir."

Johann crunched a few paces over the wreckage.

"Well, Henry, who do you think it was?"

"*Who*, sir? I don't understand."

Johann waved his hand impatiently. "Who lit the torch, or threw the bomb, or whatever it was that razed this place to the ground?"

"You think it was arson, sir?"

"Well, don't you?"

Henry Keith looked uncomfortably around. "I'm not sure, sir."

Johann shook his head slowly. There was a sooty smudge on his cheek.

"This gas station burned because somebody wanted it to burn, Henry. It burned because there's somebody around who wants to see our retail gas sales go to the wall. Somebody who wants to keep the gas market to themselves."

"You really think that, sir?"

"I wouldn't say it if I didn't really think it. Jesus Christ, Henry, if I was in their position I'd probably do the same thing."

Henry Keith shook ashes from his foot and looked unhappy. "I could always get some detectives onto it, sir."

Johann eyed his aide from the shadow of his hat. "Detectives won't help us. We need someone clever. Someone who knows the gas-station market better than us. I feel too much like an innocent in Paradise."

"Oh, I wouldn't say that, sir."

"Well, that's because you're prone to attacks of dumbness, that's why. The only way to get on top is to admit to yourself what you don't know, and I don't know this gas-station business any better than I know the length of a piece of string."

At that moment, the city fire marshal came striding toward them in his big yellow rubbers. He had a scorched, weathered look to his face, and a bristly mustache.

"Mr. Cornelius, sir?"

Johann nodded.

"We've, uh, sifted through most of the wreckage now, sir."

"And what have you found?"

"Well, there ain't no evidence in favor of arson, sir, but on the other hand, there ain't no evidence against it, neither."

"I see. Well, that's good enough for me."

"You mean you believe it was done deliberate?"

Johann prodded at the black ruins with his foot. "The moment I heard what had happened, I knew it was done deliberately. The only question remaining in my mind is who did it."

The fire marshal took off his helmet and wiped his forehead with the back of his hand. "Can you think of anyone who don't like you too much?" he asked, trying to be helpful.

Johann almost laughed. "Hundreds," he said in a husky, amused voice.

The fire marshal stood there for a while longer, nodded and sniffed, and then went back to his new red-painted Plymouth PE DeLuxe, complete with shiny brass bell. Johann and Henry Keith trod gingerly over the ashes until they had reached the sidewalk, and then Johann said: "I want you to put the word out."

Henry Keith tugged down his rumpled coat and tried to look intense.

"The word, sir?"

"That's right. Put out the word that anyone who feels like helping us out, as far as gas stations are concerned, can expect a lifetime pension for their trouble."

Henry Keith jotted that down. "Right, sir. I'll do that right away, sir."

Johann clapped him on the back, too hard for comfort. "That's a good boy, Henry. Let's make sure we get this bastard, whoever it is, and let's make sure we sew him up for good and all."

Johann was dining in his hotel suite that evening, around eight o'clock, when the telephone rang. Henry Keith answered it while Johann sat there with a mouthful of duck terrine. The hotel room, the best they could find in Shreveport, was decorated with fading yellow flowers and various etchings of Shreve's Cutoff and Mack's Bayou, all rendered with a vaguely depressing dedication to reality.

Henry Keith said: "Yes?" and Johann swallowed his terrine with a mouthful of Sauternes. He hated wines with any trace of sweetness, but this was the best and the driest the hotel stocked.

On the telephone, Henry Keith said: "You're kidding." Then: "You're kidding." Then: "When did this happen?"

Johann said harshly: "Who's kidding? What the hell's going on?"

Henry listened for a while longer, then put his hand over the mouthpiece.

"It's our office at Austin, sir. They just had reports from the Texas Rangers and the local police that three of our gas stations went up during the afternoon. At Tyler, Waco, and Temple, sir."

Johann pushed away his wheeled table and stalked over to the telephone, wiping his mouth with his napkin. He snatched it from Henry's hands and said loudly: "Who's that?"

"My name's Irving, sir," said a nervous voice on the phone.

"Well, Irving, what the hell's going on?"

"I just got the news, sir. Three gas stations were burned down,

300

and one of our staff killed. Two others got bad burns trying to put down the flames. The fire people say it's almost certainly arson, sir."

"Jesus, Irving, that's four in two days!"

Irving didn't sound at all happy. "Yes, sir, it is, sir. I'm afraid that it is."

"Irving," said Johann darkly, "I want guards on every single gas station we've opened. I want them armed and I want them now. If anyone, anyone at all, tries anything funny, then they've got specific orders from me to shoot. Do you understand that?"

"Yes, sir. Right away, sir."

Johann put down the phone. He rubbed his eyes for a moment, and then he said to Henry Keith: "Fetch me the gas-station file."

He pushed aside his dinner and laid out maps and lists. With his gold-nibbed Larkwood pen he marked with a cross all the four gas stations that had been attacked, and then he sat back in his chair and stared at them. Henry Keith said: "Are you looking for some kind of pattern, sir?"

Johann shook his head. "Whoever's got the nerve to go around bombing gas stations isn't going to worry about whether he's doing it systematically or not. Hell, I just want to know *who.*"

"I put the word out, sir. We may get an informant."

Johann leaned forward glumly and peered at the maps. "Don't count on it," he said in a soft, almost reflective tone. "Whoever's involved is pretty sure of himself, and pretty sure of us."

"Do you think they'll go for more gas stations? Or do you think they're just trying to warn us off?"

Johann raised his eyes at Henry and there wasn't the slightest trace of humor on his face. He would be sixty-one this year, and that was exactly the age he looked. The creases around his eyelids were deeply scored, and his thin hair was a shade of yellowish gray. He had established himself as one of the fiercest and most autocratic oil billionaires in the country, and he was still spreading himself through petrochemicals, shipping, and any kind of business he could lay his hands on. He and his ever-more-complicated corporations were spinning denser and denser webs of influence through American life, taking advantage of a struggling economy and mid-Depression despair to invest everywhere at rock-bottom prices. Before 1929, and the Great Crash, he had amassed sufficient liquid funds to see Cornelius Oil over the worst. This was partly because of financial naiveté and partly because he believed more in himself than he did in other people. Whatever it was, he had remained rich, though less rich, while others went broke. Now he was reaching out to acquire himself food chains and gas stations and hotels and factories. He had put up twenty-four gas stations through Texas, Louisiana, Alabama, and Mississippi in twenty-two months. But now, quite obviously, someone had sat up and taken notice, and whoever that someone was, they didn't like what they saw.

Johann was mellowing with age. There was no doubt that he wasn't the same hard-faced tycoon who had wrestled against financial desperation and impossible pressures to build Cornelius Oil up from the ground. He wasn't even the self-controlled, philosophizing creature who had bought Robinstown from guileless and greedy men so that he could rip away the soil for coal. He still felt energetic, still felt expansionist; but he was also beginning to take into account the personal price that his business and private life had cost him. Sometimes he sat at his desk for hours on end, staring out at the rain that dribbled down his office windows, and he would shake his head and reflect, almost with disbelief, on the way that everything, whether it was oil or money or love or hatred, had its own exact toll.

Now, at nearly sixty-one years, he was gradually beginning to appreciate what his self-suppression had done. It had rendered him almost incapable of offering affection to anyone else at all, even Hester. And yet now, for the first time since his days in Amarero, he was feeling the need to love. He could picture himself as a marble statue, against whose feet wreaths and offerings were laid, and against whose chilly lips kisses were often pressed. But he was incapable of returning any of this devotion, and he remained emotionless and petrified. Even for four hundred million dollars, it may have been too high a price to pay.

Henry Keith said: "You're worried?"

Johann coughed, and shook his head. "Not at the moment. But if this continues, I could be. So today it's gas stations. What's it going to be tomorrow? If they think they can run us out of the retail business, how long is it going to be before they try to run us out of the wholesale market? And how long before they start blowing our rigs up?"

Henry Keith tried to look as pessimistic as possible. Johann said: "What are you looking so damned miserable for?"

"I thought the situation warranted it, sir."

302

"The situation never warrants a face like that. Now, what the hell are we doing about finding out who did it?"

Abruptly the phone rang. Henry blinked and sat up straight, and Johann flicked a glance across at him that meant "answer it—quick." Henry picked up the earpiece and said: "Yes?"

There was a long pause. Henry could tell that there was someone there, and yet this someone didn't seem to feel like answering straightaway.

Then the voice said: "You're not Mr. Cornelius, are you?"

"This is his secretary," said Henry Keith. "Mr. Cornelius is busy right now."

Again there was a quiet pause. Then the voice said: "What's he busy doing? Throwing pails of water over his gas stations?"

Henry Keith frowned. "Listen," he snapped, "who is this?"

The voice sounded placid. "You'll find out. Do you want to find out? The word seems to be that you do."

Henry Keith said crossly: "Listen, whoever you are. If you have some information on those gas stations, I reckon you'd better come out with it."

The voice was unworried. "What if I don't?"

Henry Keith didn't quite know how to answer that. He covered the phone and hissed at Johann: "It's some guy who knows something about the gas-station bombings."

Johann raised an eyebrow. "How much does he want?"

"I didn't ask him."

"Well, *ask*. Why the hell do you think he's calling?"

Henry Keith uncovered the mouthpiece and said: "What's your price, mister?"

There was another lengthy pause. Then the voice said: "My price is negotiable. Ask Mr. Cornelius, if he's there, whether he remembers a picture of Loch Lomond."

Henry Keith said: "What? What are you talking about? I can't ask him that."

"Ask him."

Henry laid the phone down again. He said: "I'm sorry, sir, but he says to ask you if you remember a picture of Loch Lomond."

Johann was in the middle of estimating what four new gas stations were going to cost him. He said: "How the hell should I know?"

Henry Keith went back to the phone. "I'm sorry, mister. He

doesn't know. Now, why don't you just give me your name and your number and I'll—"

"Ask him if he remembers a railroad whistle. A boy, and a railroad whistle."

Henry Keith said: "Sir? He's crazy. Now he wants to know if you remember a railroad whistle. Look, shall I tell him to—"

Johann's face rose from his maps and his papers like a gray shroud coming out of a washing machine. He whispered: "*A railroad whistle?*"

Henry Keith didn't know what to do. He nodded dumbly. Johann got up from his chair, walked across the room, and took the phone out of Henry's hands. He said in an almost inaudible voice: "*Yes?*"

The voice at the other end of the line seemed to know at once it was him. It asked, with obvious satisfaction: "Ah! So you *do* remember it!"

"What of it?" said Johann.

"Not a great deal. But enough to make it worthwhile we meet. I'll tell you where."

"Here is okay. Suite 501, the Shreveport Inn."

"There is *not* okay, I'm afraid. Those people who are giving you so much trouble know you're there. They know whom you meet, and they know where you go. Today you were out on Jewella Road, looking over that burned-out gas station of yours."

Johann said: "Of course I damn well was. Any lamebrain could have guessed that."

The voice replied: "It doesn't make any difference. I don't want to meet you at the Shreveport Inn. There's a seat on the south side of the main entrance to Querbes Park. I'll meet you there at a quarter of ten tomorrow morning, and I want you to come by yourself."

Johann rubbed his forehead for a while, and then he said: "How shall I know you?"

The voice almost seemed to smile. "Oh, you'll know me. There's an old Latvian saying which says: 'Friendship brings you close; marriage brings you closer; but a shared secret is a mingling of blood.' "

The phone at the other end was laid down. Johann held the receiver in his hands for a few moments, and then put it back on the cheaply varnished side table as if it was a precious family heirloom.

Henry Keith asked: "Are you all right, sir?"

Hester had remained at Lynwood's Island. It was Hope's fifteenth birthday party that weekend, and fifty or sixty of her friends from school were coming up to celebrate the occasion with champagne punch and dancing on the jetty. Roderick was away at college, but John had taken a week off school, and Stainer, the butler, who had an aged sister quite close to New Paltz, had driven him home in the maroon Rockne sedan which Johann had bought for the servants.

John was seventeen, and at the peak of his athleticism. He was doing better at school than when he was younger, but he was best at relay running and throwing the javelin. Whenever he came back to Lynwood's Island, he spent hours sculling, and on the day that Johann was inspecting his burned-out gas station in Shreveport, John was rowing up and down the river with long, systematic strokes, while Hester and Hope stood on the jetty and watched him, the way that women do. The bright bunting that had been strung from the jetty for Hope's birthday was popping and fluttering in the wind, and Hester had to place one hand lightly on her wide staw hat with its long blue chiffon band. The other hand rested equally lightly on Hope's shoulder.

"Doesn't he scull well?" said Hester. These days, at the age of forty-two, her prettiness was fading in the way that a pressed flower fades between the pages of a Bible, but she still had the style and self-possession with which Johann had first fallen in love. Her daughter was not half as pretty; but fifteen was the swollen age of hips and breasts and puppy fat, and hair that flopped lankly over her forehead no matter how frequently she washed it, and blushing too much, and the curse.

Hope said: "I hope his friends at school don't think he's a showoff."

Hester waved to John as he sculled past them. The surface of the river was glittering like hammered glass, and John's sculls worked their way across the reflected light in energetic angles. He couldn't wave back, of course, but he grinned.

"Boys have to show off," said Hester. "It's their nature."

"Daddy doesn't show off."

"He's a man, darling, not a boy. And in any case he doesn't have to."

"Will he be back for my birthday?"

Hester said: "I don't know. He's had a great deal of trouble

305

down in the South. He called me this morning and said his gas station at Shreveport was completely burned down.''

"I hope he comes back. I've got a present for him, too. I made it myself."

John was almost out of sight now, behind the overhanging trees that came down to the river's edge. It looked as if he was going to scull himself around to the boathouse and come ashore, so Hester gently guided Hope away from the jetty and back up the garden toward the house. It was warmer away from the river, and the old trees frothed and danced in the late-spring wind.

Hester said: "Do you love your father, Hope?"

Hope stopped, and stared at her mother in surprise. "Of course. He's my father. I've made him a foot-warmer to wear in his airplane. You can put both feet into it at once, and it's made of felt. I sewed his initials on it."

Hester looked reflective and sad. The band around her hat rose and fell in the breeze.

"He never uses anything else you've ever made him," she said. "Why did you make him this?"

Hope pushed her hair back away from her forehead. "I don't know. I suppose I keep on thinking that one day he will."

"He's not a sentimental man, Hope. Not even with his family. That's what a lot of people don't understand."

"But he loves us, surely?"

Hester smiled. "Yes, of course. Well, yes, I suppose so."

They carried on walking up the neatly raked gravel path. As they climbed beyond the trees, they could look back toward the boathouse and see John dragging his scull up the duckboards.

"I sometimes think that Daddy's upset about something," said Hope.

Hester didn't answer at first. She couldn't tell her daughter that the very same thought had occurred to her the night after she had married Johann, and that after twenty-three years of marriage she was still no nearer finding out why. She said: "Oh, I'm sure he's not, darling," and waved to John to hurry up and join them.

John was out of breath by the time he caught up. He was sweating, and he had to dab his face with his rowing towel to mop it up. Hester said: "You were wonderful, John! I've never seen you scull so well!"

John looked pleased. "I hope to make the team this season. They're pretty picky, though. Even Laurence didn't make it, and you know how good Laurence is."

"I know how much money his father makes, if that's any criterion."

John followed his mother and sister into the square central hallway of the house, with its mock-Roman mosaic floor. His sports pumps squeaked as he walked. He said: "Is Dad coming home tonight?"

"Not for a couple of days, dear. Maybe the weekend, if he can get away."

John thoughtfully rubbed the back of his neck with his towel. "Well, in that case, do you think you could spare me a half hour this evening? I guess I've got something I need to discuss."

Hope glanced at her mother, but Hester's face showed only motherly calm. These days, it was rare for John to confide in his parents. He occasionally mentioned that he wanted to go into law, or that he was going to try for the swimming six at school; but the rest of the time he behaved as if the only things that ever entered his head were sports and jazz and racing cars. Hester had suspected for a long while that John's closest friends were probably his schoolmates, and that he told his most personal thoughts only to them. She knew why, too. Ever since he was young, he had been brought up by his father to believe that the only way a man could survive in the world was to keep his most sensitive side turned away from other people. Whenever John had tried to be affectionate toward his father, he had been met with nothing but remote, lukewarm smiles, and as far as his family was concerned, he now thought that this was the only way to behave.

Hester said: "I've got some spare time now. Why don't you come into the sewing room? Hope, I'll see you later. Are you going out to Lynwood tonight to see Sally? Or are you staying in? It's salmon for dinner, I think."

Hope said: "That's okay. I'll stay." Then she went off to change, while Hester took her son's muscular arm and walked with him into the oval sewing room. She closed the door firmly behind them and pointed to one of the elegant balloon-back chairs.

John said: "I'm kinda sweaty. Maybe I'll stand."

Hester said: "Whatever you wish," and perched herself upright and precise on her favorite sewing chair. Beside her was an embroidery frame with an almost completed cushion cover of riotous rhododendrons.

She asked him: "You're not in any kind of trouble?"

John didn't answer at once. He went over to the window and looked out over the back of the house. The peacocks were sweeping the lawns with their tails, and a gardener was busy digging in plants.

He said: "It's pretty hard to explain, really. I mean, it's pretty hard to find the right words."

"Try me."

"Well—I guess it's usually the kind of thing a guy would bring up with his father."

"Yes?"

"I mean, I would have . . . I *would* have talked to Dad about it —but he isn't here too often—and in any case he's not really the kind of . . . well, I don't want to sound as if I'm insulting him . . ."

Hester lowered her eyes. She picked at a stray thread on the embroidery frame. "John," she said, "I know exactly what you're trying to say."

John was embarrassed for a moment, and acted a little goofy. "Yeah, well, if you know what I mean then it's okay. . . ."

Hester said: "Is it to do with sex?"

John went very red. He hadn't realized that his mother could use the word "sex," that she could actually let it pass her lips. He mumbled and muttered, and then at last he said: "Well, kind of."

Hester held out her hand. "John, come here."

John didn't want to come at first, but then he reluctantly stepped over and laid his young perspiring hand in the dry middle-aged palm of his small and elegant mother. On her fingers were emeralds and diamonds that, auctioned, would have bought half a block of Manhattan real estate.

"John," she said, "I love your father in my way, and my way is a way that nobody else can understand. I will never tell you that he is a cold man, or an inconsiderate man, or a cruel man. He has done cold, and cruel, and inconsiderate things. You know that for yourself. But I have been married to him for long enough to know that there is something else inside him, shut away, that in all his years he may never reveal. He is just as capable of love and happiness as the rest of us, but for some reason, perhaps lots of different reasons, he has declined to let love and happiness have much of a part in his life."

John pulled up a chair and sat down. He hung his towel over the back of it, and looked at his mother with the kind of earnestness that only a seventeen-year-old with a sex problem could muster.

He said: "I guess you love him pretty much, huh?"

Hester nodded. "Yes," she said, "I do."

"Well," said John, "I love Hazel pretty much as well."

There was a small silence, during which the Delft porcelain clock on the sewing room's light walnut side table ticked with delicate patience.

Hester said warily: "Hazel? I don't think you've mentioned any Hazel before."

John grinned in embarrassment. "No. I haven't, as a matter of fact. I kind of met her in Poughkeepsie. Me and Jim Walach went to the movies one night, and that's when I kind of met her."

"You kind of met her?" asked Hester coolly. "What does that mean?"

"Well, we went to see *Meet the Baron* with the Three Stooges, and then we went to a soda fountain, and that's where she works."

Hester stared at her son as if she could hardly believe what he was saying. John shuffled his feet and said: "She's real pretty, Mom. She comes from a real good family, too. Her pop sells insurance. I guess he probably sells some of Dad's insurance, too. I mean, I guess most insurance salesmen do."

Hester said: "Do I understand you correctly? Are you trying to tell me that you've fallen in love with a soda jerk?"

John protested: "Hey, Mom, she's not exactly a soda jerk. You couldn't call her a soda jerk."

"What else would you call her? And for goodness' sake stop using that awful language. I am not 'Mom,' and I never will be."

"I'm sorry, Mother. But Hazel's a real nice girl. We went out together a couple of times on weekends, and you can take it from me she's bright and she's intelligent. She only works at the fountain to make a little extra cash to help her through school."

Hester rose from her chair as if by mystic levitation. Then she went across to the glass-fronted bookcase and peered into it like someone consulting an oracle. John could see her face dimly reflected in the glass, and somehow she looked like a young girl. The words she spoke, though, were far from young.

309

"I know what you think of us, sometimes, your father and me. I know that you choose to confide in others, rather than us. But don't you really think that the blame is as much yours as it is ours?"

Hester turned and faced him. He could see now that he had made her very angry.

"Your father worked his way up from nothing to build one of the greatest business empires this country has ever known. There is nobody in the whole of the continental United States who does not know your father's name and what it stands for. My own family was of high quality and breeding, and between us your father and I gave to our children the very finest elements of aristocracy and industry. You children—Roderick and Hope, and you, John—should be the elite of America."

"Mom, the whole *thing* about America is that we're *equal*. That's how Dad made it, and that's how I'm going to make it. Hazel is equal to me and I'm equal to her, and what's more, Hazel is equal to you, too!"

Hester took one convulsive step forward and slapped her son's face.

"How dare you!" she breathed. "How dare you speak of your mother in the same breath as a common working girl!"

John didn't answer. It hadn't been a hard slap, but it had taken him completely by surprise. He had never seen his mother so furious before, and he didn't know what to say or how to explain what he felt. Hester turned away from him and stood by her embroidery stand as if it was a lectern from which she was going to preach.

"I thought we had taught you well. I know that you have had trouble with your father, but I thought we had taught you well. I thought that you were the bright one, the one who was going to be clever and perceptive and friendly. Instead, you don't seem to have understood a single thing about your position, your responsibilities, or what you're going to have to do when you mature. Equal! How can you say such a thing? Do you really believe that gardener out there is equal to you, or that he's ever going to do more than grub in the soil for your appreciation?"

"But, Mom—"

Hester gave a brief shake of her head to show that she wasn't prepared to listen. "We are all equal in the eyes of God," she said,

310

"but we are none of us equal in the eyes of society. Good Lord, John, you might just as well have dated a nigger!"

John wiped the sweat away from his upper lip with the back of his hand. Then he said quietly: "Well, that's it, Mom. I have."

The silence was like cracked ice. Hester said: "What?"

John coughed. "Hazel is colored, Mom. She's a colored girl."

There was one second of paralyzing tension, and then Hester threw back her head and laughed. John could see her gold bridgework and he looked away.

"John, you *fool*!" Hester continued laughing. "You and your practical jokes! I should have known as soon as you mentioned the Three Stooges! Oh, I'm so sorry I lost my temper! What an idiot you must think I am! The whole idea!"

John, embarrassed by his mother's laughter, couldn't help smirking as well, and Hester took that as a plain indication that he was making fun of her.

"But just remember," she said, getting out her tray of silks in readiness for sewing, "it's all very well to play a joke on me, but your father might think differently. He doesn't quite have the same sense of humor."

In a small, congested voice, John said: "Mother, it's true."

Hester sat down and started to thread her needles with shining peacock blues and greens. "Yes, dear. I'm quite sure that it is. Are you staying in for dinner tonight? Do you know something, you had me so *mad* for a moment . . ." She smiled indulgently, and put down her sewing to lay a hand on John's arm. "You're a funny boy. You always have been. Do you remember the time you put those earthworms in poor Hope's rubbers . . ."

John found it impossible to speak. His throat was choked up, and he knew that if he didn't keep a tight rein on himself, he was probably going to cry.

"Mother," he said, on the brink of tears, "you have to understand that it's true. Hazel is colored, and she's a real girl, and it isn't a joke. We're in love."

Hester was still smiling, but the humor was leaking out of her smile like ink spreading across a damp letter. "You realize what you're saying, of course?" she asked John frigidly. "If this really isn't a joke, you realize what you're saying?"

"Mother, I can't help it. I love her."

"You can't love colored people. It's ridiculous. Nobody does."

311

"Mother, I love her! We want to get married!"

Hester let out a short, testy sigh. "John, you are seventeen years old and you are the son of Johann Cornelius. Not only are you far too young to marry anybody at all, you are certainly never going to marry a nigger who works in a soda fountain! You must tell her that it's all finished between you, and the sooner you do it, the better. I won't have it. The very idea!"

John's eyes were filled with tears now. He felt as if his insides were being torn down like layers of wallpaper. He said: "Mother, you can't stop us! We've already made up our minds!"

"What do you mean, I can't stop you? Of course I can stop you! You're far too young to marry, and that's all there is to it. And in any event, I refuse to have a nigger for a daughter-in-law. Think of the embarrassment!"

John kicked his mother's embroidery frame, and it tipped over sideways in a confusion of threads and silks. "*Will you stop calling her a nigger*!" he shrieked.

Hester stood up. Her eyes were wide with fury. "You pathetic boy!" she snapped. "You silly, senseless boy! What in the world do you think you're trying to prove?"

John went down on his knees and gathered up the silks. He set the embroidery frame straight again. But he didn't look at his mother, and he didn't answer her question. He said, instead: "I'm sorry. I didn't think you'd get so mad."

"You didn't think I'd get so mad? What was I supposed to do? Give thanks to the Lord that my youngest son has been dating a colored girl? I don't know how you can bear to kiss her! I suppose you've kissed her?"

"Yes."

"The idea of it! It sends shivers down my spine! You must tell her at once that you're finished, do you understand me?"

"I can't, Mother."

"You can and you will."

"It isn't as easy as that."

"Oh? And why not, pray?"

"She's having my baby. She's pregnant."

Hester believed him this time. She looked at him, how young he was, in his sweat-stained sports shirt and his scuffy white rowing pumps, and she raised her hand and gently ran it through his tousled hair. John couldn't quite understand why she was being so gentle now, and he thought for a moment that she was going to give in, and let him marry Hazel and raise their child. He whispered: "Mother . . .?"

His mother slowly, slowly shook her head. "My poor young boy," she said, in a voice so soft he could scarcely hear her. Then she turned and walked over to the telephone and picked up the receiver. "Stainer?" she said. "Will you get me Dr. Nash?"

John frowned. "Dr. Nash? What does Dr. Nash have to do with it?"

"Sit down, John," said Hester, and he sat. Then she brought her chair nearer and sat down, too.

"John," she told him, "you must tell me where Hazel is. What her address is. Does she live in Poughkeepsie? Or does she live someplace near?"

"She lives in Poughkeepsie, but—"

"Then you know the street, and the number?"

"Sure, but—"

"It's no use, John. Whatever you say, the best thing will have to be done. It's better for . . . Hazel . . . as well as yourself. I'm afraid that there's no getting away from it."

John said: "But Hazel's here, Mom. I mean, she's in Lynwood, staying at the Lakeshore Hotel. I told her to come up here, so that when I'd explained what had happened to you, or maybe Dad, then she could . . ."

"She could what?"

He smeared the tears away from his eyes with his hands. "Well, she could meet you. You know?"

Hester gave a small deprecating laugh. "No, my dear, I don't know. How could you think of it? Really, John, I would have thought better of you."

John said: "But she's there, Mom. She's waiting. Mom, she's having my baby."

Hester raised her hands. "It's completely out of the question. She is not to have your baby and that is why I have telephoned Dr. Nash. Do you know her room number?"

John stared at his mother disbelievingly. "Mother," he said, "it's my baby! It's a person! It's a person that Hazel and I *made*!"

"You're talking to a woman who has had three children," replied Hester. "A baby is not a person until it is born, and even then it can be less than a blessing. Your colored friend is simply pregnant, and that is all there is to be said. Dr. Nash will do everything he can to terminate her pregnancy as painlessly and as

313

promptly as possible. There! That's the telephone! That will be Dr. Nash now.''

John, frantic, said: ''Mother . . . you can't!''

Hester went over and picked up the receiver. ''I can,'' she said firmly, ''and I certainly will.''

Then, as John listened in silent despair, she said: ''Dr. Nash? It's Mrs. Cornelius. I have a favor to ask you of the utmost discretion.''

She began to explain what had happened, but John didn't stay to hear the end of the conversation. He left the sewing room and went outside to the front steps, where he sat beside a stone lion and watched the May breeze ruffle the grass, and the sparkling waves of the endlessly flowing Hudson. He didn't cry anymore. He was beyond crying. He simply sat there with his chin in his hands while the afternoon went by, and nobody, on Hester's explicit instructions, disturbed him.

She knew that he would get over it.

At ten o'clock the following morning, in Shreveport, Johann Cornelius and Henry Keith were seated side by side on the green-painted park bench at the south side of the main entrance to Querbes Park. Johann was dressed in a fawn spring suit with chalk stripes, and a fawn felt hat. Henry Keith, as usual, looked as though he had slept the night in the back of an Okie's pickup. The morning was overcast, although the sky was breaking up in the west, and Johann was growing increasingly annoyed and impatient.

''He said quarter of ten, didn't he?'' he said, opening his gold half-hunter.

''That's what you told me, sir.''

''Well, if he said quarter of ten, why the hell can't he get here on time? What does he think I've got? Money to burn?''

They waited another ten minutes, and almost as Johann was about to give the rendezvous up and go back to the Shreveport Inn, the gates of the park swung open with a squeak and a plump middle-aged man in a dark suit and a fawn hat came in and walked over toward them. As he came closer, Johann saw that he was neat and smart, with a pink expressionless face, and glittering near-together eyes. He looked, in a way, rubbery, like a bothersome baby in a business suit. His nose, at first glance, could have been a large French snail having a rest on the slow journey up his face. His hands and feet were doll-like, and he smelled of cologne. He stopped right in the front of them, clicked his well-polished heels, and said: "You must forgive me. It isn't easy to get away."

Johann looked the man up and down without changing his disgruntled expression. "I hope you know you've kept me waiting for nearly a half hour," he said hoarsely.

"Please," said the man, "forgive me."

Johann sniffed. "Well, there's not much else I can do. Are you going to sit down?"

"I thought we'd walk. It's more difficult for people to overhear when one is walking. There's an old Polish saying which says: 'The cuckoo that calls in the same nest every day is soon snared.' "

Johann said: "There's an old Texas saying which says: 'If you've got something to tell me, you'd better spit it out.' "

"Very well, then," said the smooth-faced man. "Let's walk."

Side by side, the three of them strolled around the crisscross paths. They could have been nothing more than old friends discussing their schooldays. The morning grew hotter, and Johann had to stop to wipe his hatband with his handkerchief.

"I still don't know your credentials," he told the pink-faced man. "I don't even know your name, although you very obviously know mine."

"I was coming to my credentials," the stranger said calmly. "I assure you that they're very good."

"You said something on the telephone about a railroad whistle."

"Of course," said the man. "That's my trump card."

"You know Daniel Forster?"

"I met him by chance. He came to us for money when his railroad was low on funds. He told me how well you looked after him."

Johann mopped the perspiration from his neck. "Did he say why?"

The man, with his eyes slitted against the glare of the sun, looked around the park. "Oh, yes," he said. "He told me all about that."

"Why should he?"

"Because he wanted money. Everything has its price, you know."

Johann said, with irritation: "You're telling me that?"

315

"Not really. I don't need to. But if you want any further proof that I know just what I'm talking about, then think of people like Kyle Lennox and Carina."

Johann stopped wiping his face and stood completely still. Then he turned to the pink-faced stranger and said: "What do you know about Carina?"

The man beamed. "More to the point," he said, as if he was very pleased with himself, "what do I know about the Excelsior Hotel?"

Henry Keith was looking baffled. "Excuse me, sir," he broke in. "I'm not entirely sure that I—"

Johann hushed him. "You'll find out soon enough. That's if this gentleman has his way. Or perhaps this gentleman would like to tell us his name first, and why he's acting so smart?"

The man beamed even more. "Of course. My name is David Bookbinder, and I run the legal department of Colton Oil. My master, if you can seriously call him that, is Percy F. Colton."

"*Colton!*" barked Johann.

David Bookbinder raised an eyebrow. "I thought you might be interested to hear that name again. Especially since you've been having such trouble with your gas stations."

Henry Keith said: "Are you trying to say that Percy Colton's behind these bombings?"

David Bookbinder prodded at some wastepaper with the tip of his cane. "Not in so many words. But it would seem logical, wouldn't it? Colton has one of the largest chains of gas stations in the South and Southeast, although not all of them are openly trading as Colton Oil. There's Texas Star, Abilene, Golden Power— more than half a dozen—and they're all his. What would you do if some upstart billionaire like Mr. Cornelius here started opening newer and better gas stations right in your own backyard?"

Johann stopped walking, and stood for a while in the shade of a tree, fanning himself with his hat.

"Very well," he said, "supposing it's Percy Colton. What's your price for stopping him?"

David Bookbinder smiled. "It's not quite as easy as that. I want more than a price. I want to take over Cornelius Oil."

Johann let out a sharp bark of obvious disbelief.

"Well, that's out of the question, of course."

David Bookbinder didn't seem to have heard. He said: "I want one percent of the equity, and a permanent position as chief executive."

Johann said: "You're crazy. That's completely out of the question. Do you realize how much one percent of the equity in Cornelius Oil works out at?"

David Bookbinder nodded. "That's why I'm asking."

Johann sat down on a sawn-off stump. "All right," he said quietly, "what do I get in return?"

"You get a lot," answered David Bookbinder. "You pay a lot, but you get a lot."

"Like what?"

"You get to take over Coltons and stop them once and for all. You also get to hear nothing but wonderful silence from that long-forgotten railroad whistle."

Johann put his hat back on his head. "You think I care about that?"

David Bookbinder started beaming again. "Of course you care! Why else would young Daniel Forster find himself so handsomely set up in the railroad business at such a tender age, and why else would he find ten thousand dollars a year deposited in his bank by anonymous donors? Come on, Mr. Cornelius, I've talked to Daniel Forster and I know just what happened in 1903. It was all very regrettable, and it was all very unfortunate, but it's better to let bygones stay that way, don't you think? Especially now you're handling so many government contracts, and sitting on the board of overseas trade. What would Eleanor say if she knew what one of her favorite NRA supporters had been up to?"

Henry Keith didn't understand any of this, and he looked at Johann worriedly, as if seeking tacit permission to kick this persistent busybody right out of the park. But Johann showed no signs of anything but thoughtfulness, and when he answered David Bookbinder, his voice was unusually subdued.

"I was thinking only the other day that everything in life has its price," he said quietly.

David Bookbinder said: "Yes."

"How can we stop Colton?" asked Johann bluntly.

David Bookbinder took a cigar from his breast pocket, peeled off the band, and clipped a sharp V in the end of it with a gold cutter. Then he stuck it in his mouth and searched for his matches.

"I believe we're going to have to do it on two levels. One, we're

317

going to have to hit back at *his* gas stations, so that he knows you're prepared to do battle. And two, we're going to have to creep up behind him and purchase ourselves a voting majority in Colton Oil. There's a Romanian folk saying which goes: 'When you're fighting the cat, remember the claws.' In other words, we're going to bite him in the front and claw him in the back.''

Johann said: "You seem very confident that I'm going to agree to all this.''

"Naturally. That's because you have several motives to do so, any one of which is irresistible. First, you'd like to get your own back at Colton for trying to squeeze you out of Houston-West. Oh, yes, I know about that. It's all in company minutes. You have to read between the lines, of course, but I also talked to Arnie Styvers, and I have a fair idea of what they did.''

"Second?" asked Johann baldly.

"Second is simple. Second, you'd rather keep Daniel Forster quiet. After that Robinstown business—''

"What the hell do you know about that?''

David Bookbinder smirked. "My dear fellow, I not only know about it, I did it. When poor old Oswald Stone was told to soften up some irksome fellow in the Asquahanna Valley, back in 1927, well . . . there was only one person they could go to. I don't want to sound as if I'm bragging, Mr. Cornelius, but years ago I realized that big business could flourish quicker and more effectively if it had the strength to enforce its desires as well as express them.''

"Are you saying what I think you're saying?''

"Of course. Right from the early twenties, I've made a point of cultivating gang leaders and mobsters as personal friends. I know most of them intimately, and most of them know me. We work together hand-in-glove, and whenever we want something done, we get it done. Colton had a strike in November out at Greensboro, North Carolina. Well, we put some pressure on some of the strike leaders and their families, and it was all over in three days. That's what I call effective action.''

Johann stopped at the the side gate of the park and looked at David Bookbinder for a while. The plump lawyer puffed at his cigar in the midmorning sunlight, and waited with complete equanimity for Johann's comments. Anyone with the young Riccione brothers as bosom friends could afford to.

Johann said: "All right, what's the third irresistible motive?''

Bookbinder smiled. "The third motive is that you need me.

318

You're expanding faster than you know what to do with yourself. I agree with your expansion, but you're going to have to be careful. You need more care, more strategy, and more friends.''

Henry Keith said: "Does that mean we have to get to know gangsters?''

David Bookbinder shook his head. "Just leave that side of it to me. You'll meet them, of course, when the time's right. But first let's get Percy Colton out of the way before he does any more damage.''

"You mean bomb his gas stations?'' asked Henry Keith nervously.

David Bookbinder looked pleased with himself. He sniffed the Shreveport air as if it was a place that he liked to be. "You might think about hitting Colton first right where he hit you,'' he said affably. "He's got a Texas Star station out on Youree Drive.''

"And who's supposed to throw the bombs?'' asked Henry Keith sarcastically. "Us? In gift-wrapped parcels?''

David Bookbinder shook his head. "I know a local Grand Dragon and a couple of Night Hawks who'd be pleased to assist.''

"The Klan? I thought you were Jewish.''

"I am. But friends in need are always friends indeed, no matter what their religious priorities. And in any case, the Youree Drive station is operated by coloreds, which gives the KKK an added incentive. It will also make it look like a racist attack, rather than a spot of business, which will take some of the suspicion off you.''

Johann lowered his eyes. Even though it was early, he was feeling hot and exhausted, and he badly needed a brandy-and-soda. He leaned against the park's green railings and said: "Mr. Bookbinder, you'll have to give me time to consider this. One percent of Cornelius equity is worth at least five million dollars at today's prices, and I don't think even Rockefellers give that kind of money away to strangers. Not in Querbes Park, anyway.''

Bookbinder sucked his cigar. "That's all right, Mr. Cornelius. I'm not pushing. But just remember that every day that goes by is going to see another gas station go up, and that if you *do* finally refuse to accommodate me, the balloon goes up as well. Daniel Forster may be happy to keep his mouth shut for ten thousand dollars and a few threats against his job and his family, but I'm not. All right?''

Johann nodded. "I understand,'' he said quietly. Then he said: "Blackmail's always an ugly thing, isn't it, on both sides?''

319

David Bookbinder carefully molded the ash of his cigar against the point of the railings. "Yes," he answered, equally softly. "But I have a feeling we'll be together long enough for you to say that again to me, several times."

Henry Keith glanced at Johann, and Johann looked at David Bookbinder. Then David Bookbinder said: "I'll call you," and walked quickly out of the park and across the sidewalk to a fawn Buick club sedan, which had been waiting by the curb with its engine ticking over.

The black girl had been sitting for most of the morning on a hard rush-seated chair which she had placed right in front of the hotel window. She had lifted the net curtains away from the glass so that she could see better, and she had draped them around her like a woman in a bridal veil. She was unaware of the irony; but then, she was still waiting for a telephone summons from John.

Her name was Hazel Seymour and she was the daughter of Charles Seymour, whose father had been a slave in Richmond, Virginia, when he was a boy. Charles Seymour's father, coincidentally, had belonged to the grandfather of Edward Secker, who was later to marry Hope Cornelius. It was almost as if some unfinished business had yet to be settled between the two families, one way or another.

Hazel was studying to be a mental nurse at Rockland State Hospital. She was financing her studies by working during the evenings at Zee's Creamy Sodas & Drugs in Poughkeepsie, which was where her folks lived, in a shabby-respectable house in the less elite part of town. She was sixteen years old.

Maybe it was the fixed idea that you just didn't love whites that had lulled Hazel into being so open and receptive to John. One evening, when she was tired and hot, and her candy-striped apron was sticky with syrup and ice creams, John had sloped into Zee's with another kid the same age and they had parked themselves on chrome stools at the counter. But it was only when John had handed over a twenty-dollar bill, which was the biggest bill that Hazel had been given all evening; and it was only when she caught him looking at her and smiling across the counter while she was pouring raspberry syrup for a raspberry milk shake, that she began to think that he was inter-*esting*, as her poppa used to say. She smiled back, uncertainly, and spent the rest of the evening wondering why in the world she had.

He had been waiting for her, alone, when she left the soda fountain that evening at half-past eight.

And he had followed Hazel four blocks, protesting the upright and innocent quality of his interest in her. He only wanted a *date*, and what was so all-fired awful about a *date*? In the end, flattered, she had agreed to go on a picnic with him on Saturday afternoon, which was her only free afternoon. She told her momma, of course, that she was going out walking with her friend from the neighborhood, Leila Miller, and she had made sure that John picked her up from Zee's, and not from home. The whole idea of talking and having fun with white people made her feel peculiar inside, although when John arrived outside Zee's that Saturday in his own bright red Hupmobile convertible, the one that Hester had given him for his birthday, and when Hazel saw the basket packed with hams and pies and fresh fruit and wine, and particularly when John gave her a flowering corsage to match her dress, her feelings took a double dip and she didn't know whether to sit up in the car with her nose in the air like an African princess, or crouch down so far behind the dash that nobody could see it was her.

It was a day of strong blue skies and mountainous white clouds, and they drove the little red car into a field of yellow mustard, and talked and ate as if they were rich folk stranded in somebody's dream. Around four o'clock it grew chilly, and the clouds built up heavy and metallic, so John put up the car's canvas top, and they sat in green-and-yellow gloom while rain rhumbaed on the roof and dribbled tearfully down the windows. It was then that they first kissed, and having first kissed, there was no keeping them apart, and even after the fresh California peaches and the Kentucky ham, they almost devoured each other. Hazel went home that night to her parents' home with the dingy brown wallpaper and the sepia photographs of Charles Seymour in a rigid white collar and derby hat, and she quietly ate her supper of burgoo and cornbread as polite and tame as ever, but inside her emotions had gone completely wild, and she knew she had fallen in love.

Now she waited in her small room at the Lakeshore Hotel, patient and pregnant, expecting not only John's baby but his family's friendship as well. The management had been reluctant to provide accommodation for a darkie at first, but it was hard for them to resist the wishes of any Cornelius, no matter how junior. Anybody who did business at Lynwood's Island stayed at the Lakeshore at one time or another, and Johann and Hester occasionally ate there.

Just after two, when Hazel was beginning to feel hungry for lunch, a long silver car drew up outside the Lakeshore Hotel, its tires inscribing semicircles in the white gravel. Hazel leaned forward, and saw one of the rear doors of the car being opened by the Lakeshore's porter, and John step out. He stood there for a moment, and it looked as if somebody inside the car was giving him last-minute instructions, for eventually he nodded, and walked up the steps and went inside the hotel.

Hazel found herself shaking. She pushed aside the net curtains and put the chair back in the corner of the room. She didn't want John to think that she had been staring out of the window all morning. That would make him feel anxious; and she didn't want to make the father of her baby anxious. She took off her shoes and sat down on the bed with a copy of *Vogue* that John had bought for her, and tried to look as if she was calm and relaxed, and as accustomed to wealthy living as he. On the first page she opened, she saw a long gold evening dress for one hundred and thirty-five dollars, which was almost exactly what her father managed to bring back after two months' work.

There was a subdued knock at the door. She said: "Who is it?" She quickly patted her hair in case the net curtain had disturbed it.

John said: "It's me. Can I come in?"

"The door's open."

He walked in, and somehow he looked different. In Poughkeepsie, he had always been young and fun and fashionable. But now he was wearing an expensive gray double-breasted suit, and his hair was combed with unaccustomed neatness, and he had a fragrance about him too that she didn't recognize. He came over to the bed, leaned over, and kissed her. It was meant to be a lingering kiss, but somehow they didn't feel like lingering very long. John sat down on the edge of the bed.

"Well," he said, "how are you?"

She shrugged. "I'm fine. I've missed you."

"I've missed you too. I'm sorry you had to wait so long."

"That's all right. Just so long as you fixed your folks."

John nodded, and didn't answer.

"You did fix your folks okay, didn't you?" she asked him.

He let out a short laugh. "I sure fixed 'em!"

"You don't sound very certain."

He laughed again. "Of course I am."

"Well, what did they say? What did your momma say? When you told her? She must've said something."

John took her hand between his, and smiled at her. She wished he wasn't smiling. He usually smiled only when he thought something was funny, and what was funny about any of this?

"Mother was . . . surprised, of course."

"Surprised, or shocked?"

"Well, a little shocked. It's her first grandchild, after all, and she wasn't really expecting it!"

"I guess not. But I am."

"Well, we all know that. But in any case, everything's going to be fine. We're going to take you right now to see Dr. Nash, the family doctor. He's got a clinic here, and he can check you over and make sure everything's fine."

Hazel said: "Right now?"

John grinned. "The sooner the better, huh?"

"John, that's real nice, but I'd appreciate some lunch. I haven't eaten since dinner last night. I'm real hungry. In fact, I'm so hungry, I could eat a white man."

John laughed some more. Why was he laughing so goddamned much? It seemed like he was frightened of something, or embarrassed.

Hazel said: "John . . . everything's all right, isn't it? There isn't anything wrong?"

John shook his head. "Hazel, everything's perfect. All we have to do is get along to Dr. Nash, and then we can go get ourselves something to eat."

Hazel frowned. "I don't want to see Dr. Nash. I don't *need* to. I saw my own doctor in Poughkeepsie. He says it's six weeks gone and everything's fine."

John bit his lip. Then he said: "Dr. Nash is the finest in the whole country. That's why we use him. He's a really nice guy. Wait till you meet him. I mean, he's the country's best."

"John—"

John gripped her hands strangely tight. He said: "Listen, Hazel, just for me. Go see Dr. Nash just for me. Will you do that? Now, look, it's almost two, and I said we'd be round there at ten after."

Hazel got up from the bed and walked across to the wardrobe. She could see herself in the mirror, dark and tall, and in the angle of light that fell behind her she could see John sitting, his head bent and his knees together, like a man waiting in a cell.

She said: "You're worried about something. Why are you worried? Was your momma real mad?"

He looked up with artificial brightness. "Mad? No, she settled down to the whole idea pretty well. She's a very understanding person."

Hazel said: "Do I get to meet her?"

"Oh, sure. Well, I guess so."

"You only guess so? I'm going to marry her son, and you only guess so?"

"Well, Hazel, it's . . ."

Hazel turned around. Her voice was calm and sad, but there were no tears in her eyes. The way she was standing, one hand on her hip, her head bent slightly to one side, made her into a dark silhouette that was as soft and sorrowful as anything by Renoir. The room was lit only in grays and browns, with a rectangle of reflecting mirror from the wardrobe.

She said: "There's something wrong, isn't there? Your momma didn't like this one little bit."

John clenched his knuckles. "Really, Hazel, everything's fine. Now, all we have to do is—"

Hazel slowly shook her head. "Don't lie, John. I can take anything you've done to me, but not lies. Why don't you just tell me what truly happened, the truth, no matter how bad you think it's going to be?"

John said: "You weren't supposed to know."

She laughed, softly and forgivingly. "No, I guess that I wasn't. What de darkies don't know cain't hurt 'em."

"Hazel—"

"I'm sorry. I know you've never been like that. But it's your momma, isn't it? I should've known. If I'd've had any sense, I wouldn't've even come this far. She doesn't want her dear young baby boy mixing with coloreds. What she especially doesn't want is a half-caste grandchild. She doesn't want to have to order up chitterlings for one while the rest of the family is having *pâté de foie gras.*"

John stood up. She could tell that, two or three hours ago, he had probably been crying. But between that time and now, he had made up his mind about something, and whatever it was, it wasn't in her favor, nor in favor of the baby that was growing inside her.

"I've let you down, haven't I?" said John.

Hazel went to the window, pulled back the net curtains, and looked down at the long silver car in the drive.

"Yes," she said, "you have. But I guess the pressure must be more than most people can stand."

"What pressure?"

"Oh, the family, and the fortune. I can't expect a young boy like you to give up hundreds of millions of dollars just for love. And in any case, you don't really want to, do you? If you married me, and if we had this baby, you'd have to spend the rest of your life fighting the snobs who wouldn't invite you to dinner because you'd be bringing a black wife, and the kids who'd make this baby cry its little heart out because it wouldn't be black and it wouldn't be white and it wouldn't know *where* it belonged. You'd have to fight your family and your money and your own self, and I can't rightly ask you to do that. One colored girl from Poughkeepsie is not worth that."

John reached out and touched her arm.

"Hazel," he said, "I love you."

She turned and smiled.

"You thought you did, once. Don't lie, John, it's not worth it. I can see by your eyes that you've made up your mind. I'm not going to force you."

"Oh, Hazel, I'm so sorry. I don't know what to say. I thought if I talked to Mother she'd understand. I thought if I . . ."

Hazel let the curtain fall. She went over to the wardrobe, opened it, and took out her suitcase. It was a new brown leather suitcase that John had bought for her specially. They had taken care when they chose it, because John had said she could take it on her honeymoon, too. That was only two or three days ago, but now it was nothing more than a new suitcase that she almost wished she didn't have. She started to pack her few belongings, her dresses and her hairbrush and her red shoes.

John remained by the window, staring silently out at the grounds of the Lakeshore Hotel. He couldn't understand why he felt so little emotion. Perhaps he had already cried himself out for one day. It was in the night, that night, that it was going to start hurting.

Hazel clicked shut the suitcase locks and went to get her coat from the back of the door.

"John?" she said, as she put it on.

325

John didn't answer.

She came closer, and looked at him with such tenderness and regret on her face that, if he had turned toward her, he would have understood far more about her, and maybe something about himself, too. But he kept his eyes on the driveway outside, and on the impatient fingers he could just discern drumming on the silver car's steering wheel.

"John," she said again, "I can't say I won't be sad, and I can't say that I won't miss you, because I love you more than anyone I ever knew, and this wrench is going to hurt me so bad. I'm going to cry for you, John, when I'm in private, and by myself, but I'm not going to cry in front of you. If you don't want me, and you don't want the baby we made, then I'll just have to do the best I can."

John said quietly: "What are you going to do about the baby?"

"What do you *think* I'm going to do? I can't expect my momma and poppa to look after me while I sit around the house getting fat, can I?"

"If it's money . . ."

Hazel looked at him. He lowered his head in embarrassment.

"Well," he said, "if it's money . . ."

She almost smiled. "You're ashamed of saying that, aren't you? Well, there's no need. I'm going to get rid of this baby, and since it's your baby as well as my baby, I'd appreciate some financial help."

John turned around at last. "I'm sure that Dr. Nash—"

She shook her head emphatically. "No white man is going to touch me. Not to take away my baby. And in any case, that was the way you planned it, wasn't it? You and your momma were going to take me to see your wonderful Dr. Nash, and your wonderful Dr. Nash was going to take a look, and all of a sudden, my *God,* what's *this,* an unexpected miscarriage! Oh, Miss Seymour, we *are* sorry. We *do* apologize. How clumsy, to give you an accidental D-and-C like that! Come on, John, I'm studying to be a nurse. I'm also a woman, and a pregnant mother. And I'm black. What you wanted to do was bad, and it was cruel, but I know why you planned to do it, and I know just how terrible your load must be."

"Load? What are you talking about?"

"The load you have to bear on your shoulders, John. My cross is that I'm colored, but your cross is heavier than mine. You're *rich.*"

326

John listened to this with a perplexed expression that showed he didn't grasp it at all. How could wealth be a burden? Money was the universal lightener of loads, the lifter of heavy weights. When you had money, you could afford to hire somebody to carry your cross for you. He turned back to the window, his mouth pursed as if he had sucked a candy and found it had a center of liquid vinegar.

Hazel said: "Will you give me a ride to the railroad station?"

John glanced at her. "I can't make you change your mind?"

"What choice do I have? To lose my baby in Lynwood, or to lose it in Poughkeepsie? They're not that far apart."

"Maybe I can talk to Mother some more."

Hazel smiled sadly. "No, John. You know it's no use. I came up here with a crazy dream that couldn't ever come true. I guess I knew it couldn't happen, right from the start. One day you'll find yourself a nice white lady from a nice respectable family, and you and she will settle yourselves down together and live the way your momma always wanted."

John lifted her suitcase off the bed. She opened the door for him, and as he passed her by on his way into the hall, she said: "Besides . . ."

He stopped. "What do you mean, 'besides'?"

She leaned forward and kissed his forehead. It was a dry, chaste kiss. "It doesn't matter," she told him.

"No—tell me, please."

She dropped her eyes. "All I was going to say was that when I find a man to marry, and a man to give me children, I'll want a man who stands by me, no matter what, and a man who stands by his baby. That's all."

They stood there in silence for almost a minute. Then John hefted the suitcase and went downstairs to the waiting car. Stainer opened the trunk for him, and he stowed it away. He wouldn't let anyone else carry it. He wanted to understand what a load was. Hazel came down, pulling on a pair of beige gloves, and Stainer opened the rear door of the car for her to get in.

Hester was sitting in the front seat. She looked severe and elegant in a dark gray suit, with a spray of diamonds on her left lapel. She turned and said to Hazel: "I'm sorry, we haven't been introduced. But John has told me all about you."

Stainer started the motor, and the car scrunched out of the

hotel driveway. Hazel sat with her arms held tight around her, as if she was cold. The inside of the car was five degrees warmer than it needed to be, and it was fragrant with leather and perfume.

John said: "Hazel just wants to go the train station, Mother. She doesn't want to see Dr. Nash."

Hester turned around in her seat to look at Hazel. "Are you *sure*, my dear? Dr. Nash is one of the finest in the country. We'll quite happily pay."

Hazel was watching the trees flicker past. She shook her head without looking at the woman who was never going to be her mother-in-law.

"I just want to get home, thank you, ma'am."

Hester said: "Please yourself, my dear. We're only trying to help."

John put in: "You can still change your mind."

Hazel turned her head and looked at them both. "Help?" she said, with a taste of bitterness in her voice as sharp as the pith of a fresh-peeled lime. "You wealthy white people have never helped anyone except yourselves, and you never will. Charity begins at home, doesn't it, Mrs. Cornelius, and what's more, you make sure it stays there."

Hester said airily: "You can be as rude as you like, my dear. You'll be on that train in ten minutes."

John said, as if he were reciting the label of a patent-medicine bottle: "Did you know that this is a Pierce Arrow 'Silver Arrow' saloon, and that it was one of only five made for the Chicago World's Fair last year? It has a V-12 engine that develops 175 horsepower and it cost upwards of ten thousand dollars."

Hazel, who hadn't meant to, wept. John wept too, but only because he realized what he had actually been able to inflict on another human being without the benefit of money, and that within a few days his first baby would be lying dead and bloody in a hospital trashcan, unable even to dream of wealth and Pierce Arrows and dull days like this on the banks of the Hudson River.

The Grand Dragon of the Shreveport Ku Klux Klan lived in a tidy white-painted suburban house with ranch-style fences and floral curtains drawn back and tied like the curtains of a doll's house. He was standing outside in his front yard when they arrived in David Bookbinder's fawn limousine, with a contented expression on his

328

broad, sunburned face that reminded Johann disturbingly of Kyle Lennox's face, thirty-one years and a dozen centuries ago. It was as if David Bookbinder had deliberately selected this man to nudge his memory and remind him of his buried trespasses.

The Grand Dragon came forward to meet them as they climbed out of the car. He was physically enormous, like a huge side of bacon from a prize-winning pig. He wore a very starched white sport shirt and very crisply pressed khaki pants, and sandals that revealed two rows of toes as pink and orderly as prawns.

"How do you do, David," he said, and squeezed David Bookbinder's hand. "And these are your friends, right?"

The day was glary and hot. Johann wore sunglasses and a straw hat, and Henry Keith had almost dissolved into perspiration and crumpled linen.

Johann said: "Johann Cornelius," and took the Grand Dragon's hand. Then he said: "What do I call you? Your Dragonship?"

The Grand Dragon guffawed. "Now, you don't have to do that. The name is Chesley Crowther. And in any event Johann, it ain't considered particularly diplomatic to mention the Klan names around here no more, on account of the official line against it. But come inside. There's some beer on ice, if that takes your fancy."

They trooped inside. The house was small and furnished with cheap light-varnished chairs and tables in the Grand Rapids style, but it was kept conspicuously clean, and there was a new icebox humming and whirring in the kitchen. Chesley went to open the beer while Johann sat himself down and looked around. On one wall was an embroidered sampler which said "God Is White," and on the opposite wall hung a photograph of Chesley Crowther and twenty other heavily built citizens of Shreveport on a fishing trip.

"Well, now"—Chesley grinned, handing out glasses of Old Milwaukee—"it's a long time since you been down this way, David. Just as well, considering you ain't strictly one of us."

He sat himself down, swallowed a long gulp of beer, and then fastidiously wiped the foam from his upper lip with a pressed white handkerchief.

"David is our one exception to the rule," Chesley told Johann, leaning over with a confidential wink. "And that's because David is a powerfully interesting and influential fellow, ain't you, David? He's our latter-day Judah Benjamin."

David Bookbinder sipped his beer and then put it down on the table.

"It's a question of expedients," he said calmly. "There are times when business interests and political interests override racial feelings. Personally, I think Chesley here is an inexcusable bigot, but he knows I think that, and we've decided to share the same bed from time to time, no matter how uncomfortably."

"I thought the Klan was pretty well broken down here," remarked Henry Keith. "At least, that's what they say in the North."

Chesley Crowther laughed, and swallowed some more beer, and patted his upper lip, and laughed again.

"Saying the Klan is broken is akin to saying the church is broken," he said. "As long as folks believe in the supremacy of the white man, and so long as folks won't tolerate communism, and welfare, and mixing of the races, and letting the nigger despoil what we have in this pure country of ours, then the Klan will stand strong. We've got a heritage to protect, Henry, and we're going to protect it if it means shooting every nigger and every bleeding-heart liberal in the belly!"

Johann said dryly: "What I really want to know, Mr. Crowther, is whether you can mount an effective and confidential campaign against Colton gas stations. The racial politics really don't interest me."

Chesley turned on him. "They don't interest you, huh? Well, let me ask you something. If you found your son or your daughter had been mixing and mingling with niggers, what would you feel about that?"

"I don't know. It's never happened, and I don't suppose it ever will."

Chesley waved his meaty arm in a dramatic sweep. "That's what you say now! But unless you fight all those who seek to prove that the Negro masses ain't biologically inferior, then the Negro masses are going to rise up against you, and they're going to mix and mingle with your sons and your daughters. How would you like a nigger for a son-in-law, or a daughter-in-law maybe? How would you like a half-breed mutt as your grandchild and your heir? I have pride in what I am, Johann, and I hope to God that you do too."

David Bookbinder looked across at Johann for one brief moment, and in that moment Johann wondered just how much this quiet and curious man knew about his past. He felt almost as if his entire character were laid open for Bookbinder's inspection, like a soldier's kit.

He said to Chesley: "Mr. Crowther, I know where the Klan's sympathies lie. But there is no possibility that any of my children will fall in with blacks, and if they did I would do my level best to make sure that they pretty promptly fell out again. Now, do you think we can talk about business?"

Chesley raised his hands in a conciliatory gesture, and parked his big, well-laundered bottom back in his chair. "What you're asking is whether I can cause some ruckus round at the Colton gas stations, and make it look like a regular Klan ride?"

Johann nodded. "Mr. Bookbinder here has given you most of the details, I think? We want the gas station on Youree Drive burned flat."

Chesley scratched his ear. "That sounds easy enough. But what happens if we get any trouble from Dan Gibbons?"

"Dan Gibbons is the local police chief," explained David Bookbinder. "We have him very tame, Chesley, don't worry. I paid him a visit at home last night, and he's looking forward to a new car. He won't come around until you're well away."

"That sounds regular enough," agreed Chesley. "And what's the main fee for the night's work?"

"Ten thousand dollars," said Johann. "All in used bills, all paid immediately after the job's done."

Chesley liked the sound of that. These days, the Klan was divided, weak, and desperately short of funds, and when the time came for a new Grand Wizard to be elected to preside over the Invisible Empire, Chesley knew that cash in the bank would give him a fighting chance at the polls. He said: "I'll drink to that," and raised his glass.

They talked for a little while more, discussing the details of the night's raid, and then Chesley showed Johann the Klavern in the back room of the house, the dark and sacred room in which the Shreveport Klansmen met.

Johann rubbed his eyes tiredly. Perhaps the whole world was populated with endless variations of himself, and his own crippled emotions. He said to Chesley: "Thank you, Mr. Crowther. I'm sure you'll do us a fine job," and pushed his way back into the daylight.

That night, at midnight, the Klan rode again in Shreveport for the first time in almost nine years. They clattered up Youree Drive on horses, fifteen of them in white pointed hoods and fluttering white robes, yelling and screeching and waving fiery torches that roared and smoked. The streets were deserted as they rode into the forecourt of the Texas Star gas station, where one sleepy colored attendant had been sitting with his feet up reading a comic book and listening to late-night country music on his radio.

The Klansmen dismounted and burst into the attendant's cabin. The boy's name was Charlie Wright, and he was so terrified by the Klansmen's spectral appearance that he wet himself. He dropped onto his knees, and one of the Klansmen hit him in the neck with the butt of a rifle. He fell against his chair, stunned.

They rifled the cash register and smashed every window in the room. They turned over filing cabinets and ripped open drawers, scattering papers and receipts. Then one of them brought a red tin can of gasoline over from the pumps, and they splashed it over the cabin, and all over Charlie Wright as well. Backing off, they tossed matches into the cabin, and it exploded into a funneling blowtorch of orange fire.

While three Klansmen erected the traditional cross at the side of the forecourt, the rest of them rampaged around on their horses, firing their rifles into the air and hooting like owls. At last the cross was up, and they set it alight, and in the darkness of a night in 1934 the hair-raising symbol of racial purity blazed as bright as it had in years gone by.

Charlie Wright, awakened by agony, tried to stumble out of his burning cabin. The Klansmen whooped and hollered as they saw him staggering like a man of flames from the doorway. He made it as far as the gas pumps, with his hair and his clothes and his face alight. But then he dropped to the ground, and his body lay there blazing, while at his home five blocks away his mother looked up at the clock and decided it was time to put his supper on.

When the Texas Star gas station exploded, the *whump* of detonating gasoline fumes was heard four miles away, and it shattered windows a quarter of a mile in every direction. A spinster who lived across the drive thought the end of the world had arrived, and so she promptly went upstairs and climbed into her lodger's bed for a grand finale. A dog was blown through the back of its kennel, hurled across fifty yards of garden, and ended up on the dining-room table of an elderly librarian who was eating alone. At the fire station, the fire chief waited for ten minutes, as required, and then sent the engines out.

Along Youree Drive, the Klansmen galloped in frenzy and elation, ghosts in bedsheets and wizards' hats. They split up at the

332

corner of Ockley Drive, and rode off to their homes, still shouting and calling like wild banshees, while the tall cross burned by the wrecked gas station, and sirens wailed from the west.

In his hotel room, Johann drew back the drapes and listened to the clamorous noises of the night. David Bookbinder was sitting there, too, with a glass of whiskey and a last cigar. Henry Keith was in the next room, talking on the telephone to Cornelius managers and brokers in New York, preparing the plan of financial investment for the following day.

"Well," said Johann, letting the drapes fall back. "It seems we've lit ourselves quite a fire."

David Bookbinder nodded placidly. "Fire has to be fought with fire. And men like Percy Colton have to be put in their place. He's an old bird, but he's a tough one."

"Do you really believe he'll give in?"

"He has to. We already hold a seventh of Colton voting stock, and once it gets around that his gas stations are being systematically destroyed by the Klan, we'll quickly get our hands on a whole lot more."

Johann said: "You're a strange man, Mr. Bookbinder. You have strange methods of working."

David Bookbinder smiled. "Does that mean you've decided to employ me?"

Johann lifted his eyes. "I never really had much choice, did I? I made my bed in 1903, and now I've damned well got to lie in it."

David Bookbinder shrugged. "I'm pleased you can see it that way. It could have been pretty unpleasant otherwise. I hate blackmail, you know."

Johann went over to the side table and poured himself a glass of brandy. He sipped it, and closed his eyes while it soaked down his throat.

"Yes," he said, "I can almost believe that you do."

He sat down, hunched forward in his chair, with his glass held in both hands.

"Mind you," he went on, as if David Bookbinder really needed any kind of explanation, "it wasn't blackmail that finally decided me."

David Bookbinder said nothing, but pursed his lips and blew a smoke ring up at the ceiling. It rose, spun, and then dissolved.

"What happened in 1903 was something that I've never quite understood. I sometimes look back on it, you know, and I wonder if I was quite mad. I took up with a girl of twelve or thirteen, and she gave me such friendship that I think of her now as a miracle. In a way, I suppose it was me who caused her to die. Then I lost the love of a woman who was more beautiful than you could imagine, and let her fall into the hands of men who destroyed her pride and her womanhood forever. And her life, too.''

David Bookbinder said: ''You talk of love very glibly.''

Johann pulled a face. ''When I say love, I mean devotion. I'm not sure that I know what love is.''

''Of course you do. Why do you think that you felt about these unfortunate ladies the way you did? You have always been in love.''

''You mean with myself?''

David Bookbinder shook his head. ''You are in love with wealth. Of course, I haven't known you all your life, but you exhibit the symptoms of a longtime sufferer.''

''Wealth?''

David Bookbinder looked at him with what could almost have been kindness. ''That's right. It's a rare but serious disease. It's even worse than being in love with money.''

''You're talking nonsense.''

''No, I'm not. The love of money is a very specific love, and it is almost always found among those who will never be rich. If you adore the smell of ten-dollar bills, the feel of treasury paper between your fingers, then you are a financial sybarite, but you are not a lover of wealth. Real wealth is a cold and abstract goddess, Mr. Cornelius. To love real wealth you must be elevated and inspired by the *concept* of riches. Have you noticed how the rich carry no money with them? The ecstasy comes from within their minds, not from within their wallets.''

Johann eased himself back in his chair like a man settling himself into a scalding bath. ''Does the love of wealth have to make me so dissatisfied?''

''*All* love makes you dissatisfied,'' said David Bookbinder. ''That's the very definition of love.''

''But why did I let Beatrice slip out of my grasp? Why did I let her go? And Carina, I should have protected Carina night and day!''

David Bookbinder stood up and walked across to the ashtray, where he ground out the butt of his cigar.

''I'm not an alienist, Mr. Cornelius. I'm not even a rabbi. But in my humble opinion, I'd say that you were doing exactly what any man does when he is trying to control an obsessive and unrequited love. You were seeking in women some substitute for your passion for wealth. How much easier to love a woman than to love wealth! To love wealth is like following a golden mirage that you can never quite grasp. But, unfortunately for you . . ."

Johann looked up.

"Unfortunately for you," said David Bookbinder, "your women, no matter how wondrous, were not enough. You pushed them, and yourself, to the very limit of what you could take. You thought you loved them, but they became grist for the mill which has ground out your fortune. No, Mr. Cornelius, it was all very sad, and it was probably not your fault, but I suppose it was inevitable, or as the Russians say 'the return of the summer birds is no surprise.' You had to discover how little you loved women to realize how much you loved wealth."

Johann didn't answer for a long time. He sat sunk in his chair, endlessly rotating his brandy glass, his forehead furrowed and his mouth turned down.

Finally he said: "I'm going to appoint you, Mr. Bookbinder, as the chief executive of Cornelius Oil. This is on the strict understanding that none of what you know about my life in Texas is ever revealed to anyone. I will also make over one percent of Cornelius equity."

He paused once more, and then he said: "For our own personal working relationship, I want you to know that you have partly succeeded in blackmailing me, and partly failed. If I had been determined to resist you, I would have done so, and probably succeeded, no matter what scandal you dug up. But I feel that appointing you will do me some good, although quite what kind of good, I am not yet sure. I think you will probably be a permanent reminder to me of what I am, because we are not very different, you and I. Everyday I can look at you and see myself in my rawest form, and that is the only effective way I can think of to punish myself enough."

David Bookbinder smiled. "Believe me, Mr. Cornelius, your choice is wise. Now, perhaps you can do me a favor?"

"What is it? Do you want me to put your appointment to music?"

"Nothing like that. I have a friend who has had some trouble with a federal grand jury, and he's looking for someplace quiet to stay. I wonder if you have a small room or two up at Lynwood's Island?''

"What's his name?''

"Oh, you know him well. Or you should. Dutch Schultz.''

Johann swirled his brandy around. He was not happy, but at the same time he felt as if some nagging tooth had been pulled, and that tomorrow he might actually wake up and feel no pain.

"So this is how it begins, is it?'' he said softly.

David Bookbinder beamed. "Beginnings are always bedeviled by uncertainties,'' he said. "Do you want to shake hands?''

Johann looked up at his new chief executive, and then shook his head. "One day, perhaps. But not now.''

Outside, they heard the sound of an ambulance bell. It was all that was left of Charlie Wright, on his way to the city morgue.

Percy F. Colton was nearly ninety in 1934. *The New York Daily Post,* which didn't like him, frequently called him "the Methuselah of Money.'' But even though his rotund face had withered and collapsed, and even though he now attended all his business meetings with a uniformed nurse on either side of him, he still maintained a reputation for hard dealing and ruthless self-protection. It was a general assumption on Wall Street that he had something to do with the bombing of Cornelius gas stations, although nobody could quite agree on the degree of his involvement; and it was also a general assumption that Johann Cornelius had somehow inspired the Ku Klux Klan to strike back.

But what was not known anywhere was that David Bookbinder, the head of Colton's business-law department, was already working against his boss's interests, and that he was laying complex and elaborate plans for kicking the supports out from under the Colton oil empire completely.

It happened on August 2, 1934, a warm and cloudy Thursday, the same day von Hindenburg died in Germany, and the morning that the first fourteen-passenger night flight arrived in Los Angeles after crossing the continent from Newark.

On the eighteenth floor of the Colton Building on Park Avenue South, hundreds of Colton shareholders assembled at a special meeting to discuss the effects on Texas Star and Golden Power retail sales because of three months' burning and bombing by the Ku Klux Klan. Things had gotten so serious that few automobilists

336

would stop at Texas Star gas stations, for fear of retribution from the Night Hawks. Sales had dropped fifty-eight percent, and were still sliding.

Once the shareholders were assembled in the long, blue-carpeted gallery, Percy Colton himself arrived. He shuffled up to the board table on two sticks, with his white, bright, Colgate-polished nurses helping him along. Everyone stood as a mark of respect, and there was even some applause. David Bookbinder, on the far end of the board table, was clapping louder than anyone.

Percy Colton at last sat down, and handed his sticks to one of his nurses. There was a rustle of anticipation and excitement in the hall, and some of the directors looked around uneasily, as if they sensed that something unusual was up.

Percy Colton rapped his gavel. "I call this meeting to order."

There was a last buzz of conversation, then silence.

Percy Colton looked around with red-rimmed rheumy eyes. "This extraordinary meeting of Colton Oil shareholders has been called to sound out your feelings about the little problems we've been having with our gas stations down South."

Someone said: "Little *problems*? You're *kidding*!"

The heckler was hushed up, and then Colton said: "I want to tell you now that I believe we have this problem licked. Ostensibly, it looked as if the Ku Klux Klan was raiding our gas stations because of our policy of employing colored attendants. But I've been doing some investigations of my own, and I believe that we have one of our major rivals in the petrochemical industry to thank for these wanton attacks."

Another voice said: "So what are you going to do about it."

And someone else called: "Who started the bombing in the first place? That's what I'd like to know!"

Colton banged his gavel. "We're doing everything we possibly can! You have to understand that whenever one of our places is attacked, the local police and fire departments are bribed into looking the other way, and they've obviously been bribed enough to keep on looking the other way for quite some time yet. Now, the KKK doesn't have that kind of money to hush up a few local flatfoots, so that means someone with considerable financial resources is systematically destroying our gas stations."

"And why?" shouted a woman from the back. "Because *you* started destroying *their* gas stations first!"

337

There was a jumbled roar of approval, and a burst of applause. A man in a navy-blue suit and spectacles stood up from the second row and raised his hand.

"Mr. Chairman, I want to propose a motion!"

Colton banged his gavel again. "Sit down!" he snapped. "You can propose motions when I've finished speaking!"

"Mr. Chairman, I want to propose a motion right now! I want to propose that this corporation has no confidence in its chairman and board of directors, and demands their resignation as of now!"

Someone else jumped up and shouted: "I second the motion!"

Again there was a roar of approval. Colton looked angrily around the hall, and then banged three times with his gavel, until the shareholders gradually settled down into silence.

"Very well," he said caustically. "It's out of order, but if you want to vote on that motion, then I'm agreeable. Let's get this childish yowling over with, and then we can get down to business. Mr. Kharmann, will you be kind enough to count hands?"

"Yes, sir."

Colton looked around again, more slowly this time, identifying the faces he knew were friendly, and the faces he was more doubtful about. There were quite a few new faces, and many he didn't know at all. He said softly: "All those in favor of the motion please show."

At least half the hands in the hall went up. Mr. Kharmann, peering at the crowded seats through bifocals, counted as quickly as he could. "Thank you," he said at last, and the hands went down.

Percy Colton said: "All those against the motion please show."

More hands went up. Mr. Kharmann counted, and then sat down to figure out the results. The hall remained absolutely silent while he totted up share proportions and proxies.

After almost five minutes, he abruptly lifted his head. He was quite pale, and he took his spectacles off before he said anything.

Colton snapped: "Well? Let's get on with it!"

Mr. Kharmann shook his head. "We can't, sir. The motion is carried."

Colton snatched the figures from under Mr. Kharmann's nose. "Carried? Don't be so damned ridiculous!"

He looked down the list of voting shareholders, and then jabbed his finger at one of the most influential names of all—Carina Hydraulics.

338

"Who's this?" he said, his voice rigid with fury. "Who's this Carina Hydraulics? I thought Carina Hydraulics was tied up with our Kansas operation! How come they voted against us?"

The directors on the board looked at each other, nonplussed. Then one of them said: "David—you know Carina, don't you? Didn't you arrange that investment?"

Amid the hubbub and shouts, David Bookbinder stood up and faced the meeting. He raised one hand for silence, and at last got it.

"It appears," he said, "that I have made a terrible mistake."

Again there was a confused babble of voices.

"Please . . ." he said, "let me explain. I was under the impression when we sold our new share issue in June that Carina Hydraulics was a well-financed corporation that was eager to invest in Colton Oil and in whose integrity and dependability we could absolutely trust. We were going to let them use our storage and refining facilities, and in turn they were going to put several million dollars in our expansion.

"Regrettably—" he went on, but his next few words were drowned in shouts of dismay and surprise.

He lifted is hand. "Regrettably, Carina Hydraulics, although it is a legitimate corporation of the highest standard, is not exactly what you might term friendly. It is owned for the most part by Kruyper Coal, which in turn is almost entirely owned by Cornelius Oil."

There was a shout of amazement. Two reporters ran from the room at once, heading for the nearest telephones.

Colton rose from his seat as if he was a withered puppet being tugged up on a string.

"*Cornelius*?" he spat. "*Cornelius*?"

David Bookbinder did his best to look abashed. "I regret, sir, that this is indeed the case. And I'm afraid that Cornelius Oil also holds voting majorities in Hulbert Aviation Fuels, and Rockaway Properties, and Nash Lumber Corp., and Eastern Wave Insurance, all of which"—he lowered his voice respectfully—"have voted against the board today."

Percy Colton sank back into his chair. One of his nurses held a cool red-fingernailed hand against his brow. The other one shook out some tablets.

David Bookbinder said: "I can only take the blame for this remarkable rout myself. It was because of my lack of thoroughness and my inattention to detail that so many voting shares fell into the

339

hands of Colton Oil's major rival. I was remiss in that I failed to check back proxies with sufficient care, and I accept full responsibility for what has happened today. I would be pleased if you would accept not only my apologies, but my immediate resignation.''

Colton pushed away the proffered tablets. "Just get me out of here," he said harshly. "Just let me get some air."

Much later that evening, David Bookbinder arrived at Johann's brownstone mansion in Gramercy Park. He was admitted by Vucinzki, the butler, who took his homburg hat and showed him into the room where, years later, Roderick would sit and sift through the files of letters and memos that told the story of what Bookbinder was about to do. Johann was sitting in his favorite chair, with papers spread all around him, dictating replies into an Edison recorder.

"Sit down," he said. "I'm almost through."

David Bookbinder sat. Eventually Johann scooped up his papers into an untidy stack, switched off the recorder, and rang the bell for Vucinzki to come collect them. Then he turned his attention to David Bookbinder and said: "Well? That's that, isn't it?"

David Bookbinder took out a cigar. "You're pleased?" he asked with a small, provocative smile.

"I don't know. I suppose Carina got her revenge at last."

"I think we all did. In any event, it was time that old PFC went off to a nursing home and wove baskets."

Johann nodded.

David Bookbinder said: "I suppose you know that you're now the third-biggest oil producer in the United States?"

"Yes. Henry told me. He also asked me to make sure that you called off the Klan."

"I have already. The Grand Dragon was quite disappointed. He said they haven't had themselves so much fun in years."

"Some people have fun wringing chickens' necks," said Johann.

The two men sat there for a while, saying nothing. They made strange uncomfortable partners.

Finally Johann said: "I was thinking."

David Bookbinder raised his eyes.

"I was thinking that, since this is a week for revenge, I ought to do the job properly."

340

"What do you mean?"

Johann appeared to be focusing on something very far away. He said: "There's a restaurant on Fifty-eighth street. The Carbonnade."

"I know it. It used to be called Eduard's."

"That's the one. Well, I want you to buy it. When you've bought it, I want you to fire everyone there and close it down."

David Bookbinder looked at Johann narrowly. Then he said: "My guess is that years and years ago, the staff of the Carbonnade insulted you. Am I right?"

Johann didn't answer.

David Bookbinder said: "The best thing for you to do is leave well enough alone. I expect the manager and the waiters from 1903 are long gone. And anyway, I like eating there. They serve kosher beef."

Johann thought about this, and eventually nodded. "All right, if that's what you want. But if you want my opinion, Mr. Bookbinder, I think that you'll be the death of me."

David Bookbinder clipped his cigar, and in the silence of Johann's room, the cutter made a distinct *snip,* as if someone was cutting a film.

1937

CORNELIUS ANNOUNCES AVIATION PLANS

"WORLD'S GREATEST
AIRPLANE" ALREADY UNDER WAY

Roderick Cornelius, elder son of oil billionaire Johann Cornelius, and leading Cornelius Oil executive, today revealed his plans for building and flying the world's largest and fastest passenger airplane.

"What we are setting out to do here today will shrink the world," he told a conference of aviation specialists and news correspondents in Charleston, West Virginia.

—*New York Times*,
September, 1937

On dull days, the new Cornelius Oil Building on lower Broadway took on a sort of despairing magnificence, like a giant hunchback, fatuously gilded and decorated for the passing amusement of a decadent prince, squatting in a rainy palace yard. On Wall Street, it was popularly known as "Groaning Grange." Its architect was a graceless imitator of Cass Gilbert, the designer of the Woolworth Building; but where Gilbert could make a Gothic spire seem ethereal and weightless, this man could only pile one massive block on top of the other, the more titanic and overbearing the better, and then garnish his huge and heavy-shouldered creation with as many irrelevant embellishments as possible.

The building was tiresomely constructed in a muddy shade of brown granite, all thirty-five hideous stories of it, and it was as depressing inside as it was out. Every office was paneled in South American mahogany and carpeted in brown, and every door handle and radiator was molded with bronze vine leaves. There was even a rumor that the architect would have liked stained glass in the windows, but someone (probably Hester) had drawn the line at that. Lauder Greenway had called the building "a monument to everything that money can buy—and I mean *everything*." And when James Gamble Rogers visited the lobby, soon after the building opened in 1936, he took one look at the black-veined-marble walls (plagiarized from the Straus Building) and dubbed it "the most expensive funeral parlor in American history."

The Cornelius family were aware that their main office was architecturally aggressive, but "The House," as they usually called it, was the kind of bulky physical presence that they wanted their empire to have. It was a temple to their fortune and the way they had made it. As Johann said: "I want every passing banker, every passing investor, every stray Rockefeller staring out of the Standard Oil Building, to look at my building—to *have* to look at my building—and see that it stands for what we are. We're rich, solid, powerful, traditional, and arrogant. If it's ugly it's because we *want* it ugly, and there isn't a damned thing that anyone can do about it."

David Bookbinder's office was on the thirty-fifth floor, a secluded eyrie among the uppermost spires. It was humid and cloudy in New York City on June 9, 1937, but during the afternoon a few scattered showers had helped to relieve the oppressive airlessness, and David Bookbinder had been sitting in his office with the windows wide open, so that a few spots of rain fell on the papers and files he had stacked on the sills. He enjoyed the sound of the showers on the buttresses outside, and the fresh smell that breezed into his room, and he thought wryly that when his accounts department received the bills for handling, they would look as though they were marked with tears.

Bookbinder was less settled than usual, because Johann was in the city. There was a strike of teamsters over pay and working hours. Hester was in town, too. She was visiting friends for afternoon tea, and then Roderick was taking her to see Maurice Evans in *King Richard II.* Roderick was twenty-three, and inclined to be pudgy, and he was increasingly nervous because Johann had given him orders to investigate the possibility of Atlantic flying-boat routes. The day of the airship had come to an abrupt and horrifying end on a wet evening last month, when the *Hindenburg* had exploded over New Jersey. Now it was rumored in the trade that Pan American was testing out the intercontinental airplanes, and Johann wanted to make sure that Cornelius Oil had a share of whatever was going. Hester thought the idea of flying across the Atlantic was exciting, but Roderick disliked heights, and had even bet his friend Davina Beerenberg twenty-five dollars that Amelia Earhart wouldn't make it. Davina was nuts about airplanes, and had taken the bet enthusiastically.

John was on summer vacation with a friend from Harvard. They were spending some time in Florida, visiting some progressive young writers they knew on Key West, and then they were going to tour some of the Cornelius oilfields in Texas, as a filial duty to Johann. John had sent David Bookbinder a cheeky picture postcard which said: "Today I ate my first conch. I have to admit that it reminded me of you."

As far as the Cornelius empire was concerned, business was reasonably brisk; but months ago David Bookbinder's sensitive nose had begun to make him uneasy about the stock market, particularly with copper prices the way they were, and he was doing everything he could to prepare the organization for a cutback and a possible recession. He had had a long telephone conversation with Daylong Oil that morning. Their vice-president, Al Foretto, had talked about car showrooms that were crowded with unsold cars, and a public that was finding luxuries increasingly expensive to buy.

"I can't get over the way the New Dealers are blaming *us*," Foretto had said. "All this talk of the 'sixty families' pushing up prices. I had a deputation from the cracking plant only yesterday, asking if they could personally put their grievances to Mr. J."

"And what did you tell them?"

"I told them I'd pass the message on to you."

"And what did they say to that?"

"I can't repeat it."

"Repeat it," David Bookbinder had said. "I'm not a child."

"Well," Foretto had said unhappily, "they said they wanted to talk to Edgar Bergen, not Charlie McCarthy."

David Bookbinder had laughed. After all, he was in a strong enough position to find it funny. He rarely listened to the radio himself, except for weather and stock reports, but he knew about the *Chase and Sanborn Hour*'s newly famous ventriloquist act, and the idea that the Daylong workers regarded him as a wooden mouthpiece for Johann Cornelius made him chuckle.

His amusement hadn't done much to relieve his anxiety, though. He had already spoken to Henry Morgenthau, the Secretary of the Treasury, at a private reception at City Hall, and protested about the cutbacks in government spending. In his usual storybook manner, he had taken Morgenthau to one side and said: "When a man is balancing on a wire, Henry, he can only go forward, backward, or downward."

Morgenthau had said roughly: "What do you think I am? A circus act?"

Bookbinder had patted his back and said: "Maybe so. Just think about it when the situation requires you to step sideways."

At around half-past four that afternoon, it started to rain again and David Bookbinder left his desk and went to the window. He had an angled view of Bowling Green, thick with hurrying umbrellas, and when he turned uptown he could see the gray and spectral spire of the six-year-old Empire State Building, gleaming with a faint yellow wash of hidden sunlight. Traffic honked dolefully, and a light wind blew across from the Jersey shore. He took a cigar out of his thick leather case and carefully removed the band.

It had been David Bookbinder's fiftieth birthday last month, in mid-May, with a champagne party out at Lynwood's Island. At the same time, he had celebrated his third year with the Cornelius family, and Hester had given him a gold card case inlaid with lapis lazuli and studded in rubies with the number three. When he had the case valued for insurance, the broker had suggested a round $215,000.

Johann had grumbled that the gift was a waste of money, but he hadn't grumbled for long. After three years of working with David Bookbinder, he was beginning to admit to himself that, in spite of Querbes Park, and in spite of Beatrice and Carina, David Bookbinder had a way of manipulating stocks and bonds that was almost magical, and a special talent for exerting pressure on unwilling senators and congressmen. He almost wished that Bookbinder had been around in the days of Albert Fall and the Teapot Dome business, instead of Jack Field.

In three years, David Bookbinder had probably done better for himself than in the whole of the rest of his life put together, and that included his years at Colton Oil. Johann often remarked that, whatever else was wrong with David Bookbinder, at least he put his money where his mouth was.

From his undistinguished beginnings, David Bookbinder was now making well over $1.5 million a year, and paying less tax than a Pennsylvania coal miner. But he never forgot his origins, nor his luck.

The door of David Bookbinder's office opened without warning, and Johann stalked in. David Bookbinder didn't turn around. He knew it was Johann, because nobody else would dare to walk in like that without knocking. He took out his cigar cutter and clipped a V in the end of the rich closely packed Havana tobacco.

Johann flung his black homburg onto the desk and stood there in his gray summer overcoat, looking big and elderly and fierce. His jaw was working around as if he had something in his mouth that he couldn't decide whether to spit out or not.

"David," said Johann huskily, stepping forward and finding a chair for himself. "Do you think I'm getting old?"

David Bookbinder remained at the open window, with his pinstriped back to his employer. He said: "There's a saying, I forget who said it."

Johann, his arm resting on Bookbinder's desk, sighed and stared at the floor.

"The saying asks whether it is better to be rich, or better to be wise," went on David Bookbinder, turning around as he spoke, and reaching in his tight vest pocket for his lighter.

Johann looked up. Bookbinder lit his cigar, and stood silhouetted in front of the window for a moment, in clouds of smoke, like Mephistopheles freshly arrived from hell.

"I suppose you have a cute answer," said Johann.

Bookbinder smirked. "The answer's not cute, it's true. The answer is that it's better to be rich, because the wise man spends his days at the rich man's door."

Johann grunted. He wasn't in the mood for Bookbinder's folklore. He said bitterly: "That may have been true whenever that saying was invented, but it certainly isn't true today. Maybe Roosevelt was right."

"Roosevelt?" queried Bookbinder.

"Well, dammit," said Johann. "If the Supreme Court is supposed to be too old at seventy, what hope do the rest of us have at sixty-five? I'm old, David, I'm old and I'm worn out. I'm tired of business and I'm tired of oil, and most of all I'm tired of myself. I don't care if I'm rich or wise. I'm exhausted."

David Bookbinder walked around his desk and sat down. He laced his fat pink fingers together like a plateful of frankfurters and blinked at Johann seriously.

"Don't tell me," he said. "You had a bad day with the teamsters."

"Bad?" snorted Johann. "They're totally intractable! I was down there talking to the so-called boys from Local 818, and I got absolutely no place at all. They've been getting twenty-five bucks a week, which is more than almost anyone in the country, and now they want thirty-seven or nothing."

Bookbinder said: "Were the newspapers there?"

"Of course they were."

"Maybe I should have gone down in your place. I'm not quite as quotable as you. I hope you didn't say anything colorful."

Johann pulled his coat around him petulantly. "I think I've

been in this business long enough to say *what* I like to *whomsoever* I like, David. I did nothing worse than call the CIO an avaricious ratpack on the backs of honest capitalism, or something like that.''

Bookbinder sucked his cigar. "I hope you're kidding," he said in a placid voice.

"Of course I'm kidding. But I'm not taking any more of this. I want you to get Fred Durham up here first thing in the morning, and we'll start to talk about layoffs. I'm not going to be black-mailed, David, and that's final."

Bookbinder could hardly resist a small, fat smile. "Let's not forget why I'm here, Johann," he said. "And let's not be too free and easy with our aspersions. Okay?"

Johann didn't answer. He sat champing his expensive bridgework for a while, and then said: "Do you have any coffee in this place?"

"Sure," said Bookbinder. "Like a bagel?"

"Yes, why not?" said Johann. "I haven't eaten since breakfast. This must be the toughest day's work I've done in five years. The next thing we know, those teamsters are going to be sitting down like the General Motors boys."

Bookbinder shook his head. "Don't worry about it. For every General Motors there's a U.S. Steel. And for every man in work today, there are going to be two men out of work tomorrow. The way that the market's going, Johann, another recession is ab-solutely inevitable. There's no getting away from it. In two years' time, the CIO will be nothing more than a distant and rather un-pleasant memory."

"And what about our stock values? I trust *they're* not going to become nothing more than a distant and rather unpleasant memory?"

Bookbinder leafed through his accounts. "I won't say the next couple of years are going to be easy. But I've already cut way back on production, and I'm ready to unload labor if we have to. I've negotiated one or two new outlets abroad, and I think we should weather the storm without too much capital loss."

"Did you sign that German contract?"

"Of course. We have two shiploads of heavy-duty tires on their way to Hamburg right now. I'm still cool on the Mercedes-Benz contract, but it could work out okay."

Johann turned around as Stephanie came in with a rattling tray of silver coffeepots and Spode cups, and a plateful of buttered bagels covered with a crisp white napkin. She poured their coffee out for them and kept glancing nervously at Johann as he began with difficulty to munch his bagel, as if it was amazing that a multimillionaire could actually be bothered to eat anything so mundane.

When she had gone, Johann said: "It's good to see that you put profit before honor."

"What do you mean?" asked David Bookbinder, knowing exactly what he meant.

"Let's put it this way," said Johann, sipping his coffee. "Your patron Mr. Rothschild wouldn't exactly have kicked his heels in the air, would he, if he'd known you were going to do business with Herr Hitler?"

Bookbinder grunted. "I'm not the only one, Johann. There are plenty of financial worthies out there on Wall Street today who are looking at their bank balances for guidance, rather than their racial consciences. Hitler's in the market for engineering goods and tires and all kinds of stuff. He wants the commodities, we need the money. I think the Atlantic Ocean is a long enough spoon if we have to sup with the devil."

"That's what *you* think," said Johann. "One of these days, Herr Hitler is going to fly over here in his Zeppelins and take potshots at you through your office window."

"Not that the *Hindenburg* was anything to go by," murmured David Bookbinder, pointedly raising his eyebrows.

They sat for a few minutes in silence, drinking their coffee. There were no telephone calls, because David Bookbinder always left instructions that his meetings with the Almighty were sacrosanct, and that nobody was to call or interrupt. With the rain pattering against the windows, and the wind flapping the loose papers on Bookbinder's desk, they could have been shut away from the world in some timeless carpeted vessel, with no view outside but the clouds, and no sound but the faint barking of car horns as New York City came to the close of another showery summer day.

"You know something," said Johann, rubbing his eyes, "you and me ought to sit down someday and work out just what the hell we mean to each other."

Bookbinder grinned faintly. "It's a romance, Johann. Didn't you know?"

Johann snorted. "Some romance!"

David Bookbinder said nothing for a while, but he puffed out smoke in small puffs, and looked as if he was thinking seriously. After a while he cleared his throat and said: "Many great friendships start off the way that we started off together; many enduring friendships. They last because there are no illusions, and never have been."

Johann said dryly: "I could ruin you. You know that, don't you?"

Bookbinder nodded. "Of course you could. But why should you? There are some dramatic gestures that are worth the price, but that wouldn't be. That's why I believe we have a romance of a kind. We are two souls who both believe in the intrinsic virtue of capital, floating together down a tunnel of love. We have to trust each other in the dark, like sweethearts do."

Johann brushed bagel crumbs from his coat. "Why do you always have to have your windows wide open?" he asked. "Look what happened to Jean Harlow. Caught herself the winter influenza and was dead in a week."

"Would you weep at my funeral?" said Bookbinder.

Johann said: "Just about as much as you're going to weep at mine."

There was a light rap at the door, and Stephanie showed Hester in. She was dressed in a smart dove-gray afternoon suit with chalk stripes, a floppy-collared cream silk blouse, and a black crocheted vest. Her dark hair was softly waved, and she wore a small gray turban with a veil and a diamond-studded plume. She didn't like the fashion for openwork hats and peaks because they didn't show her big eyes to their best advantage.

The two men stood up, and Johann offered Hester a chair. David Bookbinder went across and closed the window.

"How were the brotherhoods?" asked Hester, sitting down and opening her pocketbook. "Tea, I can tell you, was *dreadful*."

Johann coughed. "If you insist on taking tea with those incredible old dragons, I think you have to accept the consequences. David and I have just spent the afternoon . . ."

"Romancing?" suggested David Bookbinder.

Johann squinted across at him with a narrow-eyed look that Hester missed. He licked his lips, and then nodded.

"That's right," he said. "Romancing."

"Well," said Hester briskly. "If that's all you're doing, perhaps we ought to go up to Gramercy Park and get ourselves changed. Roddy's coming round at seven, and your dinner's at half past, isn't it?''

Johann nodded glumly. "I'm addressing the Republican Finance Club on the long-term problems of relief cuts. Although after my fun and games this morning with the CIO, I'm beginning to wonder if welfare's worth it. The American worker needs a kick in the rear, not relief."

"Is Hope back from Connecticut yet?" asked David Bookbinder.

"She certainly is," said Johann. "Haven't you noticed the haggard look on my face?"

David Bookbinder leaned forward on his desk. He coughed. He didn't look directly at either of them when he said: "Are you still having . . . well, *difficulties*? With Hope?"

Hester obviously didn't know whether she wanted to tell David Bookbinder anything about Hope or not. Her relationship with her husband's chief executive was courteous, but in a very stilted way. You felt that if their financial destiny were not so tightly intertwined, they would both have gladly passed each other on Broad Street as though they had never met. Hester privately thought that David Bookbinder was little more than a Semitic mobster, and that his complexion was like some cheap candy that small boys bought at Coney Island. She had once said so, to Johann's irritation. Bookbinder, for his part, was quiet and wary in Hester's presence, and would never talk seriously about business. He wasn't entirely certain that Hester knew very much about the way in which he had taken over the management of Cornelius Oil, and he didn't intend to give anything away.

But in any case it was Johann who told Bookbinder about Hope, and so Hester didn't have to make the decision, although she sat there tight-lipped and wished that Jo would try to keep his private life private, especially from a man like this.

"I'm old for a father," said Johann. "I know that. Hope's eighteen and I'm almost sixty-four. Maybe I don't understand the younger generation, and maybe that's the trouble. But she's wild! How can you bring up a girl like that, in good homes, with plenty of everything she wants, and a good education, and discipline, too, but still she turns out wild!"

David Bookbinder took out a very large white handkerchief and tooted his nose. "How wild is wild?" he asked in a muffled voice.

"Well," interjected Hester, "she used to go around with John Roosevelt and John Drayton during the Christmas vacation, and you know what sort of horseplay *they* get up to. But now it's worse."

"Worse?" broke in Johann. "She wears short skirts, she has her hair cut like Jean Arthur, and dammit, David, she *smokes*. I wouldn't be surprised if she kept a hip flask, and drank liquor."

David Bookbinder said: "Have you tried having it out with her?"

"I would if I could understand a word of what she says! She's always talking about 'boogie-woogie' and 'killer-diller' and everything 'sends' her. She goes out every night and spends her allowance like it's going out of style. Four, five hundred dollars a week, sometimes more, on some dumb crowd of kids who spend all their spare time racing up and down the highway in sports cars, going to parties and getting up to God knows what else. I mean, do you happen to know what an 'alligator' is?"

"An alligator," put in Hester, "is a young person who likes swing music. I thought even *you* could have worked that out."

"I don't *want* to work it out," said Johann testily. "I want to speak to my daughter in English, not some foreign language that nobody's heard of. She's a wild girl, David, and she's willful, and as far as she's concerned, I'm just some antique old has-been from the older generation."

David Bookbinder smiled. "We could cut off her allowance if you wish," he suggested. "It's kind of hard to make whoopee without the wherewithal."

"That wouldn't do any good," said Hester. "Most of her friends are wealthy. They'd just advance her the money—*give* her the money—until we gave in."

"I see," said David Bookbinder. He laid his cigar on the edge of his ashtray.

"She's wild and willful, that's all," repeated Johann. "Thank God there hasn't been any gossip in the newspapers about her, but if she goes on the way she is, it's bound to happen sooner or later."

David Bookbinder looked down at his desk for a while and then said quietly: "Do you really mean she's wild and willful, or do you mean she's the only person who's ever stood up to you and gotten away with it?"

Johann slowly turned his head when David Bookbinder said

that, like a large and threatening beast looking around itself for the impudent monkey that has pulled its tail during feeding time.

"David," he said softly. "I'll pretend I haven't heard that."

David Bookbinder kept smiling. "That's all right, Johann. You pretend you haven't heard that, and I'll pretend that I haven't heard of the year 1903."

There was a curious silence that Hester didn't understand at all. Outside the window, the rain had stopped now, and dark evening clouds were gathering gloomily from the west. Hester blinked uncertainly at both men and said: "Nineteen-oh-three? What's so special about 1903?"

Johann didn't answer straightaway, but then he lifted himself laboriously out of his armchair and wrapped himself up, with slow dignity, in his overcoat.

"It's a joke," he said in a hoarse and heavy voice. "Nineteen-oh-three is a joke."

And David Bookbinder smiled at Hester, and nodded, and smiled again, as if to say that indeed it was, and a very good joke at that.

The three cars bounced and walloped over the rough country roads, their headlights jostling through the warm summer night. Even from quite a way away, you could hear the young people shrieking and laughing as they swerved from one side of the road to the other, and someone was trying to play "Don't Be That Way" on a clarinet, but was obviously too drunk and out of breath.

By the time they reached the crossroads, the three cars were almost neck-and-neck, taking up the whole roadway, and the kids were yelling and shouting to each other as they raced faster and faster toward the junction with the main highway.

"Get off, Eddie! Yayyy!"

"Ohhh, this sends me! This really sends me down!"

For a moment, two of the sports cars bumped against each other—running board grinding against the running board—but then they blared across the main road with their horns going *parpp-parrpp-parrpp!* and were swallowed up in the darkness on the other side.

They drove for another ten minutes, gradually losing speed, until they drew up at a small muddy turnoff, and killed their engines. All of the kids were laughing and joking, and someone was saying: "I sat on my hat! Would you look at that? I sat on my goddamned hat!"

Still talking and shrieking, they climbed out of their cars and stood around while one of the boys, in evening pants and shirt-sleeves, did his best to open a bottle of bourbon.

"Boy, if my mother could see me now!" One of the girls giggled. "She'd go nuts! I mean really nuts!"

"If your mother's here, I want to know about it," said the boy with the bourbon. "She's a fine woman!"

He gave a mock-lustful cackle, and everybody laughed.

After a while, the boy managed to open the bottle, and they all sat around in their dinner suits and evening dresses and made themselves comfortable on running boards or rugs, and lit up Old Golds and passed the bourbon around. The sky was a dense blue through the rustling black fingerwork of trees and branches, and a damp breeze was blowing. Somewhere far away, toward Danbury, a motorcycle sawed its way monotonously through the early evening. Their cigarettes glowed orange in the dark, and the kid with the clarinet kept on tootling the opening bars of "Begin the Beguine."

"You know your trouble, Mel," called one of the girls. "All you can do is begin to begin 'Begin the Beguine.' Why don't you ever *finish* it?"

"Nuts to you, Virginia," said Mel. "One day I'll be up there on stage with Artie Shaw, and then you'll squawk out of the other side of your mug!"

"What are you going to do? Hold his coat?"

Sitting on the running board of Eddie Kaiser's red Chrysler convertible, Hope Cornelius listened and laughed. She was feeling full of sparks tonight—bright and smart and pretty. In her clinging white silk evening dress, with its deep décolletage and feathery plumes over her breasts, she knew she looked at least two years older than eighteen. The bourbon hadn't passed around to her yet, but she was puffing assiduously on her Old Gold, and holding her head up in a very sophisticated way. She wore red lipstick, heaps of mascara, and she had plucked and penciled her eyebrows into thin curves. Her wavy brown hair was tucked into a white curved evening hat, and her only jewelry, apart from her rings, was a big butterfly brooch in rubies and amethysts.

Next to her, Eddie Kaiser was smoking his cigarette in an ostentatiously "tough" way, taking deep drags and blowing the

356

smoke out through his nostrils. He was a beefy young boy, and his overtight tuxedo and black-and-white shoes didn't make him any less noticeable.

He turned to Hope and grinned in the darkness. His hair was shaved short and prickly at the sides, with a brilliantined center parting on top. He said: "Some fun, huh?"

Hope took a little sip of smoke. "It's okay," she said carelessly. "If you like sitting in the woods on a wet night, drinking whiskey out of the neck of a bottle."

"Why, sure I do," said Eddie Kaiser. He was seventeen, and in four years' time he was due to inherit something in excess of four million dollars from his father's patent-medicine business. His high school friends nicknamed him "Pills."

"I'd like to do something original for a change," said Hope. "We're always doing the same kind of thing. We have parties, we go dancing, we go to nightclubs. I mean, that's all we ever do. I want to do something *wild* that *means* something."

"I'd like to do something *wild*," put in John Deerman enthusiastically.

"Well, *this* is wild," said Mel Herbert. Then he said uncertainly: "Isn't it?"

Hope looked around at all the young, well-fed faces. Among them, these dozen or so children were worth more than the capital reserves of some small countries, and yet here they were, sitting in a soggy wood in New York State on a showery June night, drinking whiskey and wondering what to do with themselves.

"If you think this is wild," said Hope, "then I suggest you go home and play Mah-Jongg with your mother. With any luck, you might faint from the excitement."

"Maybe we should go round to your dad's place at Lynwood's Island," one of the girls suggested to Hope. "We could play poker, and every time any one of us loses a hand, we could make it a rule that they have to take off a piece of their clothing."

"Aw, that's dumb," said Eddie Kaiser.

"You only think it's dumb because you can't play poker."

"I can too! I just think it's dumb. If I want to get a girl's clothes off, I don't have to sit down at some dumb card game and do it."

Philip Strachan called out: "Why don't you do it then, smartie? I don't recall you taking any girl's clothes off."

"You button it," snapped Eddie Kaiser. "Just because you're the Casanova of the campus."

"Hey," said John Deerman, passing the bourbon bottle to Hope, "I heard my father tell this real funny joke the other day. I mean, it's real dirty, but it's real funny."

"I don't want to hear any jokes," complained Virginia. "You're the only person who can tell a joke and make me feel sad."

Hope took a swig of bourbon from the bottle and passed it. She said quietly: "That's because J. D. is exactly like his father, nd J. D.'s father, just like *all* of our fathers, comes from a bankrupt generation."

"My father's not bankrupt," said Cicely Schweizmann. "He's rich, and that's his whole trouble." Cicely, a dark-haired girl with a camelhair jacket slung over her shoulders, was memorable for her enormous breasts. Philip Strachan used to say about her: "God thought that rich girls are always unhappy, so he gave her an extra helping to make up for it."

Hope said: "That's what I mean, Cicely. Our parents are all wealthy, but mentally they're bankrupt. They don't know anything. I mean, our whole country's been through eight years of poverty and hardship and sweat, and they still talk about brotherhoods and workers like they're some kind of rabid scum."

"Hey, wait a minute," said Eddie Kaiser. "That's John L. Lewis talk, that is."

"More like *Grapes of Wrath* talk," commented Kenny Thursgood.

"I don't care what kind of talk it is," said Hope. "Why do you think we're sitting here in these stupid woods drinking whiskey? Because we don't want to be sitting at home listening to our pompous parents talking their usual unreal garbage about the world today and how they help to run it."

"I don't think my father's unreal," put in Mel Herbert. "He's stuffy, I'll give you that. But I don't think he's unreal. You have to give our parents something. They sure know how to make money."

"That's about *all* they know," said Hope. "And do you know what their money costs the people who work for them? Do you really understand what it costs, in *humanity*, for you to stick a forkful of *pâté de foie gras* into that fat face of yours? Don't you read the papers? Don't you read about the strikes and the Okies and the struggle this country's going through?"

"Oh, come on, Hope," said Philip Strachan. "The best thing that our parents can do for this country is make money. You know that as well as the rest of us. If your daddy didn't have those oil wells of his, pumping out that lovely liquid money, about five hundred thousand people would be out of work tomorrow. What's the cost of one forkful of *pâté de foie gras* compared with what your daddy's putting into this country, and what he's doing to keep the economy strong?"

"But the CIO—"

"Forget the CIO. The CIO is a communist subversive group, and they're doing everything they can to bring this nation to its knees. Well, they won't do it!"

"Hey, listen," put in John Deerman. "Are we here for a political discussion or are we going to have some fun? Hope, you said yourself you wanted to do something original."

"Yes, come on, Hope," said Cicely. "We can't change the course of history sitting out here."

Hope stood up and brushed the seat of her dress. "Okay," she said pertly. "I have an idea."

"We stick up a gas station?" asked Kenny Thursgood. "I'm sure Philip would like to do that."

"No," said Hope. "I'd like to do something that's wild, but at the same time it's wild for a *purpose*."

"I know," said John Deerman, "we assassinate Roosevelt."

"Not that purpose," interrupted Hope. "If we assassinate anybody, we ought to knock off Hearst, or someone like that."

Eddie Kaiser said: "For God's sake, Hope. How are we going to do *that*? And what *for*?"

"I don't really mean we ought to knock off Hearst," said Hope. "But we have to do something clever. It has to look like it's a practical joke—you know, just high-spirited kids horsing around. But at the same time we have to make sure that it blows a Bronx cheer at something that our parents believe in. Do you understand?"

"My father believes in eating lightly boiled eggs for breakfast," said Kenny Thursgood. "You want me to blow a Bronx cheer at lightly boiled eggs?"

"Don't be so childish. It has to be something that shakes their very foundations. Like the class structure."

"The class structure? I don't understand."

"Well, you wouldn't. But this is what we do. We go back to the highway and we cruise up and down until we find ourselves a hitchhiker. Or maybe we stop off at a diner and look for some

359

truck driver, or any old down-and-out. It has to be someone who looks real awful, and poor. Then we pick him up, and take him with us to the Royale Country Club, and we treat him like an honored guest. We get our usual table, and buy him a bang-up dinner, and make all the waiters bow and scrape to him, the same way they bow and scrape to us.''

"Go on," said Philip Strachan. "Then what happens?"

"Well, that's it," said Hope. "Can you imagine Hugo's face when we walk in? Can you imagine all those stuffed shirts who eat there, when they turn around and see some decrepit old bum drinking his soup straight out of the bowl? I mean, don't you think that's beautiful?''

In the darkness of the clearing, the kids looked at each other in bewilderment, and then back at Hope.

"Is that supposed to be a blow for socialism?" asked Philip Strachan.

"Can you think of anything better?" Hope said.

"Well, no, I can't. But it doesn't seem like much of a blow for socialism. I thought socialists sat down in factories and stuff like that. I can't see Richard Frankensteen telling his workers to go dine at the Royale Country Club, can you?''

Hope said: "What *are* you? Don't you understand what something like this can *do*? Everybody who knows us—all our parents and everybody—they'll just think it's another practical joke. They won't get too sore about it, and they'll stay just as complacent as they always were. But the workers, the socialists, they'll see what we're doing for what it is. We're bringing down the system, a little at a time, and showing we're not made of the same rigid conservative stuff as our parents.''

John Deerman scratched his head. "I think it's a funny idea," he said. "But I don't quite see where the socialism comes in. I mean, I'm willing to go along with it just because it's funny.''

"Well, as long as you go along with it, I don't mind," said Hope. "Maybe you'll understand it when you've gotten yourself some political sophistication.''

"I don't mind doing it," agreed Kenny Thursgood. "It's better than playing strip poker, and it's certainly better than standing around here.''

"Virginia?" asked Hope. "How about you?"

Virginia shrugged. "If we're all doing it, I guess I'm game.''

Cicely said huskily: "I could be his escort. I could really wiggle in there, you know—like Jean Harlow."

"You mean like Jean Harlow used to."

"Come on," said Philip Strachan, "if we're going to do it, let's get it real well organized, so that we all know what we're doing. A practical joke is only funny if you do it well. Otherwise, you're wasting your time. Eddie . . . do you still have that spare tuxedo in the trunk of your car?"

"I think so," said Eddie Kaiser. "It's probably kind of crumpled, but I guess that's all the better."

After twenty minutes of arguing and giggling and elaborating Hope's idea, the kids agreed on a plan of action. They climbed noisily back into their three cars, with Hope and Cicely Schweizmann sitting in the rumble seat of Philip Strachan's convertible, and started up. Then they turned around on the narrow road and made their way back to the junction with the main Newburgh-Danbury highway. It was almost ten-thirty now, and the sky was lighter now that the clouds had cleared. The forecast for tomorrow, June 10, was warm and fair.

They turned upstate when they reached the highway, and after driving for only three or four minutes they found the perfect place. By the side of the road, set well back in its own cinder-strewn parking lot, was a small diner and gas station. It was a low wooden building with a green-spotted tarpaper roof and a zinc chimney that wafted the odor of bacon grease into the warm summer night. Through the lighted windows the kids could see the owner, a stocky man in a white undershirt, clearing up after the day's business. A feed truck had just pulled out of the parking lot, and its red taillights were disappearing in the direction of the Hudson Valley. At a table alone sat a gaunt-looking man in an old gray suit, with a cup of coffee and a doughnut.

The three cars drew up by the side of the highway, and Philip went back to confer with Eddie Kaiser. Then he came back to Hope and said: "We're all set. Do you want to go in and do the honors?"

Hope climbed out of the car, and Philip helped her down to the side of the road. For a moment he held her hands and looked down at her, handsome and curly-haired, with a serious face.

"You're a girl in a million, Hope. Do you know that?"

She didn't answer. She didn't particularly like standing there with Philip, holding hands by the side of the road, with all the other

361

kids looking on, but Philip was almost compulsively boring, like the Ancient Mariner, and just like the wedding guest, she could not choose but stay.

"I know you think that our mothers and fathers are pretty old-fashioned," he said. "But you have to remember that we're all looking for a brighter future. *All* of us—not just socialists and workers. The rich have rights too, you know."

Hope lowered her eyes. "For someone as bright and a well-educated as you are," she said, an octave higher than she'd wanted to, "you really don't have much vision."

Philip wasn't upset. He liked girls with spunk. "You're a rare one," he told her, smiling.

"Yes," she said.

The night wind flapped the gleaming silk of her dress against her slim ankles. She said: "I suppose I'd better get going. Just give me a couple of minutes to size everything up. I'll give you a wave from the window if I need any help. Eddie, did you find that tuxedo yet?"

"I'm just looking," said Eddie in a muffled voice from the trunk of his Chrysler.

"Good luck, Hope," said Philip, and climbed back into his car. He gave her an impossibly jaunty little wave, and then started up. Eddie found the tuxedo and clambered into his car. The three cars backed up out of sight by the trees at the edge of the parking lot, and then cut their engines and switched off their lights. Soon there was nothing but the rustle of the wind and the soft sound of the stirring trees.

Hope crunched across the cinders and climbed the three wooden steps to the door of the diner. Most of the lights inside had been turned off now, and she could see the owner wiping his hands and hanging up his apron. She opened the screen door and went inside.

The owner looked up, but the man in the gray suit, the down-and-out, kept his eyes on his tepid coffee and the last crumbs of his doughnut. Inside the diner it was uncomfortably warm, and there was a clinging smell of fat and bacon grease. A large pound cake lay under a smeary glass dome like an exhibit at the museum of fossils. An electric fan circled tirelessly and uselessly around on the ceiling, casting its flickering shadows over worn-out brown oilcloth upholstery, two rickety pinball machines and a Myrna Loy calendar.

"We're closed, lady," said the owner abruptly. He was short

and Slavic-looking, with cropped gray hair and a soiled plaid shirt. There was a row of blunt pencils in his breast pocket.

"I just wondered if I could get some help," said Hope, trying to look as wide-eyed and helpless as possible.

"What kind help?" asked the owner. Behind him, on the wall, was a faded picture of the frozen Vistula at Bydgoszcz, and a yellow rosette saying "1st."

"It's my car," said Hope. "I was just passing and it broke down. It made a noise like poopity-poopity poon-tang and just stopped."

"Well," said the owner, shaking his head. "From cars I don't know."

Hope said anxiously: "I did think of calling a garage. You know, to come and tow it for me. But a garage will take hours. I have to be in Newburgh tonight, it's absolutely essential, because my poor dear uncle is desperately sick, and supposing he dies while I'm waiting for a tow truck?"

The owner found this a little hard to digest. He shook his head again and said: "From cars I don't know. One end, other end. From cars I don't know nothing."

Hope said: "Do you think maybe that gentleman sitting over there knows something about cars?"

The owner stared at her. Then he turned his head and stared at the down-and-out sipping the last dregs of his coffee under the Myrna Loy calendar.

"Him?" asked the owner.

"Yes, *him*," said Hope. "There's nobody else in here, is there?"

The owner shrugged. Then he called out: "Hey, you!"

The down-and-out didn't realize that the owner was shouting to him at first. He continued to sip his coffee, peering into the cup as if he was making sure that there wasn't an extra mouthful hiding in there someplace.

"Hey, you!" called the owner again.

The man laid down his cup and looked up. He was haggard and prematurely gray, with the sharp pointed face and exhausted eyes that characterized all those who stood in line for soup, or hung around railroad yards, or sold bootlaces or wind-up dolls on the corners of countless city streets. His striped shirt was frayed, and his gray suit was worn shapeless. He could have been fifty, but he was probably nearer to thirty-five. There was a desperate destroyed composure about him, like a once-fashionable steamship reduced to dredging estuaries. He could have been handsome once, in a bank-clerk kind of a way, but now his face was neutral with poverty.

He said: "Are you talking to me?" and his voice was very soft and polite.

The owner said: "You think I talk to myself?"

The man said: "I'm sorry. No."

For what was apparently the first time, the man looked across at Hope. His eyes didn't seem to register any kind of surprise at seeing a young girl in a shining white silk evening dress in a cheap roadside diner at ten-thirty at night, but he did say "Good evening" to her and straightened his greasy tie.

"What you know from cars?" demanded the owner. "This lady, she's broke down. What you know from cars?"

The down-and-out stood up. He was short, and very thin, and Hope noticed that he wore no socks. He came forward, trying to walk straight, and said: "What appears to be the problem, miss?"

Hope looked at him warily. Now that her "blow for socialism" was actually happening, she felt frightened as well as excited. She had thought about it for weeks—ever since the last row she had had with her mother. The idea had seemed silly at first, but the more she thought about it, the more she liked it. She wanted to do something that made pompous people look as shallow and mean as they were; and also she wanted poor and down-trodden men like this to know that she and her friends weren't all spoiled brats, idling their time away at sailing and dancing and skiing, but that the next generation of rich would be genuinely charitable, honestly helpful, and free of the grotesque rigidity that had led them all into 1929.

It was partly a blow at her father, too. Johann Cornelius had never wanted Hope to be anything more than his pretty little daughter: bright but obedient, spirited but ready to come to heel when required. She sometimes wondered if he was trying to prove something to himself by the way he treated her. She knew how influential her mother was in his life, and he had an unnaturally gruff, evasive way of dealing with strong and independent women. All through her girlhood, Hope had tussled against his suffocating intolerance, like the time he had refused to let her join the Lynwood Girl Scouts because he was adamant that she should be a pretty girl, a feminine girl, and that she would hate fending for herself. He had shouted at her: "Pampered? Of course you'll be pampered! I won't have it any other damned way! What do you think I made all my money for? Why do you think I struggled? Some girls would give their right arms to change places with you!" Hope remembered him saying that because her mind had conjured up a disturbing impression of a strange girl sitting in *her* chair, in *her* frilly frock, but with only one arm—the price this girl had paid to change places with Hope.

Now this emaciated down-and-out stood wearily in front of her, an unsuspecting champion for her rebellious cause. He gave a hoarse, hollow cough, and raised his hand in front of his mouth. She noticed how dirty his fingernails were. Crescents of cheesy black. He sniffed.

"My . . . my car's broken down," she said quickly. "I think it must be something quite simple. It isn't a flat or anything like that. Perhaps I flooded the engine. I sometimes do that. I wonder if you'd be kind enough to . . . take a look for me."

Her voice seemed to dwindle away very small. The down-and-out looked at her with washed-out eyes, and she noticed for the first time that one was blue and the other hazel.

"Miss," he said courteously, "I am, or I *was,* an insurance man. I'm afraid automobiles are a mystery to me, just as they are to this gentleman here."

The diner's owner nodded, as if that was the wisest remark he had heard in several years, and hung up his dishcloth.

"From cars," he said, "is mystery."

Hope was growing anxious. She said: "Well, couldn't you just come out and see? It's only just outside. Maybe you can think of something to get it running."

The down-and-out tugged at his nose. "Well," he said, "I still think a tow truck is your best bet, but I'll come and have a look. How much do I owe you, Mr. Leszno?"

"Ten cents."

Hope opened her white jeweled pocketbook, reached inside, and took out a ten-dollar bill. She said: "Let me pay for that."

The down-and-out eyed the bill suspiciously. He already had the dime ready in his hand, and he laid it carefully on top of the cash register with an audible click.

"That's all right," he said quietly. "I still pay my way."

Hope flushed, and put the bill back in her purse. "Well, please yourself," she said. "I didn't mean to suggest that—"

The man waved his hand as if to say that she should forget it. He said: "Good night, Mr. Leszno," and walked with Hope to the screen door and opened it. The shadow of the electric fan windmilled over their backs as they stepped out into the night.

Hope said: "It's just over there, by the trees. I was lucky to get it off the highway."

As they walked across the parking lot, Hope said: "By the way, my name is Hope Cornelius. Would you mind telling me yours?"

The man looked across at her. In the blue gloom of the evening he seemed almost spectral. The darkness clung in the hollows of his eyes, and his cheekbones were as narrow as a rat's. He said: "Why do you want to know?"

"Well—she shrugged—"I like to find out what my Galahads are called, in case I ever need them again."

The man coughed. "Do you think it's ever likely that our paths will cross in the future?" he asked.

"You never know."

"Well, I don't think so," he said. "Whoever you are, Miss Cornelius, you're obviously a very wealthy young lady, and I am nothing more than a vagrant who used to sell insurance. I don't spend a lot of time in Palm Springs, you know. In fact, I mostly work this area doing packing and odd jobs for the local stores. I earned two dollars yesterday, cutting cords of firewood from dawn until midnight."

Hope frowned. "Haven't you heard of the CIO?"

"Oh sure," said the man, sticking his hands in his pockets. "But it's no use belonging to a brotherhood of workers if you're not a worker to begin with. Besides, I don't agree with communism."

"They're not communists. Their whole purpose is to protect people just like you."

The man stopped walking and stared at her.

"You're pretty unexpected, you are," he said. "If you don't mind my saying so."

"What do you mean?"

"You're wealthy. Is that your car there, under those trees? Wealthy people don't generally hold with brotherhoods."

Hope said: "The point is, I know what it's like to be rich. My father's rich, and because he's rich, he's lost all his humanity. That's why I hold with brotherhoods, because I want to see some humanity."

The man coughed again. They reached Eddie Kaiser's red Chrysler, standing empty under the rustling trees. The man walked around it once, examining it, and then went around to the front.

"Well," he said, "I guess we'd better take a look under the hood."

He peeled off his jacket, folded it in half, and laid it carefully on the ground. Then he rolled up the patched sleeves of his shirt and started to grope for the catches that held the hood.

"I hope it's nothing too serious, Mr. . . . ."

The man looked up. "Bausor, if you must know. Lewis Bausor, from Yonkers originally."

"That's a nice name," said Hope. "Do you mind if I call you Lewis?"

"Do whatever you want. You've got the money to."

Hope leaned against the side of the car. "Now, come on," she said. "You know that isn't true."

"Isn't it?" asked Lewis. He lifted the Chrysler's hood and peered inside. The engine was highly polished and immaculate. The cylinder heads had been plated in chromium, and there was the soft gleam of brass and machined aluminum everywhere.

"This is some engine," said Lewis. "I'm not sure I know where to start looking."

"Maybe there's nothing wrong with it," said Hope.

Lewis wiped his hands on his pants. "Well, if it won't start . . ."

Then he stood up straight, and looked at her across the raised hood.

"What do you mean?" he asked. " 'Maybe there's nothing wrong with it'?"

Hope twirled her pocketbook. "Just that. Maybe there's nothing wrong with it. Maybe I brought you out here for some different purpose altogether."

"Like what?" said Lewis defensively.

There was a giggle, and a shuffling sound in the shadows of the trees. Out of the darkness stepped Philip Strachan and Eddie Kaiser and Virginia and Cicely and Mel and all the rest of the kids. They came and gathered around the car, while Lewis Bausor stood there in his neatly rolled-up shirtsleeves, looking from one to the other in complete bewilderment. Philip, all gleaming white dickey front and gleaming white teeth, came right up with his hand out in welcome and said: "Hi."

367

Lewis turned to Hope. He said: "Who are these people? Would you mind telling me what's going on?"

"They're my friends," said Hope with a smile. "It's a surprise. Everybody . . . meet Lewis Bausor, from Yonkers!"

Philip Strachan shook Lewis' hand and said: "How do you do, Lewis? I'm Philip, and this is Mel, and that there's John Deerman, and if you'd just like to come around here I'll introduce you to everyone else."

Lewis lifted his hands as if to protect himself from this torrent of sociability.

"Now, hold on, please," he said. "Just a minute. Would someone mind telling me what this is all about?"

Philip Strachan put one arm around him. An immaculate black tuxedo sleeve and white laundered cuff against worn-out stripes.

"Lewis," said Philip intimately, "it happens every so often that our secret society of socialites meets in the rural reaches of New York State."

Lewis frowned but didn't say anything.

"When we meet," said Philip Strachan, "we select for one evening a deserving member of the public, and we treat him to a night of feasting and merrymaking. Our philosophy is that even though the laws of wealth are immutable, which prevents us from distributing our property freely and without let across the entire nation, we can at the very least take single and individual Americans of lesser means and give them a fleeting taste of the joys of being rich."

Lewis Bausor licked his lips. He looked as if his mouth had gone dry, and next to Philip's well-fed bulk, he appeared on a smaller scale altogether, like the villeins in medieval paintings who are always drawn tinier than their feudal lords.

"Mr. Bausor," explained Virginia, "what Philip means is that we're going to take you out for a meal. As a kind of gesture."

Lewis Bausor bent over and picked up his folded jacket. He turned to Philip, and said in his soft voice: "I appreciate your thought, sir, but I'm afraid that I just ate."

"A cup of coffee and a doughnut isn't *eating*," put in Hope.

Lewis shrugged. "Maybe not to you. But that was all I could afford."

"That's precisely the point," put in Eddie Kaiser. "That was all *you* could afford, but *we* can afford more, and we want you to *have* more. We want you to have one real good six-course dinner that you can remember for the rest of your life."

"Oh, say yes," said Cicely Schweizmann. "Please, Mr. Bausor, *do* say yes!"

Lewis Bausor said: "Six-course dinner?"

"That's right," enthused Kenny Thursgood. "With turtle soup, and prime steak, and fresh trout, and all the hot biscuits you can eat."

Lewis lowered his head. He coughed. They waited and nudged each other and giggled while he made up his mind. After a while he looked up again and said: "I suppose really you're doing this to ease your conscience?"

Philip Strachan pulled an exaggerated face of mock horror.

"Conscience, Lewis? How you misjudge us! I don't blame you, of course. Everybody misjudges the wealthy. But let me tell you that no man can have a conscience if he makes money in the service of his country. We have no conscience. All we want to do is to share some of our good fortune around."

Lewis looked again at Hope, with a questioning expression, as if trying to check that it was all right to say yes. Hope nodded, and grinned at him; and, reassured, he grinned back. "All right," he said. "If it's going to make you all happy, I accept. You know, I haven't had a good dinner like that in three years. The last good dinner I had was in 1934, on Thanksgiving night, when a man picked me up just outside of Poughkeepsie and took me back to his home. That was my last good dinner."

Eddie Kaiser came forward with his spare tuxedo.

"You'll have to wear this, Mr. Bausor. The place we're taking you, they don't allow business suits."

One of the girls tittered at the idea that Lewis Bausor's worn-out gray outfit could be seriously regarded as a "business suit." Philip Strachan said: "Quiet, please! This is going to be a very dignified occasion." The girls all *shushed* each other, and giggled some more.

Eddie took Lewis Bausor around the back of his car to change into his tuxedo, while the rest of them got themselves ready to leave. Hope, for some reason she couldn't quite understand, felt subdued and quiet, and she waited by the side of the red Chrysler, staring out across the parking lot to the diner, where the lights at last went out, and Mr. Leszno locked up for the night.

"Tarantara!" trumpeted Eddie Kaiser. They all turned around, and out of the shadows came Lewis Bausor, dressed in Eddie's tuxedo. He was smiling sheepishly, and tugging down the black coat to try to make it feel more comfortable. Considering that Eddie Kaiser was a tall and hefty young man, and that Lewis Bausor was undersized and scrawny, the fit wasn't too bad. The coat was a little dusty and crumpled from lying in the trunk of Eddie's car, the white dickey was already spotted with soup, and the pants were so long that they concertinaed over his shoes, but as Philip pointed out, he didn't have any socks on, and the long pants would help to hide that omission from the Royale's maitre d', who was pretty punctilious on matters of dress.

Lewis Bausor came toward Hope, pressing down his straggly gray hair with the flat of his hand.

"How do I look?" he said hoarsely.

Hope nodded, and gave him a half-smile. She felt something tightening her throat, almost as if she wanted to cry. She knew that crying was quite ridiculous, and she knew that what they were doing was a real blow for socialism, but all the same it was hard to keep her eyes from blurring, and when she spoke she sounded as hoarse as he did.

"Lewis," she said, "you look just fine."

They climbed into their three cars. Lewis shared the rumble seat of Philip's car with Kenny Thursgood. They set off, with a roar of over-revved engines and a salvo of horns, for the Royale Country Club. Mel Herbert produced his clarinet once again, and serenaded them as they sped through the moth-laced night.

It took twenty minutes of chaotic driving to reach the Royale. They sped in through the impressive wrought-iron gates, and slewed their cars around on the circular gravel driveway. Although it was late, the club was still brightly lit and crowded, and there were Cadillacs and Packards and Chryslers glistening like schools of expensive fish in the parking lot.

"Well, old man," said Kenny Thursgood cheerfully, helping Lewis Bausor out of his seat, "what do you think of it?"

Lewis Bausor, in his crumpled tuxedo, stood on the perfectly raked gravel and lifted his eyes slowly upward—up from the semicircular sweep of marble steps, up to the massive open doors and the glittering hallway inside, up to the columns and porticoes and ranks of shining windows, up to the ledges and shutters and stone acanthus leaves.

Hope came around the car and took Lewis Bausor's arm. He was standing there with such a white face that he could have been dusted in flour. It was only in the light of the driveway that Hope began to see how worn-out and sick he looked, and how incongruously the tuxedo hung on his bony body. He should have been in the hospital—not making an entrance at the Royale Country Club. But she squeezed his thin arm through the thick folds of his coat and said: "Come on, Lewis. This is going to be beautiful."

As they reached the door, Philip Strachan, with Cicely Schweizmann on his arm, caught up.

"I'll go first," he said. "I'm sure I can soft-soap Hugo. Anyway, I don't think he'll dare."

"Who's Hugo?" asked Lewis Bausor.

"Oh, he's the maitre d'," said Virginia. "A very particular man, if I might say so. So make sure you hide your ankles."

They went through the doors into the lofty, brightly lit hallway. The floor was a dark mirror of highly polished Italian marble, and there were yew shrubs in decorative green-and-yellow ceramic pots all around. Ahead of them rose a maroon-carpeted staircase, and the foyer above that led to the principal restaurant. Even from the hall, they could hear the lilting sounds of the orchestra and the low murmuring of conversation.

"Better than Joe's greasy spoon," said Kenny Thursgood. "In fact, better than *anybody's* greasy spoon."

They trod upward through thick carpet, and crossed the foyer. Above them, floating in pastel clouds across a cupola dome, were nymphs and goddesses and overweight cherubim. With Hope clutching Lewis' arm tighter and tighter, they approached the tall doors of mahogany and engraved glass that led into the Royale's restaurant. Hope could already see Hugo, the small, dark-haired, ruthlessly particular maitre d', and her heart beat in irregular bounds. She didn't dare to look at Lewis Bausor, who was shuffling along beside her with his pants trailing on the carpet.

Inside, the restaurant was decorated in red velvet and plush, with a hundred gilt tables all crisply laid with white linen, solid silver cutlery, and rococo candelabra. At one side, the orchestra played on their rostrum, fiddling their way through endless elegant chamber music. At the other side, double doors opened into the kitchen, and dinner-jacketed waiters hurried in and out of these like bees flying in and out of their hive, carrying silver trays of salmon and pâté and oysters and the *pigeonneaux royaux, sauce paradis* for which the Royale was renowned. Not only was there an aromatic mingling of sauces and fruits and liqueurs and *filet de boeuf*, but there was an equally aromatic mingling of conversation, with the well-bred vowels of New England spicing the broad, flat, languid language of sunbelt profiteering. The restaurant, as usual, was crowded.

Hugo spun on his patent-leather shoes as they walked in, and gave his customary unsubservient bow.

"Monsieur Strachan," he said. But his eyes flicked over Philip's shoulder, and checked out everyone else like a gunfighter checking his chances of survival.

"Good evening, Hugo," said Philip. "Crowded tonight?"

Hugo's round French face twitched in something like a smile. "As always, Monsieur Strachan."

"Well," said Philip, "I want a table for fourteen."

"All members, Monsieur Strachan?"

"That's right."

"And the gentleman with Mademoiselle Cornelius?"

"Oh, I forgot him. Yes, he's a guest."

Hugo produced the guest book as if he had been hiding it under his dickey. "You will, of course, sign for him, Monsieur Strachan?"

Philip blushed slightly, and hesitated. "Well, actually," he said, "he *is* a guest of Miss Cornelius."

Hugo didn't budge. "Lady members, sir, cannot sign the register on behalf of gentlemen visitors." All this time, he was keeping his eyes on Lewis Bausor, and taking in with meticulous observation the lopsided dickey, the hurriedly tied bow, the sagging jacket, and the trailing trousers. Lewis Bausor leaned on Hope's arm with the dispirited collapse of total pessimism, and she felt as if she were taking the Scarecrow in to see the Wizard of Oz. He coughed once or twice, but suppressed it as much as he could.

Philip Strachan shrugged, and held out his hand for a pen. Hugo had it uncapped and poised as instantly as if he had plucked it out of the air. Philip signed, and turned back as he did so to give Hope a humorless and well-boiled smile.

Conversation in the restaurant subsided as Hugo led them all between the tables to a long banquette by the window. Most of the diners were friends of their parents, and they waved and smiled as they went. "Good evening, Mrs. Vanderhaugh." "Good evening, Mr. Sharp." "Good evening, Miss Gaylord."

As Hope passed one table, she heard Mrs. Vanderhaugh, the lubrication widow, say in her usual piercing whisper: "Who on earth, my dear, is *that*? Has he come off a *raft*?"

Hugo seated them all at the long table. Lewis Bausor sat uncomfortably next to Hope, and gave her a nervous grin. Kenny Thursgood and Virginia sat opposite, and Philip Strachan sat at the head of the table on Hope's left. The orchestra began to play a rather inaccurate version of the Trout quintet, and the surrounding conversation began to rise again. Only once or twice did diners at nearby tables cast worried looks at Lewis Bausor, but Hope was too happy to care, and Lewis Bausor was far too anxious to notice.

The wine waiter came and asked them if they would care for an aperitif or a cocktail. Lewis Bausor looked around him, biting his lips, as everyone ordered. Then the wine waiter said to him: "Sir? Your pleasure?" and he almost shouted: "A dry martini!" Hope thought to herself: He's done well, he's coping, and she tried not to think about his sockless feet.

They sipped their aperitifs in awkward silence. On his second martini, growing flushed, Lewis Bausor began to talk more, and gain some confidence, and they listened to him with a mixture of indulgence and disquiet. Hope could sense the tension all around her, and she kept glancing over to the velvet rope where Hugo stood, in case she caught him telephoning her father.

"I can tell you," said Lewis Bausor, picking up his fish knife and buttering his bread roll with it, "that I've seen things on park benches that would make your hair curl. You think you've seen life? You wait until you see the bums that hang around the Bowery, the way they live. Stinking drunk on wood varnish, crawling with lice. And some of them respectable men at one time, bankers and the like! And women, too! I remember in thirty-five, when I was in the Midwest, I saw women who would do anything a man cared to for fifty cents, except they were usually so filthy that you would have given them fifty cents to go away. I was on the Chicago elevated railroad, and I saw a woman, no doubt a respectable housewife before the Depression, raise her skirts and administer a pessary, clear in front of the whole car!"

At the next table, Mrs. Edwin Daumier, wife of the New York investment chief, raised her hand to her brow as if she had a headache. She was a porky little woman with a hooked nose, in a low-cut black dress, and Hope was aware of her reputation as one of the Royale's most snobbish and most tiresome members. She had obviously heard every word that Lewis Bausor was saying, and it wasn't doing much to improve her enjoyment of her *suprême de volaille Jeannette*.

Hope touched Lewis' arm and said: "Please, Lewis, you mustn't talk so loud. They're kind of sensitive here about the raw side of life."

Lewis turned to her. His eyes were pink and watery, and Hope suddenly realized that on two martinis he was already drunk. His stomach had been empty, except for a cup of coffee and a doughnut, and he probably hadn't touched gin in years.

"Sensitive?" he asked. "Of course they're sensitive! That's why you kidnapped me, isn't it, and brought me along? You wanted to show all these stuffed pigeons in here that you were liberal and free-thinking, isn't that right? I knew that all along. *I* came for the six-course dinner, but *you* invited me here for the sheer pleasure of shocking all these old turkeys, didn't you?"

"Lewis, *please*," said Philip Strachan in an urgent whisper. "Keep it down, will you?"

Lewis coughed, and wiped his mouth with his folded napkin.

"I don't understand you kids," he said, shaking his head. "You're not made of much, are you, except sugar and spice and all things nice?"

Hope said: "I don't know what you mean. Don't you realize what a first this is, bringing you in here? Don't you see that you've just broken through the whole barrier of wealth and snobbery?"

Lewis Bausor almost laughed. "I haven't broken through anything! The only reason they let me in here was because I was with you. I couldn't have gotten in here by myself in an ice age."

"But you're here, all the same," said Kenny Thursgood.

"Oh, sure, I'm here, but you're making damned sure that nobody knows about it. Keep your voice down, Lewis! Don't make a mess with your bread roll, Lewis! What's the point of dragging me in here if nobody knows?"

Hope said hotly: "The papers are going to know, tomorrow, because we're going to tell them!"

The waiters were bringing the hors d'oeuvres. On Hope's recommendation, Lewis was having chilled Mediterranean prawns and plover's eggs. It was laid in front of him by a waiter who could

374

scarcely suppress his disapproval of serving a man who looked, and smelled, like a hobo in borrowed finery, and it didn't help when Lewis picked up his fork and prodded the elaborately arranged dish so hard that one of the little eggs rolled off his plate and halfway across the tablecloth.

Hope was having turbot soufflé, and Philip Strachan was making do with Parma ham. They all started eating, but it was apparent that, all of a sudden, they didn't have much appetite. The wine waiter brought a crisp and fruity German Moselle, and Lewis swallowed glassful after glassful. Across the table, Kenny Thursgood gave Hope an unsteady grimace, as if he was definitely beginning to regret the whole thing.

"Well," said Lewis, cramming prawns and plover's eggs into his mouth and tearing off some more bread, "what are these papers going to say? 'Down-and-outs get hungry like the rest of us, and need to eat'? Is that what the great breakthrough is? Discovering that losers are human beings too, and that people with no money need to eat just as much as people with lots of money? Is that it?"

"Of course not," put in Mel Herbert. "Everybody knows that a down-and-out is a human being. That's not the point of the joke."

Lewis Bausor stopped chewing. A prawn tail hung from one side of his mouth. He said softly: "Joke? What joke?"

"Well," said Mel, "you have to admit that the whole idea is kind of amusing. I mean, you coming in here, and all. I mean, it's pretty wild. You have to admit that."

John Deerman said: "Every practical joke makes a serious point, Lewis. Behind every laugh, there's a cry of pain. Behind his smiling makeup, every clown cries."

Lewis Bausor stared at him with his thin, ratlike face, his eyes glittering with drink. He said: "Is *that* what this is all about? It's a *joke*? Hope . . . is that right?"

Hope felt confused. She said: "It's not *exactly* a joke, Lewis. I mean it's not a joke on you. It's more a kind of charade. Can you see what I mean? What we're trying to say by bringing you here is that rich people live like that all the time. In charades. But it's not *you* that looks absurd. It's all these people here. By having you sit down here, eating their food, drinking their wine, sharing their restaurant, you're showing just how selfish and inhumanitarian they are."

The waiters were clearing away the hors d'oeuvres plates and bringing the fish. Trout, delicately steamed in herbs. Philip

375

Strachan said: "Try the fish, Lewis, the fish is terrific," but Lewis Bausor was too wound up now to turn his attention to food.

"You don't know anything, do you?" he said loudly and incredulously. "None of you kids know shit!"

At the next table, Mrs. Daumier raised her hands to her ears, and her escort, Señor Perova from the Spanish embassy, signaled with a wave to Hugo that something was wrong. Hugo began to weave toward them through the white tables like a little speedboat making its way through the sea.

Lewis Bausor said: "How the hell can *I* make *anyone* here look ridiculous? You expect *me* to make *her* look stupid?" He pointed wildly toward Mrs. Daumier. "She looks stupid already, but I will always—*always*—look more stupid than her, because I'm poor and she's rich! You can't touch anyone who's rich! Don't you understand that? You're rich yourselves and you don't even know the simple facts of money! You may be fools, but nobody's a bigger fool than us bums and us down-and-outs, because we worship what you've got, and because of that we worship *you*, more than saints, and that's the whole truth!"

Señor Perova, a heavy-shouldered man with a frilly white evening shirt and a drooping black mustache, came over and tapped Lewis Bausor on the shoulder.

"Sir, I suggest you apologize!" he said thickly.

Lewis Bausor looked up at him with unfocused eyes and said: "Go suck yourself. I was leaving anyway."

Señor Perova, without any further argument, hit him on the side of the head. There was a general gasp. Lewis Bausor tipped backward off his chair and fell against the window, cracking one of the panes. Philip Strachan leaped up and held Señor Perova's arm.

"Please . . . señor! It's not his fault! I'm terribly sorry! Mrs. Daumier . . . please accept my personal apologies! This man is my guest, and I take full responsibility. I'm afraid it's the drink, he's not used to it! Kenny, will you give me a hand to get him out of here!"

Hope was kneeling down beside Lewis Bausor. There was a raging red bruise on his cheek, and he kept putting his hand to his mouth as if he thought his teeth might have been broken. Hope looked up and said: "No, Philip! He's my guest and he's staying! That's the whole point of it! They only have to see someone like him, and they turn into wild beasts!"

"What do you mean, 'they'?" snapped Philip. "These people

aren't 'they'! They're *us*! It's this guy who's 'they'! Now, let's get him out of here before he causes any more trouble!"

Hope was crying. "It wasn't his fault, Philip. He just didn't know what he was supposed to do. He just didn't know how important it was!"

Hugo had reached them by now, and he was clucking and fussing around, and straightening the cutlery and rubbing his hands.

"You must leave!" he said. "Please . . . you must all leave! This is most distressing!"

"I'm not leaving," said John Deerman. "I haven't finished my dinner yet."

"Well, this person must leave," insisted Hugo, gesturing toward Lewis Bausor, who was now sitting up on one elbow. "He must leave absolutely at once."

"For what reason?" challenged Hope, her eyes blinking with tears. "There's been an argument, it's over, everybody's satisfied. Why does he have to leave? He's my guest and I want him to stay."

Hugo rolled his eyes upward, and looked away as if his mortal dignity had been mortally offended. "*Immm*-properly dressed," he said curtly. "That is all. *Immm*-properly dressed."

"He has a tux," pointed out Kenny Thursgood, who had returned to eating his trout. "You can't deny he has a tux."

Hugo pointed a rigid finger toward Lewis Bausor's ankles. His pants had ridden up in the scuffle, and there, in plain view, were his gray naked shins.

"No hosiery," said Hugo. "There is, in existence on his feet, no hosiery, and the rule is plain. Without hosiery, dinner is refused."

Lewis Bausor painfully climbed to his feet. The restaurant was silent now, and everybody in the room was staring at him with hostile curiosity. He whispered to Hugo: "Help me out, please, will you? I don't feel so good."

Hugo turned away. "You must help yourself out. I decline to touch you for reasons of hygiene. I have my diners to consider."

Hope said: "Come on, Lewis, I'll help you," and she lifted his arm across her shoulder. She looked at Philip Strachan, but Philip Strachan stood with his arms by his sides and still didn't move. Slowly, jerkily, they made their way back across the restaurant, back toward the tall glass doors, and as they passed each table, it seemed that their passing stirred up conversation again, and by the time they had reached the velvet rope, where Hugo watched them imperiously as they left, the restaurant was lively with chatter and laughter, and the orchestra was playing Rimsky-Korsakov, and out of the kitchen doors came a fiery silver tray of crabmeat *crêpes louise*.

"Miss Cornelius," called a somber voice as she helped Lewis through the swing doors. It was Gordon Eames, the Royale's secretary, a big glossy man who looked as if he polished himself all over every morning with beeswax. He had small pince-nez, and he was peering at her through them with an expression of considerable pain.

"Good evening, Mr. Eames." She was out of breath. She didn't look up, because she knew that her mascara had run.

"Miss Cornelius, it has come to my attention that you were responsible for introducing this person into the club."

"Yes, Mr. Eames."

"In that event, I shall, of course, be obliged to inform your father. I am sure that we, the committee, can be lenient; but I am not at all certain how your father will consider your conduct."

Mr. Eames signaled to two of the green-jacketed footmen who stood by the side of the foyer, and they came forward and took Lewis Bausor by the wrists. Lewis himself did not resist, or even stir, but leaned against the wall with his face pale and his whole body stringless and slack.

"You may return to your party, Miss Cornelius," said Mr. Eames. "I will see that this person is expelled."

For a moment, Hope hesitated. She turned to Lewis Bausor and reached out her hand to him, but he wouldn't or couldn't lift his head, and when she said, "Lewis . . . I'm sorry," he didn't even appear to have heard her. She left him there and went back into the restaurant, where Hugo had considerately ordered that her trout should be kept warm on a chafing dish. It wasn't until weeks later that she realized how predictable a girl she must be, for nobody more perceptive than a restaurant waiter to know, infallibly, that she would return to her meal.

The two footmen took Lewis Bausor out into the night. They marched him silently between them up to the end of the graveled driveway, to the decorated gates which stood at the country club's entrance. Once they were off country-club property, in the shadows of the highway, they proceeded systematically to beat him up, punching his face and chest and kicking him savagely in the groin and legs. He lay there on the road for most of the night, with a broken jaw and four fractured ribs, his face resting in half-digested prawns and plover's eggs.

A week later, on an afternoon of deep blue sky and idle clouds, they sat in a sloping pasture of oxeye daisies and long grass a few miles outside of Charleston, West Virginia. They were visiting Roderick's new orange-brick Queen Anne mansion to join him for a birthday picnic, and also, discreetly, to scrutinize Roderick's new girl friend, Celia Lulworth, whom he had met just two weeks before at one of Davina Beerenberg's parties, and about whose charm and beauty and "*wit*, mother!" he had been enthusing ever since. Hester had found it quite a bore to go to the theater with Roderick in New York, because he talked about nothing else except the wonderful Celia, and how rippingly well they got on together.

A warm breeze was blowing from the southwest, a soft and sleepy wind that some of the local folks called "the used-up breath of Kentucky." The daisies nodded, and butterflies flickered through the grass all around them. Lester, Johann's traveling valet, had laid out a cream-colored damask cloth on the ground under the shade of some old Virginia oaks, and the Cornelius party sat there in their pretty and decorative summer clothes, sipping tulip glasses of Dom Perignon, and nibbling at upland plover, soft-shell crabs, steak-and-truffle pies, as well as ripe English cheeses and small crystal dishes of *soufflés glacés*.

Johann, whose white-painted twin-engined flying boat was moored on the placid blue lake only half a mile from the house, had flown down from Lynwood's Island with Hester that morning, and he was sitting in a folding chair with his feet in the sun and his face plunged in shadow, munching his pie as if he had something on his mind. He wore a white barathea suit that seemed incongruously *sportif* for him; he was tanned, and grizzled by oncoming age, but he still looked like a man who had spent most of his adult life in smoke-filled offices.

Hester, in a lemon-yellow dress with a ruffled collar and a print of pale pink flowers, was wearing a wide yellow hat with a soft chiffon veil, which she had tucked up while she ate her soufflé. She was speaking in unusually guarded tones, mainly because she wanted to see what Celia had to say for herself. She knew that her son's new friend was the only daughter of Henry Lulworth, the adding-machine millionaire, but she had also heard stories about the Lulworth's family's sanity. There were tales that William

Lulworth, the second son, was able to work out applied calculus in his head, as long as he kept his eyes shut, and that he spent entire weeks solving such obscure problems as the very hour when the residents of Butte, Montana, would next see an eclipse of the moon, for fun.

But Hester had to admit that, on first sight, Celia was proving almost more than suitable. She was a tall, pretty girl, with china-blue eyes and lips that were so full and red that they didn't need lipstick. Her blond hair was fashionably waved, but her style of dress was formal enough to meet with Hester's approval. She wore a pale pink pleated summer skirt, and a soft silk top in white, with strings and strings of pearls around her neck. She spoke brightly and wittily, but never too precociously, and she managed to converse and eat simultaneously without the usual difficulty that Roderick had.

Hester could sense that Celia, though sparkling, was also very strong, and although she herself was always antagonistic to other women as confident and capable as herself, she knew how important it was going to be for Roderick to have a woman with both elegance and steel. Johann, she thought (as she gently stroked the leg of his white ducks), was growing old. It wouldn't be long before Roderick had to take over his fortune and his problems, and she had seen too much of Johann's agonizing struggles with the government, the unions, the price of raw materials, and the price of working with David Bookbinder to think that Roderick had the stamina to carry such a weight on his own.

Roderick, looking plump and hot, his hair stuck down with pomade, was sitting cross-legged at the far corner of the tablecloth. He had taken off his garish red-and-green-striped blazer and was hacking away at a piece of cold poached salmon. Hope, who was in an unsociable mood these days, had taken her glass of champagne and was sitting a little way away on the crooked arm of a tree, swinging her legs and staring out over the gently falling grassland toward the lake.

Lester came around with more pies, warm and crusty from his portable straw-lined hotbox, and the warm afternoon seemed to roll softly around them like all the summer days that ever were.

"Don't you think Roddy's house is coming on well?" asked Hester, looking down toward the square orange-brick mansion. The sun lit it up as she spoke, and then faded again.

Celia smiled. "I do rather," she said. "I'm so looking forward to seeing it finished. I must say, though, it's difficult to say what the *hallway* is going to turn out like, with all those blue drapes all around."

Hester smiled back, without really smiling at all. "They do make the hallway cooler, you know. It gets intolerably hot here in summer."

"It's a very unusual blue," remarked Celia. "It reminds me of mackerel, when they're not too fresh."

Hester's mouth pursed. "I chose it myself," she said. "If you knew anything about it at all, you would know that it's called Skagerrak blue, and that it was used by the royal house of Sweden to decorate many of the rooms at Drottningholm, the queen's summer palace."

"Skagerrak blue?" said Celia with an interested nod.

"It *cools*," explained Hester. "It is an icy blue, a Scandinavian blue, and that is why it has such a cooling effect."

Roderick had a mouthful of salmon. He said: "If you ask me, the whole place would've looked better in red. Now, there's a color to cheer you up. Red."

"Nobody *did* ask you, Roddy," said Hester, buttering herself a small crumbly cracker.

"It's my house," pointed out Roderick.

"Well, that's as may be, but it's going to be decorated in *my* taste. If I let you have your way, the whole place would look like a mixture between a bordello and a garage."

Celia couldn't help laughing. "Your mother's quite right, Roddy," she said. "I mean . . . just look at your blazer. Red and green! I didn't know whether I was going out with the heir to the Cornelius fortune or a downtown traffic signal."

Hester raised her head. She looked piercingly calm, an expression which Celia found disturbing but also impressive.

"I assure you," said Hester, "that you are going out with the heir to the Cornelius fortune, and it would probably be just as well if you did not forget it."

Johann was wiping his mouth with his napkin. "I'm stuffed to bursting," he said. "That was a good spread, Lester. Remind me to have those steak-and-truffle pies again sometime."

"Thank you, Mr. C.," said Lester. He was gray-haired and stooped now, but he had been serving Johann Cornelius on planes and boats for almost sixteen years, and he wasn't planning on immediate retirement. Lester was the only man around that Johann seemed to treat with any degree of kindness and consideration. Everybody else was expected to anticipate Johann's whims and instructions at least an hour in advance, and have everything he wanted tied up and settled by the time it first crossed his mind.

"Well, Roderick," said Johann, sitting back in his folding chair and lacing his big fingers together, "how's the airplane side of things?"

Roderick glanced at Celia, and gave a grin. "That's how we kind of met, really, Celia and me. You know Dee Beerenberg has learned to fly solo? Well, she gave a big party up at her parents' place, and that's where we first bumped into each other."

Johann glanced at Hester and nodded. Hester said: "I think your father was really inquiring about the transatlantic routes you were working on."

"Oh, them! Oh, they're all in pretty good shape now. But I think we may have to do some kind of cooperative deal with Pan American to begin with. It's a question of available know-how, and available engineering. There are so few people around who can give you a feasible estimate on transatlantic routes that everything you do is pretty much a shot in the dark."

Johann, concealed in shadows, didn't raise his head. Sitting as he was in the bright afternoon sunlight, Roderick found it difficult to see his father's face beneath the trees, and he had to squint.

Johann said: "Did I ever tell you the story of how I started Cornelius Oil?"

"Well, sure, sir, lots of times."

Johann nodded again. "Of course I did. And what did I tell you? What did I say was the one most important thing that kept me going—the one most important thing that made me rich instead of poor? Why am I rich, Roderick? Can you tell me that? Why am I rich when poor old Joe Schmoe in the street doesn't have two red pennies to rub together?"

Roderick looked uncertain, but Celia took his hand to reassure him. The gesture didn't escape Hester's attention, and she noted it down as a plus in Celia's favor. She knew the girl had deliberately teased her over the decoration of Roddy's house, but she was mature enough to understand that they had simply been going through the time-honored ritual of son's girl friend challenging son's mother. In a matriarchal society—which, as far as she could see, *every* civilized society was—it was a necessary stage in a young man's journey through life. He was passed on from mother to wife like a Christmas parcel, quite oblivious of the complex and wary examinations that went on between them.

Roderick said: "One of the things you told us, sir, was that you should always be bold. Always grab hold of the chance when it comes, because good chances never come twice."

There was a long silence. Far away, by the lake, a reed warbler started whistling, and the breeze ruffled the grass and the flowers like a mother passing her hand over the hair of her favorite child.

"And?" said Johann at last.

". . . and, well, that's about it," stammered Roderick. "I mean, it's all a question of chances. And of seizing those chances. Quickly, you know, and not letting them go."

Johann sniffed. Then he said: "Don't you think that the transatlantic air business is something that we ought to seize right now? While the chance is still here? Can we *beat* Pan American, instead of cooperating with them? Can we build our own airplanes? Can we become the first corporation to fly a scheduled weekly airplane service to Europe? Is *that* a chance worth seizing?"

"Why, sure it is!" said Roderick overenthusiastically. "We could get in there straightaway. That's if it's something you really want to do."

Johann rose from his chair and stood for a while under the tree, his hands in his pockets and his back bent with age.

"Roderick," he said, "it's not a question of whether *I* want to do it or not. This is *your* project. It's up to *you* to decide if you want us to invest in airplanes for transatlantic flying. I will always have to give final approval to your budget, and so will David, but unless you learn to stand or fall by yourself, then what am I going to do when it's time to hand all this huge corporation over?"

Roderick was deeply embarrassed, especially in front of Celia. He said thickly: "I'm sorry, sir, I didn't mean that. I just meant that if the corporation's overall policy—"

"There *is* no overall policy, not on air flight! I gave you carte blanche to *create* a policy. Now it's up to you to tell me what you want to do!"

"Johann," admonished Hester. "This is Roddy's *birthday*. Do we have to talk about business? I'm sure you're boring Celia to death."

Johann turned around. For the first time that afternoon, the sun fell across his face, and Celia saw his pale glistening eyes, his thick nose, and his sagging jowls. His white collar looked too tight for him, but he stood in such a way that it appeared to be the only thing that was holding him up. He was a heavy, old, ugly man, but he had a sense of suppressed energy that held Celia's attention completely.

"This young lady isn't bored," said Johann. "I've been watching her, and I know she's not bored. She's a young lady who understands wealth, and young ladies who understand wealth are always interested in finance, with some exceptions."

He raised his eyes momentarily and looked over at Hope, who was now lying on her back in the grass twenty yards away, making daisy chains, and swinging her bare feet.

"I'd like to hear you opinion, Miss Lulworth," said Johann. "You know about flying, don't you? You've been around with the Beerenbergs and the Earharts. What do you think we ought to do about transatlantic flight?"

Celia lowered her eyes and smiled modestly. "I'm afraid I'm not an expert, like Roddy."

"All the same," insisted Johann, "tell me what you think."

"Well," she said, "I think it's probably wiser to play it safe."

"What do you mean by that?"

"I mean that flying itself, actually running your own air fleet, seems so uncertain. Look at the Zeppelins! Up until last month, everybody thought we were going to go back and forth over the Atlantic by airship, but now you wouldn't get most people up in one of those things if you offered them a free flight and a thousand dollars spending money."

"Well, you're probably right," said Johann. "But what's your suggestion? I'd like to get *some* money invested in aviation."

"I think you ought to place your money in all the services that people who fly are going to need, no matter *how* they fly. Things like carrying cargoes, and catering for passengers while they wait for suitable weather to fly. People always eat and drink when they travel! And what about things like filling up airplanes with fuel? It must take hundreds of gallons to fly the Atlantic. If you can monopolize all the services on the ground, you can let the air fleets take all the risks with airplanes and crashes and explosions, and you can sit there taking in a steady profit without any of the dangers."

Johann listened to this, and then chuckled. "You have a wise head, Miss Lulworth. I've a good mind to kick out David Bookbinder and hire you instead."

384

"There speaks the voice of an optimist," said Hester, a little bitterly.

Johann ignored her. He turned to his son Roderick and said: "Well, Roddy, you've heard what Celia has to say about flying. Now what about you?"

Roderick stood up and walked around to the shade of the oaks, shaking his head.

"I have to admit it's a very sound theory," he said, "but it's not exactly the stuff that Cornelius fortunes are made of, is it? I mean, you can't call air freight the gold mine of the future, can you? How much freight can any airplane carry? Only a few hundred pounds, at the most. And the cost! Who's going to pay a thousand dollars to send a couple of tires to Europe when for eighty dollars they can send a whole car by sea? No, if there's any money in the air it's in passenger airplanes, and I'd like to see the Cornelius name on our own machines."

"Our own machines?" said Johann. "You mean . . . build our own airplane?"

"Well, that's right."

"You seriously want to do that?"

"Sure. In my opinion, it's the only way. If you have your own airplane you control all the ancillary things, like freight and so forth, and you can name your own prices for them."

Johann took out his handkerchief and slowly dabbed his forehead. The wind had dropped, and it was ninety-five degrees in the sun. The reed warbler called again down by the lake, and Lester was collecting the plates.

"Roddy," said Johann slowly, so that only Roderick could hear. "When did all of this come to you? It wasn't just this minute, was it? Because of what Celia said?"

"Of course not! I've been working a couple of weeks on this."

"And you really believe that it would be a good idea for Cornelius Oil to go into aviation?"

"Absolutely. I mean, one hundred percent."

"Well," said Johann, "the best thing you can do is write me a report. Include all the figures, all the finance, and make sure it's sitting on my desk at Lynwood's Island by Friday next."

Roderick blinked in unexpected pleasure. He lifted his hands as if he were going to clasp his father's arms, but Johann simply grunted and turned away.

"Sir, I—"

Johann coughed. "Don't say a word, Roddy, not one word. This is your test, and if you say any more, you might make me change my mind. Sooner or later this business is going to be in your hands, and I want to make sure that if you have two or three or more million dollars to invest, that you do it properly. If you want to build an airplane—well, I'll give you the money and you can build it. But, by God, it had better be the best damned airplane that ever was."

Roderick glanced at his mother. She reached up a hand to him, and he held her fingers for a moment, and then let go.

He said to his father: "I won't let you down, sir. I promise."

Johann beckoned to Lester to fetch him his stick. He said: "No, Roddy, you won't."

Roderick went back to Celia with a grin. He didn't notice the look that passed between Celia and Hester, the look of shared understanding about the true implications of what had just happened. It was, in fact, the first look in a series of looks that were the negotiations and the discussions in the gradual handover of Roderick from one woman to another; a look that he himself was too involved with his new airplane project even to notice, let alone comprehend.

Later that evening, when Hope sat in her bedroom overlooking the woods that curved around one side of the house, there was a rap at the door. She said: "Come in," and Hester came in, still dressed in the formal blue evening gown she had worn for dinner, but with her hair let down ready for bed. Hope was sitting in a large green wing chair by the window, her bare toes on the sill, reading *Vein of Iron*. She said: "Hullo, Mother."

Hester sat down on the end of Hope's mahogany bed and put her hands together in the way she always did before she made a serious announcement.

"I suppose you're going to tell me off for sitting on a tree all day, instead of talking about boring old airplanes with you and father?" said Hope.

Hester said: "I hope we're not that severe a family."

"It depends on your mood, Mother, if you must know."

"Well," said Hester, "it isn't that."

"Oh, I thought it was. Well, what is it? What other heinous crimes have I committed?"

Hester said: "Look at me."

Hope sat up and looked at her. She said: "It must be serious. Who am I supposed to have murdered?"

Hester said quietly: "You haven't quite murdered anyone, you'll be pleased to hear, but this morning your father had a telephone call from the newspapers. Apparently a vagrant was picked up by you and some of your friends a week ago and taken to the Royale Country Club, where his behavior caused grave offense to many of the members. He had to be ejected from the club, this vagrant, and while he was being ejected, he became violent, and it was necessary for the club's footmen to use physical force against him."

Hope said quietly: "Go on. What happened?"

"He ran away, apparently," said Hester in a toneless voice. "He ran away and disappeared into the night."

"I don't understand."

"That isn't all. He was found two days later in a field not far from the club. He had obviously dragged himself there. He was dead from hunger and exposure."

Hope stared at her mother, and tears dropped from her eyes and onto her open book.

"Not Lewis," she said. "Not Lewis Bausor. Please."

"You know his *name*?"

Hope covered her face with her hands. "Oh, God," she wept. "Oh, God, I feel so awful."

Hester said: "Hope . . . you must listen to me. Do you mean to say that you actually *knew* the man? You were consorting with a down-and-out?"

Hope tried to answer, but couldn't. Her mother handed her a small lace handkerchief, and she dabbed her eyes and blew her nose. Her mother said: "It's all right, I don't want it back."

At last Hope lifted her head, wiping away the last tears with the side of her hand. She said: "I only knew his name. I think he came from Yonkers. I never knew him before. Oh, God, Mother, I feel so guilty. I feel like I killed him myself."

Hester said coldly: "Perhaps, in a way, you did."

Hope sat there biting her lip and staring at her mother with reddened eyes. She knew that Hester would always do whatever mothers were supposed to do, and more. She said all the right words, at all the right moments. She never forgot birthdays or special treats. She always attended school events, and she dressed as every girl hoped her mother might dress. But somehow it was impossible to penetrate Hester's motherliness any deeper than that. It was seamless and beyond criticism, and yet because of that it seemed like an act. Real mothers are occasionally imperfect, but Hester never was.

"I'm not going to ask you to explain yourself until you want to," said Hester. "That is *not* because I wish to spare your feelings, but because I want you to dwell on what has happened, and consider your part in it, and then come to your father and myself and tell us the truth in the spirit of contrition which you should."

"Mother," said Hope, "I am *not* contrite! I did it for a reason!"

"What reason could there possibly be? You dragged an unfortunate man of no social standing into the Royale, and you not only humiliated him but you made a fool of yourself. I understand from Mr. Eames that Philip tried several times to dissuade you, but you insisted on carrying on with your idiocy. You couldn't even listen to your friends!"

"Mother," said Hope, "it wasn't *like* that! I took Lewis Bausor to the Royale because I wanted to show that even rich people can have compassion. Or don't you understand what compassion is?"

Hester remained still and upright. A shuddering crescent of light, reflected from a gilt Louis XV mirror on Hope's bedroom wall, shone on her right cheek. Outside, the gardeners clattered their barrows and lawnmowers back to the stables. Someone was whistling "Stormy Weather."

"My dear," said Hester, "I may not be up-to-the-moment, as you are. But I do know that holding a vagrant up to ridicule in one of the most select country clubs in the nation is not, by anybody's standards, a compassionate act."

"Mother, I—"

"Don't interrupt! *Think*, instead of interrupting! Think of how selfish you were! You wanted to prove that you weren't rich and spoiled? What a way to do it! Did you once consider this unfortunate man's feelings when you took him into the Royale? Did you once consider that he might have his own dignity and pride, no matter how mean and poor he looked to you? By what right did you treat him as your plaything? Or were you so blinded by the glory of your little crusade that such things didn't enter your mind?"

Hope couldn't answer. Two more tears ran down her cheeks, and she felt a deep, choking pain in her throat.

388

"This man's death isn't the only tragedy you've caused," continued Hester. "If you'd taken any interest in your father's affairs, you would have known that he is engaged in delicate negotiations with the Brotherhood of Teamsters. A great deal of money and many jobs depend on the outcome of these negotiations, and if he cannot persuade the union to compromise, he may have to throw hundreds of men out of work."

Hester reached forward and raised Hope's chin. "Look at me," she said. "How is your father going to negotiate with workingmen if his daughter has treated one of their number with such contempt that he has died?"

There was a long silence. Hester eventually stood up and went to the door. She looked across at her daughter for several minutes without speaking, and for the first time in her life, Hope found it impossible to read what her mother was thinking at all. Hester's expression was remote, and yet touched with something that might almost have been pity.

"In the morning," said Hester, "you will have Nora pack your case. Your father is going to fly you to Connecticut, and you will stay there with the Landseers for as long as your father and I wish you to. The Landseers have already been telegraphed, and they have agreed to have you. While you are there, you will see none of your usual friends. Neither will you smoke cigarettes or drink liquor. I want you to understand that this is a punishment."

"The Landseers?" said Hope. "Oh, Mother, please—"

"It could have been worse," said Hester. "It was all I could do to persuade your father not to disinherit you altogether. He is very angry, Hope, and it will take him some time to get over it. He said . . ."

There was a pause. Hope looked up, and for some reason her mother looked suddenly confused.

"He said that *all* life, especially innocent life, is sacred, and that you must never abuse the power over life that money gives you. Do you understand?"

Hope whispered: "Yes, Mother. In a way."

Hester took a light breath. "I hope, for your own sake, that you do."

1938

COSTER REVEALED AS SCHULTZ ALLY

McKesson & Robbins Head and
Gangster Were Partners in
Bootleg Operations

Arthur (Dutch Schultz) Flegenheimer was not only aware
that F. Donald Coster was an ex-convict named Philip
Musica, but was associated with him in illegal liquor
dealings from 1927 until the gangster's murder eight
years later, it was revealed yesterday. Federal investigators are still uncertain, however, how Musica could
have remained undiscovered for so long, and are continuing their search for an unknown ally or allies in the legitimate world of corporate business.

—*New York Times,*
December, 1938

It had just stopped raining when Celia arrived at the airfield in her cherry-red Bentley and parked outside the office door. She stepped out of the car in her French-styled linen suit and tugged at her gloves as she walked across the puddly concrete apron toward the main hangar. There was a fresh breeze blowing from the east, and the clouds were tumbling away to leave the sky blue and clear.

She went into the open doors of the hangar, and was surprised at the silence. For once, the huge half-finished airplane that stretched from one end of the gloomy building to the other was resting in peace, unattended by fitters, riggers, welders, and electricians.

She called: "Roderick?"

There was a cough from the far end of the hangar. Roderick appeared from the tail of the airplane, dressed in greasy white coveralls, with a cheese sandwich in his hand.

"*Roderick*," said Celia. "What *are* you doing?"

He came over. "Sorry, my darling. I was having lunch with the boys."

"You promised to take me over to the Hunting Lodge for lunch or had it slipped your mind?"

"Oh," he said, surprised. "I thought that was tomorrow."

"I can't possibly go tomorrow. You know that. I have a planning meeting with Denis Mulligan tomorrow at the Bureau of Air Commerce."

Roderick looked sheepishly at his cheese sandwich.

"Well, it's too late, now," said Celia. "You might as well finish it now you've started it."

"It won't take me long to wash up," said Roderick. "We can be there by two."

"I don't *want* to be there by two. I don't *like* lunching late. I like to have time for a cocktail, and anyway, I can't spend the rest of the afternoon sitting over lunch."

"Well, I'm sorry," said Roderick. "I guess I got involved in the

C-1 again. You know something, we've really licked those engine-mounting problems now. This baby is going to fly like an angel."

Some of the fitters came out now, wiping their mouths after their impromptu lunch, and picking up their wrenches and screwdrivers to carry on with their work. They had been assembling the C-1 for three months now, and Roderick planned for a first proving flight in the middle of September.

"I just wish you'd spend a little less time messing around with oil and wrenches and a little more time on the business of selling airplanes," complained Celia. "You don't seem to understand that you're wasting your own money doing all this yourself. You're *far* more valuable in the boardroom. As it is, I've had to see the British by myself, and Pan American, and after I've seen Mulligan tomorrow I'm going to have to talk to the Hughes people."

Roderick had a mouthful of sandwich. "I'm sorry, darling. I just think that you're the best person for the job."

"Of *course* I'm the best person for the job. But it shouldn't *be* that way. *You* should be doing all this. These airline people hardly know you, except from what they've read in the papers. You ought to make personal contacts. It's all very well having a wonderful airplane to sell, but if you haven't prepared the groundwork, you'll find that Curtiss or Boeing or one of those other people have gotten in before you."

"Darling," said Roderick, "I know you mean well, but there is no point at all in trying to market something which I don't yet have."

"Of course there is! You're not thinking ahead! An airline has only so much money to spend on planes, and if they've already committed it to someone else while you've been fiddling around with the final screw-tightening and propeller-polishing, then you're sunk, aren't you? You've committed Cornelius Holdings to twelve million dollars on this project, and if you don't sell it, then you're twelve million dollars down."

Roderick slapped his hand against the C-1's aluminum nose.

"This airplane is going to speak for itself. And I wish for once that you'd let me do things my way."

Celia sighed and turned away. Sometimes she despaired of Roderick. He was so well-meaning and gentle, and he always remembered to bring her flowers and jewelry, but his mind was like layers of kapok. It took so long for any intuitive ideas to penetrate that she usually gave up and put them into action herself. It was simpler, and saved hours of futile argument. Besides, ever since their unsuccessful wedding night, when too much Dom Perignon had left Roderick floundering and flaccid, she had promised herself (and him) that she would give him all the direction and courage that he usually lacked.

"I would really like you to come tomorrow," she said. "Denis tells me that he has a very good test pilot in mind."

"A test pilot? For the C-1?"

"What else?"

Roderick wiped his hands on a piece of rag. "I was thinking we might persuade Corrigan to do it."

"Oh, forget about Corrigan. He's too worked up about this transtlantic flight he wants to make."

"He sounds like a good pilot, though," asserted Roderick.

A tall young man with a small mustache and a droopy tweed suit that hung around him in billowing folds came walking across the hangar with an armful of blueprints. This was Lem Cosnett, the chief designer of the C-1, and Roderick's closest adviser on aviation. Roderick had chosen him because he had barnstormed through Indiana and Ohio for six years, and knew more about the quirks of civil airplanes than most engineers would learn in a lifetime of sitting at a drawing board.

"I'm still worried about the stalling speed," he said to Roderick in his twangy voice. He caught sight of Celia, and said: "Hallo, Mrs. Cornelius. How are you?"

"Busy," said Celia. "How are you?"

"Well, I'm worried about the stalling speed," he repeated. "If this bird takes off with a full payload, and if we can't get those engines to build up power a little quicker, then we're going to end up flat on our tail."

"I thought they'd beefed the engines up," said Roderick.

"Well, they did," replied Lem. "But you have to realize this is a big airplane. I mean, it's bigger than I really wanted to build it."

Celia said: "It's big that's going to pay. There's no commercial point in building anything smaller."

Lem glanced at Roderick, but Roderick simply shrugged.

"Maybe I can get Rolls-Royce to quote for engines," suggested Lem. "Oppenheimer tells me they're building a first-class rigout for Vickers. That could give us some more horsepower."

Roderick shook his head. "I'm sorry, Lem. There isn't time. Mrs. Cornelius needs a February delivery date at the latest. She's already had three penciled orders from the Pentagon, and tomorrow we're going to see the director."

Lem took out an Old Gold and lit it.

"Well," he mused, "if you're prepared to take the risk . . ."

Celia said: "What risk?"

Lem opened out his plans and held them against the nose of the plane. "When you build any new airplane," he told her, "you come up against certain imponderables. You find that the plane behaves different in the sky than you thought it was going to. It's a question of design, and balance, and the whole relationship between your power plants and your airframe. I can only calculate up to a certain point how the C-1 is going to behave, and the rest is guesswork. Well, my guess is that we may have trouble on takeoff because of the unusual weight of this baby. The motors may not be able to develop sufficient power quickly enough to take it up."

"You mean it would crash?"

"Not necessarily. But it might mean that it's limited to certain airfields which have very long runways. That cuts out short-haul freight work from local airfields around the U.S."

Celia looked testily from Roderick to Lem, and back again.

"Why didn't we know this before?"

"Well, Mrs. Cornelius, it's a brand-new airplane, and we just couldn't foresee what was going to happen."

"I don't think that's any excuse at all," snapped Celia. "Do you have any idea how much money we've already invested in this machine?"

"Yes, but—"

"It's not a question of 'but'! We're not in business to build airplanes for our own amusement. We're in business to make this airplane pay. And if it's going to pay, it's got to be capable of flying out of every airfield in the continental United States, as well as half the airfields in Europe."

Roderick coughed, embarrassed. "Celia," he said gently, "I really think we ought to wait until the C-1's completed, and then we can test it and see for ourselves."

"Don't you realize how *expensive* that would be?" asked Celia. "I'd rather abandon it now if it's not going to pay its way, and cut our losses."

Roderick was about to say something, but stopped himself. He said to Lem: "I'll be back in a moment," and then he took Celia's arm and led her out of the hangar into the fresh July sunlight. Celia waited until they had reached her parked Bentley, glittering with raindrops, and then she turned around and said: "I suppose you're going to go into one of your wounded-bull-elephant routines now."

Roderick was angry. He looked like his father when he was angry—big and liver-lipped and fierce. He said: "If you talk to me like that again, in front of the staff—"

"Don't be ridiculous," she said. "The staff have as much responsibility as you do. You shouldn't even be down here, anyway, dressed up like a monkey on a stick. If you behave like a laborer, you'll find you get treated like one."

"By *you*? My *wife*?"

"Of course not. But you really must sort your ideas out. We're not playing games anymore. Your father gave you this money to invest in a plane, and if it doesn't work, you're in real trouble. I'm only trying to help you out of a fix."

Roderick walked moodily around to the front of the car and laid his hand on the solid-silver mascot of a flying Mercury. In the distance, across the scrubby airfield, a V-shaped flock of ducks rose from the Ashland marshes and wheeled into the wind.

"You've changed, you know, since we married," he said almost truculently.

Celia looked at him. "Yes," she replied. "I suppose I have."

"You have to realize," he said, without turning around, "that a man has certain drives—certain ambitions. My ambition is to build a plane that's better and more exciting than any plane that's ever been built before."

"You know what your father always says. Making a profit, by definition, is exciting."

"But it's not everything," protested Roderick. "There's more to life than making a profit."

Celia sighed. "I wish you wouldn't persist in being so incorrigibly naive. Of *course* there's more to life than making a profit. But making a profit is the essence of business, and that's what this airplane is. It's not an Erector set, it's a piece of commercial speculation."

Roderick stared at his bride across the reflecting hood of the car. She *looked* the same as the laughing young girl he had taken down the aisle three months ago in New York. The wedding cars, Lincolns and Hispano-Suizas, had stretched for eleven blocks, and it had taken a whole city refuse truck to clear up the confetti. But she didn't talk like a pampered young girl anymore. She had turned out to be a hard-bitten businesswoman—impatient, ruthless, and unwilling to admit that anything was more important than the right percentage. What he failed to understand was that she was protecting her position in the Cornelius family hierarchy by protecting Roderick, and that she was keenly aware that her own influence and success were inextricably enmeshed with his. It wasn't that she didn't love him. She didn't, as a matter of fact—not wholly and passionately. But she had never looked for love in the men she knew. What she really wanted was *command*.

Roderick saw none of this. He just saw a pretty young girl with a peekaboo hat, her blond wavy hair blown by the afternoon wind, and he was perplexed and hurt that she was being so intolerant toward him. He wondered vaguely if he was giving her enough presents.

"You never wanted me to build this plane, did you?" he asked her. He sounded like a small boy. "That day at the picnic, you made that pretty clear to all concerned."

"Don't be so ridiculous, darling. I was just saying that there's more financial risk in the airplane industry than there is in freight shipment and servicing."

"Oh, God. You talk like J. P. Morgan on a wet Tuesday."

"Roddy!" she said in a shocked voice. "How *can* you say that? After all I've been doing to help this project along!"

Roderick was confused. He came around the car and held out his arms apologetically, but he was still wearing his greasy coveralls, and she held her arms up to protect her pale linen suit like a mother protecting her infant from a leering stranger.

"Celia," he said. "*Please*. We seem to be arguing all the time these days."

"*I'm* not arguing," she said haughtily. "It's *you*."

He sighed. "All right, it's me. I'm sorry. Maybe I should leave the fitters for a while and get back to my desk. Maybe I'm working too hard."

"It doesn't seem to me that you've been working hard at all. You seem to spend most of your time tinkering with oily bits and pieces and eating sandwiches."

Roderick pointed toward one of the motor housings on the wing of the C-1. "You see that?" he said abruptly. "I made that. I actually made it. With my own two hands."

Celia looked briefly and nearsightedly toward the hangar. "Did you, darling?"

"Yes."

"Well, that's nice. Now, if you take off your dirty things, I can give you a ride back to the house. If you're actually going to make the effort to come see Denis Mulligan with me tomorrow, then you'd better do your homework on the flight schedules and the operating costs. And, *please*, don't let anyone start spreading rumors that the plane can't lift itself off the ground. That would be disastrous."

Roderick looked at his wife for a moment, and then thoughtfully smacked the fist of his right hand into the palm of his left.

"Give me five minutes," he said in a voice that sounded more than a little defeated. "I have to tell Lem what I was doing this morning. Just for the progress chart."

As he walked back to the hangar, she said: "Was it a worthwhile morning's work?"

He stopped. He said: "Yes. I put in the rudder." And then he disappeared under the shadow of the C-1's wing to go tell Lem.

Johann was sitting in a cushioned basketwork chair by the swimming pool when David Bookbinder and his dark-suited young companion arrived at Lynwood's Island. The pool was enclosed by glass, with a dome that on hot days could be opened up like the leaves of a transparent water lily, allowing the summer breeze to circulate inside. There were rare plants growing in pots all around, many of them flowering and scented, and some of them trailing right down to the water's edge.

Johann was wearing a large red-striped bathing suit, and was sitting back reading the paper. There was a gold-trimmed telephone on the bamboo table next to him, and a silver tray with brandy-and-soda. Birds flittered and chirruped in and out of the dome, and a quiet fountain played among the leaves.

The pool was one of Johann's favorite haunts in the summer, when the pressure of business eased off. He didn't swim much, but he liked to feel that he might take a dip if the mood took him. There was a view through the windows across the wide back lawns of the house, toward the woodland and the rhododendron garden, and the sprinklers were making glittering rainbows across the grass.

He wasn't a gardener, but he was relaxed and eased by gardens, and he'd once told Roderick's business tutor that "no garden, however small, should be without a swimming pool and a couple of acres of woods."

David Bookbinder came around the edge of the pool, followed closely by the man in the dark suit. Their footsteps echoed inside the greenhouse, and their reflections dipped and wavered in the water. Johann put down his paper and watched them approach.

David Bookbinder said: "This is Merrett Kale."

Johann reached out his hand without getting up. "How do you do, Mr. Kale. You'll forgive my casual apparel."

"It's a pleasure to meet you, Mr. Cornelius. I've heard a great deal about you."

"Who hasn't?"

Merrett Kale grinned, and sat down uncertainly on an upright basketwork chair opposite Johann, while David Bookbinder dragged over a daybed and lay back with his hands folded over his potbelly like Buddha on his summer vacation.

Johann reached over for his brandy-and-soda and inspected Merrett Kale without saying a word. Kale was one of the smart young breed of new Navy Department executives, with a crispness about him that made you think he even starched his underwear. His face was lean and fit in a Buster Crabbe way, and he wore a prickly little mustache that didn't suit him. His hair was cropped short, except for a sandy curl at the front that he obviously considered dashing. His shoes were polished like black glass, and he wore a blue polka-dot necktie with a tiny knot.

"Well, Mr. Kale," said Johann slowly. "I hope you had a pleasant flight up."

"Yes, sir! That's an impressive airplane you have there. I don't think I've ever flown in anything quite like it."

"No, you haven't. It's the only one there is."

David Bookbinder said comfortably: "I hear John Livingston's in trouble. Dewey's trying to tie him in with Hines."

Johann said: "I heard. Our friend on the grand jury had a word in my ear the other day. What does Walter say?"

Bookbinder unwrapped a large Havana cigar. "He's not sure. Cooper told him they may be making arrests in a couple of days."

"Arrests? I don't know what's the matter with these people. They see rackets behind every bush."

Bookbinder flicked his lighter and fed his cigar to the flame. "You have to admit the electrical business was getting a little out of hand," he said, puffing smoke.

Johann shrugged. He'd known for some time that Thomas Dewey was going to try to corner Livingston. After all, it was one of the largest electric companies in the country, and with the grand jury investigating collusive bids between electrical contractors for private and municipal work in New York City, a confrontation had been trembling in the air for months. Johann's own electrical division, Allen Voltage Corp., was lying particularly low at the moment, with all the books in the hands of his certified accountants.

Johann turned to Merrett Kale. "You look like an ambitious kind of a fellow," he said in a toneless voice.

Kale flapped his hands like two pale puppets. "Well, yes, sir . . . I guess I am."

David Bookbinder said, without taking his cigar out of his mouth: "Mr. Cornelius wants to know *how* ambitious."

Kale coughed. "Well, sir, I believe I'm *very* ambitious."

"In other words, you want to get to the top?"

"Yes, sir!"

"The top of what? The Navy Department?"

Kale smirked. "Actually, sir, I'm more interested in politics."

"I see," grunted Johann. "So you'd like to be President?"

"Not quite, sir. But I'd like to find myself someplace where I can have some real influence."

"You don't think you have influence now?"

"In some respects."

"In what respects?"

"Well, sir, I'm involved in the contract department. Contract evaluation is my line."

"You mean when someone puts in a bid to build something for the Navy, it's your job to evaluate how cost-effective it is, and whether it's the right kind of tender?"

"That's correct, sir. I don't have the last word, of course, but my comments are always taken seriously. I was an honors graduate in marine engineering, sir. Best of 1931. I'm kind of a blue-eyed boy in blue."

Johann sipped his brandy. His eyes never left Kale's face, and after a while the young engineer found himself looking at the

401

mosaic floor of the swimming pool, involuntarily avoiding the relentless stare of a man who had a dollar for every minute that Merrett Kale had lived.

A peacock, shining like a blue enamel brooch, strutted through the iridescent spray of the lawn sprinklers, and a warm summer draft blew in through the open windows of the greenhouse. In the distance, there was the silly, conspiratorial warbling of doves.

Johann said: "You've come here because you have something to offer. I presume that what you have to offer bears some relation to your tasks at the Navy Department."

Merrett Kale took out his handkerchief and patted perspiration from his neck. His starched collar was cutting into his skin and making him sore.

"Well, sir," he said, "I've always felt that industry and government should cooperate more closely. I know that the law requires defense contracts to be put out to tender, but quite often it's obvious who the best contractor for the work is going to be, right from the start. Unfortunately, because of the red tape and the committees, the best contractor isn't always selected. Maybe his price is a little high, or maybe the secretary doesn't like his face."

"I think you can spare me the explanatory prologue," remarked Johann. "Would you please just explain what you have to sell?"

Merrett Kale blushed. "It's not as easy as all that, sir. But it so happens that the last session of Congress provided for four 35,000-ton warships for the Navy. The same basic type as the *Washington* and the *North Carolina*. That's a twenty-eight knot ship with nine sixteen-inch rifles in three turrets, and an armored belt about fifteen inches thick."

"And?"

"Well, sir, they're coming up for offers."

Johann nodded thoughtfully.

Merrett Kale said: "They could be very profitable contracts, Mr. Cornelius. Very profitable indeed."

Johann looked at him.

"There's talk of Congress giving the go-ahead on 45,000-tonners, too," added Kale. "We have plans in preparation already."

Johann said dryly: "The President is talking about disarmament. He says that war contracts are only of passing value to the economy."

402

Kale shook his head vigorously. "That's just what he says for public consumption, sir. At the Navy Department we don't have any doubts. One way or another, this country has got to get itself ready for war."

"You think so?" asked Johann.

"I'm sure of it, sir. And in any case, the President isn't going to be *that* reluctant to start placing war contracts. Passing value is better than no value at all."

David Bookbinder tapped a chunk of ash on to the floor. He said: "Tell Mr. Cornelius your offer, Mr. Kale. He likes things blunt."

"Well, sir," explained Kale, "it so happens that if your shipping people want to bid for these four warships, my department will be involved in vetting your tenders."

Johann almost smiled. Then he said: "How much do you want?"

"If your bids are accepted, a quarter of a million dollars."

Johann glanced across at David Bookbinder. Bookbinder simply shrugged, as if to say that any decision was entirely up to Johann.

Johann couldn't quite make up his mind. He'd seen hundreds of men like Merrett Kale—men who'd done well in their chosen profession and then found that their chosen profession wasn't as glamorous or as lucrative as they'd hoped when they were milk-fed college graduates. They'd approached him from every major corporation he could think of—from Tide Water and Standard, from Chrysler and Du Pont—and the story was always the same. They'd been wrestling for months, sometimes years, with the fantasy of selling their souls for what they considered was real wealth, and when the moment actually came, they invariably sold themselves more than cheap.

Thoughtfully Johann said: "How do I know I can trust you, Mr. Kale? For all I know, you could be an agent for the grand jury."

"You can check my credentials if you like," said Merrett Kale. "I'm sure you have the means to do it."

"We do," put in David Bookbinder. "And you can bet your life that we will."

Johann said: "It's too much."

"You mean a quarter of a million?"

"That's right."

Merrett Kale bit his lip. "I'm sorry, that's the price."

"I'll give you half that."

"I'm sorry, I can't risk it for less than two-hundred-fifty thousand."

"I'll give you half that, with ten thousand dollars cash in advance, nonreturnable."

Merrett looked up. "Nonreturnable? Whether you get the contracts or not?"

"That's what I said. You can have it right now, cash in your hand."

Merrett Kale hesitated. He knew that $125,000 was too cheap a price for helping Cornelius Shipping win the warship contracts, but at the same time ten thousand dollars, to him, was a great deal of money, and if it was nonreturnable he could walk out of here and keep it without even having to compromise himself. If the contracts were fortuitously awarded to Cornelius, he could take the credit and collect the rest of the money, and if they weren't, it was too bad. He would still be ten thousand better off, and he wouldn't have risked anything.

He looked at David Bookbinder, and then at Johann.

"All right," he said emphatically. "It's a deal."

Johann picked up his telephone and said: "Henry? Yes, it's me. I want you to take ten thousand dollars in cash out of the safe and bring it out to the pool. . . . Yes, right now."

The three of them waited in silence for several minutes. Now that the deal was concluded, Merrett Kale couldn't think what to say. He was embarrassed at having accepted a lower offer, but at the same time he was quite pleased with himself for having out-maneuvered the great Johann Cornelius into giving him ten thousand dollars for nothing. It was money for old rope. Money for jam. He felt like smiling, but obviously couldn't.

"Do you swim, Mr. Kale?" asked Johann.

Merrett Kale said: "I'm a sailor."

"I know that, Mr. Kale," said Johann. "What I meant was, 'do you swim?' as opposed to 'do you sink?' "

Merrett Kale didn't know what to make of that remark, and said, instead of answering: "I admire your pool, sir. It's very fine."

"Yes," said Johann. "It's the only one there is."

Henry Keith came out of the house in his shirtsleeves, carrying a manila envelope. His hair was thinning on top, and he had dark mulberry-colored circles under his eyes, but he had survived twelve years of Johann Cornelius remarkably well. It was probably because he had never been ambitious. Johann always said that he liked his employees to set their sights high, but Henry Keith knew that meant setting their sights slightly below Johann or any of his family. He had seen too many aggressive young executives come and go to have any illusions about that.

Henry nodded to David Bookbinder, and then passed the envelope to Johann. Johann opened it up and riffled through the bills.

"The usual procedure on these?" he asked Henry.

"That's right, sir. The usual."

"Here you are, then, Mr. Kale," said Johann, and passed him the money. Merrett Kale took it, and flicked through it himself.

"You don't trust me?" Johann smiled.

Merrett Kale colored. "It's just a habit, sir. I didn't mean to suggest—"

"It's a good habit," said Johann. "Always look your gift horses right in the mouth. You'd be surprised at how much bridgework is missing."

Merrett Kale stood up. "Well, sir," he said. "I'd better be leaving. I don't want anyone asking questions."

Johann nodded. "One of my chauffeurs will take you out to the railroad station. I believe there's a train for the city every half hour."

"Thank you, sir. It's been a real pleasure to do business."

"Anytime, Mr. Kale. Let's keep our fingers crossed for those ships, shall we?"

"I'll be in touch with Mr. Bookbinder, sir, and I'll keep him informed."

"I'm sure."

Henry led Merrett Kale out of the swimming pool and back to the house. After they had gone, David Bookbinder sat there with his fingers laced together, puffing placidly at his cigar and enjoying the sunshine.

"You know something?" he said.

"What's that?"

"I believe I've finally converted you."

Johann took a long swallow of brandy-and-soda. "Converted me to what? Systematic skulduggery?"

Bookbinder laughed. "There's an old saying, you know, which sums this occasion up perfectly."

Johann said: "I was afraid there might be. What is it?"

"It's Polish. The market gardeners used to use it, in Lwow. They used to say, 'Even the largest apple on the tree, no matter what it promises the woodcutter, will fall when the branch is snapped off.'"

Johann thought about that. Then he said: "I think I see what you mean. You're ahead of me, aren't you?"

"I think I'm paid to be ahead of you."

Johann picked up his telephone again and said: "Henry? Has that gentleman left now? . . . Good. What train did he hope to catch? The three-thirty-two . . . That's excellent. What time does it get into Grand Central? . . . All right. That's fine. Now put me through to Eddie Corcoran, will you? . . . That's correct, in Norfolk."

He laid the phone back, and sat there for a moment with his eyes closed, listening to the soft slopping of the water in the pool, and the squittering birds.

The telephone jangled, and Johann reached over and picked it up.

"Eddie? This is Johann Cornelius. . . . I'm fine, how are you? . . . Listen, Eddie, I have a little problem here, and it's causing me some embarrassment. I thought you could maybe help me out. . . . Yes, that's right. Well, it's one of your Navy Department people. I don't like to tell tales out of school, but there's a lot of money involved, and I don't like to see people take advantage. No, quite right. Yes. His name's . . . What's his name, David?"

"Merrett Kale."

"Eddie? His name's Merrett Kale. I believe he works in your contract division. Young guy, quite bright. That's it. Well, he came around here this afternoon and all but promised me the work on four 35,000-ton warships. Cornelius Shipping, that is. All I had to do was pay him a quarter of a million bucks, and the contracts were in the bag. . . . Well, that's right. I know you can't believe it, Eddie, but that's the way it was. I stalled for time, and paid him ten thousand in advance. My secretary has the serial numbers. Yes, in cash. He's carrying it with him now, on the three-thirty-two from Lynwood, gets into Grand Central at five-seventeen."

David Bookbinder listened to Johann talking, and thoughtfully sucked at his cigar. A ragged cloud was moving across the sun outside, and the lawns went suddenly dull. All the sparkle went out of the sprinklers, and he wondered if it was going to rain.

"There's one thing more," said Johann, on the telephone. "Well, I'm afraid that's right. The mood that the government's in right now regarding rackets, you can't be too careful. We don't want rackets in the Navy Department, do we? But what I *do* want to do is put in for these ships all the same. Maybe not the whole four. But two. If I can wrap up two of them, then there's no need for any disappointment, is there? . . . Come on, Eddie, you know what I mean by disappointment! *I* don't want to be disappointed by missing out on some patriotic defense work, and *you* don't want to be disappointed by having this treacherous bum Kale blot your record. Now, isn't that a fair definition of disappointment? . . . Good. I knew you'd understand. . . . All right, call me back. But don't forget, that's five-seventeen at Grand Central. All you have to do is ask him where he got it, and see what he says. . . . Terrific. Good-bye, Eddie."

"Short and sweet," remarked David Bookbinder as Johann put the phone down.

"We've got him by the balls and he knows it," said Johann gruffly.

Bookbinder said: "Yes, I guess we have," and eased his bulky body up from the daybed. He sat there watching the pool for a while, and then he stood up and brushed down his jacket.

Johann said: "You're going straight back to the city?"

"I guess so. We have a meeting of Kruyper Coal at eight."

"I was hoping you might stay for dinner. Hester's away in Vermont for a couple of days, and I wanted to talk."

Bookbinder put away his watch. "Was it urgent? What you wanted to talk about?"

"It could be. It's just that I'm kind of concerned about our involvement in rackets."

"You're scared of Dewey?"

"Aren't you?"

"Why should I be?" asked Bookbinder. "Tom's a good friend of mine. And any involvement we have with organized rackets is entirely for our own protection. We've been through this before. Any business on the scale of Cornelius Industries needs to keep complete control of all of its manufacturing and distribution, right down to the last truck. And let's not kid ourselves the police can protect us. I worked out that by cutting in Gizzi on the railroad contract, we saved ourselves almost three-quarters of a million last year from the decrease in pilferage and hijacks."

"Suppose someone decides to unburden their soul? Someone like our good friend Merrett Kale?"

"Oh, come on, Johann, you're getting chicken-livered in your old age. We can always have Walden Farrow to lunch.''

Johann rubbed his face tiredly with both hands. ''I suppose so. It just seems to me that wining and dining the Justice Department isn't much of a substitute for keeping our hands clean.''

Bookbinder stared at Johann with a beady, riveting look that could have been surprise but was probably disgust.

''Don't you get holy with me,'' he said in a soft voice.

Johann turned away. Sometimes he felt such a bristling dislike for David Bookbinder that he could hardly bear to look at him. Bookbinder was like some goading younger brother who followed him around all day, worrying him and nagging him and enmeshing him in hopeless complications. He could see himself in David Bookbinder, and that's what made it worse. All the less pleasant traits of his own personality, which he normally kept firmly repressed, were openly buzzing around David Bookbinder like a swarm of blowflies.

Johann said: ''Have a swim before you go.''

''A swim?''

''I find it refreshing. It washes off the contamination.''

Bookbinder looked at Johann in silence for a minute or two, and then grunted a small, fat laugh. He said: ''I might at that.''

The Landseers were holding a garden party at their place in Connecticut, and John awarded himself the weekend off from his summer school at Worcester and drove down there in his green Buick convertible. He hadn't seen Hope since her banishment from Lynwood's Island, although they'd spoken on the telephone a couple of times, and he was looking forward to chewing the fat. The prospect of a Landseer garden party wouldn't usually have been sufficiently compelling on its own to bring him all the way down to Hartford, but apart from Hope, he knew that Susan Grainger Steadman was going to be there, and there was quite a lot about Susan Grainger Steadman that tickled his fancy. She was dark and vivacious, and he understood from Philip Strachan that she was not averse to ''third base.''

The Landseers were such tedious people that John often used to think that they held special family meetings to decide how they could make themselves even more boring than they already were. They lived in a large ugly half-timbered mock-Tudor house on a nine-acre estate outside of Hartford, most of which was lawns but some of which was neatly cultivated woodland. Mr. Landseer was a senior partner in the old Connecticut law firm of Higgs Chandler Askew, and he was renowned for his thoroughness but not his haste; he had managed to prolong one complicated claim for damages for eleven years, and the way the case was proceeding it looked as though it would take another eleven years to settle it. The defense had several times protested to the bench that Landseer was trying to bore them out of court, and the bench had yawned and openly agreed.

Martin Landseer, their only son, was the model of his father. He was twenty-three now, and he was studying corporation law with the promise of a good position at General Motors. He was a sloping-shouldered young man with fair hedgehog hair, steel-rimmed spectacles, and a protuberant Adam's apple. His white ducks always seemed to be mangy, and his shirt collars curled up like stale sandwiches. He was a well-known jerk.

A shower had just passed over when John drove through the brick arch at the head of the Landseers' driveway and sped down toward the house. It always rained when the Landseers held a garden party, and the servants spent more time rushing in and out with tarpaulins to cover the tables than they did serving drinks. There was a marquee, with bedraggled bunting, and a brick barbecue that was smoking heavily. Everyone was clustered on the veranda of the house, talking and laughing loudly, and some of them waved as John tooted his horn.

As he climbed out of his car, a rather stuffy sun was coming out from behind the clouds, and people began to wander back onto the lawn. A seven-piece band was there, in red-and-white-striped blazers and straw skimmers, and they were busy wiping off their kitchen chairs with their handkerchiefs. John straightened his tie and walked across to the veranda to say hello to Mr. and Mrs. Landseer, and see if he could find Hope.

"Well, how are you?" said Mr. Landseer, squeezing John's hand and forgetting to let go. "You sure look top-notch, if I can say such a thing."

"Is Hope here?" asked John.

"She certainly is. As a matter of fact, this party is really being given for her."

"That's kind of you. I'm sure she's thrilled."

"Not so thrilled as we are, I can tell you."

John said: "I don't quite understand."

Mr. Landseer winked, and his monocle dropped out. "It's supposed to be a secret, really. They're going to announce it later."

John managed to retrieve his hand. Behind them, the band started to play "Tiger Rag." "Announce what?" he asked.

"Well, I really shouldn't say it, but I must tell you that I'm real proud, and happy as a boy's father could be."

At that moment young Martin Landseer came up and said: "Father, I think Harris wants to know when he can start serving the cold lobster."

"Hi, Martin," said John.

"Oh, hi, John. Glad you could make it. How's the summer school?"

"Pretty tough. Is Hope around?"

"Sure. Has father told you the news?"

Mr. Landseer said: "Not me, son. I've kept my lips sealed as tight as a jar of pickles."

"Did you get the job?" asked John. "The legal thing at General Motors?"

Martin nodded his head. "I guess you're related, so you ought to know first. Hope and I are middle-aisling it. This is our engagement party."

John blinked at Martin Landseer in total surprise. Of all the jerks that walked the northeast United States, Martin Landseer had to be the jerkiest. Hope knew that. Hope had even said so herself. She had once seen Martin Landseer in his bathing costume on Long Island, and called him "a kipper in a brown woolly bag." How could she think of marrying him? He was boring, like all the Landseers, but one could forgive him an inherited defect. It was his whining, smarmy, ineffectual personality that annoyed John, let alone the fact that he rooted for Yale and thought that Max Schmeling should have won his rematch with Joe Louis. John couldn't understand what Hope could possibly see in him. Perhaps he had hidden talents, like a very long thing, but he couldn't see Hope giving up fun and parties and social adventure for a *thing*, no matter how magnificent.

"Well"—Martin Landseer grinned—"aren't you going to congratulate me?"

John held out his hand. Shaking hands with Martin Landseer

was like wringing out a wet dishcloth. How could Hope actually let hands like that fondle her body?

"Have you . . . fixed a date?" asked John, hot and cross.

"Sure." Martin winked. "We're aiming for next spring. I can tell you, your sister has made me a really happy man."

"She's made *all* of us happy," put in Mr. Landseer, dropping his monocle. "Mrs. Landseer calls her an angel, and I think that's about the right word for a girl as charming and composed as your sister, Hope."

John said: "You're very kind."

Martin Landseer slapped him awkwardly on the back. "We'll be brothers-in-law! Don't you think that's something!"

John gave a wan little smile. "How are your sausages?" he asked.

Martin Landseer said: "Fine!" but then realized he didn't understand what John was saying, and said: "I beg your pardon?"

"Your sausages. They look like they're getting pretty well grilled out there."

The Landseers' cook, a painfully thin woman in a tall white hat, was trying to prod cutlets and wieners on the brick barbecue. Smoke was billowing out across the lawn, as thick and foul-smelling as last month's Quackenbush fire out in Paterson, New Jersey.

Instead of going to help his future brother-in-law to bring the barbecue under control, John dodged off around the back of the house to see if he could find Hope. The first thing he wanted to know was what this nonsense about marrying Martin Landseer was all about. She could have had her pick! He knew for a solid gold fact that Philip Strachan was gaga about her, and even Eddie Kaiser said she was a doll. So why had she chosen Martin? Out of perversity? To punish Mother and Father for sending her away? Or had she really been smitten?

He walked around the back of the house and found Hope on her own, sitting at the far end of the veranda, eating strawberries and whipped cream with a spoon. The spoon flashed in the smoky sunlight. Her head, in a white feathery hat, was bent down over her crystal bowl, and she didn't see him at first; she was gently rocking herself in a swing seat and tapping the veranda rail with the tip of her toe every time she rocked. As he came toward her, he thought she somehow looked like a photograph of herself; and when she turned and saw him, and smiled, he was convinced that he would never forget seeing her like that, across the clipped lawn and jostling marigolds, behind the white-painted veranda rail, in her white hat and her loose white embroidered summer dress.

He came up the three steps onto the veranda's wooden floor and said: "Hi."

Hope reached out a hand. There was a sparkling engagement ring on her finger, but he pretended he hadn't noticed it.

"Do you like it?" she asked.

He nodded. "Sure. It's a nice ring."

"Nice? It almost broke the Landseer family for the next hundred years. Eighty thousand, if it's a dime."

"Since when did you count the cost of things?"

Hope was licking her spoon clean. She stopped licking and looked up at John with a clouded face.

"You don't sound like you're very enthusiastic," she said carefully.

"Well, to tell you the truth, I'm not."

"You don't like me counting the cost of things?"

"That's part of it. Have you counted the cost of marrying Martin?"

Hope put down her strawberry dish. "I don't know what you mean."

"Sure you do. What happened to the kipper in the brown woolly bag?"

Hope shrugged noncommittally.

"You don't love him, do you? I can't believe that. What about you and Philip?"

Hope looked away. "Philip's just a dumb preppie, that's all."

"Oh, that's ridiculous!" said John. "Philip's very fond of you, and what's more, Philip's a bright guy. At least he doesn't look like a refugee from a thrift store!"

Hope stared at him fiercely, and he saw something in her face—something hard and decided but also self-destructive—that he had never seen in her before. He sat down on the veranda rail and folded his arms and said: "I just don't see what you're trying to prove. Martin won't make you a husband—not in a million years."

"Martin's very sensitive."

"Oh, sure. Like a marshmallow."

412

"You don't understand. He's kind and he's gentle and I feel sorry for him. He'd do absolutely anything I asked him to."

John frowned. "And that's what you want in a husband?"

"I just want it in somebody. There's never been anyone like that in my life. It's either been Father, who's totally dedicated to his business; or Mother, who's so goddamned relentless; or Roddy, who's spending all his time crawling around Father; or you."

"And what's my trouble?"

Hope tapped at the rail with the toe of her shoe. "Your trouble is that you're too damned honest."

"You think that's a fault?"

"It is in our family."

John sighed, and reached into his pocket for a tin of Balkan Sobranie cigarettes. He offered one to Hope, and they lit up. The smoke from the barbecue was now hanging thickly around the side of the house, and the sunlight was falling through it in shifting spokes. They could hear the band playing, and the shouts and laughter from the rest of the guests.

Hope said: "I have this desire to look after people weaker than myself."

"Don't you think Father has that?"

"Yes, I do. But he's buried it someplace inside of him. I sometimes think that he cares very much. I think I inherited this feeling from him. But because of the business, and because of what we are, we're not allowed to show it."

John said: "Is that why you're marrying Martin? Just because you want to be kind to someone less fortunate than yourself?"

Hope watched some small boys in white knickerbockers running around and around in the smoke; and heard their nurse calling to them from somewhere out of sight. The nurse said: "Montmorency! Montmorency!" in a high piping voice.

Hope said: "Is it wrong to be kind?"

John tapped his ash into the flowerbed. "Of course not. But you have a duty to be kind to yourself, as well. I'm not trying to tell you how to run your life, Hope, but consider what you're doing before you do it. I mean, think about it. Martin Landseer isn't exactly Clark Gable."

"He's not Johann Cornelius, either, thank God."

John looked at her acutely. "You don't dislike Father that much, do you?"

Hope kicked at the veranda. "You bet I do!" she snapped. But

413

then she let the momentum of her kick squeak her backward and forward on the swing, and die away, and then she said: "No, I don't really."

John said: "Whatever Father says—I know he's kind of gruff sometimes—but whatever he says, he loves you."

"I don't know whether he loves anybody. Least of all me."

"Hope," insisted John, "you don't have to marry Martin Landseer just to prove something to Father. That's the wrong reason completely."

Hope gave the garden swing one last push and then stood up. She reached over and kissed John on the cheek, almost absentmindedly, the way a distracted mother kisses her son on his way to a college football game.

"I want to marry Martin Landseer because I want to see what it's like to be charitable and kind. I want to see what it's like to devote your whole life to someone weak, and give them strength. It didn't work with Lewis Bausor,—you know, that poor man who died. But I know that I *could* do it if I really tried."

John said: "You're more like Father than you even know."

Hope smiled as though she didn't believe him. But she didn't say any more, because Martin Landseer came cantering around the back of the house in his yellow suspenders, his white ducks smudged with smoke, and a black smut on the end of his nose. He was calling: "John! John! It's getting out of control, John! You'll have to come and help!"

While John and Hope had been talking, they hadn't noticed that the rolling smoke from the barbecue had grown even darker and thicker, and that it was now almost impossible to see down to the end of the garden. From the lawn at the side of the house they heard coughing and shouting and the band trying to strike up another tune with the ragged uncertainty of men who don't know whether to play or run.

John stripped off his coat and followed Martin back through the smoke to the brick barbecue. It looked like a cocktail party on the battlefield at Gettysburg, with elegant young things standing around with martinis while the clouds of war rolled past in dense and choking billows. From the veranda Mr. Landseer was shouting apopletic directions to his servants, who stood at a hesitant distance from the blazing barbecue, holding pails of water and looking miserable.

"Don't drench it, or there's no lunch!" he was shouting. "And

414

don't throw water on the meat! Watch the meat, will you, for God's sake!"

"John! What can we do?" panted Martin. "You're good at this kind of thing! What can we do?"

John looked at this flapping, useless young man with the smut on his nose and felt almost sorry for him. But he didn't feel *that* sorry. A jerk like Martin Landseer needed teaching a lesson, especially when he came sniffing around John Cornelius' sister. He put his arm around Martin's shoulder and said confidingly: "I'll tell you what to do. Impress your friends. Do what they used to do out on the Cornelius oilfields when they had a gusher that caught fire."

"What was that?" asked Martin anxiously.

"They snuffed it out with dynamite. Just snuffed it out. You won't need water, and you won't spoil the meat."

"But we don't have dynamite. At least, I don't think we have."

"You have some kerosene, don't you? There's a can of kerosene right there."

Martin looked worried. "Yes . . ."

"Here's what to do. Screw the lid on tight, and throw the can of kerosene into the barbecue. One bang, and you'll snuff that fire right out, and save your party."

"Do you think it'll work?"

"Of course! They used to do it on the Cornelius oilfields all the time. They had roustabouts who did it for a living!"

Martin Landseer took off his spectacles and wiped the soot off them on the tail of his shirt. "Well, okay, if you think it's going to work."

John said: "You go ahead. I'll just wait here and make sure everything's all right."

"Okay." Martin nodded and skirted around the thickening smoke of the barbecue to the far side, where the can of kerosene stood on the small pavement patio along with the charcoal and the skewers and all the rest of the cook's paraphernalia.

He called out: "It's okay, Father! I'm going to try something! Just keep your distance!"

The servants looked relieved that they weren't going to be called on to throw their pails of water. Mr. Landseer shouted: "You be careful, there, Martin! That's two hundred dollars' worth of good meat there!"

Hope came around from the veranda with her handkerchief

over her nose and mouth. John saw her and ushered her back again. "I should stand well away if I were you. Martin's doing something with kerosene. I'm not quite sure what."

Nobody could quite believe it when Martin Landseer picked up the can of kerosene, tightened the lid, and scuttled up to the brick barbecue with it, shielding his face from the guttering flames with his upraised arm. The band had been playing "Ah, Sweet Mystery of Life," but as the cornet player and the banjo plucker saw Martin with his can, their music dwindled away like water down a bathtub drain, and they scattered from their chairs.

Martin awkwardly heaved the can straight into the fire, and then, only five or six yards away, turned around and clapped his hands over his ears. Mr. Landseer bawled: "*Martin! What the devil are you doing?*" but neither he nor anyone else had the time or inclination to rush into the smoky epicenter and rescue his reckless son.

There was a sound like warping tin, and then immediately afterward an immense bellowing bang. Wieners and chops and T-bones sprayed through the guests in a greasy hailstorm, and the brick barbecue itself was thrown straight up into the air like a handful of jacks. There was a lot of screaming from the girls, and hoarse exclamations from the men, and above all of the hubbub you could hear Mr. Landseer shouting: "Martin! Martin! Are you all right?"

John ran around through the rubble and scattered meat, worriedly trying to locate Martin. My God, he'd had no idea that the fool would be dumb enough to *stand* there! Supposing he was dead, or terribly hurt? Supposing he was lying among the sausage links with his head blown off?

He found Martin standing a little way away. The Landseer boy was smiling shakily. His hair was standing on end, and his spectacles were hanging from one ear. He had no clothes on at all except for his shoes and his socks.

When he saw John, he reached out his hands and mouthed: "John . . . I can't hear! I can't hear very well! I can't hear!"

John shouted: "I'd better find you a pair of pants!"

"I can't hear you!"

Martin nodded, and John went running back toward the house, through milling and babbling guests, his face set as tight as he could manage, to stop himself from laughing.

Mr. Landseer caught his arm as he reached the veranda. "Where's Martin? Is he alive? Where is he?"

"He's okay, Mr. Landseer. He's kind of shocked. Look, he's over there. Can you tell me where his room is, and I'll get him some pants."

Mr. Landseer seemed to be as deaf as his son. He hurried off across the wrecked and smoky lawn, one hand raised like a father in a Greek tragedy, muttering as he went: "My God, the meat. My son, the meat. My God."

It was only when John glanced along the shaded veranda to the back of the house and saw Hope standing there with her face pale and her eyes wide with anxiety that he thought he might have played the wrong sort of joke altogether. He began to wish he'd kept out of it and gone looking for Susan Grainger Steadman instead.

Roderick wasn't altogether happy about the test pilot that Denis Mulligan had suggested for the C-1, but today was too late to do anything about it. It was the last weekend in September, 1938, rainy and stormy for the most part, and Roderick had been obliged to divide his time between the last-minute preparations for the C-1's maiden flight, struggling in the small hours of the morning with landing-gear pistons that stuck and four Pratt & Whitney motors that refused to cough in unison, and his office desk. In New York, the Republican State Convention had predictably selected Thomas Dewey as candidate for governor, and David Bookbinder had been rearranging and redistributing Cornelius interests with a bad-tempered feverishness. He was forever calling Roderick on the telephone and asking if he could warehouse canned meats and liquor in Charleston, or whether he could move his tobaccos to Ashland, or if it was possible to reregister Cornelius corporations in other states.

The test pilot's name was R. S. Fairbanks, and he used to fly coast-to-coast sleepers in the early days of the Douglas DC-3, in 1936. He was a bony, taciturn man from Harrisburg, Pennsylvania, with weary-looking eyes and a thin mustache. He habitually wore a brown leather flying helmet with the strap undone, a dusty black cavalry jacket, and riding breeches. He spoke in dry and oblique sentences, and had told Roderick that he thought the C-1 was "no better and no worse than a Sikorsky Clipper, and that ain't saying nothing."

Just before dawn on Saturday morning, October 1, Roderick drove down to the Ashland airfield in his laurel-green Pierce Arrow, one of the last Pierce Arrows to be built before the company went bankrupt. He parked outside the main hangar and stepped inside the building through the small access door in the huge sliding portals which protected the C-1 from the rain and the salt-marsh winds. All the lights were blazing and the hangar was noisy with stammering drills and shouting men and the whine of compressors. Lem Cosnett, sweaty and tired in a fawn pullover with unraveling sleeves, came over and shook Roderick by the hand.

"Is she fit?" asked Roderick. He tried to sound as matter-of-fact as possible. A doctor inquiring after a young girl's health. But they both knew how much this date meant. They'd been working frantically for weeks to make sure the C-1 was ready on time, and on Monday night Roderick had even driven all the way to Cincinnati and back to pick up a set of instruments for the start of Tuesday morning's construction. What's more, instead of his laundered blue coveralls, he was dressed today in a dark wool double-breasted suit and a crimson silk tie, and even though it was only five-thirty, he had already shaved. He was prepared, psychologically and sartorially, for the C-1's first triumph.

Lem Cosnett leafed through his clipboard. "I guess we're all fixed except for a couple of checks on the landing gear."

Roderick reached out and touched the airplane's plain aluminum elevator. "You know something, Lem, she's beautiful."

Lem had been checking off his last-minute list of procedures. He looked up at Roderick and wiped his forehead with the back of his hand.

"As far as I'm concerned, sir, she doesn't get beautiful until she flies."

"Flies?" asked Roderick. "Oh, she'll fly, all right! She'll fly like a bird."

Lem lowered his eyes again. "Jack's still not sure about the motors. He's done what he can, but he's still not sure."

Roderick took his hand off the elevator. His fingertips had made dabs of condensation, which gradually melted away.

Lem said: "It's kind of a short runway, after all."

Roderick thought about that, and then shrugged. "You know what Mrs. Cornelius said. If we can't lift her off from short runways, then she's not a commercial proposition."

Lem nodded, not particularly joyfully. "Yes, sir, I know that."

Roderick stared at him hard. "What you're saying is that you know that, but you're still not sure about the motors."

"It's forty-one tons of airplane, sir. It's as big as a Clipper, and it's going to take a lot of runway."

"That's Mr. Fairbanks' job, isn't it? It's up to him to get her into the air."

"He can't do it without the power, sir."

Roderick turned away and walked around the tail of the airplane, inspecting the paneling and the control surfaces. "What you don't seem to understand, Lem, is that Mr. Fairbanks is the finest pilot in the world, according to Mrs. Cornelius, and also according to Mr. Denis Mulligan. He's such a fine pilot, in fact, that he could get the C-1 off the ground if it had no motors at all."

Lem said: "Yes, sir."

Roderick looked back at him across the reflecting tailplane, so that he seemed like a man standing chest-high in the sea. "I don't believe that, and I'm sure you don't believe it, either, but it's the official line, and since Father appears to subscribe to the Fairbanks fan club too, we're stuck with things the way they are."

"Yes, sir."

"Okay, Lem. Let's get around this baby and see what the boys think of her chances."

Together, Roderick and Lem went on a short tour of the C-1's hangar, talking to riggers and aero engineers and mechanics. To each, Roderick put the same question: "How do you think she's going to fly?" Most of them thought good. Some of them said: "Okay, I guess." But he still kept on asking, until he was satisfied that every man in the hangar believed that the C-1 was going to climb up into the rainy skies this very morning, and wheel over West Virginia like a silver albatross.

They drank coffee out of enamel mugs, and waited around for R. S. Fairbanks. The test pilot arrived at eight, wearing his accustomed flying helmet and black jacket, but this time he was sporting his medals as well. He came straight up to Roderick and said: "I gather we're ready."

Roderick cleared his throat. "We believe so. I want to take off at nine."

Fairbanks blinked his noncommittal assent, and then turned abruptly on one heel. "Is there any coffee left? I'm as parched as a possum's ass."

Roderick looked down at his shiny black Alan McAfee shoes

with their almond-pointed toes and punched decorations. He said: "You know what to do if you run out of airfield and you're still short of power."

"I know the orders, yes," answered Fairbanks, spooning four sugars into his coffee and stirring it.

"You'll throttle back?"

"If necessary."

"This is a small field. Remember that. It's probably going to be close."

Fairbanks swallowed his coffee in three big mouthfuls, put down his mug, and wiped his mouth with a folded handkerchief. "Ready when you are, Mr. Cosnett."

With R. S. Fairbanks in the cockpit, they went through the final routine of checking every flap and trim tab on the whole airplane. Rudders and ailerons opened and shut like the lids of magician's boxes. Then, at eight-thirty the hangar lights were switched off, one by one, and two mechanics rolled back the sliding hangar doors, allowing the gray grimy light of an overcast day to filter over the polished metallic skin of the C-1. A Ford pickup was backed into the hangar and linked to the airplane's tail wheel. Slowly the giant machine was towed out of the hangar backwards, a huge glistening salmon caught by the tail.

Roderick stood in the chilly wind with his hands in his pockets watching the airplane drawn out onto the airfield. He checked his Cartier wristwatch. It was a quarter of nine now, and he hoped his father and mother would arrive in time for the first takeoff. Even if they didn't, he could have Fairbanks fly this baby over and over and over again, for his father's benefit, or to show off to his mother, or for anyone who still needed proof that he wasn't the dogged and obedient elder son any longer, strong on devotion but lacking in flair. He wasn't the awkward asthmatic who couldn't keep his pencils sharp. He was the airplane maker, the man who was going to take America into the streamlined future, the dapper confidant of Howard Hughes and Charles Lindbergh and Bennett Griffin. This year, almost 200,000 people would fly by air, and next year, thousands more. Roderick had a dream that scores of Americans, rich and poor, would soon be girdling the globe by Cornelius Airways. He could picture it clear in his mind—a world teeming with airplanes, all winging their way hither and thither, with smiling families peeping from every porthole—mothers and fathers and uncles and aunts—happily traveling through clouds and sunshine in a miraculous aerial future which he, in his beneficent industrial genius, had created for them.

It started to rain. Celia's cherry-red Bentley appeared around the corner of the hangar and stopped. Their English chauffeur, Wilkinson, opened the door for her and held an umbrella over her head as she walked across toward Roderick, severe but faultlessly elegant in a gray cape and turban hat, and holding her toy silver-haired poodle, Fortescue. Fortescue had just had a permanent wave, and Roderick thought that he looked like Harpo Marx's toupee on legs.

Celia offered her cheek to be kissed. She didn't look at the airplane. She said: "Are we ready to start, darling? You know we have the general coming down this afternoon for the Army Air Force, and at three there's Commander Armbruster. You haven't forgotten, have you?"

"No, I haven't forgotten. Where's Father?"

"Oh, he'll be here. Your mother couldn't quite decide on the mink or the silver sable. Personally, I think they're both much of a muchness."

"I suppose you've had another row."

"Of course not. More of a *contretemps*."

"What was it this time?"

"Oh, Roddy, it's too boring. Your father wanted David Bookbinder to come, but your mother said she detested him, and *no*. So then your father made his usual speech that if it wasn't for David Bookbinder, the world would have long ago collapsed into economic ruin. That's when I told both of them to stop bickering and finish their breakfast, and of course your mother said she wouldn't have *anyone* speak to her like that, and so on and so on. But they'll be here later, don't fret. Your father won't let you squander twelve million dollars on an airplane that won't fly, and he won't believe it can fly until he sees it for himself."

Roderick said doggedly: "Of course it's going to fly. What the hell does he expect?"

Celia tickled Fortescue under his curly chin. "That's what we're here to find out, isn't it? Whether it flies or not?"

Roderick didn't answer. He was watching Lem Cosnett taking a last prowl around the C-1, his clipboard on his arm, checking the tires and the landing gear. Now the plane was out in the open air, it appeared deceptively small, even though its wings spanned 151 feet, and it was 160 feet from its streamlined nose to its tall tail.

Roderick actually found himself wondering whether it *was* going to fly, or whether he was guilty of absurd delusions and self-aggrandizement. He looked up and the frayed yellow clouds were hanging very low, with only a faint dirty-yellow light seeping through them from the early-morning sun. A piece of newspaper tumbled across the grass and caught itself on the wheel of the C-1, flapping and damp, until a mechanic hurried over and fastidiously removed it.

Celia remarked: "You seem depressed, Roddy. Are you?"

Roderick looked at her. He sometimes wished she wasn't so pristine and beautiful. She wasn't pretty; no one could call her that. But she had a cold perfection to every part of her face that had once made him believe she was a goddess. Perhaps she still was. But he knew now that it was less than easy for a mere mortal to cohabit with a goddess, especially one as relentlessly devoted to success as Celia.

"I'm not depressed," he said flatly. "I'm a little anxious, that's all."

"I thought you would have been magnificently pleased. Full of your own achievements. There it is, Roddy. A big, beautiful airplane, and you built it yourself."

"Yes," he said. He didn't sound very convinced.

Celia laid Fortescue down on the grass, and the toy poodle stood at the end of its slender studded leash, quaking like a powder puff with chronic pneumonia.

"Have you heard any more about Hope?" asked Celia. She was deliberately changing the subject, but Roderick didn't altogether mind. He was too nervous about the C-1 to talk about it, or whether it was going to fly. It was enough that it was actually *there*, parked on the grass a few yards away, a dull silver torpedo with looming wings. It was enough that he could smell the oily odor of airplane fuel, mingled with the salt tang of the marshes. It was enough that he could hear the dry bark of R. S. Fairbanks from the cockpit window, calling: "Oil pressure normal, flaps normal, fuel normal, landing-gear indicator normal, hydraulics normal."

A small flock of birds flurried overhead in the slanting wind. Roderick took out his clean handkerchief and blew his nose.

"Hope?" he asked, absentmindedly. "She's still planning on marriage, as far as I know. John sees more of her than I do. It's still a sensitive subject around here."

"What does your mother think?"

"I don't think she's particularly pleased. But Martin Landseer's an honest wight."

"A what?"

"It's medieval for 'guy.' I guess it's the only word you can use for someone like Martin. Slow but well-meaning. If there was still hay to be forked in the world, Martin would be the kind of fellow forking it."

"I see," said Celia a trifle coldly.

"Well, *you* may," Roderick told her, "but Mother certainly doesn't. Nor does Father. They both believe she'd marry the first person available to spite them for all that fuss last year."

"You mean the man who died?"

"That's right."

"I don't see the connection."

"Neither do I, frankly, but John believes that she's obsessed with the idea of looking after the world's lame ducks. She didn't succeed with that vagrant in New York, so now she's turned her attention to Martin Landseer."

"Is he that much of a lame duck?"

Roderick coughed. "Let's put it this way. When he was at college, the frat told him to steal a lady's drawers as an initiation. He came back a couple of hours later with the drawers out of a dressing table."

Celia didn't allow herself to smile. She said: "There's nothing we can do, is there? I mean, she's not stupid. She must know what she's getting herself into."

"I don't know."

"Well, *I* know, even if *she* doesn't. You would have thought that the man who died would have taught her a lesson. When the wealthy mix with the not-so-wealthy, no matter how benevolent their intentions, they usually wind up destroying them. She'll end up doing the same thing to Martin Landseer, you mark my words."

A midnight-blue Rolls-Royce limousine, with whitewall tires, its bodywork polished like a starry sky, appeared around the corner of the hangar. The chauffeur opened the door and Johann and Hester stepped out, regal and slow, and stood for a moment to make quite sure that everyone was aware of their arrival. Roderick went over to greet them, but Celia kept her distance and made an unnecessary fuss over the wretched Fortescue.

Hester was looking pale, and was wearing an ankle-length black fur coat. She extended a limp arm to Roderick, and he grasped her

423

hand and briefly kissed it. Johann appeared tired, too, and he was masked like a bandit in a plaid scarf. On the lapel of his long vicuna overcoat, he wore a carnation with a sprig of fern.

"I'm so glad you could make it," said Roderick, taking his mother's arm. "This is going to be the most terrific day of my life."

Johann said: "So that's the airplane, is it? Is it ready to go?"

"Almost, sir. We're just making the last checks now."

"What are you going to call her?" asked Hester. "Not just the C-1, I hope?"

"I'm going to wait until she flies first," said Roderick.

Hester said: "I think you ought to call her Eastward Ho! That sounds so romantic, doesn't it?"

Roderick smiled uncomfortably. "Yes, I suppose it does."

Lem Cosnett came over and inclined his head respectfully to Johann and Hester. Then he murmured in Roderick's ear: "It's no use."

Roderick frowned. "What do you mean?"

Lem Cosnett said "Excuse me" to Johann and Hester and led Roderick aside by the arm. He said quietly: "There was too much rain last night. The airfield's sodden. If I was sure of the power, I'd say okay, but I'm not. If the plane runs into the marshes, it's going to take days to get her out."

Roderick bit at his fingernail. He looked irked.

"I'm sorry," said Lem, "but that's the way I feel about it. I'd rather wait until the weather dries out."

Roderick said: "When's that going to be? What's the forecast?" He knew what the forecast was.

"Stormy."

"Then it's going to get worse, isn't it, not better? Are you seriously suggesting we've got to hold this twelve-million-dollar airplane all winter, just because the grass is wet?"

Lem Cosnett looked unhappy. "I have to give you my opinion."

"All right," said Roderick, "you've given it. Now let's talk to Fairbanks, and see what *his* opinion is."

He walked across the grass toward the C-1, ducking under the fuselage and rapping on the hull just below the cockpit. The window slid back and R. S. Fairbanks stuck his head out. "Yes, sir?"

Roderick said: "Mr. Cosnett here believes the ground is too wet for a takeoff. How do you feel about it?"

R. S. Fairbanks pulled a face and thought about it. Then he called back: "I once took off from Casper, Wyoming, in a force-eight gale, with lightning striking all around, and the soil was flooded six inches deep with rain. What's worse, my wheels caught a fence on the way up, and I flew all the way to Scottsbluff, Nebraska, with fifty yards of barbed wire, three fence posts, and a wooden feed trough flying behind me."

Roderick still wanted to make sure. "So you believe you can fly today?"

"Mr. Cornelius, I'm ready for off."

Roderick turned to Lem Cosnett. "There's your answer," he said quietly. "He can do it, and that's good enough for me."

Lem Cosnett held his clipboard to his chest. He didn't agree, but he knew that he was going to have to give in. He nodded and said: "All right, if that's what you want to do. I'll get myself aboard."

Roderick went back to Johann and Hester. Johann said: "Is everything all right? It's cold out here. I don't want your mother catching pneumonia."

"Everything's fine, sir. They're ready to roll."

They stood in the soggy and persistent wind as one by one the motors spluttered and the propellers turned over. Lem Cosnett climbed into the plane and closed the main door. Roderick held Celia's arm, but she seemed more interested in Fortescue than she was in him and after a while he let go. Johann and Hester both appeared preoccupied and quiet, and Roderick began to wonder if any of his family were really interested in him or what he did at all. The motors were revved up faster and faster until the airplane was shuddering and all conversation was sawn away in a droning torrent of noise. Hester held her hands over her ears and Roderick felt almost embarrassed that he was causing his mother so much discomfort.

In the distance, the windsock stood stiffly toward the northeast. The huge plane began to roll slowly across the grass, and then turn its nose into the breeze. From where they were standing, they could see R. S. Fairbanks lowering his goggles. He was a pilot of the old school. He liked to fly with the windows open.

The grumbling roar of the motors grew louder still, and then R.

S. Fairbanks released the wheel brakes and the airplane began to move off along the bumpy grass. Hester clapped her hands, excited now, and cried: "It's off! Look, darling, it's off!"

Trundling away from them faster and faster, the C-1 gathered speed until its tail wheel lifted from the grass, and it was running on its two main wheels. Roderick found he was digging his fingernails into the palm of his hand, and that his face felt as rigid as a plaster mask. He could hear Fairbanks gunning the motors until they were screeching, and held his breath as one main wheel lifted off the ground momentarily and then sank back again.

None of them spoke as the airplane ran on and on over the grassy airfield. Roderick was tensely aware that if Fairbanks didn't get it off the ground in the next three or four seconds, then he was going to have to throttle back and call the flight off. He heard the motors rise to a throaty howl that he had never heard from them before, not even during their weeks of punishment testing, and he knew that Fairbanks was giving his takeoff every ounce of power possible.

"Oh, God, fly," he whispered. Only Celia heard him, and she touched his shoulder with her hand; not comfortingly, but as if to reassure him that, yes, the world was very hard.

Even when he saw spray rising in clouds from the airplane's wheels, and knew that Fairbanks had run it into the marshes, Roderick still believed that it would rise miraculously off the ground. Fly, you bastard, fly! But then he saw showers of mud, and the sound of the motors suddenly dropped off with a sinking, complaining whine.

"He's botched it!" cried Roderick in an oddly effeminate voice. "He's run it into the mud! For God's sake, did you see that? He's run it straight into the mud!"

Roderick, heavily, began to run across the airfield in the direction of the marsh. The airplane still hadn't come to rest, and he looked like a man chasing a plane that he had just missed by a minute or two. Johann and Hester and Celia stayed where they were, watching him gallop awkwardly through the wet grass in his celebration suit.

The airplane appeared to sink sideways, with its tail in the air and one wing broken. Then, without warning, one of the motors made a flat walloping sound and burst into flames. The wallop echoed back to Roderick from the hangar behind him.

He stopped where he was. Panting, he turned around and began

426

to run back to the buildings. He shouted to Celia: "The car! It's quicker! Get in the car!"

The riggers and mechanics were already running past him with fire extinguishers. He climbed clumsily into the Pierce Arrow and started it up, driving erratically across the muddy ground. One of the riggers saw him coming and jumped onto the running board as he passed, and climbed in beside him.

One wing of the airplane was blazing fiercely. Already a dark spiral of smoke was staining the gray sky, and marsh birds were wheeling and turning all around it. Everything was unnaturally quiet, except for the engine of the Pierce Arrow and the sound of tires slithering in the mud. It was only now that Roderick appreciated how heavy and wet the airfield really was.

They reached the edge of the marshes and the car refused to go any farther. They climbed out into the shallow water and ran in long splashing strides toward the burning plane. It had run almost a hundred yards into the marsh before its wheels had sunk into the soft ground and its undercarriage had collapsed. The bright orange flames were reflected in the wind-ribbed waters, and there was a strong aroma of airplane fuel.

Roderick splattered around the burning wing to the nose. He could see R. S. Fairbanks sitting there, apparently unconscious. He called to the rigger: "Can you get the door open? It looks like they were knocked out!"

The rigger, shielding his face from the heat of the fire, tried to locate the main door. He called: "I got it! But it's too hot to touch!"

Roderick ran back around the wing to the side of the plane. The fire was out of control now, peeling back polished aluminum from blackened spars and ribs, and charring the sleek motors into dark carcasses. The main door was within reach, but the rigger was right. Roderick tried to touch it and the tips of his fingers were seared into blisters.

He yelled: "*Lem! Can you hear me? Lem!*"

He listened, but there was no response from inside the plane.

The rest of the mechanics and riggers were now splashing toward them across the marsh, and they had fire extinguishers and crowbars.

"The main door's red-hot already!" shouted Roderick. "Get it open—fast!"

The fire began to twist and lick at the fuselage, making a soft

427

funnely roar as it fed on wood and upholstery and airplane fuel. The riggers banged at the main door with their crowbars, and tried to prize it open, but one by one they had to step back, their faces bright red from the heat, and their best shirts scorched brown.

"Can we get in through the cockpit?" yelled Roderick. He was panicking now. The flames were spitting and crackling all along the fuselage, and at any moment the gallons of aviation fuel in the starboard wing could explode and burn all of them.

They circled around the charred wreckage of the port wing to the cockpit. They knew they were too late. The fire was already so far advanced that a man would have to be suicidal to try to rescue Lem Cosnett from the airplane's roasting shell. Once inside, he would probably never get out.

The windows of the cockpit were as brown and smoky as the mica door of a household furnace. Roderick shouted to two mechanics: "Give me a lift up here! Maybe I can get the pilot out!"

The mechanics gripped their hands together to form a step, and lifted Roderick up against the hot curved aluminum of the airplane's nose. He peered inside the open window, and he could see R. S. Fairbanks sitting almost peacefully in his seat. He shouted out: "Fairbanks! Fairbanks! You have to get out!"

He shouted again and again, but then the airplane's skin grew too hot to touch, and the mechanics had to let Roderick down onto the marshy ground again.

"I think Fairbanks is dead already," he said, his face white. "At least I hope so. I can't get him out of there. There isn't a chance."

One of the mechanics, a stocky man with wavy white hair and bright blue eyes, said: "I think we'd better move back now, Mr. Cornelius. The whole shebang's going to blow herself up in a moment."

Reluctantly Roderick said: "Okay." They splashed way through the muddy waters and tufted grass, feeling the heat of the fire on their backs, and then they stood fifty or sixty yards away to watch twelve million dollars of airplane and two lives burn into ashes. The smoke piled heavily into the sky, and the plane's framework steamed and crackled as it steadily sank into the marsh.

Almost a minute had passed when they heard what sounded at first like a bird whistling. Then they suddenly realized it was a very high-pitched human scream. Roderick felt as if he was being frozen, or as if he was numbed by whiskey. He didn't seem to be real at all. The flames were mirrored in the waters of the marsh, and someone inside the airplane was still alive!

"It's Fairbanks!" said the white-haired mechanic hoarsely. "I'll swear that's Fairbanks!"

None of them moved. They were airplane builders and they knew that there was nothing on earth they could do. The open window of the cockpit was far too small to extricate the burning pilot, and the main door of the airplane was now buckled and twisted and impossible to open. Two of the riggers actually knelt down in the waters of the marsh and prayed, and the rest of them stood with their heads bowed, hoping that R. S. Fairbanks wouldn't scream for too long.

"That fuel's going any second," warned the white-haired mechanic. "Watch it now! It's going any second!"

Through the rippling heat, Roderick could see something moving. He thought it was a fragment of burning fuselage. But then he saw it waggling up and down, and he understood—coldly and in total fear—what it actually was. By some superhuman effort, R. S. Fairbanks had actually forced his head and his shoulders out of the tiny cockpit window, and was trying to escape from the agonizing heat of the blazing plane. He had torn his scalp and his face as he pushed through the sharp aluminum frame, and one of his ears was almost severed. All the time, he was shrieking, in a voice of such desperation and pain that Roderick started to shake with terror. The fire must already be burning Fairbanks' legs, and yet his blind will to survive was so compulsive that he didn't consider that he was turning himself into a bloodied and mutilated cripple in order to escape it.

One of the riggers started to run toward the plane, but Roderick bellowed: "No!" and just as the man hesitated, the fuel in the starboard wing exploded, and chunks of fiery aluminum sprayed into the air. Roderick felt a flying fragment of hot metal graze his face, and he clapped his hands over his eyes to protect his sight. There didn't seem to be any noise—just a compression of the surrounding air, which tightened and then released itself.

Roderick walked back to his abandoned Pierce Arrow. He sat himself in the front seat and started to cry. He clutched his arms and swayed backward and forward like a child, with tears streaming down his face, and his lips curled down in a blubbering howl. He called for his mother, over and over, and after a while his mother came, driven across the grass in state in her midnight-blue

Rolls-Royce. She held his blistered and smutty hand with her own cool fingers, and let him rest his pomaded hair against her black fur coat as he twisted his necktie around and wept. "Oh, Mother, oh, Mother, oh, Mother . . ."

Johann stood a little way off, regarding with a solemn face the last few fires that flickered across the marsh. Celia stood a pace or two behind him, stroking Fortescue. At the moment, she preferred to leave her husband in the tender care of the womb that had borne him.

Johann said, without turning around: "You suspected this would happen, didn't you? It's a tragedy."

Celia stopped her stroking and raised a beautifully plucked eyebrow. "I'm not sure that I know what you mean."

Johann shrugged. "It's no use pretending. I knew what you were the day I first met you. A strong lady. I've met them before, you know. I'm even married to one. You wanted to put money into air freight and ground services, and Roderick wanted to fly planes. You were right and he was wrong. And now two innocent men have died."

"It might have flown," said Celia. Johann looked back at her over his shoulder and was both satisfied and disturbed to see that her face was quite deadpan. He grunted.

Celia stepped forward, until she and her father-in-law were side by side. "It might even have been a *success*," she said softly.

Johann shook his head. "Success comes from getting things right. From getting everything right. The motors were wrong, the decision to fly on this field was wrong, the leadership was wrong. Sooner or later, something like this was inevitable. This airplane would have died a quiet death even if it hadn't died a noisy one. I'm sorry it was so noisy."

Celia said: "It was well-insured. Overinsured, in fact, with Lloyd's."

Johann nodded. He poked his cane into the soft soil and watched muddy water fill the hole he had made.

"I'm interested in everything that happens within the Cornelius business," he said. "I took the trouble to have your order books examined. I saw, to my surprise, that you hadn't been selling airplanes at all."

Celia gave a faint smile. "I wondered when you'd notice."

Johann looked at her. "It's my business to notice."

"And are you angry?"

"Why should I be? At least you've salvaged something out of this fiasco."

"I thought you might be angry," said Celia. "I thought you might think that I wasn't giving Roderick a fair chance."

Johann took out a handkerchief. The wind and smoke had made his eyes water, and he dabbed at them carefully. "There are no fair chances in business," he said calmly. "This was Roderick's test, this airplane. It was a test of his commercial perception, but it was also a test of his ability to survive."

"He hasn't come out of it very well, has he?"

Johann pulled a face. "That depends on how you look at it. According to your books, Cornelius Airways has air-freight orders for—how much is it?—something over a million dollars. That's a twelfth of my capital investment defrayed already, apart from insurance."

Celia said: "It just seemed like a terrible risk, putting all of your investment on one airplane. That's why I went around selling air-freight services, whether we were going to ship on our own planes or someone else's."

"You're a smart lady."

Celia stroked Fortescue in a slow, almost bemused way. "I don't quite know how I'm going to break it to Roderick. But I suppose I'll manage."

"He should be pleased," said Johann.

"No, he won't be. Not at first. He'll think I didn't believe in him. He might even try to make out that it was my fault the plane didn't fly."

Johann tapped his cane against the ground. A fire wagon was jouncing across the grass, but it wasn't hurrying, and the firemen weren't even sounding the siren. Most of the fragments of the C-1 could be stamped out underfoot.

Celia said: "Does this leave Roddy stranded?"

"In what way?"

"Are you going to pass control of the business to John?"

"Why should I? He didn't come out of it very well, but *you* did. Because of you, I don't see why Roddy shouldn't take over the business when the time comes. I just want you to understand that when he does, David Bookbinder and all the senior staff will know that every decision he makes has to be discreetly vetted by you. Roddy will never know about that proviso himself. He is my son, after all, and he has little enough left to be proud of."

"Doesn't that make you feel . . . I don't know, *deceptive*?"

"Does it make *you* feel deceptive?"

Celia turned away. She didn't want to answer that question. Johann gave a short, humorless laugh and said: "There are times in all of our lives when we are deluded by others for our own good. Don't you agree?"

Celia said: "I suppose so."

Over in the Pierce Arrow, Roderick was still sobbing. Johann heard him and grimaced. Celia laid her hand on his arm and said gently: "Don't be too hard on him. It's not his fault entirely. He was trying very hard to impress you."

Johann nodded. "You're a good girl, Celia. I wish I were free to give you more."

"Free?"

Johann lowered his head. "You'll understand one day."

Celia was about to ask him when, and how, but he turned away and walked over to the car. Roderick was now patting his reddened eyes with his handkerchief and trying to tidy himself up. Hester said: "I think he'd better go home. It's been a dreadful shock. Those poor men."

Johann stared down at his son for a long moment. Then he said: "Roderick?"

Roderick kept his eyes averted and didn't answer. When Johann spoke again, his voice was a harsh, slow baritone.

"A long time ago, Roderick, I wept tears like you are doing now. But I wept them because someone had sacrificed something for me which they valued beyond price. You must never weep for yourself again. It is a luxury that not even people as rich as we are can afford."

Johann didn't wait for his son to reply. Roderick couldn't possibly have anything to say which would interest him, in any case. He walked back to his mud-splattered Rolls-Royce and disappeared inside. Hester kissed Roderick briefly on the forehead and followed him. The chauffeur closed the door. It was like a door that had closed in 1903. As they backed up, turned, and drove away, the smoke from the burning C-1 dirtied the skies behind them, and the last few fires glowed on the marshes like the fires of a primitive settlement. It rained again, harder this time, a faceful of wire rods, and Celia had to drive the Pierce Arrow back toward the hangar, with Roderick sitting numbly beside her in the front seat.

Raindrops hung on the tip of his nose and the lobes of his ears like three diamond pendants.

On the first day of April, 1939, in the same week that President Roosevelt approved the plans for two 45,000-ton battleships, Hope was married in Hartford, Connecticut, to Martin Landseer. After the ceremony, thirty-five cars took two hundred and fifty guests back to the Landseer house, where they danced on the lawn to most of Benny Goodman's orchestra, which had been dressed for the occasion in yellow blazers and white ducks, which they had to give back later. Hope appeared to be joyously happy, although Philip Strachan did say that perhaps she was hysterically happy. She twirled her way from guest to guest, laughing and chattering and drinking too much champagne. Martin trailed around after her with a bashful smile, and he was asked by one bitchy young thing with kiss-curls and an off-the-shoulder dress: "Haven't I seen you in *Snow White*?"

Hope wore a fashionable crinoline dress with flounces and bows, and as she circled the lawn, her head thrown back and her eyes alight, she looked as if she was starring in a glamorous movie of her own life.

Johann was testy and irritable that day. He disliked weddings intensely, and he particularly disliked the Landseers. It was only because his own daughter was getting married and because Mrs. Landseer was a long-standing friend of Hester's that he came at all. When he stood in church and gave Hope away he looked as miserable as Robert Taylor when Greta Garbo died in *Camille*, and afterward, when a fussy fat woman told him that he hadn't lost a daughter but gained a son, he said: "Madam, I would rather have contracted hepatitis."

There was a five-tier cake, with silver horseshoes and silver bells, and photographers with Kodak plate cameras popped off flashbulbs like Chinese firecrackers. A cub reporter from the Hartford papers asked Hope how she was going to spend her time now she was Mrs. Hope Cornelius Landseer, and she answered with a voice as pealing and gentle as a nunnery bell: "I'm going to look after my husband, in every way."

There was a curious feeling in the air. The clouds were as thick and high as cliffs. Johann and Hester had flown over Flushing Meadow in their private DC-3 on their way to Connecticut, and had looked out over the glittering sprawl of the New York World's Fair, all ready for opening in three weeks' time. The Trylon had cast its seven-hundred-foot shadow like the pointer of a sundial. Now Johann was standing on the veranda of the Landseer house in a gray top hat and morning suit, masticating a slice of wedding cake as if it was baked from dust. Beside him Mr. Landseer was pink around the ears and telling Johann endlessly and tediously that they were both fathers-in-law together, correct, and how they ought to play regular rounds of golf out at Hurstview Golf Course, because Mr. Landseer was a member, and it was a fine course. Johann said he knew it was a fine course because he owned it. He then asked Mr. Landseer why he didn't buy himself a monocle that didn't keep dropping out. The band played "In the Mood." One of the young men at the reception had fought in Spain and was telling a butterfly crowd of girls how he had ridden horseback through the bombs and shrapnel at Caldetas and just reached the harbor in time to catch the *Omaha* as it steamed away with American evacuees. Hope went around in her crinoline dress like the clockwork doll on the top of a jewelry box. The sun went in and out behind the clouds, so that the afternoon was sometimes as flat as a newspaper picture, and sometimes bright and sparkling with flags and trumpets and bottles of champagne. In spite of the sunshine, Johann knew that America was preparing to lay down two of the world's biggest battleships, at a cost of ninety million dollars each, and that there was probably going to be war.

United States Attorney Godfrey K. Prescott was in his long steamy greenhouse when his wife came to the door and called him. He was a dahlia fanatic, and he grew the best blooms that New Rochelle had ever seen. He regularly won prizes, and his red-brick chimneypiece was clustered with rosettes and honorable mentions.

"Can't it wait?" he said irritably. "Can't you get the fellow to call back?"

"Dear, he said it was quite urgent. It's to do with McKesson & Robbins."

Prescott sighed and peeled off his rubber gardening gloves. He walked back to the house in his striped apron and went into the sitting room through the French doors. Sunlight fell in bright trapeziums across the velvet-covered antique furniture, and the silver presentation cigarette box winked at him from the table. He picked up the telephone and said: "Yes?"

There was a crackly silence. Then a low, hoarse voice said: "Is this Mr. Prescott, the U.S. attorney?"

"That's right."

"Well, I have some information for you. I guarantee it's good stuff. I'd like to meet you someplace and talk it over."

Prescott ran his hand through his black wavy hair. "Can't you tell me now?" he asked his informant. "Are you calling from home?"

"I'm calling from a bar in New York City. I can't tell you too much right now."

"Give me a general idea."

The man coughed. Somewhere in the background, Prescott could hear the sounds of music and laughter.

"Just a rough outline," insisted Prescott.

"Well, it's about Phil Musica. You've been asking what his outside connections were."

"That's right."

"I can name his main connection. I can prove it, too."

"What else?"

"I can definitely tie Musica in with Dutch Schultz, and I can tie Dutch in with Musica's main connection."

Prescott reached across to the cigarette box and took out a Lucky Strike. He lit it awkwardly with the Regency-style lighter, and puffed blue smoke across the slanting shafts of sun.

"What kind of evidence do you have there?"

The man said: "Wait one." Then, after a pause he said: "I got letters and papers and contracts. But it's worth something."

"How much is something?" asked Prescott.

"Five g's."

Prescott sucked at his cigarette. "That's a lot of lettuce for one name."

The man said: "It's a big name, Mr. Prescott. It's worth every penny."

Prescott thought for a moment. Then he said: "All right. Where can we meet? Can you get yourself out of the city without attracting attention?"

"I think so."

"Get up here right away, then," said Prescott.

"You'll have the money?"

"Not right away, but if the information's good, I'll give you a personal check and a signed guarantee."

The informant didn't say any more, but promptly replaced his receiver. Prescott held his telephone in front of him for a moment, as if he expected it to say something else, but then he laid it back on its cradle and went back outside. His wife, reclining on a striped deck chair, said: "Anything interesting, dear?"

He shook his head. "I don't know. The fellow's coming here later, and then I'll see."

His wife said in mild exasperation: "Not another gangster? I don't think the neighborhood's gotten over that awful Gizzi man yet."

Prescott smoked his cigarette. "It's to do with Philip Musica. It could be a break."

"I see, dear. Well, I just hope the man's not too rough, or too flashy, or something."

Prescott went back to his greenhouse. He had been working on the Musica case ever since the McKesson & Robbins scandal had broken, and he was still convinced that Musica had had secret connections in big business. Masquerading under the name of F. Donald Coster, the onetime gangster Musica had used the reputable drug house of McKesson & Robbins as a front for embezzlement and the export of airplanes, armaments, food, and blankets to foreign countries. At one time Coster-Musica had tried to export two million rifles.

In spite of the scale of his rackets, the seemingly respectable head of McKesson & Robbins had fooled bankers, investors, and accountants for years; and Prescott was convinced that somewhere along the line he had taken expert guidance from some *éminence grise* with a genius for swindles. Musica was undeniably a major-league embezzler, and during the early 1930's he had close connections with Dutch Schultz, but it took style and imagination and limitless resources of ready money to do what Musica had done, and Prescott knew that Musica had none of those assets at his disposal. There had to be a contact in Wall Street.

Musica's own version would never be heard. When police had arrived to arrest him in January at his stately house in Fairfield, Connecticut, he had promptly committed suicide. Godfrey Prescott often considered that Musica might have felt it more prudent to silence himself painlessly than to have his big business contact do it the hard way.

During the length of the afternoon, he potted fresh plants, and the sun dropped down behind the gabled roofs of his house. At five o'clock he checked his watch and began to tidy up for the day. As it turned out, his informant never arrived in New Rochelle, and Prescott never heard from him again. During the days and weeks that followed, Prescott often sat at his desk and wondered what the man might have had to say; but like all officers of justice, he was patient and calm and inured to the casual and constant presence of sudden death.

1940

President Roosevelt tells us that there is always give-and-take when it comes to allocating military contracts. Well, let me ask him this: Who's doing the giving, and who's doing the taking?

—Senator H. K. Hubslager,
April 12, 1940

A warm spring wind was ruffling the palms along the driveway as the long white Cadillac Imperial sedan swept silently toward the house. It circled the ornamental fountains, watched with hushed anticipation by the assembled staff of thirty footmen, maids, cooks, and cleaners, their white jackets and overalls starched as crisp as cuttlefish shells, their hair combed and gleaming, and their eyes screwed up against the morning sun. The sedan came to a stop in front of them, and they stood as stiff and straight as they could while the fawn-uniformed chauffeur smartly opened the door and lowered the carriage step.

Johann, the leg of his light gray suit raised far enough to reveal the oddly endearing sight of his summer combinations tucked into the top of his silk socks, stepped heavily and carefully down from the car, and then supported himself on his cane while the chauffeur helped Hester. He was looking sallow and tired, and hunched, and he put on his hat with the slow care of an old man.

Hester took Johann's arm, and turned to face the staff with a bright smile. She had reached the age of forty-eight with energy, strength, and that radiant dignity that is peculiar to the wealthy and the self-assured in middle age. She wore a simple spring coat in primrose-colored wild silk, and a wide-brimmed hat to match. Her eyes were hidden behind dark sunglasses, but only because she found it impossible to sleep on airplanes, and they were red from eyestrain.

They looked, as they stood there on the raked brown gravel, like a proud and happy old couple, and the staff spontaneously greeted them with a spatter of applause.

Radec, their butler, came forward in his swallowtail coat and bow tie, and dipped his big round head respectfully.

"Nice to see you, Radec," said Johann in a thick, warm voice. "How's the chili today?"

"I hope, better than ever," answered Radec, displaying two ranks of glittering white dentures. "Miguel has been fussing here, fussing there, meat, chilies, vegetables, ever since he heard sir was

441

coming. And madam, too, forgive me. You are looking as beautiful as ever, madam."

"I could use a brandy-and-soda," said Johann, and he leaned on Hester to help him toward the house. "I feel as dry as a hole in the desert."

Behind them, Max Wemmer, the vice-president of Cornelius Oil California, was waltzing about in his red-and-white blazer and white golf cap like an animated barber pole, directing the removal of Johann and Hester's sealskin luggage from the trunk of the Cadillac. A visit from the Almighty himself was an exciting and nerve-wracking rarity these days for the Cornelius staff out on the Coast, especially since Johann had been kept busy in New York for over a year by the worsening of Hitler's war and all the complicated business problems that went with it. There was sunken shipping to worry about, trade embargoes to worry about, requisitioned warehouses and goods to worry about, and it was only now that Johann had allowed Hester and his doctors to persuade him to take a short vacation at Carina Mia, his secluded twenty-five-bedroom Spanish palace outside of Pasadena.

Inside the house, it was cool and dark. Their footsteps echoed on the polished marble floors. There was a soft rustle of palms from the gardens, and the plashing of waterfalls. The staff were chosen, and well-paid, for their quietness and their discretion, and they hurried here and there in a busy hush.

"I'll take my drink on the balcony," said Johann, handing Radec his hat. "Are you going to freshen up, my dear?"

Hester took off her dark glasses. "I want to take a bath and lie down for a while, unless you need me. Radec . . . can you get Maria to open the green bedroom? It won't be so hot there."

Johann leaned forward and kissed Hester on the forehead. He clutched her hand and squeezed it. "I'm going to do what you asked," he told her. "I'm going to sit down and have myself a good peaceful vacation. I guess I deserve it."

"You're not the only one." Hester smiled. She had spent the last six months feverishly fund-raising for one of Eleanor Roosevelt's welfare committees, and the prospect of relaxing at Carina Mia, with its Turkish baths and pools and restful rooms, seemed like bliss.

Max Wemmer came in, his heels clicking on the floor, his vacation smile tacked firmly into place.

"Okay, sir, that's everything. If you need me, I'll be downstairs in the office. I'm just going to sort out the day's trading figures for you, and then get those oil estimates you asked for."

Hester looked at Johann rather sadly. "You asked for oil estimates?" she said.

Johann coughed and tapped his cane on the floor, abashed. "I need to know what the rest of the fellows are doing, even if I don't do anything myself."

"Well, you take care," chided Hester, and kissed him. Maria, her red-haired and elegant Italian secretary, had arrived now, a divine Botticelli in a pale green linen suit, and curtsied a greeting, and so Hester said: "I'll see you later, when I feel less like a stranded lobster."

Johann, fastidiously escorted by Radec, walked across the wide hall to the elevator, and he stood patiently still while they rose to the second floor.

"It's been more than a year now, hasn't it?" asked Johann, as Radec rattled back the gold-painted trellis gates.

Radec nodded. "We understand, sir. We don't feel abandoned. All the staff were very pleased with their Christmas gifts, sir."

"I gave you a gold Larkwood pen, didn't I? Do you like it?"

Radec bowed his head in pleasure. "It's very fine, sir, but it's even finer that you remember what you gave me."

Johann smiled without answering. Every head butler in every one of his houses had received a gold Larkwood pen; but winning the confidence of his personal staff, the people who actually cared for his clothes and his food and his aging body, was becoming an increasingly pertinent pursuit. He would be sixty-seven this year, and he was beginning to feel increasingly weary and increasingly short of breath.

"We have a print of *Ninotchka* in the house, sir, if you want to watch it sometime," said Radec.

"Yes, I might," said Johann. "Isn't that the picture with Garbo laughing?"

Radec walked with him along the marble-flagged upper corridor, in which was hung one of the largest private collections of Goya sketches in the world. Through the yellow-tinted Spanish glass, Johann could see the distorted outlines of the San Gabriel mountains, and the deep blue sky was turned to watery green. He had always liked this house in Pasadena; it was spacious and secluded and almost monastic. It would be easy to spend the rest of his life in its cool rooms, meditating and sleeping, and listening at night to the soft katabatic winds from the mountains.

The butler opened the double carved doors that gave out onto the balcony room. This was one of Johann's favorite retreats, one of the few places where he could sit and relax and relish being rich. It was decorated in rich Mexican colors—reds and greens and golds—with a dark blue mosaic floor that had been taken piece by piece from the sixteenth-century Church of San Carlos del Rincón in Oaxaca and reconstructed here. Along one wall was a deceptively simple oak table, waxed to such depths that Johann always felt he could drown in it, set with white ceramic dishes of guava, papaya, and pineapple. The story went that the table had been sawn from the deck boards of one of Sir Francis Drake's galleons, and that it was stained in English sailors' blood.

It was the view from the balcony itself, though, that made the room so serene. It looked out over the subtropical gardens that surrounded Carina Mia, an eighty-acre paradise of roses and orchids and magnolia, with glades and waterfalls and winding pathways. In the distance were the tiled rooftops of La Canada, and the sandy-colored mountains, and the haze of a California morning.

Johann walked to the edge of the balcony and propped his stick against the pierced-stone balustrade. He took a deep breath of mountain air and closed his eyes.

"You're tired, sir?" asked Radec solicitously. "Your drink is coming up right away."

Johann opened his eyes and looked out over the gardens. A sprinkler was twirling around and around, shedding diamonds all over the closely shaved lawns. He gave a small, wry smile.

"Tiredness is only relative to how much work you have to do," he said in a husky voice.

"You can rest here, sir, surely? For a week or so?"

"Well, I'm supposed to. But this war is keeping us pretty busy. We're caught between the government on one hand, pushing for all the nitrates we can produce and all the oil we can pump up and all the ships and airplanes we can build, and the Germans on the other hand, confiscating our goods in Europe and sinking half our consignments and blowing up what they don't steal. I just heard this morning that the Luftwaffe bombed the Savage Hotel in London last night—bombed it flat. Apart from the fact that it was the only hotel in London worth staying at, I happened to own sixty-six percent of it.''

Radec went across the balcony and brought up Johann's chair, a big rattan peacock chair with its seat upholstered in Mexican tapestry. Johann eased himself into it, and sat there for a while in silence, a small reflective smile on his face, listening to the gentle sounds of the garden. One of the footmen came in with a glass of brandy-and-soda for him on a silver tray and set it down beside him with a dish of salted black olives.

"It's just like I remembered," Johann said quietly.

Radec nodded. "It's yours, sir, and it always springs to life when you come back here."

Johann said: "Did I ever tell you why I called it Carina Mia?"

Radec coughed politely behind his fist. He had started his career as a waiter at the Hotel Tarnow, in Warsaw, where Polish aristocracy had once eaten, in one evening, four hundred quail in black-currant sauce, and danced polkas on the tables, and he knew how to cope with the oblique conversation of the rich.

"Yes, sir. I remember it was a touching story."

"It wasn't completely true, the way I told it."

"No, sir?"

Johann picked up his glass. He paused for a while, his eyes staring blankly at the bubbles that rose to the rim. Then he said: "I don't suppose it matters, though, what's true and what isn't. Not after thirty-seven years."

Radec waited, immaculately posed, for Johann to say something else, but when he didn't, and it was plain that he wasn't going to, the butler softly clicked his heels and prepared to withdraw. He had almost reached the door when the telephone rang. He diverted himself toward it like a deflected torpedo, and lifted it out of its gilded cradle.

"Mr. Cornelius' residence."

He listened for a moment, and then placed his hand over the receiver.

"It's a call for you, sir. Said to be personal."

Johann shook his head. "I'm not taking calls now. Take a message and give it to Max Wemmer."

Radec spoke into the phone again, and then said: "It's Mr. Jack Field, sir. Apparently he's calling from the front gatehouse."

"Jack Field? I don't believe it! Give me that phone!"

Radec brought the telephone over and set it on Johann's table.

He tugged a clean linen square out of his breast pocket and quickly buffed up the receiver before handing it over.

Johann said: "Jack? Is that you?"

There was a crackle, and then a familiar voice said: "Hi, Johann. I just dropped by to pass the time of day. Can I come on up?"

"You came to Pasadena to pass the time of day? I thought you were based in Washington now."

"Well, that's right. But your office told me you were here, and I was kind of anxious to see you."

Johann smiled. "The way I hear it, you don't have *anything* to be anxious about these days. They tell me you're doing pretty good."

Jack laughed. "No complaints. But listen, if this is a bad moment, I can come back in the morning. I didn't realize you'd only just arrived."

Johann shook his head. "No, Jack, you come on up. I'll have the guard open the gate, then what you do is drive around to the left side of the house, around by the fountain, and park there. It's about a half-mile. What do you feel like drinking?"

"My throat tells me a collins."

"I'll see you in five minutes."

Johann set down the phone, and then dialed the house switchboard to put him through to Hester. She was soaking in the tub, but every bathroom at Carina Mia had a telephone.

"What's so urgent?" she asked him.

"Guess who just arrived, unexpected?"

"Don't tell me David Bookbinder. I couldn't bear it."

"No, no, nobody like that. Jack Field."

"Jack Field? But that's wonderful! I must come on down. Did he say why he called?"

"Just a passing visit, as far as I can tell."

"Is Ellie with him?"

"I didn't ask."

"Oh, Johann. That's typical of you. You're quite useless."

Johann grunted. "Maybe I am. But you're the only person in the world who's allowed to say so."

In a while Johann heard a short, discreet knock at the door. Radec went to answer it, while Johann reached for his cane and lifted himself strenuously to his feet, his brandy-and-soda in one hand, his back as straight as he could manage. Jack Field, in a snappy double-breasted white suit and a black-and-white-striped tie, came breezing in with a wide smile.

"Johann!" He grinned and took Johann's arm in a firm, friendly grip. "It's real good to see you. Real good."

Jack Field, in his early fifties, was fit and tanned as a yachting instructor, although his wavy brown hair was graying now, and his cheeks were engraved with the lines of a man who had fought very hard and very bitterly to get what he wanted. Johann saw the struggles of Jack's career marked on his face, but he also recognized that tensile bearing that comes with great confidence and great success. From an awkward and muddled beginning in 1921, through near-bankruptcy in 1929, Jack had built up one of the finest law practices on the eastern seaboard, Field-Babson-Field, with Oliver Babson, the eccentric genius of tax law, and his own son, Randy Field. Jack Field's personal fees for a business brief were now so high that *Fortune* remarked laconically that "it is probably the greater economy to defend your own case and lose than have Jack Field as your advocate and win."

The footman brought in drinks and nuts, and Jack and Johann settled themselves down on the balcony, smiling at each other with the kind of shy pleasure that comes from meeting an old friend. They hadn't seen each other for over three years, although they still exchanged Christmas cards, and Hester occasionally met Ellie at charity committees.

"Is Ellie not with you?" asked Johann.

"No, no. She's spending a month in South Carolina, looking up relatives. She's just as lovely as ever, I'm pleased to say."

"And Randy?"

"He's okay. He's doing pretty well. In fact, he's thinking of moving out here to California. Either Los Angeles or San Francisco."

"You still look as if leaving Cornelius Oil was the best thing that ever happened to you."

Jack stirred the ice in his drink. "I don't regret it, Johann. Any of it."

Johann coughed. "I'm glad of that. They tell me you're a very high-powered fellow these days. What's next? The Supreme Court?"

"Not for me. I'd rather argue than decide."

Johann raised his glass. "I'll drink to that."

There was a small silence. They smiled at each other. Then

Johann said: "I suppose I ought to be using your services, seeing as how you're the best damned lawyer around. Do you give discounts to friends?"

Jack laughed. "Do *you*?"

"Certainly. Anytime you need a few thousand barrels of crude, just let me know."

Jack smiled at that, but the smile didn't stay on his face for very long. He took a taste of his drink, and then he looked at Johann seriously and worriedly. A breeze made the palms in the garden rustle and hiss, and the flowers nodded in crimson agitation.

Johann said: "You've got something on your mind."

Jack pulled an apologetic face.

"Well," said Johann expansively, "I guess it's kind of hard to visit your friends these days for the sake of friendship alone. We're all too busy."

Jack said: "What I've come for . . . well, I hope you'll see that it *is* friendship."

Johann didn't look at him. Instead, he narrowed his eyes and peered across the valley at the mountains, as if he was expecting a smoke signal or a heliograph message from distant peaks.

"The truth is that the government is looking for some kind of scapegoat right now," said Jack.

"Scapegoat? What for?"

"It's the war, I guess. There's been a lot of pressure from the left about kickbacks and racketeering on military contracts. It's public money, after all. And there's a pretty determined group of senators who want to make a name for themselves by catching some big corporation paying out bribes to Army and Navy and Air Force officials."

Johann nodded reflectively. "I think David Bookbinder mentioned something about that. Senator Hubslager was one. David calls him the Whining Example."

"That's the man. Well, he's determined to make a public circus out of prosecuting half the Pentagon and any big business concerns he can catch with egg on their face. He says we can't criticize the Germans and the Japanese until we put our own morals in order."

"Who does he think he is? Saint Peter?"

Jack shrugged. "It doesn't matter if he thinks he's God. He's chosen the right moment to kick up about corruption, and Roosevelt would rather toss him a small fish to keep him quiet than stir up a lot of mucky water trying to deny that defense contracts have occasionally been awarded on the basis of golf-club memberships and vacations in Bermuda, instead of by open tender.''

Johann frowned. Jack, looking at him, thought how tired and old he was these days. The balcony was so quiet that he could hear his watch ticking.

Jack said uncomfortably: "Last week—at the end of last week—I was approached by Senator Jorkins. He and Hubslager have been crusading together for years. Jorkins asked me to put together a draft prosecution case against two leading corporations, so that they could assess which case they could most effectively proceed with. One of those corporations was Rehoboth Engineering.''

Johann looked up. Rehoboth Engineering was building six motor torpedo boats for the U.S. Navy and over thirty landing craft for the U.S. Marines. It was owned jointly by Cornelius Shipping and Kosket Finance, both of which were major Cornelius companies.

"What's the other corporation?" asked Johann.

Jack shook his head. "I'm sorry, but that's confidential.''

"You're not proceeding with the cases, are you?''

"Of course not. I had to declare my interest in Cornelius corporations and turn the whole thing down. It's gone to Usher-Oppenheim-Clark, as far as I know.''

"Did Jorkins tell you what kind of angle they're going for?''

Jack nodded. "That's why I flew here today. I think you're in for a rough ride. They know about your deals with Eddie Corcoran in the Navy Department over the 35,000-tonners, and they also know about Admiral Messenger.''

"What about him?''

"Well, I expect you recall what he said to the Navy specifications people. 'I'd rather face the Germans with one motor torpedo boat built by Rehoboth than fifty built by Norfolk.' ''

Johann couldn't help smiling. "Yeah, that *was* pretty exaggerated, wasn't it? But everybody knows that Admiral Messenger has his own way of putting things. He's a national hero, and if you're a national hero, you're allowed to be eccentric.''

"Eccentric, yes—corrupt, no.''

"What do you mean?''

"I mean that Hubslager knows that you paid the admiral twenty thousand dollars to build a new vacation home at Narragansett.''

Johann thought about this, and then spread his hands as if to say: Well, what's twenty thousand dollars between friends? "If a big corporation happens to build a home for a great and respected American, what's wrong about that?" he asked rhetorically.

Jack sat up and fixed his eyes on Johann with all the intentness that Johann could still remember from the day he had quit Cornelius Oil.

"It's not the house, Johann. You could have gotten away with that. You could have come clean, and said you made a genuine mistake, and contritely given the house to some needy old widow instead."

Johann smiled. "You're still the same old Jack, aren't you?"

"Not quite," said Jack. "Because I don't have any ideas at all about how you're going to explain away the boys."

Johann didn't move, didn't speak, as if he was expecting Jack to say something more. Then he raised his eyes and said dryly: "What boys?"

Jack stared at Johann blankly, trying to work out if he was joking, or lying, or playing some kind of elaborate game.

"You really don't know?" he said, and his disbelief was plain.

Johann shook his head. "If I knew, Jack, I wouldn't ask you. We've known each other too long for hedging. Besides, I have to say that you're the only man alive to whom it is no pleasure at all to lie."

Jack stood up and walked to the balustrade of the balcony. As he did so, two ground doves flew up from the bushes, their wings flickering red in the clear sunlight. He sat on the balustrade and reached into his inside pocket for a brown envelope, which he carefully opened.

"If you really don't know about this," he said quietly, "I'm afraid that you're due for a bad surprise."

"Not much surprises me these days," retorted Johann, and held out his hand for the envelope.

He took out a dozen black-and-white photographs, obviously taken under difficult lighting conditions. They showed a shadowy bedroom with a wide four-poster bed, on which lay an elderly man and three young boys, none of whom could have been older than fifteen. They were all naked, like plucked guinea fowl, and the photographs showed them in one sexual pose after another. The most graphic picture of all showed the elderly man lying on his back, deeply penetrating a young boy who lay on top of him with

450

his legs held up in the air by his friends. The elderly man was clearly recognizable as Admiral Messenger.

Johann numbly returned the photographs to their envelope and handed them back. He said in a tight voice: "You'd better explain."

Jack tucked the pictures back in his pocket. "It's very simple," he said. "In return for his help in securing the motor-torpedo-boat contract for Rehoboth Engineering, Admiral Messenger was not only given a house by his good friends at Cornelius Shipping. He was given some houseguests as well. These three boys were procured by one of your executives and driven around to Narragansett one weekend for your great and eccentric national hero to play with. The only problem was that Senator Hubslager had your executive tailed by private detectives, who took these pictures. Worse than that, two of the boys have been traced, and are quite willing to say in court that they were forcibly abducted, that they were forcibly seduced, and that it was a Cornelius Shipping man who arranged it."

Johann swallowed as if he had a cactus in his throat. He said: "I didn't know about this, Jack. I didn't have any idea."

"Would it have made any difference if you had?"

Johann glanced up sharply. "Do you want an honest answer to that, or a moral one?"

"You don't have to answer at all. It's not my place to judge what you do. I've probably done worse myself, morally speaking."

Johann ran his hand tiredly through his hair. "The honest answer is that I might have considered it. But I can't believe those boys were anything else than just what they look like. Young whores. I don't believe anybody got themselves abducted or seduced, forcibly or otherwise. Those boys went because they were paid, and they probably enjoyed themselves as much as Admiral Messenger. That doesn't mean to say that it doesn't sicken me, or that it doesn't disgust me, because it does. It makes my flesh creep to think that we had anything to do with it. But how the hell can Hubslager expect to make an example of Cornelius Shipping if all he has to show is dirty pictures and two male whores?"

Jack slowly shook his head from side to side. "You're wrong, Johann, and you know it. By the time those two male whores get put up in front of a court of law, they're going to have their hair perked up and their Eton collars on, and if they tell the judge that the dirtiest thing they ever did before meeting your wily Cornelius

Shipping man was trip over their hoops and muddy their knickerbockers, then he's going to believe them. And so is every decent Christian parent from Narragansett, Rhode Island, to Gravity, Iowa. This prosecution isn't just a case of business corruption. That's nothing to get the public worked up about. It's to do with morals, and scandal, and it's been a long time since the public had a good meaty scandal to get their virtuous teeth into. This is going to be very bad news for you, Johann, and that's why I came to warn you."

Johann took a deep breath. "Well," he said gently, "I appreciate it."

"I'm just returning a great many old favors." .

Johann called: "Radec!"

"Yes, sir?"

"Get Mr. Bookbinder on the telephone, right away."

Jack said: "I don't want you to do anything rash, Johann. They haven't made up their minds if they're going to go ahead yet."

"What do you mean by rash?"

"Well, nothing. But I've heard that David Bookbinder tends to take . . . well, overdecisive action."

"Overdecisive?"

"Oh, come on, Johann, you know what I mean. There are one or two stories around about what happens to people who get in his way."

Johann finished his drink and then swirled the ice around in his glass. "Yes, I suppose there are. But you needn't worry. If anyone is going to take overdecisive action in this particular instance, it's going to be me."

"Why don't you call Hubslager direct? Maybe you can mark out some middle ground."

"Middle ground? The only ground I'm going to mark out with him is the ground I'm going to bury him in. Politically speaking, of course. If he has the goddamned self-righteousness to—"

"Johann," interrupted Jack. "This is serious. Really serious. You could find yourself out of Washington, out of society, out of all your committees, out of shipping, out of government contracts, you name it. This country will turn any number of blind eyes to bribery, and extortion, and graft, but it won't tolerate anything to do with sex. Even if those boys are shown up for the male whores they very probably are, you still can't win! They'll say that you corrupted a grand old sailor for the sake of your own grubby profits, that you buy and sell children for sex, that you're a pimp and a pervert! You can't take that kind of publicity, Johann; nor can your business reputation. You can beat up strikers, you can even have business rivals assassinated. But if you get the mark of sexual corruption on you, it's going to take years and years to wash it clean."

Johann said nothing. His chin was lowered on his stiff white collar, and his mouth was creased downward in serious thought.

Jack said: "If nothing else, Johann, think of Hester. Think of Roddy and John and Hope. If you don't come to some kind of compromise with Hubslager, if you don't give him some kind of concession, he's going to make sure that he drags all of you down. How could Hester walk into a charity-committee meeting with the papers full of that kind of stuff?"

Johann raised an eyebrow. "Hester's a strong woman," he said simply.

"I know that," said Jack kindly. "But she doesn't have to go through something like this. I'm thinking of all of you, Johann. I really am."

Johann toyed with an olive. "What kind of concessions do you think Hubslager would find attractive?"

"I'm not sure. But he might be persuaded to look more favorably on Cornelius Shipping if he's promised some kind of future support."

"What kind of future support?"

"Campaign contributions might do it. Or it might be enough if you promise to ease off your political opposition to organized labor."

Johann's eyes widened. "And he's trying to take *us* to the cleaners for corruption?"

Jack said: "That's the way of the world, Johann. Corruption is only what the other fellow does."

"Have you talked to Hubslager personally? You're not mixed up in this, are you?"

Jack shook his head. "As far as I'm concerned, the whole thing stinks like a dead catfish. But we're friends, Johann, you and I. You got me started, you paid me well, and you never stood in my way when I really wanted out. You're much more appreciative of people, and much kinder, and much more sensitive, than most of your staff or your friends will ever realize. And I guess that's why I'm here today, saying what I'm saying now."

Johann lifted his head. Then, slowly, he held out his hand, and Jack took it. For a long time they clasped hands together, looking into each other's eyes, partly with comradeship, partly with mystification at their own selves and their friendship, and partly as a recognition that they could only hold hands for a brief moment before each of them would have to face the consequences, bitter or happy, of his own life.

"Okay," said Johann. "But I'm still going to bury Hubslager. Deeper than a goddamned sugar-pine root."

Just then the door opened and Hester came in, wearing a long silk robe and a red-and-yellow head scarf.

"Jack," she said, holding out her arms. "Such a pleasure to see you!"

After dinner that evening, Johann retired to bed early and left Hester and Jack in the drawing room. They sat on the rich leather Chesterfield in the shaded light of Mexican brass lamps, finishing their coffee and liqueurs and talking quietly. Around them, on the shadowy walls, hung dark portraits of Spanish heroes, bewhiskered and cuirassed, and plants in hanging baskets. Through the half-open doors they could hear the soft hesitant sound of a plectrum-plucked guitar, as one of the trio who had entertained them during dinner played a gentle romantic melody.

"It's almost too restful for comfort," said Jack. "I bet you wish you could stay here forever."

"Sometimes." Hester smiled, pouring him another cup of coffee. "But I think I'd miss the cut-and-thrust of New York society, wouldn't you? You have no idea how keenly it sharpens the mind, all that social skulduggery."

Jack, looking handsome and oddly boyish in his tuxedo and black tie, said: "You never seem like the kind of woman to bother with etiquette and pecking orders and bringing out your daughter."

"On the contrary, I adore it. My mother gave dozens of parties when I was a child, and she always used to keep me up-to-date on who was acceptable, and who wasn't, and why. Johann wasn't at all acceptable when I first met him, but I suppose that was part of the attraction. I was a very forward young girl, you know, and the idea of having a very rich husband with the manners of a sodbuster rather appealed to me."

She smiled at the memory. "He seemed very masculine after all those Harvard lounge lizards, and I suppose I thought I could tame him. I did, in a way. But I never wanted him to get *too* civilized. Hope says that I must have had a Fay Wray complex, whatever that is. I suppose she means that I preferred King Kong to King George."

Jack laughed. "You'd better not let Johann hear you say that."

She brushed back her hair. "He wouldn't mind. He does have a sense of humor, you know, even if it is a bit biblical."

"He seems tired."

Hester nodded. "It's the war. He's been working too hard. I wish he'd delegate more, but he won't. Roderick's been pleading to take over the chemicals side, but I don't think Johann really trusts him. He's on the airplane and boat side now, Roderick, and I'm sure he's underemployed. Compared with Johann, anyway."

"Does Roderick run Rehoboth Engineering?"

"I believe so, yes. Yes, he does."

"Since when?"

"A year or so, maybe longer. Why?"

Jack rubbed at his cheek thoughtfully. This was going to be difficult to put into words, and he wasn't even sure that he ought to try. But he was already worried that Johann was going to be far too inflexible with Senator Hubslager, in a situation that could be solved only by compromise and crocodile tears. He said a little uncertainly: "How much notice does Johann take of what you say?"

"*Notice*?" said Hester. She looked at him curiously. Her diamond pendant earrings caught the lamplight for a second, two sparkling showers of brilliant gemstones. She was wearing a fashionably wasp-waisted evening dress in pale lavender satin, and there was a fragrance about her that made Jack realize how much he missed Ellie.

"I didn't mean to be rude," Jack said hastily. "What I meant was, if there was a difficult problem that needed very special handling, do you think you could persuade Johann to treat it with a little less than his usual zeal?"

Hester put her coffee cup back on the silver bird-cage tray. She had suspected that Jack's visit wasn't entirely social, and now she knew she was right. Very quietly she said: "You'd better tell me what's gone wrong."

"Well, it's early days yet," said Jack. "But it looks like Senator Hubslager is putting together a bribery-and-corruption case against Rehoboth Engineering and Cornelius Shipping."

"Bribery and corruption? But what are they supposed to have done?"

"I can't tell you all of it. It's too damned nasty. But it's a lot to do with kickbacks and rigged tenders for military contracts. All I *can* say is that it's potentially dynamite, and that's why I had to come and talk to Johann personally. I wanted him to understand that lowering his head and charging straight for Senator Hubslager's solar plexus is the worst possible thing he could do."

Hester's eyes darkened a little. They were very brown, very intense. She said: "How nasty is too damned nasty?"

"Nasty enough to make the name of Cornelius take on the social odor of soiled laundry."

"Well, *what*? I'm not a child, Jack. I do know something of the world's less savory side."

Jack colored. "I know that, Hester. It's just that if Roderick's running Rehoboth, then he's ultimately responsible for what happened, and it's kind of hard for anyone to tell a mother that her son has been ultimately responsible for something as bad as this."

Hester was sitting very upright. In the next room, the guitar was picking out the sad melody of "Aguascalientes," and a spidery shadow revolved across the whitewashed wall as a soft draft turned one of the plants in its basket. She said in a measured voice: "I would never say this to anyone else, Jack, but Roddy is not ultimately responsible, in any real sense, for very many of his own decisions. Roddy's a builder, you know. A dreamer. But he's not a decision-maker. Most of his really important policy comes from Celia. She's a very hard, capable girl, and I'm afraid that she often takes the place of Roddy's spine."

Jack was embarrassed. He hadn't wanted to force Hester into having to say anything like that, either about Johann or any of her children. He liked Roderick, although he was quite aware of how soft he was, and Ellie got on well with Celia. But even if Roderick hadn't been personally responsible for sending those boy whores to Admiral Messenger, his weakness had enmeshed his mother and his father in what could turn out to be the worst big business scandal in years.

Jack said: "Whoever was actually responsible, the whole Cornelius organization is going to have to carry the can back, and that means Johann. Someone bribed Admiral Messenger into supporting Rehoboth's tender for motor torpedo boats by procuring three young boy prostitutes for him. Senator Hubslager has full details—even photographs—to prove it."

"And of course Johann wants to tear Senator Hubslager's head off," said Hester.

"You're not shocked?" asked Jack.

Hester held her hands demurely in her lap. "No, Jack, I'm not shocked. I might have been ten years ago. But times have changed. I remember the first time I found out that Cornelius Oil had provided a young lady of the night for some French customer's personal entertainment. I was horrified. But different people have different prices, Jack, and I suppose that when you're running a successful business, you have to be aware of what those prices are."

"I just wish the press and the public shared the same view."

Hester brushed her dress straight. "I'm not saying that I'm not revolted, Jack, because I am. But I'm not shocked. What did Johann say?"

"He was outraged, of course. He hadn't known anything about it. But what concerns me is that he's going to challenge Hubslager to bring it out in the open, and Hubslager has so much evidence he can't possibly fail to wipe the floor with all of you. Unless you can get Johann to ease off, Hester, you've got big trouble."

"Well," breathed Hester, "I'll try my best. It's just that Johann is a little funny about sex."

She lowered her blue-shaded eyelids. "I don't know why, and it has never been any good asking him, but Johann seems to feel that sex is for the reproduction of children and the occasional release of temper. There, I shouldn't be telling you that, either. But we've been friends a long time, Jack."

"Hester . . ."

She shook her head. "You don't have to say you're sorry. I wouldn't tell you if I didn't want to."

She stood up and walked across the polished parquet floor, her lavender dress mirrored in the dark wood so that she looked like an ice skater on a mysterious pool. She crossed her arms across her breasts as if she was trying to keep warm.

She said simply: "Being married to Johann has been a very strange experience. He can be so spontaneously generous he can almost make you cry. He can be affectionate, in a gruff kind of way. But I don't think that he has ever actually loved me, or, come to that, anyone. Perhaps there *was* someone, once. I didn't meet him until he was thirty-six, so I suppose he must have known some young ladies. There was a very old photograph among his belongings when we moved to Lynwood's Island—a girl in a feather boa. But I only glimpsed it once, and I think he must have hidden it or thrown it away."

Jack sat still and alert, his fingers tautly laced together, hoping that Hester would spare him the most deadening details of her twenty-nine years of marriage. He didn't want to be put in the position where he would have to make a choice between them, because he loved them both. He said: "All I really need to know is how much you can persuade him to hold off on Hubslager. An investigation of all this Admiral Messenger business can wait until later, when we're sure we're out of the woods."

Hester looked across at him a little sadly. "Yes," she said. "I think I can persuade him to keep his temper."

They were silent for a few minutes, while the guitar played an old Mexican love song that was almost absurdly romantic. Then Hester said: "I should have married a man like you, really. Younger, and less complicated."

Jack didn't say anything. He lowered his eyes and looked down at the floor, and wished that life wasn't so damned involved. Hester walked back to the settee, her skirts rustling, and stood beside him. She hesitated for a moment, and then she laid cool fingers on the back of his neck, and massaged him with strong, sensitive strokes.

"I sometimes feel that I threw my womanhood away. Not my intelligence, or my personality, because Johann has never abused either of those. But he never makes me feel like a woman and nothing else. It makes me so frustrated sometimes, because he's so masculine and so physically attractive. He may have had the capacity to love when he was younger, you know, but if he did, he lost most of it on the way."

She knelt down on the rug in front of him and clasped her hands around his neck, so that he was looking straight into her wide brown eyes. Even at forty-eight, she was still pretty, and her dress was cut low enough to show the cleavage of her small, rounded breasts. The laugh lines around her eyes, those that hadn't been smoothed away by Dr. Carlsson and Dr. Michael, only softened the pertness of her heart-shaped face.

458

"Do you know what the words of this song mean?" she said, as the guitar music strung its Spanish passion through the rooms.

Jack cleared his throat and whispered: "No."

Hester's tongue moistened her lips. "They talk of a young girl from Cuatro Ciénegas who hears that her lover has died in the war, and gives him up for lost. In fact, he was only wounded, but when he returns to find her, she has already married someone else, a merchant she secretly despises. She sings this song standing on the veranda of her house as she watches her lover walk down the street arm-in-arm with her younger sister. The chorus says, 'I sold my adoration for a thousand thousand pesetas, but all the tears in Coahuila cannot buy it back.'"

Jack looked at her carefully. He said: "You're lying. This song is 'The Flowers of Tulancingo.' Ellie has a record of it."

Hester smiled, and then bent forward and kissed him warmly on the lips. "If I were Ellie," she whispered, "I'd be proud of you for saying that."

By the time they had bicycled through the long grass and down to the edge of the lake, they were thoroughly out of breath and laughing at their own unfitness. Hope got there first, but then Philip had the picnic hamper on his handlebars, and he was red in the face and sweating when he finally dismounted.

"At least you won't have to carry it all back." She laughed. "We'll have eaten it all."

"Just because it's going to be *inside* me instead of *outside* me, that doesn't mean it's going to weigh any the less," protested Philip.

They propped their bicycles up against a shady shell-bark hickory, and Philip unstrapped the hamper and laid it down on the long grass. He spread out the plaid blanket that had been neatly folded on top of the food, and then turned the hamper around so that Hope could take out the cold roast chickens and fruit.

She passed him the chilled champagne, wrapped in paper to keep it cool. "That's your department," she said. "And I think I could do with some now. That is absolutely the last time I take up any suggestion of yours. 'A gentle cycle down to the lake.' My God! It was more like the Tour de France."

"We made it, didn't we?" retorted Philip. "A fainter heart would have given up on Taghkonic Hill."

"It's not my heart I'm worried about," said Hope, "it's my

459

legs. I'm going to have calf muscles like a Russian ballet dancer."

Philip untwisted the wire from the champagne bottle. "*One* of you has to have muscles," he teased her, "and Martin doesn't seem to be playing his part."

"Oh, Philip!" she said, and tossed a peach at him. He ducked, laughing.

"I'm not trying to be rude," he told her. "It's just that the last time I called around at Gracie Square, I accidentally hung my skimmer on Martin's nose instead of the hat stand."

Hope pursed her lips, but didn't answer this time. She set out the fruit and busied herself with arranging the picnic plates. Philip looked around the raised lid of the hamper and said: "Hope?"

Again she didn't answer. He said: "You're not cross, are you? Come on, I was only joking."

She glanced up, and he could see by her eyes that she wasn't really annoyed.

"Just remember this," she said, opening the pickle jar and forking out a warty green pickle, "there's only one person around here who's allowed to criticize Martin, and that's me. He's my husband, and I'm his wife, and whatever I think about him in private is my business. Apart from that, he doesn't *mean* to be skinny and stupid."

Philip twisted off the champagne cork and lifted two long-stemmed glasses in his left hand so that he could fill them up to the brim with *brut*. "Martin's not *that* stupid," he remarked, waiting for the fizz to settle. "He's eastern sales VP for Chrysler, he's found himself an apartment on the river, and he's married to you. There's a million guys a hell of a lot smarter than Martin who would have given their front teeth for all of that."

He passed one of the glasses to Hope. "Mind you," he added with a grin, "I have to agree that he's skinny."

They ate their chicken and fruit, and drank their champagne, and then sat back against the trunk of the hickory, feeling sleepy and contented. It was a hot, hazy day in New York State, not far from Kent, Connecticut, where Philip Strachan's father had a small summer retreat. It was only a half-hour's drive from the diner where, just three years ago, Hope had picked up Lewis Bausor; but everything that had happened that night now seemed like nothing more than a movie they had once gone to see, so long ago that they could scarcely remember who was in it.

Three years hadn't done much to mature Philip Strachan's wit or deflate his pomposity, but they had certainly improved his looks. His face had lost that precocious rich-kid look, and his hair was shorter and less cherubically curly. By the time he was thirty, he was probably going to look just as rugged and heroic as his father, Senator William Strachan, and undoubtedly bore the pants off people twice as readily. He was finishing his studies in banking and accountancy before entering the family brokerage firm as a junior partner. He could be very boring when he talked about the market.

But Hope, sitting by the lake in a gauzy print dress and white shoes, her broad-brimmed straw hat lying beside her on the grass, was not particularly interested in conversation. She was lonely for the companionship of a man who didn't always remember to bring her flowers, who didn't always agree to do whatever she wanted, visit whichever restaurants or theaters she wanted, buy her whatever gifts she pined for. She was lonely for a man whose body felt hard like a man's, who smelled like a man, who acted as roughly and impulsively as a man could. She drank champagne and orange juice too early in the morning, flirted with too many husbands at too many soirees and dances, drove her De Soto coupé through so many stop lights that her glove compartment was crammed with unpaid tickets, and twice already, when Martin was away on business in Detroit, had made love in the back of automobiles to men she had tipsily picked up at dinner parties.

Martin was in Boston this weekend, planning a special sales boost for the new $895 Chrysler Royal. To begin with, Hope had considered that it might be dutiful to visit his parents in Connecticut, but on Friday evening Philip Strachan had called and asked if she wanted to join him upstate for a picnic the following day. She remembered, quite out of the blue, what he had said to her that night they had taken Lewis Bausor out. "*You're a rare one.*" So—perhaps to see if he really meant it—she said yes.

Leaning on his elbow in the grass, Philip took out a cigarette and lit it. Across the glittering surface of the lake, a tight flock of white-winged scoter ducks flapped and flurried. Philip said: "Are you really as unhappy as all that?"

Hope rested her chin on her knees and gazed wistfully out at the water. "I don't think I really know what happiness is."

"Well, neither do I. It's a state of mind, right? But I know what *un*happiness is."

She sighed. "Do you have a cigarette?" she asked him. He

461

passed her his, and she took a long drag and then passed it back. She puffed out the smoke in an impatient narrow stream.

"To tell you the truth, Hope, I don't know why you married Martin in the first place. You knew that you wouldn't get along."

"Oh, we get along all right. He's really quite friendly, in a doglike way."

"But don't tell me you want to stay married to a *dog*. I could have let you have King. He's a thoroughbred, and what's more he's handsome, and I bet he would have made a damned sight more interesting husband than Martin."

"Philip, don't insult him. I don't want to hear it. I don't even want to discuss it."

Philip shrugged. "It seems crazy to me."

"What does?"

"Well, why stay married when divorce is so easy? You could get yourself free in six weeks with a good lawyer. Tell the judge that Martin's been cruel to you. Going off on business trips and leaving you to fend for yourself. All that kind of stuff. The courts love it. And if you sob into your hankie a couple of times, they'll award you the whole apartment in Gracie Square and fifteen grand a year."

Hope took the cigarette from him and inhaled the smoke deeply. "I don't need money, Phil. And I don't particularly care if I never see the inside of that pokey little apartment ever again."

Philip said: "More champagne?"

She held out her glass. "I only married Martin to show Father that I was independent. A big act of defiance. If you send me off to the Landseers as a punishment, then I'll damned well make it look as if I loved every minute of it. My God, what a price to pay. Do you know something, I can look at Martin standing there in his pajamas, all ready for bed, and I can think to myself, look at you, you awkward little worm. I wish a huge great bird would come swooping down and carry you off in its beak."

Philip loosened his tie. "It could be arranged. I'll have a word with the Audubon Society."

Hope smiled, and shook her head. "I have a terrible feeling that I'm never going to get rid of Martin Landseer as long as I live. Maybe that's my punishment for Lewis Bausor. I can't conceive of God doing anything worse to me, can you?"

Philip said: "Cheer up, this is supposed to be a picnic."

"You should have brought a gramophone," she told him. "At least we could have had some music."

"A gramophone? By bicycle? And I suppose I could have balanced the records on my head?"

Hope stood up and took a few steps down toward the rushy brink of the lake. "You're not like Martin," she said. "Martin would have carried a five-piece jazz band on his shoulders if I wanted him to."

She kicked off her shoes. "It's so hot," she said. "It's like being in Africa."

"We could go for a swim," suggested Philip.

"We haven't brought towels."

"We could lie on the grass and let the sun dry us off. That's what they must have done before towels were invented."

"Nobody invented towels. How can you invent a towel?"

Philip stood up, too, and began to unbutton his white shirt. "Somebody must have. You don't think that Neanderthal men came down to the waterhole with Turkish towels over their arms and back brushes, do you?"

Hope turned around. The sun reflected off the water that lapped in between the rushes and lit up her face with curves of light. Her eyes were clear and pale. She said: "All right, then. Let's swim."

She bent her head forward, and Philip unbuttoned her dress down to the waist. As he loosened the last button, he leaned toward her and kissed the back of her neck, just where her wavy brown hair came to a fine downy point. Out on the lake, two or three of the scoter ducks flustered up from the water, but then settled back down again.

Hope's dress fell to the grass, around her ankles, and she stood in her short oyster-colored satin slip, her head still lowered, her arms down by her side. Philip came up even closer behind her, and nuzzled at her hair, and held her around her waist with his lean, muscular arm. He whispered: "If only you'd taken more notice of me before."

She let her head fall back against him, and he kissed her forehead. "If only *you'd* taken more notice of *me*."

His hand reached and cupped her soft breast through the thin slippery fabric of her slip. He gently rubbed her nipple between his finger and thumb, until it was crinkled and stiffened. She said, even more softly: "We ought to swim."

He didn't answer, but lifted her slip over head, while she raised her arms to help him like a surrendering Victorian nymph. The slip fell to the grass, and was caught by the warm summer breeze, and blew over and over.

She turned around, wearing nothing now but her French step-ins and her gold bangles. She put her arms around him, and he squeezed and fondled her breasts with his strong fingers until she shivered, and bit at the muscles of his chest with her teeth. They kissed, so deeply that she felt as if she was being swallowed alive, and the only times she opened her eyes she saw his tanned cheek, his lashes, his curly hair, and the spangled green sunlight that danced through the leaves of the hickory tree.

He reached his hand inside the loose leg of her French step-ins and touched her. She knew that she was moist, like a ripe peach that someone has just bitten into. His fingers parted her, and then worked deeper and deeper inside, until his hand was slippery enough to force his index finger, right up to the knuckle, in her tightest place, and he could slide his thumb in front. She gasped and shivered, but he tugged at her, gently and sensuously and insistently, his finger caressing the ball of his own thumb through the sensitive membrane that divided them, until all she could do was plead with him to stop, to go on, to pull her into thousands of tingling fragments. He was so close that she could hear his breath roaring in her ear, and feel his hardness against her leg. But a moment came when it seemed like the whole day was giving way beneath her, and she buried her face in his chest, her eyes tight shut, and she could feel his fingers inside her like fingers of buzzing electricity, touching every nerve in her thighs and her stomach, and she held him tight, tight, tight and gasped: "*Ah*!"

He stroked her, caressed her, and said: "Hope. My own darling Hope."

She stayed close, shuddering, weak. But then the feeling began to ebb away gradually, and she raised her head to look into his eyes. "No," she said in a wobbly voice. "Not *your* darling Hope."

He touched her forehead. "Do you think it could be? Ever?"

She smiled, glancing away toward the grass where her slip lay discarded. "I shouldn't think so. But you never know. The future always leaps out at us by surprise."

464

Without saying anything else, she unbuttoned his white summer pants and helped him to take them off. His thin knee-length cotton undershorts clung to his hardened penis like the sheet around an unveiled statue. She tugged them down, and held his rearing erection in one of her small, well-manicured hands, her diamond and topaz rings glittering against the dark red of his swollen flesh. She stroked him once or twice, up and down, and he gripped her shoulders and murmured something which she couldn't hear but could easily understand.

From across the lake, even though the haze of midday heat, they could be seen quite clearly. Hope, naked, clinging to the scaly trunk of the hickory tree, while Philip stood behind her and pushed himself into her. You could even have heard them gasping and laughing, and Hope's high-pitched squeal when Philip at last reached his climax. Then, bare and brown as two children, they splashed through the rushes into the cool water, and swam for almost twenty minutes, their heads bobbing on the still surface. Philip could be heard singing "The Yellow Rose of Texas," and Hope joined in the chorus with an exaggerated trill.

Afterward they lay on the grass until the sun was nibbled by the tops of the water oaks around the lake, and the breeze began to blow cool, and then they dressed and gathered up their blanket and their picnic hamper and mounted their bicycles to go home.

The late sun fell orange through the turning spokes of their bicycle wheels. Hope had given her French step-ins to Philip as a lighthearted memento, and he had tied them to his handlebars so that they fluttered as he rode. There was a warm scent of early-summer evening. Hope was so happy, and yet so unhappy, that her eyelashes were sparkling with tears.

They said very little else. They stopped once, before they reached the driveway up to the Strachan house, and Philip touched her hair and her lips with gentle fingertips.

"Do you think that it might be any use?" he asked her in a throaty, uncertain tone.

"I don't know," she told him.

"Can we meet again?"

"Not like this. It would have to be secretly. Martin would never suspect, but his parents would, and so would mine."

He looked down at her thin wrist, with its heavy gold bangle.

"You wouldn't mind if I called you? Maybe soon?"

"Philip, I don't know. You mustn't stampede me."

He swallowed. "I know. But I love you."

She reached out and stroked his cheek. "No, you don't. You just imagine you do."

He shrugged. "Maybe you're right. But you know what they say about imagination. It can move mountains."

"Not imagination. Faith."

"Doesn't Faith go with Hope?"

She kissed him, quickly and affectionately, and then mounted her bicycle again. "So does Charity," she called back, and she was halfway down the driveway before Philip could catch up.

Jack met Ellie off the Carolina train at Union Station, and helped her carry her parcels and hatboxes to where their navy-blue Buick Phaeton convertible was parked outside in the sun. It was a sweltering day, but Ellie looked fresh and cool in a green lawn dress and a white hat with green ribbons. Jack opened the car door for her, gave the porter a quarter for stowing her suitcases away in the trunk, and then climbed into the driving seat.

"No chauffeur?" she asked.

He started the motor. "What's the matter with *me*?"

"Nothing. I just hoped Lloyd wasn't sick."

"I gave him the day off. I felt like collecting you myself."

He pulled away from the station concourse and steered the Buick out through the congested, glittering traffic. The sun beat down on the back of his neck, and he put his hat on.

"How was California?" she asked him, searching in her pocketbook for her powder compact.

"Hot. How was South Carolina?"

"Hot, too. But it was so nice to see everybody, I didn't care. You should see Rose's children now. It was only last year they seemed like babies. Now they're all in grade school, and Billy has no front teeth at all."

"Umh-humh."

Ellie raised her compact and quickly powdered her nose. Jack turned down Louisiana Avenue toward Constitution Avenue, and the dome of the Capitol flickered into view behind the trees.

"How's Randy?" she asked him.

"Randy? Oh, well, he's fine. Just fine. He's working on a case for the Department of Agriculture right now. Could be a good step forward, if he wins it, and I think he will."

Ellie closed her pocketbook and smiled. "Do you remember when he wanted you both to be railroad engineers?"

"What brought that up?"

She looked across the car at him. "I don't know. Maybe I was just thinking of way back when."

"You sound like you're still nostalgic for South Carolina," he told her, without turning his head.

"Maybe."

They drove in silence along Constitution Avenue, past the Ellipse and the White House, and out toward Theodore Roosevelt Bridge. It was breezier once they were out over the Potomac, and Ellie took off her hat and fluffed out her hair. In middle age, much of her prettiness had been erased, and she was plumper now, and there were faint crisscrossing crow's-feet around her eyes. When she wore sunglasses, she looked like Bette Davis would in twenty years' time.

"Are you tired?" Jack asked her.

"Only slightly. Why?"

"I'd like to drop by Senator Karlbeck's house to pick up some information he promised me."

Ellie shrugged. "As long as I don't have to socialize. Is it important?"

He checked his mirror and pulled out to overtake a huge diesel truck with "Manassas Transport" emblazoned in dirty red letters down its flanks. He said: "It's to do with Cornelius Shipping."

"You mean the corruption prosecutions you were telling me about?"

Jack nodded.

"Is it serious?" she asked.

"So-so."

"Well, how serious is so-so?"

Jack glanced at her, and pulled a face. "Disastrous, if you must know. There was a chance that Senator Hubslager would go for Brookline Industries instead of Cornelius Shipping. But this business with Admiral Messenger was too juicy for him to resist. They've dropped their intended action against Brookline, apparently, and now they've got three law firms working on files for the Senate committee on government contracts and the New York district courts."

Ellie reached across the seat and laid a gentle hand on his knee.

"Do you really have to get involved?" she asked him. "It won't do you much good if it comes out that you've been supporting Johann—especially if he's found guilty of corruption."

"He saved my life once."

"I know that, Jack, but you can't go on repaying someone for saving your life forever."

Jack gave her hand a quick, affectionate squeeze. "He saved my life and I was able to spend my life with you, and that's why I'm quite ready to do whatever he needs me to do whenever he needs it."

He signaled right, and turned down the quiet, wide tree-lined stretch of Patuxent Drive, where Senator Karlbeck lived.

Ellie said: "Do you know how much you flattered me by saying that?"

Jack smiled. "I wasn't flattering you, my darling. It's the truth. It's the way I feel."

They pulled up beside a scrupulously neat brick-and-weatherboard house with lawns of unnatural emerald brightness and rows of umbrella magnolias that stood as stiff as terrified children. Outside the white-painted front porch, a tall elderly man with a gray flat-topped crew cut, heavy spectacles, and a baggy brown cardigan was trimming creepers to grow in severely parallel rows.

Jack let Ellie out of the automobile, and they walked up the swept flagstone path. Jack called: "Good morning, Senator! How's the garden?"

The old man hung up his clippers on the creeper trellis and peeled off his gardening gloves. "Good to see you, Jack! How are you, Ellie?"

"We can't stay long," explained Jack. "Ellie just arrived from South Carolina, and she's looking forward to resting up. She did the grand tour of the aunts and the cousins and the nephews back home."

Senator Karlbeck scratched the back of his prickly neck. "Fanny's been threatening to drag me off on a tour like that for years, back to Montana. I was almost delighted when war broke out, because that meant I was too busy, and couldn't go."

"Now, then, Senator," said Ellie.

Senator Karlbeck grunted in amusement. "It won't make no difference when the time comes. Fanny always outvotes me, no matter what. I'll tell you something—if my pals in the Senate could

468

see the way that she badgers me and bullies me about, why, they'd pass a National Henpeck Act in sympathy."

Jack smiled guardedly. "Did you get the information?" he asked.

Senator Karlbeck threw a questioning glance at Ellie, but Jack said: "Don't worry about it, Ellie knows. I told her all about it when Hubslager first approached me."

"Well, as long as you both realize that this is top-security stuff," advised Senator Karlbeck. "If it ever came out that I'd told you, I'd have to deny it most strenuously, and you'd be the one who'd wind up holding the baby."

"I know that, Senator," said Jack.

"Well, then," said Karlbeck, pushing his hands into his pants pockets, "I can tell you for starters that Hubslager is dead set on prosecuting Cornelius Shipping and all of its responsible executives. But he's not going to move until late September or early October, when the election is just cooking up nicely. Then he's going to blast the trumpets, bring up the curtains, and hope to catch as many people as possible with their pants down."

Ellie inquired quietly: "Does the President know?"

Senator Karlbeck shrugged. "It's hard to say for sure. But Hubslager had a half-hour meeting with FDR two weeks ago, and I can't think of anything else which a no-hoper like Hubslager could discuss with the President, can you?"

"So what's his angle?" asked Jack, gently touching one of the white, cup-shaped flowers of the magnolia.

Senator Karlbeck rubbed his chin. "There are several possible angles. But you might be interested to know that some Communist group was hawking a list around Washington a few months back, and that list contained the names of all those major corporations which were secretly paying substantial campaign contributions to the GOP. And when I say substantial, I mean millions."

"One was Cornelius Shipping?" asked Ellie.

"You guessed it," said Senator Karlbeck. "And my guess is that Hubslager got hold of that list, and only brought his bribery-and-corruption investigation to bear on those particular corporations that were marked on it. He isn't so much interested in industrial morals as he is in getting FDR elected for a third term. If he can prove that the GOP candidate has been financed by profits from sexual corruption, why, that's as damning as saying that the man's a pimp. Roosevelt couldn't lose."

"What's Hubslager's motive?" Jack wanted to know. "Apart from being a Democratic senator?"

Senator Karlbeck looked glum. "What's the motive that makes any of us do anything? Personal ambition. Hubslager's forty-six now, but he's never held a government post more important than fish-and-fowl protection. If he can show that the GOP and Cornelius Shipping are as queer as a three-dollar bill, then FDR is obviously going to be grateful, come inauguration time."

"I thought Johann got along fine with the President," interrupted Ellie.

"Sure," said Jack, "and Hester's like Eleanor's favorite sister. But that's only because Johann doesn't take political sides in public, and if he does make any contributions, he does it in secret. If you ask me, most of Cornelius Shipping's contributions were okayed by David Bookbinder, anyway. Bookbinder's pretty anxious to keep on the right side of Dewey."

"What a mess," said Ellie.

"Sure it's a mess," agreed Senator Karlbeck, "but then, politics always is. And apart from that, you may—just may—have a lever."

"What's that?"

"It's not going to be easy, and you're going to have to find your own way of working it. But there's one thing that could silence Hubslager, and that was his own involvement in 1938 with the Welfare Investment Plan."

Jack raised an eyebrow. "I remember that. But he got good publicity out of it, didn't he? He raised millions of dollars for old folks, and everybody said what a great charitable guy he was. Mr. Charity, they called him, didn't they? At least for a month or so."

"One of my colleagues in the Senate has some pretty solid information that shows Hubslager and Jorkins diverted nearly three hundred thousand dollars of the Welfare Investment Plan into their own pockets."

"You're kidding! Who?"

Senator Karlbeck pulled a wry face. "I can tell you, but it may not do you much good. It's Senator Strachan, and Senator Strachan is ambitious and far-sighted enough to have his eye on the forty-four elections."

"What does that mean?"

"It means that he's still gathering witnesses and affidavits and facts. He's taking his time over it, you see, because he's counting on Jorkins running for President in forty-four, and he wants to make sure that he's got a real humdinger of a scandal to drop right down Jorkins' chimney when the forty-four primaries start.''

"You mean he won't release the information now?"

"Not for all the whiskey in Paradise. And especially not for something as petty as discrediting Hubslager. As far as Senator Strachan is concerned, Hubslager is the nearest thing that a human being ever got to a chitterling, and he certainly doesn't want to waste his prize scandal on a creature like that."

"Have you asked him?" said Jack.

Senator Karlbeck nodded. "Oh, yes. We had lunch last week at the club. But he's keeping it close to his chest. The only reason I found out about it myself was because he needed my affidavit on a whole lot of investment transactions."

Jack looked thoughtful. A dusty wind rustled through the magnolias and set the blossoms bobbing. Across the street, a chauffeur was buffing up a black Cadillac Sixty Special, watched by a solemn small boy in a striped T-shirt. The blue summer sky was streaked with high cirrus.

"Do you need some money?" Jack asked Senator Karlbeck. "Did you have to pay anyone off?"

The senator shook his head. "Just take it as a favor. It won't do you much good in any case if you can't persuade Strachan to give you what he's got."

Ellie said: "Is it really worth pursuing? I don't want Jack to get himself tied up with something that's going to damage his reputation."

Senator Karlbeck laid an affectionate arm around her shoulders. "I'll tell you something, Ellie. If the day came when I didn't put my reputation on the line at least once, then I'd pack my bag and take myself back to where I came from. Risking your reputation is what your reputation is all about."

"It still worries me," she said. "I mean . . . it could be a terrible scandal, couldn't it?"

Senator Karlbeck shrugged, and started to put his gardening gloves back on. "I guess it could be. But remember that the only difference between a political scandal and a normal piece of day-to-day Washington business is that the newspapers got to hear about it."

"You're an old cynic." Ellie grinned and kissed the senator's cheek.

They talked for a while about the forthcoming elections, and then they said their good-byes. On the way back to the car, Ellie said: "What on earth are you going to do now? We've never met Senator Strachan, have we? Isn't he supposed to be incredibly hard-baked?"

Jack opened the door for her. "Hard-baked or not," he said, "he must be open to some kind of persuasion. It looks like the only chance we've got."

Ellie said: "You don't have to do this, Jack. You could drop it right now and nobody would mind. Not even Johann. He'd understand."

Jack closed the car door and sorted out his ignition key. "I know that," he told her quietly. "But I guess I've committed myself. And you know what you once told me. You said that if I ever gave in to thieves and carpetbaggers, then I'd really disappoint you; and I don't ever want to do that."

Ellie was about to say something else, but Jack said: "The senator's waving good-bye," and they both turned to wave back. Then they pulled away from the curb and drove back down Patuxent Drive to the main highway. It was dusty and glaring hot now, and Ellie untied her thin silk scarf.

"I love you," she said. "Just as much as ever. Even more than ever."

Jack looked at her. "I love you, too."

She reached across the back of the seat and gently touched his graying hair.

"You're worried about something, aren't you? Something you're not telling me."

He shrugged, as if it was nothing.

"You're not just doing this to pay Johann back for saving your life, are you? You haven't even thought about that shipwreck for years."

He turned the Buick south, and they drove into a blur of golden sunlight and bright concrete highway. "It's one of those things. Suddenly you feel like settling old debts."

"Not you, Jack. And not this way. You know Johann's guilty, don't you? Even if he didn't know about Admiral Messenger personally, his corporation knew and that makes him morally responsible. And I'm sure he knows about every other bit of bribery and chicanery that goes on. Come on, Jack, you don't even *like* him particularly."

472

"I don't *dis*like him."

"You said yourself only two or three months ago that he looked dignified and elderly and respectable, but that was only skin-deep."

"Well, that's true."

"Then why are you getting yourself involved in all this? I don't understand it. I know that it's dog eat dog and cat eat mouse, and Senator Hubslager's no more honest than Johann or anyone else, and I know that you feel you owe Johann something, but not this much, surely?"

Jack said: "I owe Randy something. I owe Randy some kind of commitment. Something to say that I understand."

"Randy? What does Randy have to do with it?"

Jack drove in silence for a while. Ellie said: "Jack?"

He turned and looked at her with a face made tired by sadness. "There's a roadhouse just along here," he told her quietly. "I think we'd better talk about this over a drink."

They pulled off the road and parked in the parking lot. The roadhouse was mock-Tyrolean timber, with a hedge of dusty firs, and a neon sign that said "GO DEATS." A fat man in a tiny panama hat was sitting in a pale green Hudson Eight, devouring a whole poloney and listening to the baseball scores. A truck flashed past with a mournful doppler sound.

It wasn't the best place to talk about anything so sensitive or dear. They sat at a small smeary table by the window, where blowflies buzzed and rattled against the glass, and a hostess in a red velour jacket and a pillbox hat brought them two tasteless collinses. Behind the bar, the bartender was carrying on a long nasal harangue against anyone who felt we ought to stay out of the war, but of course *he* couldn't go fight the Germans personally since his grandfather came from Dresden.

Ellie whispered: "What's wrong, Jack? You've been talking so strange today. What's happened?"

Jack couldn't speak at first, couldn't get the words to rise past his larynx. He looked down at his drink, and then he said: "It's Randy. He took me out to lunch a couple of days after you left for Carolina."

"He's all right, isn't he? I mean, he's not ill?"

"No, no, he's fine. It's nothing like that."

"Then what did he say?"

Jack raised his head. Ellie was amazed and disturbed to see that

473

his eyes were glistening with tears. Tenderly she reached out and touched them, and they sparkled on her fingertips.

"I don't know what kind of a parent I've been, not to have noticed," Jack said miserably. "I don't know how I could have let him suffer like that. He tried to tell me before a couple of times, but somehow he didn't think I was listening, or he got scared."

"*Jack*," said Ellie. The tears were sliding down his cheeks now, and a red-haired woman sitting opposite them turned and stared.

"He said that when he was young, it didn't matter so much. He thought it was some kind of a phase that everybody went through. But by the time he was seventeen, he knew for certain. He was very unhappy round about then, do you remember? Very confused and argumentative. Didn't seem to know what he was or what he wanted out of life."

Ellie breathed: "Yes. Yes, he was."

"Well," said Jack, taking out his handkerchief and wiping his eyes, "he managed to come to terms with it, in a way. Managed to work hard, play hard, and keep his mind off it. He still went through agonies, trying to keep it from me. From us. But he managed."

There was a terrible silence between them. Outside in the parking lot, they could hear the fat man's car radio faintly playing "A Tisket, a Tasket."

Then Jack said, with such pain that Ellie had to take his hand across the table: "This time he couldn't hold it back any longer. He's fallen in love, and he says that his love is returned. It's Maurice Ritchie, his clerk."

Ellie stared at him. She had guessed what he was going to say, almost as soon as he had started to tell her, but she had tried to believe that it was something else, anything else, but that. She said: "Oh, my God," and put her hand to her mouth in overwhelming grief.

"He wants to go away," Jack continued quietly. "Someplace where people don't know who he is, or who he belongs to. He wants to set up house with Maurice and then start his own law firm. He talked about Los Angeles or San Francisco. He said he was sorry."

"Sorry?" wept Ellie. "Oh, my God, *he* doesn't have to be sorry. It's us! The perfect parents, weren't we? Or we thought we were. And we didn't even guess. Oh, Jack . . . oh, my God."

Jack sipped his drink. "That was part of the reason I got involved with this Hubslager business. I suppose it was dumb, but I felt that if maybe I showed that I could understand people like that, maybe protect them, then Randy would see that I . . ."

He rested his head in his hands.

"I don't know what Randy *would* see," he said in a desperately unhappy voice. "But he's my son, and I don't know what else I can do."

Ellie said: "Please, Jack. Let's go home."

Jack nodded. The bartender was saying: "Mind you, if I could afford to dress like Robert Donat, I would." And outside, in the lot, the radio played "When the Moon Comes Over the Mountain."

Senator William Strachan's secretary, Florence, who was known throughout Washington as the girl whose eyes said "bed" and whose legs said "piano," opened the varnished door of his office and announced: "Mr. Henry Keith, sir. You're expecting him."

Senator Strachan didn't take his well-polished Alan McAfee shoes off the desk. Instead, he looked up at Henry over his horn-rimmed half-glasses and shouted harshly: "How are you, Henry? Take a seat."

Henry tugged up the pants of his creased blue suit and then perched himself awkwardly on a small chair next to an overweening rubber plant. "I'm real pleased you could fit me in, Senator," he said with an uncertain grin. "I'm sure you must be pretty busy these days, what with November and everything."

"That's right," growled Senator Strachan. He was a handsome, large-headed man with closely cropped gray hair and a Harvard tie. He was one of those uncompromising and slightly unhinged Republicans from whom Johann usually tried to stay away. Extreme views may have been fine for winning elections, but they caused nothing but ructions in industry, and apart from that, Johann preferred quiet company these days, and that was why he surrounded himself with moderate men.

"I don't know how much Mrs. Cornelius told you on the telephone," said Henry.

"Nothing. She simply said it was urgent and important. And I can tell you now that it had better be."

"Oh, it is."

Senator Strachan stood up and paced stiffly around his desk. His office was paneled in light oak, and hung with half a dozen amateurish oil paintings that his wife had given him for Christmas. On his desk was a photograph of Philip on his graduation day, a saintly smile on his lips; a family crest with the motto "Brains & Brawn" beneath it; and a scale model of the U.S. submarine *Squalus*. He kept the *Squalus* there to remind himself that out of the worst disasters, something good could always be salvaged.

Outside the window, there was a scrubby lawn and a view of the back of the Justice Department. It was another hot, hazy day.

Senator Strachan said: "I can't say that I've ever had the opportunity to talk to Mrs. Cornelius for long."

Henry Keith opened his briefcase and gave a little hiccuping cough like a sick chipmunk. "She's a very pleasant lady, sir. She knows her own mind. But most pleasant."

"So I believe," replied Senator Strachan flatly.

Henry sorted out an untidy heap of papers, dropped a lot of them, then fished in his pocket for a handkerchief. He blew his nose loudly, then collected up his papers again. "Summer cold," he explained.

Senator Strachan sat on the edge of his desk and waited impatiently.

"Right, now, here we are," said Henry. "There's a long report from the Greenbaum Detective Agency, and something from Pinkerton, and one or two random bits and pieces from Judd."

Senator Strachan put his magnificent head to one side and looked down at Henry with a sour, gritty expression. "*Judd*?" he asked, as if he had a sudden mouthful of bile. "*Greenbaum*?"

"Yes, sir. They're both pretty reputable private-detective agencies up in the New York–Connecticut area. They weren't hired by us, I hasten to tell you, but by Mr. Martin Landseer."

"Landseer? That was the fellow that Hope Cornelius married, wasn't it? Bit of a milksop, if my memory serves me."

"Well, sir," sniffed Henry, "you could say that."

"All right, then. So Mr. Martin Landseer hired some private detectives. What does that have to do with me?"

Henry wiped his nose again. "Well, what Mr. Martin Landseer wanted to find out was whether his wife, that is, Mrs. Hope Cornelius Landseer, was being entirely, well, loyal."

"Isn't that why *any* man hires a private detective?" put in Senator Strachan gruffly.

"I guess so. It varies. In this case, though, we have some pretty clear evidence of adultery. It seems, I'm sorry to say, that Mrs.

476

Hope Cornelius Landseer has been having a pretty constructive relationship with your son, Philip.''

Senator Strachan folded his arms. "Where did you dredge up this so-called evidence?" he demanded.

"Mr. Landseer supplied it. He's considering divorce."

"And that means he's going to cite Philip?"

"Well, that's right."

There was a silence. Senator Strachan walked back around his desk, sat himself down, and stared at Henry from under his bushy gray eyebrows. Henry smiled back, a little nervously, and wiped his nose again.

"What's the alternative?" asked Senator Strachan at last, resting his chin on his square fist.

"Well, sir—"

"I gather there *is* an alternative. I mean, you haven't flown here from California just to tell me that Martin Landseer is citing Philip."

Henry put his papers away untidily. "Mrs. Cornelius doesn't want you to feel that you're being pressed, sir. But she does have a suggestion."

"Go on."

"Mrs. Cornelius said that she could dissuade Martin Landseer from citing Philip by agreeing to pay the Landseers a substantial divorce settlement."

"And what would I have to do to ensure that *that* happened?"

Henry rustled and bustled in his briefcase again, and brought out more paper. "Well, sir, Mrs. Cornelius understands that you have some information relating to the Welfare Investment Plan of 1938, in which Senator Jorkins and Senator Hubslager were pretty substantially involved."

Senator Strachan raised an eyebrow. "Word gets around, doesn't it?"

Henry smiled. "It sure does, sir. Even walls have ears."

"Well," said Senator Strachan, "even if I did possess such information, what about it?"

"Nothing at all, Senator. Except that Mrs. Cornelius would really care for a copy of everything you have on the matter, on the understanding that she could use it or release it whenever she wanted."

Senator Strachan stared at Henry Keith balefully for a long time without saying a word. Then, abruptly, he shouted: "*Hah!*"

477

Henry Keith blinked, and sniffed.

Senator Strachan rose from behind his desk like a rhinoceros topping the crest of a hill. In a voice that was powerful, deep, and almost steady, he said: "Mrs. Cornelius wants information on Senator Jorkins and Senator Hubslager? Mrs. Cornelius does, does she? Well, you can go back to California and you can tell Mrs. Cornelius that if she wants information on anything she can get it the way that I got it. The *hard* way."

Henry Keith looked abashed. "You don't want to cooperate?"

"Cooperate? This is extortion! The usual grinning, oily, Cornelius extortion! I'm supposed to save my son from public scandal by giving Mrs. Cornelius valuable political information? Just imagine if the whole damned country were run that way! No, sir, Henry, I'm telling you that if Philip has been misbehaving himself with Hope Cornelius Landseer, then Philip has got to take what's coming, no matter how much it hurts him or his family, because nobody in the world, and especially not Hester Cornelius, is going to blackmail me for anything. Not for *anything*, do you understand?"

Henry Keith sat tight and silent. It was only when Senator Strachan had thumped his fist on his desk and sat down again that he ventured to speak.

"Is that what you want me to say?" he asked meekly. "That you don't care what happens to Philip?"

"Does Mrs. Cornelius care what happens to Hope? Can she really exploit her daughter's sexual adventures for the sake of business? What kind of a mother can do that?"

Henry coughed and looked down at his scruffy brown shoes. "Well, sir, I have to tell you that the consequences of this are going to be pretty serious. If we don't solve this problem with Senator Hubslager one way, we're going to have to solve it another."

"Well, you just damned well *solve* it another way," grated Senator Strachan. "Because this information is mine, and it's going to stay mine, and I wouldn't help you or Hester Cornelius if you were hanging on my window ledge by the tips of your fingers."

Henry Keith shrugged. "Okay, sir. But just remember that you *are* on the first floor."

Senator Strachan pushed a button on his desk, and Florence appeared at the door like a wooden woman out of a weather house.

"Mr. Keith is just leaving us," the senator said harshly.

Henry Keith closed his briefcase and stood up, getting himself

478

entangled in the rubber plant. "You sure you won't spend some time reconsidering?" he asked quietly.

Senator Strachan shook his head, tautly and almost imperceptibly; and so Henry shrugged, and said "Okay," and winked at Florence as he ambled out.

They met in Morningside Park, under the shadow of the Cathedral of St. John the Divine. It was so hot that Philip had to take off his coat and fold it over the back of the bench. Hope, in a light gray pleated skirt and a pale yellow silk blouse with padded shoulders, kept fanning herself with a *Ladies' Home Journal*. The forsythia bushes looked brown and dusty in the unnatural heat.

"I suppose your mother told you what happened," said Philip, unfolding his handkerchief and patting the sweat from his forehead.

Hope kept her hands demurely in her lap. She said: "Yes."

"I'm proud of Father, anyway," said Philip. "At least he wouldn't be swayed."

"That doesn't make any difference to us, does it?" put in Hope.

Philip shrugged. "Was there ever any 'us,' really?"

"You said there was. Perhaps I misheard you."

Philip leaned over toward her. "No, when I said 'us,' I meant . . ."

Hope turned away. "It doesn't matter. Whatever you meant then, if you don't mean the same thing now, then it doesn't matter. You're not my husband."

Philip said: "Well . . ." and looked embarrassed. Across the park, an old man was scattering bread to the pigeons as he walked, like a sower of seed in a biblical picture.

Hope said: "This has to be the last time, you know. We can't meet anymore."

"Don't you *want* a divorce?"

"It looks as though I'm going to get one, whether I like it or not."

"But surely your mother wouldn't—"

"Wouldn't she?" interjected Hope. "You don't know Mother."

Philip looked glum. "I've never been cited before. I suppose it's going to appear in all the worst newspapers."

"And the best," said Hope.

Philip gave a queasy little smile and nodded. "I guess you're right."

Hope sat quietly for a few minutes, nervously twisting her diamond rings around and around. Then she said: "Did you try persuading your father?"

"Oh, yes. Of course I did. But he said that America always comes first, which, being translated, means Senator William Strachan's political career always comes first. He won't give your mother anything on Hubslager—not a single sausage—not even if she tells him that my grandmother's been sleeping with half of Congress."

"But *why* won't he?" asked Hope.

Philip pulled a face. "Because he's impossibly stubborn, being Irish, and because he won't have a woman telling him what to do, not even Hester Cornelius, and because if he lets your mother have this information on Hubslager now, he's throwing away one of his best weapons against Jorkins in forty-four."

"Surely the Welfare Investment Plan is going to be stale news in forty-four. That's even if Jorkins is nominated. Personally, I'd rather nominate a warthog."

Philip sighed and brushed back his hair with his hand. "I agree. But just try telling Father."

There was another long pause. High up in the vivid blue sky, a silvery transatlantic Clipper droned by, its wings catching the sunlight. It was almost lunchtime, and the first few office workers were venturing into the park with sandwiches and flasks.

"I wonder what that detective said?" said Hope.

Philip frowned at her.

"According to Mother, Martin's had me followed for *months*," Hope went on. "Ever since we went to the Manuccis for Twelfth Night, and he came out into the conservatory and caught me kissing Robert Scheinhorn. I think it's repulsive. Exactly the kind of repulsive thing that Martin would do. I mean, if your own husband can't trust you . . ."

Philip said: "Yes," in a flat, disinterested voice.

"Thousands of people do it these days," insisted Hope. "It's nothing to get divorced about. Nothing to send private detectives out about. Martin's so damned old-fashioned."

Philip leaned back on the bench and closed his eyes. "It's your

480

mother I can't get over. What an opportunist! When Martin came creeping around with that stuff about you and me, she must have thought the gods were smiling on her. Just what she needed to squeeze my father—'Give me the dope on Hubslager or else I'll make sure your son gets publicly cited in my daughter's divorce.' She doesn't give a damn about anyone, does she? Not you, not anyone.''

"Not me especially," said Hope with gentle bitterness. "She's always considered that I'm too much competition, and that's why she's always made sure that she keeps me out of the way. Don't worry, Philip, I'm used to it.''

"How can you ever get used to a mother like that?''

"People have worse mothers. People have mothers who beat them, or flirt with their boyfriends, or get drunk.''

Philip nodded, and then said: "What are we going to do now?''

"I don't know," admitted Hope. "I guess it's up to Martin. He's gone to stay with his parents for the time being, and I suppose they'll work out whether he's going to divorce me or not.''

"You don't care?''

"Of course I care. My God! My mother's tried to use my own body to buy my father out of a prosecution. What's even worse, she's failed. God knows what's going to happen now.''

Philip took her hand. He looked into her eyes with a serious if slightly preppie expression.

"Hope," he said gently, "I want you to know that I'm very fond of you.''

She put her head on one side and smiled. "Fond? That's not even worth a divorce, really, is it?''

"I don't know. I wasn't trying to hurt you.''

She lifted her face to him and kissed him. "Oh, Philip.''

He smiled. "I guess I'll see you in court. I don't suppose it'll be that painful.''

Hope, quite unexpectedly, began to cry.

"Being rich is always painful," she told him.

At Carina Mia, at evening time, Johann was sitting on the balcony with a last brandy-and-soda. The air was warm and soft, and from time to time he almost fell asleep.

Hester came in from the bedroom, wearing a long dressing

gown of black silk that swept noiselessly over the mosaic floor. She bent over and kissed him on the forehead, and whispered: "Johann?"

He opened his eyes. "I was thinking," he said gruffly. "I wasn't asleep."

She pulled over a small rush chair and sat down beside him. "I just talked to Senator Strachan again," she said quietly. In the dusk, Johann could see her elegant profile as a soft silhouette.

"Well?"

"He won't change his mind. He said that if Martin wants to cite Philip as corespondent, then that's tough on Philip. Can you believe it? He said he can't mollycoddle Philip, any more than *his* father mollycoddled *him*."

"Have you spoken to Hope?" asked Johann.

"Well, briefly. She knows what's going on."

"And she's not concerned about it?"

"I don't know. She can't stand Martin, so I don't suppose she particularly cares."

"She didn't tell you?"

Hester stroked his forehead. "I don't think she wanted to."

"Well," said Johann, "it looks as if we're going to have to deal with Hubslager the difficult way."

"Do you think I ought to speak to David Bookbinder?"

"You?"

Hester shrugged. "I may dislike him, but I have to live with him. And even the worst people can be useful sometimes."

Johann rubbed his watering eyes. "I sometimes wonder what we're trying so desperately to protect around here. Our reputation? Who cares what anybody thinks about us? Maybe our souls? Don't ask me, Hester. I think I'm too tired to worry."

Hester said: "It's all right. I'll call David tonight. He's in Jersey, isn't he?"

"That's right. But tell him to think about it first, before he gets anything done. I don't want anything ill-considered."

She kissed him again. "Nothing ill-considered," she promised, and left the balcony room to make her call.

On the night of July 9, 1940, a black Plymouth sedan carrying four passengers was involved in a collision with a gasoline truck at the junction of Ditmas Avenue and Flatbush Avenue, in Flatbush, New York. The gasoline truck exploded and all four passengers were trapped in the blazing Plymouth, out of reach of passersby and firemen. They died, according to the local fire department, "horribly."

The passengers were later identified as Lieutenant E. N. Scargas, of the New York police; Mr. Gorton Tighe, a New York attorney; and two boys of fourteen and thirteen, Antonio Carlo and Francisco Delray, both of Brooklyn. The truck driver was never found. *The New York Times* suggested that the boys were vital witnesses in a rumored corruption prosecution, and that they were on their way to be interviewed by New York investigators about their involvement in what may have been "an important scandal."

A spokesman for the New York district attorney's office refused to confirm or deny these suggestions, but agreed that the boys had been involved in a forthcoming case as "quite important witnesses" and that the case would now almost certainly have to be dropped.

Five weeks later, on August 14, 1940, Admiral Peary Messenger went for an early-morning swim in the ocean off Narragansett, Rhode Island, and disappeared. An intensive search by the Coast Guard during the afternoon had to be called off because of the failing light.

1945

We are having our little troubles now—a few of them. They are not serious. Just a blowup after a letdown from war.

—Harry S. Truman,
Gilbertsville, Kentucky, 1945

Those days, in the first fall after the Second World War, in those strange breezy times of demobilization and peace, in the beginning of the Truman era, with the boys coming home from Europe and the baseball fans looking forward to a season when games would be played without war cripples and 4-Fs; in those times of Toots and Caspar and Thimble Theater and Ginger Rogers in *I'll Be Seeing You*, the Cornelius family rarely visited the House at all. The only consistent exception was Roderick. He had always fancied himself as a Wall Street man, and even though he had very little to do except mooch around the offices and set everybody's teeth on edge, he enjoyed the suppressed bustle of financial paperwork and the endless tapping of ticker-tape machines.

He was there, at the House, on a rainy Thursday in October, 1945. He was sitting in a creaky leather armchair in the gloomy penthouse office on the thirty-fifth floor, where David Bookbinder sat behind his enormous desk the size of an aircraft carrier and directed the day-to-day flows and transactions of Cornelius money.

Bookbinder had been busy all morning. It was one of those curious days when the market still showed signs of depression psychosis, but was just beginning to catch the light-headed fever of boom times. He was rearranging some of the Cornelius holdings in war-related industries, but he was reluctant to turn too much over to peacetime production, particularly with the news from Europe of "Soviet encirclement." While he talked endlessly on the telephone, Roderick had been drinking his Scotch.

As lunchtime neared, there were fewer phone calls and more paperwork. Bored, Roderick stirred his Scotch whiskey with his forefinger, and then absentmindedly sucked it.

"You shouldn't do that," said David Bookbinder, without looking up from his papers. "It reminds me of Foster."

Roderick blinked, vaguely surprised. "Does Dulles do that?"

Bookbinder nodded.

"I thought you liked him," said Roderick a little suspiciously.

Bookbinder methodically ticked off stocks and holdings, and then tossed the papers into his pending tray. "I do," he said, screwing the top on his Waterman pen. "But you couldn't say that style was Foster's strong suit, could you? Even Janet's sick of his socks."

"I never noticed his socks."

Bookbinder clipped his pen into his vest pocket and stood up. "I knew Foster when Bill Cromwell was paying him fifty dollars a month, and that was fifty dollars better than most law clerks used to get in those days. Foster was such a hick we used to call him the Kansas Kid. He could put on a Brooks Brothers suit, and in five minutes flat, he could make it look like one of Charlie Chaplin's castoffs."

Roderick said reflectively: "I don't mind what he does with his suits. I just wish he'd play the game a little more *our* way and a little less *their* way." He nodded in the vague direction of the Standard Oil Building.

"It's all a question of connections," said Bookbinder. "As it happens, they've put far more money into their connections than we have."

"Is that *your* decision?"

"Not entirely. Personally, I'd much rather have Foster as an ally than an enemy. He's going to wind up Secretary of State one of these fine days, and if we're not buddies by then . . . well, you can use your imagination."

"Father says he's a saboteur in savior's clothing," said Roderick.

"What makes him say that?"

"I don't know. Maybe he's just prejudiced. Father never liked what Dulles did with American Oil, and I guess we've all been biased against him ever since."

"American Oil was centuries ago."

"Sure. But Father has his favorite hates, and Dulles is one of them. He says he's gotten too spiritual, and I don't think Father believes in spiritual economics. He says there's only one thing worse than an idealistic Communist, and that's an idealistic Republican. As far as Wall Street goes, they're a total frost."

"Wall Street," sniffed Bookbinder, "is suffering from terminal mediocrity. And *now*, of all times!"

Roderick shrugged. He took a clean white handkerchief out of his dark blue double-breasted suit and patted a few clear drops of perspiration away from his neatly clipped sideburns.

"Well, sure, it's mediocre," he said, "but I don't think that's necessarily bad. Maybe we *need* to be mediocre. Father says that the whole secret of managing a complicated corporate budget is to have a highly developed sense of the wishy-washy."

Bookbinder laughed roughly. "Don't you worry what your father says. Your father used to prod cows for a living."

"And now you're upset because he prods you?"

"Your father's growing old," replied Bookbinder flatly. "Sometimes, for old times' sake, he tries to provoke me. I used to be a boxer at law school—did you know that? I was very athletic. Your father used to enjoy riling me up at important meetings, just to watch me clench up my fists. He used to say: 'David, what I'm waiting for is the day when you punch Howard Pew straight in the nose!' "

Bookbinder walked over to the window and looked down thirty-five floors into the rainy streets of lower Broadway. The sidewalks were beetled with shiny black umbrellas, and a tangle of Checker cabs and limousines were honking at each other dolefully.

"I sometimes believe, Roddy, that your father made his fortune as a kind of revenge."

This sort of conversation was too mystical for Roderick. He opened his gold half-hunter and checked the time. "Are you coming for lunch?" he asked. "I promised to meet Celia at the Plaza."

"You had lunch there yesterday."

"I know. But Victor likes to ride in the hansom. And apart from that, Celia has this . . . *thirst* for Gouron's cream-of-chicken soup. She says she gets it every year, as soon as the weather turns cold. If I didn't believe that lightning can only strike in the same place once, I'd swear she was, well, expecting."

"Pregnant?" said Bookbinder, raising an eyebrow.

Roderick frowned. "*Expecting*," he corrected carefully. "But she's not, of course. It's just the soup."

David Bookbinder went over to the coat stand and took down his dark gray pinstripe coat. There was a fresh pink carnation in the buttonhole, wilting a little in the office's seventy-degree heat, and he sniffed it ostentatiously before he put the jacket on.

489

"You should wear a carnation, too," he said to Roderick. "Your father's garden produces the finest carnations in the whole state. A mark of pride."

"I can't stand carnations," replied Roderick distastefully, swallowing the last of his Scotch. "They remind me of funerals."

Bookbinder looked at him. "That's why you should wear one," he said.

Roderick, for some reason that he couldn't understand, found that remark distasteful. He said: "You're a pretty morbid bird today."

Bookbinder tugged his vest down over his plump stomach. "Better to be a morbid bird than a plucked duck," he remarked enigmatically.

"If you trust my driving, we'll go in the car," suggested Roderick, shaking himself into his dark Chesterfield coat.

Bookbinder was lighting a cigar. "You drive *yourself*? Is this the new democracy? Is this why we fought the Japs?"

"I like driving," said Roderick. "I brought the Lincoln down this morning, and she's a real dream. V-12 L-head engine, and a Liquamatic gearshift. I parked her downstairs."

Bookbinder grunted. "If you knew as much about finance as you know about those damned automobiles of yours, I could die a happy man."

Roderick went red. He usually went red when he was put out, or embarrassed. At thirty-one, he was a big, heavy-boned young man, with a wispy blond mustache that he had started to grow when Celia was away in the hospital giving birth to Victor. He looked more like his father than ever these days, and his expensive clothes never seemed to sit on him comfortably. His hats always looked too small, and his overcoats billowed around him in copious folds. His big feet were laced up in shoes like black polished barges.

The two men walked side by side through the outer office.

"I'm going for lunch, Miss Kaminsky," said Bookbinder.

They reached the high black marble lobby and stepped across its echoing oval floor to the garage entrance. Several passing employees raised their hats or said "Good afternoon, sir." Roderick acknowledged them with a hasty, embarrassed smile, but David Bookbinder didn't even turn his head.

The Lincoln, a white 26H coupé, was parked at the foot of the stairs. Roderick unlocked the doors, and they climbed in. It smelled of rich new hide upholstery and Celia's perfume. A large yellow teddy bear with a wide leer on its face was propped up in the back, along with Victor's teething ring and rattles. Roderick started the engine, and the car bounced on soft suspension up the garage ramp and into the street.

It was October, and it was chilly and wet. Impatient business executives stood at street corners waving their umbrellas at passing taxis, and stenographers and office boys crowded the sidewalks. Burned-smelling smoke drifted across Broadway from bagel stands, and there was still the odd postwar feeling in the air. It was regretful, as if a dream were over, and now we had to forget about fantasies of glory and struggle and our boys overseas, but it was also elated, in a peculiarly practical kind of way, because now we could think about housing, and new cars, and jobs, and television sets, and front-runners at Aqueduct. James Thurber would be fifty-one in two months' time and he had just published *The White Deer*—the story of a prince who had to find a thousand jewels in ninety-nine hours.

Roderick, steering the Lincoln uptown, said: "I give up."

"You give up what?" said Bookbinder.

Roderick looked at him. "I give up on the plucked ducks."

"Well, forget about the plucked ducks. Think about the carnations."

Roderick pulled up at a red light. A young veteran in Army uniform, with one empty sleeve safety-pinned up, came across and tapped at the window.

"Our glorious fighting forces," remarked Bookbinder sarcastically.

Roderick wound the handle down. "Yes?"

The vet was only about twenty-one or twenty-two. He was thin and scraggy, with an unshaven chin and eyes that were red from sleeping on Broadway doorsteps. He said, very politely: "Is it possible that you might have the price of a bowl of soup?"

Roderick turned to David Bookbinder. "Do you have any change? I'm penniless."

David Bookbinder patted his pockets, and then shook his head. "I'm sorry. I haven't carried a billfold in six years."

Roderick searched his own coat again, but he had nothing at all. He said to the veteran: "I'm sorry. We'd like to help, but we don't have any money."

The veteran stared at them. He had rain on his eyelashes. He stared at Roderick's expensive Chesterfield, and Bookbinder's fragrant cigar. He said: "You don't have any *money*?"

Roderick was embarrassed.

The veteran said: "How can you sit there and tell me you don't have any *money*?"

Roderick said: "Well—"

"I don't want any, not now," said the boy. "I just want to *know*."

"Well," said Roderick lamely. "It's just that . . . we don't have any use for it."

The veteran was still staring at them when the light changed and Roderick thankfully pulled away. He said to Bookbinder: "Remind me to carry some change with me in the future. I don't want that to happen again. Better still—you carry some."

Bookbinder reached into his coat and took out a wad of bills. He ruffled through them and said: "My dear Roddy, I always do."

Roderick glanced over at the bills. Then he stepped hard on his brakes and pulled into the curb. A taxi blasted its horn at him, and the driver yelled: "Ya brainless bastard!"

David Bookbinder pretended to look surprised. "What's the matter? Why have we stopped?"

Roderick said: "Just give me the money!"

"What do you mean? *All* of it? There must be four hundred dollars here."

"Just give me a twenty. Come on, quick."

David Bookbinder said: "You're making a mistake, Roddy!"

"I don't think so. Now, give me the twenty."

David Bookbinder sighed, and peeled off the bill. Roderick snatched the money, climbed out of the car, and ran back along the sidewalk in the rain. He bumped into women with bags, men with briefcases, umbrellas, and strollers. He reached the traffic light, and the young soldier was still standing there, waiting for the red. Roderick ran across the street and tapped him on the shoulder.

The boy turned. He was so much shorter and thinner than Roderick that he made Roderick feel like a huge overfed giant. Roderick held out the twenty-dollar bill.

The vet stared at it. "What's that for?" he said.

"My friend found it in his coat. I wanted to give it to you."

The boy stared at the trembling bill in Roderick's hand, and then he looked up into Roderick's eyes.

"Please," said Roderick, "take it."

The vet looked down at the money again.

"Take it," urged Roderick.

The boy said carefully: "I don't have change."

"Change? What change?"

"A bowl of soup, with bread, is five cents. I don't have change for a twenty."

"Well, take all of it. Have a hundred bowls of soup."

The boy lowered his head. "Mister," he said, "I've lost my right arm, and I've lost my job, but I don't think I've lost my pride."

"You can't eat pride," said Roderick. It was raining hard now, and he was getting wet.

"No," said the vet. "And you can't buy pride, either."

Roderick impatiently pushed the bill into the boy's top pocket. "Pride or no pride, take it anyway. Take it as a favor to me."

The boy took the twenty out of his pocket with his good left hand. Then he put it up to his mouth and tore it into shreds with his teeth. In the rain, the fragments stuck to his lips.

Roderick looked at him. For some reason, he felt alarmed. He said to the boy quietly: "Are they all like you? All the boys who came back?"

The vet brushed dollar confetti from his mouth and turned away. Roderick reached his hand out to touch the boy's shoulder again, but then changed his mind. He was being elbowed and buffeted by passing shoppers and he was getting soaked. He went slowly back to the Lincoln, opened the door, and climbed in.

David Bookbinder was waiting for him patiently.

"Well?" he said, sucking his cigar. "Did he take it?"

Roderick didn't look across at him. He started the engine and pulled the car out into the lunchtime traffic.

"What makes you think he didn't?"

David Bookbinder chuckled, and tapped his forehead with his forefinger. "Psychology, Roddy, that's what. The psychology of money."

"I didn't know money had a psychology. I thought psychology was all about dirty dreams."

"And you your father's son? Tch-tch!"

Roderick shrugged. "I guess I'm a disappointment, huh? Just tell me how you put a share certificate on a couch, and then maybe I'll understand."

"It's very easy," said Bookbinder, sticking down a wayward leaf of tobacco with spit. "You just demonstrated the psychology of money in its purest form with that one-armed bandit at the street corner."

"Goddamned jaywalkers! How's that?"

"You offered the kid too much. A twenty-dollar bill was too abstract for him. He's probably never had one before in his whole life. To him, it was just so much paper—Monopoly money. The same goes for most of the people out there. The reason they're never going to get rich is because they don't want to. No—it's true. As soon as you start talking money in zeros—as soon as you start talking about bonds and stocks and options—most people go glassy-eyed with boredom."

"Maybe that's just as well," said Roderick, slowing down for another red light.

"It is," agreed Bookbinder. "All most people want are *things*—like a house and a shiny car—and *prestige*—like a fancy executive title and a key to the first-class washroom. You don't have to offer them money. If you give a guy a name like 'corporate vice-president,' he won't even worry that you're paying him five thousand dollars a year less than you could be. Give him a company car instead of a raise. He'll love you for it."

Roderick nodded. "In other words, don't offer a man the price of a case of champagne when all he wants is a bowl of soup."

"Exactly," said Bookbinder.

They crossed West Eighth Street and continued uptown on Broadway. The windshield wipers purred backward and forward like two nodding cats, and the rain pattered onto the Lincoln's convertible roof. On a street corner two cops stood next to a soggy poster for Hitchcock's *Spellbound*, with rain dripping from their caps.

"I'm beginning to wonder what all this is about," said Roderick. "First of all it's ducks, then it's carnations, now it's psychology and management."

David Bookbinder puffed his cigar quietly. "I did want you to be properly prepared. I didn't mean to be devious."

Roderick grunted. "I don't think you can *help* being devious. Father says that . . ."

Roderick suddenly stopped. In Bookbinder's eyes he detected the faintest flicker of emotion. It was the telltale widening of the pupils when the stud-poker player spreads out a winning hand—the nervous telegraph that gives away boxers before they strike.

"It's Father," said Roderick. "You're setting me up to say something about Father."

David Bookbinder nodded.

"Is he all right? I mean . . . there's nothing *wrong*, is there? His health's okay?"

David Bookbinder said: "I tried to keep this for later. This isn't exactly the time and the place to tell you."

Roderick said anxiously: "David—please. I have to know."

"Well," said David Bookbinder, "your father's been having tests."

"I know that. He was up at the sanatorium last month. He told me that everything was fine, and Dr. Clarke said he was one hundred and five percent."

David Bookbinder looked out of the car window. Droplets of rain clung to the glass and dribbled shakily downward.

"Your father was trying to protect you from distress. He was also trying to protect the whole of Cornelius Oil. The last thing we wanted to happen was a run on shares, particularly now. But the truth is, Roddy, that your father is a sick man."

"Sick? How sick?"

"It's his heart. It's weak, and it's diseased. Dr. Clarke diagnosed it last Thursday, and Dr. Scheiner gave a second opinion, and agreed."

David Bookbinder was silent for a moment. When he spoke, his voice was steady and flat, but there was something regretful in it, too—the kind of gray nostalgia that blew through New York for a war that had just finished, and a dream that had just faded away.

"He's been feeling breathless and suffering pain for almost two years now. For everybody's sake, he's kept it quiet. Your mother knows, but nobody else. If he takes life easy, he could survive for a while, but there's no real chance of curing it."

Roderick was driving slowly and mechanically, and almost ran a red light.

"I don't know what to . . ."

"I know," said David Bookbinder. "It's a tough break."

"Isn't there some way of . . . I mean, David, the family can afford to give him the best treatment in the world! Surely *someone* can help? Some specialist? What about that Swiss doctor that mother went to? The one in Basel."

Bookbinder dropped his cigar out of the window, and shook his head.

"They've given him six months at the outside. The treatment just doesn't exist. Even if your father was twice as rich as he is now,

495

he couldn't do anything about it. You can't buy what doesn't exist."

"But, Jesus, can't we . . .?"

David Bookbinder shook his head again. "The best thing we can do is keep it under wraps. I didn't want to tell you about it just yet, but I guess you had to know. John doesn't know, though, and neither does Hope. I advised your father against telling them."

Roderick was very pale, and he didn't answer.

"The thing is, Roddy," said Bookbinder, "that I'm worried about what's going to happen next. Your father's illness is very tragic and it's very sad, but we must make calm arrangements for the future. Unless we're very careful, we're going to find ourselves in a sticky situation, particularly with the market the way it is."

"Don't you think that John and Hope have a right to know?" asked Roderick flatly.

Bookbinder coughed. "Well, of course they do. Watch that truck, Roddy. Of course they have a right to know. But the reason I suggested that they didn't find out just yet was because of all the problems over inheritance."

Roderick said: "We don't have any problems. All three of us have enough trust accounts to sink the *Missouri*."

David Bookbinder took out his handkerchief and coughed into it.

"That's quite true, Roddy. But what we have to think about now is whether those trust accounts are in the most profitable posture."

"What's that supposed to mean?"

Bookbinder was obviously searching for the most delicate way to phrase his next remark. He said slowly, with his tiny hands coming together to form a protective cup: "Every fortune, when it's passed from father to son, is at risk. Inheritance tax is one risk, sure. The Fords found that out. Until they set up the Ford Foundation, they were faced with 91 percent inheritance tax on Henry Ford's 58½-percent holding, and 91 percent of nearly $700 million isn't two slices of lemon Danish.

"But there are other problems as well. If you disperse your fortune to avoid inheritance taxes, you run the risk of that fortune never coming together again as a single political and financial force. Too much stray money goes into too many odd foundations and trusts, like it did with the Rockefellers, and that kind of thing has a debilitating effect on the power of the central fortune. I don't think we'd like that to happen with the Cornelius fortune, would we?"

"I still don't see what you're getting at."

Bookbinder smiled distantly. "Not yet you don't. It does require a little explaining, and it also requires some gentle rearrangement of funds. But let me put it this way for now. Wouldn't you rather see all the Cornelius trust accounts and stock holdings legally and bindingly arranged so that all came under one controlling force—instead of being split up into fragments?"

Roderick's forehead furrowed, and he didn't reply.

David Bookbinder leaned over toward him. "Wouldn't you rather have your hands on the reins of the whole team, for instance, instead of allowing John and Hope to gallop some of the best horses into any old mire they felt like? Don't you think that's wiser? Don't you think that's safer for all of us?"

Roderick looked across at Bookbinder and tried to read what was happening behind those small, intent eyes.

"I guess the principle's right," he said uncertainly. "But what about the technicalities? And what would John and Hope have to say? The money's theirs, after all. Maybe they're younger, but they're not stupid."

Bookbinder sat back. "I didn't say they were. But I do believe, Roddy, that if anyone has the guts and the go to manage this fortune, its you. Look at you—you're the spitting image of your father. Do you think he worked all his life, created this empire with his bare hands, just to have it dissipated?"

They were driving east along Fifty-ninth Street to the Plaza. The sky over Central Park was thundery gray, and the trees rolled and rustled like frothing horses in the rainy wind. Roderick drew into the carpeted sidewalk and pulled on the Lincoln's hand brake.

"I don't know, David," he said. "Let me think about it, huh?"

David Bookbinder buttoned up his coat. "That's okay. Give it a couple of days. But remember your father's condition, Roddy. You can't leave it forever. There just isn't that much time."

That same rainy afternoon, in a small and quiet apartment in the East Fifties, John Cornelius was lying on the blue silk quilt of a double bed smoking a Turkish cigarette. He could hear the rain pattering against the glass of the window, and the echoing sound of car horns and traffic, but he seemed almost completely at peace, watching the thin ribbon of smoke rise to the apartment's decorative plaster ceiling.

He was naked. He was short and stocky for twenty-eight, with a darker complexion than his brother Roderick, and a sharp, muscular face, like a football player from Notre Dame. His body was yellow with fading suntan, and patterned with whorls and eddies of black hair. There was a coarseness about his appearance that wasn't unattractive—a heavy shadow on his chin, and stubby, hairy fingers. But there was refinement as well. He was relaxed like a swimmer floating on the ocean at an expensive resort, and he had grace and accuracy in every movement.

Around him, the apartment was bijou but luxuriously furnished. Thick brown carpets, walls covered in pale shot silk. A rose-period Picasso hung by the bedroom door, showing a sad-faced *saltimbanque* on a horse. The bed was French, made of carved mahogany, with elegant wooden flowers and petals twining around the headboard. There was a persistent fragrance of Guerlain perfume and exotic tobacco, mingled with that well-heated smell that pervades the apartments of the wealthy all over the world.

A girl's voice called from outside the bedroom: "John! Where are you now?"

John reached over to the silver art-nouveau ashtray beside the bed and crushed out his cigarette. "I'm at Getty's. Right this very minute, I'm putting a very interesting proposition to J. K. Carter about refining facilities at Port Arthur. He's looking at me with his well-known puzzled expression, and he's nodding his head like the jackass he is."

There was the sound of someone walking unevenly in wood-soled mules. The girl appeared at the bedroom door, a small Slavic-looking creature with dark curly hair, slanting brown eyes, and a finely defined jaw. She was wearing an embroidered silk negligee in shiny pink, and she carried a highball glass in each hand, clinking with ice and cold gin. Her name was Mara Malinsky, and this was her third week on the East Side. Her small breasts wobbled under the silk as she walked toward the bed.

"Does J. K. Carter *accept* the proposition?" asked Mara, sitting down beside him with the two frosty drinks in her hands. "Or does he say, 'John Cornelius, get back to your love nest, and treat Mara Malinsky to everything she deserves, and a few things she doesn't'?''

John rubbed his chin, mock-thoughtful. "No," he said at last. "He accepts the proposition."

In gleeful retaliation Mara pressed both highballs firmly against John's hairy nipples. He yelped, and rolled over, splashing cold martini all over himself. Mara set the glasses down on the marble-topped bedside table and threw herself on top of him, laughing and struggling. They tussled and kissed and fought, and then John suddenly found himself with his hands around her bare bottom, her negligee raised up around her waist, and he was looking into those eyes the color of unskinned almonds, and her lips were almost parted, moistened, as if ready to kiss him. Gently he lifted his head and touched his mouth against hers. She ran her hand through his thick dark hair. Then she kissed him back, licking his teeth like a child after rock candy.

He stared at her for a long time. There was a strange photographic light in the room which made the whole afternoon seem like a long romantic movie. The scene where the lovers tangle in the sheets. Lips touch and tongues softly click. The scene where the young mistress walks naked across the room, thin and delicate, with wrists and ankles slender enough for the smallest bangles. The sound of the bidet running as she squats to douche away his semen.

"Shall I play some music?" she asked. "Are you in the mood for music?"

John grinned and touched the tip of her nose with his finger.

She got up from the bed, straightening her negligee. She was not yet used to being wanton. This was, after all, only the fifth time they had "been" together, and she was still uncertain of herself. She walked across the bedroom to the polished mahogany Victrola and opened the lid. He watched her through half-closed eyes, idly stroking his own hairy belly.

"You know what you remind me of?" he said.

She looked up. The dim October light caught one of her eyes, and made it transparent like a carnelian.

"No," she almost whispered. "What?"

"You remind me of a woman I once saw when I was visiting France with my mother. I was only ten years old. Ten or eleven. We went to the beach at Arromanches. It was quite cold and gray, and you couldn't see very far out to sea. There was a woman sitting in the sand dunes with a scarf around her head. She had a husband in a striped blazer and a very yappy dachshund. She was eating strawberry cakes and drinking wine from a plain tumbler. I fell in love with her straightaway, and it's only just occurred to me that you look exactly like her.''

Mara lowered her head to read the label of the record she was putting on.

"Have you fallen in love with me?" she asked. She wound the handle round and round, and raised the heavy pickup arm to check that the needle was still sharp. She didn't look around.

John sat up on his elbow. "Would you believe me if I said I had?"

She thought about that. Then she said: "No. I don't think I would, really."

"Would you *like* me to fall in love with you?"

She shrugged. "What I would *like* and what I can *get* are two different things, aren't they? But, anyway, I don't think you would. You're very *different* for a trillionaire, but you are a trillionaire, aren't you? You talk romantic, but you do some very trillionairish things."

"Like what? What have I done lately that's trillionairish?"

Duke Ellington crackled into the room, playing "Ev'ry Hour on the Hour I Fall in Love with You." Mara twirled around the bed, lifting her negligee so that its long sleeves floated through the air.

"You've ensconced me," she said, "in this dreamy apartment. You've bought me a car. And you've made sure that my slightest whim is attended to, and always pronto! I only have to say fried baby clams, and I get them!"

John laughed. "That's not trillionairish. Listen, come here, and I'll tell you what trillionaires do. You really want to know?"

She swooped onto the bed beside him. "I bet it's boring," she said, blinking at him cheekily. "I bet that being a trillionaire is such a yawn that you have to hire special people to put their hands in front of your mouth for you."

"If you're talking about my brother, Roddy, then you're absolutely right. Roddy is the staunchest, most conservative trillionaire that ever breathed. He's stingy, too. He steals stationery from cheap hotels, and towels from bus stations. He's the only trillionaire who's got 'Property of U.S. Treasury' printed on his toilet paper. He collected a few rolls on his last visit."

"You're kidding again," said Mara. She reached for her

highball and took a long drink. Then she turned over on her back and stared at the ceiling. "I'll bet your brother, Roddy, is the kindest, most generous guy in the whole world."

John sniffed. "You're right, as a matter of fact. He is. He'd give his last doughnut to Earle McAusland."

"I get the feeling you resent him."

"No, no," said John, swallowing cold gin. "I don't resent him. Why should I? He's the kind of older brother that some younger brothers would give their left legs for. What you have to understand, *ma chère* Mara, is that when you're an heir and an executive in a corporate entity like Cornelius, you support your family no matter what. You can't tell where blood ends and money begins."

She turned over and examined him from close up, as if he was an unusual sculpture.

"Don't you ever get lonesome?" she asked.

He shook his head. "That's one of the great fallacies that people with thin wallets like to believe about people with fat wallets. It isn't lonesome, being rich. Not unless you're a real recluse. I mean, I guess my father isn't very sociable these days, but he used to be, when he was younger. When you have bottomless reserves of money, you can meet whoever you want, you can have parties and dinners whenever you want, and you can fly hither and thither whenever you want. Did you know that I have my own plane?"

"Your own? You mean it belongs to you personally?"

"It sure does. But that's nothing. Roddy has five. He has them all parked in a big shed down at his place in Virginia, and whenever he's down there, he goes and ogles them. He's kind of an airplane nut."

She sat up. "Would you like to hear another record?"

"Sure. Anything you like."

She padded over to the Victrola again. As she was sorting out what she wanted to play, she said: "I really find it frightening."

"Frightening? What?"

"All your money. It scares me."

"I don't wave it at you, do I?"

"You can't."

He didn't answer that. Instead, he reached over for his gold cigarette case and carefully removed an oval Turkish cigarette. He lit it with his glittering lighter and puffed out blue smoke.

Mara laid the steel needle into the groove of "I Can't Put My

501

Arms Around a Memory." There was a small smile on her lips when she turned back and looked at John—half-wistful and half-resigned.

"I knew when you picked me up that you couldn't take me around. But it all seems so strange. You must be rich, because you're John Cornelius. Yet I can't experience any part of your life, and I can't see what it is that makes you rich, or why you enjoy it. I have to sit up here in this . . . ivory tower, and the only time I see you is when you're stark naked."

John blew out smoke. "In that case, you see me at my best."

She pretended to be exasperated. "You're so conceited. I'm sure that you look quite presentable when you're dressed."

He smoked thoughtfully for a while. Then he said: "You're a strange girl, Mara."

She didn't look up. She was watching the record label go around and around as the needle hissed its way through the faint strains of trumpets and trombones.

He got off the bed and walked across to where she stood. Naked and hairy, he kissed the back of her neck. They were momentarily knotted together by thin strands of curling cigarette smoke, like printed lovers on a Valentine's Day card.

"I promise," he said. "I promise that when Irene and the girls go south, I'll take you out. First stop—the Starlight Roof at the Waldorf. Now, how about that?"

She turned around, pouting. "You're mocking me," she said "You never go there."

"I do too. I was there last week, and I cut a rug with Hedy Lamarr."

"You're a liar."

He grinned. "Well, maybe I am. But there are plenty of places we can go, and not be recognized. I'm not a movie star, you know. The common rabble in the street don't know me from Adam."

"Nor do I," she said. "You're always as naked as Adam when you're with me."

She stroked his shoulder, her fingertips circling softly around. She was gazing sadly across the bedroom as if she could already detect the shadows of a heartbroken future. She sighed.

"I guess I came too late," she said. "I can borrow your body, but that's about all. I can never be part of your life."

"You don't have to be jealous of Irene," he said, frowning.

"But I am. She can share your life, and your home, and your

502

children. She can stand by your side at parties, and go riding with you, and what can I do?''

John went across to the ashtray and tapped his cigarette. The afternoon light was growing dimmer, as if it was being filtered through layer after layer of white muslin. At almost the same moment he tapped the cigarette, Roderick was drawing into the curb outside the Plaza, and pulling on his hand brake.

John said: "When Irene goes south, there's no reason why we couldn't hold a dinner party. I have a place on East Eighty-second Street, and a cottage out at the Hamptons.''

"You mean a discreet dinner party?'' asked Mara. "A few well-trusted friends?''

"Who do you think I meant? The editor of the *New York Post*?''

Mara said: "John, don't treat me like a child. I'm twenty-one. I'm a woman and I have the instincts of a woman. You can't shut me up here for the rest of my life, and just use me when you want me. I have to be able to participate in what you're doing. You have to give me the chance to give you something back. I can't do that when you hide me here.''

"Well," he said uncertainly, "I'm sure we can work something out.''

She looked perplexed. "Don't any of your other friends have mistresses? Kept women? Surely it wouldn't shock them that much?''

"Mara, it's not a question of shocking people.''

"Then what? If it's not a question of shocking people, why can't we have a dinner party with your usual friends? Just wait until Irene's gone south, and have a dinner as normal. You can always say I'm your long-lost cousin from Holland, or something like that.''

John sat on the edge of the bed. He ran his hand tiredly through his hair. "Mara,'' he said, "do you have any idea who my usual friends are?''

She put her head on one side. She wanted him to look up at her, to give her a clue, but he didn't.

"Rich people, I guess,'' she said lamely. "Du Ponts, and people like that.''

John nodded. "Last week," he told her, "I had a small informal dinner for eighteen people. The Duke and Duchess of Windsor were there, and so were Clara Bell Walsh, Harvey

Firestone Jr., Sir James Dunn and Lady Dunn, and a sprinkling of other people you might recognize. Howard Hughes, for instance. Those are my usual friends."

Mara stared at him. "The Duke and Duchess of Windsor? You know them?"

John at last looked up. "I met them through Roddy. The duke's very partial to Scottish haddock, and Roddy knows an airline pilot who can fly them in special."

"Haddock?" said Mara unbelievingly.

"That's right. And broiled woodcock, if you're interested."

"You're mocking me again. You're avoiding the issue."

John said: "There is no issue. I'm very fond of you, Mara, and I want to keep you around. But I can't stroll around town with you hanging on my arm, because I have responsibilities to my family and my stockholders and everybody else who's associated with me because I'm known to be respectable."

She rubbed at the soft carpet with her mules. "You make it sound . . . very heartless, somehow."

She could see he was annoyed. He was sensitive, and he hadn't wanted to say what he had, but she had cornered him into it. They both knew that his money and his reputation were inescapable facts of life, and that everything they did—every laugh, every kiss, every act of love—would have to be conditioned by them. She reached over and kissed him gently on the side of the face. "I'm sorry," she whispered.

He smiled wryly and took her hand. "It's not your fault. You feel that way because you're generous, not because you're mean. You're a lovely girl, Mara, and however long I can hold on to you, I shall."

"Am I that different from Irene?"

The record was finished, and it was circling around with a breathless *click-hisss-click-hisss-click-hissss*. The way that the early-afternoon darkness was crowding into the room made John feel like switching on the lamps, but for some reason he was reluctant to. It was almost as if, once he did that, he was admitting that their hours together were nearly over. A small Swiss carriage clock chimed lightly from the drawing-room mantelpiece, and he knew it was half-past two. Rain pattered against the window like someone throwing a handful of raisins.

"I thought Irene was so beautiful," said Mara. "I've seen her photograph so many times. She looks so serene."

John nodded. "Yes, she is serene. But you can carry serenity too far. If you carry serenity to its ultimate limits, you wind up mummified."

"Isn't she very . . . relaxed?"

John stood up and walked over to the Victrola. He watched the record scratching around without making any move to turn it off.

"She believes in recreation," he said. "She swims, she rides, she plays tennis. She does all the right strokes with all the right folks. She's a bright hostess, and everybody says how wonderful her taste in wallpaper is. She's a good mother, too. She dresses the twins beautifully, and if they were old enough to speak, they'd ask to go play with the Vanderbilts."

Mara's slanted eyes dropped.

"Then why me?" she said.

There was a soft silence. John said: "I know what *you're* thinking."

"What am I thinking?"

"You're thinking I'm a frustrated husband who's been temporarily displaced by his newborn babies, looking for a little entertainment after hours."

She couldn't help smiling. He came over and knelt down in front of her, his penis hanging between his hairy thighs like a curious species of fruit.

"You're thinking that I don't really love you at all, and that as soon as I've gotten tired of you, I'll toss you by the wayside and go on to some other floozy. You're thinking that I'm specious, caddish, and villainous, not to mention sex-starved."

She leaned forward and they rested their foreheads together, gazing in close-up at each other's eyes. She touched his ear.

"That's right," she said. "That's just what I'm thinking."

They stayed like that for a while, face to face, and then John stood up.

"If you'd like to change the record," he said, "I'll fix the celebration drink."

"What's to celebrate?"

"I don't know. You and me, I guess. The weather. President Truman's new hat. Anything that takes your fancy."

She held out her hands for John to help her up from the floor. He lifted her, and embraced her closely in his arms. She had a thin, almost childlike body, but there was something intensely erotic about her as well. There was a contrast between her slightness and

505

her fierce appetite for lovemaking that aroused him. It was as if a child had just discovered sex, and was overindulging herself without any qualms of conscience or morality. To John, brought up under Johann's regime of regular churchgoing and Hester's dislike of any song or story that was remotely suggestive, this was something to make his nerves tingle and jump alert, and his hair rise up on the back of his neck.

"You do things to me," he said, quiet and amused.

She kissed him. "You do things to me, too."

He patted her small behind as she went to change the record. "This drink I'm going to mix you is the ultimate drink of all time," he said, reaching for his green silken bathrobe and wrapping it around himself. "It was invented by His Majesty King Alfonso of Spain, at the men's bar of the Paris Ritz."

He disappeared briefly into the kitchenette, and returned with a silver tray. On the tray was a Georgian silver wine cooler crammed with crushed ice and containing a dark green bottle of Moët & Chandon's Dom Perignon Cuvée 1934. Beside the cooler were two half-liter goblets of chilled and misted silver, and a bottle of Remy Martin vintage cognac.

Mara, choosing a record, said: "Champagne? Where in the world have you been hiding that?"

John laid the tray ceremoniously down on a small Bauhaus table and grinned. "I hid this in the saucepan cupboard when I came in. All the time we've been spooning and crooning, this beauty has been steadily chilling."

He took the champagne out of the ice, unwrapped the foil, and popped the cork out. The foam, as dry and astringent as a mouthful of prairie dust, surged into the silver goblets, and when they were brimful, John added three good-sized measures of cognac to each.

"Wait . . ." he said. "I nearly forgot the strawberries!"

Mara laughed with sheer pleasure. "Strawberries? And champagne? You have to admit that *this* is trillionairish!"

John came out of the kitchen with a woven wicker basket tied with pink ribbons and crammed with fresh strawberries.

"This isn't trillionairish," he said. "This is what we rich folk call *piggish*."

They sat on the bed while slow, treacly jazz hissed out of the Victrola. John handed Mara her goblet and picked up his own. She looked down into it, and the reflections of silver and champagne made flickering patterns on her face.

"It smells absolutely beautiful," she whispered. "Like liquid money."

"It's called the King's Death," said John. "You're supposed to drink it in three or four swallows, and then gorge yourself on strawberries."

She giggled. "Shall we try?"

"We have to. It's the only way to drink it."

"Is there anything you have to say before you drink?"

John shook his head. "The drink speaks for itself. You can say 'I love you,' if you like."

Mara swirled the goblet gently around, and watched the scintillating bubbles rise from the surface.

"I think perhaps instead I'll make a wish."

"Okay. What will you wish?"

"It's a secret. But I expect you know what it is."

He drank. The champagne was cold, and foamed in his mouth as if his teeth were turning to froth. Then the cognac warmed its way down his throat, and smoothed away the dryness.

"Yes," he told her. "I know what it is."

By the time Roderick had finished his lunch at the Plaza, and Celia had persuaded him to take young Victor around the park in Pat Rafferty's hansom, John and Mara were wet-eyed with drink and seized by a lewd and unreal passion that led them to make love over and over, sometimes collapsing on each other breathless when they were only halfway through, sometimes teetering on the very brink of it—but kissing with wide-open mouths and salacious tongues, and clawing at each other as if they wanted to scratch and bruise their flesh, and finishing up slower, slower, with the pace of the Twentieth Century Limited coming to rest, with a long bout of self-inflicted cruelty which left Mara facedown on the shiny blue quilt, weeping out loud from pleasure and agony, and John panting against the cold glass of the window, his cigarette burning away untouched in its ashtray.

Hope, as usual, was feeling brittle and annoyed. She had come in and out of the morning room five times, and each time Edward was sitting in his big brown brocade armchair, *The Wall Street Journal* raised in front of him like the sail of an old schooner, reading his slow and considered way through the market digest.

Finally, huffing in temper, she banged at the paper with her fist.

"Is there anyone in?" she snapped. "Or have you all gone to sleep in there?"

Edward, unperturbed, shook his newspaper back into shape. "We are not asleep in here, Hope. We are reading."

Hope clucked her tongue. "I suppose the fortunes of the Ohio Oil Company are far more interesting than what we're going to eat for dinner tonight."

Edward didn't stir.

Hope snapped: "I suppose the closing prices of Sears, Roebuck are more attractive than your own wife."

Edward folded down one corner of his paper and looked at her. "I'm catching up with the news. Is that such a crime? A man can't catch up with the news in his own house?"

Hope tossed her head impatiently. "Well, that's just dandy," she said. That's just wonderful to know. At least you've made it clear where I stand."

"And where do you think that is?" asked Edward.

"I damned well *know* where it is! I have to organize the whole of this evening's dinner, and all the entertainment, and all you can do is sit on your rump and read yesterday's paper. That's where I stand, Edward the Second!"

Edward shrugged, and went back to his reading. But Hope stood over him, tapping her foot on the parquet floor, her arms folded and her eyes sharp with anger.

Eventually Edward couldn't ignore her any longer, and he dropped the corner of his paper down again.

"Did you want something?" he asked courteously.

"Oh!" she said. "You've noticed I'm here!"

"Yes," he said slowly, "I *have* noticed you're there. In fact, I'd have to be deaf, dumb, blind, and paralyzed not to notice you're there. Now, what is it you want?"

"God," she said, spreading her hands in a histrionic appeal to the ceiling. "You're impossible!"

Edward put down his paper altogether. "I'm not impossible, Hope, I'm just trying to have ten minutes' reading. Is that too much to ask?"

"Edward," said Hope, "how long have we been married?"

"Why—do you think it's too long?"

"It's four months," said Hope sharply. "Four months last Thursday."

"And?"

"And you're sitting here reading the paper when you could be helping me! That's not young love, is it?"

Edward carefully scratched one eyebrow. "It could be," he said. "It depends how closely you equate love with money."

"I don't equate them at all!"

"No, well, maybe you don't. But then you've never had to worry about money, like I have."

"What's that supposed to mean? I just don't think that love equals money, or money equals love, that's all. And I think I have enough experience of both to speak with some authority, don't you?"

"I wouldn't deny it."

"So what do you mean? What does young love have to do with dollars and cents? Or is that the way you usually measure it? Are you a man, Edward Secker, or are you an adding machine?"

Edward picked up the paper again. "There's some interesting news in here about Daylong Oil, of Ohio."

Hope stared at him as if she could hardly believe he was real. She blew out her cheeks in exasperation and clapped her hands to the side of her head.

"I knew it!" she said. "I married a financial maniac!"

Edward smiled, but without much humor. "If you'd *listen* for a change, instead of jumping to uncomplimentary conclusions, you might understand what I'm trying to tell you."

"I don't have *time* to listen," rapped Hope. "I have to organize the terrapin. I have to make sure the partridge has arrived, and I have to demonstrate to that dummy of a cook the simplest possible stuffing for mongrel goose. Not that you care."

Edward shrugged. "Okay, if you have to go, you have to go. I'd hate to think we had disorganized terrapin in the house. I'll be down later, just as soon as I'm through with the paper, and I'll sort out the wine."

A pale-faced girl in a long white apron appeared in the morning-room doorway. She knocked shyly and said: "Excuse me, Mrs. Secker. There's a telephone call from your mother."

Hope gave Edward one last hot-and-bothered look and stalked off to the phone. Edward watched her go, half-amused and half-affectionate, and shook his head like a fond father.

His marriage to Hope had been one of those tangential and unexpected matches that seem to work because of their very unlikeliness. Hope was still in hiding when he first met her, isolated from society by her parents and friends until the last sickly memory of her scandalous divorce from Martin Landseer faded away. Hope

509

had spent most of her exile at Lynwood's Island and in Boston, dressing whenever she went out in severe black and navy-blue suits, and almost always veiled. Like many women who have fallen from social grace, she attempted to make public atonement by working for charity; and it was while she was chairing a meeting of the Veterans' Aid Society out at Lynwood that she had met Edward Secker.

Edward was thirty-six; a tall, large-boned man with a slight stoop and a dry way of talking. When he wore his reading glasses he reminded people of FDR, because he had that same big face, placid forehead, and those same small, intense eyes. Hope used to say, when she first met him, that he was so lengthy and angular that he had to fold himself up when he sat down, like a carpenter's rule.

He came from a reasonable, hardworking family—the Seckers of Virginia, specialists in fine tobaccos. His father, a one-legged planter with huge gray mustaches, had sent him through Harvard Law School, and he was now a junior partner in Donleavy, Settle, the Wall Street lawyers. Edward was conscientious and businesslike, but he had a kind of clean-cut gusto that had appealed to Hope in those suffocating and funereal days after her divorce—an enthusiasm for sailing and swimming and golf that had blown through her life with refreshing ingenuousness.

The refreshment was wearing off a little, but the marriage had done more for Hope than she realized herself. She had been twenty-six in May, and was a classically tempestuous Gemini. She was petite and still very pretty, just like her mother had been, and the only obvious Cornelius characteristic she possessed was her awkward temper. But there were dark smudges under her wide brown eyes, and her triangular face seemed to have a haunted quality about it—a worried shadow that passed over it in photographs and at odd, unguarded moments.

Hope always dressed beautifully. This morning, as she made the arrangements for tonight's family dinner party, she wore a dark green woolen dress with a V neck, square shoulders, and short sleeves. Her chestnut hair was swept up and held with green combs, and around her neck she wore a simple emerald choker. She usually spent two or three hours every morning getting ready for the day, and at Marchings, their twenty-bedroom house on Long Island, they always changed for dinner. Edward was boisterous, but he was also traditional, and insisted on what he called "manners."

They had an unusual social life. It was alternately busy and

510

remote. Some weeks they had guests every day, and glittering dinner parties for lawyers, business contacts, movie people, publishers, artists, and visiting acquaintances from Europe, and they always made the society pages, even when Hope was doing something as mundane as shopping for hats on Fifth Avenue.

At other times, though, they lapsed into isolation, and Hope would go for long walks in the grounds with their two red spaniels, treading through the wet leaves and brushing her way through overhanging trees and bushes. The gray fall skies hung very low over their white L-shaped mansion, and there was a sad smell of winter in the air. Those were the times when Hope began to wonder what marriage to Edward was really going to be like. His humor and his energy might have helped her to put the Landseer scandal behind her, and soothed her emotional fears, but what would happen when she was completely cured? Would she turn around and look Edward in the face and realize that it was nothing but overwhelming weariness and frailty that had caused her to marry him, and that their relationship was really nothing more than the affectionate bond between a doctor and his patient?

As she once confided in her friend Faith Schickman, the opera singer: "I don't want to spend the rest of my life in a hospital for broken hearts. Once I'm healed, I want out."

Edward was friendly and affectionate enough, though. He liked making love, although he wouldn't take off his wide-striped pajamas; and he would often kiss Hope very demonstratively in front of other people. He liked riding and he enjoyed cigars, and he was planning on taking her south to Virginia for their first vacation. There had been no honeymoon because of the pressure of Edward's work, but he was always talking about taking her to Europe—"and I'll make love to you under the Vienna moon."

Right now, on this wet October day, he seemed more preoccupied with business than usual. He had chosen to stay at home and finish up his backlog of paperwork rather than go into the city. He had already spent several hours on the telephone, and Hope had never seen him scrutinize the paper so thoroughly. She didn't care for business very much. To her, money was money regardless of its origin, and you spent it on clothes and houses and parties. It smothered you in fine jewelry, and sometimes it protected you from great harm.

She was in the big, high-ceilinged kitchen, going over the dinner arrangements with the cook, Mrs. Polanski, when Edward

511

eventually came down. There were heaps of vegetables all over the solid pinewood table: broccoli and earthy potatoes, pale rooty parsnips and speckled squashes. Already the polished copper saucepans and decorative molds were assembled, and the black kitchen maid, a pretty, cheerful girl with the unlikely name of Yolande, was scraping and slicing potatoes and grinding herbs. The old sink and range had been replaced by the Seckers with an up- to-date stove and dishwasher from Westinghouse, but the kitchen hadn't lost its antique charm.

"Well," said Hope sharply, "have you finished the funny papers?"

Edward nodded, and stole a red currant from a white enamel bowl.

"I've finished all right. Unfortunately, they're not so funny."

"What's that mean? That's okay, Mrs. Polanski, the nuts can wait until later. What's that mean, Edward?"

Edward stuck his hands in his pockets and looked around the kitchen.

"Can we go someplace else? Just for a minute? I think there's something you ought to know."

"Is it really that urgent?"

"It's . . . essential."

Hope sighed. "All right. Can you cope with that, Mrs. Polanski? I won't be too long."

Mrs. Polanski, a puffy-faced woman with great red forearms like Popeye, squinted at Edward suspiciously and nodded.

"I cope," she said thickly. "You just tell me the hows and the why-fors, and I cope good."

They went upstairs, and Edward opened the door of his study—a small book-lined room just off the main hallway. There were Harvard pennants on the wall, and an oar from Edward's sculling days. On the desk, which was littered with open books and heaps of paper, was a silver statuette of an athlete in rather long drawers. Edward said: "Sit down," and pointed to a fat ugly chair with a brown cushion on it. Hope, quite stiffly, sat.

Edward shuffled through the papers.

Hope said: "I feel as if you're about to tell me something awful. Something I don't want to hear."

Edward said: "Uh-huh. I am."

She sighed impatiently as he went on shuffling paper. "You're not a bigamist, are you? Or is that too much to hope for?"

512

Edward ignored her. He pulled out a long scribbled list of names, crisscrossed with arrows and figures and percentages, and said: "Here we are!"

Hope sat back and crossed her legs. She was always elegant, but there was often a nagging tension and impatience about her, and her friends frequently felt she was bored, or tired, or anxious to get on to her next appointment. Only Edward was impervious to it, because Edward was linear in his thinking and dogged in his progress, and if he knew that there was no logical reason why Hope should be bored, tired, or anxious, then he presumed that she wasn't, and didn't concern himself about her twitchiness at all.

Edward held the list up and waved it slowly back and forth, like a doubtful small boy waving at a Shriners' parade.

"I don't have proof yet," he said emphatically, "but I do have a pretty clear suspicion."

"You have a pretty clear suspicion of what? I wish you'd make sense."

He made a steeple of his hands. The dull daylight reflected from one lens of his spectacles, turning it blind.

"It's very hard to explain," he said, "and if I wasn't me, and if I didn't happen to be married to you, then I don't think I ever would have noticed at all. But when you look at what's been happening from our particular point of view, it all starts to smell pretty unusual."

"*Edward*," said Hope testily.

"No, no," put in Edward. "Just let me tell you. It's important to both of us, and it's especially important to you. After all, it's *your* money. If someone tried to pick your pocket, you wouldn't let them get away with it, would you? So don't let them pick your inheritance."

"I beg your pardon?" said Hope. She had been idly fondling the long-drawered athlete, but now she turned around.

"Your inheritance, Hope. I know it sounds absurd. But someone is trying to squeeze you out of your inheritance."

Hope put her hand to her mouth and let out a small affected laugh.

"Edward! What a ridiculous idea!"

Edward wasn't abashed. "It is ridiculous, I agree. But you take a look at these papers. Whether it's ridiculous or not, it's happening, and it's happening right under your nose. Daylong Oil is a particular instance."

"Daylong? But I control that company, don't I? I'm the largest stockholder, anyway. You know that as well as I do."

"Well," said Edward, "you *think* you're the largest stockholder."

"What's that supposed to mean?"

"Look here. You own 23.2 percent of Daylong stock. The remaining 76.8 percent of stock is divided among fifteen other stockholders, and the largest individual share that any of those stockholders owns is nine percent."

"So what's the problem?"

Edward took off his reading glasses and rubbed them with his handkerchief. He looked big-faced and nearsighted without them—like a large carp staring out of a bowl on the sideboard.

"The problem is that one of the minority stockholders has just sold four percent of stock to the Williamsburg Associated Bank."

Hope shook her head, uncomprehending. "What does that mean? Four percent isn't much."

"No, it isn't. Except that seven of those fifteen other stock-holding companies are controlled, in their turn, by banks or trusts or oil corporations which, in *their* turn, are controlled by Cornelius Oil—and specifically by the Cleveland division."

Hope frowned. "That's Roddy's division, isn't it? I mean—Roderick manages Cleveland?"

"He certainly does. Now let me tell you something else. Up until this Williamsburg bank transfer, Roderick's holding companies owned 19.1 percent of Daylong common. But it so happens that the Williamsburg Associated Bank is controlled 63.5 percent by Schuster Mills of Chicago, and Schuster Mills of Chicago, apart from reciprocally owning 2.05 percent of Daylong stock, is itself controlled by Cornelius Oil Cleveland."

Hope stared at Edward in disbelief. "Edward, are you telling me that Roddy actually controls my company? The company that Father gave to me?"

"It certainly looks that way," said Edward. "But I'm afraid that isn't the worst of it."

"What could be worse than that? I mean, what on earth is he trying to do?"

"Let me tell you. During the past month, there have been dozens of subtle sales of small percentages of stock in almost every corporation and fund in which you have an interest. Each time, no

514

matter how many deceptive holding companies and banks are involved, the result is the same. Roderick takes control.''

Hope was silent. Then she said: "Give me a cigarette."

Edward passed her an inlaid wooden box with a brass tennis racket for a handle. He lit the cigarette for her with a silver lighter, and she blew out an unsteady stream of smoke.

"Edward," she said, "if this is some kind of a prank . . ."

Edward looked at her and said nothing. He simply shook his head, and she knew that he was speaking the truth. Edward liked to boast about the shark he once caught off Florida, but he never exaggerated about money. His law firm was known for its dryness.

"All right," said Hope. "What about David Bookbinder? He's supposed to manage the family money and protect us from things like this. Surely he knows what's going on."

"I'm sure he does," said Edward. "In fact, he's probably instigating the whole operation. I don't like to be rude about your brother, but can you really see Roderick working out a deal like this, and carrying it off without a hitch? It's only a fluke that *I* found out."

"But what about Father?"

Edward put his glasses back on and squinted at Hope with a serious, sympathetic face.

"I don't believe your father knows. But I do believe that your father has something to do with it."

"I just don't understand," said Hope. The cigarette burned between her long, emerald-painted nails, and she felt unsafe and uncertain. She hadn't felt as bad as this since her divorce. This morning, everything had been reasonably secure and composed, but now she felt that familiar dropping sensation beneath her feet, like discovering that your best friend really hates you, or that a love affair has suddenly and inexplicably gone sour.

"It took me a long time to work it out," said Edward. "There were several possibilities—several reasons *why* Roderick should suddenly want to take control of all your interests—but only one fitted the bill."

He looked down at Hope's high-heeled crocodile shoes. He seemed to be searching around inside of himself for words, like someone in a bookstore who can't make up his mind which book to buy. Then, looking up again, he said: "Your father isn't a well man."

Hope's cigarette paused an inch away from her parted lips.

"He's been up to Lynwood Sanatorium to have a checkup," said Edward. "Apparently he's been feeling bad for a long time. I happen to know one of the specialists up there. His brother went to Harvard Law School with me, and I was kind of friendly with the whole family. They owed me a favor, so they did something a little unethical and told me what your father's test results were."

"Go on," said Hope hoarsely.

"I know your father told the family he had a clean bill of health, but the truth is that he's suffering from heart disease. They expect him, the doctors that is, they expect him to be dead in about six months. Maybe sooner."

Hope didn't move.

Edward said: "I'm sorry I had to break it to you like this, but it seems that nobody else was going to tell you. David Bookbinder's known about it for days, and so has your mother. For some reason, they didn't want you to find out."

"Does Roddy know?"

"Well," said Edward, "I expect so. That's why we're having this quiet game of proxies. He and Bookbinder are obviously trying to get their hands on the whole fortune before your father actually passes away."

Hope said: "It doesn't seem real. Father's been around for*ever*. What's it going to be like when he's not there anymore? I can't imagine it."

Edward reached for a cigarette himself. He didn't often smoke cigarettes, but right now he felt he could do with one. It had been hard enough keeping his discoveries quiet, but now he knew he was going to be locked in a vicious and unequal battle between Hope's family and her own financial protection. For an outsider, that wasn't going to be all flowers and candy. He knew what the Cornelius family had done to Hope's first husband, Martin Landseer, and the story of Johann Cornelius and Daniel Forster was one of the great Wall Street mysteries. As the saying went: "Never cross a Cornelius." He lit up, watching Hope's worried face and wondering if he ought to be equally worried himself.

"What about John's interests?" asked Hope. "Have you found out anything about those? Are they trying to do the same to him?"

"I don't know yet," said Edward. "I don't have complete lists of stock proxies yet. But, logically, I'd say that they were. In some cases you and John hold stock in the same corporations, and they'd

516

obviously want to stop you two from joining forces and outvoting them. It's been a very sneaky, very cleverly managed operation, and the reason they're doing it now is so that they can take full advantage of your father's condition. They want his seal of approval on the whole thing.''

"He'd never give it! He'd burst a blood vessel if he even knew about it!"

"Not necessarily. It depends how they told him. Listen, Hope, your father's seventy-two years old and he's not the businessman he used to be. He's old, and he's staid, and he forgets things. He's put far too much trust in David Bookbinder lately because he can't remember what's happening from one day to the next. If you ask me, Roderick and Bookbinder are going to wrap up the whole thing by persuading your father to sign over his controlling interest in Cornelius Oil Cleveland to Roderick personally, which will mean that directly or indirectly Roderick will own or control eighty percent of the family's oil and chemical and shipping interests. He's already a heavy stockholder in Cornelius Oil itself and Cornelius Oil New Jersey. That doesn't include Hester's slice of it, but then I presume that Roderick is Hester's favorite baby.''

Hope nodded. Her cigarette was burning her fingers, and she crushed it out in an ashtray with "Gleneagles Golf 1937" engraved on it.

"There's something even more sinister," continued Edward, "but I don't know whether I'm letting my imagination run away with me.''

Hope said baldly: "You'd better tell me, whatever it is.''

"It's a question of trust funds," said Edward. "As far as I can make out, there are dozens of trust funds set up for you and John and Roderick, right? Now, I don't know the conditions placed on all of these funds, but I get the impression that most of them are subject to the arrangement that you can draw interest from them for the rest of your life, but you can't touch the capital.''

Hope said: "Yes, that's right.''

"Well," said Edward, "if you can't touch the capital, then the capital presumably passes to your children, and to John's children and Roderick's children.''

"Yes," whispered Hope.

"But what happens if you don't have children? I mean, here's hoping, but supposing you don't? Or what happens if you have children and they die before they reach the age of maturity?''

517

Hope frowned. "In that case, the capital continues to be held as a trust fund by the central Cornelius Fund, and the interest is payable to the Fund."

"Which is managed by David Bookbinder?"

"Yes, but—"

"But *nothing*, Hope! Those are the facts!"

"Are you seriously suggesting that—?"

"I'm not suggesting anything, but I do think that the situation is potentially dangerous. If Roderick and Bookbinder can put the squeeze on all your inherited common stock, and if they can make sure that they hold the whole of Cornelius Oil in the palm of their hand, then you don't think they're going to balk at taking over the trust funds, do you? How much are those trust funds worth? Two hundred million? Three hundred million?"

Hope touched the emeralds around her neck. "But they *can't* take them over," she said. "Not unless . . . well, not unless they . . ."

Edward raised one meaningful finger. "Not unless you and I remain childless, and the twins don't live long enough to collect."

Hope was silent for a moment, but then she said: "Oh, that's ridiculous! I know Roddy's a bit weak when it comes to finance, but . . . well, that's *absurd*! He'd never do anything to hurt anyone!"

Edward puffed his cigarette awkwardly. He didn't inhale, and he let out the smoke in little round clouds, like the cartoon train in *Dumbo*.

"I don't think that Roderick's anything to worry about. He's your brother. If you ask me, he doesn't really understand what's going on. But David Bookbinder disturbs me a lot."

"David's a big fat Jewish teddy bear! He's been looking after Cornelius money for years!"

Edward shook his head. "Don't let his jolly fat looks fool you. I saw Lucky Luciano once, and he was the most ordinary and respectable-looking guy you could hope to meet."

Hope stood up and walked over to the window. The rain was still sliding slowly down the glass, and the trees and bushes of their small estate were clinging with mist.

"I don't know what to say," she said. "You've knocked the bottom out of everything I've ever believed."

Edward stared at the floor. "I can't prove it yet. You know that. But I had to warn you."

"Yes, I suppose you did. But what can I do now? They're all coming to dinner tonight. Even David."

"Well, for the moment you'll have to make out that you don't suspect them at all. But we must get your father aside and see if we can break it to him. Once he signs over that Cornelius Oil Cleveland stock, we don't stand a chance."

Hope traced a pattern on the window with her fingertip. "Do you think he'll believe you?"

Edward rubbed the back of his neck tiredly. "No, I don't. But he'll believe *you*."

She turned. "You don't expect *me* to tell him?"

"Someone has to."

There was a long silence. Then, from outside, there was a hesitant rap at the door. Edward said: "Come in!"

It was the pale-faced maid. She said: "Mrs. Secker, there's been an accident."

Hope glanced at Edward and then snapped: "Accident? What accident?"

The maid was confused. "It's Mrs. Polanski. She let the terrapins out by mistake, and they've crawled under the Frigidaire!"

Hope stared at the maid for a moment, and then gave a loud burst of nervous laughter. "Oh, my God," she said in her most overdramatic voice. "They'll mate!"

It happened so quickly that, years afterward, Irene could never remember whether it was Ally who had cried out first, or whether it was Clara. She couldn't even recall if it had been raining or not (it was), or where her mother-in-law had been standing when she first ran out into the street.

They were spending the day at Johann's heavy brownstone house overlooking Gramercy Park. John was downtown, negotiating refinery facilities with Getty Oil, but later in the evening they were all going to drive out to Hope's place on Long Island for dinner. Johann and Hester would continue in the evening to Lynwood's Island, while David Bookbinder's chauffeur was going to drive everybody else back to the city.

Irene didn't much care for Cornelius family gatherings, but she

519

liked Hope and Edward, and nobody expected her to participate much. Even John these days seemed to have eased off his earlier pressure to "get yourself involved" and to "think Cornelius." Life seemed to be settling down again, and because John was away so frequently on business, she could recultivate some of her old friends, and spend hours of play and leisure with the twins.

That afternoon—the same afternoon that John was having his "Getty Oil meeting" with Mara—Irene was sitting in the library at Gramercy Park, embroidering herself a flowery dressing-table mat. The sky outside was brown and gloomy—the sky from an early newsreel—and she had to wear her spectacles to see what she was doing. She didn't like to switch on the light, because Johann was snoring softly in his library armchair, almost buried in the shadows of his bookshelves and in the gathering darkness of an October day, and Willkie, his black Labrador, was sleeping around his feet like a fitful puddle of India ink.

Irene was a beautiful woman even if she wasn't a sensual woman. She was tall, and she carried herself with such poise and inbred dignity that bell captains never questioned her carefully measured tips, and strange men in the street raised their hats to her. She had a perfect oval face, with precise little lips, and immaculately arched eyebrows. Her eyes had once been described by Fiorello La Guardia, who quite often came to dinner at Gramercy Park, as "visionary." In fact, they were very pale gray, and only looked visionary because she was marginally nearsighted.

She had met John Cornelius three years ago, when he was twenty-five and she was twenty-three. It was 1942, and New York was still in a guilty, frustrated flummox about the war. John had wanted to go to Europe and save Holland single-handed from the Nazis, but Hester had insisted that her two sons were "captains of commerce" and shouldn't go. Johann, in a surprisingly surly mood, had grumbled that if they went, the government would commandeer his oil and his ships and his chemical plants, and if that happened, they needn't bother to come back. So the boys had half-reluctantly remained in the States to keep the pumps pumping and the factories turning out airplanes, ammunition, canned foods, and waterproof capes, not to mention record profits.

Irene, brought up in a repressive Bostonian atmosphere, where she had always been required to dress in sober colors and walk two steps behind her mother, had only begun to open her petals after a year at finishing school in Switzerland, and even then she was one of the palest flowers in the garden. It wasn't surprising that John, in 1942, had impressed her deeply. He was active, stylish, energetic, and good-looking. He always drove open convertibles, even when it rained, and he swam and rode and played terrific golf. They had met one summer night at a party at Grosse Pointe Shores, Michigan, and because he was drunk and she was happy, and the orchestra was playing "I Found a Million Dollar Baby in a Five and Ten Cent Store," they had sworn undying love.

The twins, Ally and Clara, were now eleven months old, and nearly walking. Right now, at half-past three in the afternoon in October, 1945, they were upstairs at Gramercy Park, sleeping. They would soon wake up and want their supper (soft-scrambled eggs and milk).

Johann, old and dry in his library chair, began to stir. From where she was sitting, Irene could only see his stubby-fingered hand with its brown liver spots, and the glisten of his old eyes somewhere in the shadow. He cleared his throat thickly and leaned forward.

"You still sewing, Irene?" he called. He liked Irene. She was one of his favorites; and he always spoke to her gently. Irene looked up.

"It's growing too dark now, Father," she called back. "I think I'll have to stop."

Johann took out his handkerchief and dabbed his mouth. "Am I going to see my babies before you tuck them in for the night?"

"We're taking them out to Long Island with us, Father. You can see them at Marchings."

"Well, I always like to see them when I can. The way I feel these days, I wonder if each time I see them isn't maybe the last."

"Father! That's no way to speak!"

Johann reached across with stiff fingers and switched on the table lamp next to his chair. A circle of electric light illuminated his age. He was a big man who had collapsed and shrunk with the passing years. There seemed to be nothing inside his green cardigan and his gray flannel trousers but the loosely assembled parts of an old bedstead. He was bald except for a few untidy white wisps around his ears, and his skin was tanned into that pale parchmenty color that passes for health among the very old and the very sick. His blue Dutch eyes had been rinsed of color, and his cheeks were like wrinkled beets that had been left to dry in the sun.

521

He cleared his throat again and sniffed.

"Oh, I shall be around for a little while yet." He smiled. "I didn't make my pile just to please my children. I want to enjoy some of it myself."

"I always knew you were a playboy at heart," teased Irene. She stuck her needle through her embroidery, laid it aside, reached over, and kissed his softly withered cheek.

Johann held her hand for just a moment, and ran his thumb over the sapphire and diamond rings.

"It's a strange thing about wealth," he said, watching the diamonds sparkle and the sapphires wink.

"What is? You can't blame yourself for being wealthy."

"I don't. But it's strange all the same. No matter where you get your money from—even if you lie and you cheat and you steal—it doesn't matter at all once you've got it. A gangster can rub elbows with anyone he likes if he's rich enough, and everybody will say how virtuous he is, and how temperate."

"But you're not a gangster, are you? How can you say that!"

Johann stared across the room at the sepia shadows of the passing clouds.

"No," he said quietly. "I'm not a gangster. But I'm not a holy saint, either. Some of the money I made wasn't as clean as it might have been, and some of it, the making of it, caused other people great pain."

Irene, still bent over him, frowned at the freckles and blotches on his bald head.

"Father . . ." she said. "Is anything wrong?"

He looked up. "Should there be?" he said.

"No, no. I didn't mean that. It's just that you seem to be . . . well, you're very reflective. You're not usually as thoughtful as this."

Johann shook his head. "No, there's nothing wrong. I'm just exercising an old man's prerogative, and rambling on."

"You're not worried about anything?"

"Worried? When you get to my age, you don't worry about a thing. It isn't worth the effort, whatever it is. No . . . I'm just thinking about the things I've done and the things I haven't done . . . and wondering whether they were good or bad . . . or whether I should have done better."

Irene looked at him for a while, and then quite spontaneously brushed her fingertips across his forehead.

522

"You won't think I'm impertinent, will you, if I say something?" she asked him.

He shook his head. "When you and I get together, Irene, we're best buddies, and best buddies can never be impertinent. You tell me what you've got to say, and I'll do my best to answer."

She said: "Well . . . I just wanted to ask if you were lonesome."

There was a silence. Johann didn't answer and he didn't stir, but his eyes seemed to lose their perception of the present, and stare back year by year, over decades and quarter-centuries and long-lost times when things were different, and carriages rattled in the sunlit streets of Broughton, Texas—streets that were now busy with automobiles, and crowded with stores. Irene, for one moment, thought she had gone too far and asked him a question that went too deep, but when the moment had passed, he looked up, and smiled at her, and stroked her wrist.

"Everyone gets lonesome sometimes," he told her. "But with you, and with Hester, and with those babies of mine, those twins, I could never stay lonesome for long."

What she didn't know, though, was that inside his mind as he spoke he was firmly closing a front-parlor door. Click. And sealing away the old mahogany furniture, and the decorated drapes, and a night that he had thought about many times in forty-two years.

"All right, Father," she said. "I'd better go and get the twins ready. Hope expects us out there by eight."

She left him, even though she had to pause at the door and look back to make sure he was all right. She had a feeling he might be crying, but he wasn't. She wasn't to know that he never cried. She closed the library door and went quietly upstairs on the plush green carpet, up to the nursery room that Johann and Hester kept for the twins.

Ally was already awake. She was lying on her back, cycling her legs in the air and chatting seriously to herself. Clara was still fast asleep, a bubble between her lips, one chubby hand tucked under her cheek. Both twins had cornsilk hair and big blue eyes, and an odd look about them that was one hundred percent Cornelius. Their nursery was wallpapered with flowers, and they slept in two identical cribs, hand-painted in France with tiny roses and cupids. Today they both wore long cream nightdresses of Brussels lace, underlaid with coffee-colored silk linings. Their nanny, Miss

Bendizzi, was already with them, laying out their traveling clothes for the evening. They were going to wear their brown tweed velvet-collared coats, their brown corduroy button-up leggings, and their dark brown berets.

Miss Bendizzi was a madonna, too, in her own way, but a Modigliani madonna, all olive skin and green eyes and big breasts. She wore a crisp white uniform and a white cap, and she spoke appalling English with almost religious sincerity.

"I give them eggs for just a moment," she said as Irene came in.

"That's all right," said Irene. "We're leaving at around six-thirty; so there's no need to rush. And how are my little angels? How's my beautiful little Ally?"

Ally lifted her hands and smiled with pleasure. Clara, in her crib, began to open her eyes and stir.

"This one does pooh-pooh," said Miss Bendizzi. "If you can leave yourself outside, I make everything clean."

"Thank you, Miss Bendizzi," said Irene. "Just give me a call when they've finished their supper, and then bring them down to the day room. Their grandfather wants to see them while they're still awake."

Clara was crying now. Her face was red, and she clenched and unclenched her fists. Miss Bendizzi clucked over the crib, and lifted her out.

"You don't cry! You be happy! Everything for you is won-derful!"

Irene kissed her twins and went downstairs to her own bedroom. It was just a little after five now. Hester was already bathing for the evening, and the faintest smell of gardenia bath oil wafted down the upper landings. Johann had gone to be shaved, and Jack, his valet, was pressing his dinner suit. As Irene sat at her wide mirrored dressing table, taking off her makeup and waiting for the colored maid Suzie to finish drawing her bath, she thought about Johann, and hoped that John wouldn't be too late back from his meeting. He had promised to catch up with them if he was delayed, but she knew how involved and endless oil negotiations were.

She bathed, using glycerin soap for her sensitive skin. On the fourteen-karat gold faucets, elaborately designed by German goldsmiths in the 1890's, drops of condensation formed, and ran cool down her bare toes. She sang psalms under her breath (it still embarrassed her to sing out loud) and wallowed back in the warm soft water and thought how lucky she was.

"Consider the lilies, how they grow . . ." she recited to herself as she soaped her little breasts.

Her own maid, Letty, a dark-skinned Andalusian girl with nails like Count Borgia's unwashed daggers, had laid out Irene's evening gown. It was a new creation from Gerard Watkins, her favorite designer, and it had just the kind of haughty simplicity she wanted. It was made of shimmering white watered silk, with a deep but narrow neckline that was framed in V-shaped pleats, like the leaves of a book folded back. The shoulders were fashionably padded and square, and the skirt fell with perfect simplicity.

In front of the mirror she gave herself silvery Betty Grable eyes, a bright red rosebud mouth, and subtly rouged her cheeks. For jewelry, she wore a brilliant star-shaped diamond pendant that Hester had given her on their first anniversary, and a whole cluster of diamond rings, including the $555,000 Newport Stone.

By six-fifteen, almost everybody was ready. They assembled in the day room while the servants brought their hats and coats and wraps. Hester was still upstairs, changing her mind about her green shoes, but the twins were there, and Johann had Ally on one knee and Clara on the other, and he was singing an old Dutch farm song to them, about how the rooster lost his temper with the silly hens, and crowed and crowed all night, and the little girls giggled with every cracked crow.

Vucinzki, the butler, came in to announce that the cars were outside, and that he had umbrellas for everyone, because it was raining hard. Just then, Roderick and Celia arrived, and there were kisses and greetings and loud helloes. Roderick was looking flushed after drinking too much whiskey at lunchtime, and Celia was icy and charming as usual, particularly when David Bookbinder came in, dripping wet from the rain, like a pink porpoise that had just flopped in from Marineland.

In the early-evening darkness outside, the cortege of black shiny Cadillac limousines, jeweled with raindrops, was waiting. There was lots of laughter as the servants held umbrellas over their heads, and car doors slammed and lights lit up and V-12 motors purred politely into life.

It happened, like all tragedies, with absurd quickness and at a time when hardly anybody was actually looking. Hester had arrived in the hallway, and everybody had turned in her direction to say "Good evening" and "How are you, Mother?" Irene was carrying Ally, and was about to hand her to Letty, so that Letty and Miss Bendizzi could sit in the back of the last limousine together and care for the twins. Miss Bendizzi was carrying Clara, and because there were no spare umbrellas, she had stepped out into the road, covering Clara with her coat. The chauffeur was holding the door open for Letty on the curb side, and so Miss Bendizzi had to open the street-side passenger door herself.

A dull gray Buick sedan, splashing through the puddles of Gramercy Park, skidded almost gracefully toward the line of parked limousines and struck the door of the last Cadillac just as Miss Bendizzi was placing Clara carefully inside. Everyone turned at the sudden *bosshhh*! of colliding metal and the curious silence that followed. Then Miss Bendizzi wailed, with pain and with hideous shock, and they rushed around to see what had happened. As they did so, the Buick reversed, pulled away from the wreck, and skewed off into the night with a howl of tires.

Irene, in her white silk dress, fell on the road in complete collapse. There was blood everywhere, and glass. The Buick had struck the limousine's half-open door and crushed Clara between the door itself and the door frame, as well as smashing four of Miss Bendizzi's fingers. Little Clara's body, in its brown tweed coat and its button-up leggings, was almost torn in half.

They carried and dragged Irene back into the house. She lay on the settee in the day room, shivering and almost unconscious with shock. She had lost one of her white satin slippers in the street, and the police cars and ambulances that arrived later ran over it several times. Roderick rang the Getty Oil people to try to find John, and discovered that he was not at Getty at all and that there was no meeting about refining facilities at Port Arthur, and never had been.

Almost unnoticed in the confusion and the horror, Johann, in his black dinner suit, carefully and slowly climbed the stairs. He was tall, but he was bent and old, and his face was suddenly blue. As he climbed each step, his hand clutched for the banister rail, and he heaved himself higher and higher without knowing why he was doing it or where he was going. He just had the feeling that if he made it to the top of the stairs, he would survive.

He looked upward toward the bright French chandelier hanging over the first landing. It sparkled and glittered in front of his eyes. It was like a Holy Grail, floating and twinkling above the peak of a holy mountain. Behind him, he heard sirens, and slamming doors, and the sound of someone crying.

He knew he could never make the top. He thought he would stop to rest. It was so difficult to breathe, and nothing seemed to be clear or comprehensible.

He said: "Oh, Clara," and fell sideways. His face was pressed against the soft stair carpet. He could see every detail of it, it was so close. Every scratch on the brass stair rod, every mark on the nails that had fastened it into place. It seemed quite amusing to him that a man rich enough to have a view of the whole world should end his life with a view so completely restricted.

He said: "Oh, my little Clara."

He only wished it were possible to shed tears.

Four days later, while Johann was still deep in a coma in his private rooms at Lynwood Sanatorium, Edward Secker met David Bookbinder, by prior appointment, at the front bar of the Colony on Sixty-first Street. Edward had to wait half an hour for Bookbinder to arrive, and he sat tense and unhappy with his dry martini, reading a folded-up copy of *The New Yorker*. Outside, the day was crisp and cold and bright, and the Colony's lunchtime trade came in with heavy overcoats and red cheeks.

Eventually Bookbinder arrived. He shook Edward's hand with his own cold, plump fingers. Marco, the barman, took his order for a Scotch on the rocks, and Bookbinder sat himself down, breathless and overweight, and said: "I'm sorry I'm late. They're digging up the streets again, and it's murder."

Edward, lean and lanky in his dark pinstripe business suit, raised his eyebrows at that.

"Is it?" he said. He was wearing a black armband and a black necktie. David Bookbinder wore a dark club tie with a gold crest on it.

"Have you seen Irene?" asked Bookbinder. "John's thinking of sending her away for a while, maybe down to Roderick's place in West Virginia."

"I saw her briefly," said Edward. "She seemed all right, but I don't even know if the shock has really sunk in yet."

David Bookbinder sipped his drink and nodded. "It does usually take a few weeks," he said heavily. His beady eyes were looking around the bar for anyone he knew. He seemed uninterested and bland to the point of boredom, and Edward was beginning to wonder if he'd made the right decision, bringing him here.

"I . . . er . . . I don't suppose you know how Johann is?" asked Edward.

Bookbinder didn't look at him. "All right," he said. "The last I heard."

"They think he'll pull through?"

"They don't know yet. He needs a lot of rest. It was only a minor seizure, but when you're that age . . . well . . ."

Edward said: "I suppose you're right. And he does have a history, doesn't he, of heart disease?"

Bookbinder didn't blink, but he still kept his eyes away.

Edward said: "You knew that, of course, didn't you? About the disease? You knew how little time he had left?"

Bookbinder swirled his glass around so that the ice clinked against the sides. The bar was filled with the mingled murmur of wealthy New Yorkers in the process of sharpening their lunchtime appetites. The rich smell of roasted meat mingled with the bouquet of dry sherry and gin, and someone said: "Come on, Jerry, let's eat."

Edward leaned forward. "Aren't you going to answer me?" he whispered to David Bookbinder. "Or are you thinking up an alibi?"

Bookbinder at last looked him in the face. "I don't have to answer anything that *you* say," he said with a small, puckered smile. "I'm only answerable to Johann Cornelius."

"Wrong," contradicted Edward. "You're also answerable to Hope, and to John. You manage their money, and that makes you very answerable."

David Bookbinder's smile was slowly drained of its satisfaction, but it still clung to his face, like a price tag on a cheap suit.

"You're being very irregular," he told Edward, his eyes following the laughing, chattering people who were going in to eat.

"I don't think *you* can speak to *me* about irregularity," Edward answered quietly and tersely.

"Oh, no?"

"Not when you're shifting stocks around like cattle on the Chisholm Trail."

David Bookbinder grunted in amusement.

"Not when you're trying to take control of the funds and corporations that are my wife's rightful inheritance," persisted Edward.

Bookbinder reached into his pocket for a fat hide cigar case and took out a long Havana. He offered one to Edward, but Edward said: "No, thanks."

"Please yourself," said Bookbinder. He clipped the end of the cigar, and lit up. He was wreathed for a moment in clouds of blue smoke—a financial Caesar in rapidly vaporizing laurels.

"It's my opinion," said Edward, "that you are trying to use Roderick as your stooge. You're working through Roderick's stock and Roderick's corporations to put the squeeze on every block of stock that John and Hope inherit, so that the only person who will ever have any say in the way the Cornelius fortune is organized is *you*. Well, you're found out."

Bookbinder ·sucked his cigar thoughtfully. Then he said: "Edward . . . you must think I'm unusually naive."

"I don't think so at all. I think you've done this whole thing very well."

"Of course I have. I didn't mean that. What I meant was that you must think I'm naive if you suppose that your finding out is going to make the slightest difference."

Edward looked at Bookbinder sharply. "What do you mean by that?"

"Precisely what I say. You've laid your cards on the table—very good, then I'll do the same."

"What cards?"

"*What* cards? My dear Edward, I always have cards. You don't survive on Wall Street for as long as I have without keeping something in reserve."

Edward raised his glass to the barman for another martini. Bookbinder's Scotch was still half-full.

"You've made it plain to me that you disagree with my financial policy," said Bookbinder. "You've also placed me in an awkward position as far as the market's concerned, because I'm still in the process of negotiating for stock, and if the word gets around that I'm buying, then most of the prices will go up by a great deal more than I particularly wish to pay."

"So?" said Edward. "Give me ten minutes, and I'll give the story to *The Wall Street Journal*."

Bookbinder laughed. "Oh, you wouldn't do that. Because one story deserves another, and if you give my story to *The Wall Street Journal*, I'll make sure that Hope's real story goes to the *New York Post*."

Bookbinder said this in such a jocular way that for a few moments Edward didn't even realize how much he was being threatened. Then he turned around and stared at Bookbinder in total disgust.

"You'd really do it, wouldn't you?" he said. "You'd really, actually do it!"

"Yes," said David Bookbinder. "I would."

Edward, when Bookbinder had first walked into the bar, had decided not to raise the subject of trust funds. But when Bookbinder said that, he was so furious that he couldn't hold it back any longer. He leaned forward and hissed right in Bookbinder's smooth pink face: "What about Clara?"

Bookbinder drew back.

"Clara?" he said, unsure.

"Yes—what about Clara? And what about Clara's trust funds? And what about Ally's trust funds, if Ally accidentally happens to wind up the same way?"

Bookbinder screwed up his little eyes. "Are you seriously accusing me of what I think you're accusing me of?" he said unsteadily.

Edward nodded fiercely. "That's lousy grammar, but yes."

Bookbinder scratched a small fragment of cigar leaf from his golden front teeth.

"In that case," he remarked, "you're a bigger fool than I thought you were."

He reached into his briefcase and took out a copy of the afternoon paper. He laid it on the bar, and pointed with his pudgy finger to a news item at the foot of the front page. It said: "Cornelius Baby Heiress Death: Hit-and-Run Driver Charged."

Edward read through it quickly. A construction worker from East 169th Street had been arrested in the Bronx after his gray Buick sedan was seen by a traffic cop to be damaged. He was accused of driving while drunk and failing to report an accident. His

530

name was William Peebles, and he was forty-eight.

"Does that sound like a hit to you?" asked Bookbinder, his voice tight but controlled. "Do you honestly believe that anyone could be *that* callous, and *that* avaricious? Even me?"

The telephone behind the bar rang twice. Marco picked it up and talked into it for a while. Then he passed it over to David Bookbinder and said: "Call for you, Mr. Bookbinder. Your office."

Edward watched David Bookbinder's face as a tiny, tinny voice spoke to him on the other end of the line. For the first time ever, he felt he was in the wrong financial division. David Bookbinder had too much money and too much power, and all Edward could do was hop and scream and protest. He was quite ready to believe that Bookbinder was capable of systematically wiping out the next Cornelius generation, but he knew that belief and suspicion were useless. Even facts, even evidence, might not be enough. To force David Bookbinder's hand, he was going to need to work carefully, subtly, and with months of proper preparation.

David Bookbinder laid down the phone. He was perspiring, and he wiped his plump neck with his handkerchief.

"That was the House," he said in a low voice. "Johann's bad. They don't expect him to last the day."

"Do they want us up there? At Lynwood?"

"Right away. My car's outside. We can go in that."

Edward swallowed his drink, stood up, and buttoned up his coat.

"David . . ." he said, before he signed the check.

"Yes?" said Bookbinder.

'I want to forget this for now. But I have to say, I have to warn you, that I'm not going to let it rest. You can't lean on Hope's inheritance, and that's all there is to it."

David Bookbinder reached for his overcoat and his homburg. With his cigar in his mouth, he reminded Edward of an old-style racketeer. As he buttoned up his coat with his tiny pink hands, he stared across the bar as if he were thinking of something else altogether, like what he was going to eat for dinner, or the halcyon days of the gold standard.

"Well," he said absently, "that's your privilege."

A little way apart, they walked into the front lobby. Next to the glittering Van Cleef & Arpels showcase, David Bookbinder stopped for a moment and faced Edward squarely for the first time. The reflected glitter of diamonds was all around him, as if he had suddenly become celestial.

"I myself am like a species of sea urchin," said Bookbinder. "I may be soft inside, but you have to chew your way through a mouthful of prickles before you'll ever find that out."

Edward didn't say anything. A woman in a gray square-shouldered suit, fragrant with Chanel, raised her eyebrow at him as she passed. He turned away.

"That," added Bookbinder, taking his arm, "is a word to the wise."

The slanting sunlight caught them as they stepped out onto Sixty-first Street, and across town they could hear the roompity-boompity sound of a marching military band playing "Anchors Aweigh" as yet another division of marines was welcomed home from the war. The sound echoed flatly against the buildings as the band paraded slowly up Fifth Avenue, passing the smoking bagel stands, the ghostly plumes of steam, and the throngs of shoppers who were looking forward to their first Christmas at peace.

1954

BOOKBINDER QUITS CORNELIUS

"Reasons of health" says oil exec

Wall Street Reporter

David Bookbinder, the 67-year-old supremo of Cornelius Oil, has announced his retirement "as of now." Known for his three decades in the oil business as the man with the golden smile, Bookbinder denied suggestions that he had been ousted by pressure from the Justice Department because of his involvement in big business graft in the 1920's.

> —*New York Daily News,*
> September, 1954

It was the year that TV dinners were invented—turkey, sweet potatoes and peas on the same compartmented tray. It was the year that Bill Haley released "Rock Around the Clock." It was also the year that Lucille Ball appeared pregnant in *I Love Lucy*, the year that necklines plunged to daring new depths, and the year that Nash and Hudson combined to form the American Motors Corporation. The Comics Code Authority banned horror comics and demanded that "all lurid, unsavory, and gruesome illustrations be eliminated." At the movies, Rock Hudson starred in *Magnificent Obsession*. Two million Americans were out of work, and during the early summer, children ran around the streets crowing "Point of order, point of order," in imitation of Senator Joseph McCarthy.

It was 1954. Cadillacs began to sprout tiny fins, Dwight D. Eisenhower was President, and David Bookbinder resigned as chief executive of Cornelius Industries.

Bookbinder was carefully packing away framed letters in a brass-bound trunk, along with his gold cigar box and his pigskin memo pad, when Roderick rapped loosely at the half-open door and walked in. David Bookbinder didn't look up. Cornelius executives had been shuffling in and out of his office all morning, picking over the remnants of twenty years with the company. He reached over and took a small ivory statuette from his desk and packed that alongside his memo pad.

Roderick parked himself on the arm of Bookbinder's leather chair. He said: "How are you doing?" in a concentratedly offhand way. Bookbinder said: "Okay," and stowed away some blue-backed law books.

Roderick hummed a tuneless tune and folded his arms. He was trying not to show how relieved he was that David Bookbinder had actually decided to surrender without a fuss, but at the same time he was still anxious that he might change his mind at the very last moment and stay. It was impossible for Roderick to imagine what Cornelius Industries was going to be like without David Bookbinder, and until that bald head had actually disappeared down the corridor for the last time, he wasn't going to let himself believe it.

He said: "Do you have any plans yet? Vacation, maybe?"

Bookbinder grunted. "Maybe."

Roderick nodded. "I hear that Hawaii's pretty nice this time of year. Have you ever thought of Hawaii?"

Bookbinder paused in his packing and stood straight. He glanced across at Roderick as if he were someone who had momentarily caught his attention in the street. "No," he said tiredly. "I have never thought of Hawaii. Right now, I'm too busy thinking about Washington, D.C."

Roderick said: "I thought we could take a ride."

"A ride? That sounds like a James Cagney picture."

Roderick blushed. "I didn't mean it to. There's a restaurant out in Connecticut I'd like to try. It's only an hour's drive. I thought we could maybe go over some of the final details there."

Bookbinder said: "I don't usually go for business lunches."

"Well, I know that," said Roderick. "But it's a fine day, and I guess the circumstances are kind of . . . well . . ."

Bookbinder thought for a while, with his pudgy hands on his hips. Then he said: "Okay. When do you want to go?"

It was September. The sky was a crisp pottery blue, and the leaves in Connecticut were beginning to turn. They drove in Roderick's green-and-white Oldsmobile Ninety-Eight, with the top down. David Bookbinder wore a black homburg hat and sat with his hands crossed in his lap. Roderick was dressed in plaid tweed, with a jaunty Tyrolean hat with fishing flies on it.

As they drove, Roderick said: "There are one or two things I'm going to have to know."

"Yes," answered David Bookbinder flatly. "I guess you'd better."

"I have to know some of the names, and what the connections are."

"Of course. The connections are aware of that, too."

"You mean, they're ready to discuss some kind of settlement? I presume they'll want some kind of settlement."

David Bookbinder took out a cigar. The Oldsmobile's Rocket engine swept them across deserted intersections, past peeling country stores, through curves of wooded highway. Behind the flickering trees, stretches of lake water gleamed like half-hidden mirrors.

Bookbinder said: "You're going to have to be sensible, you know."

"What do you mean by that?"

"Well," explained Bookbinder, reaching out and pressing the car's cigarette lighter, "you're not dealing with high-school societies. You're dealing with wealthy and organized businessmen who have helped Cornelius Industries for over twenty years. Most of that help was perfectly legitimate. Some of it was less so. But you have to understand that in two decades, a nation's interpretation of what is legitimate and what isn't inevitably alters. There was a time when organized labor was the filthiest phrase in the book. It didn't matter if you leaned on the CIO. These days, you have to be careful. *More* careful, anyway."

Roderick stared through the curved windshield at the sun-flecked highway ahead. A new white Corvette zipped past them, its radio blaring "Shake, Rattle and Roll," and disappeared up ahead.

He said slowly: "What about the killings?"

Bookbinder peeled the label off his cigar. "Well," he said, unperturbed, "we don't exactly call them that."

"It's still the same, though, isn't it, whatever you call it?"

Bookbinder smiled reflectively. "I guess it is. But your father could always see it my way."

"What way's that?"

"He could always see that any business of the size of Cornelius Industries, as it moves through the years, has to come up against opposition, and eliminate that opposition as it arises."

"Is that a fancy way of saying that you knock off anybody who gets in your way?"

"Of course not."

"Well, explain it to me."

Bookbinder held the cigarette lighter against the end of his cigar and sucked in smoke. When he was lit up, he said: "I can't stand smoking in the fresh air. It makes a good cigar taste like Christmas wrapping paper."

Roderick didn't answer. If David Bookbinder didn't want to discuss his disreputable past in detail, then that was his privilege. But it was desperately important for Roderick to know what had been committed in the name of Cornelius Industries over the years, and what underworld connections the business still had. He couldn't pretend that he wasn't alarmed; but he genuinely felt that once Bookbinder was gone, he could ease the Cornelius corporations out of most of their criminal connections, and return them to legitimate working.

He asked: "Was it true what he said, that old man from Pennsylvania?"

Bookbinder smiled. "That was a long time ago, what happened in Pennsylvania. That was in 1927, before I started work for your father. I'd only met your father once. A strange man, your father, that's what I thought when I first met him. That was in 1925."

"I didn't ask for a history lesson. I just wanted to know if what the old man said was true."

Bookbinder shrugged. "It was true in a way. He was setting up the Robinstown open-cast mine in those days, up in the Asquahanna Valley. Some of the folks there were ready to sell out right away, because they were hard times then, for farmers, in 1927. But there was a little local opposition, and your father wanted it painlessly removed. It was a risky operation, you see. Everyone thought he was setting up a dye works, including the county authorities. They didn't know he was set on stripping every square inch of turf for ten square miles."

Roderick took a right fork, and the Olds bounced its way down a small dusty side road. Branches tapped and squeaked against the car's bodywork, and birds fluttered and jumped in the trees.

Roderick said: "It bucked up the town's economy, though, didn't it? That's a prosperous place even today, Robinstown, last time I checked the figures."

"Sure," remarked David Bookbinder. "It's kind of changed, of course. In 1927 it was all grass and cows."

"So what about this local opposition? How did you 'painlessly remove' it?"

Bookbinder sighed. "It was all pretty roundabout. I had a call from a friend of mine in Pittsburgh. His name was Joey Divine and he distributed bootleg liquor. He said that some young character had approached him with a contract on behalf of someone named Johann Cornelius, and did I know who Johann Cornelius was. As it happened, I did. As I said, I'd met him first in 1925, at some reception or other. I told Joey to leave the contract to me, and I had a word with Arthur."

"Arthur?"

"Arthur Flegenheimer. Dutch Schultz to you. He was a friend of mine in a manner of speaking. There's an old Turkish saying which talks about 'the two pebbles which roll down the same dry

538

watercourse, and knock each other along.' It's a way of describing occasional help from someone you don't see too often. That was how Arthur and I used to work.''

Roderick slowed the car down for a tight tree-lined bend. They emerged by a sparkling river, where a white-painted Colonial-style restaurant stood between the rusting autumn trees and the reddish-brown rocks of the creek bed. There were several other cars already there, and Roderick parked alongside them.

Before he opened his door, he turned to David Bookbinder and said: "Dutch Schultz was murdered, wasn't he?"

Bookbinder nodded. "That's right. The year after I joined Cornelius Industries. They caught him in a chop house in Newark. He was in a coma for hours, but all he spoke was babble, and he never told the cops who did it. It was a cheap hoodlum called Charlie Workman, as a matter of fact.''

Roderick said: "Did you—?"

But David Bookbinder raised his finger to his lips and closed his eyes. "Don't ever ask it," he said gently. "It's one of those answers that won't ever do you anything but harm.''

They climbed out of the car and went up the rustic wooden steps that led to the restaurant's entrance. A toothy girl in a red plaid suit showed them to a small table by the window, where they could watch the river rushing over the stones. Farther upstream, Roderick could see an old cottage with smoke trailing idly from its chimney. He ordered clams and entrecote steak.

As they drank their cocktails, Roderick said: "So what the old man said was right? Someone from Cornelius Oil really did kill the Robinstown sheriff?''

Bookbinder's eyes were hooded. "In a manner of speaking.''

Roderick let out a deep breath. "No wonder Walter was so insistent you resign.''

"He was, yes. He's been a good friend, Walter has. But I guess that fate put him in an awkward spot. I don't blame him. At least he's kept it out of the papers, and away from the FBI.''

Roderick said: "Who else?''

"Who else what?''

"Who else has died in the same way? Did you 'painlessly remove' anyone else?''

Bookbinder looked slowly around the restaurant to make sure that they were not overheard. He could see the waitress coming with their clams, and he paused until she'd set them down. He tucked his napkin into his collar, and squeezed lemon over the grayish shellfish with complete equanimity.

"There were one or two."

Roderick frowned. "One or two? When? What do you mean, one or two?"

David Bookbinder stared up at him. "Before you start getting too excited, don't forget that pilot of yours, Fairbanks, and that Cosnett fellow. If Walter hadn't had a word with the Bureau, you might have found yourself in considerably more embarrassing trouble than me."

Roderick said tensely: "I'm not trying to sound off. I just want to know the facts. You mean you actually took out contracts on people who opposed you?"

Bookbinder swallowed a clam. "We're not the only corporation with a record of physical enforcement," he reminded Roderick mildly. "I think you might remember the Baldwin-Felts men at Ludlow, and you might remember Harry Bennett at Ford, with his six hundred armed thugs, and you might remember Frank Costello and Joe Adonis and Ben Siegel."

Roderick sat back. "Christ, David, I knew we had some protection on a small scale. I mean, you have to look after your trucks and your warehouses. But what you're talking about is organized crime!"

Bookbinder took a sip of water. "Don't be naive. You know damned well that every major business in the entire country has to have some connection with gangsters. A billion-dollar enterprise without its own enforcement arrangements is no safer than a whale stranded on a beach. Obviously we've kept our major connections as quiet as possible. Most of them were made through me. We've kept you well out of it so far, but now you have to know."

They sat in silence while the waitress took away their empty clam dishes and brought their steaks.

Roderick said: "You mean to say that my father knew all about this? Every detail?"

"Not every detail. But he knew. Your father and I and Dutch Schultz went to see *She Done Him Wrong* together, did you know that?"

"I never saw it," said Roderick.

Bookbinder wiped his mouth. "Arthur loved it. Your father didn't. He said that Mae West was too mature. That was the word he used. 'Mature.'"

Roderick didn't seem very interested in his steak. "David," he said quietly, "I want to know how many people have died."

"It's not too many," answered Bookbinder, munching. "Do you think we could have some wine?"

When he returned to the house at Gramercy Park that evening, he was withdrawn and thoughtful. After his lunch with David Bookbinder in Connecticut, he had spent most of the afternoon combing through the company's files and lists of connections, with Bookbinder sitting a little way away in his leather armchair, placidly smoking his cigar and filling in Roderick's background knowledge with pertinent comments and explanations.

"You knew Philip Musica?" Roderick had asked, with eyebrows raised, as he held up a sheaf of correspondence from McKesson & Robbins, dated 1935. Bookbinder had nodded. "Sure. In its way, it was a very useful arrangement," he explained. "The only trouble was, Philip wasn't smart enough to keep himself out of the limelight. Sad, that. You know he committed suicide?"

Roderick, tight-lipped, had answered: "Yes."

Now, in the quiet drawing room of his own home, he called for old Vucinzki, the butler, to bring him a whiskey, and he sat down in a high-back Jacobean tapestry armchair, his father's favorite, and opened up a buff file in which he had brought home all the most pertinent letters and documents relating to David Bookbinder's cooperation with racketeers and Cosa Nostra. There were letters from the 1920's, soft with age and typed in purple ink, from men like Lucky Luciano and Big Jim Colosimo. There was a complicated correspondence with Michael Ahern, one of Al Capone's attorneys, on legal matters relating to tax. Throughout all the years that David Bookbinder had controlled Cornelius Oil, and its sister industries of shipping, insurance, coal mining, air freight, and foods, its negotiations with almost every union had been characterized by threats of violence, its prices had been fixed by payments to government officials, its trading monopolies had been protected by skillful bribery, and its occasional legal errors wallpapered over by policemen, judges, and attorneys who were prepared to be lenient in return for a brand-new set of fancy golf clubs. There was no question that David Bookbinder had been clever, conscientious, and thorough. Everything he had done had been undertaken in the best interests of Cornelius Oil. Roderick, feeling a small twinge of embarrassment, even recognized that

Bookbinder's attempt to corner a voting majority of Cornelius Oil stock for himself and Roderick in 1945 had probably been the most efficient and practical step to take. As it was, his father's death had forestalled any further transfer of stock, and Hope's husband, Edward, had made quite certain that the remainder of Hope's inheritance remained intact. John, too, although he had chosen exile in Washington, had kept a close eye on his Cornelius shares, and there was no chance that either of them could ever be dispossessed again.

What Roderick found unsettling was that almost every letter and document in the file he had brought home was, from a business owner's point of view, both realistic and sensible. If your corporation was in danger of Senate investigation for breaking antitrust laws, didn't it make sense to treat a couple of leading senators to free vacations in the Bahamas, and a Cadillac Biarritz apiece? If the CIO was threatening to shut down your chemical plants, wasn't it good business to send a few persuasive pugilists around to encourage the workers to change their minds? And if there were profitable contracts to be had, like warships or airplanes or fuel supplies, where was the harm in making sure that the men who awarded the contracts were in no position to give them out anyplace else? This, surely, was what free enterprise was all about. It was the name of the game. And although Roderick didn't approve of Bookbinder's connections with racketeers, he had to admit that they had been used sparingly and shrewdly, too, and that they had never dominated the essential business of discovering and refining oil, building ships, and carrying cargo. Cornelius Industries, as far as Roderick could make out, had never trafficked in bootleg liquor or drugs, or been party to fraud or embezzlement. But with an elaborate but discreet network of bribed officials and sympathetic gangsters, David Bookbinder had simply ensured that Cornelius corporations had burgeoned and spread over twenty years without any hindrance from government, law, tax men, or petty extortionists.

The only thing that mystified Roderick was why his father had allowed David Bookbinder such extensive control for so long. Maybe it made good sense to have underworld connections, but from what Roderick could remember of his father, the old man had been quite capable of forming his own. Roderick sat in Johann's chair for two or three hours, while the sky grew grainy and dark outside in Gramercy Park, and he still couldn't work out why

David Bookbinder had ever worked for Cornelius Oil at all. Even now, at the very end, with the threat of the Robinstown murder hanging over his head, Bookbinder had only resigned because Walter Grossmith, their most influential government connection, had insisted. There had been too much pressure from the Justice Department for him to do otherwise.

Roderick was still sitting there when Celia came back from her afternoon appointment with Trans World Airlines. She laid her pocketbook on one of the antique occasional tables, peeled off her fawn gloves, and said: "*You* look morose."

Roderick stretched. Some of the papers fell off his lap. "I'm worried," he said. "And I'm baffled."

Celia tinkled the bell for the butler. "In that case," she said, "it's business as usual."

Roderick ignored her. He collected up the fallen papers and said: "I was talking to David today. We had lunch at the Waterside Inn."

"How nice."

"We went over this Robinstown business. You know, the homicide disclosures, all that."

"Did he squeal?"

"David doesn't squeal. He's not the type. But he did give me a pretty thorough rundown on every connection he's had for the past twenty years. It's all here. I was staggered when I read it. Did you know that Cornelius Oil actually paid twenty-five thousand dollars to Enzo Torino to protect their meat-packing interests in Chicago? Did you know that?"

Celia took out her long cigarette holder, and lit a cigarette. "When was that? Eighteen years ago? What does it matter?"

"It matters because Enzo Torino is still alive. He might be locked up, but he hasn't lost the power of speech. And that isn't all. We have business arrangements and shipping deals with people like Frank Gizzi and the Riccione brothers and every gangster you can think of. Not thirty years ago. Not thirty days ago. Today."

Celia didn't appear at all disconcerted.

"You know that George O'Hare protects our air freight. You can't call him a shining angel of purity, can you?"

"Celia, George O'Hare is a minor thug. These men are known public enemies. Major-league mobsters."

Celia said: "Where on earth is Vucinzki? I'm dying for a martini."

"Celia, listen!" snapped Roderick. "Gizzi and the Ricciones and Albert Hagermeyer are gangsters. Organized criminals! How can we possibly justify having a concern like Cornelius Industries tied up with people like that? Not just tied up! We use their outlets, their couriers, their finance systems, their muscle, everything. We use them to bribe State Department officials to fix foreign contracts. We threaten unions and newspapers, and we even paid a TV company to forget about a program on Anastasia. Celia, we're up to the neck in cahoots with some of the worst gangsters in the whole United States!"

Celia tapped her ash placidly. "I don't know what you're flapping about. They're on our side, aren't they? The time to flap is when they're not."

Roderick stared at her. He was about to say something, but at that moment Vucinzki came creaking in and asked her what she would care to drink. They waited in silence until the old butler had considered her request for a very dry martini with his usual deep, pondering sighs, and shuffled off to get it. Then Roderick said: "I think you *knew*."

"Knew what, my dear?"

"You know damned well what! You've known all along!"

Celia turned away, irritated. "There's really no need to shout. I'm not deaf."

"You're not blind, either, or stupid."

"Well, what's that supposed to mean?"

"It's supposed to mean that you've been doing most of the practical day-to-day business, while I've been nodding and waving and generally behaving like a dumb figurehead; and that if you've been doing most of the practical day-to-day business, then you must have known about these people all along! Christ, Celia, you must have *met* them!"

Celia sat upright, her eyes as cold as pebbles. "Are you that pathetic?" she asked him. "Are you that . . . *numb* to what goes on around you?"

"I've been trying to run a multinational corporation!" yelled Roderick. "I've been trying to run one of the country's largest oil producers, and one of the country's largest wholesale-food chains, and the country's third-biggest shipbuilder, and one of the country's major air-freight corporations, as well as chemical companies and pharmaceutical companies and insurance companies, and so many goddamned enterprises I don't know what they all are! I found out yesterday we've owned the Larkwood Pen Company since 1931, and all my life I've been *buying* the damned things!"

Celia stood up. She was dressed in a brown-and-red Dior day dress, clinging around her hips and elegantly split up each side. Her modern diamond brooch, in the stylized shape of a flying hawk, winked at Roderick in the last fading light of the day.

"Roddy," she said, "you're forty years old this year. Don't you think it's time to grow up?"

He stared at her. "Time to grow *up*?"

Celia lowered her eyes, but not in humility. She was reciting something that she had known for years she would eventually have to recite, and she was trying to recall those careful words she had been putting together for just such a moment as this.

"On the day that the C-1 crashed, your father explained what he was going to do," Celia enunciated quietly.

"Explained? Explained to whom?"

She glanced up. "Explained to me."

"*You*? What do you mean?"

She sighed. "Oh, Roddy, it's so damned obvious. Your father gave you one big expensive opportunity to prove what you were made of. He invested millions of dollars in testing your mettle, because there were billions more at stake. You couldn't expect him to give you control of Cornelius Industries if he thought you were too weak to manage it."

Roddy was pasty, and his jowls were shaking like a frustrated dog's.

"Weak?" he said hoarsely. "*Weak*?"

He turned on his heel and then turned back again.

"*Weak*?" he repeated, as if he wasn't at all sure what the word meant.

Celia looked away. If there was one spectacle which displeased her more than Roderick when he was being affectionate, it was Roderick when he was trying to make a histrionic scene.

"If I'm . . . weak . . ." snapped Roderick. "If I'm *weak* . . ."

"Oh, don't stutter, Roddy, for goodness' sake."

"Listen!" bellowed Roderick. "If I'm weak, then why did he hand it all over to me when he did? Why did he put me in charge? Why does it say on my door 'Roderick Cornelius, President'? Why does it say that? That's what I'd like to know!"

Celia raised her neck up and up as if it were on an endless crank.

545

"Of course you're president," she whispered. "But even presidents can be puppets."

She lowered her eyes again, but she still had that stiff, arched posture that frightened Roderick so much. He felt sometimes that Celia was not a real woman at all, but a brand of sarcastic robot. He watched her in genuine horror and fascination as she explained what for sixteen years he had never suspected.

"Every single decision of major policy which has affected every single branch of Cornelius Industries since Johann died has been taken jointly between David Bookbinder and myself," said Celia precisely.

"You have not written one memorandum, one report, one suggestion, one instruction, or even one check that has not been vetted by one of us or both of us. That was your father's explicit instruction to both David Bookbinder and myself, and that was exactly what happened."

Roderick opened his mouth, said nothing, and then closed it again.

Celia stood up. "Your father loved you, in his way, and he wanted to maintain the pride of the family name. But he was not a believer in dynastic rule for its own sake. He didn't believe that a son necessarily inherits his father's abilities. That's why he tested you with the C-1, and that's why he made sure you never really laid your hands on any power or money at all."

Roderick went over to the window. He seemed to have aged fifteen years in fifteen minutes. The strained light made his face look haggard and ancient.

Celia said: "Perhaps you think it was wrong of me to agree to do this behind your back. Well, perhaps it was. But I did it because I wanted money and power for myself, and I wanted the same for you, and if this was the only way to get it, then that was the way it was going to have to be."

Roderick said softly: "You and David Bookbinder. What a combination."

Vucinzki rapped on the door, and then came in with Celia's martini. She took it off the silver tray and dismissed the old butler with a wave of her hand.

"There was no love lost between me and David Bookbinder," she said. "But at least he was the kind of twisted personality I could trust."

She sipped her freezing martini, and then walked over and laid a cool hand on her husband's shoulder. He looked at it; at the sapphires and diamonds on every finger; and then he turned back to the night.

"I knew all about David Bookbinder's little plan to corner John and Hope's inheritance," she said evenly. "He didn't do it to protect you, or even in the best interests of Cornelius Industries. He did it entirely to keep me out of things, so that when Johann died there would be only one puppet-master instead of two. He wasn't only buying out John and Hope; he was tying up their shares in a holding company that would have made it impossible for me to exercise any influence over them."

Roderick said dully: "Then poor little Clara didn't die in vain."

Celia held Roderick's shoulder for a moment longer, and then released it. "No," she said almost inaudibly.

Roderick turned. "I don't suppose you know whether it was an *accident* or not," he said in a curiously bland tone of voice. "You seem to know everything else."

Celia frowned. "Roddy, you're not suggesting . . ."

Roderick walked tiredly over to his chair and sat down. He rubbed his face with his hands. "I don't know. You seem to know enough gangsters."

She pursed her lips. "I don't know *why* Clara died," she said coldly. "I believe it was an accident, a genuine accident. It only seemed suspicious afterward because David Bookbinder turned it to his own advantage. I suppose you can say that was immoral in itself. But he loved the twins, in his own rather repulsive way. He wouldn't have harmed them."

"But once Clara was dead, it was all right to use her death to make himself a little more money? Is that what you're saying? My God, he may not have killed her, but he certainly acted like a gangster once she was gone."

Celia sipped her martini.

"Well, that's the whole point of this conversation, isn't it?" she said. "Your . . . moral compunctions about employing the mob."

"Is it so strange to have moral compunctions about consorting with criminals?" asked Roderick. "Or is it acceptable behavior these days? Maybe you should explain it to me. I've been a puppet for so long, I think I've lost the facility to think for myself."

"Roddy, please!"

547

"No, Celia, tell me! Tell me about these people! Tell me who they are, and what they do, and how often you see them! Are they fun? Are they witty? Do they make jokes about beating people's brains out and crushing little girls in automobile doors? What do they like for supper? Can they dance well? Do they buy their jewelry or do they steal it?"

Celia took three stiff paces across the room, swung her arm, and smacked Roderick across the face. He jerked back in his chair, but he didn't attempt to retaliate. He didn't even raise his hand to the three lacerations on his cheek where nearly two and a half million dollars' worth of gemstones had cut his skin.

"I see . . ." he said slowly. "You've learned their techniques as well as their names."

Celia turned away, furious, clutching her crossed arms.

"God, Roddy, you're such a fool! What do you think America is? The heavenly land of opportunity? There is one rule that keeps a big business alive in this country today and that is the rule of suppressing your competitors. The market for oil is only so big. If we want a bigger share, we have to take it from someone else. And that someone else certainly isn't going to stand by and let us do it without a fight. Yes, of course we're in league with gangsters. Some of them are ugly and vicious and stupid, but most of them are extremely cultured, extremely sophisticated, and know more about this business than you do. They know the realities of life, Roddy, and they're set up to deal with them."

Roderick reached down to where his papers were untidily stacked on the floor. He lifted one up at random and read from it.

"In 1952," he said, "we were indirectly responsible for the bombing and closure of seventeen rival gas stations in Louisiana, Texas, and Arizona."

He picked up another sheet, turned it the right way up, and squinted at it.

"In 1950 we paid the Ricciones one thousand dollars to send a man to burgle the offices of the Department of the Interior, so that we could acquire vital papers which would enable us to bid successfully for development land."

He shuffled for another one, but Celia said: "That's enough."

Roderick looked up. "Enough for what? Enough to make you feel guilty?"

Celia shook her head. "It's enough, that's all. You've made your point. Now I think you'd better face the truth."

548

"Face the truth?" asked Roderick. "What the hell do you think I'm doing?"

Celia turned around. "I mean *really* face the truth. Face to face. I want you to meet Ricardo Riccione, in person."

Roderick lowered the sheet of paper he was reading, and their eyes met over the top of it with the strange caution of two people meeting for the very first time.

David Bookbinder's retirement was not a long one. He never made it to Hawaii, although he did get as far as Key West, where he rented a shady wooden house three doors down from the house which Ernest Hemingway made famous, and he walked along the quiet streets, through the fingery shadows of palms, wearing a wide straw hat with a blue band around it, and long khaki shorts. They make leather sandals on Key West, and he bought himself a pair of those, as well as a big straw bag to take picnics of cold lobster and chicken around the island. Some days his stout crimson figure was seen on the flat white beach by the airfield, staring out at the flat blue ocean. Other days, he sat on Conch Quay, wearing black sunglasses that didn't suit him, and read back issues of *The Wall Street Journal*. Or he'd stand at the corner of Waddell and Vernon, stock-still, in his droopy shorts and flowery red-and-yellow shirt, as if he was receiving a message from God, and had to stop to hear it through.

Two weeks after he had left New York, on a windy Thursday afternoon with a hint of hurricane in the air, he returned to his rented house to find the front door open.

He paused for a long while at the front gate. The garden was lush and green and overgrown, with palms that nodded and fragrant tangles of wild orchids. A flurry of tiny parakeets shrilled and twittered over his head.

David Bookbinder turned slowly and looked down the placid street. His nose was red and peeling because he had spent the morning on the white sands of West Beach. Under his arm was a folded copy of *Metallurgical Review*. He took off his sunglasses and bit his lip. Across the road, a black man slept at the wheel of a two-tone Packard Patrician. The palms rustled and dipped.

He could have, and probably should have, walked away. But instead he went through the gate and stood for a moment on the path, peering into the darkness of the old, elegant house. He could see the blue-black shine of the floorboards, and the shadow of an ugly little Chinese table that stood in the hall. He called the name of his cleaning woman: "Cristobel?"

There was no reply. He climbed the steps of the veranda. He waited at the doorway for a moment or two, and then went inside. He laid his creased magazine on the hall table.

They were waiting for him in the drawing room. They seemed to have no doubt at all that he would come; or that when he saw them, he would make no attempt to escape. They were relaxing in two of his wicker armchairs, smoking hand-rolled cigarettes in black paper, and when he appeared at the door one of them simply said: "Come on in."

The room was cool and civilized, with large dark paintings behind reflecting glass, and small brass tables from Kashmir. The two men didn't seem to belong there at all; like two helmeted football players at a croquet tournament. One of the men was tall and heavy with a blond crew cut and horn-rim spectacles with one cracked lens. He wore crumpled light gray slacks and a yellow short-sleeved shirt. The other man was younger, hipper, with curly black hair and a big greasy nose. He wore a loose-fitting T-shirt and patched denim pants. His faded sneakers shifted and shuffled on the floor, tapping out the beat to some unheard rock-'n'-roll song that was playing in his head.

David Bookbinder stood there in his leather sandals and his shorts and said: "Who are you? Who sent you?"

The crew-cut man didn't even look up. He sucked at his cigarette, and kept his eyes on the floor as the smoke leaked out of the side of his mouth. He asked solemnly: "Are you Mr. Bookbinder?"

David Bookbinder stayed where he was. He said: "You'd better get out of here, quick."

The young hip hoodlum glanced at his crew-cut friend, and his feet kept dancing. The crew-cut friend said: "We ain't going no place." Then he took one last drag at his cigarette, and nipped it out between his finger and his thumb before tucking it thriftily back into his shirt pocket. He stood up.

David Bookbinder felt a surge of fright in his stomach, but he was too experienced to run. If you ran, they hit you straightaway. If you stayed where you were, there was always a chance that whatever irrational processes went on in their distorted, deprived minds, they might consider it more amusing to have mercy than to kill. The crew-cut man came around him and gripped his wrist with such viciousness that he said "Ah!" but that was all.

Conversation was pointless. These men had no idea why they were here, and they probably had no idea who they were working for. They led him down the passageway, past foxed and fly-specked prints of privateers at anchor, and out of the back door with its green-and-yellow stained-glass panels to the garden.

They descended the wrought-iron steps into the luminous emerald shade of palms and acacias. A lizard ran across the path in front of David Bookbinder's feet. Somewhere in the trees, a bird sang a repetitive and complicated song that sounded like "Here we go again, boys, here we go again." It was sultry and stifling in the garden, and sweat ran down David Bookbinder's neck.

The three of them walked around the back of the house until they reached the dilapidated, peeling shed where the garden tools used to be kept. A tangle of gourds, speckled and warty, grew down one side of the wooden roof.

The young man with the curly hair forced the shed door open. Inside it was musty and dark, with that pervasive smell of tropical mildew. The man with the crew-cut ushered David Bookbinder inside, and they stood there for a while, as their eyes grew gradually accustomed to the dim light, amid broken seedling pots and rusted shears, and a roller with a cast-iron handle that must have dated from seventy years ago. The young man closed the door behind them and bolted it.

"What are you going to do?" asked David Bookbinder.

The crew-cut man coughed. He said: "I guessed you kind of *knew*."

David Bookbinder was an old man. He said: "Can you make it quick?"

The crew-cut man shrugged. "That depends on you. We gotta do it the way we was told."

There was a silence. The young man with the curly hair was rummaging around with something that sounded metallic, but he was out of David Bookbinder's line of sight. David Bookbinder said: "Can I have a cigar?"

The crew-cut man said: "It's too late for that. What do you think this is?"

David Bookbinder said nothing. Then the crew-cut man said: "Anyway, cigars is bad for your health."

551

The young man with the curly hair heard this remark and laughed. The crew-cut man said: "Shaddup."

David Bookbinder kept thinking that those who live by the sword must die by the sword, but all the same he wondered whether he really deserved *this* kind of death. He had always exercised violence with the utmost discretion and tact, and his own hit was the first that he had ever experienced first hand. He hoped and prayed that it would be abrupt and not bloody.

Those who had paid the two men, however, had not specified abruptness. They had specified a sort of homicidal joke. To carry it out, the young man with the curly hair dragged an old wooden seed box across to the door of the shed, and the crew-cut man made David Bookbinder walk over and stand on it, with his back to the door. When David Bookbinder saw the young man take up a handful of six-inch nails and a heavy carpenter's hammer, he realized, with terrified fascination, what they were actually going to do.

They forced a rag into his mouth so that he couldn't scream. Then the crew-cut man pinned him against the door with the weight of his body while the young hoodlum with the curly hair seized his left hand, dug the point of a nail into the flesh of his palm, and hammered the nail right through into the wood with four hefty blow

David Bookbinder tried to struggle, but then they grabbed his other land and nailed that to the door, too. His eyes were bulging with pain and fear but he couldn't speak. They knelt down and unbuckled his new leather sandals, and then they crossed his feet over each other, and drove a third nail straight through his plump arches and into the door. The young man with the curly hair kicked the box away and admired his handiwork.

The crew-cut man said: "It looks like he's too heavy. It looks like those nails are going to tear out of his hands."

The other young man nodded, and picked up more nails from where they were scattered on the shed floor. With a couple in his mouth, he banged two more into each of David Bookbinder's arms, one through the muscle of the forearm and the other straight through the flinching bicep. By the time he had finished, David Bookbinder was almost unconcious.

The crew-cut man said: "Don't forget to bring that hammer along. Wipe it clean and throw it off the quay."

"Okay, Jackie."

The crew-cut man sniffed, and reached in his shirt pocket for the cigarette butt. "Okay, let's go."

They swung the door open and for a brief moment David Bookbinder saw sunlight again. Then they closed up the shed, and locked it, and he was left with arms and feet of fire, hanging in the musty twilight.

He went through fifteen hours of agony. He wept, and sometimes he prayed. It never ended. He prayed that he would die. He tried to spit out the rag so that he could call for help, but he couldn't. The pain was so great that he slept, and then dreamed about it, and then woke up to find that it was real. He didn't dare move in case the nails tore through his sinews and hurt him even more.

Just after dawn on Friday morning, his bald head dropped between his shoulders and he died. The birds outside sang "Here we go again, boys, here we go again." The roller with the cast-iron handle, coincidentally, had been purchased on the same day that David Bookbinder was born.

His body was discovered eight days later by a Martinique-born handyman who was clearing out the house in preparation for new tenants. The police already knew what had happened, and had been well-paid to deal with it quietly. The coroner declared that he had died from a seizure, not at all uncommon in a man his age. Then he was cremated without publicity and his ashes were thrown, at night, into the dark and fluorescent waters of the Gulf of Mexico.

In 1954 the water commissioner of Toledo, puzzled for months by dramatic drops in the level of his reservoirs at unexplained times of the evening, suddenly realized what was going on. The citizens of Toledo were rushing to their toilets during TV commercials, and flushing their cisterns in simultaneous three-minute Niagaras.

Something else happened in 1954. John Cornelius, the president of Cornelius Armaments, came home early one evening from work and saw a red-and-white Chevrolet Bel Air parked in his hedge-lined driveway in Georgetown, and the white lace curtains of his upstairs bedroom drawn. The advertisements said about the Chevrolet Bel Air that it wrung more power out of every gallon, and that it was a long way from "full" to "empty." A recent *Washington Post* feature on John Cornelius had called him "that individualistic and pugnacious arms supremo."

Tonight he wasn't pugnacious. As soon as he saw the red car on his sloping driveway, he glanced in the mirror of his own white Cadillac convertible and pulled out into the traffic. The evening sun was falling across the street in crisscross patterns of telephone wires and trees. He checked his rearview mirror just once more, and glimpsed his home, a stately Colonial six-bedroom house of dark brick and white pilasters, disappearing behind a passing moving van.

John didn't know whether he suddenly suspected Irene of having a lover or not. He had had a mistress himself, of course, but his relationship with Mara Malinsky was so unique, and so oblique, that he couldn't see how Irene could possibly get herself involved in anything similar. Still, he had to admit that she had a tacit license to take another man to bed. All the gossip and the scandal about Mara must have been hard for her to take.

He took the folded handkerchief out of his breast pocket and dabbed his forehead. It was quite warm this evening. He was dressed in a light gray double-breasted suit and a white shirt with a polka-dot tie. If it hadn't been for the luxurious white Cadillac, you could have mistaken him for any one of the conformist and conservative middle-management men who poured out of Washington evenings and made their way home. In 1952, he had grown a small bristly mustache, which made him look five years older than his thirty-seven years. It was a kind of protection against the scandal and disapproval that he had faced from his family and his friends. Irene didn't like it much and called it his "infernal Fuller."

It was a half hour before the scarlet-and-chrome tail of the Bel Air began to back out of his driveway and into the street. John had been listening to a quiz show on the radio, and the Chevrolet appeared just as the quizmaster asked: "And do you, Ed, know just what brand of hosiery your wife wears?" John switched the radio off and reached over to start the Cadillac's motor.

As the Bel Air passed him by, he raised his hand against his face so that the driver wouldn't recognize him. But he peeped through his fingers and caught a half-second glimpse of the man who may or may not have been his wife's lover. He was prepared for almost anything—prepared to identify a business friend or a golfing partner or a dinner guest. Afer all, lovers were rarely strangers. But what he wasn't prepared for was the man's color. The driver of the

Bel Air was black. A heavily built West Indian with dark sunglasses and an expensive lightweight suit.

Maybe he had thought of tailing the Chevrolet and confronting the driver with what he knew. But his hand stayed numbly on the gearshift, and he didn't move. The evening street seemed suddenly too windy and public and cold for a convertible, especially when a middle-aged woman in a print frock stopped beside him with a bulging A&P bag and said: "Do you mind if I rest this on your automobile for just a moment?"

He told the woman: "I'm just leaving." He checked his mirror and saw his worried eyes. Then he released the parking brake and swung the Cadillac out across the street in a wide U-turn.

When he turned the corner and arrived outside his house again, the bedroom curtains were open. He nosed the Cadillac down the driveway, tugged the brake, and climbed out. He pushed his way past the dusty box hedge that lined the drive, and took out his key to open the blue Georgian front door.

Irene opened it for him. She was wearing a loose Japanese robe of pale green silk, loosely tied around the waist, and she looked even taller and saintlier than ever. On appearances alone, accusing Irene of adultery was like casting grubby aspersions about the private life of Saint Agnes. John paused in mid-step, his brass doorkey poised on the end of a gold chain that came from his pants pocket. He looked like a life-size ornamental lamp that was trying to plug itself in.

Irene said: "Hello. You're back early."

John looked at her. "That's right."

She stepped back, and he entered the house. He laid his papers and briefcase on the hall table. There was a hush inside the house that gave a curious theatrical quality to any sound or talking. Irene's silk robe, as she walked behind John toward the living room, was rustling like sad trees.

John looked around. The television was on, without any volume. The room had rows of windows that faced north over the garden. It had always been a chill, shadowy garden. Stone people stood around outside with mossy and petrified patience. The living room itself was neutral and tasteful, with large chesterfields in pecan-colored hide, and Victorian armchairs covered in brown velvet. It was, of course, very Boston.

"You seem rather quiet," said Irene. "Would you like a drink?"

John shook his head.

"I've had another boring day," Irene continued. "But then, I don't really suppose you're interested."

John walked over to the marble mantelpiece and opened a silver cigarette box. He took out a cigarette and lit it thoughtfully.

"Of course I'm interested." He kept his eyes on the television, where a woman was doing something complicated with two boxes of soap powder.

"You don't seem to be."

"Don't I? I'm thinking."

Irene picked at the back of one of the chesterfields with her long pearlized nails. "You still haven't said whether you want a drink yet."

"I'm sorry. No, I don't, thank you."

"I'm having one."

John glanced at her, but shook his head again, and said nothing. Irene went over to the cabinet, took down a heavy Waterford crystal glass, and poured herself a large gin-and-tonic. It was Lewis' day off today. Usually she tinkled the little silver bell. She cupped the glass like a child with a mug of milk, and walked slowly back toward him. He puffed unsteadily at his cigarette.

"You're, un . . . not dressed," said John.

Irene blinked at him, and then gave a funny little laugh. "No," she said in a high voice.

He felt as if he were sinking in an elevator. He despised himself for what he was thinking, and what he was about to suggest, but at the same time he knew that what remained of their marriage was not going to survive for very long unless he knew. Perhaps his guilt needed bathing with the cool knowledge that he wasn't alone in his need for someone outside their relationship to support and console him.

"Is this how you usually look when you have visitors?" he asked her. "Is this how you usually . . . dress?"

There was a silence. Then Irène said: "What do you mean? I don't have visitors."

"No," said John. "But you did."

There was another silence, longer and colder. Irene took a deep, wavering breath.

"I came back a half hour ago," John said dully. "There was a car in the driveway, and the bedroom curtains were drawn. I waited down the street and watched the car when it left."

Irene said: "You've been *spying* on me?"

"I don't think so. I don't think satisfying my curiosity about a strange male visitor who for some reason causes you to draw your bedroom drapes at four-thirty in the afternoon is spying. I think it's husbandly interest."

Irene went to the window and pulled back the net curtain. A few yards away, an encrusted, bird-spattered statue of the Venus de Milo stared armlessly back at her.

"Your husbandly interest isn't usually as noticeable as this," she said, without any attempt to conceal her bitterness. "In fact, you're hardly ever here to display it."

John lowered his eyes. "I'm not trying to condemn you, Irene. I just think I've a right to know the truth."

"What truth?"

"What truth do you think? The truth about you and this man."

Irene shrugged. "What do you want me to say?"

"You could start with his name. I think I'd like to know who I'm sharing my bed with."

Irene turned around. "Oh, I see. You automatically assume that he's my lover."

"As a matter of fact, I do. What else am I supposed to think?"

"Why don't you try thinking nothing for a change, instead of squalid little suspicions?"

"Squalid!" snapped John. "The man's black, and you call me squalid!"

Irene's pale eyes widened in shock. When she spoke, her voice was quavering with suppressed outrage.

"So that's it! You object because he's *black*! My *God*! John Cornelius, the fun-loving energetic liberal! The only good guy out of the whole rotten family! You don't mind strange men seducing your wife as long as they're the right color! My God!"

She stared at him for a moment longer, and then she said: "You disgust me. You make me squirm."

John threw his cigarette into the empty grate. "You make me feel the same way. It was your choice to stay after you found out about Mara. You could have divorced me. You could have walked straight out of the door. I told you what the terms were, and you were prepared to take them. You wanted to be a Cornelius wife, and a Cornelius wife you stayed.''

Irene came across the tapestry rug toward him. "I didn't know there were *rules*," she said. "I didn't know that I was only permitted to take a certain variety of lover. Perhaps you'd better tell me what other objections you have. Is it all right if they're ginger? What about profession? Do you object to dentists, or tightrope walkers? Any religious scruples? No Jews? Come on, John, you'd better tell me so that I know! I'm sure there must be something else that sets your teeth on edge apart from darkies!''

John seized a leather cushion from the chesterfield and hurled it across the room. It knocked a small Staffordshire figure of a miserable shepherd off a mahogany sidetable, and shattered it.

"You whore!" yelled John. "You stuck-up Back Bay whore! You played around with a black man in my bed, and you have the brass face to turn around and mock me?''

Irene looked at him with an odd smile. It was like the smile of a simple-minded child, or someone who is suffering from extreme shock. But she was neither simple nor shocked; it was a smile which meant that however much John insulted her, however much he bellowed and shouted, he was only doing what she wanted him to do at all times, and at any cost, and that was to take notice of her.

"I didn't take him to bed," she said in her immaculate and aristocratic tones. "He came to look at the air-conditioning.''

"In a mohair suit? Who are you trying to kid?''

Irene kept on smiling. "He came, first of all, this morning, and when he came he wore coveralls. I took a fancy to him, and I asked him to call back this afternoon, when the maid had left. When he returned at three, he had taken a bath and put on a clean shirt. He picked me up in his arms as if I was a child, and he penetrated me standing up in the kitchen doorway.''

She loosened the tie of her robe. "If you like, I can show you his semen.''

John turned back to the mantelpiece and took out another cigarette. As he lit it, he glanced up, and saw Irene's reflection in the gilded French mirror above him. Her robe was open, and he could see her small breasts and her pale body. He looked down at the grate, and didn't look up again.

"I think we had better revise our agreement," he said quietly. "I think that if we are going to stay together we had better protect ourselves from the wild animals that we are capable of turning ourselves into. From now on, I will tell you nothing about what I do, and I want to hear nothing about any of your sexual escapades, either. For Ally's sake, I am prepared to live with you as long as you like, but don't ever expect to be touched by me again.''

He turned and faced Irene, and his expression was grim and gray. She smiled at him benevolently.

"Oh, don't worry." She smiled. "I'll make you touch me. Whatever you say, I'll make you touch me.''

John didn't answer. He felt overwhelmed by frustration and fears. He was feeling jealousies that had never troubled him before. His affair with Mara had finished, for all practical purposes, nine years ago. But he was still haunted by guilt and he could never quite work out why. Was it guilt for the emotional injuries that Irene had sustained in the family row that had followed, and their self-imposed exile in Washington? Was it guilt for Clara's death? Or was it guilt for Mara and for Ally? Whatever it was, it made him feel numb and chloroformed from reality; as if he would only be allowed to return to normal happy life when he had paid a long but unspecified penance. He was a naturally honest and sensitive man, but in the company of a woman like Irene, whose weakness was her greatest strength, he was almost powerless.

Perhaps his deepest guilt was that, for his own sake, he should have left her years ago.

He said: "I think I'll have that drink now.''

Irene didn't move. She said: "In that case you'd better get it yourself.''

He stayed where he was for a moment. Then he went over to the drinks cabinet and poured himself a small glass of Jim Beam bourbon. He drank it where he stood, the way that people stand at their bedroom washbasins and drink water.

"Quite frankly," he said, "I don't know whether you're making this up or not.''

"Making it up? Why should I do that?''

"I don't know. Perhaps you want to punish me.''

Irene pouted in mock sympathy. "Oh, darling . . . how could I ever punish you?''

"Very easily. You punish me every time you throw my love for you back in my face.''

Irene sat down on the chesterfield and spread her Japanese robe around her so that she looked like a big pale pear-shaped bee sitting on a shiny flower. She said: "To tell you the truth, John, I think you stopped loving me a long time ago. I don't think you've loved me since the war."

"And that's your answer, is it? To fornicate with Negro handymen in the kitchen doorway?"

"Handy*man*, darling. There was only one."

"You're making it up."

"Am I?"

"Of course you're damned well making it up! It just doesn't happen! And in any event, what the hell is a black air-conditioning mechanic going to see in a Boston bluestocking like you? A man like that wants somebody sensual. He doesn't want a prim white wife in Bergdorf Goodman underwear!"

Irene raised an eyebrow. He couldn't tell if he had hurt her or not. She sipped her drink and said: "Prim, am I?"

There was a moment's pause, and then she said: "I don't know why you married me if you thought I was prim."

"I don't know either."

"Do you really regret it that much?"

"Oh, Christ, Irene, I don't regret it. I just regret the damage I did, and I regret Clara's death, and I regret the way we've been limping along for nine years with nothing between us but mistrust and bickering."

Irene lowered her eyes. Her eyelids were made up in a rather unpleasant shade of pale blue. "Well," she said, "it wasn't my fault."

"Does it really matter, now, whose fault it was?"

She looked up. "You can say that because it was you—you and that Polish woman who didn't even have the decency to stay away from another woman's husband. It wasn't *my* fault and you know that it wasn't my fault, and now you're trying to say that it was."

"I'm not saying anything of the kind. I'm saying that after nine years, it doesn't matter anymore."

Irene's eyes began to get crowded with tears. "If it doesn't matter, why do I still feel like this?"

"Like what?"

"Like being *horrible* to you. I can't help it. I love you, John, but I have to be horrible to you to make sure you still love me. I think that if I hurt you, but you still love me, then your love must be real."

John stared at her. She was as saintly as ever, but now she was older, her saintliness was less visionary and magical and more like the pious rigidity of those painted plaster figures that Mexican women keep on their dressing tables next to the shell-backed hairbrushes.

He said huskily: "You didn't do it, did you? That thing with the black man?"

She wept, and the tears dripped steadily onto her Japanese silk. John felt that he ought to put his arm around her, but for some reason he was disinclined to. He was probably put off by what she had said about *making* him touch her. And apart from that, crying did nothing to transform her into a soft and gentle wife who was desperately in need of his protection. She remained stiff. He felt it would have been like putting his arms around an effigy.

"I'm going out," he announced quietly. "If anybody wants me, I'll be down at the Republican Club."

She nodded, and sniffed. She said: "I'm sorry, John. I didn't mean to."

He stood by the door trying to think of something to say; something that would make her understand that they were probably lucky to be able to live together without too much friction; and that passionate love was the last thing he wanted from her. He would have been quite happy to be left alone. But she sat there with her sad face, wet and weeping, and all he could do was turn away, and close the door behind him, and hope that while he was out she wouldn't do anything absurd, like swallow too many pills or bake him a chocolate angelfood cake.

As they reached the gates of Nineveh, Ricardo Riccione's estate out at Thornwood, New York, the last ragged clouds of a summer shower had just passed toward the Kensico Reservoir, and the fresh sun made the roads steam. Roderick, looking paler than usual, was driving his green-and-white Olds Ninety-Eight and wearing a charcoal-gray suit and a gray homburg hat. Beside him, Celia was as calm and cool as ever, in an ice-blue suit and a veiled hat to match.

Nineveh's gateheads were built from dressed granite, with black-painted gates of decorative iron with gilded leaves. Through the ironwork Roderick could see nothing but mature oaks, with an immaculate asphalt drive leading away behind them. As he drew up to the gates, a tall man in a well-fitting dark blue uniform appeared from a green-painted sentry box and walked over toward them.

"Mrs. Cornelius," said the guard, leaning across the car. "It's good to see you."

Roderick's expression tightened. Celia said: "This is my

husband, Mr. Roderick Cornelius. I expect you'll be seeing some more of him soon."

The guard nodded. He looked very Italian, with long sideburns and dark eyes. Although he was friendly, he could break a man's neck with a single violent twist of his hands. He said: "Pleased to know you, Mr. Cornelius. I've read your name a lot. My name's Contini."

Roderick grunted. "Can we go in now?" he asked impatiently.

The guard wasn't at all fazed. "Sure. Mr. Riccione's expecting you. Take the car down to the end of the driveway, as far as the rose gardens, and someone will park it for you. Mr. Riccione's in the gazebo right now."

Celia waved and said: "Thank you, Contini," but Roderick remained annoyed and unsmiling. Contini saluted and went over to pull the switch that opened the high black gates.

They drove down between rustling leaves that irradiated them in lemons and greens. Roderick said nothing. The drive seemed to wind along for miles, and they smelled the rose gardens before they actually reached them: a dense and almost delirious scent of Sutter's Gold and President Herbert Hoover. Then they turned the corner and it seemed as if the grounds had effervesced with thousands and thousands of flowers.

He parked the car and climbed out. When he walked around and opened the door for Celia, she said: "Isn't it divine? This really is the divinest place."

Roderick helped her out. "What is he? Some kind of horticultural maniac?"

Celia said: "Ssh, don't be so provocative. The gazebo's this way."

"Oh, so you've been there before?"

Celia linked her arm through his, and together they walked with guarded aplomb between the snow-showers of roses. Roderick was sweating, and he would have done anything to take a breath that didn't hang heavy with the scent of floribunda.

"You can see the gazebo from the house," Celia remarked, almost like a professional guide, as they mounted a small slope between rhododendron bushes and bergamot. "I've never actually *been* there, but I've *seen* it."

As they came around the bushes, the gazebo came into view. It was built of white stone, with a cupola roof, and decorative stone balustrades all around. Behind it were the untamed woods of

Riccione's estate, shady and cool. But in front, and below, all his ornamental gardens were stretched out with privet hedges and winding paths, and fountains that glittered and sprayed in the afternoon sun. His house itself was a severely classical twenty-bedroom house of pinkish Italian stucco.

The man himself was sitting in the gazebo painting in oils at a small easel. He was physically diminutive and very dapper, and he wore tiny gold-rimmed sunglasses. He could have been Al Capone's cousin, although several of his more politically minded friends remarked on a flattering resemblance to the Little Flower. Ricardo would have been delighted to have been christened Fiorello. He had an extraordinary sense of humor which relished the contrast between the sensitive culture and the total ruthlessness of crime.

Riccione, of course, was not alone. Twenty yards away, sitting mournfully on a small marble seat, a man in a pale blue suit and a fedora hat kept a restless eye on the surrounding woods and trees, and drummed his fingers on the high-powered rifle that lay across his lap. There were probably other guards around, too, concealed behind the rhododendrons, but you wouldn't find that out unless you were rash enough to reach suddenly inside your jacket for a cigarette.

As Roderick and Celia approached the gazebo, Riccione laid down his brushes and stood up. He raised his hat and held out one small plump hand to assist Celia up the gazebo steps.

"My dear," he said, kissing her. Then he turned to Roderick and smiled with a row of little white teeth, like a baby's milk teeth. "And you, Mr. Cornelius. How glad I am to know you."

Roderick shook hands. He felt extremely nervous. When Riccione dragged over two white-painted garden chairs for them to sit on, the squeak of the metal feet against the stone floor of the gazebo made him feel depressed and alarmed.

"What are you painting?" asked Celia. "It looks like a sort of rose."

Ricardo nodded. It was impossible to see his eyes behind those maliciously small sunglasses.

He walked over to his little painting where it glistened wet on its easel. "I think I have a talent for this, you know. If only I had more time. I am a great admirer of Beatrix Potter, the English lady. She painted flowers, and they came alive."

Celia said: "My husband has a talent for shipping things by air.

He was an air pioneer, you know. He has a great talent for that."

Roderick looked uncomfortable. He said: "I'm a businessman, Mr. Riccione. A businessman, plain and simple."

Ricardo raised one eyebrow from beneath his dark glasses. It was like a black crow taking off from a black lake.

Roderick told him: "It was a complete surprise, as a matter of fact, finding out that we did business with you. For one reason or another, mainly to do with my family and the way it works, I didn't know until now that your world and mine were so closely linked."

The mobster nodded. He was so mild and courteous that Roderick found it increasingly difficult to sustain his annoyance. Ricardo Riccione was the kind of man to whom children came in distress, and around whose feet birds and squirrels clustered in the hope of crumbs. It was easy to suspend one's mistrust, and to forget that he and his late brother, Giorgio, were reputed to be responsible for more than eighty-five violent murders. He said quietly: "And what did you feel, Mr. Cornelius, when you did find out? Were you anxious?"

Roderick looked up slowly. "Well, I don't think 'anxious' really describes it. It was more like finding out that your mother has been having an affair with the local rat catcher."

Ricardo obviously liked that analogy, and smiled.

"Yes," he said.

Together they watched the servant scale the last few yards of the slope with his silver tray. When he reached the gazebo, he spread a crisp linen tablecloth with a practiced snap, and laid out silver knives and forks and condiments. There was a chilled bottle of Chablis Grand Cru in a silver cooler, and under fresh linen napkins were small salads in the shape of flowers, with tomatoes, anchovies, blanched capsicums, and a concoction of smoked trout and cream.

Roderick watched with a severe face as these appetizers were laid out. After the servant had uncorked the wine, poured each of them a glassful, and retired to a respectful distance, he said: "What's this?"

Ricardo seemed surprised. "You won't eat with me?"

Celia glanced at Roderick in displeasure.

"Mr. Riccione," said Roderick tersely, "I came here to argue, not to eat."

"Does one preclude the other?"

Roderick was mopping his neck with his handkerchief. "What

564

I'm saying, Mr. Riccione, is that I find it difficult to break bread with people I don't admire.''

There was a pause of some moments. Riccione puffed out his little cheeks and tapped his little fingers on the arm of his garden chair, as if he were trying to think of a way to deal with a nephew who had expressly been told not to crawl under the strawberry nets.

"Well, Mr. Cornelius," he said at length, "you don't have to eat. I cannot sit you on my knee like an infant and spoon it into you.''

Celia said: "Roddy, please, there's no need to make this more difficult than it really is.''

"It's difficult, all right," said Roderick. "And accepting Mr. Riccione's hospitality isn't going to make it any easier.''

Riccione stood up. He walked to the rail of the gazebo, and then he turned around and spread his hands appealingly.

"You do not like me?'' he asked. "Is that it?''

"Don't be ridiculous," snapped Roderick. "I hardly know you. But I know your reputation, and it's your reputation that we've got to talk about today.''

"You mean you want to talk about roses?''

"You can stick your roses up your ass. I want to talk about mobs.''

Celia said: "Roddy!''

But Riccione waved her into silence. He shook his head and walked back toward Roderick with an expression that may have been one of regret and consolation if it had been possible to see what his eyes were doing behind his sunglasses.

"I'm sorry, Mr. Cornelius, but you're quite right. We should get down to brass tacks at once. Obviously we cannot be pleasant until each of us knows where he stands.''

He sat down, and sipped at his glass of wine. Then he said: "I think it regretful that we did not meet earlier. You seem like a man who could have contributed much to our relationship with Cornelius Industries. But I know how it was with your father, and I also know that a series of unfortunate events led your father to pass the business to your wife and Mr. Bookbinder, God rest Mr. Bookbinder's soul.''

Roderick frowned. "That's a little premature, isn't it? David Bookbinder's in Florida, on a long vacation. He may have retired, Mr. Riccione, but I don't think he's counting on dying just yet.''

Ricardo Riccione shrugged. "None of us ever do.''

"Are you speaking as an expert?"

"I am speaking as a man who enjoys his life and all the gifts of God to the fullest."

"It seems you've also enjoyed extorting most of our clients to the fullest."

Ricardo laid down his glass. "Well," he said equably, "you can call it extortion if you want to. But terminology is not reality. The words of crime, and of business, and of politics, are all interchangeable. I do not see the distinction myself. We are all of us concerned with the quality of life, and that is all."

"What kind of quality does your life have?"

Riccione smiled. "A very pleasing one, I like to think."

"And what quality of life can a trucking corporation boast if it refuses to handle Cornelius goods before any other? Or a longshoreman who doesn't make a point of ripping open a few sacks of Du Pont fertilizers, or short-weighting Kaiser Cement in favor of Cornelius Cement? What quality of life does an insurance salesman enjoy when he doesn't return ten percent more Cornelius business in any six-month period than any other? Or a wholesaler who won't push Cornelius foods in front of all the rest? Can you tell me that?"

Ricardo wasn't at all troubled by what Roderick had said. "Mr. Cornelius"—he smiled—"what quality of life would one of your secretaries enjoy if you paid her to take letters and she never did?"

"She'd get the sack."

"Of course. Now, these people I look after for you—all these truckers and dockers and wholesalers and salesmen—they are being paid by you, too. But supposing one of them fails to perform his tasks, what can we do then? We cannot sack him. We have no legal hold over him because his very usefulness to us is that he works for someone else. The only hold we have is what I call the *forceful suggestion*."

Roderick flicked a quick look at Riccione and then looked away. "I can guess what that little sugar-coated expression means," he said dryly.

"Perhaps you can," said Riccione, "but you probably imagine torture and beating up and bricks thrown through the window at night. That is what most people outside of this business imagine. I had a very famous young movie star for dinner last week, and she persistently asked me to show her my revolver. Well, Mr. Cornelius, I haven't owned a revolver since 1922."

Celia said: "Ricardo isn't a hoodlum, Roddy. He's not like Dutch Schultz or any of those."

"That's right." Riccione nodded. "When my people apply forceful suggestion, they simply make a character evaluation of the transgressor in question, and they apply psychological pressure to his weakest point. If he's been doing badly at work, for instance, they will suggest that it will be much safer for the man's job security if his boss doesn't know just how bad he's been. If he has a sick relative in the South Bronx, we might suggest that life would be easier all around if this relative wasn't evicted. We rarely have to take these steps. We have found that the fear inside a man's mind is a far more potent weapon than a blackjack."

Roderick licked his lips. "The reports I read from you and your brother mentioned that four men had been killed in 1950 for holding back shipments of Haymann Drugs, which are ours, in favor of someone else's. They also mention Jimmy Hoffa and a few other choice names. Now, did these men die for real, or did you just make a forceful suggestion that was more forceful than suggestive?"

For the first time, Ricardo Riccione removed his dark glasses. His eyes were wet and myopic, and he appeared to be staring at something that was hovering over Roderick's head, although Roderick was quite sure that he was really focusing straight at him.

Riccione said softly: "I do not understand what you are trying to impute."

Roderick said: "Isn't it obvious? I'm putting it as plain as I can. I want to find out exactly what sins you've committed in my name, with my money, and I want to put a stop to it."

Celia ·vas about to say something, but Ricardo raised his hand to show her that he was fully in control of the situation and that she needn't take sides against Roderick just for the moment.

"You are a strange man, Mr. Cornelius. For a businessman, you're really most unusual."

"I happen to have morals, if that's what you're suggesting."

"Oh, it is not so much that you have morals. All of us have morals, of one variety or another. It is just that you fail to perceive what morals really are."

He restored his tiny dark glasses to his nose, and sat back to look at Roderick with disconcerting interest.

Roderick blustered: "If you've got something to say in your own defense, you'd better say it. Otherwise, I think we can say that the whole Cornelius-Riccione arrangement is off. And I mean o-f-f.''

Ricardo laughed. "Why should I defend myself? This is what you fail to understand about morals. We are both in the same business, you and I. We are both in the business of making as much money as possible with the minimum amount of effort. Quite often this means that we have to exert pressure on people, and sometimes it means that we have to kill them. Although you were evidently not aware of it, there were many times in the past nine years when you asked for things to be done that could only economically be achieved by violence or assassination. Those four men who died in 1950 died because you—*you*, personally—insisted that Haymann Drugs speed up their distribution in the Midwest. That was what you wanted done, and although we had been reasonably content to let the situation ride in the past, that was what we did.''

Roderick turned to Celia. "What's he saying? You told me that all my instructions were vetted by David and you!''

"That's right, darling. In this case, we happened to agree with you. It was a good idea.''

"But, Christ, Celia, you knew that they'd have to—''

"Yes.''

Roderick stared at his wife, but in her ice-blue suit she was as composed and perfect as ever. The Madonna of the Dollars. He blinked, and there were drops of perspiration on his eyelashes. The salt of it stung his eyes. He reached over and picked up a glass of white wine and drank some. It was crisp and fruity, and probably cost eighty dollars a bottle, but he might just as well have been drinking water.

He said: "I asked David Bookbinder how many people had died, and he wouldn't tell me.''

Ricardo Riccione shook his head. "It is better that you don't know.''

"But what the hell am I going to do? What happens if the same situation comes up again?''

Riccione got up from his chair and came to sit on the balustrade right next to Roderick, and he laid his hand on Roderick's shoulder. Roderick glanced uncomfortably at the pale pink fingers, and wondered, not for the first time, why everybody talked down to him, as if they were party to some secret knowledge that he was incapable of understanding.

"Mr. Cornelius," explained Riccione gently, "we are simply

working in two different departments of the same store. You are the big chief upstairs, and I am running your dispatch department. I cannot work without you, but neither can you work without me. If what I am doing is a crime, then what you are doing is also a crime, because you cannot survive unless I help you."

"What do you mean?" asked Roderick, trying to turn his head around. "Are you trying to suggest that I'm a criminal?"

"I am just demonstrating the unalterable truth. You can certainly run your business any way you please. You can run it on Quaker lines if you wish. Some corporations do, although I would be interested to see how Quaker their tax returns are.

"You can be as upright and as decent as a saint, but if you are, you must be prepared to pay the price for it. You will be penally taxed by a revenue service that never gives a sucker an even break. You will be undercut and cheated by your competitors and your own dealers. Your trucks will mysteriously find themselves with flat tires on crucial delivery dates. Your factories will burn down. Your goods will be stolen. Your books will be juggled. In fact"—and here Riccione leaned forward and almost whispered in Roderick's ear—"you will be eaten alive."

Roderick sat for a long, long time in silence. Ricardo Riccione went back to his own seat, tucked a napkin into his collar, and began to fork up salad, watching Roderick all the time. Celia started nibbling, too, and sipping wine, but she obviously didn't have much appetite.

Roderick sighed. Then he said: "I came here today knowing that everything you've told me was true. Maybe I just didn't want it to be true. Maybe I had a dream."

Riccione munched, and nodded. "We all have dreams, Mr. Cornelius. What we must *not* do is allow other people to prevent us from fulfilling them."

Roderick kept his eyes on the ground. His annoyance had abated altogether, and now he felt nothing but depressed. Perhaps he had known all along that he could never extricate Cornelius Industries from their involvement with men like Riccione, but it was more than painful to face up to the reality of his own weakness. He finished his wine, and when he looked up, the servant was standing at his side to pour him some more. He lifted his glass.

"I will tell you a last something," said Riccione. "It may sound grandiose to your ears, but it is quite true. There is not a single person living in this continent who is safe from us. That shows you

569

how much power your money can buy, Mr. Cornelius. We can exert pressure on anyone you like; or, if it is unfortunately necessary, kill anyone you like. And I mean *anyone*."

Roderick gave Riccione a lengthy, assessing look. He said: "I presume when you say *anyone* you're excluding the President."

Riccione looked surprised. "Of course not! Who knows, we may be called upon to remove a President one day. Not that there is any chance of a Democratic President for a few years yet. But, yes, it could happen, if enough men like yourself got together and decided they disliked the President enough to pay the sort of prices I would have to ask."

Roderick grunted mirthlessly. "And what's the asking price on a President?"

Ricardo Riccione swallowed wine and smiled. "Ask me when the time comes, Mr. Cornelius. I am sure we can work something out."

Celia said brightly: "Are you going to show Roddy your new roses?"

They walked around the gardens and the house until a gong summoned them for lunch. Riccione showed them his personal mutations of Peace, and a new rose that he was trying to grow in memory of his late brother, Giorgio. Giorgio had died of leukemia seven months ago, at the height of an investigation into his connections with the Justice Department. Ricardo sniffed the new rose sadly, and had to turn away for a while to blow his nose. Roderick looked at Celia impatiently during this small display of fraternal emotion, but Celia's expression was inscrutable.

The dining room was white, with a floor of polished red Mexican tiles, and an indoor fountain that bubbled and gurgled and made it necessary for Roderick to excuse himself from the table at least twice. The house was more like someplace in Italy or Los Angeles than New York State. Ricardo joked that if he had a mortar he could fire shells from his front steps and straight into the Rockefellers' $200,000 playhouse at Pocantico. "And wouldn't that be a harsh reminder that crime is always at the rich man's door."

Five servants brought them fresh crabmeat frosted with avocado; quails roasted in bourbon; stuffed flounder; quenelles of veal and rosemary with asparagus; and strawberries. Beside them, rose petals floated in gold finger bowls, and the reflected light from their glasses of Bollinger champagne wobbled in curved patterns on the high ceiling.

Roderick ate very little. He felt as if he were being initiated into criminal society without any consideration for his own feelings. But if Cornelius Industries was going to survive intact, what else could he possibly do? For the first time in his life, he began to understand the price of money, something which his father had known from the very beginning.

"Ricardo," he said, as he laid down his gold fruit spoon, "I want us to come to an understanding."

"I am very pleased." Ricardo beamed. "Understandings are the stuff of happiness."

"I want an understanding about murder. There's nothing very happy about that."

"Murder? My dear Roderick."

Roderick laid his crumpled napkin on the table. "It's important, Ricardo. It's important to me, and it's important to the whole future of myself and my family and all the thousands of people who work for us. I want it clearly understood that nobody is to be murdered to implement any Cornelius policy."

Ricardo pulled a thoughtful face.

Roderick went on: "I also want it understood that if any forceful suggestion is going to be necessary, then I want to know about it in advance, and I want to know exactly what it's going to be."

Celia's eyes went from Ricardo to Roderick and back again.

Ricardo smoothed down his silver pomaded hair with the flat of his hand and said: "You must see that we are not exactly employer and employee. What I am trying to say is that I do not work for you in the sense that I am your hireling. Your business is in partnership with mine, and is inextricably interlinked with mine. Many of the trucks you use belong to me, and most of the wholesale outlets you utilize on the East Coast are completely under my influence, even when they are not actually mine."

There was a silence. Ricardo smiled, almost shyly. Then he said: "If I deem it necessary, for the good of our joint interests, to eliminate some persistent opposition, then I shall do so. You are in no position to protest."

"But—"

Ricardo raised a hand. "No buts, Roderick. You do business your way, and I will do business in my way."

"You're making me—and Celia—and everybody at Cornelius Industries accessories before the fact. Do you realize that?"

"Of course. You are also accessories *after* the fact. You knew what David Bookbinder had been involved in, and yet you made sure that he was protected from arrest and scandal. Isn't that, ordinarily, a criminal action?"

"It's no use trying to blackmail me, Ricardo."

"But of course it is. What else can you possibly do? Are you going to allow an industry the size of Cornelius Oil to collapse like a poorly cooked soufflé, just to salve your own conscience? They would put you in prison—not because you were involved in homicide, but because you renounced the capitalist way in favor of some namby-pamby social idealism. Anyway, you are not that sort of man at all. You are not a suicide."

Roderick pushed away his plate ferociously. "Dammit, Ricardo, I don't want any more people to die! I don't want to be tied up with murder and extortion!"

Ricardo began to lose his patience. He took off his little dark spectacles again, and his eyes, though myopic, were anything but kind. "Now you're being ridiculous," he snapped. "You have been tied up with murder and extortion all your life. The whole of Cornelius Oil was founded on murder and extortion, just like every other so-called respectable big business in the United States."

Roderick didn't answer. He didn't really have anything to say. He knew, to his own discredit, that his protests were as hollow as papier-mâché puppets. He was frightened by killing, and the criminal underworld unnerved him. But he also knew that the strength of spirit he would need to cast off Riccione and all his kind was beyond him. As Riccione had said, he was not a suicide.

He said at last: "I think you must give me some time."

"How much time?" asked Ricardo.

"A day or two. I need to turn this over in my mind."

"Of course."

Celia said: "Don't worry, Ricardo. Roddy will come around, won't you, Roddy? He's not as impetuous as he first appears."

Roderick shook his head. "I just want to think, that's all."

"Of course," repeated Ricardo, like a psychiatrist telling his patient that *of course* there were vultures perching on the end of the couch.

After lunch Riccione showed them his business suite. It was an endless room of thick carpets and deep leather chairs, with paintings by Stubbs and Gainsborough along the walls, and a group of Italian bronzes. Roderick was thoughtful and worried for the rest of their visit, and when a small Italian chauffeur brought their green-and-white car to the front of the house for them to leave, he said nothing at all to Ricardo Riccione except: "Thank you."

On their way back to New York, as they drove through the late dusty sunlight toward the shining spires of Manhattan, Celia said: "Don't you think he's perfect?"

Roderick glanced at her. "Perfect? You mean Riccione?"

A warm wind was blowing off the East River. They cruised southward down FDR Drive amid shoals of Kaiser Manhattans, Dodge Firedomes, and Checker cabs. Taxi fares were twenty cents for the first quarter-mile and five cents for every succeeding quarter-mile. The sky was very pale and high. Roderick said nothing more until they got back to Gramercy Park, but on that summer day in 1954 he felt quite sorely that he had lost something of himself, and when he went upstairs and saw all the files and papers that David Bookbinder had given him, he no longer felt inclined to open them, and he knew that he would probably leave them fading and undisturbed for the rest of his life.

There was a family barbecue at Hope and Edward's place on Long Island that weekend. Roderick hadn't seen Hope for weeks, and he was surprised how pale she looked, even though it was late summer. She wore a gray cotton dress that made her look grayer still. Edward was a little worried about her, but said that it was probably tiredness. They were due to fly to Europe in a week for a vacation in Venice, Florence, Switzerland, and the Rhineland.

Roderick and Celia brought Victor with them. Victor was eleven now, and Roderick didn't like him a great deal. He was a plump, precocious boy with a particularly irritating line in sneering, uninformed conversation. Roderick sometimes watched his son talking to friends, or playing tennis with his big flat feet and his big fat thighs, and he wondered sorrowfully if *he* looked like that to other people, or whether it was something that Victor had inherited from Celia's side of the family.

Freddie and Tess were playing with new German rocking horses that Edward had bought them. Freddie was seven, and all arms and legs and gappy teeth. Tess was five, and losing her little-girl prettiness. Despite the big candy-pink bow in her hair, she looked exactly like Edward. The rocking horses were glossy and gray and almost life-size, and the children rocked endlessly backward and forward on the grass, while Victor stood a little way away and pretended that he didn't want a turn, because rocking horses were for kids.

John and Irene were supposed to have brought Ally up from Washington, but Hope had gotten the impression from Irene that they had quarreled over something, and they had called at the last minute to cancel. None of the rest of the family minded all that much, because John had a talent for making them feel awkward. They sat around the lawn on white-painted benches, while the servants brought them tasty little hibachi snacks, and the birds warbled and rustled in the overhanging trees. It was the kind of hot summer day when you could lie back in a hammock, close your eyes, and the world would change around you without you even noticing.

Later, when it was cooler, Roderick took a walk with Hope around the grounds. Hope was smoking, and lighting one cigarette from the butt of the other.

They stopped at a small grove of trees where a stream ran down into a goldfish pool. The water was dark green, and the bright orange fish stirred through shafts of green sunlight. Water boatmen sculled their way across the pool's meniscus.

Hope sat down on a mossy stone.

Roderick said: "You'll spoil your dress."

Hope said: "It doesn't matter."

Roderick coughed. "I don't like to seem nosy," he said.

Hope looked at him and blew cigarette smoke into the shifting rails of sun.

"Well," she said, "you're my brother, after all."

Roderick said: "You don't seem happy."

"Does it show that much?"

"Well . . . Celia noticed it."

"Celia's very sharp. I mean, she's very perceptive."

"I guess."

Hope dipped the tip of her cigarette in the pool and it fizzled out. There were mauve smudges under her eyes as if she hadn't been sleeping well.

"It's not Edward, is it?" asked Roderick uncomfortably.

"Edward?"

"He's not making you unhappy or anything? I don't want to pry, but you know how it was . . . well, with Martin."

Hope gave a wan smile. "Yes, I know how it was with Martin."

"I've never seen you like this. Are you ill?"

Hope said: "It's not altogether Edward. I don't love Edward, you know. I never have. I suppose when I married him I was trying to find something that Martin could never give me. You know what they say. If you marry wrong once, you'll marry wrong twice. You should never marry anyone to correct the mistakes you made before. If it hadn't have been for Lewis Bausor, you know, this never would have happened."

"Lewis Bausor? Who the hell is Lewis Bausor?"

Hope smiled sadly and reflectively. "He's the workingman getting his revenge on the rich. It's very ironic, really."

"Hope, I don't understand a word you're saying."

Hope took out another cigarette and lit it.

"It doesn't matter. It's just a silly idea of mine."

"But what the hell is this all about? Did Lewis Bausor do something to you? Is he blackmailing you? Listen, if he's blackmailing you, I can . . ."

Roderick stopped in mid-sentence. He suddenly thought of Ricardo Riccione. "*We can exert pressure on anyone you like; or, if it is unfortunately necessary, kill anyone you like.*" He looked at Hope behind the shafts of sunlight as if she were a vision in a holy grotto. She didn't seem quite real anymore; as if part of her soul had already decided to fade into the ground.

There was a silence. Hope said: "Lewis Bausor died years ago. What I did to Lewis Bausor led to Father sending me off to the Landseers'. That was all."

Roderick said: "You're ill, aren't you? There's something wrong."

"Yes."

"Don't you want to tell me what it is?"

Hope smoked and watched the insects on the pond. "Can you face the truth?" she asked him.

He frowned.

"Well," she said, "the truth is that I have cancer. In four or five months from now, I shall be dead."

Roderick couldn't believe what he was hearing. He reached out a hand and laid it on Hope's shoulder, but through the gray cotton of her dress she seemed to be as insubstantial as a vision wrought out of steam or clouds. "*Hope*," he said with a croak in his voice.

She blew out some more smoke. "I haven't told Edward yet.

Edward thinks I'm just overworked or under the weather. I didn't want to tell him until we'd come back from our vacation. I guess I should, in a way, but then, I didn't want our last vacation together to turn into a wake."

Roderick said: "Are you sure?"

Hope looked up at him quizzically.

"Are you sure it's cancer?" asked Roderick. "Have you been to a specialist? I mean, you could have radiation treatment."

"I've been to eleven specialists," answered Hope. "And that includes Dr. Ray Parkwin and Dr. Kulpeper. I've been to London and I've been to Ontario. I'm afraid the answer is always the same. I have cancer of the liver that has advanced so far that it would be hopeless to try to eradicate it. It's painful now, but an operation would be even more painful, and it wouldn't do any good at all."

Roderick stood there numbly. Then, quite unexpectedly, he found himself crying. He shook and trembled, and the tears rolled out of his eyes and almost blinded him.

"I can't understand it," he sobbed. "You must be wrong. They must have made a mistake. Surely they can do *something*?"

Hope lit another cigarette and smiled. "No, Roddy, they can't. It's all over, and I just have to accept it. I'm doing my best to enjoy what's left."

"Oh, Hope, I'm so sorry. Hope, I can't tell you."

She looked at him with a gentle, sisterly expression. "You don't have to be sorry, Roddy. Out of everybody, you've always been the kindest. I mean that."

He took out his pocket handkerchief and blew his nose.

"I've always been the softest. That's what you mean."

"Well," she said quietly, "is that always such a bad thing? Softness?"

He mopped his eyes and then blew his nose one more time. He still had a lump in his throat, but Hope's total calmness was helping him to pull himself together. "I don't know," he said unhappily. "I guess it is when being soft means that people might die."

"You mean me? Don't be so silly."

"No, no. I didn't mean you. I mean the whole Cornelius thing with gangsters and Mafia and people like that."

Hope raised her eyebrows. "So," she said, "you've found out about it. I was wondering when you would."

"You knew, too?"

576

"Not for sure. But Edward always suspected it. He knows some people in Arizona."

Roderick said: "David Bookbinder told me. It was David's connections with some murder in 1927 that forced him to leave. We had a lot of flak from the Justice Department, and they said they'd only cover up if David quit. I guess I was pretty naive, but I didn't even suspect. I just gave out the orders and didn't question how they were carried out. Celia knew. I'm not sure how I feel about that even now. But I suppose she was only trying to protect me. The less I knew, the less likely I was to jeopardize the family. I guess I can accept that. Father knew what he was doing. But I still find it hard to swallow this whole thing of killing people, actually killing people, for the sake of business. I still find that very hard to swallow."

Hope stood up and walked around the pool. He followed her, and together they made their way out of the grove of trees, up a small slope, and across a long meadow with a view of the silvery-gray strip of Moriches Bay and the distant dark Atlantic. The air was fresher here, and Hope stood with her face to the wind, her hair blown back and her eyes narrowed.

"What are you going to do?" she asked him.

He kicked at a divot of grass. "I've been thinking. Celia and I went to talk to Ricardo Riccione the other day, out at Thornwood."

"Riccione? Is he involved?"

"He's a mainstay, on the East Coast at least. But Albert Hagermeyer and Frank Gizzi are tied up in the whole thing too. I don't know how to tell you. The whole of Cornelius Industries has been run by racketeers for twenty years."

"And they've killed people? People who've gotten in the way?"

Roderick nodded.

They walked in silence down through long swaying grass and flickering flowers. There was a smell of the sea in the air, and for the first time Hope tossed away her cigarette and breathed in as if she really enjoyed it.

"Well," she said, "whatever you decide to do, you can always think that all those poor people who died got themselves one of us in return."

Roderick stared at her in disbelief. "You don't mean that."

"Yes, I do. Do you really think our family could have expected

577

to survive with impunity after everything we've done? One of us had to lay down her life as a punishment. And as it turned out, it was me."

"Hope, you're talking crazy."

She turned on him. Her face was streaked with windblown tears. "I wish to hell I was. Don't you believe in fate? Don't you believe in the meek inheriting the earth, and the wicked being punished in hell? Or have you forgotten yourself as much as Father did, and David Bookbinder, and Celia? Oh, Roderick, we deserved to be punished, and we were!"

Roderick started weeping again, too. The two of them stood in the meadow, and Roderick held his sister close, his thirty-five-year-old dying sister, and he realized as he held her just how little he knew her.

"Hope," he said, as he stroked her hair. "What can I do to help you?"

She looked up at him. Her eyelashes were stuck with tears. She shook her head and said: "Nothing, darling, nothing."

They stayed that way for a long time, but then Roderick heard a rustling in the grass, and when he looked up, he saw Victor.

"Victor?"

The boy looked guilty. Roderick suddenly realized he must have been hiding in the long grass not far away. He gave Hope's hand a quick squeeze, and then walked over to where Victor was standing. Victor wouldn't look at him but put his hands in his pockets and tried to whistle.

"Why are you whistling?" asked Roderick.

"I don't know, sir."

"You don't know?"

"No, sir."

"Were you hiding in the long grass?"

"Me, sir?"

"Well, who else? Who do you think I meant?"

"I don't know, sir."

Roderick snapped: "Don't you know anything? And take your hands out of your pockets when you talk to me!"

Victor did so, and stood there, plump and sulky. He was about to go to school in England, and he knew that there he would be able to do whatever he liked; because he was American, because he was rich, and because his stupid father wouldn't keep nagging him. He thought of his father as a kind of tiresome pet who never seemed to grow up, but which one keeps around out of a sense of duty. Even at the age of eleven, Victor had a sense of duty.

"I want to know what you heard," demanded Roderick.

"Heard, sir?"

"Yes, heard, dammit! How many times have I told you not to eavesdrop? You've got ears like a damned rabbit! You're a damned rabbit, do you understand?"

Hope came over and touched Roderick's arm.

"It's all right, Roddy. Victor won't tell."

Victor turned to her with his big crimson face and said: "I will tell, so there."

"Tell what?" Roderick wanted to know.

Victor was silent.

"Tell what?" bellowed Roderick.

"I'll tell Uncle Edward that Auntie Hope is going to die, and then you'll both be sorry!"

Roderick smacked Victor's face with a sweep of his arm that knocked the boy flat on his back on the grass. When he sat up again, Victor had a nosebleed, and he was gasping for breath.

"You vermin!" yelled Roderick. "Don't you dare talk to me like that! You little rat! You disgusting little vermin!"

He pulled Victor onto his feet again by his collar. The boy was blubbering and trying to catch the blood from his nose in his hand.

"You will apologize to Aunt Hope!" Roderick shouted. He was almost screaming with rage. "Go on—apologize!"

Victor stood there for a moment sobbing, but then he pulled himself free from Roderick's grip and ran back across the meadow and disappeared into the grove of trees in the direction of the house. Roderick watched him go, and then, panting, he sank to his knees and squatted down on the grass. Hope stayed beside him, her hand lightly touching his shoulder.

"I sometimes wonder how I ever conceived such a repulsive child," Roderick said in a hoarse voice. "There are times when I could drown him."

"The child is the mirror of its parents," said Hope, not unkindly, but pointedly.

Roderick shook his head. "Well, he may be a mirror of Celia but I don't see what *I've* done to make him like that. I'll tell you something, Hope. When Cornelius Oil passes to Victor, it will be as crooked, and as devious, and as twisted as it was under David Bookbinder."

Hope was silent for a while. Then she said: ''I expect you're right. It's sad, isn't it? But in some ways I've always preferred an out-and-out crook to a hypocritical angel, haven't you?''

She bent over and kissed the top of his head. Then she walked away in the direction where Victor had gone. Roderick stayed there for two or three minutes, but soon moved when he realized he was kneeling on an ants' nest.

1967

HELICOPTER CRASH KILLS CORNELIUS HEIR

A private helicopter carrying Cornelius Armaments tycoon John Cornelius, younger son of the late oil billionaire Johann Cornelius, crashed at Casper, Wyoming, late last night, after reportedly striking power lines. Cornelius and his three companions, one of whom remains unidentified, were killed instantly.

—The New York Times,
March, 1967

He was standing on the corner of Howard Street in a beautifully pressed lightweight suit of pale blue nylon jersey. He was tall, and slim for his age, and his gray hair was cut as crisp as a carpet. He was smoking a cigarette in an amber holder, and his hand was resting in an unconsciously self-revealing pose on his hip.

He was feeling in one of his beatific moods today. It was one of those days in San Francisco when the morning sun has a golden haze to it, as if it's shining through milky glass, and the city becomes strangely transfigured, like a ship of carefree friends floating off into the foggy Pacific.

He was pleased about his newly acquired house, a Gothic-style mansion off Mission, which he was having restored and redecorated. He was pleased about the outcome of his latest and longest lawsuit, in which he had defended the Sausalito Artists' Workshop after an obscenity bust at their last exhibition. But perhaps he was mostly pleased that he was meeting Irene's daughter, Ally, after so many months. The older members of the Cornelius family had been uncomfortably diffident about him for years, but it seemed that the younger generation were far more forgiving.

He recognized Ally from a long way off, through the colorful crowds on the sidewalk. She was walking toward him with her Indian-braid bag slung over her shoulder, and the fringe of her poncho swinging, and as she reached the opposite corner of the street, she had to screw up her eyes, because the light was so bright and diffuse and photographic.

A friend of his had called Ally the Cornflower Kid. He could see what his friend had meant. She looked clean and precious and shining. She had straight blond hair, a pretty, almost Victorian face, and sky-colored eyes that could have been cold if they hadn't been so expressive and alive. She wore a poncho that looked fresh and clean, and well-fitting jeans that were bleached and blotchy but quite new. On her feet were Moroccan-leather sandals, all thongs and straps, with little silver bells on.

He raised his arm and waved to her. She waved back, and came running through the traffic. She took his hand in both of hers, and held it, and said: "Look at you. Just look at you."

He pretended to be put out. He pulled a face, and looked down at his immaculate suit, and said: "What's wrong? Did I leave my fly open?"

Ally laughed, and squeezed his hand, and kissed his cheek. "I can see why Mother disapproves of you," she said, linking arms. "In her book, flies are those things that buzz around horses' ears."

He smiled. "I promise you, my darling, I have never let *my* flies buzz around *any* horse's ears. But that's Irene all over. A charming lady, Irene, but very literal. Back Bay, Boston, all over."

"You haven't changed a bit," said Ally, almost dancing beside him as they walked along Howard to Fourth. "You don't even look older."

"I wish Douglas agreed."

"Are you still with Douglas? I used to adore Douglas when I was a little girl. Did you know that Douglas can cut out pieces of newspaper and make those lines of dolls, all strung together?"

He raised his eyes upward in mock exasperation. "Don't I, just. It's the only intelligent human response that anybody has ever been able to get out of him."

"Are you happy, still?" she asked.

He looked down at her, and patted her hand in an oddly fatherly way.

"Yes," he said, "I'm happy. I'm doing what I want to do, the work I like, and I'm doing it with all the people I like. That, to me, is very close to paradise."

She brushed back her long blond hair. "I'm glad," she said in a soft voice. "I just wish I could say the same."

He nodded. "It's going to take some time, isn't it, getting used to the fact that he's not around anymore."

"It was all so silly. I can't bear it, thinking he died in such a silly way."

"Nobody's death is silly," he told her. "Especially not your father's. He was doing what he enjoyed doing, and apart from that, he died honest. He always held out for what he believed."

"I don't think Mother always thought so."

They stopped at the curb, waiting for the walk signal. Beside them, a black-haired girl in a purple T-shirt was standing with a transistor pressed against her ear, listening to the distorted tinny sounds of "She Loves You." He said: "You have to make some allowances for Irene. I think she tries her best to cope with being a Cornelius, but I don't think she always manages."

Ally's eyes dropped. "I guess that's right. She's gone off to Europe now, with her cousin, to mourn. That's what she says, anyway. If you ask me, she's gone in search of some ravishing Italian count, now she's free."

He said: "You mustn't be cynical. Whether she really loved your father or not, that wasn't her fault, any more than his. None of us are free to choose the people we love."

He pointed toward an office building a few hundred feet farther up the street. It was a shabby eight-story building with peeling pink paint and faded 1930's embellishments around the windows. "I'm on the sixth," he told her. "Let's go up."

As they stepped into the Lysol-smelling shade of the lobby, she saw his name neatly lettered on the office directory, between *Farrer Yorty (Holdings)* and *Fogarty Waste Oil.* It read *Field, Randolph K., Attorney-at-Law.*

His office was neat and fussy, with crowds of potted plants on the windowsill, shelves of leather-bound law books, and a reproduction of Seurat's gray, impressionistic view of the sea off Gravelines. He sat down at his tidy, leather-topped desk and opened up a silver cigarette box.

"Smoke?"

Ally took one, and he leaned forward to light it for her. She perched herself on the edge of his desk, one leg swinging, and blew out smoke. He sat back and watched her for a while as he fitted a new crystal filter into his cigarette holder.

"I guess nobody else could tell you this and get away with it, but you're looking prettier and sexier every time I see you," said Randy.

She turned to him and smiled. "Why, thank you, kind attorney."

"I guess you didn't just call me up for the compliments, though," he said, fitting a cigarette into his holder and reaching for his matches.

"I wish I had, Randy. I wish I could say that I remembered how long it was since we last got together, and called you up because I wanted to see you."

"You don't have to feel guilty," he said, leaning back in his chair and crossing his hands over his trim stomach.

"I do. I can't help it."

"But I'm an attorney. If it's an attorney you need, then I'd be very offended if you didn't come to me."

She glanced at him with affection. "You always know the right thing to say."

"That's what makes me a *brilliant* attorney."

She stood up and walked across the quiet carpet to look at his painting of Gravelines. It was a sad, misty picture; the English Channel on a cold day of watery sunlight and edgy wind. She said softly: "It's a friend of mine, a boy. I've only known him a couple of weeks, but we've had such an incredible time together. He's in terrible trouble. I just didn't know what to do."

"Police trouble?" asked Randy. He took a sharp HB pencil out a blue glass jar and opened up the first page of a fresh notepad.

Ally nodded. "They stopped him three days ago on Market. They searched him, and found a lid. He's been locked up in a cell ever since, and the public defender who came to see him was just awful. He's already been in prison once, for six months, and he thinks they're out to get him this time. You know, really put him away. I'm so frightened, Randy."

Randy wrote a few careful notes, while Ally watched him seriously. He still looked like his father, except for a softer and more sensitive mouth, but he had a tired gentleness about him that Jack Field had never had. Jack Field had died in 1956 after three years of kidney failure; and Ellie, grieving, had died the following year. Ally, as a girl of eleven, had first met Randy at Jack's funeral, and she was so struck by the way that he had stood on his own in the dry brown grass of the cemetery, carefully avoided by both Cornelius relatives and Field relatives, that she had walked over and introduced herself, helplessly watched by a wincing Irene. From that day, Randy and Ally had been irregular but close friends, in the way that an uncle is close friends with his niece, and she had often written to him, telling him what she was doing at Vassar, and he had sent her colorful postcards of San Francisco in return.

Now, she was older, and she had decided on the course that her life was going to take; but that eleven-year-old girl in the expensive summer coat who had befriended a middle-aged man who was burying his father in ostracized silence was still within her.

Randy looked up from his notepad. He said, gently: "Can you tell me the boy's name?"

"He calls himself Destry. Everybody does. I don't know whether that's his real name or not."

"Does he know who you are?"

Ally shook her head. "I'm incognito."

"Incognito? What for?"

She lowered her eyes. "Do I have to tell you? I mean, can't you just fix Destry's bail?"

Randy put down his pencil. He looked amused, but concerned as well. "My darling, you don't have to tell me anything. I'm just interested in everything you do, that's all. You're my favorite Cornelius, remember. Don't tell me you're thinking of doing a Rockefeller, and opting out of your riches."

"Would that be so terrible?"

"I don't know. What do you feel?"

She tapped her foot against the side of his desk, and the silver bells on her sandals softly jangled.

"I don't know," she said. "But I've done it. That's the reason I'm here, in San Francisco. I'm not just here visiting. I'm here for keeps."

Randy sat up straight. "You mean you're serious? You've really given it all up?"

"I haven't given it up. I've just left it behind," she said, folding her arms under her breasts. Her blue eyes were empty of regret, but still sad, and Randy couldn't help noticing. He had given up himself one of the most treasured experiences of his whole life, a successful law partnership with his father, and he knew what it was to leave your family and your friends and your very self behind you.

"Do you want to talk about it?" he asked her.

She shook her head. "Not now."

"Well, would you like to have dinner tomorrow, and talk about it then? Come round to my house. It's a real Gothic pile. I could cook you some tamale pie. It's my specialty."

"I'd like that."

There was quiet between them, and down in the street they could hear the wailing of sirens. Then Randy said: "If you've really left it all behind, then I think the best thing you can do is stay right out of Destry's problems."

"You mean you won't help him?"

"Of course I'll help him. But without involving you. All we

587

need is for some eagle-eyed crime reporter to spot you in the court, and your whole new life is going to be blown wide open. Apart from the distress that *you'll* suffer, my darling, it'll be bad news for the whole Cornelius family, and I do think you have to consider their feelings, too.''

She twisted the ends of her hair around her fingers. "I suppose so," she said reluctantly.

Randy stood up and came around his desk to sit down beside her. He asked her softly: "Does your family know where you are?"

"Not exactly. Mother doesn't care anyway. She's too busy spending her inheritance on Flemish painting and feeling pleased that she kept Mara Malinsky's family out of the will.''

"Come on, Ally. You love your mother, don't you?"

Ally shrugged. "I guess so. I just don't think she ever got over Dad not loving her. After she found out about Mara, she didn't seem to want to love anyone or *be* loved by anyone. That's what grandmother told me, anyway."

"Ally," said Randy comfortingly, and he put his arm around her thin shoulders. She could feel the tears starting, even though she didn't want them to. She hadn't imagined how beautiful it could be, to be anonymous and free; to meet people and talk to them on doorsteps and beaches without impatient chauffeurs waiting in the middle distance, or maids hovering with clean towels and fresh makeup; to stay up all night listening to records and drinking cheap wine and listening to the delighted squeals and squeaks of people making love, without parents or butlers or security staff eavesdropping at the doors. Her first month in San Francisco had been hard, and sometimes painfully lonesome; but the very hardness of it, the mundane daily tasks of taking her clothes to the Laundromat, of wandering around supermarkets with a wire basket looking for cans of tomatoes and detergent, of making her bed and ironing her jeans, had for Ally a magical pleasure that she had never experienced before, because she had never touched a washing machine in her life, nor stepped into a supermarket. Going out and gathering the basic ingredients for a meal had, for her, been some strange brightly colored ritual, distinguished by *oohs* and *aahs* of surprise and wonder, that she had seen only in television commercials. It was mainly Irene's fault. Constantly and neurotically aware that Clara had been killed by a construction worker, Irene believed unshakably that the poor were conspiring against the rich, and she had made sure that Ally had grown up in hot drawing rooms and closeted limousines, served by carefully selected maids and valets and schooled by private tutors.

It was this claustrophobic existence, far more than her third share in the Cornelius oil and airplane fortune, that Ally had wanted to escape. All those stiff-necked dinners and social quadrilles; all those airless boardrooms and soundless apartments; all the suffocating, coddled attention of being rich. She had left because she desperately needed to breathe some real, smoggy, fresh, unfiltered air.

She had left, too, because her father had been instantly killed in March in a helicopter accident at Casper, Wyoming; and when that happened the Cornelius family had breathed a sigh that could have been sorrow but sounded suspiciously like relief. Cornelius Armaments, his personal division of Cornelius Industries, had been absorbed back into the family amoeba, and Irene, who had been living with him for the past twenty years in a hostile tizzy of doubts and hysteria and endless surrealistic fears, had at last been granted the release which she had pined for so long, and yet had longed for so little. Fulfilled in her role as a martyr, she had taken herself off to Europe to get over the mitigated tragedy of his passing, and to be photographed in black hats with veils on the Appian Way by Norman Parkinson.

For Ally, the tragedy had meant something quite different. Ally and her father had had something special between them; something which was encapsulated for Ally for all time in a memory of the hard winter of 1950, when he had taken her out secretly, buttoning her leggings himself with his stubby fatherly hands, doing up her coat, and carefully brushing her hair, and then slipping out on exaggerated tippy-toes by the servants' door, so that they could run with frosty breath to the pond out by the highway and skate, bumping and jostling with ordinary folk in cheap coats and woolen mufflers, and then sitting on a park bench afterward eating hot chestnuts from a paper poke, while a man in a frayed overcoat patted his own skinny daughter's head and told John Cornelius that if *he* had a million dollars, he'd buy himself a hog-raising business, and that was the way to make money, and John Cornelius, net worth 150 million dollars, had nodded and listened with an expression on his face that Ally had never once seen on any other Cornelius face, and which she realized years later was respect.

Now, in 1967, in San Francisco, she was trying to find that

589

expression again, so that she could wear it on her own face. Being nothing more than herself, renouncing her money and her connections, was essential to her quest.

Randy took out a pristine white handkerchief and gave it to Ally to wipe her eyes. "Would you like some coffee?" he asked her.

Ally nodded.

"Do you want to tell me some more about this boy? Destry?"

Ally blew her nose, and then shrugged. "There's not much to tell. I met him at the Pizza Kingdom, of all places. I made such a mess of my Mexican omelet one night that I went out to buy some fast food instead. And there he was, standing in line. He's young, and he's really good-looking. Kind of thin, you know, with one of those faces like a tragic Norse god. Curly hair. Brown. Really wiry. What can I say? I almost fell in love with him at first sight."

Randy gave a small, private smile. "*That* doesn't surprise me."

Ally took out another cigarette and lit it. "We got talking," she said, "and then we shared a pepperoni pizza."

"Greater romances have sprung up around lesser things," said Randy poetically.

"Randy, if any romance has ever been greater than this one, it certainly wasn't one of mine," Ally told him. "I mean, we hit it off together right from the start. He *values* things, you know? He has a box made out of tiny seashells that somebody gave him in prison, and he really takes care of this box. I can see him respect his belongings like that, and then I remember some of the boys that Mother tried to get me hitched up to, and you're not talking about the same kind of human being."

Randy's intercom buzzed, and he asked his secretary for two cups of black coffee. Then he leaned forward thoughtfully and said: "I have to ask you this. It's not squealing, or anything like that. But I have to know if you were aware of his possession of drugs."

"Of course I was. We smoke a couple of joints every evening. More, if there's a party."

"Did he actually buy and sell drugs, or was everything he got hold of kept for his own consumption?"

Ally brushed back her hair. "He used to deal, in a kind of amateur way. Mainly to friends. Grass, hashish, speed, that kind of thing. But I don't think he does it now. He's not a *criminal*, Randy, any more than ten thousand other people out there are criminals."

"Have they charged him?"

"I guess so."

"Do you know for sure? If they haven't, we can have him out of there in two minutes flat. *Habeas Corpus*."

"Well, I don't know. You'd have to check with the police."

Randy scribbled a note. "I intend to do that."

Ally laid her hand on the desk. Randy glanced up and saw it resting there—five short fingernails, unlike any other Cornelius fingernails, and three Indian silver rings.

"Randy . . ." said Ally.

There was a pause. Randy was pretty sure what Ally was going to say. He found himself hoping, really hoping, that it was true.

"I love him, Randy. He's the best thing that ever happened to me. Please help him, won't you?"

Randy reached across his desk, and took her hand, and nodded. "I'll get right on it," he told her warmly. "Perry Mason won't have nothing on me. I promise."

She went reluctantly back to her apartment on Brannan Street to wait for news. Randy was understanding, consoling, but firm. Until Destry was out of jail and onto the streets, he didn't want Ally anywhere near. If the newspapers got wind that a Cornelius heiress was trying to rescue her hippie lover from prison, a simple matter of arranging bail would turn into a nightmare of television cameras, reporters, crowds, and public inquiries. Even when Ally insisted she could face up to anything, Randy still ushered her out of his office, kissed her forehead, and told her to go.

"Remember what you've decided to be," he told her gently. "If you've given up the Cornelius family, then you've given up all your Cornelius influence, too. You can't have it both ways. Not if you want to stay sane."

She walked slowly up the narrow, uncarpeted stairs of the old rundown three-story house where she lived. Her own apartment was on the top landing. As she took out her key, she looked out of the smeary window at the buildings and rooftops outside, and at the high stately clouds that sailed in from the ocean.

She opened the door into her bed-living room and slung her braid bag down on the floor. The room smelled of waxed pine and coffee. There was a high brass bed with appalling springs and a patchwork cover, a marble-topped washstand with a blotchy mirror, and a sadly collapsed settee. On the walls were dozens of psychedelic posters for the Grateful Dead and Bob Dylan and Jefferson Airplane, and in the thick of those posters, poignantly small amid the golds and the greens and the luminous pinks, was pinned a black-and-white Polaroid of a thin-faced young man with curly hair and a frown.

She walked through into the kitchen and put the chipped enamel pot on the gas stove for coffee. The sun was beaming through the thin flowery-patterned drapes, and the kitchen was lazily warm. There were jars of wooden spoons and butter molds, flaky strings of garlic, colanders and spice jars, and three old-fashioned copper saucepans that she'd picked up at a garage sale in Mill Valley. She sat down at the rough-scrubbed wooden table and took off her poncho. She shook out her last cigarette.

She was only beginning to realize how difficult it had been to ask Randy for help. It was something that had required more strength than she could have imagined possible. As Ally Cornelius, she could have spoken to any heavyweight West Coast lawyer she liked, and had Destry out in half hour by sheer legal and political bludgeoning.

The coffee began to bubble and she turned down the gas. There was a knock at her door, and she went to answer it. It was Galina, the Czech girl who rented the room across the landing. Galina took Ally for what she said she was, and never questioned her unnerving innocence about pressing her clothes, shopping for food, or cooking even the most rudimentary meals. From the day she was seventeen, when Irene had first allowed her to wear cosmetics, up until the week she booked her flight to freedom in San Francisco, Ally had never made up her own face. After she'd appeared four or five times with shakily drawn eye pencil and smudged lips, it was Galina who had patiently showed her how to do it.

"Any news of Destry?" asked Galina.

Ally shook her head. "I haven't heard yet. I went to see the lawyer this morning, and he said the best thing I could do was stay home and wait."

"*Wait*? Did Lenin wait?"

"I don't know," Ally confessed. "Did he?"

"I don't know, either. You'll never meet a Czech who knows anything about Lenin."

Ally smiled. "You'd better come in and have some coffee. I hate to talk in doorways."

Galina came in.

"Does he think he's going to get Destry out, this lawyer?" she asked, pulling out a kitchen chair and sitting down with her legs crossed like a cossack.

"He's ninety percent sure. It's a pretty minor kind of a bust, and he doesn't even know if they've booked him. He's down there now, trying to fix bail."

Galina took out a cigarette and lit it by striking a match against the sole of her boot. She tossed the pack across to Ally.

"These narcs are unbelievable. They're picking up kids with half an ounce of grass, and all the time there are guys selling horse on the street corners like it was sticks of rock candy."

Ally took down two pottery mugs and poured out coffee. The sun had gone in now, and it was oddly dark.

"I've been feeling so helpless," she said quietly.

Galina shrugged. "That's the way the fuzz want you to feel. That's the way the whole of straight-up America wants you to feel."

"It just seems so unfair. If you knew what went on when some of these big corporations . . ."

She stopped herself. Galina looked up at her.

"When some of these big corporations what?" asked Galina.

Ally looked away. "Well, who knows for sure? But I guess there are people stealing a hell of a lot more money and doing a hell of a lot more harm in the name of legitimate business than there are on the streets."

"Well, right."

Ally lit her cigarette and took two or three long, steadying drags before she spoke again.

"I know that Destry's been in prison before," she said in a soft voice. "But he said he was straight. He said he wanted to stay straight. I mean, where's the harm in smoking grass? He wasn't selling it. He just wanted to feel good, and do good, and be good. But just because they remembered his face, they busted him. It seems insane. It seems like they actually want to drag people down."

Galina sipped her coffee. She grimaced.

"What did you make this with? Ground tarpaper?"

"I'm sorry. I've got some cream here, if you want it."

Galina poured half a carton of cream into her mug, and two spoonfuls of brown sugar, and stirred it vigorously.

"At least it'll taste like tarpaper with cream and sugar."

Ally said: "It's really thrown me off, this bust. It was so beautiful this last week, Destry and me. It was only Wednesday we went down to the ocean. We spent the whole day swimming like a couple of kids. I can't tell you. He's so . . . *natural*. He doesn't demand anything. He doesn't keep laying some heavy number on you. He just sits there and smiles and make you feel good."

Galina nodded. "I know. It's hard. But if this lawyer's any use, he'll have him out in a couple hours."

"Oh, God. I hope so."

Galina watched Ally for a while, smoking, and then she said: "Did you ever get involved with someone as much as this before? A boy?"

Ally cast her eyes down, and picked at her nails.

"Just a few. Not like Destry."

"That goes without saying. There aren't any like Destry."

Ally glanced up. "They were all boys my mother wanted me to marry. Short hair and tapered pants. If they didn't look like Alfred E. Neuman, they had bad breath and played golf."

Galina pulled an understanding smile. "Six kids and a Country Squire before you could say 'suburb.' I know the score. My mother was a little crazier than that, but believe me, it was equally urrgh. More like a goddamned nightmare."

The telephone rang out in the hall. Ally jumped nervously, and then put down her coffee mug and ran out to answer it.

"Well?" said Galina when she came back.

"Wrong number. Guy wanted the Imperial Dragon Restaurant."

Galina sniffed. "I don't recommend he comes here, unless your chow mein's improved."

Ally sat down again and held her mug cupped in the palms of her hands. She was silent for a while, and then she said: "Galina?"

"Umh-humh?"

"What's going to happen when . . . well, if . . .?"

"When, if, what?"

"Well, what happens if Destry and I stay together for a long time? What happens then?"

Galina frowned. "What do you mean, what happens then? What do you think happens then?"

Ally bit at her knuckle uncertainly. "It's just that . . . well, what happens if I want to get married?"

"Married?" asked Galina, surprised. "You've only known the

594

poor guy a couple of weeks, and apart from that, he's still locked up in the slammer."

"I know. I know that. But I can't help thinking about it."

Galina crushed out her cigarette. "I don't understand you. I mean . . . why do you feel the need? You can live together for as long as you like, with no complications, you're both free."

She pulled her chair in closer to the table and leaned forward confidentially. "Look," she said, "I know that the whole parent-society bit still weighs down on you. It does that to everybody when they first leave home. You feel guilty because you rejected what your parents have got, you feel guilty because you disobeyed them, you feel guilty because you hurt them. But you got *free*, and that's what's really important. Don't you think that? You did actually get free. And no matter what guilt you feel, what hang-ups you have, you owe it to yourself, and to Destry, and to everybody your own age who feels shut up and trapped and depressed, you owe it to them to stay loose. I mean, what are you really leaving behind? A small house in New Jersey, a family car, church on Sundays, boys who look like Alfred E. Neuman, and twenty dollars a week allowance. It's not exactly paradise, is it?"

Ally thought for a while about what she had really left behind. Houses like vast châteaux, fleets of glossy black limousines, parties and dances and banquets, and glib boyfriends drawn from the most eligible ranks of Harvard and Yale. She whispered: "Yes."

They stayed together, Galina and Ally, while the day drew on. They smoked a joint, and played the new Beatles album over and over, and once or twice friends dropped by to ask how Destry was. The phone remained silent.

At around three, they heard footsteps on the stairs outside, and a sharp knock. Ally went to the door, her head light with pot, humming "Strawberry Fields Forever," and opened it. There, on the landing, in a black summer overcoat and black hat, in a strange and striking replay of another time, another era, when someone else had arrived at a door in black, and irrevocably disturbed the life of another Cornelius, stood Victor.

Ally said: "*Victor*? Is that you?"

Victor planted one black glossy foot across the threshold. "Well," he said loudly with a big pink grin, "it looks like we've tracked down our dropout at last."

Ally retreated as Victor came into the room. He smelled strongly of 4711 cologne. She hadn't seen him for six months, but he didn't change. He was *overinflated* rather than heavily built, swollen with wealth and drink, and there was an orchid pinned to his lapel. He himself was so bulbous and big, and the orchid was so delicate, that it looked as if someone had pinned it on him for a joke. He walked uninvited into the kitchen, red-faced and perspiring, and dabbed at his face with a white handkerchief. Galina stared first at him, and then at Ally, with her cigarette dangling from her lower lip in complete surprise.

"Who's this?" she wanted to know. "Mr. Magoo?"

Ally was white. She demanded: "What do you want? How did you find me?"

But Victor was fatly unabashed, and he pulled out one of the kitchen chairs and sat himself down. One of his pants legs was pulled up, revealing a pale chubby calf and black silk socks. He said: "Aren't you going to introduce me?"

Ally felt her whole life sinking away like water down a washbasin. If there had been some way to vaporize Victor where he sat, melt him away like a carton of butter on a hot day, she would have given six months of her life to have it. The past, fat-bottomed and overbearing, had suddenly come and sat itself down on the rare and delicate future.

Galina raised her eyebrows.

"I'm Galina," she said, sticking out a hand. "I'm Czechoslovakian."

"Pleased to know you," said Victor. "They make some pretty good ball bearings in Czechoslovakia."

"Oh, I don't come from there. I come from De Kalb, Illinois."

Victor looked a little confused. "De Kalb? Can't say that I know it."

"Really?" inquired Galina. "It's the seat of Northern Illinois U, among other delights too numerous to mention."

Victor glanced up at Ally. "I think she's putting me on," he said with a knowing smile. "De Kalb, Illinois? That's rich."

Galina was about to say something, but then she sat up straight and shook her head. She could hardly believe that this apparition from Wall Street, with its short prickly Eisenhower-generation haircut and its excruciatingly narrow lapels, was actually living and breathing. She stared at Ally, then back to Victor, as if she was trying to grasp how and why Ally could possibly be involved with such a waxwork.

Ally said: "Is it something important? Well, it must be, mustn't it, if you have to come pushing right into my life like this."

Victor reached into his inside pocket and took out a gold-and-alligator cheroot case. "Oh, sure, it's important. And I have to tell you that it was the devil's own job to find you."

"Then you were suited to it," said Ally coldly, and went to stand by the window with her arms folded and her face hard with disappointment and anger. She felt used and unpleasant, as if her hair was dirty.

Victor lit a cheroot and puffed out blue smoke. He said to Galina, with an intimate wink: "Mother doesn't like these, you know. But since we're going hippie . . ."

Galina looked amazed. "Oh, sure," she said, unsettled.

Ally didn't turn around from the window. She said: "I left a box number. Why didn't you write? You didn't have to track me down."

"Well, we do like to keep tabs on the family," said Victor. "It's just a question of insurance."

"Insurance?" asked Galina.

Victor nodded. "That's right. The insurance people get a little edgy if anyone of us drops out of sight altogether. So does the stock market, of course. And understandably. There's a great deal of money at stake."

Galina smiled without humor. She glanced at Ally again, but Ally was keeping her head turned away, wishing that Victor would say what he had to say and disappear.

"I kind of guessed why you left," said Victor, turning to Ally. "I mean, I can sympathize. But I think you have to understand that you can't dump all of your responsibilities overnight like that, no matter how much you feel you want to be free. Your name's on a whole lot of stock, Ally, and we can't transfer that stock or convert it or do a single goddamned thing with it unless we have your signature."

"I appointed a proxy. Rick Heller has power of attorney."

"Not now. We had to let him go."

"You fired Rick? What right did you have to do that?"

"We didn't have any choice. He was dragging his heels over the Asquahanna deal, and when it came to foreign trading, he was in over his ears."

"You fired him because he was voting on my behalf, and that made him almost as powerful as you. That's why you fired him."

Victor peeled a fragment of cheroot leaf from the tip of his tongue, where it had stuck.

"Well, you're entitled to your opinion," he said blandly. "But the truth is that you can't just walk off and leave forty-seven million dollars' worth of stock lying around unattended.''

Galina's eyes widened, and she looked from Ally to Victor in disbelief.

"Forty-seven million dollars' worth of stock?" she said, her lip curled in jokey disbelief. "You're saying that Ally owns *forty-seven million dollars' worth of stock*?"

Victor took out his pocket watch and checked the time. He looked at Galina as if he couldn't quite understand why she was asking such a mundane question, as if he'd asked Ally about nothing more than change for a dollar. "That's right," he said matter-of-factly. "Give or take a few million. Oil's fluctuating these days."

Galina took a long and shaky drag on her cigarette. "Well, if Ally owns forty-seven million dollars' worth of stock," she said, "what's she doing here?"

Ally rubbed her eyes tiredly. "She's trying to escape," she said softly. "She's tired of servants and limousines and board meetings. She wants to get some clean air and meet some real people."

Victor turned his head to look at her. There was a patronizing expression on his face, as if he was thinking: Ah, well, they all go through this stage, but it'll pass. They soon come to realize that money is what makes America live and breathe.

Galina said: "You walked out on forty-seven million dollars? You mean that? Were you *crazy*?"

Ally shook her head. "I would have been crazy to stay. I had about as much freedom as a rat down a well."

"Oh, come on now," Victor joshed her. "It wasn't as bad as all that. Look, I'm having your house at Corona del Mar redecorated, so you can spend a few weeks there before you go back to Washington. Or you can stay at White Point if you like. Freddie's away in Europe."

"White Point?" said Galina. "White Point is that fucking great palace out at . . ."

She stopped herself. She looked at Ally as if something magical was happening, as if Ally was gradually changing into a sparkling statue of solid gold and platinum in front of her eyes. The cigarette smoke drifted in blue rags across the table. Ally's eyes had caught the sinking afternoon light, and they were paler and sadder than Galina had ever seen them before.

In the second-floor apartment below, a record player was playing Country Joe and the Fish.

Ally pushed her hair back away from her face. "You might as well know it," she said. "You would have guessed it someday, anyhow. My real name is Ally Cornelius."

Galina nodded slowly and understandingly. "I knew it," she said. "I knew it had to be something as bad as that. The whole way you've been talking. Jesus Christ. And this is Victor Cornelius, right? One of the richest young men in the whole wide world. Jesus, I don't believe it. Ally, you're a zillionaire."

"Yes," whispered Ally. She felt the tears prickling her eyes.

In the silence that followed, Ally could sense the walls closing in again. The soundless gulf between Galina's poorness and Ally's wealth was already blurring and disfiguring the way they saw each other and talked to each other, as if they were trying to speak over hundreds of miles on fading Marconi sets. Now, when Galina looked at Ally, she saw *rich*. Ally was pretty, and friendly, and thoughtful, but all of these qualities were obscured by a glittering unscalable mountain of money.

Victor said: "Are we going to talk business or not?"

"What do you want to talk about?" said Ally in a dull voice.

"Well, everything. We need to know what you're going to do. Are you going to stay here forever? It took six detectives to find you. You know that? Six! You can't carry on this way. Apart from the fact that it's unfair on me, because I have to manage most of your investments, we need to know what you're doing and where you're living so that we can administer the trust funds properly. Then there's your dividends. We have to make sure they're held in escrow under the correct terms until finally you get tired of this hippie farrago and come on home."

Ally turned to Victor and looked him full in the face. "Victor," she said, "I don't want the money held in escrow. I don't *want* it. You can do what you like with it. This is not an illness I'm going through, that's going to pass. I've made a lifetime choice that this is the way I want to be. You can do whatever you like with the money."

Victor's cheroot had gone out and he relit it. "You're really being very selfish," he told her placidly. "Your inheritance is arranged the way it is to save the whole family tax. If you're going to continue to take this attitude, which I'm sure you won't, but if you *do*, then you're going to make it necessary for Dick Marini and me to transfer your stock, and that could cost us a fortune, as you're obviously aware. Anyway," he said, looking pointedly at Galina, "don't you think we ought to talk this over in private?"

Galina lifted her head aggressively. "I don't think I want to leave, *signor*, unless Ally asks me."

Victor rubbed the back of his neck. "This is pretty confidential stuff, Ally."

"Oh, dammit, Victor, I don't care," Ally snapped back. "As far as I'm concerned, this is ancient history. I've renounced it. If you've got something to say, then say it. If you don't want to, then get out."

Victor spread his plump hands innocently. "You don't have to be so aggressive. I'm only asking for your approval on a contract."

"Well, then, ask for it. You don't think Galina's a covert agent for Dow Chemical, do you?"

Victor shrugged. "Okay. But I'll have to ask Alex in. He's waiting on the landing with all the papers."

"How very servile of him."

Victor went to the outside door and whispered something. He returned with a tall, blue-chinned man in a dark suit and a radiantly white button-down shirt. Victor sat down at the kitchen table again, and the blue-chinned man opened a brown leather briefcase for him and stood patiently by while he sorted out the papers he needed. Victor spread heaps of letters and draft contracts all over the tabletop, and then nodded to Alex to leave them. Ally recognized the man from the San Francisco offices of Daylong Oil, and it was as remote and unreal as recognizing a stock actor from a 1950's movie.

"What do you want me to do?" asked Ally.

"I just want you to countersign a couple of these contracts, that's all."

Galina looked from Victor to Ally and back again like a solitary spectator at a practice tennis tournament. Ally took one of her cigarettes, lit it, and said: "What's it for? Napalm? Guided missiles? I'm not signing for any of those."

"Funding, that's all," said Victor. He pushed the contracts across the table. "There, and there, and there at the back."

Ally, in the golden light from the window, her elbow crooked and her cigarette held high, her hair shining in blond filaments, didn't answer ar first, didn't even move. But then she took the pen resignedly, nudged the contracts nearer with the heel of her hand, and quickly signed.

"Is that all?" she asked flatly.

Victor smiled, and shucked the pages straight. "That's about it. Oh . . . except we would like to know what your plans are. Are you going to stay here for a few months, or what?"

Ally lowered her long eyelashes. "I don't know," she said quietly. "I haven't made any plans."

"Well, could you let me know if you decide to move? It's just a formality. Insurance, mainly. You know how it is."

"Yes, I know how it is," said Ally. "That's why I'm here."

Victor stood up and tugged down his creased coat at the back. "There is one other thing," he said, licking his lips.

"What's that?"

"Well, it's a question of discretion. If you're going to live here, we would like to suggest that you try to stay away from anything that might prove publicly embarrassing."

"You mean she shouldn't stroll down the Embarcadero with her tits hanging out?" inquired Galina.

Victor frowned at Galina uncomfortably. "I mean drugs, and alcohol, and things of that kind."

Ally said: "Victor . . . why don't you please just leave?"

Victor sighed. "I'm not trying to tell you how to lead your life, Ally. I'm just trying to protect you."

"Forget it, will you?" said Ally.

"I know why you're acting this way," Victor told her. "You think that I'm unsympathetic, don't you? You think because I'm always up to my ears in accounts and contracts that I don't see what goes on."

"I didn't say that. Did I ever say that?"

"Maybe you didn't, but it shows in your attitude."

"Come on, *signor*," said Galina, getting up from her chair. "Why don't you leave the lady alone?"

Victor ignored her. He said to Ally: "Listen. I know what it's like to feel this thing's getting on top of you. We all feel it from time to time. It's a terrific burden, a terrific responsibility. But you don't get rid of the responsibility just by walking out of the door. The thing to do is make sure you relax from time to time, take a few days off, and then you can get back to it fresh."

"Victor, I don't *want* to get back to it."

"Look at me," said Victor, as if he hadn't heard her. "I come out to the Coast now and again. I even have a couple of girl friends out here. Did you ever see Sheila, from the Westwood Club?"

"The Westwood Club?" said Galina. "I thought only geriatrics went there. Geriatrics and rednecks."

"You can mock all you like," said Victor. "But at least I get away from work for a while and then come back to it feeling good. Maybe all you needed was a break, Ally. But you can't live like this for the rest of your life."

"Why not?" asked Ally.

Victor looked around at the two tiny rooms, the sagging settee, and the clusters of posters. "Well . . ." He chuckled. "What can I say?"

Ally moved over, and took Galina's arm. " 'Goodbye' would be nice," she told Victor softly.

Victor stood and looked at her for a long time. What made her behavior even more irritating to him, quite apart from the trouble she had caused over contracts and stock, was that she was so damned pretty, and he could have fancied a kissin'-cousins relationship without any extra encouragement at all. He dropped his eyes, and found himself looking at the way the nipple of her big, heavy breast was outlined by her cheesecloth blouse.

"Okay, then," he said, with phlegm in his throat. "But I'll have to keep tabs on you."

Ally showed him to the door. Alex from Daylong Oil was sulking out on the landing. Victor gave Ally a little fat-fingered wave, and then said: "Let's get out of here, Alex, before the goddamned rodents get us," and they disappeared noisily downstairs.

Galina was standing in the kitchen with her hands on her hips. "Well," she said, "how about you?"

"How *about* me?" asked Ally wryly. "Do you want some more coffee?"

"Do you have some wine? I think I could use it."

"Surely."

They sat at the table without talking for a while, sipping the sweet red California burgundy. Then Galina said: "What are you going to do? Go back?"

Ally shook her head.

"But how can you go on living here, when you've got all that money? I mean, it makes no sense. Why eat out of a can when you can afford the best restaurants?''

"Galina, that isn't the point.''

"Well, maybe not, honey, but it's part of it. You left the money behind, but you didn't dump it. What are you going to do—commute between a penthouse office and a cold-water walk-up?''

Ally drank her wine and looked sad.

"I'm not trying to bring you down, Ally,'' said Galina, holding her hand. "But I don't want to see you pulled this way and then that way, like you were just now. You're going to find it hard enough to discover where you're at as it is.''

Ally picked at a knothole on the table with her fingernails. "I guess you're right,'' she said disconsolately. "But I don't know what else I can do.''

"Can't you sign your holdings over to someone else in the family?''

"Not without upsetting years of trust-fund arrangements and charity foundations. It wouldn't be fair on the charities, apart from anything else.''

"Well, can't you just spend all the money you've got? Jesus, if you have any trouble doing it, I don't mind helping!''

"Oh, Galina, you're beautiful.'' Ally smiled. "But you don't even realize how rich I really am. If I bought twenty Cadillacs a day, every day of my life, I wouldn't even use up one-half of one percent of my capital. I can't spend it, or even give it away, fast enough to use up the accumulating dividends and interest. And all these trust funds and foundations are so complex, and they're so interdependent, that it would take me years and years to sign over everything I've got altogether, and by that time it would have accumulated even more. Today, right this minute, I am probably worth a hundred million dollars.''

Galina sat back in her chair, shaking her head in amazement and amusement. "It doesn't seem real. It just doesn't seem real.''

"It's real, all right. And it's like being born with a hunchback.''

Galina was going to say something else—that it didn't make any difference, that she still liked Ally in spite of her money, that she'd never feel tempted to ask her for a handout or a loan—but somehow the words didn't want to come. The rich are only different because they can have all the things they want, but that difference alone is a chasm that is almost impossible to bridge.

The sun fell across a yellowed reproduction of John Heade's *Orchids, Passion Flowers and Hummingbird*, from the Whitney Museum. Out on the landing, the telephone started to ring.

They were almost shy when they spoke, like children.

She said: "Destry?"

His voice was very soft. She held the telephone close against her ear as if it could warm her whole mind.

"Ally?" he said. "Ally, they let me out."

She stood on the landing, silhouetted by the last light of the day, with Galina watching expectantly from the half-open doorway, and she sobbed with relief. Galina came over and held her tight, and wiped away the tears with her Czechoslovakian scarf.

"Did they treat you bad?" she asked him. "Are you okay?"

"I'm fine. There was just some kind of mix-up down here. It seems that one of the detectives on duty last week had special instructions to hold me. Some mix-up, God knows why. Anyway, I'm out."

"Oh, Destry, I love you. I can't wait to see you."

"I love you too, baby. I've missed you."

Ally wiped her eyes again, on her sleeve, and said: "Did they grant you bail? Did Randy fix it for you?"

"They dropped the charges. It seems like the fuzz know this lawyer friend of yours from way back. I heard him tell them that if they didn't have sufficient evidence, he'd kick their asses all the way to hell and back again."

"I'm so happy. I can't tell you how happy I am. Oh, Destry."

"Listen," he said, "come around to my place. I have to wait here a half hour, then I can go. They want me to sign some paper or something. Come around at eight, maybe eight-fifteen, and we'll cook some food and smoke some grass and—"

"Yes," she said. "Yes."

There was a crackly silence; then Randy came on the phone. He said: "Feeling better now, my darling?"

"Randy, you're wonderful. I don't know how to thank you."

"You can pay my usual fee, if you like."

"Oh, Randy, more than that."

"Okay. You can come to lunch next week at the St. Francis Yacht Club, so long as you don't wear your Levi's."

604

She smiled. "That's a deal. Thank you, Randy. Really, thank you."

In a voice that she wouldn't have recognized as sounding exactly like his father, Randy said: "Ally, for you it's a pleasure."

She hung up the phone. Galina was standing by the window. "Destry's out?" she asked. Ally nodded.

"Oh, I'm real pleased," said Galina.

Ally hugged her. "I'm so excited! I'm going to see him at eight."

"Are you going to tell him?"

"Tell him what?"

"Well, that you're not who he thinks you are. That you're really Ally Cornelius, instead of Ally Pocznicz."

Ally looked at her strangely. "I don't know," she said in a low voice. "Do you think it makes any difference?"

"Do you?"

"I'm not sure. But I'm still the same person, no matter what my name is—aren't I?"

Galina leaned back against the landing window. "Unh-hunh. You may still feel the same, but will Destry still feel the same toward you? I mean, apart from anything else, he's suddenly going to find out that you could buy him and sell him fifty times over in the same street, and how's he going to feel then? It doesn't do much for a man's, you know, ego."

"Destry doesn't have that kind of ego."

Galina shrugged. "Don't count on it. Where I come from, every man has an ego."

Ally thought for a moment, biting her nail. Then she said: "In De Kalb, Illinois?"

She caught a taxi up to Destry's place—the first taxi she had used since she first arrived in San Francisco. She felt oddly guilty about it in one way, as if it was selling out, but on the other hand she knew she was trying to prove something to herself. If she was honest about what she was, if she faced up to her problem, then maybe she'd be able to discover herself. She was rich—impossibly and unavoidably rich—and perhaps she had to admit it.

Destry's room was in a yellow-painted wooden house on a steeply angled corner of Telegraph Hill. There were geraniums in pots, and a marmalade cat slept on the wall outside with its paws tucked in. The fading sunlight was still warm but somehow regretful. She paid off the taxi driver, and then climbed the three white steps at the side of the house and pressed Destry's bell. The card under the bell read "J. Di Maggio."

He came down the stairs three at a time, and she saw his lean outline through the hammered-glass window. He opened up the door, and there he was, lean and narrow and brown, with that Pan-like curly hair and that sharp chiseled face, and Ally felt her breath tightening and all the happiness she had never believed she could ever have come bubbling up.

They hugged each other on the doorstep, and Ally shed tears against his thin bare suntanned chest, and a black woman walking down Telegraph Hill with her shopping basket stopped at the curb to stare at them.

Destry held her away from him, so that he could look at her. He had a friendly, foxy smile that made her feel so wanted and so loved that she wished he could smile all the time, day and night. He was wearing nothing but his faded worn-out jeans, with a hefty brass-buckled belt. He kissed her, and he tasted like Chinese food and marijuana.

"You're an angel in disguise," he whispered. "Or maybe you're not."

"Maybe I'm not what?"

"Maybe you're not in disguise."

They climbed the rickety, burlap-carpeted stairs to the landing, and then stepped into his room. He had a wooden crate upended by the window, and a hammer and nails on the floor.

"I was trying to fix up some wind chimes," said Destry. "I kind of like wind chimes. They make me feel like I'm some kind of Tibetan monk."

Ally kissed him and fondly fingered his small brown nipples. "Do you *want* to feel like a Tibetan monk?" she asked him.

He shrugged. "I don't know. I picked up the chimes in a store next to the police station, when I was buying food for this evening. They just seemed like a good idea."

Destry's room was plain and spare compared with Ally's. The walls were whitewashed, and the floor was carpeted with sisal matting. He slept on a mattress covered by a plain white quilt, and cooked on a gas ring on a plain black-painted table. There were some rainbow-dragon trees in earthenware pots, and a rice-paper painting of the gate to the Temple of Confucius at Ching-hai. The room was always serene and welcoming, though, and Ally and

Destry had spent hours there, talking or making love or just sitting in silence, listening to the sounds of San Francisco at night. Faint rock music, distant ships, clanging streetcars, laughter.

Ally stood in the center of the room. Her hair was brushed and shining, and she was wearing a mini-dress of pale blue crochet. She said, very simply: "I love you. You know that, don't you?"

He grinned, and didn't answer.

"I hardly even realized what I felt about you, until this happened," she told him. "But I can't hide it."

He was still grinning. She suddenly realized he was bashful, and that he was so pleased by what she was saying that he didn't know how to act. She knelt down beside him, and touched his curly hair, and kissed his lean brown cheek.

"There's something else I can't hide," she said softly.

He raised his eyes.

"It's something important. Something I should have told you before."

He shrugged. "You don't have to tell me anything, if you don't want to. You know that. It's today that matters, not yesterday."

She bit her lip. "I know. But this affects today."

"Badly or gladly?"

"I don't know. I guess it's up to you."

He got up from the floor and climbed onto the upturned crate with a mouthful of nails. "Is that in the center?" he asked her, holding up the wind chimes over the window.

She stood up and nodded. He leveled up a nail, and started to bang.

"Destry," she said, "you have to know that I'm rich."

Destry bent the nail, and then hammered his thumb.

"Christ!" he swore, sucking it, and then waving it around in the air.

Ally watched him, looking worried.

"Destry," she said. "I'm *rich*."

He got down off his crate, hugging his thumb in his armpit. "Do you think Tibetan monks have this much trouble?"

"I don't think so. I guess they just think of Buddha, and the pain goes."

"Okay, I'm thinking of Buddha. Buddha, Buddha, Buddha. It still hurts. Maybe I need more training."

She took his wrists. He looked at her, saw that she was serious, and quieted down. "Did you say something?" he asked her.

607

She nodded. "I said that I was rich. You think I'm just ordinary, but I'm not. I'm very, very rich."

He stared at her with a half-smile, unsure if he ought to believe her or not. Then he said: "Okay, you're rich. That's okay."

"Destry," she said, "you don't understand."

"Sure I do. You have rich parents. You left it all behind. It's the old, old story. I don't mind. Ally, honey, I want you because of what you are, not what your old man's got stashed away in the bank."

She brushed back her hair. "It's not my old man. It's me. I'm not really Ally Pocznicz at all. I'm Ally Cornelius, of Cornelius Oil."

He frowned, but then his frown faded, and he laughed. "You're putting me on. Come on, you're putting me on. *Cornelius Oil*?"

She squeezed his wrists tighter. "Destry, I'm a multimillionairess. I have houses, cars, airplanes, boats, racehorses, and furs. I have a thirty-percent share in the Pacific International Building on the waterfront. I may even own this house, for all I know."

"For all you know?" he said light-headedly. "You mean, you could own a house and *not know*? Ally," he said seriously, "is this a true fact? You're not kidding?"

She shook her head. "I couldn't lie to you. I went through a bad enough time getting you out of jail. I'm Ally Cornelius. I can't help it. I was born that way."

He whistled under his breath. Then he walked up the room, and walked back down again. "You're really Ally Cornelius? *Really*?"

She nodded. "You want to see some ID? Here's my driver's license."

Grinning, he took it, and looked at it. "You're right," he said, as if he had just discovered it was Christmas tomorrow. "You really are."

He walked around the room again, and then he said: "Shit. How about that. You really are. You're actually Ally Cornelius."

She said hesitantly: "Is it . . .?"

He looked at her, still smiling. "Is it what? Is it *okay*?"

She nodded.

He came over and he put his arm around her and kissed her hair. "Are you different than you were this morning?" he asked her very gently, in her ear.

She said "No" in a small voice. She was on the edge of crying.

"Well, neither am I," he said. "And if you're Ally Cornelius, that only makes me feel proud. Me—with a multimillionairess! Don't you think that's something?"

"I've . . . well, I've kind of renounced my money," she said awkwardly.

"Renounced it? What for?"

"I guess it was too much for me. It was taking up too much of my life, too much of what I was. I mean, I still own what I owned before. I still have the same income. But I left it behind when I came to San Francisco."

Destry sat down on the crate. "I don't know what to say," he told her. "I don't know whether to ask you for a hundred bucks for a new hi-fi, or whether to say that I just love you."

Ally wiped a tear from her cheek with the back of her knuckle. "Do you think you still could?" she asked him.

He laughed. "You're kidding! You're a good-looking multimillionairess, and I can't say that I love you?"

There was an edgy pause. Then Destry said: "I'm sorry. I didn't mean it to sound bad. I mean that I love you whether you're poor or wealthy. I sometimes wish I was rich myself, but wishing isn't going to make any difference, any more than wishing is going to make you poor."

"It's going to change things, this," she whispered.

He got up, and hefted his hammer. "Sure it is. You can't expect it not to. But it doesn't have to change things for the worse, does it?"

"I don't know."

"Well, hand me those wind chimes, and let's get them up."

Destry stood on the box, and finally managed to bang a nail in straight. Ally passed up the wind chimes, and she couldn't resist touching his leg with her hand as if Destry standing on this upended orange crate were a priceless Praxiteles marble that she couldn't resist stroking.

Destry said: "It hasn't even sunk in yet. I've fallen in love with a girl, and she turns out to be someone else. I mean, you can't rush me. Listen, how many houses do you own?"

"Eight. Not including my place at Corona del Mar."

"Eight houses! Shit!"

He climbed down from the orange box. He put his thin arms around her waist and kissed her on the forehead. "I guess I'm still suffering from shock," he said tenderly. "Right now, I don't

609

know whether I'm pleased that you're Ally Cornelius, or whether I'm scared. But it doesn't matter. I'd like to stick around to find out."

Ally kissed him back. "So would I," she murmured.

They kissed deeper, and his tongue probed into her mouth. "I think I'm going to put on some music," he said quietly. "I got the new Love album today, and I think it's going to put me in the mood."

He walked across the room, unselfconsciously unbuckling his jeans. He dropped them, and kicked them away with one leg. His body was all skinny and hard and muscular, tanned as a gypsy all over, and his long penis with its smooth purple head was already half-erect.

Ally pulled her dress over her head and unlaced her sandals, but she didn't take her eyes off Destry. He was squatting by the record player like some brown faun that had trotted in curiously from the magic forest.

She took off her panties and then sat down on the floor under the tinkling wind chimes, and Destry turned around and grinned at her. "You look like that calendar that Marilyn Monroe did. You know the one? You have those same big soft tits. In fact, I think yours are even bigger."

He knelt down beside her and kissed her hair and her face.

"Does bigness matter?" she asked him.

He pulled a mock-lustful face. "Does bigness matter? That's like asking if french fries come with the hamburger."

She giggled and rolled over on the floor. He caught her legs, and held her, and nibbled and kissed at her knees and her thighs. Then he looked up at her, and his eyes were gentle but serious.

"Did any man ever go down on you before?"

She blushed. She didn't know what he meant.

"Go down?"

He parted her legs with his hands. "Down here," he said.

She said: "I don't . . ."

He grinned. His front teeth were square and white. He stuck out his pointed tongue, and then dipped his head forward. She felt something warm and wet drawing a line upward from her anus, and flickering like a cat at her clitoris. It made her shudder, and she reached down and gripped his curly hair as if to make him stop, but also to make him stay.

"Destry," she whispered, "you mustn't."

He took no notice. He licked again, and then again and again. She felt a growing sensation of tension and warmth between her legs, and after a few moments she put her hands down there and opened herself even wider for him, so that the tip of his electrifying tongue could thrum on the tip of her clitoris, and then slide between the glistening folds of skin to dip itself into the wet darkness of her vagina.

Above her, the wind chimes spun and spangled and turned, and the brown curls of Destry's head bobbed between her thighs. Love was singing.

Her orgasm came like a steel trap in her back. She was tensed and panting, her head back against the floor, her eyes tight shut and her face in a reddened grimace. She clutched her breasts in her hand, her nails digging into the soft skin, and her thumbs rapidly rubbing her nipples. It was the slowest orgasm she had ever had. Destry was licking and licking and each time she thought she was on the verge of making it, the steel trap would relax a little, and she'd have to brace her muscles again. But then the trap snapped, and she shrieked out loud, kicking and struggling to keep him away, and yet smother his face even deeper in her juices.

She lay there for a long time. San Francisco spun around her, slower and slower. In the kitchenette, she heard Destry pottering around, and the clink of glasses. The album was still playing, although she could have sworn that they had already been making love for hours.

He came back in, and sat down on the floor beside her. He laid out his lid of grass, and while she fondly watched him, he separated stalks and seeds, and prepared his joints.

"You always seem so composed," she told him.

He was licking the paper. "I wasn't always like that."

"You're open, but you're self-contained. You seem to know exactly what you want."

Destry leaned over and kissed her. "It took me four horrible years to discover how to do it. The secret is, you give whatever you can, and you don't ask anything of anybody. You don't even ask people to love you."

"Do you like it that I love you?"

"Of course. I love you, too."

"Do you mean that?"

"Yes. I wouldn't say it if I didn't."

Ally was so pleased that she practically cried. She rolled over and kissed his bare foot.

"You shouldn't do that, you know," he told her.

"Why not? I love you."

"Well, you're a rich young lady and I'm just a bum. Rich young ladies shouldn't kiss the feet of bums."

He finished rolling the first joint, and reached over for his matches to light it up.

"Were you always a bum?" she asked him.

He took a deep drag of grass smoke and closed his eyes. "I was born a bum," he told her. "My father was a railroad engineer and my mother was an office cleaner. I don't think they ever meant to have me. They were both about a hundred when I was born."

"Did you ever want to be anything? I mean, did you ever have a dream?"

Destry passed her the joint. "Oh, sure. When I was five I wanted to be an insurance salesmen. I didn't know what they did, but I knew they had fancy cars, and that's what I wanted. Then when I was ten I wanted to be an ace reporter, but my schoolwork was too bad, and my father died, and in the end I was a delivery boy for a grocery store."

"Destry," said Ally softly, "what about us?"

"What about us?"

"Well, what are we going to do?"

He rubbed his thin cheek thoughtfully. "I don't know. I guess we'll just have to work out each day as it comes around. I mean, I can't pretend that I still feel exactly the same about you. Your money impresses me. It's impressive. I can't help it. It's a natural response."

"I don't want to impress you. Not with my money, anyway. I just want to make you love me."

"Can't you do both? I mean, Ally, there's nothing *wrong* with money."

She sat up, her hands on her thighs, and looked at him close. "Oh, there is," she told him. "Money is so corrupting. Money is so damned corrupting."

Destry took back the joint, sucked at it hard, held the smoke, and then let it all out, and shrugged. "Corruption like that I could stand," he told her.

She laughed. She was getting a little high, and her laugh

sounded metallic and ringing. She kissed him, and whispered: "You're beautiful. You're beautiful and I love you."

Destry folded his arms around her neck and held her close. "In a minute," he murmured, "I'm going to do things to you that you won't even believe."

"Like what?" she whispered back.

"Just you wait and see."

He got up to turn the record over. Ally lay back on the floor again, listening to the wind chimes, and watching the reflections of automobile taillights streaming across the window, like red blood cells coursing through some darkened artery.

There was a ring at the downstairs doorbell. Destry said: "I'll get it! Where did I leave my pants?"

"On the floor," called Ally. She heard him rooting around for them, and then the rustle of denim and the sharp zizz of his zipper. Her mind seemed very far away and relaxed. His footsteps, bare feet, went out into the hallway. The apartment door clicked.

Somebody had already come up the stairs and was standing on the landing. She could hear gruff voices. She listened for a few moments, but she couldn't catch what they were saying. They seemed to go on and on for such a long time that eventually she sat up and reached over for one of the Mexican blankets to wrap around her. Then she padded out to the door to see what Destry was doing.

The glare of a naked bulb didn't seem to light the landing at all. There were two men there, and Destry was standing against the crumble-plastered wall with his hands up in the air. Ally said: "Destry?"

The men turned around. They were heavy and their faces looked as if they'd been roughly hewn out of rocks. One of them lifted a badge and said: "San Francisco Police Department."

"What's he done? What's he supposed to have done?"

"Don't you worry, Miss Cornelius. The best thing you can do is get yourself dressed."

Ally clutched the Mexican blanket tighter around her neck. "But I don't understand. He hasn't done anything."

"Ally," said Destry in an oddly hollow voice. "Just do what he says."

There was a uniformed cop at the foot of the stairs. A red flashing light from the patrol car outside lit him with a scarlet theatrical glare.

"Are you bringing him down, Lieutenant?" called the cop.

"Sure. Just wait till we've searched his apartment."

Ally said in a high-pitched voice: "I suppose you have a warrant?"

The detective held out his fist toward her and opened it. Lying there, crushed and damp, was Destry's joint. "This joker is up for illegal possession of a dangerous narcotic. Don't talk to me about warrants."

Destry said again: "Ally . . . just do it. Just go inside and get dressed."

One of the detectives said: "Shut up, Carlsson."

Ally said: "Carlsson?"

"George Carlsson," said the detective. "Also known as Curly, also known as Destry. We've been pulling him in for years. You name a goddamned low-life we haven't. Goddamned hippies."

Ally said: "I'm going to call my attorney. He's down on Fourth Street. Destry . . . don't say anything till then."

The detective said: "Miss Cornelius, I advise you to stay out of this. You have to understand that we're doing this for your own protection."

"I won't stay out. Now, give me a couple of minutes to get dressed and then I'm coming down to the station with you."

"Miss Cornelius—"

"I'm not going to argue. Just remember who I am."

She turned to go back into the apartment, but then she heard a scuffling noise. In the dim light of the landing, it seemed that Destry was holding a knife. She saw the blade of it flash as one of the detectives wrestled to get it free.

"Watch yourself!" yelled one of the detectives hoarsely. "Watch yourself!"

The knife clattered and spun on the worn linoleum. Then, in three long gelatinous seconds, the detectives stepped back, and Ally saw they were holding guns. Maybe the grass was affecting her sense of time, but she was sure that the knife fell *before* they raised their guns, and she wasn't convinced that Destry himself had even been holding the knife.

They fired once and the noise was so deafening that all her senses were blotted with sound. Two wide red splashes marked Destry's chest, and then the patrolman fired from the foot of the stairs and blew half of Destry's head away. The boy turned and collapsed, and the detectives holstered their Specials and looked down at him.

Ally tried to scream, but it came out as nothing but a squeaky, airless gasp. She found herself bending over in shock and then she was on her knees, her head against the open door, so shaken by Destry's sudden death that she felt as if every nerve that gave her body motion and meaning had been stripped and disassembled like a torn-apart television.

"You see that?" said one of the detectives. "Did you see him pull that knife?"

"They're all the goddamned same," answered the other one. To Ally's ears, he seemed to be talking from the bottom of a deep, echoing well. "Goddamned low-life."

The patrolman came up the stairs and peered at the crumpled body. There were pink lumps on the wall, and Ally realized with a kind of detached disgust that they were pieces of Destry's brain. The patrolman said: "Did you see that knife? The way he pulled that knife out? It was either him or Phil."

Ally got up from the floor and walked across the landing pale and trembling. She tugged at the sleeve of the detective named Phil. He turned around and frowned at her, as if he had never seen her before in his life.

"You've shot him," she whispered.

The detective didn't answer. Ally pushed past him, and knelt down beside Destry's body. His face was against the floor, and his eyes were open in what looked like a studious inspection of the floorboards. She wanted to close them, but somehow she couldn't bear to touch him.

"I'm sorry, Miss Cornelius," said the detective gruffly. He had near-together eyes, and a scarlet sport coat with coffee stains on it. "I really am sorry, but you saw the knife for yourself. He pulled a knife."

"He shouldn't have pulled it," explained the patrolman. "When you see something like that, you have to respond. You know what I mean?"

Ally stood up again. She said: "He had no knife. He didn't even own one."

The detectives glanced at each other. "He must have," said the one called Phil. "Maybe he kept it hid."

Ally paused for a moment, but then she turned away from the

boy who had just been her living lover, and nodded. "Yes," she whispered. "Maybe he did."

The cop said: "Lady, I really suggest you get your things together and leave this place to us. We're going to have to search it for dope, and it's better if you ain't here."

Ally lifted her head. "What about me? Aren't you going to arrest me too?"

The other detective said: "What for?"

"For possession. For smoking. I was smoking too, you know."

The detective laughed. "You were? It was his stuff, though, wasn't it?"

"Maybe it was," insisted Ally, "but you'd arrest me under normal circumstances, wouldn't you?"

The detective shook his head. "You ain't done nothing. My advice to you is to get your things and go."

The detective called Phil said: "Your cousin's waiting for you outside. He'll take you home."

It was then that Ally felt a freezing sick sensation that seemed to break everything she had ever understood about life into chips of ice. She looked from one detective to the other and said: "My cousin's outside? You mean, he came *with* you?"

"He, uh, tipped us off. He was worried about you. We've had you followed right from Brannan Street. With a hoodlum like this, I think you ought to go over and tell him thanks."

"This guy's a known hoodlum," said the other detective.

Ally opened her mouth, and then closed it again. There was nothing at all to say. She pulled the Mexican blanket tighter around herself and then went back into the apartment to dress. All the time she was putting her clothes on, she kept her eyes fixed on a blank place on the wall, and tried to close her ears to the bangling sound of the wind chimes.

She took only one souvenir. It was a piece of paper on which Destry had been writing a poem the night they had first made love. His ball-point pen was still resting on it, and she lifted the paper without touching the pen.

It said:

The day's in disguise;
It's wearing a face I don't recognize
It has rings on its fingers & silken roads in its eyes
& body & blood both speaking as old friends at a secret lunch

She crossed the street and Victor's black limousine was waiting there. Victor himself was sitting in the back, behind tinted glass, his legs crossed, reading *Business Week* with his horn-rimmed half-glasses on the end of his protuberant nose. The chauffeur, who had been hovering around the car having a discreet smoke, beetled over at once when he saw Ally and opened the door for her.

Victor looked up. Inside the car, it was cool and air-conditioned and it smelled of nothing but Victor's after-shave and hide upholstery. The chauffeur closed the door and sealed the two of them away.

Victor said: "Is it all over? Have they arrested him?"

Ally's lower lip was shaking and she found it difficult to speak. But she was determined not to cry. To cry for Destry in front of Victor was not what her tears were for. She swallowed hard, and then she said, "You know what happened. You set it up, and you paid for it yourself."

Victor took off his spectacles and stared at her. Then he noisily folded up his newspaper and said: "Now, wait a minute. You think I had anything to do with this?"

"The police told me. They told me you tipped them off."

"Yes, I did tip them off. But that was only because this person you were seeing was—"

"Was what? Was a human being who's lying dead up there? He's dead, Victor, as if you didn't know! He's lying up there on the landing with his brains halfway up the wall!"

Victor said: "You're kidding! Is this some kind of a joke? What are you trying to do?"

She turned on him, and now she couldn't stop crying, no matter what. But they were tears of anger, tears of desperation, and maybe more than anything else, they were tears for what she was—and no lover, nor flowers, nor beads, nor bells, could ever change that.

"I don't know *what* you did! I don't *have* to know! Everything this family touches turns out the same! As soon as we find something beautiful, something worth loving, we turn it rotten, or we kill it! You're a murderer, Victor, just like I am for loving him, and just like those stupid detectives are for believing what you said!"

Victor was sweating. He forced Ally roughly back against the seat and said: "Now, hold on a goddamned minute. Will you hold on for one minute?"

Ally turned away, her face wet with tears. "I don't want to

listen, Victor. I don't want to hear. It's not going to make any difference."

Victor said: "Well, you're going to hear whether you like it or not. I've put up with you and Freddie and Tess for long enough. Oh, it's terrific for you! Oh, sure! You can come and go as you please, and collect your dividends whenever you feel like it. But who the hell do you think is keeping this whole thing going? Who the hell stays up until four in the morning working out the financial policy and the tax structure and the investment planning?"

Ally whispered: "I'm sure you're doing a wonderful job. Do you want that in writing?"

"Come on, Ally, don't be smart. The truth is that one of my six private detectives tracked down this boyfriend of yours, and found out that he was a known pusher. He did a stretch in the penitentiary in Vancouver for dope peddling, and then he came down here."

Ally said: "My God, Victor, I knew all that. But he wasn't a murderer. He didn't have to pay for what he did by dying."

"No," said Victor, "he didn't. But when you're on the wrong side of law and order, you have to accept the risks. Apart from that, he was doing more damage than he ever realized by dating you."

The ambulance arrived, lights flashing and siren whooping, and bounced to a halt across the street. The rear doors opened, and two white-jacketed attendants hurried out with a stretcher. A curious crowd had gathered at the corner, and two cops were holding them back.

Ally said tiredly: "He didn't even know who I was until today."

"And he still wanted to see you?"

"Of course he wanted to see me. What do you think?"

Victor reached into his inside pocket for his cheroot case. He took one out and put it between his lips. He looked thoughtful.

"I just thought that if he knew who you were, he'd lay off. He'd understand his responsibilities. It's his own fault, you know. If you're a known criminal, you can't expect to . . . well, you know, get involved, hobnob with people like us."

Ally turned and stared at him. "*People like us*?"

"Sure," said Victor. "Can you imagine what the newspapers would have said if it had gotten out that you were dating a convicted pusher? Can you imagine what that would have done to the public-relations image of our pharmaceutical division? Ally, you own eleven percent of Haymann Drugs. Don't you understand what it would do to their business if it got out?''

Ally brushed back her soft blond hair. The street lights caught it, and touched it with filaments of pale gold. She said softly: "Victor, it's *my* life. What I do with my own life is nothing to do with Haymann Drugs or Cornelius Oil or anyone else.''

"That's where you're absolutely wrong,'' said Victor, lighting his cheroot.

"What do you mean? You mean I can't go to bed with a man because some dreary drug company in Indiana doesn't like the idea of it? Or because *you* disapprove?''

Victor nodded. His head was so wreathed in smoke that for a moment it looked as if he had no head at all. Then the limousine's air-conditioning drew it away, and revealed him serious and pink and sweaty.

"You're a very rich young lady, Ally. You didn't get rich through working, but through being born. You didn't have to do anything, and you don't have to do anything now. But nobody gets anything for nothing, and in return for your wealth you have to behave with a sense of prudence toward everyone whose livelihood depends on it. When you decided to go to bed with that drug pusher, you put the job of every man at Haymann Drugs at risk. You put millions of dollars in jeopardy. And you could have had your name, and *my* name, and your *father's* name, too, dragged through print as if it was offal.''

Ally sat back in the deep, comfortable seat of the car. She said: "I suppose it doesn't matter to you that Destry is dead.''

"Of course it matters. I don't want to see you hurt.''

Ally turned her eyes toward him. "You shouldn't say things like that unless you can sound as though you mean them.''

"I do mean it.''

"But you knew that the police were going to go after him. You tipped them off.''

"I've told you why. I just had to act in everyone's best interests.''

"You didn't act in Destry's best interests.''

"Of course not. He was the rotten apple.''

"Is that what you think he was?''

"Well, sure. I know that you can't see him that way, but—''

"You're damned right I can't see him that way! Whatever he

619

was, whatever you thought he was, you had no right to judge him! How you can sit here and decide if a man's going to live or die without feeling disgusted with yourself, I can't imagine."

Ally's voice was catching, and she was crying again. "Oh, Victor," she said, "you're such a stupid pig. You're such a blind and stupid pig."

Victor was embarrassed by her tears, and didn't answer. After a while he said: "Can I take you anywhere?"

She turned to him, her eyes red, and said: "When I see you now, sitting here, I really understand why all these hippies have come to San Francisco. You're twenty-four, Victor, and you're an old man already. You've lived your whole life in twenty-four years, and now there's nothing left for you to do. At least the hippies have come in search of some hope."

Victor took out his handkerchief and mopped his forehead. Then he pressed the intercom button and said to his chauffeur: "Mark Hopkins, please, George. I have an appointment with Goldberg."

The chauffeur started the motor. Ally said: "You can take me to Brannan Street first, and then to the airport."

Victor looked at his gold-and-platinum watch. "It's after nine. My appointment's at nine-thirty."

Ally said: "Victor, you killed my lover today. Don't you think you could at least summon the humanity to give me a ride to the airport?"

"I don't understand."

"You don't understand?"

"You said I killed your lover. I mean—yes, Ally, I tipped off the cops, but you can't possibly say that—"

Ally said quietly: "I don't mean that you killed him personally, with your bare hands. I'm grieving, Victor. Will you please just take me home?"

Victor pressed his lips together in barely controlled exasperation, and looked at his watch once more. But then he pressed the intercom button again and said: "George, make that Brannan Street, and then the airport."

The limousine made an awkward three-point turn across the street. Although Ally didn't want to look, she couldn't help seeing the attendants bringing down the stretcher through the hammered-glass door, past the wall from where the sleeping cat had now disappeared. The body was covered with a blue sheet, the color of tears on Tarot cards.

Victor said: "Are you all right for money?"

With Galina standing numbly beside her, she telephoned Randy. His secretary kept her waiting for almost five minutes, but then she got through. He said: "Ally?" in an odd, strained voice that immediately unsettled her.

"Randy," she said, "it's Destry."

There was an embarrassed silence. Then Randy said: "I know. I had a call from the captain of detectives just ten minutes ago."

"Randy, it was murder! He didn't *do* anything! He just opened the door, and they started hassling him, and then they shot him down!"

Randy didn't answer. Ally said: "I swear it, Randy. He didn't even threaten them! They were trying to make out that he pulled a knife, but it wasn't his. Randy, I can swear to that in court!"

Again there was silence.

Ally said: "Randy?"

"I'm still here."

"Is there anything wrong? You're not saying anything."

He sighed. "No, there's nothing wrong."

"But can't we *do* something? Can't we take those detectives to court?"

Randy sounded hesitant. "I guess we could, under normal circumstances. Maybe you can do it on your own. But I'm afraid that you're going to have to count me out."

Ally frowned. She could scarcely believe what he was saying. "Count you out? I don't understand. What do you mean, count you out?"

"It's really very simple," said Randy. "I had a call from someone else, too, apart from the cops. A man called Lupino, which is a name that you'd better forget. He said some pretty threatening things about Douglas."

"Randy . . ." said Ally.

Randy's voice was hoarse with anxiety and humiliation. "Ally, I'm sorry. I don't know what other course to take. I'm not going to tell you anything but the truth; and the truth is that I'm scared."

Ally ran her hands through her hair in resignation and sadness.

"Oh, Randy," she said with tears in her eyes.

"Forgive me, my darling," he asked her. "I love you, but you know what Douglas means. We've been together a long time, Douglas and me, and if anything happened, I don't really think I'd have very much left to live for."

"Randy," she wept. "You know I love you. You know that you don't have to ask me that. I could always forgive you. Always."

There was a silence, and then he said: "You should see another attorney, if you can. See if you can get some justice done. But, please, try not to bring me into it."

She said, crying: "I don't know. I'm not sure."

"But *try*," he insisted.

She shook her head. She was too upset to speak. She kept seeing that last slow-motion moment when Destry spun and fell against the wall, over and over, as if he would forever spin and fall, spin and fall, for the rest of her life.

At last she said: "Take care, Randy. Please take care. Goodbye." And the last time that a Cornelius would ever speak to a Field, fifty-eight years after Jack Field stepped aboard the SS *Galveston Bay*, passed by.

Galina held Ally close to her and whispered: "Don't cry. Come on. Rich girls don't cry."

It was early the following morning when she arrived in Washington, D.C., on the businessman's red-eye special. As the 707's shadow fled over the gleaming Potomac on its way toward Dulles, she sat by the window trying to repair her makeup in the mirror of her compact, and saw how vacant and expressionless she looked. *I wonder who I am now*, she thought to herself, *and what I'm doing here*.

She had only hand luggage, and she was out of the airport terminal in fifteen minutes. It was going to be a hot day. A blue-gray haze was gradually being dissolved by the mounting sun, and the taxi driver's radio announced that temperatures up to ninety-six degrees were anticipated.

Tired, drained, she sat in the back of the taxi as it carried her across the river and past the white reflecting spire of the Washington Monument. The taxi driver, a black man with horn-rimmed eyeglasses, said, "That's the White House there, on your left."

She nodded and said: "Thank you." She had been there for lunch once at a time when Lyndon Johnson had been trying to be nice to some of the richer and more influential Republicans. LBJ had called her "the prettiest-looking Cornelius ever." Ally had joked: "You can pick me up by the ears if you like."

The taxi driver said: "This is it, lady," and pulled up outside the Madison hotel at Fifteenth and M. Ally paid him and stepped out. The sidewalk was crowded and the nine-o'clock sunlight fell across it like pieces of mirror. The doorman tipped his cap and said: "Good morning, Miss Cornelius. I hope you're well."

She nodded almost imperceptibly and went through the doors into the foyer. A cluster of Japanese businessmen was standing around in light blue raincoats, holding brand-new briefcases and looking confused. Ally went up to the desk and signed in. The desk clerk said: "I was sorry to hear about your father, Miss Cornelius. Real sorry."

Escorted by the bell captain, she went silently up to her suite. She knew that she couldn't keep herself composed for very much longer, and when the bell captain started to demonstrate the bedside lamps and the television and the drinks cabinet, she gave him a twenty and said: "Please go. I'm very tired." He nodded and bowed and vanished like a conjurer.

In a kind of emotional slow motion she fell face forward on the bed. She cried bitterly, in deep painful sobs, for almost fifteen minutes. Then gradually she felt the shock and the distress subsiding, and she lay there in the brilliant sunshine that crossed the bed, trying to restore her mind and relax her body. Even now she understood that she couldn't mourn Destry for very long. Whether she could ever discover herself again, though, was another question. Yesterday, on that landing in San Francisco, she had lost more than a lover.

She slept for three hours and the day passed her by. At five-thirty, when the sunlight was beginning to climb the opposite wall, she had a long bath and washed her hair. Then, sitting on the edge of the bed with one towel wrapped around her head and another for a sarong, she picked up the phone and called Clyde.

"Hallo?"

"Clyde . . . is that you?"

"Sure. Who is this?"

"It's Ally. I'm in Washington."

"Ally! I didn't recognize your voice. What are you doing here? I heard from Freddie and Tess you were in San Francisco."

"I was, until this morning."

"What's wrong? You sound funny."

Ally bit her lip. She didn't want to cry on the telephone. She said: "Something bad has happened. I can't tell you now. Can you meet me here for dinner?"

"The Madison?"

"That's right. I'll book a table at the restaurant."

"That's fine. Make it seven-thirty. Are you sure you're all right?"

Ally said: "I'm okay now. I had a rest today, and I'm feeling a little bit better."

"Okay. I'll see you later on. Look after yourself."

Ally laid down the phone. Across the room, in the large mirror, she could see herself sitting on the bed in her yellow towels, pale and peaky like a painting on the wall of a woman whom nobody loves.

Clyde was probably the only person who could give her any help. That was ironic, really, because if the Cornelius family had had its way, she never would have known of Clyde's existence. They spoke of him, whenever they had to, as if he was some variety of unpleasant grippe, or a stray dog that none of them could ever quite manage to put out of the way. What made it even more irritating for them was that he was successful; he had inherited the best of his father's qualities for making money, and even though he was nowhere near the multimillion-dollar league, he was a brisk and efficient young manager, and at the age of twenty-one he was an equal partner with a young wheeler-dealer called Ulrik Schroeder in Sorensen's Fast Foods.

Ally hadn't known that she had a half-brother until she was sixteen. Then, by chance, she had seen her father in the restaurant of the Ritz-Carlton Hotel in Boston with a strange young boy—a boy with dark curly hair and a rather Slavic-looking face—and they had been talking to each other intently over lunch. Ally had been shopping with a girl friend of hers from Cambridge, and since she and her friend were both dieting, they had decided on oysters, salad, and broiled scrod. When they were ushered into the Ritz's restaurant, there was John Cornelius, her father, looking unexpectedly flushed and happy, and there was this curious boy.

She remembered walking straight over to her father's table, and the expression on her father's face when she had said: "Hello, Daddy. Is this someone I ought to know?"

John Cornelius had stood up, laid a hand on the boy's shoulder, and said seriously: "Ally, this is your brother."

It had hurt and shocked her at first, but two days later her father had spent an afternoon with her in New York, and given her tea, and explained all about Clyde and why he had kept him a secret. Somehow, whenever she thought about Clyde from then on, she remembered the taste of Lapsang-souchong and lemon, and Scottish scones, and her father's crisp white cuff with its ruby links.

"I once loved a girl named Mara," her father had said. "She was very beautiful, and we had an affair. It didn't mean that I loved your mother any the less, or that I don't love your mother now, but as you grow older you will discover for yourself that love takes many different shapes, and that it is possible to love more than one person at the same time, though not always in the same way.

"I finished my affair with Mara when Clara died. There was no question then of it being able to continue. Your mother suspected what had happened, and I myself felt guilty, because I was in Mara's arms when Clara was killed. It took me many years to get over that. But Mara was pregnant with my baby, and when the boy was born she wrote to me and told me what had happened. I sent her money, and supported the boy, and now he's grown up. I see him from time to time, and he's a boy to be proud of. He's like you in many ways."

"But why did you keep him such a secret?" Ally had asked.

Her father had looked dejected. "Your mother insisted that you never know. I had to agree. But now you've found out for yourself, and I'd like you to get to know him. He knows all about you."

Ally's first formal meeting with Clyde had been arranged by their father. They had lunch in New York. It had been snowing that day, and there was a sense of unreality about the entire occasion. Ally could hardly believe that for sixteen years she had had a brother and that she had never known. At first she had felt angry with her father, but as she talked to Clyde more and more, and found that he was enthusiastic and stable and actually happy, she came to understand that if anyone was to blame for the absurdity of their relationship, it was her mother. Ally had developed a crush on Clyde which she had never quite gotten over.

She hadn't seen Clyde for six months, and when he walked into the bar of the Madison in his sharply pressed gray suit, with a white flower in his buttonhole, she was pleased to see that he hadn't changed much. He was tanned a darker brown, and he had put on a little weight, but apart from that he was still the same Clyde Malinsky who had sat opposite her that day in New York, with the

625

snowflakes tumbling against the restaurant window, and explained to her that he wanted to be rich, like their father, but on his own terms.

"Clyde," she said, and he leaned over and kissed her. "Oh, Clyde, it's so good to see you."

He sat down, and admired her. She had plaited her hair up the way he liked it, and she was wearing a blue-and-pink chiffon evening dress with a low-cut front that showed her breasts. Around her neck was a three-strand golden choker, and on one wrist she wore a set of eight gold bangles, all different, that had been commissioned from Cartier.

"You get prettier every day." He smiled. "Would you like another drink?"

"I'm all right for now. I don't really want to start drinking."

"Are you afraid you'll never stop?"

"I'm afraid I might cry."

He reached into his inside pocket and took out his cigarette case.

"You said something awful had happened. Are you going to tell me what it is?"

"I'd like a cigarette."

When he had reached over and given her a light from his Chinese-red lacquered Hermès lighter, she blew smoke and started to explain. He watched her seriously with his dark, upslanted eyes as she told him about her experiences with the hippies in San Francisco, and about the fleeting love affair with Destry that had ended with his shooting. She didn't cry, but when she had finished telling him what had happened she raised her hands to her face for a moment as if she were trying to convince herself that it really was Destry, and not her, who had died on Telegraph Hill.

Clyde said: "Did you love him very much?"

Ally said: "It wasn't so much that I loved him. I did love him, I think. I could have loved him even more. It was just the way that he was killed. He was killed as if he was an irritation to Victor, and I suppose to society as well. Even if they hadn't shot him, he would have gone to the penitentiary for possessing drugs, and I wouldn't have seen him again."

Clyde was drinking a Bloody Mary. He took a long swallow and then said: "That really reminds me of what Dad used to say."

Ally frowned. "What does?"

"This whole thing. The way your boyfriend was killed. Dad

626

always used to say that it was dangerous to cross the Cornelius family."

"But Dad was a Cornelius, too."

"He was to begin with. But after that affair with Mother, and after *me*, he was pretty well ostracized. Well, you know that. He used to say that he never quite made it to the inner sanctum. They allowed him to run Cornelius Armaments, but all the major decisions were made by Roddy and Grandpa and David Bookbinder. Dad was always out in the cold."

Ally said: "But they weren't *dangerous*, were they? I mean, they were very powerful men. But they wouldn't have killed anybody."

Clyde reached for his drink. "Wouldn't they? I don't know—not entirely. But Dad always used to say that it was real strange that all throughout the family's history, anyone who's ever been any kind of embarrassment has wound up dead or ruined. I even wonder about Dad sometimes."

"Oh, Clyde, you can't think that . . ."

"Well, I don't know. I don't have any evidence. But I guess a helicopter accident is a pretty easy thing to arrange, if you have the right contacts."

Ally bit at her knuckle. "I can't believe that. It seems like some kind of detective story."

Clyde said: "I know. It's absurd. Well, it *seems* absurd on the face of it. But Dad was always saying that Grandpa and David Bookbinder were the kind of people it paid to say yes to."

"But Dad had something to be sore about. I mean, the way they treated him after Clara died—the way that Mother treated him . . ."

"Sure. Some of what he said must have been sour grapes and nothing else. But he was always going on about Bookbinder, and why Bookbinder had to resign, and he always used to say that if he could only find out the facts, he could give Bookbinder a taste of his own medicine."

The maitre d' came through the doors from the restaurant and informed them that their table was ready. They went through and took their seats and Clyde ordered a half-bottle of champagne to start the meal off. The Montpellier was crowded as usual, and candles sparkled on every table.

When they'd ordered, Clyde said: "I don't have any proof about this, and I could be completely off the track. But when

Bookbinder resigned in 1954, it wasn't just because of old age, like everyone thought.''

"Why not? He must have been near seventy."

"He was. But he was still active, and he was perfectly fit. What's more, he resigned just before an important oil deal in the neutral zone with the Kuwaitis, and the whole thing ended up in Getty's lap instead. Dad said that what happened was that someone tied Bookbinder's name up with a murder that had been committed about thirty years before. Apparently it was a complete fluke. One of these writers who goes around interviewing old-timers had gone to the backwoods of Pennsylvania and talked to some ancient old guy, and lo and behold the ancient old guy had said he was going to break his silence after all this time and tell who'd done a famous unsolved local murder.''

Ally finished her champagne. "Clyde," she said, "this all seems so farfetched."

"It is," insisted Clyde. "It *is* farfetched. Dad said that, too, but that's why he believed it. He said it was so farfetched you could never have made it up. It just had to be true.''

"And the murderer was David Bookbinder? Is that it?''

Clyde shook his head. "Oh, it wasn't as obvious as that. The book writer managed to track down the murderer's sister, who lived in Pittsburgh or someplace like that, and even though the murderer was long since dead, she remembered who had called him up that day in 1920-something and given him the hit job. So the writer tracked down the guy who had commissioned the killing, and as far as Dad knew, he spilled the beans.''

"What are you saying?" asked Ally with a quizzical look. "That David Bookbinder was a hired gun?''

Clyde shook his head. "Not in a thousand years. But in some way, Dad used to think that he was connected with people who were. I don't know how, or who, or why. All I know is that Dad used to say that if you added up all the people who had got in Grandpa's way, you'd be surprised how many of them had died from unnatural causes.''

"But David Bookbinder's *dead* now," said Ally. "How could this have anything to do with Destry?''

"Because I *feel* it," answered Clyde. "Because I feel that what happens to ordinary common murderers happens to organizations as well. Once they've established the criterion that wealth and power are worth more than human life, they'll continue to eradicate anyone who threatens or even provokes them.''

"Clyde," said Ally gently, "you're not getting paranoid about this, are you?"

Clyde forked up some lobster. "Well, maybe you think I am. But let me tell you some other people who irritated Cornelius Oil, or its associated corporations. Andrew Bailey, of Incorporated Electrics, and he died in a shooting in 1936. Dutch Schultz, the numbers racketeer, and he died in a shooting in Newark in 1935. And the latest one I can find is Henry F. Preston, who was the man who tried to sue Cornelius Oil for offshore pollution in 1961. He died in an 'accidental' shooting at his home in Jacksonville."

Ally said: "I don't know why you don't tell someone about this."

Clyde grunted. "Who? The government? The police? Maybe I'm on the wrong track, and I'm just chasing shadows. But supposing I'm right? How long does it take before the eradication squad gets after me?"

Ally finished her lamb and laid down her fork. "Clyde," she said, "I don't want to sound patronizing, but are you sure that it's not just your feelings about the Cornelius family that's making you think all this? I mean, maybe it's nothing more than a coincidence."

Clyde chewed his food in silence for a moment. Then he looked up and said: "Are you convinced that Victor had nothing at all to do with your boyfriend's death? Are you absolutely sure that he didn't pay those cops a few hundred bucks to finish him off?"

Ally stared at Clyde for a moment, and then lowered her eyes.

"Well?" said Clyde.

"No," answered Ally in a husky voice. "I'm not sure at all."

Clyde reached across the table and held her hand. "That's exactly the way I feel about it," he told her. "I don't have any evidence, only guessing and hearsay, but from what I know of Grandpa and Roderick and Victor—well, I wouldn't put it past them. That's all."

"Do you think we ought to tell Freddie and Tess?"

"I don't know. I don't think so. Tess is okay, but Freddie has his feet in both camps. Even Tess is kind of flippant. I don't think she'd take it too seriously."

"So what are we going to do?" asked Ally. "How can we find out more?"

Clyde said: "I don't know. I don't know what to do. Sometimes I think the whole idea is totally stupid, but the more I think about it, the more it makes sense."

Ally said: "Have you tried talking to Emma?"

He shook his head. "I don't see Emma anymore. We split up about a month ago."

"I'm sorry."

"Oh, it was bound to happen. Mutual disregard."

The waiter brought a plate of iced chestnut soufflé for Clyde, and he started to spoon it up. Ally had nothing but black coffee.

"No wonder you're putting on weight," she told him.

"It's not the food," he said. "It's the lack of exercise. I'm chained to my desk fourteen hours a day. Sorensen is growing all the time. Did you know we're now the second largest distributors of hamburger meat in the whole region?"

She grinned. "No, I didn't. But I'm impressed."

He said: "You know, I always thought it was a pity that you and me were related."

She didn't say anything, but waited to hear what he was going to say next.

"What I mean is," Clyde explained, "we always get along so well. You know, you're the first person I've been able to speak to about this David Bookbinder thing. It's been bottled up inside me, and when you can't speak your mind, you wonder if you're going crazy."

"You're not crazy. You may be wrong, but you're not crazy."

"That's what I think."

He scraped up the last few traces of his soufflé and then sat back in his chair. "Are you going back home?" he asked her.

"Home?"

"Well, back to New York."

"Mother's still in Europe. There's no point."

"And you've given up San Francisco for good?"

"I'm not sure. I think so. I had a dream when I went there, of what I was, and what I could be. But it was only a dream. Victor came along and woke me up."

"I think Victor's an unmitigated worm," said Clyde. "He's been crawling around ever since he was old enough to talk, and he's never had the guts to stand on his own two feet."

Ally shrugged. "Perhaps we shouldn't be too hard on him. After all, he's the only one who keeps the business together, as he keeps on reminding us."

"That's untrue," said Clyde. "If anybody keeps that business together, it's Celia. Did Dad ever tell you about Roderick and the airplane?''

"I don't think so.''

"Remind me to tell you sometime. It's a painful story. Now, listen . . . do you want a brandy?''

Ally reached out her hand and touched the back of Clyde's tanned wrist. "Do you think we could have one upstairs? I'm feeling kind of tired now.''

He looked at her narrowly.

"Upstairs?''

She nodded. Her eyes were misty, and the flickering white candle in the center of the table made them shine like moonstones under water.

"Ally . . .'' he said.

She grasped his wrist tighter.

"If you don't want to come,'' she said softly, "then all you have to do is say no.''

He said: "Are you sure you really want me to?''

She nodded again.

Clyde took his hand away and reached for his cigarettes. He gave one to Ally and lit them. She puffed nervously for a few moments and then said: "I suppose I shouldn't think of things like that. I suppose you think I'm still in shock.''

He shook his head. "No, I don't think that.''

"You seem to disapprove.''

"I'm not disapproving. If you must know I'm very moved.''

"Moved?''

He leaned forward across the table. "I fell in love with you the day I first met you. I never thought that you might feel the same way about me.''

"You didn't guess?''

He took his cigarette out of his mouth. "How could I? I hardly ever see you.''

"Well,'' she told him unsteadily, "it looks like we're the two misfits. The two odd-feathered birds who stuck together.''

"You're not a misfit.''

"I had a twin who died. You don't know how much of a misfit that makes me feel.''

Ally signed the check and they left the Montpellier and walked out into the hotel lobby. A bus was parked on M Street outside,

631

and more Japanese tourists were arriving in the lounge. A woman in a mink wrap was holding her toy dog and complaining to her bald bespectacled husband about the heat. Finally he snarled: "Mildred, I'm not God, dammit. If you want it to freeze, ask Him."

Ally and Clyde went up in the elevator. They were accompanied by a man in a loud plaid jacket who sniffed continually. They didn't hold hands or even look at each other.

Ally unlocked the door of her suite and they went inside. The drapes were drawn and the chambermaid had turned down the corner of the bed. Ally shucked off her shoes and went across to switch on the television. "Would you like a drink?" she asked him. "It's all in the cabinet there. The key's in the drawer."

While Clyde poured them brandies, she walked over to the window and looked out at the night. The faint honking of motor horns was mingled with the monotonous sound of the air-conditioning. She felt light-headed and excited, as if something good was going to happen to her.

The ten-o'clock news was on television. There was a protest about discrimination in Maryland schools, and a county official was trying to explain his policy to a group of disgruntled parents. One of the parents said: "It ain't natural. It just ain't natural."

Ally turned from the window and lifted her evening dress over her head. It settled on the floor like a pink-and-blue cloud. Clyde was sitting on the end of the bed with his glass of brandy, and she went up to him in bra and panties and turned her back.

He looked at her curving back, and the spread of her hips.

She said: "Please unhook it for me."

He reached up and unhooked the catch of her bra. Her breasts came free, and he put his hands around and felt the soft weight of them in his fingers. The tips of his index fingers touched at her nipples and they knurled and hardened.

She turned around and put her hands on his shoulders. He kissed her breasts, softly and lightly at first, but then he took the stiffened nipples between his lips, and sucked them against the roof of his mouth. Then he nipped her with his teeth, and she closed her eyes and sighed. She held one of her breasts in both hands, and offered it up to his kisses and his bites until she could hardly take any more.

She pulled off his coat almost violently, and then stripped off his tie and his shirt. The sleeve of the shirt tore, but neither of them

632

cared. Then she pushed off his shoes, and tugged at the belt of his pants. She was whining with excitement when his pants were around his knees, and she gripped his rigid hardness through his white shorts.

They were both panting hard when she climbed astride him and reached down to guide his erection up between her legs. Then she arched herself backward and almost lifted her knees clear of the bedcovers, so that she sank down on him with her full weight. It went up so far that she cried out, but she wanted it that way. She wanted it to be so beautiful that it hurt, and so painful that it was beautiful.

Clyde said: "*Ally . . . Ally . . .*" but after that it was nothing but ferocious kisses and the feverish strenuous coupling of two people who had to blot out the meaning of the act with the passions of the act itself.

At the moment of orgasm, Ally bit her own hand so hard that she almost wept. Then it was all over, and they were lying side by side, sweating and gasping for breath, elated and terrified by what they had done.

Ally rolled over, winding herself in the bedcovers. Clyde stayed where he was, wiping the perspiration from his face with his hand.

She said: "I suppose you know we've condemned ourselves to hell?"

He coughed. "Do you really believe that?"

"Why not? I like to think there's a reward in heaven for being good. So there must be a punishment for being sinful."

"Is that what they told you in San Francisco?"

"They don't preach anything but love and forgiveness in San Francisco. That's apart from how to roll joints and steal paperback books."

"They didn't tell you how to cope with incest?"

Ally sat up. She looked at Clyde for a long time. "Don't use that word," she said. "It doesn't describe it at all."

"That's what it's called, isn't it?"

"No. It's love, not incest."

He got up off the bed and rescued his coat from the floor. "Do you want a cigarette?" he asked her.

She watched him take two out of the pack and light them. "I wish you wouldn't call it that," she said. "We're only half-related. We don't even look alike."

"Celia thinks we do."

"I don't care what Celia thinks. Celia's a domineering old bitch, in any case."

Clyde sat down on the bed and gave one of the cigarettes to Ally. "It's not even so much what Celia thinks," he said gently. "It's what the law thinks, as well. We could be arrested for this."

She lay back and watched the smoke rise to the ceiling. "I get the feeling you're trying to make me feel guilty," she said.

"I just want you to understand the problems."

"If I love you, is that a problem?"

"Not in itself."

"But it's a problem if anybody else finds out?"

He nodded. "Perhaps we ought to agree to stay away from each other."

She said: "Could you?"

"Could I what?"

"Stay away? After this."

He shrugged. "It doesn't have any future, does it?"

"That's not what I asked."

He stood up again and walked naked to the window. She looked at his broad back and his muscular buttocks. He had the body of a man who hasn't quite reached maturity—still lean and well-proportioned, but gradually broadening and thickening across the shoulders and hips.

"I could quite easily love you so much that I would never be able to let you go," he said simply. "I told you that I fell in love with you the day I first saw you. In a way, I've loved you ever since. It's always seemed to me that we have so many secrets to share, and that we're so much alike. After I met you, I had fantasies about you. Some of them were really sexual. Now we've actually made it all come true, and it was a hundred times better than any of the fantasies. But that's the trouble. It's like everything else, isn't it? It's too good to be true. It can't happen and we both know that it can't."

There was a long silence. Then Clyde came back to the bed and sat down beside her again. She reached over between his broad thighs and held his soft penis in one hand, gently squeezing it and caressing it.

"Yes," she said, without letting go. "Yes, you're right."

They went to the cemetery where their father was buried. He had asked in his will to be buried in Washington, the city he had made

634

his home after Clara's death in 1945. The cemetery was on a tree-shaded slope not far from the parkway, and when they arrived early in the morning the wrought-iron gates had just been opened. It was still fresh, and the lawns were damp with dew, but it was going to be another hot and humid day.

Ally wore a simple black dress and a black hat with a veil. Clyde wore a dark suit with a black tie. They didn't speak as they walked up the meticulously rolled gravel path to the top of the hill where their father lay.

It was a simple white marble gravestone, and all it said was: *John F. Cornelius. 1917–1967. Beloved Husband of Irene.*

They stopped in the shade of the rustling trees. Ally knelt and laid a spray of white chrysanthemums on the grave, among the earlier flowers that had already wilted.

Clyde said: "I guess I still can't get used to it. I just can't believe it's him."

Ally didn't answer. Her eyes were filled with tears. For one fleeting moment she remembered that day on the skating pond, going around and around on the ice, with her father laughing and the sun like a dull orange bulb in the wintry sky.

Clyde turned away and looked down the slopes of petrified gravestones to the bluish haze that came up from the Potomac. He had felt desperately lonely since his father died, and coming up here did nothing to make him feel any better. His mother had suffered a debilitating stroke three years ago, and had been in a nursing home ever since. He saw her once a month, but as time went by he found he was making excuses not to go there. It was too depressing, arriving with flowers and books, to find her pale and paralyzed in her blankets, unable even to smile at him in the coffee-colored sunlight of her medicated room. His father had been his strength and his courage ever since he was small; and the thought of that warm and active man lying here in this cemetery was more than he could stand.

Ally said: "You don't think we've let him down, do you?"

Clyde shrugged. "No. We haven't let him down. He understood love, didn't he? I mean, he understood the kind of love that other people don't understand. He's probably here today because he loved someone else, instead of the person he was meant to."

"I wish I could talk to him now, about Destry."

"He'd probably say the same as me."

"What's that?"

"He'd say that it was always bad luck to cross a Cornelius, and then he'd tell you to leave the whole thing well enough alone."

Ally lowered her head. "I was thinking of going to the newspapers. Perhaps to *Time* magazine."

"What would you say? 'My drug-addict lover was shot dead in a police raid and I suspect my cousin'? You don't have any evidence."

"We know about David Bookbinder."

"We know what Dad told me about David Bookbinder. But Dad's dead. And even if we could prove it, there's no *prima facie* connection between what David Bookbinder did forty years ago and what Victor's doing now."

Ally said: "Isn't there *any* justice?"

Clyde laid his hand on her shoulder. "Against the rich, no. Especially not against Victor."

Ally looked down at her father's grave. She had wanted to come because she needed to reassure herself that he had once actually existed and apart from his letters and photographs, this was now the only tangible evidence. But she didn't believe that he was really there, lying in his gold-handled coffin under the dry soil. It seemed such a strange place for him to be.

Clyde said: "I think I have to go now. Ulrik's expecting me at ten."

Ally didn't turn around. She said: "I'll wait here for a little while. I don't know when I'll be able to come again."

"You're leaving?"

"I think so. I think it's better. I'll go and stay with Freddie and Tess in L.A."

Clyde stood there for a little while, saying nothing. "I do love you, you know," he said at last.

"I know," answered Ally. "I love you, too."

He didn't seem able to leave. He walked a short way down the path, but then he turned around and she was staring at him so sadly that he stopped. He came back again and he put his arm around her and brought her forehead close to his. Through the veil of her hat, her face was like a face in a shadowy looking-glass. He could see the tears on her cheeks, and he was so upset that he could hardly speak.

"Ally, I love you, but we can't."

She nodded, and swallowed.

636

"Please, Ally, just tell me that you understand. It isn't because I don't love you."

She lifted her head and looked at him.

"I'll find somebody else," she said with a lopsided smile. She reached into her pocketbook and took out a handerchief. "I'm sure I'll find somebody else."

He took hold of her arm. "Don't make me feel that it's my fault," he said quietly. "Just say that you understand."

She dropped her gaze to the ground. The tears were clinging to her lashes. She whispered: "I understand, Clyde. I know that we can't go on."

"And you'll find somebody else?"

She smiled sadly. "I expect so. Nobody like you, but somebody to love."

He nodded. "Well, me too."

"You'd better go now," she urged him. "You don't want to be late for Ulrik. Not when you're doing so well."

He lifted the black veil of her hat and kissed her. Her lips were warm and soft and salty with tears. Then he lowered her veil again and without saying another word, he turned and walked off down the cemetery path.

Ally stood watching him go, her hands and feet neatly together as if she was standing in church. He gradually disappeared behind the rows of trees, until all she could see was the top of his head, and then that was gone too. She thought: How small people shrink, and how quickly, when they walk away. They dwindle away as if by some extraordinary and uncanny magic, leaving me life-size and alone.

Farther down the cemetery, she saw an old bent woman in black, a posy of hothouse violets in her hand, making her way painfully and slowly toward a tombstone where a gleaming white angel stood, its arm uplifted, one finger pointing upward to the hazy sky.

1976

I stand for something that this country needs now more than at any other time in its history. Integrity in government . . . .

—John T. Russell,
Los Angeles, 1976

Halfway through dinner, Victor pushed away his mutilated plateful of fish, picked up his champagne glass, and rose unsteadily from his seat. Ariadne, who was smoking nervously at the other end of the table, said: "Have you finished?"

Victor nodded. "I don't usually eat dinner," he explained slurrily. "This was all for your benefit, anyway. I put on weight very promptly, if I eat dinner."

"Victor . . ." she said.

"Bring your glass," he told her. "I want to sit down in the library."

She looked quickly at the three servants, standing silent and attentive in the pale green dining room, waiting to clear away the wreckage of their uncomfortable meal. Then she stubbed out her cigarette and followed Victor through the carved double doors into the dim shaded light of the library.

He closed the doors, coughing. He didn't look at her. He said: "You really shouldn't have come, you know. At the moment, I'm very busy. I have a lot to do. I told you I'd get in touch."

She attempted a smile. "Victor, I came because I *love* you! I wanted to give you a surprise."

"You did that all right," he muttered ungraciously, but it was so low that she didn't catch what he said. He looked sweatily around the room for his half-finished glass of champagne.

Victor had been drinking almost all day. His big red perspiring head lay on his starched white collar like a boiled New England ham on a platter, and it was almost surprising not to see carrots and potatoes arranged around his ears. He had taken a tumbler of Calvados with his scrambled eggs at breakfast, and since then he had attended a full-scale business luncheon with a Pennsylvania coal company; a society wedding reception for the daughter of a Jewish textile importer he didn't like; and the launching of a friend's new yacht down at Sandy Bars. If there was any advantage in owning your airplane, it was the way you could be flown from one alcoholic event to another, with little unnecessary interruption.

Now he was back at Spiermont, his pillared white Colonial mansion on Cape Cod, feeling freshly drunk on top of a pounding hangover, and wanting nothing more than to be rid of Ariadne. His mother was arriving in the morning, and he had fifteen sets of investment accounts to prepare.

When Victor was drunk, which was often, he became brutally argumentative, and as he argued, his arms flailed around like windmill sails. He had a broad, bovine face, like his father's, with a fleshy nose that was cleft at the tip into two prominent bulges.

Awkwardly propped on the big red leather chesterfield, in his formal black dinner jacket and his white dress shirt, he looked like a Wisconsin spinach farmer at his uncle's funeral. In fact, the only instantly appealing point about Victor was that according to a recent issue of *Fortune*, he was the seventeenth richest man in the United States of America.

Ariadne wouldn't sit down. She paced around Victor in a possessive circle. She was not rich. She wasn't even moderately wealthy. She had flown from Los Angeles that same day on a ticket she couldn't afford, and this dinner, which was such an irritation to Victor, meant, in her eyes, the difference between a life of beautiful dreams and a permanent state of gravelly reality.

She tried to be coaxing. "You're like a *child* sometimes," she said. "Like a little boy who can't make up his mind. You need people to make up your mind for you. Can't you see that's why I've come?"

Victor shrugged.

Ariadne felt unsteady and woozy with drink, but she stayed alert. She was a tall, supremely groomed young girl of twenty-one, whose glittering earrings flashed to match her teeth and her dark, acquisitive eyes. You might have guessed she was wealthy the first time you saw her, but every spare cent she earned was invested in looks—in clothes, in hair, in cosmetics. Her tension gave her away. The rich may be a great many things, but they are rarely tense. Tension is for those who have to struggle to survive.

The mahogany doors of the library had eased slightly ajar, and as the servants cleared away the assaulted remains of the poached turbot, they listened discreetly to the blurting of Victor and the anxious coaxing of Ariadne like a radio serial they didn't want to miss. They kept their eyes on the Sèvres porcelain plates and the Georgian silver cutlery, never permitting themselves anything more than a trace of a smile, even when Victor slapped the arm of the leather chesterfield and shouted: "But that's Los Angeles! Los Angeles is a completely different fettle of kish!"

Ariadne had her back to him. She was picking at the spine of a leather-bound book with a long red fingernail.

"Is it your family?" she asked him quietly.

"It's nothing to do with my family. My family doesn't come into it. Don't pick at that book, its a first edition."

She turned. She was fraught with fear, but she tried to sound as calm as she could. This unfamiliar, offhand version of Victor, so different from the Victor she had known on the Coast, needed careful and sensitive handling.

"I just thought it might be. Your family, I mean. Maybe your mother. You told me she was very . . . well, protective."

Victor didn't answer. He wouldn't even raise his eyes. His finger went round and round the rim of his glass, making a low screeching sound.

"Victor," she said. "You're so strong when it comes to business, and everything else. People admire you, and respect you. They do what you tell them to do, and they don't feel anything but admiration. I've seen it."

He swallowed champagne. "So?"

"So why do you let your family rule your heart? Can't you make up your own mind who you want to fall in love with? Can't you do what you want to do?"

"I am doing what I want to do," growled Victor pettishly. "I'm getting drunk."

He reached behind him, knocking over a decorated glass table lighter, and lifted across a half-empty bottle of Moët champagne. He felt awkward and inflated and big, a clumsy giant fr m Jack and the Beanstalk. He wished to God that Ariadne would go away, but he didn't know how to tell her. He thought she was terrific-looking and arousing, and sexy as hell; but her bluntness and her West Coast manners alarmed him. He knew that he could no more introduce Ariadne to his Mama than turn up at a badminton tournament in black leather pumps. Victor was a man who believed in subtlety and safety. He avoided out-and-out confrontations whenever possible and at all costs. At the age of eight, from the safety of his treehouse, he had sent his younger cousin Freddie to negotiate with his nurse over the ticklish question of some stolen fruitcake. He really wished that Freddie were here now. Ariadne had been stimulating company out on the Coast, but back here, in the quiet cultured circles of Eastern wealth, she looked to him exactly what she was. An ambitious, open-minded, acquisitive hostess from a topless lounge.

He splashed champagne unsteadily into his glass. He felt frustrated and embarrassed enough to crush the glass in his fist, to squeeze it and snap it like Ariadne's mawkish, misguided sense of romance. But he controlled himself, like a trainer tugging the chain of a flea-ridden dancing bear; and he banged the bottle back on the table.

"Victor," persisted Ariadne. "Why do you think I came here? I thought you wanted me. You said you wanted me, and when I didn't hear anything, I came."

"You *shouldn't* have come," he mumbled. "I told you what I was going to do. I said I would call you, remember? I said I would call you, and then we'd see about your coming East."

"Victor, that was three weeks ago. You didn't call."

"But I was going to," he said.

She gave a twitchy little smile of desperation. "Victor, darling, you said you wanted to marry me. I thought if you wanted to marry me, you wouldn't mind. Victor, we were practically *engaged*. You said you wanted to marry me, didn't you?"

He slurped his champagne noisily. He almost shrugged a denial, but even Victor didn't have the nerve to do that.

"Let's say we discussed it," he said. "As a possibility."

Ariadne bit her lip. "A possibility? Is that all? Just a possibility?"

"Well," he conceded, trying to make her feel better. "Let's say it was a little more than a possibility. But it was just a discussion—now, wasn't it?"

"I don't know," she said simply. "I suppose I'm all right when I'm out on the Coast, but when I come here, I'm not quite the kind of girl your family likes to have around. Is that it?"

Victor didn't look up. He watched the bubbles rise to the rim of his glass. He wondered, not for the first time, where the bubbles came from. He peered underneath his glass, but as far as he could make out, they seemed to materialize from nowhere at all.

Ariadne shook her head. "Christ," she said. "You're twelve years older than me, and you're five hundred times richer, and you're just like a little kid."

She didn't know whether she felt like crying or not. All the

644

time, on the flight across to Boston, she had known deep inside her, that he didn't really want her. But it's not easy to give up a dream, particularly when you've just had one tempting taste of it to whet your appetite. She had even told her mother and father she was going East to get married and that when she came back they'd have a wonderful surprise. What was worse, when she'd opened her pocketbook on the plane to find her hairbrush, there was the faded lace garter that her mother had worn at her own wedding, and fifty dollars in creased bills. The money was a gift from her father. He was Greek, and wouldn't send his daughter away without a dowry. Standing in Victor's lavish library, surrounded by leather-bound first editions and volumes of rare prints, she felt the painful absurdity of what she was trying to do. With the whole of her dowry, she couldn't have afforded one book from one shelf.

Victor cleared his throat. "What you have to understand, Ariadne . . ." he said blurrily. "What you have to understand is that I have to think about more people than just myself. I am a man of . . . responsibility. I am an heir, you see, and heirs must give very careful consideration to the people they marry."

Ariadne took a deep breath. "In other words, you don't think I'm good enough?"

Victor rubbed his eyes. "For God's sake, Ariadne. You always oversimplify everything. Don't you see that—"

"I don't see anything. All I see is, I thought you wanted me, and now I think you don't."

Victor drank, and spilled champagne down his chin. He wiped it clumsily with his handerchief, and then mopped his sweating pink forehead. He sniffed.

"Ariadne, you're being blunt with me, so I'm going to be blunt with you."

She said softly: "Go on, be blunt." But at the same time, she came across and sat down next to him on the leather sofa, very close, with her breast against his arm, and her knee touching his. She took the crumpled handerchief out of his breast pocket and wiped champagne from his black satin lapel.

"Well," said Victor, "our family, the Cornelius family, has been part of American life for seventy years." He was trying to sound businesslike and pragmatic, like a man explaining the workings of his new lawnmower to his next-door neighbor.

"I see," said Ariadne. She caressed his knee, which twitched.

"We have interests in oil, in engineering, in airlines . . . thousands upon thousands of people depend on us for their livelihoods . . ."

"Victor," she said, leaning forward, so that her lips were almost touching his cheek.

He looked at her sideways, without moving his face. If he moved his faced toward her, their lips would touch, and that was just what he didn't want.

"What? I'm explaining it to you."

She stroked his leg. "You've explained it over and over. You don't understand. I don't want you for oil, or engineering. I don't want you for any other reason except you're Victor."

He frowned. "Look," he said. "I want you to know that I don't think you're gold-digging."

She drew back a little. She stared at him—his pink Dutch face. There was something about him—something clumsy and foolish and gauche—that made her feel frustrated and deeply affectionate at the same time. How could a man be so rich and so competent, and yet so ham-fisted in love?

Her fingers traced patterns around the heavy gold rings on his hands. The question is: Can you separate a man from his money? His money represents what he is, what he's made of himself, his background and his character. If wealth is part of Victor's character, is it immoral to want the wealth as well as the man?

"Victor," she said gently, "remember those nights in California?"

"Sure," he said uncomfortably. He was sweating like a ton of pink wax.

"Remember that time we went swimming in the moonlight? That was real beautiful, wasn't it? And remember how we went back to the room, and I dried you, and pampered you, and we made love?"

"Yes. I remember that."

"Victor," she said, curling his fine blond hair around her finger, "wouldn't you like me to do that for you always? Wouldn't you like me to do that for you *now*?"

He tried to reach past her for the champagne bottle. She pressed up against him, and kissed him, little kisses, all over his face. He screwed up his nose.

She's turning me on, he thought to himself. She's turning me on and I refuse to be turned on. She's too brash and she's too cheap, and I wish to God she'd stayed where she was. What's going to happen if Mama turns up? What's she going to say if she sees me sitting in the library with a topless dancer from L.A.? Doesn't this girl realize I have responsibilities? Look at the size of her goddamned breasts! How could I introduce a girl with breasts like that to the British ambassador, or the Parke Stanfields, or anyone? He felt like an adolescent boy caught playing with himself over a copy of *Playboy*.

"Ariadne . . ." he said, trying to fight off her kisses.

"I *know* you've got problems," she said. "I know it, darling, I know it. You've got problems with your family and problems with your life and everything. But, Victor, just answer me one question. Don't you think I'd make you a terrific wife?"

Victor felt cornered. "It's difficult to say," he said blindly.

Ariadne pressed closer. "Victor, what are you *talking* about? You told me you loved me. Didn't we have the best two weeks in the whole world? You said you loved me, Victor. You *promised* you did."

He stood up very abruptly. His white shirttail was hanging out of his dinner jacket at the back.

"What are you going to do?" she asked him.

Victor said nothing. He rang the long brocade bell pull for the servants. After a while, his neat little butler, Eustace, appeared, looking like the diminutive Italian barber he had once been. Eustace conscientiously avoided looking in Ariadne's direction, and gave his usual little bow.

"Eustace," said Victor thickly, "I want some more Moët."

"Yes, sir."

"I also want you to tell Rosen to get a car out. Miss Skouros is staying in Hyannis tonight. Book her a room at Dunfey's."

"Very good, sir."

Eustace turned and left. Neither of them noticed that he left the library doors marginally ajar. Victor was too busy simmering in his own inadequacies, and Ariadne was searching in her pocketbook.

"There," she said, holding up a crumpled handful of dollars.

Victor focused his eyes on the money like a man on the beach trying to see which one of a hundred swimmers is his drowning aunt.

"What's that?" he said.

"Money. You might as well have it. It's my dowry, from my father. It was all that he could afford."

647

Victor lurched. He couldn't keep his balance, and he had to sit down.

"Money? What do you mean?"

Ariadne was starting to cry. She wished she wouldn't. She didn't feel like crying. But somehow the tears wouldn't stop pouring out of her eyes.

"I thought I was going to marry you. It was what you said, and I believed you. I'm sorry. But you can have the dowry. You deserve it, I suppose. You've got so many responsibilities, after all. Every little bit helps, doesn't it?"

Victor's eyes bulged. "What the hell am I going to do with that? How much is it?"

"Fifty dollars."

He stared at her as if he couldn't believe that sums of money actually came that small.

"Fifty dollars? What the hell am I going to do with fifty dollars?"

Ariadne was weeping openly now. The tears were impossible to stop. They left dark streaks of makeup down her cheeks, and her eyes were blotted like a letter left in the rain.

"It's all . . . my father . . . could afford . . ." she sobbed.

Victor heaved himself to his feet again. He was almost glad she was crying, because that made her look ugly, and when she was ugly, she was defenseless. He could lose his temper with her, the way he lost his temper with inefficient tax lawyers and fumbling accountants.

"For God's sake!" he shouted coarsely.

She lowered her head. Her shoulders shook with intermittent sobs. She had no handkerchief, and she had to wipe her eyes on the backs of her hands.

"I don't understand what you want," he said impatiently. "Look at that necklace, how many girls do you know with necklaces like that?"

She dumbly put her hands behind her neck and tried to unfasten the necklace, but the clasp wouldn't open.

"I don't care about it," she wept. "If you want it back, you can have it. I'm sorry I cost you so much money."

"I don't want it back!" shouted Victor. "What's the matter with you? Just because we have a two-week affair, does that mean we have to stay together for the rest of our lives? You'd hate this life! You'd hate it!"

"And what about you?" she sniffed, looking up with a tear-blotched face. "Would you hate me, too?"

"It's not *possible*," he said impatiently.

"Why?" she said in a shaky voice. "You haven't even told me *why* it's not possible."

He spread his arms. He had an expression of testy resignation on his face. "You don't grasp what I'm saying," he told her. "It's not up to me. I have to think of the destiny of the entire family."

"Destiny? Don't you ever think about love?"

He didn't answer.

"Don't you ever think that I love you, Victor, and that you might even love me? I saw feelings inside you during that two-week affair that I haven't seen once tonight. Victor, you're a strong, emotional, loving man, but you're letting your family and your money and your own fears stand in your way."

Victor looked at her. "You don't know anything about me," he said, trying to sound cold.

Ariadne's eyes widened. The light from the heavy-shaded library lamps gleamed down her silvery skin-tight dress, as if shiny orange liquid had been poured down her body.

"I know a lot about you," she said huskily. "I know that you're sensitive when you allow yourself to be. I know that you're full of affection, when you allow yourself to let it out. I know that you're rich. I know that you don't know anything about real life at all, or real feelings, and that you're terrified that somebody's going to show you. It's very easy to be brave when you're rich, Victor. But it's only when you're poor that bravery really means anything. You're scared of me, aren't you? And you're even more scared of your family."

Victor reddened. "I think you'd better get out of here," he said. "I think you've said enough for one night."

She shook her head. "You don't even know how much I love you, do you?"

"Look, Ariadne . . ."

She stood up and walked across the shiny parquet flooring. She put her arms around his neck and she tried to draw herself in close to him. He stood sagging and motionless like a pile of pillows about to collapse on the floor.

"Wouldn't you like to give it just one more try?" she whispered. "All we have to do is leave everything and go upstairs. Even if we don't get married, we could remember this one last night. Wouldn't you like to do that? Wouldn't you like to feel me again, the way you used to, back in California?"

Victor swayed. He couldn't see properly, and he felt nauseous. I want her. I want that soft silvery body of hers, and I want to hear her moan and whimper because I'm giving her everything she craves for. But if I do that she'll still be around tomorrow, and the family are coming around for their meeting tomorrow, and what's Mama going to say about a two-bit topless dancer in a wrinkled evening dress?

He raised his arms, the same way that she had raised her arms to unfasten the necklace, and he pulled her hands away from his neck.

"Ariadne, you have to understand—"

"Victor," she said, soft and hurt.

"It can't work, Ariadne."

"You haven't even said why. You haven't even told me why. I spent all of my savings coming here, Victor, because I thought you wanted me. You haven't even said why, or anything."

He looked at her, standing there, with her smeary makeup and her huge great breasts, and he didn't even pity her.

"It's a question of fitting in," he said in a bald voice.

She didn't understand. "What do you mean, fitting in? What kind of fitting in?"

He swallowed. "Socially. It's a question of fitting in socially."

She let out a long breath. It hurt her, when he said that, but it also gave her an irrational surge of hope. He was so unsure of himself with women that he thought it would crush her, saying that. He didn't even realize that insults would only stir up her optimism. If he insults me, he must feel *something* for me. At least he's not totally indifferent. If he despises me—well, hatred is supposed to be the next thing to love, and perhaps I can do something about it.

All that was wrong with that equation was that Victor knew nothing about soap-opera psychology, and even less about sentimental love. Ariadne, on the other hand, watched, and believed, *The Waltons*.

"Victor," said Ariadne gently, "you don't even know what your own feelings are, do you, Victor? Victor, love, you don't."

Victor stood stiff and uncertain, like President Nixon in the last days of his resignation.

"It has," he said, "to be a political, family, and financial decision. I can't take it right away. It has to be thought about."

She shook her head, almost lovingly. "Oh, God, Victor, you're such a little baby."

"Look," he said awkwardly, "if you need anything to tide you over . . ."

She stared. "What do you mean?"

He stuck his hands in his pockets and looked embarrassed. "I mean, if you need any money. If you're in a bind."

He might just as well have come straight out and called her a cheap West Coast whore. She kept on staring at him, trembling, and she stared at him so long that he had to turn away from her and gaze nervously at the rows of leather-bound books.

"You're paying me off," she said in a hushed voice.

"Ariadne, it's nothing of the kind. You know what I have to contend with. How could we ever think about *any* kind of future together without thinking about it in a wider context? It has to be analyzed in a wider context than just a personal relationship."

"I won't take your money, Victor."

He turned, impatient. "It's not a *question* of taking my money. You just said yourself that you spent your savings coming here. Ariadne, I appreciate what you did. I appreciate it, from the bottom of my heart. I just want to make sure that you're not out of pocket, that's all."

"Out of pocket?" she said disbelievingly. "Victor, I love you."

"I *know* that. Ariadne, I *know* that. But, right this minute, I have to confess that I don't know what to say to you."

"Will you ever know?"

"Ariadne . . ."

"You just said we had a future together."

"That was an 'if.' "

"Well, what does that mean? Does that mean you're really still thinking about it? You have to tell me, Victor. You can't just leave me like this."

Victor closed his eyes. Through the waves of his hangover, Ariadne's voice sounded like someone speaking through a tin funnel, across a windblown baseball diamond.

"I think you'd better leave," he said quietly. "Rosen will drive you to Dunfey's."

"Victor, I can't go until you tell me."

He opened his eyes again. She was still there.

"Victor," she said. "Please . . ."

"Ariadne," he said carefully. "It's going to be very difficult. Look . . . if you want to . . ."

"What?"

"Look, you can keep the necklace."

They stood there facing each other. The big-boned millionaire in the dinner jacket with his shirttail hanging out, and the tall curvy dancer in the too-tight silver dress. They faced each other, and for a long while it seemed as if they didn't understand, either of them, why they were there or what they were doing. They looked at each other like two strangers on the Staten Island ferry.

Ariadne, stunned, reached up to touch the emerald pendant, as if it were something she had been carrying about with her all along, and which she had only now discovered to be the real cause of all her misfortunes.

She felt panic; real, sickening panic. If he really meant it, if he really made her go, then she had nothing to go back to at all. For the first time in her life, with Victor, she had walked on handmade Persian carpets, eaten off antique French porcelain with solid silver knives and forks, sipped château-bottled wines and real champagne, dressed in silk and sat on velvet. It was a world that had seemed before like a fantasy, but she had discovered that it really existed. Going back meant her deadend job in the Starlight Lounge, an emerald necklace that would just about pay for the whole trip, and two mystified and oversympathetic parents. She would turn up at her father's tool shop, alone and miserable, and they'd make a fuss over her, feed her with garlic soup and hot rolls, and in the evening she'd bury herself in her mother's arms and cry until it was too painful to cry any longer.

She stepped uncertainly toward Victor, her hands out in front of her, a newly blind woman reaching for the safety of a handrail she couldn't see. Victor gripped her wrists and held her so that she couldn't touch him. She made a funny little noise like a cat mewing.

"Ariadne," he said. "You mustn't take this thing the wrong way."

His words were tightly leashed, but his mind wasn't. He didn't know what he was going to do now. His irritation and his anxiety, aggravated by his drunkenness, were making him act like a crude man-sized puppet made of logs. He wanted to get rid of her. She excited him physically, but he preferred to feel pain at losing her, to wallow in self-pity and talk about "the terrible lonesomeness of great wealth," than to have to cope with Ariadne's passions and Ariadne's appetite for crude emotion. What she didn't realize—and what he only half-understood himself—was that he was not a whole man. He was already the victim of a crushing disaster, with terminal injuries. He had been buried, at birth, under a mountain of money.

"Victor," she pleaded. "Want me, Victor."

He mouthed "No" practically silently.

"Victor, you don't know how much I need you. Victor, what am I going to do without you?"

He let go of her arms, pushing her away from him like casting off a rowboat.

"Get a good night's sleep," he said hoarsely. "We both need a good night's sleep. I'll call you in the morning and then we'll see."

"I can't wait, Victor. I won't be able to sleep unless you tell me now."

She was crying again. Head down in deep, noisy sobs.

"Ariadne . . . I can't tell you now. What do you want me to say? For Christ's sake, let's just call it a day!"

She stood in front of him, clutching herself in her own arms, sobbing like a goose. Victor knew what you had to do in cases of hysteria. He stepped forward, quite abruptly, and slapped her face.

He didn't expect her to hit back. That was the last thing he thought would happen. But Victor had never hit a woman before; it was something he had seen in movies and read about in magazines. And he had never before provoked a girl who had spent three years of her working life in a topless lounge. Perhaps the fact that she hit him back was the most convincing reason not to marry her.

He had half-turned away in the split second after slapping her, and he didn't even see it coming. The first thing he knew, she had smacked him hard across his right ear, and pushed him violently in the hip. He stumbled clumsily over the big green library chair, and fell with a painful jolt on his right knee. A whole swarm of fear and hopelessness and rejection came flying out of her, and she scratched and pummeled and smacked him, and he had to raise his arm to protect his face.

"*God*!" she shrieked. "*You bastard*! *You total bastard*!"

"*Get the hell off*!" he roared, but she fell on top of him, breasts swinging, and they sprawled across the parquet floor, kicking and wrestling and struggling. Victor managed to seize one of her wrists, but she reached down with her other hand and squeezed him between the legs, so agonizingly hard that he screamed out loud. Enraged, he flung her over on her back and held her against the polished boards with his own weight.

"Ariadne!" he gasped. "For Christ's sake . . . *Ariadne!*"

She jerked her face to one side. She wouldn't look at him. She didn't want to hear anything but the words for which she'd flown three thousand miles.

"Ariadne," slurred Victor, pressing on her even more heavily. "Listen, Ariadne. I'm talking and I want you to listen. We had a great time together on the Coast. I'm not denying it. Don't let it ever be said that we didn't have a great time together on the Coast. But you have to see my side of the story. Can you see my side of the story, Ariadne?"

She wouldn't answer, and she still wouldn't look at him.

"Ariadne!" he snapped. "Can you hear me, Ariadne?"

In response, she simply twisted her body underneath him.

Victor was an adolescent when it came to sex. When girls came close to him, and he could feel their warmth, he responded with a directness that both excited and embarrassed him. Now Ariadne was shifting between his thighs, and the effect was immediate. He was shaking and trembling, and he could feel knots tightening up in his muscles like twisted trees. How could she be so tantalizing and so dumb at the same time? How could she lie there wriggling between his legs, being so blind and nagging and ridiculous? He couldn't marry her. Couldn't she see that? Couldn't she understand? Why the hell did she keep on nagging and nagging and nagging? Couldn't she understand English?

He despised her, and at the same time he felt a rush of lust that made him grimace with frustration. He wanted to hurt her, and rape her, and see her jump and jolt and beg for mercy and beg for more. He felt heated urges that made him almost incoherent.

"*Ariadne!*" he shouted again.

She kept her face away. He raised his arm and smacked her across the cheek—such a cracking blow that her head jerked. Her cheek was blotted with a wide scarlet mark, and tears ran out of her eyes, mingled with black eye makeup.

"*I'll hit you!*" he bellowed. "*I'll hit you again!*"

Ariadne saw sheets of red in front of her eyes, and all she felt was pain. She twisted herself around underneath him, breaking free, and tried to wriggle away like a slippery silver snake. She nearly made it, scrabbling on hands and knees on the shiny parquet floor. But Victor clawed out and caught her ankle, and he wrenched her toward him, panting and gasping.

He was shrieking, himself, with rage. They were both kneeling, and he hit her straight in the face with his fist. She felt her nose burst inside, and she banged back on the floor like a falling chair. Blood sprayed over her lips and splattered her breasts.

Victor fell clumsily on top of her. He seized hold of her silver evening dress at the back, and he tugged it with his big red hands. She whimpered and cried and hit back at him, but he tore the dress halfway up, baring her naked bottom and her curved waist. He bear-hugged her around the body, and pulled open his own trousers with one hand.

Her blood dripped quickly onto the floor in front of her. She twisted again, and tried to pull herself away, but Victor held on to her with a bitter, unremitting, clamplike grip.

"Victor," she bubbled. "Please . . ."

He pushed himself against her. He was coughing with the effort. He pushed and rubbed himself against her again and again. Ariadne, with her eyes almost closed with bruises, watched the blood splash onto her hand, and realized that Victor was trying to rape her, but couldn't. He loved her so little that he couldn't even rape her. After a few seconds, without a word he let her go. She heard him fall back onto the library floor. On hands and knees she crawled over to the table and unwound the napkin from the bottle of champagne to bathe her nose.

Victor himself felt winded and numb. He lay on the floor with his fly open, staring up at the library ceiling, a man knocked down in the accident of his own destiny. The chandelier sparkled in his eyes and reminded him of birthdays. He knew what he had done to Ariadne, but he had no idea of what he might have done to himself. Right now, right at this moment, he didn't want to think.

Ariadne managed to stand up. The napkin was dark red, but she could feel a clot forming in her nose, and the worst of the bleeding seemed to have stopped. Her head pounded, and her eyes were misty with pain. She felt like the survivor of a senseless accident, nothing else. She was shocked and quivering and a long way past tears. The greatest shock of all was not the punch, nor any of the violence. It was the final, total rejection. The millionaire was lying like a bundle of washing on the floor of his library, and he really didn't want her. She sat down on the Chesterfield, feeling faint and giddy, and then she was sick. Some of it was fish, but most of it was champagne.

Now there was no alternative—she had to stay the night. Victor called Dr. Weywood up from Hyannis, a fussy and tiresome old man with very chilly hands, and Dr. Weywood examined her face, and gave her a cold compress, and told her she was lucky she hadn't broken her nose. Before he let the doctor into the room, Victor gave Ariadne a confused speech on why she had to say that she had taken a fall from a horse. Ariadne lay in her white nylon nightie in the large French walnut bed, unmoving and still shocked, and didn't say anything at all.

Victor left her. He took a long shower, sudsing his plump body over and over with coconut-oil soap. Then, in a dragon-patterned bathrobe of ultramarine silk, he went into his office and called his personal lawyer, Dick Marini, on the telephone. Eustace brought him a tray of black coffee, which he drank in quick, scalding mouthfuls. He checked his watch and it was two-thirty in the morning.

He leaned back in his own reclining chair, swiveling around so that he could look out over the nighttime gloom of his grounds, and waited while the phone rang and rang and rang. Eventually it was picked up. A weary voice said: "Who is this?"

"Dick? It's Victor."

"Oh, hi, Victor. Do you know what time it is? Don't you whiz kids ever sleep?"

"Dick, I think I have a little problem here."

"Can it wait till the morning?"

Victor drummed his fingers on the brown leather top of his desk. "If it could wait until morning, I wouldn't have called you now."

Dick sighed. "Okay. What's wrong?"

"Well . . ." said Victor. He suddenly realized he was embarrassed. He could hardly find the words to describe what had happened; but he knew, for his own protection, that he had to. "Well, Dick, it's a girl."

"A girl?" Dick managed to keep most of the surprise out of his voice. "What kind of a girl?"

Victor blurted it all out. "She's a girl I . . . uh, met in Los Angeles. You remember that West Coast business trip I did three or four weeks ago, in April? That was the time. I just met her, you

656

know, in a club. She wasn't anything special, but, you know, we kind of got along. She stayed around for the whole two weeks and we kind of got along pretty well.''

"I see," said Dick. He was evidently taking notes. "Did you sleep with her?"

"Well, I guess a couple of times. But that's not the problem."

"What is the problem?"

Victor poured himself some more coffee. The silver spout rattled unsteadily against the cup, and he just couldn't keep it still.

"She, uh, came up here. I mean, she flew up here today. She was here when I got home, and she seemed to have the idea fixed in her mind that I had promised to marry her. I mean, Dick . . . don't ask me where she got the idea, because you know how careful I am. But that was what she was saying. She said she loved me, and she wanted to marry me, and that out on the Coast I was supposed to have suggested that I marry her."

Dick Marini sniffed. "What kind of a dame is she?"

"Er, well, she's not exactly a Bouvier."

"A hooker?"

"No, no, nothing like that. She works in one of those lounges, you know? The topless lounges. Kind of a hostess."

"In other words, a hooker."

"Well, I don't know."

Dick made more notes. Then he said: "Did she threaten you?"

"Not exactly."

"What do you mean, not exactly?"

"Well, this is the problem. She went on and on at me, and in the end I asked her to stay for dinner—I mean, just for the sake of courtesy. She flew all the way from L.A. just because she had this kind of stupid idea that I was in love with her—you know? I hardly even remembered the girl, but the least I could do was feed her. Anyway, we both got drunker than we should, and we had a kind of an argument."

Dick sounded suspicious. "What kind of an argument?"

"Well," said Victor uneasily, "she got hysterical, so I hit her."

There was a lengthy silence. Then Dick said: "Go on. You hit her, and what then?"

"She hit me back. So I punched her in the face. And that's just about it."

"You punched her in the face?"

Victor coughed. "That's about the size of it, yes."

657

"Where is she now?"

"She's right here, asleep I guess. I called Dr. Weywood, and I told her to say that she'd taken a dive off a horse."

"She did what?"

Victor frowned. "She fell off a horse. I told her to say she fell off a horse."

Dick Marini tried not to sound too exasperated. But his voice was tightly under control when he said: "Victor, you just did the worst thing you could have possibly done."

"How's that? What do you mean?"

"I mean that, as your guest, that girl was your responsibility, and you want to tell a court that you let her ride one of your horses, after a boozy dinner, in the dark?"

Victor swiveled around and leaned heavily on his desk. "What court? What are you talking about?"

"The court that every right-minded citizen goes to when someone very rich does them the slightest injury, that's what I'm talking about. So what's it to be? She fell off a horse, which makes you negligent, and liable for damages; or you punched her in the face, which makes you a sitting duck for assault charges. Either way, you're going to drop a bundle of money, and worse than that, you're going to cop some very bad press."

Victor chewed at his thick raspberry-colored lips and said nothing. He didn't blame himself for what had happened. It had been a nasty snag devised by fate and misfortune especially to trap and confuse him. He didn't even blame Ariadne. Victor had been brought up to believe that destiny and the lives of the Cornelius family were the woof and the warp of American history, and that other people were simply incidental flecks of colored wool. He thought nothing at all of Ariadne, except that she had been picked by fate to arouse his lust, and that his lust had made things go wrong. His own failings were far more important to him than any of Ariadne's strengths.

"Dick," he said carefully, "we have the election November."

There was no reply.

"Did you hear me, Dick?" he repeated.

"I heard you. I'm thinking."

"Dick, we have to keep any mention of this out of the papers. And away from Mama, too."

Dick mulled over that. "Don't you think you have a duty to tell her?" he suggested. "She wouldn't thank you if it came out later."

"I don't know. I don't know what to do. Christ, Dick, that's why I'm calling you. Give me some creative suggestions."

"Well," said Dick, "do you think she's susceptible to money?"

Victor coughed. "I'm not sure. I offered her something before—kind of expenses—but she didn't seem too interested. She comes from a pretty run-down background, though. Her father runs a garage, or a handyman store, something like that. I guess I could try waving a few conciliatory dollars under her nose."

Dick said: "Wait till I get there. I think you've done enough already. Meanwhile, don't admit to anything. Were there any witnesses? Did anyone see you hit her?"

"There was nobody else in the house."

"How about servants?"

"I don't understand."

"Victor, in court, a servant's evidence is just as valid as anyone else's. Did any of the servants see you do it?"

Victor tried to think. "Well, there was Eustace and one of the others. They helped clear up afterward. The girl had a nosebleed. But they didn't actually see me hit her. No, I mean nobody saw that."

Dick let out a short, tight sigh of relief. "Thank heaven for small mercies. Listen, go to bed now. Keep that girl around at your place. I'll come round first thing in the morning and talk to both of you. I don't want her to think that she has any grounds for complaint against you. But on the other hand, I also want her to know that if she tries to get smart, it's going to be the worse for her."

Victor swallowed tepid coffee. "I could tell her that myself."

"Victor," warned Dick, "that is not your line of country. Leave it to me. You pay me enough to do it, and I'll do it well. Meanwhile, don't talk to the girl at all, except to state simple facts like 'this is your breakfast' or 'oh, what a beautiful morning.' You got it?"

"Okay, I got it. But listen, Mama and the family are coming around tomorrow."

"All right. I'll make it early. Thanks for your call."

"Okay," said Victor, and laid the receiver down. He sat motionless, hunched, for a long while. He was beginning to feel bruised and sick and desperately tired. He still had all his investment figures to go through, and it was a quarter of three in the morning. The biweekly family meeting—once every alternate Thursday—was scheduled to start at nine-thirty, and Victor was expected to have his statistics ready. He dragged a heavy file across the desk toward him, and opened it up. The first page said: "Lubricant Equity (Panama).", He unscrewed his pen.

About an hour later, when all the servants had gone to bed, and the corridors of Spiermont were silent and dark, Victor thought he heard a car engine start. He looked up from the pool of light in which he was working, with his horn-rimmed half-glasses perched on the end of his bulbous nose, and listened. There was a kind of rustling noise from somewhere outside, but it may have been nothing more than an early-morning wind rising up in the trees. He checked his watch, shrugged, and went back to work.

By half-past five, he had finished. A gray, haggard light was beginning to strain through the office windows, and outside he could make out the shadowy shapes of the trees and the sloping lawn. He stretched, rubbed his eyes, and then reached over and switched off his desk lamp. He was tired, but he liked to work at night. He liked the idea of staying up late while the rest of America slept, toiling through figures that would keep thousands of slumbering men in employment. When the sun rose, they wouldn't even know what Victor had done to protect their jobs in the still small hours.

He stood up and walked to the window. Somehow, when the sun came up, problems didn't seem so bad. The problem of Ariadne, once Dick Marini had sorted it out, would be tidied up, parceled into a legal file, and that would be the last of it. He remembered the heated nights that he and Ariadne had spent in California, and he had a dark small twinge of regret; but as Ariadne had made her bed, so she would damn well have to lie in it. Girls from topless lounges don't marry responsible chief executives, and that was an indisputable rule of American life. Out of his top drawer Victor took a small cheroot and lit it. He didn't smoke very often, but this morning he felt he deserved it. The lighter on his desk, in the shape of an oil derrick, was a gift from his mother.

He opened the French windows and stepped out onto the wide Italian-marble patio. There were round, well-trimmed rosemary bushes in cerise marble pots, and wrought-iron tables and chairs. There was an early-morning chill in the air, and the grassy slopes were white with dew, but Victor felt he needed refreshing. He discarded his leather slippers and in his blue bathrobe walked on pudgy bare feet across the patio, down three steps, and into the grass.

A few birds chipped and cheeped in the trees, but otherwise the estate was silent, and the house was dark.

He made his way around the back of the house, where tall Doric pillars supported a stark and elegant arch. There was a wider patio at the back, with a long, hedge-lined swimming pool. The pool was entered by wide, semicircular steps, at the top of which stood a white marble statue of a naked nymph riding a giant sea horse. Victor liked the statue, because it was sexy, and fashioned with an exquisite eye for detail, but his Mama considered it "unnecessary."

The pool looked cold and silvery this morning, like a breathed-over mirror, and the hedges alongside it were sparkling dully with dew. Victor approached the pool from the slope above the back of the house, down a series of grassy steps, and admired, as he approached, the symmetry of the house's reflection in the still water.

It was only when he reached the marble patio around the pool itself that he realized the surface of the water was covered in oil. It was streaked with iridescent, curving rainbows of scum. Frowning, not understanding what had happened, he looked around the pool for signs of vandalism or oil cans. There was nothing. The white naked nymph, with her frozen erotic smile, rode her sea horse down the far end of the pool, and mocked him to say it was she.

"Eustace!" he called, even though he knew that Eustace couldn't possibly hear him. His voice sounded flat and weak. "*Eustace!*"

He stepped right up to the edge of the pool and peered through the oil into the water. Then, there was no mistaking what had occurred. Dark, flat, and distorted, the outline he saw was of a Cadillac limousine, drowned in the deep end of the pool, leaking oil and gasoline in misty clouds.

His heart thumped, and he felt desperately short of breath. He still didn't know what this meant. He went down on his hands and knees, shading his eyes against the white reflections from the house, trying to make out the shape of the submerged car. It was one of his own, one of three Cadillac Broughams he kept at Spiermont, and someone had evidently driven it across the grass, across the patio, down the steps, and into the water. He could even see the tire marks on the edges of the steps.

Victor had to lean right over the water before he could see

661

clearly enough to discover who had done it. Wallowing against the driver's window, stirred by the faint currents in the water, was a pale human arm, and the shine of a body that was silver as a herring.

He clambered to his feet, panting, and this time he really didn't know what to do.

Celia Cornelius, with an uncanny sense of occasion, had arrived in a large black hat, with black plumes. She was a tall, elegant woman of sixty, her striking face still beautiful, with a thin distinctive nose, china-blue eyes, and full, naturally red lips. Her hair was shining platinum white, tinted with an aura of pink, and her sapphire-and-diamond earrings tinkled from ears that were as soft as a young child's. In her superbly tailored black suit of watered silk, with her lean gold-knobbed cane, she looked like a wealthy raven, or the matriarchal proprietor of a fashionable funeral parlor. She spoke in high, dry tones, and lifted her hand toward people when she addressed them, as if waiting for them to click their heels and kiss it.

"The question is," she said imperiously, "why did the unfortunate girl do it? *That* is the question."

Dick Marini sniffed. He was leafing back through his notebook, trying to read his squiggles of the previous night.

"That's just one of the questions," he said bluntly. "The whole thing is a mass of imponderables. I think the best thing we can do is find out just how much we can get away with, and just how much we can't."

Celia frowned. "I don't think the Cornelius family has ever had to *get away* with things, Mr. Marini. Victor is not exactly a hardened criminal, to say the least. The poor boy has asthma."

"So did Al Capone," said Dick. "I don't remember it did *him* a lot of good."

The family had gathered. Unusually, they sat in the south drawing room, a spacious, coffee-and-white room decorated in French rococo style. There were tall windows on three sides, and the morning sun slanted through hand-worked curtains of Brussels lace, casting decorative patterns over the polished maplewood floor. Between each of the windows stood small gilded tables with curved and decorated legs, topped with Dresden vases. Above them was a series of richly colored eighteenth-century Dutch oils depicting views of Amersfoort at different seasons in the year.

The family themselves sat around the carved and gilded fireplace on an antique Indian carpet of subtle reds and blues. A rare and fascinating Fabergé clock, decorated in gold and enamels, chimed softly on the mantelpiece. In the elaborate mirror behind it, like another painting, you could see Celia Cornelius, rigid and upright in a tall-backed chair of old gold plush; Dick Marini, plump and worried, sitting next to her on a French dining-room chair; on a long rust-colored settee, quiet and casual, Victor's cousin Freddie, Freddie's sister Tess, and his other cousin Ally; and Victor himself, in a pea-green jacket that made him look even more washed-out than he really was, slumped in an awkward rococo chair eating chocolate mints.

"Sounds to me like Victor's done it again," said Freddie. He was a lean, laconic-looking young man of twenty-nine. His hair was light brown, long, and brushed back. There was something about his face that reminded people of a thin Dustin Hoffman. He wore a red-and-blue-striped blazer and white Humphrey Bogart pants.

Celia looked at him with disapproval. She always had disapproved of Hope's children, particularly when she remembered how often they had ganged up against Victor. They ought to remember that Victor had dedicated the whole of his life to the Cornelius family, from his childhood days, when he counted her garden-party guests on a nursery abacus, to the present time, without once denying his parentage, or his responsibilities, or giving up his duties. A sense of duty may be unexciting, but all of their wealth depended upon it, and through their wealth, the men and women they employed. A sense of duty was more than *Hope's* children had ever had.

"Victor has not 'done it again,' " said Celia dryly. "Victor has always assumed his full burden of duty and obligation, and that has made Victor consistently more open to pressures from outside. Which is more than we can say for some."

"I propose the first move we make is inform the police," said Dick Marini. "It's four hours now since Victor discovered the car, but we can easily say that he discovered it much later, and there won't be any material evidence to dispute that. Apart from that, it wouldn't have made any difference to Miss . . ."

"Skouros," said Victor.

"To Miss Skouros. She was dead, must've been dead, as soon as the car filled up."

"Do we *have* to call the police?" asked Celia. "Isn't it possible that we can deal with this matter in another way? I'm not talking about anything *illegal*, but I do think the family must come first. We do, after all, have the facilities to take responsible action."

Freddie snorted. "What do you call responsible action? Paying the girl's parents to swear she was drowned on the *Lusitania*?"

Dick Marini lifted one pudgy hand. "We've got a problem here that's got some kind of precedent. What we don't need, especially with Victor's election involvement, is another Chappaquiddick. I know this is different, before you all start shouting me down, but in the eyes of the public the whole thing's going to look remarkably similar. Maybe Victor isn't the candidate himself, but his name is closely linked with John Russell's, and if there's any suggestion of scandal or negligence, we're going to find ourselves up to our necks in political mud. So what I'm saying is, the first thing we do is call the cops. That's just what Teddy Kennedy *didn't* do, and that's just what he found so tough to explain."

Victor was about to say something, but he closed his mouth. His mother, in any case, had lifted her hand regally in Dick Marini's direction, and was giving her own opinion.

"I believe we ought to discuss it a little longer. The trouble with calling in the police is that the whole thing is immediately taken out of our hands. The girl is dead, and there's no bringing her back."

"Jesus," said Freddie, "I hope not. The topless dancer from two fathoms!"

"Freddie!" snapped Victor. "If you think this is some kind of a joke, then I suggest you get out of here and laugh up your sleeve someplace else. The girl happens to be dead, and the whole family's involved."

Ally, so far, had said nothing. She rarely had much to contribute at family gatherings. She wore a plain, carefully cut dark blue dress and there were dark circles under her eyes. She didn't smoke, and she sat with her hands in her lap, listening to the random conversation of her cousins with solemn intentness.

Dick Marini made a few notes and then turned around to Ally and said: "What do you think, Ally? Do you have any views?"

Ally didn't look up. She was picking at the clasp of her gold bracelet in a way that reminded Victor disturbingly of Ariadne picking at the spines of his leather-bound books.

"I think the first consideration we have is toward the parents of the dead girl," she said quietly. "I also agree we should call the

664

police. There seems to be a lot of talk about saving Victor's political reputation, but I seem to remember that this family was supposed to live by the principle of doing right by other people.''

Celia raised one elegant eyebrow. ''Ally, dear, I don't recall that anyone suggested anything different.''

Ally shook her head. ''I think,'' she said firmly, ''that your suggestion of responsible action was another way of saying that we ought to find some way to shirk our responsibilities.''

Celia pursed her lips, and she rapped the gold ferrule of her walking cane on the floor, *tap-tap-tap*, as if casting an impatient spell.

''Mr. Marini,'' Celia said tautly, ''I think you'd better explain to Ally what will happen if the press gets hold of this.''

Dick Marini pulled a face. ''There's no doubt that they'll call it Chappaquiddick II. This is supposed to be a real clean election, and on our side we've done everything we can to make sure that our candidate and our campaign staff are gleaming white and straight as arrows. This thing, this accident, this could mean the whole difference between victory and failure.''

Ally, now, did look up. Her blue eyes were slightly myopic, and they were always disturbing and bright.

''Is that it?'' she asked. ''Is that the price of telling the truth? A seat in the White House?''

Freddie blew smoke. ''Aw, come on now, Ally. You're being a little melodramatic here. The real point is, what are we going to do to save Victor's bacon?''

Ally flushed. ''I thought you were on my side,'' she said. ''I thought you believed in this family's ideals.''

''Of course I believe in the family's ideals. But what's the good of having ideals if it doesn't make any difference whether you have them or not? We're talking about a dead girl here, and as Celia says, we can't really do much to bring her back to life. I think Victor's behaved like a complete screwball, but what's done is done, and what we have to do now is see if we can minimize the problem.''

Victor reddened, but Celia raised her hand to silence him. She liked the way the tone of the argument was going, and she didn't want Victor antagonizing Freddie at such a sensitive moment.

Tess said: ''I still think we ought to call the police. The longer we leave it, the worse it's going to get.''

Ally shrugged. ''I don't mind what you do, as long as you tell the truth. I just don't see how we can continue to support a political career if we've got something like this to hide. All right, it may not make any difference to anyone else if we don't have ideals, but it will make a terrible difference to *us*."

Celia gave Ally a frosty little smile. "I do think you're jumping to conclusions, Ally, dear. When I talked about responsible action, I was very *insistent* on the word 'responsible.' What is *not* responsible is to call the police without being quite clear what we are going to say to them. I am not talking about lies. I am not talking about distortion. There will be no cover-ups in this family. We bear too much of an obligation toward the people of America for that. But it is irresponsible to inform the police and the press and the public about this incident without first weighing what its historical implications might be."

Victor nodded. He, too, believed that the Cornelius family held the reins of American history in their hands; and that if a Cornelius sneezed, the whole of Wall Street was likely to catch a cold. It was far easier for him to accept what had happened with Ariadne as a historical event rather than as a mean and embarrassing personal failure.

"Victor is not a malicious character," said Celia, appealing to the family in her dry, gin-and-tonic voice. "He is honest and hardworking, and he has dedicated more to this family than anyone since Johann himself. But while *we* know that what he did was nothing more than give way to a spate of rage, history will judge him very differently, and with very much colder eyes. It is hardly dishonest, hardly irresponsible, if we simply make sure that the public sees him as we do, for what he really is."

Freddie squashed out his cigarette in a small French porcelain ashtray. He didn't like Victor; he never had, and never would. He disliked Victor's fat crimson face, and his clumsy behavior, and above all he disliked his incongruous little-boy obedience to Mama, which gave Freddie the complete creeps. Many of their past differences had been grudgingly papered over, but Freddie still *physiologically* felt repelled by his older cousin. Unlike Victor, Freddie was not particularly fond of thankless, masochistic toil. He did not see himself, like Victor, as a kind of Carl Sandburg figure of finance, adding up 357 columns of credits and 589 columns of debits before daybreak. Freddie lost money faster than Victor, especially when he gambled on fringe stock issues and stud poker; but he also created money faster, and more ingeniously.

Despite their mutual dislike, Freddie now made up his mind to stand behind Victor and offer his practical support. It was a matter of family loyalty and financial common sense. If social and economic boats were not to be rocked, then Victor must appear blameless. Freddie didn't dismiss the political considerations, either. A Cornelius man in the White House—John Russell—would be the family's greatest coup in years. It would mean fresh opportunities for adventurous investment, and enough government contracts to underpin some of the less stable Cornelius enterprises, such as Woodward Tires. Victor was a stupid ox as far as Freddie was concerned, but right at this moment, the ox needed all the encouragement he could get.

"Celia," said Freddie, "I think it's time we stopped talking about history and started talking about practicalities."

"Very well," said Celia a little icily. She was waxing eloquent on the dutiful virtues of her only son, and she did not really care to be interrupted by one of Hope's young people. But she waved her hand and said: "Tell us, then. What practicalities?"

"The police, for a start," interrupted Dick Marini. "They're a practicality. Are we going to call them or not? I vote we do. We have to."

"Wait a minute," said Freddie. "Of course we call the police. But what we have to consider is—*to what*?"

Tess frowned at him. "What do you mean, Fred—*to what*?"

Victor inspected his cousin morosely, but said nothing.

"I mean this," explained Freddie. "As things stand, Victor will be considered to blame for this girl's action. Not legally, perhaps, but morally, in the eyes of the voting public. What we have to do is change the *appearance* of what happened, so that the voting public has a positive and sympathetic reaction to Victor, instead of a negative and hostile reaction."

Ally sighed and sat back. "Go on," she said. "Let's hear the dastardly plot."

"It's not a plot and it's not dastardly. It's a simple adjustment of focus. At the moment, it looks as though this girl killed herself in Victor's pool because he wouldn't marry her. Public sympathy goes out to the girl, because she's been rejected by a plutocratic meathead—"

"*Freddie*," said Celia coldly.

"It's no good saying '*Freddie*' like that," said Freddie. "We have to look at it the way the public is going to look at it. As far as

667

the public is concerned, Victor has denied this girl her inalienable right. The inalienable right of every small-town American girl to marry a millionaire.

"The point is . . ." said Freddie, taking out another cigarette and lighting it. "The point is that *what actually happened* is not relevant. It's not a question of telling the truth, or of not telling the truth. None of us really *knows* what occurred. Maybe it's important to find out why she did it. Maybe it isn't. I mean, it could have been a complete accident. But, at the moment, we have no way of knowing. So the only known fact, the only possible truth we can tell, is that the girl is dead."

Dick Marini checked his watch. All the time they were talking, the pool water was seeping into Ariadne's tissues, giving forensic scientists clearer and clearer information on the time of her death. If they didn't make up their minds soon, then Ariadne's corpse was going to make up their minds for them. He made a few quick notes, and some rough calculations.

"What I propose we do," said Freddie, "is stop acting like a bunch of frightened hit-and-run drivers and start acting like a family with influence and resources. We have the resources—let's use them. If we all agree that our responsibilities only stretch as far as announcing the girl's death and taking care of the girl's parents, then I believe we can work out a watertight story."

Celia lifted her beautiful elderly head. "I think 'watertight' is a rather unfortunate word, in the circumstances. But I believe you're right. This family has a far greater obligation to the nation than it does to one single person, and I don't think that the unfortunate girl herself would have wanted us to abdicate our mission simply for the sake of admitting something that, in the final analysis, was not our fault."

She did not notice how quickly she had absorbed Victor's personal problem into the family's collective conscience. Ariadne's death was no longer Victor's difficulty alone; it was a guilt that had to be borne by all of them, and absolved by all of them, for the sake of the family name. A family linked by finance is far more inextricably entangled than a family linked by love. Love ties, but wealth welds.

Dick Marini said: "I'd like to know what you mean by 'refocusing' this problem, Freddie. I'd also like to remind you that

668

we don't have a great deal of time. A police autopsy will pinpoint the moment of death to the nearest couple of hours, particularly in a case of drowning."

Ally said: "*I'd* like to know how this family manages to have a far greater obligation to America than it does to Americans. This girl might have been a topless dancer, and not very bright, but she was a living person, wasn't she? And a voter."

Celia tried to smile. "Ally, dear, let's leave the ethical issues aside until we find out what Freddie has to suggest."

"How *can* we leave the ethical issues aside?" said Ally hotly. "This whole thing is an ethical issue! We're *talking* about ethics, and about accepting our responsibilities! Just because we're rich, does that make us divine?"

There was a difficult pause. Victor coughed. Freddie finally leaned forward on the settee and said: "Money doesn't place anyone above their obligations, Ally. But it can make it easier to get around certain restrictions. You know that. You learned it the same way I did."

"Yes," said Ally. "I do know that. And sometimes I wish to God that it weren't true."

Tess said: "I agree with Ally about the ethics. But I also think we ought to listen to Freddie's suggestion. There's no point in arguing about what we *are*; it's what we decide to *do* that counts."

Dick Marini said: "I second that. And I suggest you make it quick. If we don't decide on something within the next thirty minutes or so, we're going to have to call the cops anyway."

"All right," agreed Freddie. "Here's the idea. As I said, it doesn't involve anything more than altering the framework of what happened. We just want people to view it in the right light. Victor, you'd better butt in and tell me if anything doesn't ring true, or can't be supported by what actually occurred. All we're doing here is a public-relations job on recent history."

From time to time, while Freddie spoke, Dick Marini checked his watch. But after a while he relaxed and listened instead, and when Eustace came in with coffee and *petits fours*, he hardly noticed.

Around lunchtime two of the ground staff started to drain the pool. The oily water gradually inched down the sides, leaving a ring of smeary gray grime, and the two men smoked and didn't say much at all. They had their eyes on the watery shape of the submerged Cadillac resting under the surface with its dead driver.

One of the men said: "Would you kill yourself like that? I wouldn't kill myself like that." The other man shrugged. He didn't look like the type who would attempt to kill himself in any way at all.

Inside the house, Dick Marini and Freddie were both in Victor's study making a long series of phone calls. Victor himself was excluded, on the grounds that the less he knew about the cover-up, the better it would be for him. Victor wasn't glib when it came to public relations, and the financial press treated most of his handouts with healthy skepticism. He only managed to keep his widespread image as a millionaire good guy through his lavish parties and receptions for newspaper reporters and (more shrewdly) their editors. Victor had learned that a well-placed crate of champagne was worth any persuasion in the world—at least any persuasion of which *he* was capable.

Celia had retired to the conservatory, and sat among the green frondy palms and ferns talking to Victor's father, Roderick Cornelius, on the long-distance phone. She had taken off her black plumed hat and it lay on a white wrought-iron chair like an exotic pet cat that was suffering from the heat. The midday sun glimmered through the green-tinted glass of the conservatory, shining on the blue-and-yellow Turkish-tiled floor, and Celia sat amid this tropical scenery, her back upright, with a small glass of very dry sherry on the table beside her. She could have been an exiled Italian widow living in North Africa, or a countess in Victorian England.

Roderick sounded impatient and tired on the phone. He had spent six days in Strasbourg tying up a complicated airline deal with Flugwerk GmBh. He was embroiled in a heavy set-piece business battle, and he was attempting to bring the whole deal to its grinding climax within six or seven hours. Apart from that, it was seven o'clock in the evening in Strasbourg, and he'd been working since five A.M. It wasn't hard to see how Victor inherited his doggedness.

"I don't like the sound of this *at all*," he was saying. "Can't you have a word with Santana at the FBI? I've known him for years, and he owes us a favor."

Celia said: "Darling, I don't think so. Victor brought it up, the same suggestion, but Freddie says the FBI is very sensitive about scandal these days."

"Well, I don't know. I don't like the sound of it *at all*."

"Darling," said Celia, "it does seem the best way. We've been over it in detail, and even Dick Marini agrees it's foolproof."

"What does Dick Marini know? The last time we did anything that Dick Marini suggested, we ended up with a 250,000-dollar settlement. Isn't there any other way? This sounds crazy."

"There must be plenty of other ways," said Celia, brushing a hand over her pink-tinted hair. "But we don't have any more time to think of them. It's either this or going straight to the police and telling them what really happened. It's not the family reputation I'm worried about, Roddy, it's the whole election, and everything. If people find out that Victor's been having trouble with girls from strip clubs, what kind of confidence are they going to have in John Russell?"

Thousands of miles away, Roderick gave an angry little grunt. "You wait till I get back there," he snapped. "I'll tan Victor's ass so he can't sit down for a month."

"Roddy, he's not a little boy anymore."

"Then why the hell does he behave like one? Topless dancers! What the hell's the matter with him?"

Celia sipped her drink. "Hester once told me that in 1932 you went out with a girl from a burlesque show in Denver, Colorado."

"That's ancient history. What I'm worried about is *now*. How long is this thing going to take?"

Celia glanced at her Piaget watch. "Freddie says it should all be over by six this evening. Give or take ten minutes."

"Freddie's an overconfident smartass."

"And you're tired, darling. Why don't you have a nice drink and put your feet up for half an hour? You'll feel much better."

"Better? How the hell can I feel better? I've just found out my son is a negligent womanizer and my nephew is a certifiable lunatic! Apart from that, my own wife's helping them out. What am I supposed to feel better about?"

Celia sighed. "Roddy, darling, just get some rest. I'll call you later when I know some more."

"I don't like one bit of this, and if I was over there, I'd put a stop to the whole thing. You're all as dumb as each other."

"Roddy, you don't have to be rude."

Roderick Cornelius let out a thin, exhausted sigh.

"I'll call you later," said Celia. "I promise I will. Just don't worry about it. I can't say I like Freddie myself, but he knows what he's doing."

"All right," said Roderick. "I surrender, as usual. But don't

671

forget to tell me what's going on. Don't worry what time it is. If you have some news, call. I should be at Flugwerk most of the night anyway."

"Very well, darling. Now, remember I love you. Good-bye."

Celia laid the phone down and took another sip of sherry. The taste was dry and crisp, and it warmed her. She had telephoned Roddy out of political courtesy, but she really didn't take too much notice of what he said. He was too engrossed in his freight and his airplanes and his containerization policy. He was just like Victor. They were men out of the same mold; men who stumbled around directionless until they were guided and powered by a strong woman. She sometimes considered that the true genius of the Cornelius family was to marry the kind of women who could urge them into ambitious and constructive moneymaking.

She opened up her black crocodile pocketbook and took out her diary. With a small pencil of figured gold and silver, topped with a single ruby, she wrote herself a reminder to telephone Roddy when she had some news for him.

Victor, his father's lesser shadow, now paced the lawn outside of Spiermont, like a man waiting for the birth of his first child. He wanted to smoke a cheroot, but decided against it, in case Mama saw him and disapproved. Today Victor urgently needed encouragement and approval, and he admitted, even to himself, that he was prepared to do almost anything to get it.

In the distance, he saw the two brown-overalled groundsmen draining the pool, but he didn't go near. Instead, he restricted his pacing to the velvety surface of the croquet green, whistling tunelessly and trying to look nonchalant, as if he was on vacation.

Freddy, watching him from the study, remarked to Dick Marini: "What do you think Victor's up to? He looks like a racing steward trying to make up his mind whether the going's too soft."

Marini was in the middle of a complicated call. "Don't ask me," he said. "That guy's got problems."

It was an hour before the surface of the pool had dropped low enough for the tail end of the Cadillac to emerge. By then Freddie and Dick had finished their arrangements, and they came out to watch. Celia, Tess, and Ally stayed indoors, occasionally glancing out from the sitting-room windows to see how the work was progressing, but keeping well away from the prospect of dead dancers.

One of the groundsmen lit a cigarette and offered one to

Freddie. Freddie took it, and the groundsman made a shield with his hands to protect the flame from his lighter.

"You know something," said the groundsman. "When you're dead, it don't matter a damn how much money you got."

Freddie smiled at his impertinence. "No, it doesn't," he said quietly. "But it matters to the people you leave behind."

Inch by inch, the oily water fell away from the car. Soon the whole rear end was clear, and water was gushing from the trunk. Freddie could see the huddled shape of Ariadne in the front seat, her hair in sodden rat tails, her white cheek pressed against the window. He felt his breakfast rising up inside him like a mangy dog turning over in its sleep.

"Is the tow truck ready?" he asked Dick Marini, and Dick Marini nodded.

"They brought it up the driveway ten minutes ago. They're keeping it out of the way until we get the chance to sort things out. Not a pleasant sight, is it?"

Freddie dragged deep on his cigarette and said nothing.

Soon the pool was empty, except for streaks of oil along the bottom and the water that ran out of the drowned car. One of the groundsmen put on a pair of rubbers and stepped tentatively down the greasy slope to the car's side.

"She's dead, all right," he called. It was an absurd thing to say, but he was nervous and nauseous, and it was all he could think of. Nobody answered anyway.

The other groundsman joined him, and together they opened the car's door and dragged Ariadne out. Her silver evening dress shone like crumpled cooking foil. They carried her laboriously up the slope of the pool, up the steps, and laid her on a stretcher. One of them covered her up with a neatly folded white sheet.

Freddie, smoking, walked over to the stretcher and looked down at the crisp, well-ironed shroud. Then he bent forward, and with two fingers lifted the edge of it. The girl had her eyes closed. She was a startling shade of bluish-white, like Stilton cheese, and her cheeks were puffy and swollen. There was a dark brown bruise on her nose.

"So you're Ariadne," he said. He almost expected her to open her eyes and answer. But she stayed dead, and he dropped the sheet back and stood erect. Dick Marini was standing right behind him.

"Okay," said Freddie. "Let's get this thing moving."

Dick Marini waved his hand, and there was the sound of a

heavy diesel starting up. A large orange-painted tow truck backed slowly around the side of the house and across the lawn. It was driven by Walther, Victor's heavyset chauffeur, and, alongside him, the owner of the Hyannis Circle garage. They maneuvered it up to the edge of the swimming-pool steps and halted. The garage man, a short stocky Pole in red overalls and a red baseball cap, unfastened the two hooks from the back of the truck and slithered down toward the Cadillac to fix them on. He had been paid a great deal of money, and he did just what they'd told him to do, and didn't even look around. They wanted this car out of the pool, they were going to get this car out of the pool. For five grand, you didn't ask how the hell it got here, or nothing.

The hooks were secured. The Pole shouted to Walther, and Walther gunned the truck's diesel. Slowly, link by link, the winding gear tightened the tow chains, and the Cadillac began to shift. Soon, wet tires squealing, the long navy-blue limousine was dragged up the tiled bottom of the swimming pool, bounced up the semicircular steps, and hoisted into position behind the orange tow truck. The diesel burbled, and Walther drove slowly away, the Cadillac swaying behind him, until he was out of sight around the house and disappearing down the long wooded drive.

Freddie ran his hand through his long brown hair and turned to Dick Marini with a grimace. "Well, that's the car. Now let's see what we can do with the late Ariadne."

They were still talking when Victor approached, looking tall and queasy in his light green jacket.

"How are you feeling?" asked Freddie. "It won't be long, and we'll have the whole thing wrapped up."

Victor nodded. "Is that her?" he asked, pointing to the clean white sheet.

"That's right," said Freddie. "If she meant anything to you at all, I wouldn't look."

Victor lowered his head and scuffed at the grass with his pointed Gucci shoe. "I wasn't planning to," he said indistinctly. "But I don't think she meant much."

Dick Marini and Freddie exchanged glances as Victor turned around and mooned off in the direction of the house. Then Freddie shrugged and said: "Okay, This is what we do. . . ."

By five-thirty that evening a fresh wind had sprung up, and the windsock at Hyannis Airport was stiffening and rolling. The sky

674

was still clear, except for a low bank of faded creamy clouds in the southwest, and there was a smell of newly mown grass in the air.

The Lear jet was waiting on the concrete runway, its twin engines whistling in high-pitched harmony. Not far away, a long black Cadillac limousine was parked. A small group of men in pale summer jackets were talking together, while their buff-uniformed chauffeur polished imaginary smudges from their gleaming car.

"You have the route marked out here," said Freddie, pointing to his windblown chart of the northeast coast. He was wearing dark polarized glasses, and it was impossible to see his eyes. "When you reach this point, you will radio a routine weather report. If we respond in the affirmative, you carry on flying until you reach here. Then you send a Mayday. You got that?"

The pilot, a lean sad-eyed Belgian with a sandy little toothbrush mustache, nodded agreement. He stood hunched up, with his hands jammed deep in his windbreaker pockets, shuffling his feet in a complicated waltz of his own invention.

"Right," said Freddie. "Fifteen seconds after you send the first Mayday, you begin your dive. Send two or three more Maydays, but don't forget to bail out here. Don't forget to activate the pressure switch, either, or the plane won't explode. We'll alert the Coast Guard, and you should be picked up within five or ten minutes. You got all that?"

"Sure," said the pilot. "I done this kind of thing before."

Freddie checked his watch, and looked across at Victor and Dick Marini.

"It's five-thirty-two. Anyone got any doubts, any reservations? Because now is the time to say so."

Dick Marini shook his head. "Let's just get it over with."

Victor nodded ambiguously. He was red-faced and nervous, even in his elegant pale blue mohair suit by Themy of Paris. His thin hair rose and frayed in the afternoon breeze.

Freddie touched the pilot's arm. "All right, then. Get going. And don't forget to signal in the right places at the right time, otherwise this whole thing's dead as the dodo."

The pilot gave a lopsided grin. "Dead? I think that's what you want, huh?"

Dick Marini was blowing his nose. "No wisecracks, thanks," he mumbled. "We just want a job well done. I guess we'll see you later on."

The pilot gave a mocking little salute and began to stroll toward the jet. Victor whispered worriedly: "How much do you think we can trust a fellow like that? Supposing he flies straight to Boston and calls the police?"

"We can trust him," said Freddie coldly. "He knows damned well who we are, and he knows damned well that if anything goes wrong, he's never going to work again, not on any airline, anywhere. Apart from that, he was recommended by Boaz."

"That's not a bad recommendation," agreed Dick Marini. "I just hope he's got good luck, as well as a good reference. You know something, this allergy's going to kill me one day."

"It's the hay-fever season," said Victor.

The Belgian pilot climbed into the Lear jet and they saw the door close. He didn't even wave. After a few minutes the plane's engines began to whine louder and higher, and it moved away from its parking place with a slight shudder and a bounce of its wheels. Victor, Freddie, and Dick Marini, their hands over their ears, watched it move away like a white shark into the wind.

"I hope this works," shouted Dick Marini. "That jet cost the best part of half a million."

Freddie leaned over and yelled back: "If this works, it'll be cheap at twice the price."

Victor—as he had all day—remained obstinately silent. It was humiliating enough to have messed up his handling of Ariadne without having his cousin sort out the situation for him. To him, Freddie was unreliable, changeable, and feckless, and the idea of being in Freddie's debt gave him a lumpy pain like indigestion.

At 5:45 the Lear jet received clearance for takeoff. It whistled off down the runway and, quite abruptly, climbed into the sky. They shaded their eyes against the late sun as they watched it turn in a wide circle and then head toward the southwest.

"Okay," said Freddie when the sound of its jets had dwindled away in the distance. "I think it's time we got ourselves back to the house. In about an hour from now, those phones are going to start ringing."

Walther opened the limousine's doors for them, and they climbed in, like mourners leaving a funeral. Victor cleared his throat and said: "Home, Walther."

Victor's private secretary, Douglas Schuman, was waiting for them when they got back. He was a young, round-faced business graduate from Yale, with a shiny Captain Marvel forelook and an

676

inexhaustible wardrobe of dark suits with narrow lapels and tapered pants. He had been working on Victor's tax assessments with the IRS in Chicago, and he had flown into Boston at a moment's notice. As Victor's limousine crunched to a halt on the gravel drive outside Spiermont's imposing pillared portico, he came forward with a wide grin and his hand held out.

"Victor!" he called. "Hi!"

Victor, slightly dazed, shook Schuman's hand and said: "Hello, Douglas."

Douglas beamed. "It's great news, sir. It really took me by surprise. I can't tell you how thrilled everyone is. Terrific news."

Victor looked at him. Nothing had been great or terrific or thrilling all day as far as Victor was concerned, and it took a full thirty seconds before understanding began to sink into his mind. Freddie, when summoning Douglas from Chicago, must have told him the cover-up story. Douglas only knew the "refocused" side of things.

"Yes," said Victor baldly. "It's great news, isn't it? I'm very happy."

"I can't tell you how thrilled everyone is," said Schuman. "Everyone is really thrilled. Mrs. Kabotnik tried to get you some flowers, but she didn't have the time. It's wonderful news."

Victor, as they walked into the house, turned to Freddie and raised his blond eyebrows in questioning worry. Freddie, hidden behind his dark glasses, simply wiggled his fingers in a discreet wave.

"Is Mama still here?" Victor asked.

"She's dressing for the evening," said Schuman. "I guess she'll be down in an hour. Miss Tess and Miss Ally are still here. They're in the music room."

Dick Marini said: "I guess I'll freshen up too. Am I staying for dinner?"

Victor didn't answer. Freddie nodded to Dick and said: "Sure. Stay. We're going to need you."

Victor walked through the high-pillared hallway, his footsteps echoing on the red-streaked marble floor, past the curve of the magnificent white staircase, and into the music room. It was a pale eggshell blue, this room, with a highly polished parquet floor and a glorious French chandelier. A dark Steinway piano stood near to the white-curtained windows, and there were matching chaise longues, covered in dark blue velvet. Tess was sitting at the piano,

677

playing Debussy, her cigarette holder held between her teeth. Ally was relaxing on a chaise longue with her shoes off, her eyes closed.

Victor said: "Well, that's taken care of that."

Ally opened one eye. She didn't reply. At this moment, she didn't know whether to feel pity or disgust for Victor, and she didn't want to say anything that would reveal either one. The family had decided to gather round and solve Victor's problem together, and that was all that mattered for the time being. She didn't like Freddie's plan, but she had agreed to go along with it for the sake of their business and political interests. Reluctantly, Ally had to admit that the family's interests were her own, regardless of the ethics, and regardless of Victor's guilt. Ally had been through enough pain and heart-searching on her own account to know that social morality is one thing and survival is something else.

Tess stopped playing and flicked her ash into a small porcelain saucer.

"Are you frightened?" she asked him, turning around on her stool.

Victor frowned. "Frightened? Why should I be?" He walked heavily over to the window, parted the white lace curtains, and looked out.

"Well," said Tess, "there's always the chance of getting caught."

Victor shrugged.

"And there are always ghosts," said Tess. "You know, invisible shades that clank their chains in the night."

Victor turned around. "You and Freddie, you both came out of the same cookie jar, didn't you? You don't know the difference between serious and sick. The way you talk, you'd think I did this on purpose."

Tess made a moue. "Right now, it doesn't really matter whether you did it on purpose or not. Right now, you're being pulled out of the mud by your nearest and dearest."

Victor coughed. He reached in his pockets for a handkerchief, couldn't find one, and rang for Eustace.

"The trouble with you and Freddie is that you don't have any sense of proportion," he said. "Where do you think money comes from? You think I go out every morning and pick greenbacks off the trees? You've lost sight of real life, that's your trouble."

"Real life?" Tess laughed. "That's rich. If you think you've been living real life all these years, you're in deeper trouble than I thought. If you want to see real life, Victor, you ought to try doing what we did—Ally, Freddie, and me. Get out there, out on the streets, and meet people in the raw."

Victor didn't look at her. "You came back, didn't you?" he said. "You met people in the raw, but you came back."

Ally lifted her head. "Better to have come back than never to have been at all," she said quietly.

"That's bull," said Victor. "There's just as much reality in a column of figures as there is in a crowd of people. People and figures, they're the same thing. The whole of society, the whole reason we're here, is based on the making of money. The desire for money is the constant motivating force behind great art, great literature, great works. Kindness is money. Generosity is money."

"Love is money?" said Tess.

Victor didn't answer. Instead he said: "This family has got together and this family has helped me out. The situation wasn't my fault, but I was man enough to tell the truth about what happened and take the responsibility for it. I want you to understand that, Tess. And you, Ally. If I'm going to be hounded by this for the rest of my life . . . well, you'd better tell me now. I made an honest mistake. I got myself mixed up with a girl that I shouldn't have, and it went sour. I admit that. Now stop preaching about it, and gloating over it, and let's get things back to what they were."

Freddie, Dick Marini and Douglas Schuman came in, followed by two of the staff in white jackets, with four bottles of Moët in silver coolers. As the corks popped and the crystal tulip glasses were filled with effervescent wine, Celia came down, dressed in a flowing Dior dress in a mixture of violets and dusty pinks.

"What's the celebration?" she said, looking alarmed. "Victor, darling, what's happened?"

Douglas Schuman intervened. "This is my idea, Mrs. Cornelius. I thought we ought to break out some champagne to toast the happy news. Does everyone have a glass? Don't you think this is the most thrilling thing that's happened all year?"

Victor, biting his lips, said: "Douglas—"

"It's wonderful," interrupted Douglas. "The whole staff in Chicago knows about it already, and they're wonderfully, wonderfully pleased. This is a great day."

Freddie ran his fingers carefully through his long brown hair. He looked across at Celia and gave an imperceptible shrug that meant "What can I do about it?" Celia returned the shrug, and then turned away. Freddie may have helped Victor out of a spot, but that didn't mean that she had to like him.

"Come on, now," said Douglas. "Let's drink a toast. Let me propose this. Lift your glasses, please. Come on, lift your glasses. I want to propose a toast to Victor, and to the lovely girl he's going to marry. What's her name, Victor?"

Victor couldn't speak. Dick Marini whispered: "Ariadne."

"That's beautiful," said Douglas. "To Victor, and to Ariadne. May they have all the happiness that a long life can bring them."

There was an excruciating silence. Then Freddie raised his glass and said loudly: "To Victor and Ariadne," and everyone else muttered "Victor and Ariadne" and drank.

At a little after six, the captain of the tanker *Esterbrook*, making its way down the coast of Long Island, heard a noise like material ripping. He looked up from his paperback book just in time to see a small white airplane tumbling through the blue summer sky, and then a dark puff of smoke. There was a bang no louder than someone slamming a door.

Immediately the captain ordered the tanker turned. The engines slowed, and it began to circle to port in a wide, foamy arc. Churning through the glassy blue sea, it took the *Esterbrook* eleven minutes to reach the oily debris of the little white jet. Pieces of wing and spar rose and dipped in the calm water, but there was no sign of life at all.

They circled the wreckage for nearly fifteen minutes more before they saw the orange smoke from a signal flare, about half a mile away. Nosing through the fragments of jet, they came up alongside a man in a life jacket, his watery parachute floating beside him like a silky squid. The man kept calling out: "The girl! Did you see the girl?"

The captain leaned from the rail as rescue nets were lowered down the side, and two seamen clambered down to lift the pilot out of the sea. "No girl!" he called back. "No sign of any girl!"

Victor wore a black suit and a black tie. Dick Marini, sitting next to him, wore a gray suit with a black armband. Victor's pale face looked even whiter in the glare of the television lights.

The press conference was hushed and subdued. It was held in the billiards room at Spiermont, and CBS technicians had helped

680

the staff arrange purple drapes across the room to serve as a suitably somber backdrop. Victor and Dick Marini sat at a long polished table, with microphones in front of them, while the twenty or thirty press people sat facing them on dining-room chairs.

"Mr. Cornelius," asked a sympathetic woman reporter with upswept glasses and a husky voice, "did you have a wedding date planned?"

Victor shook his head. "No, not yet."

"Mr. Cornelius," said another reporter. "Is this the greatest personal tragedy that has ever happened to you?"

Victor swallowed. "I can't think of anything worse. All I can say is, it must be God's will, but I'm heartbroken."

"I understand you've donated ten thousand dollars to the dead lady's parents."

"Yes, I have. I never met them, but they're sharing my grief."

The woman reporter said: "Mr. Cornelius, do you have any idea what happened yet?"

Victor shook his head. "She left Hyannis Airport just before six. I went there myself to say good-bye. She was flying back to Los Angeles to tell her parents the good news. Then about an hour later, when I was celebrating my engagement with my family . . . well, I heard the news."

One reporter stood up. "Mr. Cornelius," he said, "on behalf of the *Massachusetts Post-Dispatch*, and I guess on behalf of everyone here, I want to offer you our sincere condolences."

Victor lowered his head. "Thank you," he said quietly. "You've all been very kind."

Dick Marini, on the corner of his notepad, was doodling, like an illuminated manuscript, the word "refocus."

The day after, Victor received his first letters of sorrow from a grieving public, and a misspelled cable from Mr. Theodoros Skouros, thanking him "from the deeps of my hearts" for the ten-thousand-dollar token of condolence. The same day, the last pieces of his Cadillac limousine were cut up by the Hyannis Circle garage, and sent, jumbled up with the rusted parts of dozens of other cars, to the Cohen Scrap Foundry in Boston. Douglas Schuman, puzzled but obedient, sent out several large checks, drawn on West Virginia Investments, Inc., to the proprietor of the garage, to the pilot of the Lear jet, to several members of the staff at Spiermont, including Eustace and Walther, and to Dick Marini. He also sent a cable to Roderick Cornelius in Strasbourg, on Celia's instructions, saying, "All tidied up. Love, C."

Victor that night ate dinner alone, chewing at his lamb like a horse, and wondering what he could possibly say at the funeral, if and when Ariadne's body was ever washed ashore.

1976

RUSSELL WITHDRAWS CANDIDACY
CITES HEART COMPLICATION
By Gerry Simons

In a shock announcement last night, Republican candidate John T. Russell said that he was dropping out of the race for nomination for President because of heart complications. He said he was "deeply grieved" that he was unable to continue his campaign, but said "it's better to be a live nonentity than a dead President."

—*Washington Post,*
1976

Victor was just blotting his monthly stock-assessment book when the telephone rang. It was two or three in the morning, and he was sitting alone in his oak-paneled office, his desk heaped with papers and folded IBM readouts. He picked up the phone and said: "Yes?"

"Victor? This is Dick Marini."

"Morning, Dick. You're up early. Or late, whatever it is."

"Victor, we've got ourselves a problem."

Victor tucked the receiver under his chin and continued to tot up figures. "Okay . . . shoot."

"They found Ariadne Skouros. Her body was washed ashore at Fire Island, the Pines or thereabouts, and two gay skinny-dippers rushed off and told the Coast Guard."

"When was this?"

"Well, this was yesterday morning."

"Yesterday *morning*? How come we didn't find out until now?"

"I guess the police didn't realize who she was at first. But they traced her pendant. You know, the emerald pendant you gave her? They traced it back to Cartier, and Cartier told them you bought it."

Victor sniffed, and sat back in his leather swivel chair. Outside his windows, the night was still impenetrably dark. He could see a reflection of himself sitting out on the patio.

"All right, so they found her. What's the problem?"

"The problem is that they've handed the investigation to homicide."

Victor picked at a stray thread on his shiny blue mohair pants. He said: "Have you talked to Henry?"

"I can't get hold of him. I only just heard myself."

"Well, will Henry fix it?"

"I don't know."

Victor sniffed again. He felt he had a head cold coming on.

685

"What do you mean you don't know?" he demanded. "He's always been helpful up till now."

"Sure, but it's election time, isn't it? And I know for a fact that he doesn't like John Russell too much."

"What am I supposed to deduce from that?"

Dick Marini was doing his best to sound optimistic, but at the same time he was anxious not to let Victor feel that Ariadne's discovery was just another situation that he could buy his way out of. There was a chilly draft blowing under the door in Washington, and Dick was growing worried that Victor's blatant financial and moral support for the West Coast Republican clique was going to leave him politically isolated in the upcoming elections. Ever since the days of the New Deal, the Cornelius family had managed to perform a curious but effective political quadrille which involved supporting the Republicans but courting the Democrats; but Victor had either refused to understand the subtlety of the family's political posture or had simply closed his eyes to the reality of Jimmy Carter and the Southern left.

Dick Marini said: "If Henry doesn't fix it, you could be implicated in a homicide inquiry, and if you're implicated in a homicide inquiry, then it's Chappaquiddick times ten, and John Russell doesn't stand a dog's chance."

Victor sat up rigidly in his chair. "Are you trying to tell me that Henry Chapman would do that deliberately?"

"I'm sure of it."

"Well, how about the local police? What do they have to say about it?"

"There's a captain of detectives named Styles. He's a pretty awkward customer. We checked him through on the FBI computer, and he's a staunch Democrat. What's more, he originally came from De Soto, Georgia, which is in Sumter County, just like Plains, where Carter comes from."

"That's all I need. Can't you buy them off? How much will they take?"

"Victor," said Dick Marini patiently, "they won't be bought."

"Don't give me that," snarled Victor. His cold felt worse. "Find out the price, and I'll write you a check."

"Victor, it won't work."

"What the hell do you mean it won't work! It's always worked! From time immemorial it's always worked! What's so goddamned holy about this present generation of cops that they can't be bought?"

Dick Marini was silent. Victor was sweating and red in the face, and he felt that he could do with a drink. He rang the bell for Eustace.

Dick Marini said: "I'm telling you, Victor, as honest as I know how, that you may have to come clean on this."

Victor was silent for a moment. Then he said: "Dick, I want to tell you something in return. I paid three-quarters of a million dollars to fix this situation. I don't expect it to get fouled up now. That's three-quarters of a million dollars, Dick."

"Yes, Victor, I know. But it wasn't the cover-up that went wrong. Least, I don't think so. The whole deal with the Lear jet and the crash and everything was perfect."

Eustace still hadn't arrived, and Victor pressed his bell impatiently again.

"Perfect, was it?" he snapped to Dick Marini. "Then why are they calling it homicide?"

Dick Marini sighed. "It seems like someone called them up."

Victor frowned. "Someone called *who* up?"

"The homicide squad. Someone called the homicide squad and told them it could have been murder."

"Well, who the hell did that?"

"We don't know. But I was talking to Jack Manners from the Massachusetts paper, and he said that they were just about to break a story on the homicide squad's secret informant."

Victor banged his fist on his desk. "But I didn't *kill* her, for Christ's sake!"

Dick Marini sounded resigned. "I know you didn't, Victor. But that's not the point, is it? Any breath of scandal and John Russell is sunk. I'm sorry, Victor, but there's nothing I can do."

Victor rubbed his face with his hand. He felt exhausted and anxious, but he was still determined that he wasn't going to be licked. His grandfather would never have given in. Well, neither would he. He would fight the bastards until he dropped. That was what being a Cornelius was all about.

"Dick," he said quietly, "I want you to think about this, and I want you to think good. I want you to call up Dino Riccione at Thornwood, and I want you to ask him for a quick hit."

Dick Marini didn't answer at first. Victor said: "Dick? Did you hear that?"

"Sure," said Dick Marini. "I heard it."

"Well, what's wrong?"

Dick's voice was dispirited. "Oh, come on, Victor, it's no use.

You might just as well come straight out with the whole thing. You can't go hitting people these days, not like you could when your father was young. If you hit people, you get reporters swarming all over you like goddamned flies. Every reporter in the whole of the continental United States wants to be Woodward and Bernstein, and you don't stand a chance. In any case, who the hell are you going to hit? Captain Styles?"

"No. Henry Chapman."

"Victor, you want to assassinate an assistant attorney general? You're out of your mind!"

Victor, in a sudden burst of temper, shouted: "I'll get rid of anyone I damned well choose!"

"Victor—"

"I can buy and sell Henry Chapman seven times in the same street! What's more, I can buy a better attorney than you, so I suggest you get off the phone and consider yourself out of work!"

"Victor, for Christ's sake!"

Victor was boiling with fury. His voice was almost incomprehensible with sudden rage, and one of the maids upstairs thought that someone was screaming with pain. She was well-trained, though, and she turned over and went back to sleep. What the rich did was none of their domestics' business.

"*Dick*!" shrieked Victor. "I will not have you stand in my way! If the way to get out of this is to hit Henry Chapman, then so help me I'll hit Henry Chapman. And the President, too, if that makes any difference!"

There was a long silence. Victor held the phone as if he was trying to crush it in his hand. His head was bent, and he was panting with emotional exertion. Finally Dick Marini said: "If that's what you want, Victor, then I quit."

"What do you mean, you quit? You're under contract! You can't quit!"

"You can stuff your contract."

Victor was about to answer, but then he changed his mind. Instead, he banged the phone back on its cradle, and stood there for several minutes with his face working in suppressed temper. His cheeks were suffused red like boiling wax. He pressed the button for Eustace again, and then picked up the phone and dialed his mother's private number. It rang and rang twenty or thirty times before he gave up and laid the phone down again.

It was only then that he realized why Eustace was not answering his calls.

The gold-colored Cadillac Seville drew up outside Golden Gardens Park, in Seattle, and the chauffeur turned off the windshield wipers. It was a heavily overcast day, and curtains of rain were washing across the city from Puget Sound. Inside the car, concealed by tinted glass and trickling raindrops, insulated by thick carpet and Tchaikovsky in quad stereo, sat Ally Cornelius. She wore a severe gray suit that made her look older than she was, and her hair was drawn back from her face. Her only jewelry was her diamond earrings—two clusters of finest De Beers stones that sent rainbows of light through the dull rainy day.

The chauffeur sat still and said nothing. Ally had asked him to be as quiet and as discreet as he knew how. He had a blue shine on his chin and a black shine on his shoes, and there wasn't a single speck of dust on his cap. His hands rested in his lap in gray kid gloves.

After a few minutes, a black Buick Riviera drew up behind the Cadillac and stopped. A young man climbed out of the driver's seat, ran quickly through the rain to the gold-colored car, and tapped on the door. The chauffeur immediately got out and opened the door for him.

The young man sat down, breathing hard, and brushed the rain from his hair. Ally kept away from him to begin with, but when he raised his eyes and they really looked at each other for the first time in nine years, she let out a small and painful sob, and reached out for him with both hands, and with devouring kisses, and with tears.

"Ally," he whispered. "Oh, my God, Ally."

She couldn't speak for a few moments. She was too choked up. But then she sat back and held his arms, and took in his tanned face and his English suit and everything about him, and she was laughing and crying both at the same time.

"Oh, Clyde, it's been so long."

He had to take his handkerchief out and blow his nose. They both laughed at the noise he made.

"You haven't changed," he told her. "You haven't changed one little bit."

She shook her head. She was hardly listening. She could hardly believe that it was actually him, and that he was actually sitting beside her.

"Even if I have changed, it doesn't matter. I still love you just as much."

689

He lowered his eyes.

"Don't you still love me?" she asked him.

He nodded. He managed to say: "I can't talk," and then the tears ran down his cheeks and he had to turn his head away and cover his mouth with his hand. She gently touched his face, and stroked his hair, while his shoulders shook and he did whatever he could to control his emotions.

"That's ridiculous," he said at last, in a voice that sounded as if he had a bad cold. He blew his nose again. "I don't think I've cried like that in years."

Ally kissed his lips. "It doesn't matter. You're beautiful. It's nothing to be ashamed of."

He said: "How long are you here in Seattle?"

She shook her head. "Just as long as you are."

"You mean you don't have a schedule?"

Ally reached out and touched the Cadillac's window, and traced the path of a dribbling raindrop with the tip of her finger.

"I've given up schedules," she said. "I've made up my mind that I want to be happy."

"You're staying?" he said.

She nodded. "If you'll have me."

He sat back and took out his cigarettes.

"I can't believe it," he said. "I know you're real, but I can't believe it."

The rain blew across Shilshole Bay, and across the trees of Golden Gardens, and washed their car. Ally said: "I guess I knew all the time that I'd come back and find you. I guess there are some things you just can't forget."

Clyde looked at her gently. "It's been a long time, Ally. I mean, nine years is a long time."

She said: "In a strange way, it was Victor who decided me."

"Victor?"

She smiled. "It's strange, isn't it, how you can accept a situation for years and years, and then all of a sudden you see it for what it is. Like, the scales fall from your eyes."

"Victor did that?"

"Oh, he didn't do it deliberately. But you know this business with him and this girl who died? The girl in the plane crash?"

"Sure. It was on TV."

"Well, I was there at Spiermont when the family decided what they were going to do about it."

Clyde blew out smoke. "What do you mean, 'what they were going to do about it'? What *could* they do?"

Ally said: "The girl didn't die in the plane crash at all. She died the night before, at Spiermont."

Clyde stared at her in complete surpise.

"You're kidding! You mean that Victor *killed* her? Is that what you mean? Come on, Ally, Victor couldn't kill an ant!"

Ally said: "He may not be able to kill one, but he could certainly rough one up. Apparently this girl was some topless dancer he'd been messing around with in L.A., and she flew to Cape Cod and tried to persuade him to marry her. They had a fight, and the next morning he found her sitting in one of his limousines, right down in the deep end of his swimming pool."

Clyde was amazed. "You mean they fished her out of there . . . out of the pool, and then they took the body . . . and they . . . Jesus Christ!"

He stared at her. "You mean they crashed that plane on *purpose*?"

Ally nodded. "Spendthrift, isn't it? But Freddie thought that nobody would ever suspect that anyone would throw away a half-million-dollar airplane, just to get rid of a Greek girl that nobody knew. Not even Victor Cornelius."

"Well, Freddie was damned right."

"He was right, but he must have forgotten to spread enough hush money around. As it was, the whole thing was a waste of money. Someone talked."

"Do they know who it was? Hey, how about that? The Deep Throat of Spiermont!"

Ally shrugged. "It could have been anybody. Do you mind if I have one of your cigarettes?"

"Of course not. Here."

He clicked his gold Dunhill lighter and she fed her cigarette from the flame. Then she took a deep breath, blew out smoke, and relaxed.

"What I learned from Victor," she said, "was what Dad nearly learned years and years ago."

"And what was that?" asked Clyde.

"I learned that no matter what I did—no matter how much the Cornelius family might frown on me—I couldn't ever do anything as fundamentally immoral as any of them."

Clyde watched her in silence. She said: "Our love, the love that

691

I feel for you and the love that you feel for me, is purity itself compared with them."

Clyde said: "You found out more about David Bookbinder, and all those killings? Is that it?"

She shook her head. "I don't think anybody will ever find out. There are too many important people implicated. But if those killings were done in the way that this business was done, then all I can say is that this family is rotten to the core, and always has been."

"Do you think that's what Dad nearly got to understand?"

"Oh, I think he always knew they were rotten. But he was like the rest of us. Well, like Victor and Freddie and Tess and me, anyway. It was always easier to be rotten than to be poor."

She watched her cigarette smoke unfurling upward. Then she said: "What he almost saw, but not quite, was what Victor showed me in San Francisco with that boy Destry, and what he clearly showed me at Spiermont. In his way, Victor killed them both—Destry *and* Ariadne Skouros. And he did it simply because to him, and to the rest of the family, money is more important than human life itself."

Clyde said: "You're a Cornelius yourself, Ally, and you're not poor."

Ally gave him a smile like bitter chocolate. "I know. I tried to shuck it all off once, and I found that I couldn't. It's a curse I've got to live with. I won't pretend that it isn't a benefit, too. There are times when I thank God that I'm wealthy, although I daren't think about the people who died to help me stay that way. But the best I can do is try to be happy, and try to stay away from Victor and Celia, and use my money the best way I can."

She reached out and touched his face. "I've wasted nine years, Clyde, because I believed I had a duty. I don't want to waste any more. People can think and say what they damned well like."

Clyde crushed out his cigarette. He said: "How did you know I was in Seattle?"

Ally smiled. "I have my sources."

"Did they tell you how I was doing, these sources?"

Ally shook her head. "They just told me your telephone number, that was all. And *that* cost me five hundred dollars."

Clyde nodded. He took out another cigarette and lit it. Ally felt warm and happy all over, and she knew that they could make it now. After nine years of missing Clyde, after nine years of trying to deny how she felt about him, she had come to her decision, and now he was here, as good-looking and beautiful as he was that day she first met him, the son of her father and her father's mistress, Mara Malinsky.

"Clyde . . ." she said. "You're doing okay, aren't you?"

He looked at her. "Oh, yes. I'm doing well. It's Malinsky Fast Foods these days. One-point-five-million-dollar turnover. We supply the whole of King, Pierce, and Snohomish counties, and that includes the city, too."

She touched his hand. "I'm so glad to see you," she said. "I don't know how to tell you how glad I am to see you."

Clyde nodded. The rain drummed on the Cadillac's roof, and they sat at the curb by Golden Gardens Park, three thousand miles away from Cape Cod, Massachusetts, and it seemed to Ally that nine years had elided into nine hours. But even nine hours, of course, could always be nine hours too long.

She noticed the sparkle of tears in Clyde's eyes. She knew then that there was something wrong, although her tenderness toward him was so strong that she couldn't guess what. She touched his wet eyes and said: "Clyde . . . what's the matter?"

He let his chin drop on his chest and he wouldn't look up. He said: "I was hoping they might have told you."

"Who?"

"Your private detectives. The ones you hired to find my telephone number."

"I don't know what you mean. What *should* they have told me?"

He sucked at his cigarette. "Maybe they should have said that I was married, with two young daughters."

Ally raised her head. She found herself looking at the Cadillac's roof. She seemed to stay that way for a long time. Then she lowered her head, but she didn't cry. She said: "I didn't know. I just didn't even guess."

"How could you? I'm not a celebrity. And, let's face it, we've been keeping ourselves apart."

Ally turned to Clyde, and when she spoke there was a slight shake in her voice, but not much. She said: "Your daughters, they must be beautiful."

Clyde said: "Yes."

"And you're happy? Please say you're happy."

Clyde tried to smile through his tears.

"What are their names?" asked Ally. "Do you realize . . . I'm an aunt, and I didn't even know it!"

Clyde said: "There's Janie, she's six; and Elizabeth, and she's two. They're both a couple of tomboys. We live out east of the city near Clyde Hill, if you can believe it."

Ally said gently: "With you, I could believe anything. Do you remember the day we first met in New York?"

"Sure. The snow. The waiter with the gimpy leg."

"And that evening in Washington, at the Madison?"

"The good old Madison. Yes."

Ally was silent for a while. Then she started to cry—silently but unstoppably, her mouth clenched tight. Clyde tried to touch her, but she waved him away and said: "Go."

"Ally, I—"

"Go," she wept. "Please, my darling, go. I love you so much. Please go. Please!"

Clyde waited for a minute or two, but Ally couldn't stop crying, and so he leaned forward and gently kissed her forehead. Then he opened the Cadillac's door, and stepped out into the lancing rain, and ran back to his Buick.

The last he ever saw of Ally Cornelius was her pale face at the rear window of her car, tinted blue, and streaked with rain from Puget Sound that fell and fell and fell on Golden Gardens.

On the golf course at Kenwood, as the amber evening light touched the distant trees, and the shadows of the golfers strode long and narrow across the grass, Roderick Cornelius stood for a moment and sniffed the air like an old hunter sniffing a trail. Beside him, the assistant attorney general, Henry Chapman, adjusted his red peaked golfing cap and swung his club in preparation for an awkward shot around the rough.

"This course doesn't get any easier," Chapman remarked in his deep, gravelly voice. He was a stocky little man with a bristling white mustache and a face that looked as if someone had sandpapered it. "Either that, or I'm sore out of practice."

Roderick said absentmindedly: "I haven't played here for years."

Chapman took a couple of swings. "It's okay if you're concentrating, and you think. It's one of those courses you need to *think* your way around.''

Roderick said: "Umm."

There was a moment's silence, then Chapman called "*Fore!*" and clipped the ball badly into the tufty grass. His black caddie took off his hat, wiped his forehead, and looked as if he wished he'd been a riverboat minstrel instead. Chapman handed over his club, and they started to walk.

Roderick said: "I guess you must know that I'm not just here for the golf."

"Well, I know you wanted to talk."

"And I guess you know what I wanted to talk *about*."

Chapman said nothing. He was one of those lawyers who preferred his clients to come out and say what they meant. In his court days, he was rarely guilty of leading his witnesses, and rival attorneys often claimed that it was what he judiciously omitted, rather than what he actually said, that gave him most of his legal successes. One disgruntled opponent had dubbed him "The Angry Silence."

Roderick said: "I've been talking to Victor about what happened."

"Oh, yes?"

"He's assured me that there's no question of homicide, and certainly no foul play."

Chapman thought about this. Then he said: "Someone must have believed there was. Otherwise they wouldn't have tipped off the police."

"I'm sure it's just an old employee with a grudge. You know how servants are."

Chapman stopped walking, and stared at Roderick with rheumy eyes. "I don't want to know how servants are," he said harshly. "What I want to know is what their masters think they're doing."

"Well . . ." said Roderick, embarrassed. "It was all a mistake."

"A mistake? *The Massachusetts Post-Dispatch* is suggesting that Miss Skouros was dead before the plane hit the water. In fact, they're even implying that she was dead before it took off."

"Henry, that's absurd. Do you seriously think that we'd crash a five-hundred-thousand-dollar airplane just to dispose of a cadaver?"

Henry Chapman rubbed his mustache. Then he said: "Yes."

Roderick looked away. The sky was fading into a pale violet color and in the distance a few clouds idled away the late afternoon like curdled thick cream. He said heavily: "You're right."

Chapman grimaced. "I thought I was. I've known you Corneliuses longer than most. You're rich with a capital R. An airplane like that grows on trees as far as you're concerned."

Roderick said: "But it still wasn't homicide."

Chapman raised a bristly eyebrow. "What was it, then? A sudden fatal attack of indigestion?"

"Henry, it isn't funny."

"At five hundred thousand a shot, I should say not."

Roderick said: "The girl killed herself. She drowned herself in the swimming pool at Spiermont. She was upset with Victor, and it seems like they'd had a fight the night before. Victor . . . well, Victor confessed that he punched her. Almost broke her nose."

Henry Chapman sighed. "Why didn't he come out with this in the first place? Why didn't he tell the truth? It's the easiest way, you know. I've had confirmed killers let off the hook because they told the truth."

"Come on, Henry, use your common sense. Victor is John Russell's biggest supporter. If any of this gets out, Russell is absolutely dead."

Henry Chapman pulled a face. "That's no skin off of my nose."

"Maybe it isn't. Maybe it's no skin off *any* of our noses. The way things are going right now, we'll be lucky to get anyplace at all."

"You mean Carter can swing it?"

"I don't know. But things a damned sight stranger than that have happened."

"In that case, Roddy, what are you worried about?"

Roderick sighed, and ran his hand over his balding head. These days he seemed to have trouble getting through to people, making them understand what he was saying. He didn't look like a man on the wrong side of sixty; but then he didn't look young, either. There was a stiffness about him, a haphazardness about his thinking, and a way of lifting his head and attending to some distant, long-forgotten time, all of which gave him away. His life had almost gone by, and he was still trying to remember what he'd done, and why, and whether there was anything important still to be achieved.

He said: "Henry, we've always been friends, you and I."

"That's correct."

"You know what Victor means to me."

Henry Chapman had arrived at the clump of grass where his ball was buried. He knelt down and inspected the lie of the land.

"Actually, Roddy, I don't know, no. You've never told me. In fact, as a matter of honesty, I've always gotten the impression you don't care for Victor too much."

"Henry, I'm asking a favor."

Henry Chapman slowly stood up. He looked Roderick square in the face.

"Roddy," he said, "you can ask me a great many things, a great many favors, and I'd do my best to oblige. But don't ask me to cover up your son's involvement in whatever this business is, because I won't."

"Henry, it's vital. If there's a single breath of scandal right now, John Russell's candidacy is totally washed up. Jesus, Henry, it's bad enough with the *Post-Dispatch* spreading rumors. This thing has to be contained."

Henry Chapman grunted, and smiled. "Someone else said that, not too long ago, and look what *he's* doing today."

"Henry, this isn't Watergate."

"No," said Henry Chapman, "but it still amounts to a conspiracy to obstruct justice. A criminal offense has been committed, and you're asking a member of the administration to use his influence to prevent due process of law."

Roderick stared at Henry Chapman for a moment, chewing at his lip. Then he said: "Henry, you've got to help me."

"Why?"

"Because I'm *asking*, Henry. And because of what you've done in the past."

Henry Chapman smiled at Roderick mildly. "Is this blackmail?"

"Oh, come on, Henry, of course it's not. But you've helped us out before, and we've paid you off, and you've got to admit that gives us a certain amount of leverage."

"Does it? I wonder. I think you're in a worse position than me. In fact, I think you're in a terrible position. If I don't help you,

Victor's in for trouble; and what are you going to do about it? Tell the press that you've been paying me off? Not in a thousand years. If John Russell ever stood a chance before, he certainly won't stand one then."

Roderick sighed. He was conscious that the caddies were waiting, and that the light was failing fast. In a half hour it would be too dark to play any more. A flock of birds rose up from the distant trees like coal dust shaken from a mat.

He said: "Henry, I'm asking you for help. No pressure, no blackmail, no nothing. As your friend, I'm just standing here and asking you."

Henry Chapman beckoned his caddie. He said: "Niblick."

Roderick waited patiently for Chapman's answer. The light seemed to sink even deeper, and a cool breeze rustled across the grass from the direction of Wood Acres. It was on evenings like this that he became aware of just how vast a continent he was standing on, and how tiny a thing he was in the whole of America. He felt like a speck on an endless map, speaking in a tinny transistorized voice.

Henry Chapman hefted his golf club. Then he put it down and turned to Roderick with a friendly but regretful face.

"Roddy," he said, "I'm as guilty as hell of taking your money, and I've done some bad, unethical things in my time. But I think maybe that a reckoning's due, not just for me but for all of us, and that's why I'm going to say no."

Roderick was silent for a long time. Then he said: "I see."

Henry Chapman said: "If you want to scratch this game, I'll quite understand."

Roderick gave a faint, quick smile. "No, Henry. Let's go on. The least you can do is give me the chance to lick the hell out of you."

Henry Chapman nodded. "Okay, if that's what you want, I guess you might as well. After all, Celia's going to lick the hell out of *you*, ain't she?"

The morning she came around to say she was sorry there was a feeling of unsettled weather, and rain. The towers of the World Trade Center were dissolved in cloud, and across in Jersey the showers were falling in ragged gray sheets.

His intercom buzzed, and Freddie said: "Yes?"

"Mr. Secker, sir? There's a visitor."

"What kind of a visitor?"

"It's Mrs. Marini, sir. She says it's important."

"Mrs. Marini?"

The secretary's voice was apologetic. "I tried to tell her you were busy, sir, but she wouldn't take no for an answer."

Freddie bit at his thumbnail. Then he said: "Okay, Jeannie. Just have her wait for a couple of minutes."

He switched the intercom to hold. On the six silent television screens banked on the opposite wall of his office, Jimmy Carter was alternately frowning and grinning, Olive Oyl was sleepwalking along a high-rise girder, a black housewife dressed up as a hula dancer was frantically trying to guess the price of a yellow Pinto, and a posse of cowboys rushed hell-for-leather toward Sesame Street and a Wrigley's Spearmint commercial.

He tiredly rubbed at his eyes. He had been trying to work all morning on a new oil-storage system. The company's supertankers were delivering crude and processed oil in such gargantuan quantities these days that many of their smaller customers were unable to cope. But he hadn't been able to concentrate on oil. He'd been feeling restless and edgy, as if people had been walking on his grave. He took out a cigarette and went to the window to look out over Wall Street.

This was the same thirty-fifth floor eyrie from which David Bookbinder had looked out during his days with Cornelius Oil. The decorations were more artistic now, with Flemish tapestries hanging on the walls, and a Louis Quinze commode that had cost as much as the combined annual telephone accounts of every citizen and office in Granite City, Illinois. But the atmosphere hadn't changed. There was still that heavy charge of wealth and influence; and an almost medieval sensation that, from here, a whole empire of oil and shipping and airplanes, a whole army of secretaries and vice-presidents and pilots and roustabouts, a whole torrent of dollars and share certificates and fiscal notes, were all directed and orchestrated to rise up in the morning, to busy themselves all day, and carry on their profitable whirl and flurry far into the night. David Bookbinder used to remark that it wasn't the view of the Hudson that attracted company presidents to penthouse offices, nor the idea that they might be marginally closer to God. On the upper floors, it was easier for them to picture the world below them as a map which stretched from horizon to horizon, and over whose colorful and many-textured surface their

699

staff and their customers flowed industriously and obediently to and fro.

Freddie stood by the window, the cigarette dangling from his lip, his eyes narrowed against the smoke. Although he couldn't have known it, he looked almost uncannily like his mother had looked on the day she had stood in the wind overlooking Moriches Bay on Long Island and told her brother that she was dying. Freddie was too thin for his height, and his white silk shirt and well-pressed 1950's-style pants made him seem strangely frail. One of his girl friends, a moist-eyed romantic with bushy pre-Raphaelite hair and a muscular father in waste mercury, had told him he looked just like Byron would have looked if Byron had been Michael Douglas' brother.

He checked his wafer-thin gold wristwatch. He couldn't keep Helen waiting too long. He hoped she didn't have much to say, wouldn't scrape at the scabs of their recently closed wounds. He was going to have to leave the office in a half hour anyway and take his helicopter up to Lynwood's Island. The whole family was due to gather this afternoon at three, to celebrate Hester's award from the American Women's League for her outstanding services to American womanhood. For lots of reasons, he wasn't going to miss it.

Eventually he pressed the intercom buzzer and said: "Jeannie?"

"Yes, Mr. Secker?"

"Send Mrs. Marini through, please."

He walked across the soundless carpet to the far side of the room, where it was darker. Beside him, the television screens jumped and flickered. He kept his eyes on the office door, waiting for it to open. He was trying to keep his heart from beating too hard, his respiration from quickening. But her quiet knock surprised him anyway, and when she stepped in through the door, he couldn't think of anything to say but: "Hello, Helen. How are you?"

She stayed by the half-open door. She was the same Helen, but different—the way that lovers always are when you meet them again after weeks of parting. He had remembered her hair the way it was two months ago, in a beautifully cut bell that had just covered her ears. Now her hair was curly and wavy, and her eye makeup was darker. He had remembered the navy-blue suit she had worn the last time he saw her. But now she was dressed in a pink summer coat, and she smelled of some fragrance that was unfamiliar. She was small, and still just as pretty, with those high cheekbones and those wide sad eyes; but no matter how often he had once kissed those cheeks, and no matter how often his lovemaking had caused those eyes to close, they had never been his.

"Come on in," Freddie told her. "Close the door."

She smiled at him. "You're not afraid of being compromised?"

"No more than I ever was."

She pushed the door to, but didn't quite close it. Then she walked across to the French chaise longue and sat down carefully on the edge of it. The light from the television screens moved across her face like a Siamese shadow play. Freddie opened the French stained-glass cigarette box on the table and held it out to her.

"Thank you," she said, and took a cigarette.

There was an uncomfortable pause. Freddie went to his desk and brought over a table lighter. He flicked it alight for her, and she leaned forward to feed from the flame.

"I didn't expect to see you again," he said quietly. "At least, not in private."

She blew out smoke, and looked up at him with her wide brown eyes. "I guess I didn't either."

He sat down opposite her, in a revolving leather and hickory-wood chair, and watched her smoke. He said: "It's hard to believe how far apart two people can get, after they've been so close."

"Do you think we're far apart?"

He nodded. "I used to share your bed, Helen. But now I couldn't even touch you, any more than I could touch Jeannie, or any other woman who didn't love me."

Helen frowned. "I never said I didn't love you."

"You said you didn't want to see me again. Don't you think that's good enough?"

She looked at him sadly through the trailing smoke of her cigarette. "I guess it is," she admitted, "if you want to look at it that way."

"Well, Helen," said Freddie, "I don't think I had much of a choice."

She stood up and walked across to the row of television screens. Brutus was stomping on Popeye, and *Gilligan's Island* was just starting. She said: "Don't you ever switch these off?"

701

Freddie took out another cigarette. "They're a guide to popular taste, and popular taste is something the Cornelius family seems to have lost sight of."

"How about the Marini family?"

"How should I know? I'm not Mr. Marini, and I've been given the brush-off by Mrs. Marini."

She turned and looked at him, and the regret and concern on her face was so plain that he found himself turning away and searching for his lighter.

"It couldn't have worked, Freddie, could it?"

"Well, I don't know about that. I was never given the opportunity to find out. Maybe it couldn't, maybe it could. But listen, what are we talking about it for, anyway? It's over, right? We've wrapped it up. We put it all down to experience and faced the future with a happy though tearstained smile."

"Freddie . . ."

He clicked the lighter but he couldn't get it to catch. He said: "Helen, it's no damned use. If you don't love me, I can't force you."

"But, Freddie . . ."

He gave an exasperated sigh. "But Freddie, what? But, Freddie, I want to start all over? But, Freddie, I think we had a good thing going? Come on, Helen, you told me it was through. You couldn't take the strain of deceiving Dick any longer. You couldn't stand lying to your children. You couldn't face your friends in case any of them secretly knew. Helen, you just weren't cut out for illicit affairs, and neither was I. So let's leave it like that."

She pressed the back of her hand against her forehead.

"Freddie," she said softly, so softly that her words fell like dead birds during a heat wave, "I came to say that I was sorry."

He left his cigarette, unlit, on the edge of the desk. He came across and held her shoulder, and looked at her in silence for a long time. In the shadows his lean, angular face looked tired. He said: "Sorry? What for?"

"Sorry for everything. I never should have let it happen in the first place."

"Oh, come on," he chided her. "You didn't *let* it happen. It just happened. These things are always happening. It's what you decide to do about them that makes for all the heartache."

"All the same, I was wrong. I didn't want to hurt you. And I'm sorry."

"That was all you came to say?"

"I came to say that I still love you," she said, raising her chin in a slight but unmistakable challenge.

He didn't answer, except to turn away and shrug.

"I came to say that if you want to go on, if you think you could stand the strain of going on, then I'd rather go on than quit. It can't work, but that isn't what's important. I know that now."

She crossed her arms over her breasts, and sucked at her cigarette as if it was oxygen. Her left hand, with her thin gold wedding band, was clutching nervously at her pink linen sleeve.

"I couldn't leave Dick," she told him. "I couldn't stand a divorce. But I've had a chance to see it all in perspective. I've had a chance to rest. And I miss you, Freddie. I miss you desperately."

There was a silence on which their lives turned. There were tears in Helen's eyes, but she refused to cry. She wasn't going to win him by weeping, she had already made up her mind about that. If he still loved her, if he still wanted her, then she was prepared to make love with him whenever and however she could. But she didn't expect his pity, or his guilt, to make up his mind for him.

She thought of the moment—the very instant—when he had first grasped her hand at a summer party on the jetty of Lynwood's Island, and how they had danced across the boards, with an eighteen-piece band playing a schmaltzy version of "I've Been Loving You Too Long to Stop Now," while colored lights reflected and dipped in the dark water of the Hudson like drowned Christmas trees. Dick had been tied up for hours in a tedious caucus with Victor, and so Freddie and Helen had danced together until the band stopped for a beer and a smoke, and then Freddie had led her down to the side of the river, among the overhanging trees that rustled and whispered in the dark. They had sat on a sawed-up log, sipping champagne and listening to the laughing and chattering of guests on the jetty and up among the fairy-lighted trees and bushes.

She had never really spoken much to Freddie before. She had always thought him cold and a little arrogant. But when he talked about his mother, and how he had tried to grow up within the Cornelius family without being crushed by the insensitive ambitions of Victor and the overweening matriarchy of Celia, she

703

began to understand this remoteness was only a device to protect his unconventional beliefs about business and money and the management of other people's lives. Freddie was quick and perceptive, and when it came to money he was prepared to take hairraising risks. But he was also unfailingly considerate to the men and women who worked for him, which was the strongest characteristic that he had inherited from his father, Edward. Helen had sensed that sympathy on the first night they had been together, and it had drawn her compulsively.

They had slept together one Thursday night when Dick was away with Victor on a business trip. She remembered that, just before dawn, Freddie had said: "Is this the way you fall in love with people?"

And she had said, stroking his hair: "We mustn't."

Now, in the gloom of Freddie's office, she stood waiting for him to say that they must.

The intercom buzzed. Freddie leaned across the desk, flipped up the switch, and said: "Yes?"

"Your helicopter's ready, Mr. Secker. So whenever you're ready . . ."

"Thanks, Jeannie."

Helen said: "You're leaving?"

He nodded. "I have to go up to the island. Grandmother's being decorated."

"What with? Candles?"

He smiled. "You don't change, do you? Too sharp to love, too soft to lose."

She looked a little sad. "I guess I have to protect myself, like everybody else."

Freddie sat on the edge of the desk. "Maybe you should come up and join in the celebrations. It's the American Women's League. They're presenting Grandmother with some kind of a plaque, in grateful acknowledgment of everything she's done for American womanhood."

Helen didn't say anything, just stood cradling herself as if she was feeling the cold.

"Of course, most of what she's done for American womanhood has been financial," said Freddie, trying to be breezy. "Part of a long-term tax-reduction scheme that Victor worked out. Like the Hester Cornelius Institute of Domestic Craft, and the Hester

Cornelius Day Schools, and the Hester Cornelius Memorial Library.''

He finally got his lighter to work, and he lit up his cigarette. ''But it's more than just money, you know. She's eighty-four, and she's managed to make herself into a figurehead. The grand old lady who dismisses women's liberation as Communist subversion, and upholds the right of the suburban housewife to whiten her laundry, bake her tollhouse cookies, bring up her kids with clean faces and short hair, and kiss her husband before he leaves for work.''

''Is that so bad?'' Helen smiled.

''I didn't say it was. John Wayne said that Hester Cornelius was the only heroine that America has left. Mind you, Frank Zappa said she was the Empress of Shake'n'Bake.''

Helen came over and rested her hand on his. ''What are we going to do?'' she asked him. There was no resentment in her voice, only plain and simple needing to know.

He looked at her. The soft gray morning light made her look almost magical. He knew that he loved her. He had loved her right from the very beginning, with a love that had stayed with him day and night, a tune that wouldn't fade, a fragrance that wouldn't die away. But whether he could go through all the uncertainty again, and all the pain of parting, he didn't know.

He said gently: ''If I asked you to leave Dick, would you come?''

She stroked the back of his hand in an absentminded way. ''You know what would happen if I did that. Dick would refuse to confide in you anymore, but Victor would refuse to sack Dick, and even if he did, it would look as if the Cornelius family were deliberately axing him because Freddie Secker had happened to fancy his wife.''

''Let them think what they damned well like.''

''You know you couldn't let it happen, Freddie, not that way. Think of the harm it would do.''

He watched her fingertips tracing patterns along the veins of his hand. He said: ''It's a grown-up world, Helen. Dick's got to face up to it sometime. If it isn't me, it's going to be somebody else.''

She shook her head. ''It could never be anybody else. Not for me.''

''Then leave him.''

There was a pause, but then she whispered "No," and he knew that she meant it. "I'll be your mistress, Freddie, for as long as you want me and as long as we can. But I can't leave Dick, not now."

He thought of the way she used to smell, in the early early mornings, when they were both lying naked on the wide curtained bed at his house in Charleston. It was a mingling of Gucci and drying sexual juices, of grass from the west wind and flowers from the gardens. He could almost picture her breasts, with their wide nipples roused by the cool that came off the lake, and the feel of her hair against his cheek. He remembered that one morning he had woken up to find her gone from the bed beside him, and he had walked through into the music room to see her sitting nude at his white Steinway piano, her back straight, her face silhouetted against the fuzzy light of the rising sun, playing Mozart.

He crushed out his half-finished cigarette and stood up. "Okay." He shrugged. "If you can't leave Dick, then you can't leave Dick."

She looked at him anxiously. "Then you won't . . .?"

He touched her cheek, and then ran his long fingers into her hair. "I couldn't resist you," he told her, his eyes steady and dark. "Whether it's wrong or right, whether you can leave him or not."

She could hardly believe what she was hearing. "You mean you'll forgive me?" she asked him.

He held her hands tight between his, and nodded. "There's nothing to forgive. You don't ever have to forgive anyone for loving you."

"Freddie," she said, and the tears slid suddenly down her cheeks. Freddie held her tight, and even though her perfume was strange, and her curly hair was unfamiliar, she was still the same Helen Marini he had held just as tight in New York and Washington and Charleston, during nights that always had mornings, and afternoons that always grew dark too soon. He kissed her, and she tasted of salty tears, and he could feel the wet on his own eyelashes as well.

"Why don't you come up to Lynwood's Island?" he asked her. "I could have the helicopter take you back to your home by two."

"I couldn't. I told Dick I was shopping."

"So what? Say you had lunch at the Pierre. It takes about as long to get served as a helicopter round trip up the Hudson."

She smiled at him through her tears. "You never change. You're always so damned impetuous."

706

"Better to be impetuous than moribund."

She kissed his cheek very softly and said: "All right, then. When do we leave?"

He checked his watch. "Two and a half minutes flat. I never like to be late for any Cornelius function. Not since Victor paid off Isaac Hayes just before a party we had at Carina Mia, in Pasadena, because he said he didn't like rock 'n' roll. Can you believe that?"

"Of Victor, yes."

They kissed again, slowly, with the relish of people who haven't kissed for a long time. Then he said: "Helen, I'm glad you came. I don't know what the hell's going to happen now. But I'm glad you came."

"I'm glad, too. As long as it doesn't hurt too much."

He shrugged. "It might. It probably will. But I guess there isn't much that's worth having that comes easy."

Freddie's intercom buzzed again, and Jeannie said: "I don't want to rush you, Mr. Secker, but the helicopter's waiting. If you want to get up to the island by one-thirty . . ."

"Okay, Jeannie," he told her, smiling at Helen. "And please inform Captain Kroscek we'll have one extra passenger."

There was a silence. Then Jeannie said: "Mrs. Marini, sir?"

"That's right."

He switched off the intercom and looked at Helen wryly.

"Jeannie's very protective." He smiled. "Almost motherly."

"Do you need a mother?" asked Helen.

He lifted his black Yves St. Laurent blazer from the back of his chair. "I had one once," he said. "I guess I didn't ever get to know her too well, but I certainly had one."

He brushed back his hair, straightened his tie, and opened his desk drawer to take out a bottle of Balenciaga after-shave. "I can remember her funeral more than anything," he went on. "It was very simple, one of the simplest funerals I guess this family ever had. I stood there and it was such a beautiful day, I could just imagine her spirit fluttering out of the grave and flying off into the sky, like a dove or something. I was glad, in a way, she was free. She was always so frustrated, and sad. She was like someone who got on the wrong train, and wound up at some strange terminus, and wandered around the streets of this strange place and never found out where she was really supposed to go."

Helen turned her face away. "That happens to more women than you'd even imagine."

707

He touched her arm. "Did it happen to you?"

She looked wistful. "I was one of those unfortunate people who discover that life is like that joke about the Polish concert. Admission is free, but they charge ten dollars to get out."

Freddie said: "Helen, you can still go back home. I don't want to mess up your life."

She shook her head. "Life isn't worth living unless it's nicely messed up. I tried to get over you, Freddie. I think I even tried to make you hate me. But I guess I couldn't bear it if you did. Just think about it. I'm the wife of a prosperous and hardworking young attorney who may just get to the top of the heap one day. What happens when I meet a man like you? You're handsome, and you're young, and you're sympathetic, and you're sitting on more money than Dick will ever see in ten lifetimes. If I said that I preferred a staid, safe marriage to an affair with you, I'd be ready for the funny farm."

Freddie reached for another cigarette, lit it, and blew out smoke.

"Your mother died of cancer," said Helen.

Freddie nodded.

She took the cigarette out of his mouth and crushed it in the ashtray.

"I love you," she said, putting her arms around him. "And that's all I can say."

The door opened, and Jeannie came in with Freddie's briefcase, packed with carefully arranged work for the next twenty-four hours. She was a short girl from Pittsburgh with wiry auburn hair that flew up from her scalp as if she had just stuck her fingers in an electric socket. She wore clashing turtlenecks of pink and red, and she treated Freddie as if he were precious porcelain. She gave Helen a quick, cautious glance and said: "Everything's here, Mr. Secker. You won't forget the insurance assessments for Daylong, will you?"

Freddie said: "I won't," and as Jeannie turned to go, he called: "Jeannie?"

She paused. "Yes, Mr. Secker?"

He gave her a gentle grin. "Thanks, Jeannie. You're very good to me."

Jeannie colored. She said: "Enjoy your flight, won't you?" and then bustled quickly out of the office as if she had an urgent appointment.

Helen said: "She's in love with you. Can't you see that?"

Freddie looked embarrassed. "She's a terrific secretary, I know that much."

They left the office and took Freddie's private elevator, decorated inside with rococo gilt mirrors, to the uppermost floor. Then it was a short climb up plush-carpeted stairs to the roof exit and the helicopter pad. As they stepped out of the elevator car and mounted the stairs, they could already hear the roaring of the helicopter motor and the whistle and drone of its downdraft.

"Hold on to your hairstyle," cautioned Freddie as he opened the door onto the pad.

Amid a deafening whine of turbines and the flack-flack-flack of idly turning rotors, the huge white-painted Sikorsky helicopter was waiting for them, a glistening albino dragon in the gray cloud of a humid Wall Street afternoon. The top of the Cornelius Oil Building roof had supported a radio tower in the 1930's, but Roderick had ordered it removed in 1955 to allow helicopters to land there, although it had taken three years of tussles in the district courts and eleven special legal dispensations before the pad had first come into use.

A staff member in an orange fluorescent helmet and green coveralls ushered them quickly across the pad and into the open door of the helicopter. Then he closed the door behind them, gave the thumbs-up to the pilot, and the twin-rotored monster rose from the roof and tilted away toward the northwest.

Inside, the helicopter was warm and extravagantly decorated. The main cabin was carpeted with a thick shag-pile rug in rich burgundy, and the walls were padded and lined with white moiré silk. There were deep-buttoned leather chairs, a wide leather-topped desk, and a divan draped with long-haired furs.

From the rear of the helicopter, balancing himself against the turbulence, came Freddie's flight director, Eric Peterson, a stocky Vietnam veteran with a peppery crop and a face as chunky as Barre granite. He was dressed in a smart light gray suit, but he looked as if he would have greatly preferred to be kitted out in khaki fatigues. Behind Freddie's back, he referred to the white Sikorsky as "the hovering whorehouse."

They shook hands. Freddie said: "Mrs. Marini is just along for the ride. I'd like you to take her back to Manhattan as soon as you've dropped me off at the island."

"She's not staying for the celebrations, sir?"

"She has to get home to Mr. Marini, don't you, Helen?"

Helen felt uncomfortable, but she nodded briefly. Beneath their feet, the helicopter angled and sloped as it turned away from Manhattan and began to beat its way northward past Englewood Cliffs, and up the foggy Hudson.

Eric Peterson scratched the back of his ear with his silver pencil. "Beg your pardon, Mr. Secker, but Mr. Marini's up at Lynwood's Island, too. He flew up this morning with Mr. Victor Cornelius."

Helen said: "What?"

"They left about ten. I don't think Mr. Marini was planning on going up there, Mrs. Marini, but it seemed like Mr. Cornelius and him had a lot to talk over, and they decided to carry on with their meeting on the way."

Helen glanced at Freddie anxiously. But Freddie simply laid a comforting hand on her shoulder and said: "Well, that's fine. A nice cozy family gathering, huh? Now, how about some cocktails, Eric? Then Mrs. Marini and I have a few problems to talk over in private."

Eric looked at Freddie and then at Helen, and back again. His eyes closed no more than a snake's do, and he nodded. "Very good, sir. Tell me what you want and I'll have Zim bring them through."

They ordered a screwdriver and a Scotch on the rocks, and then sat in armchairs by the window, looking out at the fragments of cloud and the shadowy outline of the river beneath them. Freddie held Helen's hand, but she was so nervous now that she had to take it away.

"Do you have a cigarette?" she asked him.

He went over to the desk and brought across the gold-and-enamel cigarette box.

"There's no reason for Dick to find out you're here, you know," said Freddie. "When we land, all you have to do is sit away from the window, and they'll take this thing up and off again the moment I've climbed out."

She puffed smoke. "It's just beginning to remind me of what it was like before. All that lying, and all those nasty little deceptions."

"If you like, you don't have to come up to Lynwood's Island at all. I could have us turn around and deliver you straight back home."

"That would be silly. And in any case, you'd be late. I don't want to make you late."

"Helen . . ."

She shook her head. "It's all right. I'll hide. I'm used to hiding."

"Is that what you really want to do?"

"I don't know what I want to do. But as long as Dick doesn't find out, it doesn't really make any difference, does it?"

Freddie frowned. "But Dick doesn't suspect anything, does he? What does it matter if I give you a ride up to the island? Suppose you just dropped by the office, and I was my usual impetuous self and offered you a trip for the hell of it?"

She stood up, and paced across to the other side of the cabin. "There's the Tappan Zee Bridge," she remarked.

Freddie said: "Helen . . ."

She turned.

More quietly he said: "Helen, does Dick *know* about us?"

She came back and sat down beside him. Her eyes were misted and her expression was sad. The smoke poured from her cigarette in an endless dribble. She said: "Yes, he does. I'm sorry. He asked me point-blank one day. I was so surprised that I told the truth."

"And that was when you broke it off?"

She nodded. "He said that if I didn't promise to stop seeing you there and then, he'd make sure we had the most muckraking divorce since . . ."

Freddie glanced up. "Since my mother?"

"Yes," she whispered.

Freddie let out a long, taut breath. For a minute or two he didn't know what to say, and he gazed down at the dim shores of the Hudson with a feeling of dull resignation.

Helen reached out and stroked the back of his hair. "I knew that I shouldn't have told him. But I didn't know what else to do. And he said that as long as I kept away from you, he wouldn't say a word to anyone, and that he'd go on working with you as if nothing had happened."

"It takes a pretty tough man to make a promise like that."

"Dick isn't only tough, Freddie. He's forgiving, too. And you can't say that he hasn't kept to his word. He's been quite normal when he's talked to you, hasn't he?"

"Oh, sure," agreed Freddie with a hint of bitterness. "Very magnanimous, considering that I've been screwing his wife."

"Freddie, please."

"Oh, for Christ's sake!" snapped Freddie. But then he turned away, lowered his head, and said: "I don't know, Helen. What's the damned use of it all?"

She looked at him wistfully. "The use is that we love each other, don't we?"

He raised his head. "I guess so. But you're right. We haven't been together for more than a couple of hours, and it's started all over. Cheating, and lying, and playing hide-and-go-seek. If you're going to have to hide, Helen, I'm not sure that I can go through with any more of this. It has to be out in the open or nothing."

"Freddie, I *can't* leave Dick. Not now."

He turned and looked at her steadily and strongly. "Helen, you're going to have to make up your mind. This is too much of a strain for both of us. For *all* of us. Maybe it wouldn't be so bad if I didn't love you so much. We could meet now and again, and fuck, and leave it at that. But I *do* love you, and I don't want to go on pretending that I don't. Sooner or later, it has to be me or it has to be Dick. You know that as well as I do."

"I thought we could carry on for just a little longer," she said quietly. "It isn't easy to pluck up the courage to tell someone like Dick that you're walking out for good."

"But it has to be done, Helen," insisted Freddie. "It has to."

"Even if he rakes up a terrible scandal?"

"I can survive scandal, and so can you. Maybe Hester won't like it, and I'm sure that Roderick won't, but they've all had their share of dirty linen aired in public, and it's never done *them* any lasting harm."

Helen gave a quick, uneven smile.

Freddie said: "I'm not asking you to leave him if you really can't. You know that, don't you? I can drop you off home right now, and we can forget that today ever happened. But I can only say that because I really love you. I want all of you, Helen. Not just a part."

She turned and looked down the length of the cabin. "Does that door lock?" she asked him.

He frowned. "Sure."

"Then, if we made love, nobody could come in to interrupt us?"

Freddie paused, and then nodded.

She said: "I've never made love in a helicopter before."

"Helen . . ." he said.

712

But she held out her hands for him and whispered: "Please, Freddie. It's been two months."

He stood up and held her in his arms. She looked up at him, and there were tears in her eyes. He peeled back her pink summer coat, and it fell softly on the thick-carpeted floor. Underneath she was wearing a simple gray lawn dress with a loose bodice and a thin cord around the waist. The overcast lunchtime light that strained through the helicopter's windows cast a faint shadow of her bare breast beneath the thin material.

He kissed her for a long, silent time. His right hand caressed and squeezed her left breast until she let out a small sharp breath. Then she kissed him again, almost savagely, and bit at his ear. His pants did nothing to hide the rearing hardness he felt for her, and he quickly tore away from her and went to lock the cabin door, stripping off his shirt as he went.

He came back to her, and unzipped her dress. They were both panting, like runners reaching their stride in a cross-country race. The dress slipped off her, and underneath she was wearing only her panty hose. Her breasts were small and pointed, with nipples as tight as puckered lips, and between her thighs the seam of her tights clung deep between the plump labia which she always kept shaved and childlike.

They seemed to fall back on the fur-covered divan a thousand times, a blur of arms and legs, an action replay over and over. The divan bounced under their weight with bionic slowness, and the fur rippled and shook itself. Freddie felt the soft bearskins enfold his naked back, silky and ineffably sensual, and then Helen was on top of him, her warm weight naked except for the golden crucifix that dangled between her breasts. She kissed him and licked him, and then he rolled over on top of her, and pushed himself into her with a hard, impatient thrust. She snuffled, and her fingernails bit into his shoulder. He pushed harder, his head bent down so that he could see where they joined, his rigid dark-red flesh immersed in her pink bare glistening flesh. He thrust quicker and harder, harder and quicker, and she lifted her bottom and thrust against him. He felt so stiff that he could hardly believe he wasn't touching her womb, her stomach, even her throat. For her part, underneath him, she felt smothered in fur, pressed down by his muscular body, and filled up, completely filled up, but she wanted to be stretched wider and wider, stretched by one man or two men or three. She

713

could fantasize six men at once, their erections tied together like fat red asparagus, forcing their way inside her.

All the time, the Sikorsky helicopter bucked and swayed and tilted underneath them as they flew, oblivious, over Highland Falls and West Point, into a misty summer afternoon.

Freddie came much too soon. He pulled back too far, and slipped out, and white warm translucent droplets smothered her thigh.

Helen, in a high-pitched voice, said: "No! No, Freddie, no! Oh, no!" and tried desperately to smear the fluid between her legs. She was so frantic that she was trembling.

Freddie, ecstatic one second and shocked the next, sat up on his haunches and stared at her.

"Helen?" he said, a haunted query, almost unheard in the thrumming vibration of the helicopter's cabin.

Her hand was still cupped between her thighs. She looked up at him, her eyes wide with alarm.

"Helen?" he demanded, louder this time.

She was tense for a second, her face drawn and electrified. Then she clamped one hand over her mouth, and turned away so that she was buried in the fur. Freddie saw her ribs convulse under her soft skin, and heard her sob.

He leaned forward and said softly: "Helen?"

She lay still, the tears squeezing out of the corner of her eyes and forming a clear pool against the bridge of her nose.

"It's something else, Helen, isn't it? It's not just Dick and me."

She nodded miserably.

He stayed there for a moment, and then he got up off the divan and went to pull on his pants. Over the RT, Captain Kroscek announced: "*Six minutes to Lynwood's Island, Mr. Secker.*"

Freddie went back to the divan. He lit two cigarettes, and offered one to Helen. She didn't move at first, but then she sat up, pushed her hand through her wavy hair, and took it.

"You're going to have to get dressed in a moment," he told her gently. "We'll be landing in a few minutes."

She closed her eyes and nodded. "I know. I'm sorry."

"You don't have to be sorry."

"Don't I? I came to say I was sorry this morning, but all I seem to have done is make everything worse."

Outside the window, there were dark green forests and silver

714

rivers and fragments of cloud. The helicopter began to bank around, and Freddie knew that Lynwood's Island was probably in sight.

"Get dressed now," Freddie advised. "Then I'll have Eric fly you home."

Helen nodded dumbly, and got up off the divan to find her dress and her panty hose. There was a polite knocking at the cabin door, and Freddie called: "Just a moment, Eric!"

Helen, buttoning her dress, said: "I suppose you've guessed."

"I don't know," answered Freddie. "Perhaps you'd better tell me."

"Well," she said, "I guess it had to come to this one day. Desperation has its own reward."

He looked at her and didn't reply.

Helen said simply: "They shared a taxi home, you know, Dick and one of your office gossips. That's how he found out about you and me. Well, I just thank God I was only two months pregnant then, and it didn't even show."

"*Pregnant*?" said Freddie. He knew it, and yet it still came at him like a Greyhound bus.

Helen put on her sandal. "I got rid of it, of course," she said. "It was very easy, and it didn't even hurt. I cried for a week, but that wasn't difficult to explain. Tears of joy, you see, to be back from my walk on the wild side. I don't know whether Dick believed me, but I suppose he had to. At least I wasn't seeing you anymore and that was enough."

Freddie licked his lips. He felt as if he needed a drink.

"You were *pregnant*? he asked hoarsely. "You had my child, and you got rid of it?"

She took a long drag from her cigarette and set it down on the ashtray. "You mustn't think that I don't love you," she said, so unhappy that she could barely keep from crying. "I love you more than you'll probably give me credit for."

"But *why*?" he wanted to know. "If you want to stay with Dick, why do you want *me* to make you pregnant?"

She lifted her chin as proudly as she could. "Dick's my husband," she told him. "I love you, and I mean that. But what I have with Dick is very deep and very special, and I know that I'll never leave him. The only trouble is, he can't . . ."

There was a long pause. The helicopter was coming down now,

715

and they both felt pressure on their ears. When Helen spoke again, her voice was flat and distant, like someone speaking into a kapok mattress.

"We both had tests two years ago. I'm ovulating perfectly well, but Dick has what they call a low sperm count. It's *possible* for him to father a child. That's what they told us. But not very likely."

Freddie felt an emotional pain like washing himself all over with ground glass. It was almost as if he couldn't breathe, or think, or talk.

"So you looked for a suitable father?" he asked her unsteadily and he didn't even sound like himself.

She shook her head. "I didn't have to look. I was head over heels about you already. If there was anybody in the whole world I wanted to give me a baby, apart from Dick, it was you."

Freddie took a deep breath. He said harshly: "I don't know whether to be flattered or nauseous."

Helen rested her head on her hand and started to weep. Silently, but with obvious agony.

"So today was a second try, was it?" asked Freddie. "When Dick found out about us the first time, and you had to abort my fetus, you decided you'd have another go? Say you were sorry about last time, and string me along for a couple of months so that you could get yourself knocked up?"

Helen couldn't answer. Over the RT, Captain Kroscek announced: "*Landing in one minute, sir. Please take your seats.*"

Out of the windows, Freddie could see Lynwood's Island and the stately symmetrical house. He sat down in one of the armchairs and smashed out his cigarette in the ashtray.

"You thought you'd acquire some good stock in your family, did you?" he yelled, over the sudden roar of the helicopter's turbines. "A good strain of millionaires?"

Helen lifted her head and looked at him, her eyelashes spiky with tears. "Oh, Freddie," she wept. "Oh, Freddie."

The helicopter pivoted slowly, and settled on its wheels. Captain Kroscek cut the turbines, and then there was no sound but the mournful whistling of the rotors as they spun slower and slower and slower. Eric Peterson emerged from the rear cabin, and without even an inquisitive glance at Helen, operated the door-opening lever and put down the steps. He stood, silent and at-

716

tentive, while Freddie sat with Helen, and Helen cried. A faint warm breeze blew in from outside.

"I want you to do one thing," said Freddie quietly. "I want you to fly back to Manhattan, and then take a taxi home, and I want you to forget that you ever thought anything about me except that I'm one of the men who employ your husband."

He stayed for a few more moments. Then he collected his briefcase and climbed out of the helicopter without a word. Helen called: "*Freddie*!" but he didn't turn around.

"What if I'm pregnant?" she asked him bitterly. "What happens if I'm pregnant?"

Freddie paused. The summer wind blew in his hair, and she thought he looked so beautiful that to let him go was like losing days out of her life. He said in a clear voice: "Tell Dick. He'll be happy."

As he walked toward the house, he saw Dick Marini standing close to Victor among the yew shrubs on the terrace. He saw Celia and Roderick, Ally and Tess. And behind him, the white helicopter rose into the gray summer skies and lifted Helen away, pregnant or not, its rotors flick-flacking along the Hudson Valley until their sound was nothing but echoes, and then even the echoes themselves were lost.

Celia was feeling particularly bitchy, and Freddie's punctual arrival did little to mollify her. She had considered herself the grande dame of the Cornelius family for years, and when any attention was lavished on Hester, she became shrill and argumentative, sending the servants on awkward errands (today she wanted a bottle of Swiss eyedrops that were almost impossible to find in Lynwood), and tying up the switchboard with endless calls to Germany and South America. She was dressed in a flouncy scarlet dress that did very little for her but emphasize her age, and when Freddie arrived on the terrace she was sitting on an upright gilt chair like a bright, exotic, but decidedly elderly bird, a dry sherry on a garden table beside her, her cane tapping impatiently on the stone flags.

Victor stood behind her, as sullen as a raincloud; and for the first time in months Freddie noticed Dick Marini, plump and beady-eyed, and he thought how remarkably Dick resembled a young, though much duller, Mario Lanza. He tried not to think about Dick Marini's sperm count, but it did fleetingly strike him as

717

unaccountable that a woman like Helen should find such depth and love in him. Well, no, perhaps it didn't. He was being unfair.

Tess came over and took Freddie's hand. She was wearing a loose filmy dress of printed cotton, and dozens of gold bangles. She kissed him as a sister kisses a brother, and a little bit more besides. Ally, wearing dark glasses and looking pale, kept her distance.

"Good flight?" asked Victor disinterestedly.

"I've had worse."

One of the footmen came out of the open French doors and asked Freddie what he wanted to drink. He ordered a Jack Daniel's, straight up, and Tess raised an amused and inquisitive eyebrow.

"I'm feeling tired, that's all," said Freddie. "Is the old lady down yet?"

"She's having her *medication*," put in Celia archly, as if she didn't start each day herself with two handfuls of vitamins and tranquilizers and natural health tablets.

"What time are the guests arriving?"

"Most of them by Lear jet at two-thirty," said Victor. "One or two by train and car. The usual gaggle of hysterical women, I suppose. Just like the year that Mama won the award."

Freddie's drink arrived, and he raised it up, as if he were about to propose a toast. But then he said: "I didn't know you won an award from the American Women's League, Celia. What was it for?"

Celia turned her sharp profile away impatiently. "Services to our country's womanhood," she replied as coldly as she possibly could.

Freddie felt oddly reckless. He looked Dick Marini straight in the eye and said sharply: "That's very good. I'll drink to that. The servicing of American womanhood."

Celia said in tones of infinite distaste: "You're just like your father. *And* your mother."

Freddie laughed, a brittle laugh that didn't have very much to do with humor, and he kept his eyes on Dick Marini. "That's more than some people can say," he observed, although he wished almost immediately that he hadn't. It wasn't Dick Marini's fault. The man was trying to hold on to his career and his wife, both, and you couldn't take him to task for that. It was just that, emotionally and physically at least, he seemed so vulnerable, like an upturned turtle on a hot beach.

Ally, who was sipping a dry martini, said: "I would go up and see Hester quite soon if I were you. She knows all about the Skouros thing. I don't think she's particularly amused."

"She's eighty-four," said Tess, taking out a cigarette. "What does it matter if she's not particularly amused?"

Victor, who was dressed in a bottle-green velvet suit that made him look like a pale fat Las Vegas croupier, paced across to the stone balustrade of the terrace and looked out over the sloping lawns.

"She may be eighty-four," he said with exaggerated patience. "She may not even be *compos mentis*. But legally and financially she holds you and me and everyone else in this family by the throat. Until God in His infinite wisdom decides that He wants her back, then we're stuck with her, and don't you forget it."

"Spoken with your usual grace," said Freddie artlessly.

"Oh, for goodness' sake," Celia interrupted.

Freddie knocked back his drink and set the empty glass down on the balustrade. Then he went into the drawing room through the French doors, and walked through to the elegant oval hallway. A squat man in a three-hundred-dollar pinstripe suit and a black beard was just coming down the stairs.

"Dr. Nathan, isn't it?" asked Freddie.

The doctor came down to the bottom stair, clicked his heels, and gave a small bow. "Mr. Secker. I'm pleased to see you again."

"How's Grandmother? I was thinking of going up to say hello."

"Yes, you can do that," Nathan told him. "She's not as sharp as she used to be. She has trouble remembering small things, you know. But she's in excellent health for a woman of her age. Really excellent health."

"This won't be too much for her, this presentation this afternoon?"

Dr. Nathan shook his head. "When you get to that age, the only things that are worth avoiding are repeats on television and radishes. I like to advise my patients to lead a full life. Dr. Pellen and Dr. Weiss are of the same opinion."

"Will you come with me?" asked Freddie.

"Surely," assented Dr. Nathan. "She's up in the gallery."

They climbed the curving staircase, with soft turquoise carpet underfoot. Then they walked along gloomy corridors flanked by oil paintings as dark and glossy as tabletops. They passed long-case

719

clocks that ticked and chimed. Through the windows, they occasionally caught glimpses of the gardens, green and mysterious, like gardens seen in dreams or through the keyholes of doors with no keys.

Eventually they climbed another wide flight of stairs and walked along a marble-floored gallery which ran the length of one entire wing. The gallery was glazed with yellow-tinted windows, and looked out over a bare lawn with croquet wickets, where Freddie and Tess and Ally used to play when they were children. Freddie hadn't come up to Lynwood's Island in a long while, and he was disturbed by the sense of wealthy neglect. Everything was clean and orderly and polished and in good repair; yet everything was untouched and unused, and the only sound these corridors heard was the footsteps of nurses and doctors, quietly and discreetly protecting the frail existence of the richest woman in America. The yellow glass gave the whole place a curious effect of the light, so that he felt as if they had arrived in an old photograph.

At the extreme far end of the gallery, sitting in an elaborate wicker chair, her legs covered by a wool blanket, was a white-haired old woman in a white dress. As they came nearer, they could see that her face was the color of laundry, and that her hair, although it had been plaited into a white ring, was sparse. But her dress was embroidered with white silk and edged with Nottingham lace, and on her withered fingers were white diamond rings that had cost millions of dollars. Beside the old woman was a small marquetry table, on which rested *The New York Times*, *The Wall Street Journal*, a copy of Shakespeare's *King Henry V* bound in white kidskin, a hand bell, and a glass of water.

Dr. Nathan approached the old woman first. She didn't look up at him to begin with. Her eyes were the color of pale pebbles, and seemed to be almost blind. Dr. Nathan said: "Freddie's here. He's come to see you."

The old woman nodded. "Come a little closer, Freddie," she asked in a thin voice like the rustling of tissue paper.

Freddie coughed and stepped forward. He bent down and kissed the old woman lightly on the forehead.

"Hello, Grandmother."

The old woman reached up and tugged at his sleeve. "You're a bad boy, Freddie. You must come to see your grandmother more often."

Freddie said: "I'll try. I've been pretty tied up."

720

"Try to untie yourself then," she said with a faint smile. "I'd rather see you than anyone."

Freddie grinned, and nodded. "Okay. That's a promise."

"We could play a game of backgammon," said Hester. "I'm hot stuff at backgammon, aren't I, doctor?"

Dr. Nathan grinned. "Your grandmother pastes me at backgammon every Thursday without fail."

Freddie said: "You're looking pretty well. Are they kind to you?"

Hester shrugged. "They're as kind as they can be."

Dr. Nathan said: "She's had three transfusions this month, to try to restore the balance of her corpuscles. It hasn't been easy for her."

Hester smiled. "I really sometimes wonder if it's all worth it. If it wasn't for these industrious gentlemen, I would have been lying in my grave years ago."

Freddie hunkered down beside her chair. "But you're happy, aren't you? You've got all this Women's League work. I mean, you're not *un*happy?"

Hester said: "I have a reason to live, if that's what you're trying to say."

Freddie picked up the white kidskin Shakespeare. "I see you're reading *Henry V*."

Hester nodded. "You can learn a lot from Shakespeare. You ought to persuade Victor to read it, as a daily task."

"I can't get Victor to read anything. I lent him *The Great Gatsby* four years ago, and he hasn't gotten past the title page."

"It doesn't surprise me. But there's a phrase in *King Henry V* that sums up Victor rather aptly."

"Grandmother," said Freddie, although he couldn't help smiling, "you shouldn't upset yourself."

"I'm not upset. You mean I shouldn't rock the family boat. Shouldn't take sides."

"Well, I don't know. But I guess if you have something you want to say to Victor, you ought to tell him straight to his face."

Hester ignored him. "Fluellen says it," she remarked brightly. "He says of Captain Macmorris: 'By Cheshu, he is an ass, as in the world: he has no more directions in the true disciplines of the wars, look you, than is a puppy-dog.'"

Freddie said: "Victor can't help the way he is."

Hester looked serious. "But *you* can."

There was an uncomfortable silence. Freddie licked his lips.

After a while Hester touched Freddie's shoulder and said: "I have arranged my estate so that, when I die, you will be the principal beneficiary. You will have more control over Cornelius Industries than anyone. But I must admit that I nearly canceled my will when I heard how you handled this ridiculous business of Ariadne Skouros. It was a silly scandal that could have been forgotten in a day. Instead, you've blown it out of all proportion. You've amplified it and advertised it, and you've lost John Russell his chance of election."

"There's still time," insisted Freddie.

"No," said Hester. "Victor was destructive and stupid, but *you* allowed yourself to be panicked; and if there is one luxury you can never allow youself in this kind of business, it's panic. There is too much at stake."

"If Victor's butler hadn't gone to the police, nobody would have ever found out."

That's precisely the kind of half-baked thinking I'm talking about," retorted Hester. "If Victor had been an employer who treated his staff as they were supposed to have been treated; if Victor had been the kind of man who inspired loyalty and trust, then this butler of his would never have tattletaled behind his back. And if *you'd* known what you were doing, you would have realized that one of Victor's servants was bound to talk. It was the first thing that I thought of, and I'm eighty-four."

Freddie said: "We're still waiting for an autopsy on the Skouros girl. If there's no indication that she died in a swimming pool, we might still get away with it."

Hester pursed her lined lips. "I've spoken to Dr. Weiss. He says that if the police examiners are any good at all, they'll undoubtedly find traces of chlorinated water in her body tissues."

Freddie bit his lip and glanced across at Dr. Nathan, standing patiently and quietly by.

"It's still not entirely certain," he said. "I guess we're still in there with half a chance."

Hester closed her eyes for a moment and then opened them again. "It's about time you realized that your money does not make you divine," she told him. "Your grandfather began to understand that—perhaps too late— but he understood it all the same. It is the combination of great wealth and great personal humility that makes a rich man great."

Freddie didn't answer. A bay-breasted warbler perched on the branch of a tree outside the tinted window, and he could hear it singing a thin, slurred song.

"I know what you're thinking," said Hester. "You're thinking that I'm senile, and that I've been sitting here in my chair devising all kinds of heresies to irritate you and make your life difficult. But I know what's going on, Freddie. I know that you keep in touch with public opinion, but I read everything, watch everything, and I talk to more people in a day than you talk to in six weeks. You can't get away with cover-ups like this anymore. John Russell can't put himself up for election with this business unresolved, because as sure as the wrath of God, Ariadne Skouros will rise right out of her watery grave and drag him down. One day, if not now."

"Grandmother," said Freddie, "if men like John Russell don't lead the country, then who will? I believe he's honest, and he's bright, and what are we going to do? Throw him on the scrap heap just because of some damned fool mistake of Victor's?"

Hester looked at him coolly. "The President is elected to look after the least of the American people," she said. "If John Russell gets to the White House on money donated by Cornelius Industries, and if he appoints Victor to some government office or other, which he surely will, then where is the sanctity of the least of the American people?"

"The least?" asked Freddie. "What about the greatest?"

"You think that *you're* the greatest?" the old lady retorted.

Freddie said quietly: "No."

"Well, I'm glad you said that," Hester told him. "Because whatever Victor and Celia think, your grandfather didn't think it, and I'll show you why." -

Freddie looked up. "I don't understand you."

Hester tinkled the bell on her marquetry table. "You'll see. You may not understand still. But as least you'll see."

Dr. Nathan said: "I don't want you to get yourself excited, Mrs. Cornelius. You've got a hectic afternoon ahead of you."

"Dr. Nathan," said Hester with heavy patience, "nothing has excited me since Victor Mature came to visit in 1954."

A door at the side of the gallery opened, and two nurses came through, in white uniforms and starched headpieces. One of them was as plain as a small rowboat, but the other was busty and blond, and she gave Freddie a coy glance as she walked in.

"I wish to take Mr. Secker through to Mr. Cornelius' *special*

723

room," announced Hester. "I will take Mr. Secker's arm, but you will accompany us along the corridor in case I feel faint."

Dr. Nathan said: "Do you need me any longer? I have to go check on that new plasma centrifuge."

"No, no, you run along," said Hester. "Freddie will look after me."

Freddie helped her rise from her chair and grip onto his arm. He was amazed to feel how light she was, as if her bones had all dried up to paper and her skin had been mummified. But she stood quite erect, and although she walked with careful, pedantic steps, she was just as feminine as she had been when she first sat in the foyer of the Plaza and said to Johann Cornelius: "Texas it is."

They went along the gallery, and then turned a corner to the north side of the house. Through the window, Freddie could see an angled corner of the glass-covered conservatory pool, where Johann had talked to Merrett Kale. Then they passed through a shadowy part of the corridor, lit by teardrop chandeliers and hung with Early American paintings, including three original art-nouveau poster designs by Louis Rheade that Freddie had never seen before.

"Here is the room," said Hester, steadying herself. "Now, wait a moment while I find my key."

The door looked like any other door on the upper floors of the house. It was polished beaded mahogany with brass doorplates, with a gilt number painted discreetly in one corner. But the two nurses stood well back from it, as if Hester were opening up a chapel, and it was obvious that Room 347 had a significance and an atmosphere that was almost religious, at least in the Cornelius canon.

Hester produced the key and gave it to Freddie. She rested her dry, withered hand on his and said: "You are the only member of the family who has seen this room, apart from me. I want you to understand that you must regard it as a privilege. Now, open the door."

Freddie inserted the key and turned it. Then he pushed the door a little ajar, and stood back for Hester to precede him into the room. There was a vague smell of mothballs and must.

"No, no," insisted Hester. "You go first. Just walk in. I'll wait here. The nurses will look after me."

Freddie gave her an uncertain smile. Then he pushed the door wide open and stepped inside.

It was gloomy, this room, because the windows were so heavily draped; and in any case it was foggy outside. But as he walked into it, he was aware of more than gloom; there was the shadowy presence of years and years of memory as well. He looked around it, taking it all in, but he couldn't understand what it was or what on earth it meant. Hester had called it Mr. Cornelius' *special* room, but what was special about it, except that it was so musty and antique and unlived-in?

There was an odd lingering smell of stale potpourri which pervaded everything. It seemed to hang in the wine-colored drapes, cling in the lace curtains, which were embroidered with baskets of roses, and saturate the grotesque Gothic furniture.

The room was impossibly crowded with turn-of-the-century American furniture: wine tables, china planters, china cabinets, cake stands, and standard lamps. The mantelshelf was draped in bottle-green velour, and crammed with knickknacks: cheap pottery statuettes, clocks, sepia photographs, brass souvenirs. On the brown-wallpapered walls were dozens of watercolors, etchings, and silhouettes.

One photograph caught his attention immediately. It was standing in a small oval black-enamel frame on a table by itself. It was a portrait of a wistful-looking woman in a feather boa, a woman who, even by modern standards, was remarkably beautiful. Freddie picked it up and peered at it, and as he did so, he became conscious that Hester was standing in the doorway.

"Is this you?" he asked, lifting the photograph up so that she could see it.

She shook her head. "No. It isn't me."

Freddie set the photograph back on the table again. "I don't really understand what this is all about. The room looks like something out of an old-time western."

Hester sat herself carefully down on one of the ugly carved-oak armchairs. "It is," she said.

"But what does it mean? What's it all about?"

Hester's pale face was like one of the watery portraits on the wall. She couldn't even begin to explain to Freddie how much this room haunted her; how long she had tried to grasp what it was and why it was here. In a faint, faded voice she said: "I always knew this room existed, all through my marriage. But Johann told me it was somewhere to keep some particularly special antiques, and he never encouraged me to come up here. Sometimes he disappeared for hours on end, and I suppose he sat here and meditated and relived whatever this room meant to him."

"You have no idea? He never told you?"

Hester shrugged. "It was only after his death that I began to understand it was a shrine. In his will, he asked for the whole room to be destroyed, but I managed to have that overruled. I wanted to know why he wanted to have it destroyed, and I can only imagine that he felt it might cause me distress. The only possible clue is that photograph. It has written on the back, 'J. from B.' But I don't have any notion who B. might be."

Freddie walked around the room and then stood by the window.

"Does it matter?" he asked. "He loved you, didn't he? Does it really matter if he had some lingering memory of some other woman?"

Hester smiled. "No, of course it doesn't matter. I don't think now that Johann loved me with all his heart, but we were happy enough. He was a passionate man, your grandfather, and fierce, but he was easily influenced, too, as many rich people are."

"Grandmother, why did you show me this room?" asked Freddie. He was beginning to feel claustrophobic, as if his dead grandfather's life was pressing in on him from all sides.

Hester looked up. "I wanted to show you that Johann eventually grew to understand something that Victor will never understand, and that Roderick and Celia have only accepted with such impatience and intolerance that they will never be able to tell him about it. Our wealth gives us power over other people, but if we use that power without consideration, then we are repaid for our trespasses against others a hundred times more painfully than the pain we have actually inflicted."

She closed her eyes and sighed.

"It always amuses me that Communists and liberals want to punish the rich. The rich are already punished. Roderick was punished very young, I'm sorry to say, when his airplane crashed and killed his friends. Your mother, Hope, was punished, mostly by her own conscience. Poor John was punished hundreds of times over, and I suppose you might say that he died a rich man's death. Irene was punished, and Ally was punished, and so was Tess. I don't know whether anyone has punished you yet, Freddie, but they will. As for Victor, he is storing up for himself the greatest

726

retribution of all. But who knows? He might come out of it human.''

Freddie said huskily: "This room? Was this Grandfather's punishment?''

Hester nodded. "I think so. For some reason, long before I met him, a room like this was vitally important. Something must have happened in it that he regretted for the rest of his life. Maybe it was something to do with 'B.' I shall never know. But all I can say is that I want you to grow up intelligently and wisely, and I want you to behave like a human being, no matter how superior or wealthy you are; because otherwise you'll leave a room like this yourself when you die, or something very much like it.''

Freddie looked around. There was nothing more to say. The room was silent and dead and inexplicable. He said quietly: "All right, Grandmother. Let's go join the others. They must be starting the presentation soon.''

Hester smiled tiredly. "You're quite right, Freddie. I must try to enjoy myself. That's what Sir James Charles said to me once, when we had dinner on the *Aquitania*. He was a tremendous eater, you know, and a bon vivant. He said that if you didn't drink as much as you could, and eat as much as you could, and laugh as much you could, then you might just as well suck cough drops and live in Cleveland. I'm not *quite* sure what he meant, but I think I caught the gist of it.''

There was a polite knock at the door. It was Mrs. Dubuque, Hester's lady's maid, a practical, bustling woman with a well-groomed silver-gray bun and an infallible eye for dressing old ladies with style and dignity.

"Your gown is laid out, Mrs. Cornelius," she said. "And Mr. Roderick says the presentation is due to start in forty-five minutes.''

"Freddie," said Hester, "I'll have to hurry. Now, be a good boy and see if you can have a word with Roderick and Celia before the guests arrive. Particularly before John Russell arrives. I want him to announce his retirement from the presidential race this evening.''

"Grandmother . . .''

Hester, rising from her chair, paused and looked at him.

"You've got troubles of your own, haven't you, boy?" she asked him.

727

He lowered his eyes. "Nothing serious."

She held his arm. "All problems are serious, but you're going to have more, particularly when the medical examiners find out that Miss Skouros drowned in a swimming pool. So do your best, my dear, and I'll see you later."

Freddie watched Hester walk slowly off toward her dressing room, accompanied by Mrs. Dubuque and her two nurses. The blond nurse with the big breasts turned shyly around as the small procession turned around the corner, and Freddie gave her a quick grin. Perhaps he could find some consolation there for Helen.

He went downstairs, and found the rest of the family assembled in the small ballroom. It was decorated in gold and gray, with a glossy maplewood floor, and tall windows that overlooked the south rose gardens. The fog had begun to disperse, and sunlight fell in triangles through the glass onto the parquet, glittering with specks of dust. The far wall was clad entirely in mirrors, and so a looking-glass family, uneasy and strange, was standing in the middle distance, occasionally casting surreptitious glances at the real family. A buffet lunch of cold Kentucky hams, cold turkey, artichokes, asparagus, fruit, and cheeses was laid out for the expected guests. The cutlery shone like shoals of sardines.

"Well," said Roderick as Freddie came in, "how's she feeling?"

"Very spry," answered Freddie.

Celia pursed her lips in irritation. "She's been feeling spry for the past forty years."

"She's also determined," added Freddie.

Victor caught the tone of his voice and turned away from the buffet table, where he'd been spreading a small cracker with a huge blob of Beluga caviar. His mouth was still full from the last one.

"Determined? Determined about what?"

"About you, mainly," Freddie told him. "But about all of us."

"You're not in *league* with her, are you?" asked Celia.

"*Celia*," protested Roderick ineffectually.

Freddie put his hand in his pocket and looked relaxed. "Don't worry, uncle. I'm not particularly ashamed of being in league with my own grandmother, who also happens to be the conglomerate's largest single stockholder."

"You have to admit that she's getting pretty senile, darling," said Tess.

Freddie shook his head. "She's old, that's all. A lot of the time that makes her wiser, not dumber."

Victor brushed cracker crumbs from his green lapels. "So what particular sparkling gem of wisdom has she come up with now?"

Freddie looked across at Ally, who was standing by one of the windows in a gray suit with a pleated skirt, smoking and staring out over the gardens. He said: "She's decided that John Russell should withdraw. She wants it announced this evening."

Celia went white. "*She's* decided? *She's* decided?"

Dick Marini said: "It's out of the question. If John Russell quits now, that's tantamount to admitting Victor's guilty of homicide. You might just as well wire him up to the chandelier and have done with it. I think we all agree that he *may* have to, but—"

"It's impossible," put in Roderick. "I won't agree to it. I'm not having Victor made into a scapegoat. Not for you, not for her, not for anyone. Who the hell does she think she is?"

"She's your mother," remarked Ally quietly, without turning around. Roderick, stung, ignored her.

"It does seem kind of premature," said Tess. "I mean, they haven't even finished the forensic tests yet, not properly."

Freddie stood his ground. "It's what she said."

Celia gave him a look like a snap of ice. "And I suppose you agree with her, like you always do, in the ever-improving hope of reaping the profits of her bequest? It may surprise you to learn that business and politics aren't *all* opportunism, my child. There are occasional moments when we have to lay the lust for personal gain aside."

Dick Marini said: "It's going to look so bad in the courts."

"Courts?" snapped Victor. "It won't even get to the courts. There isn't any reason at all why we can't clear this up with the police, and why John Russell can't get into the White House the way we planned. I've already laid out six million dollars for this, and I'm not about to give up now."

"I'm not so worried about the money," said Roderick guardedly. He remembered his fruitless, evasive conversation with Henry Chapman. "But I *am* worried about putting Victor's neck on the block."

"Maybe it would do Victor good," said Ally.

Celia shook her scarlet flounces and lifted her profile like an irritated turkey. "If you have nothing more to contribute than common insults, Ally, I suggest you leave. We're discussing a mature problem here, in a mature fashion."

"You're discussing how to save your spoiled brat's hide," Ally retorted, turning away from the window. Her eyes were still concealed by dark glasses.

"Come on, now, Ally," said Tess.

"No, I won't 'come on.' It's true. It's no longer a question of preserving the family's integrity, of upholding our so-called historic role. We tried to do that before, tried to convince ourselves that we could alter the appearance of what had happened so that we would all appear to be the aggrieved instead of the aggressors. I'm disgusted with myself for being a party to that airplane crash. I'm disgusted with myself for believing that my position in life set me above the law."

"Now, look here," interrupted Dick Marini, "nothing illegal's happened here. Well, not *prima facie* illegal. Victor could well have been flying Miss Skouros' body home to her parents, in which event he's only guilty of failing to report her death to the authorities. There's no evidence of foul play."

"No evidence of foul play?" said Ally scornfully. "You're deceiving yourselves more than the police and the public put together."

Freddie lit a cigarette and put away his lighter. "I'm afraid I agree with Ally. I know that the airplane crash was my idea. I know that I'm just as responsible for what happened as any of you. But we have to stop the whole thing right here before it gets out of hand. In my opinion, John Russell has to withdraw, for whatever pretext, and then we have to sit down with the police and the district attorney and see what we can do to get Victor out of a hole."

Victor banged the table so hard that the cutlery jangled.

"Freddie, it's my damned money, and John Russell is my damned candidate! You would have chipped in quick enough for your share of the goodies if they'd elected him, right? You wouldn't have preached about the law if you'd come in for some nice fat government contracts, right? So don't you, or you, Ally, or anyone else stand there and damned well pontificate at me. John Russell doesn't withdraw, and that's it!"

Celia looked with acid satisfaction from Freddie to Ally and back again. There was an awkward silence.

Freddie calmly smoked his cigarette. "I think you're forgetting something, Victor," he said in a quiet voice.

"I don't think so," said Victor irritably.

Freddie smiled. "I think you're forgetting that while you have a majority shareholding in one or two of your corporations, over sixty percent of them are subsidiaries of Cornelius Oil or Cornelius Shipping."

Roderick rubbed his cheek nervously. He could see what was coming.

"Any major donations to political candidates from any of those corporations can be vetoed by the stockholders of the parent companies," said Freddie. "Article seventy-six of the corporations' charters, if you feel like looking it up."

Celia rapped her cane on the floor. "So what do you propose?" she said frigidly. "A show of hands?"

"That isn't a bad idea at that," said Freddie. "All those in favor of John Russell withdrawing his candidacy say 'aye.' "

"Aye," said Freddie and Ally together.

Victor laughed. "It's preposterous. Even with Grandmama on your side, we still outvote you."

Tess said: "Aye."

Roderick coughed. "I hope you're not serious, Freddie. You know what this could mean."

"I'm extremely serious," said Freddie. "I want us to come slap-bang face to face with what we are, don't you? Face the fact that we're all Corneliuses. Even if it splits us up."

"You're out of your mind," said Victor. "That's the most half-assed thing I've ever heard. Who the hell do you think keeps this business running? What the hell good am I going to be in Attica?"

"They won't send you to prison," said Freddie. "You let a poor dumb girl drown herself in your swimming pool. That's not exactly a five-to-ten."

Outside, they heard the high, distinctive whistle of an approaching Lear jet. Roderick looked at his watch and said: "That must be the first of the guests. I think we'd better adjourn this impromptu board meeting and finish it later."

"No," said Celia sharply, raising her hand. "I want to know where we stand. I want to know if you'd really vote against us, you three. I want to know if we're friends or enemies."

"I stand with Victor," said Dick Marini, looking at Freddie. There was a bitter wealth of meaning in the way he spoke.

"And we stand against," responded Ally. "We're serious, Celia. We own too much of America, we have control over too many people's lives. There's too much of our own money at risk, too. If this cover-up is discovered in three or four years' time, who on earth is ever going to trust us again?''

She took off her dark glasses. There were circles under her eyes, from lost nights of sleep over Clyde, and maybe over Destry, too, and Clara.

"I think it's time this family came clean," she said simply.

There were footsteps outside, and a burst of laughter. A footman came into the ballroom, leading an excited party of women from the American Women's League, all dressed up in their summer finery. As if they were all worked by the same switch, the Cornelius family turned toward the ladies, and their frowns of anger, of determination, of opposition, of resentment, were all magically replaced by welcoming smiles.

That evening, when a soft summer darkness was clotting in the brances of the trees, and the warblers were calling across the lawns, Freddie went upstairs to see Hester. The old lady was sitting at her dressing table, and Mrs. Dubuque was brushing out her hair.

Freddie looked at her wan reflection in the dressing-table mirror.

"You were magnificent," he told her. "The ladies all loved you."

"Oh, I didn't do anything much," said Hester. "I just gave them a great deal of money."

Freddie raised his eyes and gazed out toward the river. All he could see was a silver patch of light. He looked back at her dressing table, crowded with jars of night cream and skin restorer and expensive perfumes.

"You know that John Russell has declined to withdraw," he told her.

"Yes," she nodded. "But he will."

"Are we going to make him?"

Hester shrugged. "That means putting pressure on Victor, doesn't it?"

"Sure."

"Do you want to put that much pressure on Victor?"

Freddie rubbed his eyes. "I don't want to. But I don't think we have much choice."

"It'll split the family," she cautioned him.

"Yes. But hasn't it always been split? It seems to me that

Johann was two kinds of personality, you know, and that he sired two kinds of people."

Hester smiled. She didn't say whether she thought he was right or wrong.

"Which kind are you?" she asked him.

He looked at her, and shook his head. "I don't know."

She opened a side drawer of her dressing table and took out a crumpled piece of ruled paper. She opened it out and read it carefully to herself, although she had obviously read it hundreds of times before. Then she passed it to Freddie.

"It's something your uncle John did, years and years ago. I want you to have it."

Freddie took it, and saw a few lines of childish handwriting. They read:

> My father is very rich and is the Cornelius Oil billionair. He is very old and does not have much hair. I like it when he goes away because my mother lets us have dinner in the garden room and sometimes eat squob. My father is stric and we have to do what he says. I would like to buy him a nice wig for his birthday because even though he is stric I do love him because he is my father. He has an airplan called the Ford Tri-Motor.

Freddie read it twice, and then gently folded it up.

"Johann adored that," said Hester. There were tears in her eyes. "He used to say that it was the nicest thing that anyone ever wrote about him. He was, you know, a very sensitive man."

Freddie nodded. He bent forward and kissed her. Then he said: "Sleep well," and left the room. He walked along the gallery in the dim yellow-tinted light, feeling as if Johann, and John, and everyone the Cornelius family had ever known, or loved, or hated, or done business with, were all beside him.

He heard the rumble of a Lear jet leaving the island's runway. That would be Victor, leaving for Spiermont. Roderick and Celia had already gone, closeted in their long black Fleetwood, without even a wave. Tess was leaving for California in the morning, and Ally was spending a few days with friends in Lynwood before going back to her house and her business in Washington.

He went downstairs, and across the drawing room, and out of the French doors. He stood on the twilit terrace for a while, smoking a cigarette and listening to the whistling of saw-whet owls. Then he turned and went inside for a cold supper of ham and potato salad.

Pieces of what happened were everywhere. They were scattered across America, dusty and forgotten, and they are still there today. The school composition that Hester gave to Freddie was only one small piece out of thousands; and there are many which have long since disappeared.

In a railroad collectors' store in Milwaukee, Wisconsin, lies the real railroad whistle that the Broughton stationmaster gave to Daniel Forster, and which Daniel Forster blew like crazy. Outside a suburban house in Cleburne, Texas, hangs one of the lamps from Johann Cornelius' New Orleans motorcar, and when they have cookouts the owners light it up. There are still fragments of the aluminum skin of the C-1 airplane keeping the rain out of a backyard toolshed in West Virginia; and a chicken farmer from Muskogee drives Celia's cherry-red Bentley on special occasions.

Some of the mementos are fine, while others are nondescript. Ariadne's emerald pendant was eventually sent back to her parents, who sold it after four months to raise the down payment on a new house. It now belongs to the wife of a supermarket manager in South Pasadena. The faucets from the bath in which Beatrice Mulliner committed suicide were fitted to the side wall of a gas station in Galveston, and are still used today for filling radiators. The Pierce Arrow "Silver Arrow" in which Hazel Seymour was driven to Lynwood railroad station is now a collector's item, and stands in a private motor museum in Waco, Texas.

Elsewhere, if you looked hard enough, you could find jewelry and automobiles and airplanes and moth-eaten furs. You could probably find John's Duke Ellington records, cracked and dusty, on a Greenwich Village stall; or the picture of Loch Lomond that hung in Carina's turret room in Edgar. You could find Edward Secker's Gleneagles ashtray, or David Bookbinder's leather-bound law books. Every family, every story, has its debris.

About the people, though, it would be pointless to ask questions. About Roderick, Celia, Victor, Freddie, Tess, and Ally; even about Hester, and her long-dead husband. Because you could never say that they were happy or unhappy, that they were proud or that they were ashamed. You could never say that they were satisfied, or sad, or racked with guilt. You could only say that they were rich.